KEY to HAVOC

Titles by Piers Anthony
Published by Mundania Press

ChroMagic Series
Key to Havoc
Key to Chroma
Key to Destiny

Pornucopia Series
Pornucopia
The Magic Fart

Dragon's Gold Series
by Piers Anthony and Robert Margroff
Dragon's Gold
Serpent's Silver
Chimaera's Copper
Orc's Opal
Mouvar's Magic

Of Man and Manta Series
Omnivore
Orn
OX

Other Titles by Piers Anthony
Macroscope
Conversation With An Ogre

PIERS ANTHONY

KEY to HAVOC

Mundania Press

A Mundania Press Production

Mundania Press LLC
6470A Glenway Avenue, #109
Cincinnati, Ohio 45211-5222

To order additional copies of this book, contact:
books@mundania.com
www.mundania.com

Cover Art © 2004 by Stacey L. King
Book Design and Layout by Daniel J. Reitz, Sr.
Production and Promotion by Bob Sanders
Edited by Daniel J. Reitz, Sr. and Audra A.F. Brooks

Hardcover ISBN: 0-9723670-7-1
Trade Paperback ISBN: 0-9723670-6-3
eBook ISBN: 1-59426-000-1

First Edition • May 2003
Second Edition • July 2004

Library of Congress Catalog Card Number 2003103070

Printed in the United States of America

10   9   8   7   6   5   4   3   2

CONTENTS

Chapter 1—Dragon

The boy made his way swiftly but carefully through the forest, stepping in patterns reminiscent of a game. He had a staff as tall as he was, that he used to push aside some ferns and fronds. Sometimes he braced on it for short pole vaults. It was as though there was a path that only he could see, and that it was vital that he follow it exactly, lest there be some terrible consequence. At one point he stopped before a growth resembling a giant cycad and stood as if awaiting permission to proceed. When nothing happened, he stepped cautiously inside the embrace of its tentacular fronds, climbed onto the base of the trunk and worked his way around to its far side. Then he got off, skirted the fronds, and resumed his travel.

Soon he wound down into a forested depression, an ancient sink hole with a deep pool in the center. But as he reached the water, he froze, his staff held warily before him. There was a dragon across the path. He had never seen one up close before. He recognized it immediately because of the stories he had heard about these dangerous predators. The creature was long and flat, with sleekly overlapping blue scales, but some were blistered on the upper side. It massed several times what the boy did, but might be dead. No, there was a flicker of animation, a quiver.

After a moment, the boy spoke, keeping a reasonable distance. "Greeting."

There was no discernible response. But the boy tried again: "Dragon. How were you named?"

There was a larger quiver. Then a patch of flesh at the edge of the upper side rippled and hunched and formed into a tiny tentacle. It waved, weakly.

The boy nodded. This was a signal of communication rather than combat, and could probably be trusted. He took one hand off the staff, lifted a forefinger and moved it in a series of signals. DRAGON HOW NAMED. It was the sign language that he had learned by trial and error with the smarter native species. He hoped the dragon understood.

The tentacle responded with a similar series. LACK NAME. DY-

ING. Then it sank back, as if tired.

The boy considered briefly. He was immensely gratified that his effort at communication had worked, but that solved only part of the problem. Then he signaled again, speaking the words as he signaled them: "Dragon, how can I help you live?"

The tentacle lifted and wiggled. The boy spoke the words as he read the signs. He wasn't sure he had every part correct, but thought he had the essence. "No need to help an enemy creature live."

The boy was ready. He signed carefully, for he wanted to make no mistake. The signs did not have tenses or suppositions or other qualifiers, but the context would provide enough. He hoped. "I am enemy to no creature who is not enemy to me. But even if you are an enemy, do you practice honor?"

The tentacle moved with greater vigor. "Yes, with those who understand it. Do you?"

"I think I understand it, though I am young. It means to be honest and fair, even to an enemy."

"It means more than that, but that will do. Your understanding seems sufficient for this purpose."

Havoc controlled a surge of gladness. He had established communication, but the dragon had not promised to spare him harm. "Will you exchange an oath of friendship?"

The tentacle quivered with surprise. "This is complicated."

The boy nodded again. "I know," he signaled. "But I can help you only if I know how, and if we trust each other. You must know that I will not betray you to my people, and I must know that you will not kill me. We are of enemy species; you are hurt and I am a child. I think only an oath of friendship, given with honor, can provide such mutual assurance. Give me a temporary name for you, and I will give you mine, so we can make the oath. Then tell me what to do to help you survive."

The tentacle waved weakly. "This is a significant commitment. If you enable me to live, I must enable you to live. But you may not like the manner of it. You might better let me die."

"How are you named, for now?" the boy repeated.

The tentacle shrugged. "My name is Mentor, for now. How are you named, for now?"

"My name is Havoc, for now. I offer the oath of friendship." He advanced and slowly extended his finger toward the tentacle.

The tentacle waved. "Oath accepted."

Then the boy's finger touched the tentacle. The tentacle curled around it, for a moment, then let go. In that moment a partial rapport of minds was established, confirming the significance of the oath.

"Say my name," the boy said. This would eliminate the qualifier he had used, making recognition formal.

"Say mine."

"Mentor," the boy said, naming the dragon.

"Havoc." The oath had been completed.

The tentacle waved again, but more weakly. "First, Havoc, water on my burn."

Havoc stepped carefully around the dragon, feeling his footing with the staff, and made his way to the pool. He didn't know exactly how dragons killed people, but was sure this one could have done it if he chose. There was a hollow gourd shell beside the water that he normally used as a cup for drinking. He dipped it full, then poured it over Mentor's back.

The dragon shuddered, but the tentacle waved with increased vigor. "More."

Havoc poured several more dippers of water, cooling and quenching the length of the dragon. Then he signaled again with his finger. "What next?"

"Cycad seed, powdered."

Havoc paused. Those seeds were deadly to human beings unless carefully processed. But Mentor was not human, and surely knew what he needed. Yet there was another complication. "I must have help to harvest that."

The tentacle nodded. "I release you from the obligation. I will die."

Havoc waved his finger. "No. I made the oath so I could help you live. May I bring a trusted friend to help?"

"Will that friend make the oath of friendship?"

"She will if I ask her."

"Will you ask her?"

Havoc realized that his statement had not been tight. "Yes."

"Bring her."

Havoc started to circle the dragon, then paused again. "Can you survive an hour?"

"A day, if not attacked."

"I will return with her within an hour."

He started moving again, but thought of one more thing. "It would help me to know," he signed. "What gender and age are you?"

"Male. Mature adult."

"Thank you. I too am male. My friend is female, also a child." Then he reconsidered. "Almost a woman."

"Borderline juvenile," Mentor signaled, getting it straight. "Sometimes they understand better than do adults."

Havoc thought of the attitudes of the village adults. "Yes. Sometimes."

Havoc moved back along his unmarked path, hurrying but not skipping any part of his dance-like ritual. He vaulted exactly where he had before, and pushed the same fronds clear. He paused again at the cycad, eyeing its huge cone, but did not speak to it. Then he went on, and soon reached the human village. This consisted of about twenty stone and packed-earth houses, with thatched roofs. They faced onto the street, and behind each was a fenced garden. The fences were stout, with sharply pointed posts and competent gates.

There were classes in progress in the center building, as young men and women practiced martial arts, dancing, decorative weaving, and other useful adult pursuits. Havoc ignored this and went on to a particular house. He went to the side and made a birdlike whistle.

In a moment the window opened and a face appeared. It was a rather pretty girl whose light brown colored hair and dark brown eyes matched Havoc's own in reverse: his hair was dark and his eyes light. Both had brownish white skin. She might have been his sister, but wasn't; all the villagers were similarly bland, compared to the bright colors of neighboring animals and plants, though the shades of their hair, eyes, and skin varied somewhat. "What do you want, stranger?" she asked, smiling.

"Come play," he said.

Her lips pursed. "Sex play?" She eyed his staff as if it were an instrument of such play.

Havoc did not smile at the humor. "Not exactly. But secret."

She considered, then decided. She liked secrets. "All right. If it's interesting."

"Yes." If only she knew! But he couldn't say anything about the dragon, here where he might be overheard.

"Say my name."

"Say mine."

"Havoc."

"Gale."

"Meet you at the far edge."

He nodded, and moved on. At the end of the village, where the road led away toward distant mysterious civilization, he turned, and walked in bored fashion back the way he had come. Few paid attention to a bored child. They knew that soon enough he would enter the adult realm, and have no further time for the luxury of boredom.

Gale was there at the commencement of the path. She had made her way without being noticed, as she could when she wanted to. She wore a light gray shirt untucked over a dark gray skirt, her legs bare below the knees, without shoes. They were nice legs; in fact she had always been pretty, but now was on the verge of beautiful. She had a short, slender staff of her own, and a small but very sharp knife in an underarm sheath. She stood as if expecting to be fondled. He knew why: someone was watching from a window. They would have to put on a small show.

"Who are you?" he asked.

She put on a brilliant smile. "I'm a Glamor, and I will fascinate you into utter helplessness."

The Glamors were special magicians, mythical entities of enormous powers, who were said to be able to compel instant and total love. It was supposed to be dangerous to speak of them, lest they be summoned. That made it especially tempting for children. "I'm helpless," he agreed.

"You don't show it."

So he approached her, embraced her, and kissed her, then took her by the hand and urged her down the path. She came along, holding back somewhat as if just a trifle diffident. Whoever was watching would be satisfied that the two would get out of sight, then play a childish game of Tickle and Peek.

That was one of several special boy/girl diversions all human beings knew. The boy typically wore a loose shirt and shorts, and the girl wore a knee-length skirt and untucked sleeveless blouse, without underclothing. If players were not properly attired, they had to change before they could play, or remove enough clothing to qualify. The subject would lie on the ground, legs together, arms by the sides, facing up. Generally the boy tickled the girl, in certain prescribed places, and was entitled to Peek at anything she showed or moved while reacting. If she waved her arms, he could see in through the armholes; if she kicked up her legs, he could see inside her thighs. If she curled up or turned over, he had new avenues of vision, and she had to hold the position for a count of ten while he looked. If a girl liked a boy, she could be extremely ticklish. Thereafter the girl tickled the boy, and he could laugh but not move, no matter where she touched him. She could reach inside his clothing and touch his body anywhere he had Peeked at hers, such as under the arms or between the legs. She would inquire, step by step: "Did you Peek here?" and he would answer "Yes." Then she would tickle him mercilessly for a count of ten seconds. If he said no, she had to stop. Sometimes a girl arranged to let more be Peeked than was strictly necessary, for that reason, and sometimes the boy did not protest if she went beyond anything he had actually seen. Her object was to make him move out of turn, or force him into an embarrassing reaction. It was a mutual license, and they soon became conversant with each other's private anatomy: he by sight, she by touch. Children who were not interested in each other did not agree to play the game, unless dared by others who wanted to watch. Sometimes older children would make a demonstration for younger ones, so they would know exactly how it was done. As a general rule, players had to be of about the same age, so demonstration games were a way to allow a broader range of ages. There could be currents that no one spoke of.

There were variants that got more serious, and the older children enjoyed these, because anything within the rules of the game of T&P was deemed to be technically consensual. That meant that someone might get caught by circumstance and have to show or touch more than was desired, but have no honorable way out of it, so would submit without crying foul. Sometimes the object was to push a game farther than the other would go, winning status for nerve. Girls could be just as nervy as boys, when they chose to be. That in turn gave them a cover for what might otherwise have been considered commitment, and they could pretend that it wasn't really voluntary. The correct balance of desire and deniability was essential, as touches were made by both parties, and with other than the fingers. The distinction between Tickle & Peek or Touch & Touch and full sex play became increasingly indistinct as children grew toward adult status. Adults pretended not to know that. It was all part of the natural order of growing up. No adult ever played the game with a child, on pain of banishment, because once the nominal threshold of innocence was crossed, it could never be uncrossed. This was one thing children had to explore by themselves.

When boys became men and girls became women, and showed it by their bodies and manner, they were expected to marry and procreate, not wasting time. The world of Charm was always in need of more people, and most families were large. The standard minimum was four surviving children, and no person was exempt from having such a family. This meant that men were fully occupied providing for their families, and women had little time for relaxation. Most children, observing that, were not in a great hurry to commit to adulthood. But the games were fun, and when a girl got pregnant, her days of dalliance were over, even if she was well below the mandatory marriage age of 18. She had to marry either the man who impregnated her, or another, and thereafter be true to him and bear his remaining children, with certain careful exceptions. Marriages were for the term required to raise four children, and few adults were allowed to remain unmarried even after finishing with the children. Surplus males or females had to leave the village, to return only if married. When one member of a couple of childbearing age died, the other had a month to a year to remarry or face expulsion. The children, however, would remain with the village. Childless couples were not allowed; they had to conceive or adopt, or be expelled after a reasonable interval. Even single-child families were frowned on, though tolerated for a time; then they had to adopt three more. So while childhood was for games, the approach of maturity was a time for caution, and the often free and many-partnered delights of youth became serious relationships. Some seemed to turn serious well before adulthood, and Havoc and Gale were such a case. But they had never actually spoken of the future.

When the two got out of sight of the village, they dropped the pretense. "What is it?" Gale inquired as she followed his dancing steps perfectly, and mimicked his use of the staff. He caught glimpses of her knees under the skirt, and found them intriguing, as always;

she had nice knees, and they were getting nicer.

But his answer had nothing to do with knees. "Secret."

"Secret," she agreed.

"A blue dragon in the hole."

"Blue!" she exclaimed, impressed, for that was a color they seldom saw. "How big?" They had on occasion seen small dragons of other colors, cute but still dangerous.

"Grown."

"A grown dragon? But it would eat us!"

"He's sick. Injured. As your spider was. We must help him."

"Help a dragon?" she asked, amazed.

"I made an oath of friendship."

"With a grown dragon?" She remained astonished. This whole business was hard for her to grasp, because it was so far out of their ordinary experience. Children were routinely warned never to approach a dragon, and any such creature that entered the village was killed.

"With a grown dragon," he repeated firmly. It might have seemed less remarkable with a baby dragon, because the very young of most species were friendlier and less dangerous.

She whistled. "I guess you know what you're doing. What am I here for?"

"It needs medicine, that I can't get alone. So you must make an oath too."

She paused, and not entirely because they were now before the cycad. "Are you sure it's not just a trick, because he's too hungry for just one child?"

That made him pause. "I think he's not. He's pretty badly burned. I believe he made the oath in good faith. He even warned me not to help an enemy. I think he's honest, and that his oath counts. But I can't tell you I'm absolutely sure."

"But you do believe."

"I do believe." He never said that in jest.

She pondered briefly, then angled her head in the special way she had. "I'll chance it."

He turned and kissed her for real. "Thank you, Gale."

"Well, I wouldn't do it if I didn't have a crush on you." She spoke lightly, but they were words she had never before said to him. Their relationship had started well and grown closer with time, but had remained within the bounds of juvenile friendship. This was like the game, wherein some things that were serious were phrased as otherwise, avoiding premature commitment. Probably the significance and danger of his discovery were evoking equivalently stronger emotions. Things somehow seemed more important when there was serious risk.

He pretended chagrin. "You mean I could have Peeked without Tickling? You'd have let me?"

She pretended outrage. "Of course not. Then I wouldn't have gotten my turn."

His feeling was intensifying. "You can have your turn anytime." That had always been true, and she knew it, but they had never confirmed it verbally.

They moved on around the cycad, but the dialogue would not let go. "Because I'm helping you, or because you like me?"

"Both." He did not look at her. He had seen every part of her in the past, but this was a new level of commitment. He was beginning to understand the adult belief that attitudes could count more than actions.

"If we were two strangers meeting," she said, "I might say 'Joy,' and maybe 'Adoration.'"

"And I would say 'Wonder' and maybe 'Desire.'"

She laughed. "Maybe it's a good thing we aren't strangers."

"Maybe it's good we aren't adult."

They continued dancing along the invisible path, and kept talking. "The adults say that children don't know what love is," Gale said. "You're thirteen. I'm twelve. Do we know?"

"We don't have the adult bodies yet. Maybe that makes a difference."

She glanced down at herself. "I'll have breasts in one more year, I think. Maybe sooner; they're starting. Will that help?"

"It will make a difference," he agreed. He was feeling the incipient changes in himself, in desire as well as body. "More to Peek at. But I think that's sex, not love."

"If it doesn't make a difference—not one that counts—do we know about love?"

She wanted an answer, indirect, as in the manner of the game, so that it wouldn't be on record. That avoided embarrassment. She was his tacit oath friend. Was she more? "Yes, I think we know."

She was silent, but the matter was not finished. It had to be digested, as they followed the devious invisible path. When they came to a safe spot, he stopped and turned, holding his staff aside. She embraced him and kissed him. He had not thought of her in terms of love before, because it wasn't a concept he properly understood, but now that he addressed it, he did think it was love. He felt like a man inside, and she felt like a woman. They were still friends, but this was larger. And immeasurably finer.

"Are we too young to marry?" she asked.

"I think so. The adults would laugh. But maybe we can pledge marriage, for when the time comes."

"I pledge," she said without hesitation.

He could not afford to hesitate either. "I pledge."

They kissed again. Thus suddenly, they were engaged. It might be several years before they could make it official, for bodies did not always develop quickly, but the commitment was there.

"I have no ring for you," he said.

"It can wait. I couldn't wear it anyway, until we want to be open about it."

"When I get one, I will give it to you, and you can keep it until you can wear it."

"Yes."

"Can we play house meanwhile?"

"Yes."

"I mean sexually."

"I knew that. If you can do it, so can I."

And there was another commitment, for full, formal sex, to the extent they could manage it. Havoc was sure they could. He kissed her once more, and she met him with what felt like adult passion. They had already crossed the boundary of desire. When they had opportunity, they would explore its ramifications.

"Maybe I can get a wire," she said after a moment.

He laughed, then broke off, realizing that it wasn't a joke. A wire prevented early pregnancy. She had thought this through farther than he had. They did not want to end their freedom of youth early. "Yes."

They moved on. Soon they came to the dragon. It lay blue and still, possibly dead. But as they stopped before it, the little tentacle formed and moved. "Wind," Havoc said, translating, for the girl was not as good at signs as he was.

The tentacle twitched. "Not thing. Name."

"He named me!" Gale said, surprised. "But how could he know? Did you tell?"

"No, that would be a violation. I just said a friend. A trusted female child-almost-woman friend."

"Thanks, male child-almost-man friend," she said wryly.

The tentacle moved with more vigor and detail. "The dragon can read our thoughts," Havoc said, amazed.

"Our minds!" she exclaimed. "Oh, no! Did he—?"

The tentacle moved. "Yes," Havoc translated. "Our thoughts were very strong. He knows we are pledged."

Gale blushed. "I never thought anyone would know. Until it is time."

The tentacle moved. "Make the oath," Havoc translated. "A friend will never tell."

"Oh. Yes." She stepped forward. "How do I oath him, if he can't hear?"

"Lift your finger. Let me guide it. I'll speak the words you sign, so you'll know."

"Yes." She lifted her right forefinger, and he took hold of her hand.

"How are you named, for now?" he spoke. Then, as the dragon

answered, "My name is Mentor, for now. How are you named?"

"My name is Gale," she said, and he moved her finger accordingly, with a sharp sideways motion for the strong wind.

"I offer the Oath of Friendship."

"I accept."

Then Havoc guided her finger forward to touch the tentacle.

"Say my name," she said.

"Say mine," Havoc translated.

"Mentor."

"Gale," the tentacle signed.

She turned to Havoc. "I felt his mind! He means it."

"Yes." He was glad for her reassurance, for it vindicated his own belief.

The tentacle wiggled once more. "It does feel like love."

Gale blushed again. She was getting better at that.

It was done. They were oathed. Now they had to go to fetch the cycad seed. This was another type of challenge. For not only were such seeds toxic, the plant defended them. That was why it would take two to make the harvest.

"Mentor needs a cycad seed," Havoc said as they followed the route back.

"But they're poisonous!"

"Not to a dragon, it seems. He needs powdered seed."

"This won't be easy. Those plants are dangerous."

"That's why I brought you." Then, realizing how it sounded, he qualified it. "I mean, I knew I couldn't do it alone, and I had to have help from someone I trusted."

She put on a wry face. "And I thought it was love." But then she laughed. "I hope you know how to do it."

"I can find out."

"You can find out! Who are you going to ask?"

"The cycad."

"Why should it tell you? It won't want to give up its seed."

"I hope to convince it that this is worthwhile, because Mentor needs it."

"Why should it care about a blue dragon?"

"I don't think it would care, but it might see the need. All the plants and animals have understandings with their neighbors, and with some others."

"Understandings? If we make one misstep, any of these plants we are passing will sting us or poison us or do something worse. None of them are our friends. Not really. They aren't Mentor's friends either, I think."

"We can walk where we do among the plants because we have learned their natures and come to terms with them," Havoc said. "They know us, so they don't attack us. As long as we follow the rules. If anyone else tried to use this path, if he even knew exactly where it was, they would sting him."

"I know. But letting us pass isn't the same as giving us their fruit."

"I think dragons and cycads have a deal," he said seriously. "They help each other when they have to. I bet a dragon could hurt a cycad, if it had a mind to, especially if it's immune to the poison. So maybe they do each other favors instead of fighting. Sort of a mutual assistance pact."

"Symbiosis."

"I guess. You know those terms better than I do."

"You know nature, I know words," she agreed. "So very well: maybe they cooperate. But will the cycad take your word that the dragon really needs the seed?"

"I think so, to a degree. I'll open my mind to it, so it can feel my oath with Mentor."

"Mentor—that means teacher. That's a funny name for a dragon."

"Well, we all have funny names, when you think about it. Maybe it taught somebody a lesson."

"Dragons have taught plenty of people lessons," she agreed ruefully. "Like not to mess with dragons. You know, I never saw a blue one before."

Havoc nodded. The local dragons, glimpsed always fleetingly at a distance, were yellow, red, or green, not nearly as handsome. "He must be from far away."

"I hope we can help him live. I want to know his story."

"So do I."

They reached the cycad. "You will have to take the seed," Havoc said. "While I reason with it." He was not being selfish; he related better to the natural creatures and plants of Charm, so had to be the one to do it.

Gale looked nervously at the huge plant. "I'd rather play Tickle with an ugly stranger."

"So would I! But I promised to help Mentor."

"Take my staff." She handed him her staff so that her hands could be free. He stretched his right hand so that he could hold the two together. Both staffs were made of special red wood he had found, that was not only strong, but also struck any object much harder than the wielder could otherwise manage. It wasn't just leverage; it was possible to crack stone without swinging too hard. He had made both of them, after discovering the unusual property of the wood. The staffs were good aids for traveling, for that same extra power helped with the vaulting, but were formidable weapons too. It was a similar story with their knives; they were made from chips of hard green stone he had found, and could cut much more effectively than ordinary metal blades. He had fashioned these tools because there was no getting around the fact that the wilderness was dangerous. That was why most children did not go into it at all; too many had been lost in it. Havoc's mother had finally given up cautioning him about that, as he had soon shown his competence with nature. She had said something about his being her special child. He assumed she meant he was her natural child; his younger siblings were adopted. Gale was the only natural one in her family; that was another thing that had drawn them together, at first.

Gale stepped close to the cycad. Its central body towered higher than her head, and its large long leaves writhed, orienting. It was aware of her. It had allowed her to climb around its central trunk before, but this was different. She had a mission it wouldn't necessarily like.

Then Havoc addressed the plant. He did not raise his finger, because the cycad could not see, and he did not speak, because it could not hear. Instead he thought the loudest possible thoughts at it.

O CYCAD! I AM HAVOC, HUMAN BOY. YOU KNOW ME FROM MY DAILY VISITS HERE. YOU LET ME PASS WITHOUT HARM. I MUST FETCH YOUR SEED FOR MY OATH FRIEND THE DRAGON MENTOR. READ MY MIND.

He made a mental scene of the injured dragon, and their contact.

The serpentine leaves writhed. Then, slowly, they relaxed. A way was open to the central stalk, with its huge raised seed.

Gale stepped cautiously in toward that seed, lifting her feet over the leaves on the ground.

MY FRIEND GALE IS FETCHING THE SEED. SHE MEANS YOU NO HARM. YOU KNOW HER; SHE HAS PASSED BY YOU BEFORE. PLEASE LET HER DO IT.

But the leaves writhed toward the girl. Havoc stepped in after her, intercepting them. Actually their motion was more apparent than real; it was more of a twisting in place, and erection of spines. But it was ample warning.

Gale froze in place, not trying to conceal her extreme nervousness. Havoc stepped in close behind her and put his arms protectively around her body. I LOVE GALE, he thought forcefully. I WILL HURT IF SHE HURTS. PLEASE LET HER PASS. IT IS FOR MENTOR. He envisioned the blue dragon again, lying by the pool, suffering.

The leaves relaxed again. The plant was not smart in the way of people, but it understood this type of situation. Havoc felt its acceptance of the dragon's need. "It's all right," he murmured to Gale. "Take another step."

She did so, but the leaves quivered again. Havoc felt his own limbs quiver. His contact with the plant was mental, and it could make his body react. It could send his arms or legs flinging wildly out, to bash into the erect spines and be poisoned. That was why he always paused when passing the cycad, because his best path was right beside it, within its influence, where no other plants or creatures held sway. If it let him pass, no other thing would object. But of course it was much more likely to let him pass, than to let him take its seed. The quiver in his body was continued warning. It could do the same with Gale.

"Wait, Gale," he said. She stopped immediately, holding her body in the process of stepping over another leaf. If the cycad made her move her legs, she would get stung on the ankles. If she hit only one spine, there would be a sore that made her uncomfortably sick. If she hit two, she would be deathly ill. Three or more would kill her.

He tried again. O CYCAD! WE MUST HAVE THE SEED FOR THE DRAGON. HERE IS MENTOR'S IMAGE. He summoned his mental picture, making it as realistic as possible. He showed the blistered upper surface, indicating the dragon's pain.

His body relaxed, and the spines folded back against the leaves. "Go on," he told Gale. "Use your knife to sever the stem." Then, without waiting, he resumed his focus on the cycad and the dragon. He realized that he could not afford to let up for an instant; he had to keep the plant constantly pacified. Because what they wanted of it was normally an offense requiring deadly response.

He closed his eyes, trusting Gale to tread carefully enough. He thought to the cycad, filling his image with the blue of the dragon. The color seemed to do as well as the image, so he thought nothing but blue. Every time his fingers quivered, he bore down harder. BLUE BLUE!

It seemed to continue forever. He knew that Gale was climbing the core, making her way toward the seed stem that sprouted from its top. At one point a lance of pain passed through his groin, and he feared he had stumbled against a spike. He hadn't; the pain was projected, not real. He overrode it with more blue.

Then Gale spoke. "I got it."

Havoc opened his eyes. She was standing before him, holding the huge seed in her arms. She had cut the stem; that was the pain he had felt. The cycad had let its genital be severed. It would grow another. But it was a considerable sacrifice.

THANK YOU, O CYCAD, he thought. YOU HAVE SAVED MENTOR. Then, to Gale: "Turn slowly and come toward me. We are not safe yet."

"I know." She turned, holding the seed, making only slow motions.

Even so, he felt the quiver, and saw the spines erecting. Gale paused. BLUE! BLUE! BLUE! It was dangerous to relax even momentarily.

The quiver faded, and Gale resumed her motion. She completed her turn. Then she stepped toward him.

Stage by stage, they made it out of the cycad's embrace. Havoc thanked the plant, and promised to go immediately to the dragon. They turned to begin the dance down the path to the pool.

There was a sudden shaking of the ground as something came at them. Havoc whirled. It was a green bear. The thing was not as tall as he was, but was far more massive, and its six muscular legs had awesome power. Its thick claws curled around its feet, when not sprung out to strike, and were resistant to the hazards of small plants. Thus it was able to bound across the ground with minimal pain. As it was doing now.

Havoc had only a moment to assess the situation and take action. His survival reflexes took over. The bear wanted the cycad seed, which was wonderfully nutritious for those creatures whose digestion could handle it. It could not penetrate the cycad's defenses, but now saw an opportunity to drive off the children and take the morsel. They could not fight it. It seemed that they had either to give up the seed and flee, or become further food for the bear.

But they had one thing the bear did not: intelligence. The things of Charm were marvelous, but none matched the intellect of human beings. So they could usually be outsmarted. He had a flash notion how to trick the charging bear.

"Gale! Scream and fall beside the cycad. Keep screaming."

She screamed and fell, still holding the seed. She was very good at following directions, especially when in danger.

The bear oriented on the fallen child. It was naturally attracted to terrified prey, and attuned to it before all else. So it didn't look at Havoc at all.

He stepped quickly to a safe spot beyond the cycad, leaving the way open to Gale. He lifted the two staffs, assessing vectors. This had to be done just right. As the bear passed between him and the cycad, he drove forward with both staffs pointed at the creature. He lunged, putting all his power into it.

The ends of the staffs struck the bear's middle shoulder. Their combined magnified force struck with such power as to shove the bear to the side. Not far, but enough to cause it to brush the nearest cycad leaf.

The cycad was ready. Several spines drove into the bear's side. The bear howled in pain and turned automatically to face the attack. That was stupid. It might have survived, had it bounded on out of the way, for it had a very tough hide and evidently could resist the cycad's effort to take over its limbs. As it was, it lumbered into another leaf. More spines lanced into its head and neck.

"Get out, Gale!" Havoc called.

The girl scrambled up and moved away from the cycad. Then, perceiving herself safe at last, she began to cry. Her screams had been done on order, but had had the authority of conviction; she had believed she was going to die.

He went to her and put his arm around her shoulders, comforting her. Together they stood and watched the destruction of the bear. Crazed by the poison, it was lashing wildly out at anything near—and each lash fetched in another spine. The cumulative effect was overwhelming. Soon the bear's screams sounded much like Gale's of a moment before. Then it sank down amidst the leaves and died. Its body would become food for the cycad, as it rotted and disintegrated and became rich soil.

Gale recovered rapidly, as she usually did. "Once again, you have saved me and wreaked havoc."

"I had to. I couldn't afford to let the only fiancée I ever got get blown away. Not before I got to Peek at her grown body."

She laughed, but it was as much relief as humor. She trusted him, but knew that he could not save her from every threat.

Havoc addressed the plant. O CYCAD, I PUSHED THE BEAR INTO YOU. IT WAS GOING TO EAT THE SEED.

The wildly quivering leaves relaxed. Perhaps the plant understood. Certainly it knew that the menace was over and the seed was secure for its purpose. Havoc had acted to save Gale, but also to save the seed, so this was a fair collaboration. The plant had agreed to relinquish its seed, but it was better to give it something in return. The body of the bear.

Satisfied, they turned to go along the path. Havoc took the seed and gave Gale the two staffs. He led the way, stepping and jumping from point to point, able to do it without his staff, though it was a challenge. The menaces of the small plants were not in the same class with the cycad, but there were many more of them. Missteps would get his feet stung, blistered, burned, stabbed, shocked, poisoned, or greased to become suddenly so slippery that he would be unable to stand, and would take a devastating fall amidst a combination of attacks. But he did not misstep. He had spent his life studying every plant of this route, locating those whose threats were mere bluffs, and making peace with others. Some had been in need of nourishment, and he had brought them handfuls of rich soil cadged from elsewhere. Some had been thrilled to have his chemically rich urine. Some he had intimidated, bringing a burning brand near, making clear that if they did not let him pass, he would singe them horribly. Thus at every step he had prepared his way, and could travel freely as long as he maintained relations. When new plants took root in his way, he addressed them, and either tamed them or destroyed them. It was not necessarily a nice business, but neither was survival. Every so often he rewarded those that maintained the truce, to refresh their awareness of him. He tried to make the trip to the pond at least every other day, because some plants did not have long memories.

No one else could use his trail, except Gale, to whom he had both taught it, and introduced the plants along it. She knew which ones craved special mineral dirt, and which loved urine, and they tolerated her as a non-stranger. But a real stranger not only would not know where the path was, he would not be able to use it anyway. The plants would not recognize him. The other boys of the village had discovered that early, the hard way, when they tried to gang up on Havoc and pursue him into the forest. They had thought they could imitate his dance stepping and be safe, but that worked for only three of four plants. Now they never chased Havoc, or Gale.

The two of them made it to the pool, with their special burden. The dragon was there, unchanged. The sight of Mentor made Havoc realize that perhaps he had last met a creature as smart as a person. But he wasn't sure; it would take time to verify. As a general rule, dragons didn't need intelligence, because they were so powerful in other ways. This injured dragon was no example of the powers of a well one, which was perhaps just as well. Havoc was not at all sure he could have escaped, had Mentor been healthy and hungry.

The nose tentacle formed and twitched. "I lack your intelligence, but have a great deal of memory," Havoc read aloud. Hearing himself, he realized that Mentor had read his mind again. He wasn't used to that, as most of his experience with mind contact had been with plants, which didn't have the same kind of awareness. "But I would not have pursued you, for I am beyond my Chroma, and my magic lacks force."

The children paused, confused.

The tentacle twitched again. "Disregard my last statement, for the present; I see that I spoke nonsense in your terms."

Havoc set down the seed and signaled with his finger. "We brought the cycad seed. How can we powder it?"

"Pound it on a stone. Do not breathe the dust of it." Because that would poison them.

They got to work, clearing a large passive stone—not all stones were tolerant—and fetching a smaller one for the pounding. They braced the seed carefully, and worked together to bring the pounder down on top of the seed. After several strikes of increasing force, the seed cracked, then fragmented. The fragments were easier to pound, and some of them did smash into powder. They averted their faces, avoiding the brief clouds of dust. Fortunately the debris settled rapidly.

Following Mentor's directions, they took handfuls of the powder and sprinkled it on his blistered upper surface. Almost immediately the dragon relaxed, and Havoc realized that he had been in severe pain, which was now was easing. This was good medicine, despite being toxic if eaten or breathed by human beings.

"Wash yourselves," Mentor warned them. "This substance is not good for you, even on your skin."

They were glad to oblige. They went to the edge of the pool, in the one place it was safe for them, stripped off their clothing, and squatted or kneeled in the water. They scooped handfuls of water at each other, laughing as if it were a game. Indeed, in past times they had played such a game, tickling with water instead of fingers.

Gale's breasts were just beginning to bud. She caught him Peeking and spread her arms wide to let him see. Then she lifted her knees from the water and spread them to show her clean crevice. This time he blushed. He could have Asked and she would have Shown, but Peeking without Asking was a misdemeanor. At any rate, it did seem likely that she would be a woman within a year or so. He was not sure he would be a man in that time, though his fascination with her body suggested that he was farther toward it than his body showed. Curiosity was indeed becoming desire.

They rinsed out their clothing and hung it out in the sun to dry. This was summer, the warmest of the five seasons. Vivid, the bright sun, was larger at this time, so its light and heat were strong; the things would dry rapidly. Void, the dark sun, was farther away. That was just as well, because it wasn't just the weather that could get complicated when Void was near. The adults said that the dark sun would eventually consume the bright sun, but not immediately. The adults had some convoluted theories that didn't necessarily make much sense. The plain fact was that it was warm when Vivid was near, and weird when Void was near. That was quite apart from the fascinating phases of Mystery, Charm's colorful twin planet.

They squatted naked before the dragon. The tentacle formed. "I am improving," Havoc translated. "It will take time, but if I am not attacked by another predator, I should survive. I owe it to the two of you, and now I must try to return the value. But first we should complete the exchange of names."

"But you will need food," Gale said. "You can't hunt until you are well."

"This is true," the tentacle signaled. "I was not taking a sufficiently large assessment. I am not accustomed to being helpless."

"We can feed you," Havoc said. "We can bring you meat."

"This will be necessary. But it increases my obligation, for you will be preserving my life a second time."

"We share an oath of friendship," Havoc said and signaled. "This negates obligation."

"Technically it does," Mentor agreed. "But friends do not impose unduly. I see only one way to restore balance. I must save each of you from death."

"But we're not dying," Gale protested.

"That complicates it." The dragon paused. "I now have sufficient energy to use another mode of communication. Can you comprehend sonics?"

"Do you mean verbal speech?"

"No. This." Another appendage formed, and emitted a series of rattling whistles.

"No," they said together.

"Yes, I see that is true. No humans do. Yet tentacle signaling is slow."

"You can read our minds," Gale said. "Why don't we just think at you? That should be fast."

The tentacle wiggled. "I can perceive your most immediate thoughts and emotions, and those directed to me. They focus well when you speak. Others, such as your interest in each other's exposed bodies, are normally indistinct."

Gale laughed, with some embarrassment. "Havoc, you owe me one enormous Tickle! You have Peeked at everything."

"Yes. I have seen you before, and you have seen me, but doing it this way, in the presence of another sapient creature, makes it new."

"Makes it new," she agreed, looking closely at him. But the Peeking of girls at boys didn't really count, in the game, only their touching.

"It is always new," the tentacle signaled.

"We can speak our Name stories," Havoc suggested. "Today. Another day, when you are stronger, you can tell yours."

"Agreed. I will whistle when I have a comment."

So Gale told the story of how she was named. Havoc was familiar with it, but this time it was for Mentor. As she spoke, Havoc visualized it; he was good at picturing things internally. As it turned out, this helped the dragon get a better notion.

It started innocently. Just eight years old and not yet named, she was simply called Girl. Naming was a prelude to adult status, so was not normally rushed. Her father farmed and her mother sang, and her younger siblings were normally in the village nursery, so most days everyone was out of the house and Girl was left on her own. She could go to the day care house, of course, but she was one of the smaller children there, and too often got teased by the larger ones. They ridiculed her because she was too pretty. So she preferred to be by herself, and often instead of going to the other house she hid, waited for her parents to leave, then returned and remained home alone. She would sleep, or sing, imitating her mother, though her voice was but a tiny fraction of that. She would tap her fingers on a board, pretending that it was a fine hammer dulcimer, hearing the phenomenal melodies in her mind. Sometimes she would go outside in the fenced yard, and just lie there, listening to the sounds of the world. That too, was its own kind of music.

One day she spied a tiny yellow spider who was in trouble. It had been injured, and two of its seven legs dragged. She had learned by observation and experience that most wild creatures were friendly if approached the right way, so she tried to help it. She put down her hand before it, then her face. "A greeting." She pretended that it answered "Acknowledged." She thought friendly thoughts at it. "How can I help you?" she inquired softly.

The spider paused, perhaps afraid that she was about to squish it. But then a suckerbird flew by, sucking air and insects in through its tubular snout. It would later blow their dead husks out its exhaust. It spied the spider and swooped low.

Girl moved her hand to shield the spider. "No," she said firmly. "Not this one. I am befriending it."

The bird, balked, made an angry bloop and jetted on. Girl waited long enough to be sure it was gone, then peered under her hand. The spider was there, unmoving.

"I will help you, if you let me," she said. "If you don't bite me. Will you be my friend?"

The spider seemed doubtful, but made no hostile move. Several of its tiny eyes gazed up at her.

"Go on my hand, and I'll take you inside," Girl said. "It is safe in there. No suckerbirds." She put her hand down flat against the ground before it.

The spider hesitated, so she sang it an impromptu song:

> O li'l spider, come to me.
> We'll be friends, we'll be free.

She was pleased. The song rhymed and had a nice sentiment. She sang it again, putting more feeling into it.

The spider moved. It approached her hand, then pulled itself up into her palm. It had agreed to be her friend.

"I will call you Yellow," she said. "Because I can see you're from the Yellow Zone." Their village area was a mishmash of not much color, but in the distance there were colors in three directions. One was green, another was red, and the third was yellow. The colors seemed deepest farthest away, and Girl had always wanted to go see them up close, but nobody in the village went that far. Colors, they said, were dangerous. When they traveled to another village, they followed the road, which wound carefully between colors, touching none. Maybe that was why she was attracted to the spider: it was a pure yellow, suggesting that it came fresh from the yellow zone. That made it exotic.

It? Surely this was a girl spider, because it was friendly. Because *she* was friendly. A boy spider would have bitten her. Boys were like that.

Girl closed her fingers carefully, forming a warm enclosure, and scrambled to her feet. She carried the spider inside and set her on her bed. She rummaged for a box she could close, but then realized that Yellow might not like being confined so closely. So she found a larger, open box, and put the spider there. She set the box on its side, on the windowsill. "You can get out any time you want, Yellow," she said. "But it's safer inside. Here, I'll make you a nice little yard." She got little sticks and laid them in a pattern before the box. "But don't go beyond the yard, or someone will see you and send you to daycare. You wouldn't like that; too many big rough spiders to pick on you. Because of your pretty color."

But then she thought of a problem. Spiders ate flies, and there weren't many flies inside, and anyway, how would it catch them, with two of its legs hurt? So she fetched the net her mother used to catch bugs that strayed inside, and took it out back. She swooped it through the air a number of times, until she caught a fat nondescript fly. Then she twisted the net shut, trapping the fly, and brought it inside. She set the net over the box and mock yard and straightened it out so that the fly could drop down near the spider. But the fly didn't drop; it clung to the upper portion of the net. So she settled the net down until it was almost flat on the table.

Then the spider acted. She moved along with fair alacrity, and caught the fly. She trussed the fly up with yellow thread and dragged it into the box. Then she took a big bite from one of the fly's faceted eyes. Girl's effort was a success.

Well before her parents and siblings came home, Girl hid the box under her bed. "If they see you, Yellow, they'll kick you out," she explained. "You can go where you want to under the bed, but don't show yourself beyond it. Not while they're here." Yellow seemed to understand. She didn't come out.

This began a routine that lasted for some time. Every day Girl brought Yellow out for feeding and company, and every night she hid her under the bed. Yellow was indeed good company. She liked the flies, and had interesting ways of eating them. She also liked the warmth of Girl's hand, and would sit there comfortably, listing to Girl's little songs.

The two bashed legs fell off, but new ones grew in their places. They were short at first, but Yellow seemed to manage.

One day Girl put Yellow on her head. The paleness of the spider was close to that of Girl's hair, especially where it bleached from the sunlight, so she hardly showed. When Gale grew up, her hair darkened into brown, but at this age, with all her time in the sun, it was almost blond. That enabled Girl to walk around the yard without having to carefully carry Yellow. When she was out there, a stinging fly buzzed her—and Yellow threw up a loop of web and caught it. Yellow could feed herself, now, if she had access to the outside.

"I guess that means you're better," Girl said sadly. "You can go back to your home, if you want to." She lifted her hand, and Yellow climbed on it, and she put her hand down on the ground near the fence.

But Yellow didn't go. She stayed on Girl's hand. Girl was delighted. "You like it here!" she exclaimed. "You're my friend."

So it seemed. Yellow remained, and prospered. In fact she grew larger. As she grew, her color darkened and appetite increased. She could no longer sustain herself on the flies that happened to buzz Girl's head, so had to prowl the yard herself, routing out bugs wherever they hid. As time passed, that became insufficient, so Girl opened the back gate and let Yellow out when no one was around. The spider returned by nightfall, and hid under the bed again. She was now hardly yellow at all, but her name remained.

Girl wasn't sure what Yellow found to eat out there, for the spider was now quite large: as big as Girl's head. But it must have been enough, because Yellow continued to grow. She got to be as heavy as Girl, and of course was long since past the stage of living in the box. But she was still able to squeeze under the bed at dusk. Sometimes Girl would wake at night, and put her hand down, and Yellow would touch it with a furry leg. Their friendship endured.

Yellow grew huge. Now she weighed several times as much as Girl. But she was still able to flatten herself enough to squeeze under the bed. She would go out just before dawn, and return after dusk, understanding that no one else must see her.

Girl's folks had to make a trip of several days. "The children will remain at the nursery. You can stay at the daycare house," Mother said. "They have an extra bed."

"No!" Girl protested. "I'm fine right here! I'll stay here!"

Her parents were uncertain, but she convinced them that at age eight she was old enough to manage alone for a few nights. She knew where the food was, and she would be safe.

Still, her father was nervous. "There's been news of a strange man in the area," he said. "Don't let anyone in."

"I won't." Girl knew that strangers of any type were not to be trusted.

Her folks left on their trip. Girl, honoring her promise, went to the daycare house by day, hating it; the older children were as bad as ever. But at night she returned to the comfort of her house, and locked the front door, and quietly let Yellow in the back way. "They say there's a bad man around," she said to the spider. "But I know you wouldn't let him touch me." Yellow lifted a leg and touched Girl's shoulder, agreeing.

Just the same, she kept a faint night-light lamp lit. It was easy to imagine monsters when the darkness was too intense, despite Yellow's closeness.

All was well that night. But the following day Girl saw the man. He was big and unkempt, and his piggy eyes stared at her appraisingly. She didn't like that at all. She hurried home and locked the door tight.

Late at night she woke. Something was tugging her out of bed. It was Yellow. Girl opened her mouth to make an exclamation, for the

spider had never done this before. But Yellow stroked her face with
the fur of a leg, a signal for silence. So she was quiet. Yellow pushed
her to a curtain-closet, so she stood there and hid behind the curtain.
What was going on?

Yellow squeezed back under the bed, hiding too. Why was it so
important for Gale to be away from her bed?

Then she heard the sounds. There was a faint scratching at the
front door. After a moment it creaked open. Someone had gotten
another key!

The door closed. There was the sound of footsteps. The door to
her bedroom opened, and a figure loomed in the wan night-light illumination. It was the man! He went right to the bed, where the mussed
covers and shadows made it look as if someone were still there. He
reached down to grab—and of course found nothing.

He looked up. "So you heard me coming, you little honey," he
said. "Heard me using the skeleton key, and skipped out of bed. But
I'll bet you're here somewhere. You and me, we've got a date." He
licked his lips.

He looked around, then spotted the curtain closet. "Gotcha," he
murmured. He strode across and swept the curtain aside, exposing
her. "Yes, you're the prettiest little girl in the village. I'm a connois-
seur. You'll certainly do."

Girl was for a moment too terrified to scream. Then it was too
late; the man hauled her in to him, and clapped a rough hand over her
mouth. She tried to bite, but his finger dug cruelly into her cheek,
rendering her painfully silent. He half lifted, half threw her onto the
bed. He held her down with the one hand on her head, while his other
hand caught at her nightie. He exposed her kicking legs and jammed
his fingers in between them. "What a perfect little woman!"

Then Yellow loomed before him. The man was so busy he didn't
see, but Girl saw. Two hairy legs passed over his shoulders and caught
his head. Two more hooked around his arms. The spider's head
came in to bite him on the neck. The fangs dug in.

Now it was the man's turn to scream, but Yellow flung loops of
web around his head and drew his mouth shut, stifling him immediately. It was hardly necessary; the poison was already taking effect.
The man's grip on Girl's face and crotch slackened. He fell forward
onto the bed as Girl scrambled off it. Yellow trussed him with more
loops, making the capture secure.

Then the spider paused, turning several eyes on Girl. Girl knew
that they had come to a crisis. The man was bad. He had come not
for any innocent Tickle, but to hurt and maybe kill her. But the villagers pursued and attacked anything that killed a human being. They
would come after Yellow. The spider knew that.

"You're right," Girl said tearfully. "You've got to go. I saved your
life, you saved mine. We're even. Fair parting, Yellow, forever friend."

The spider hauled the man out of the house, dragging him by a line. Girl ran to open the back yard gate. Yellow hauled the man on out, then paused, turning back.

Girl hugged the huge head, her cheek nuzzling a mandible. "I love you, Yellow. Go! Don't come back. I'll cover for you. They won't know." She let go.

Yellow dragged the body into the night. Girl knew she would never see her friend again. Tears streamed down her face as she closed the gate, swept off the drag marks, and wiped up the stains on the floor of her bedroom. Then she got back into bed and tried to sleep.

She woke in the morning, her pillow sodden. She cleaned herself up and went to the day care house. She had to pretend nothing had happened, to give Yellow time enough to get completely clear. The men would not pursue her into the yellow zone.

But it wasn't that easy. "What was that noise last night?" the woman asked her. "A neighbor reported hearing something behind your house."

Caught unprepared, Girl didn't manage an instant look of innocence. She was glad that no one had managed to scream, because that would have brought the neighbor right over. "Just some wind," she said, and cursed the stupidity of it even as she spoke.

Suspicious, the woman sent a man to check. He found evidence of a prowler, and dragging marks beyond the yard, leading into the wilds on the yellow side. But the interior of the house was clean and undisturbed. What had happened?

"A wind?" the woman asked challengingly.

Girl was stuck with it. "A big wind. A—a gale. It blew around the house something awful, scaring me."

They knew she was lying, but couldn't figure out what had happened. So the matter expired, and there was no follow-up. But thereafter Girl had her name, by the consensus of her peers: Gale.

Havoc nodded. He knew the story, of course, for they had exchanged name histories before. His own name story connected.

Mentor's tentacle wiggled, and Havoc translated: "Such friendships are unusual. Not all spiders can be trusted."

"Yellow could," Gale said firmly.

"Not all dragons can be trusted," the dragon signed.

"Mentor can," Havoc said.

"Knowledge of this experience was in your mind when you befriended me."

Surprised, Havoc realized it was so. He had had a good example of the potential reward for helping a dangerous creature. The plants were not troublesome unless approached and antagonized, but animals could move and pursue. Yet he had also learned empathy for most living things. So the approach to Mentor had come naturally.

Now it was Havoc's turn. He oriented on the story of his own naming, visualizing the scenes as he spoke. Gale, knowing the story very well, was silent.

It started, really, with Gale. After the mysterious episode of the dragging marks, he became interested in the quiet girl, and after hesitating for some months, cultivated her acquaintance. He had no name; he was just Boy, like a number of others, lacking distinction until something happened to give them identity in the eyes of the community. She was nine; he was ten. He saw that she was not well treated by other children, being a reclusive child, but there was something about her that appealed to him. She was pretty, but it was more than that.

"Will you walk with me?" he asked her. He spoke somewhat formally, because he found this awkward, and he had never properly mastered informal speech. His time in the wilderness had been at the expense of camaraderie with his own kind. He had been teased, for a time, about his "adult" phrasing. His younger siblings, in contrast, all were quite social, despite being adoptees.

"To play Tickle?" she asked.

"Yes, if you want."

"No. Let me be."

Surprised, he reassessed the situation. "I wasn't trying to Peek at you. I just meant to talk."

"Boys don't talk to girls. They Peek."

There was considerable justice in her claim. "I'm sorry. I'll let you be." He turned away.

But then she changed her mind. "Just to talk?"

He turned back, venturing a colloquialism. "Honest."

"No Tickle?"

"I misunderstood. I thought you wanted to. I don't want to do anything you don't. I just thought—maybe we would like each other."

"So you do want to Peek."

"No!" But then he reconsidered. "You're pretty. I would like to Peek. But I wouldn't do that if you didn't want to. I just thought we might be friends." It sounded like a stupid notion, now that he had said it.

"Okay. I'll play Tickle."

He was taken aback. "But I didn't mean to do that."

"You told the truth."

"Yes, but—"

"I'll play."

This was perhaps his first lesson in the unpredictability of women. They walked to a private place, and she lay down and put her arms on her head, and he tickled her in the prescribed manner with one finger on the ribs. She laughed and kicked her legs high, giving him a phenomenal Peek under her skirt. She wore no underclothing.

"You didn't have to do that," he said. "I hardly touched you."

"You saw everything," she said.

That was an exaggeration, but he didn't challenge it. "Your turn." He lay down, arms on head.

She reached into his shorts and tickled his crotch. "Did you Peek there?"

"Yes," he agreed, trying to control his extreme ticklishness in that region.

"Did you like it?"

"Yes."

"The Peek, or the Tickle?" she asked cannily.

"Both," he said ruefully.

She withdrew her hand. "So we did it, and now you can go Tell."

"No. That's not—I mean, it's fun, but not what I came for."

She studied his face. "Did you really want to talk?"

"Yes."

"Why?"

"There's something about you I like. I don't know what." Again, it was inadequate. "More than your body, I mean. I think I like—you."

"May I kiss you?"

She had surprised him again. "Yes, if you wish." He kept his arms on his head, in the position of noninterference. This was actually a kind of Touch, within the rules of the game.

She lay against him and put her lips to his. Suddenly he felt the longing. They were children, but it felt like adult business. He kissed her back.

She broke, still lying against him. "You're not just teasing me?"

"No. I like being close to you."

"You don't mind my being different?"

"If my parents hadn't adopted the children of an exiled widow, I would be a singleton, and different too."

She thought for a moment, then came to a decision. "I will do whatever you want."

That was a considerable offer, but normally there was a consequence. "What would you want in return?"

"Nothing. I will take off all my clothes, if you want, and you can Touch me anywhere, if you want, and I won't Touch you, if you don't want, and you can Talk about it all you want."

That was as much of a concession as any girl ever gave any boy of any age. It established her sincerity. He brought his arms down, without trying to touch her in any private place. "Kiss me again."

She did, with special passion. He had responded with his sincerity, asking her for affection rather than voyeurism or free license or bragging rights. He embraced her, gently, tenderly. Then they just lay there and held each other, and talked for a long time. Gale confessed that she had been aware of him before, and been attracted to him, but was afraid of rejection or cruel teasing. Boys had led her on before, only to ridicule her when she responded. So she had been doubly wary. But when it seemed he was sincere, she had gambled and trusted him.

"Let's tell others only what doesn't matter," he suggested at last.

"What they think we do," she agreed. "Peeking, Touching, laughing."

"We must decide exactly how much to say we have seen or touched, so our stories match."

"Yes. But maybe not say we kissed." Because that implied too much of the truth.

After that they started keeping company, and of course other children teased them about it, but they shrugged it off. Boy showed her the special path he had made into the wildness. He had been alone a lot, from babyhood on; his folks had discovered that he fussed less when left outside, among the plants. He had become attuned to the sights and sounds and smells of the wilds, and liked them, and the wilds seemed to like him. As he learned human speech and ways, he also learned animal and plant ways, developing affinity. He could tell when a plant or creature was friendly, hostile, or neutral; there was an ambiance. He could even talk with some, by signs he learned by observation. He discovered that other children could not listen to creatures, or sign, nor did they care; the things of Charm were simply there to be used, eliminated, or ignored. That was the adult attitude, emulated by the children. But Gale was ready to learn, and with his guidance she started attuning too, though not as well as he. At least she understood enough to appreciate his attitude. In exchange, she showed him how to attune to music.

He showed her how to win the neutrality of a thistle bush, by bringing it manure. Thereafter they could crawl under it, brushing by its points, without being painfully pricked. But that did not hold for anyone else; the thistle eased its points only for those it appreciated. She taught him the musical scales. He showed her how some animals would come forth to exchange favors, when properly signed, such as a tasty nut from a high tree for a careful removal of a burr stuck in fur. What she had done with Yellow he had done with other creatures, to a similar degree. The key was the mind: the plants and animals could distinguish the mind of friend from foe. Gale was amazed, and appreciative. In turn, she showed him how playing even simple notes on a musical instrument could enhance a spoken story, adding effect. He came to appreciate the subtle wonders of melody.

They never played Tickle and Peek again, except in dialogue, pretending they still had wonders to explore. They addressed the matter of physical curiosity early, stripping together and opening each other's bodies for viewing and handling, in complete silence. They had no secrets from each other. They reveled in their mutual trust. But when others inquired, Boy would admit that he had seen a lot of her, during Tickling, and not just under her skirt, but not quite enough yet; while Gale confided that she had once felt something solid in his pants but wasn't sure what it was and he wouldn't tell her. Neither told the truth: that they simply talked and studied nature, after voluntarily fathoming all that they cared to in the personal physical sense. Or that they kissed a lot, and held hands, and stroked each other's hair. Or that when the urge returned, as it did on occasion, they explored each other's bodies again, without pretext or denial or reservation. The sharing of minds and feelings was more important. No one would have understood. Boys and girls were supposed to be competitively interested in each other, not sharing or caring.

But there was ill feeling in other children. They had learned to be wary of Boy, especially outdoors, and left him alone. Now they resented Gale, who had gone from a shy, frightened singleton girl of nine to a satisfied and increasingly competent companion of ten. The others realized that they could hurt both of them by hurting Gale alone. So one day when a boy got hold of a stink gourd, they sprang their trap. They ambushed Gale as she walked home alone from the farthest garden, right where the forest path passed a pool, too far from either garden or village to attract adult notice. There were six of them, ranging in age from thirteen to eight, and they had rehearsed their maneuver, so she was helpless. One to each extremity, one to her head, and the leader with the gourd. The leader had in the past tried to trick her into showing him her nice body, a prelude to more; he was halfway into manhood and was feeling the early passions. He had not appreciated her curt rejection.

They gagged her with a cloth so she couldn't scream, stripped her, held her down with arms and legs apart, and prepared to rape her with the gourd. The gourd had a slimy surface gel that adhered to whatever it touched, imparting an almost indelible stench that lasted for days. While the others immobilized her, gloating and Peeking avidly, the leader, holding the gourd with his gloved hand, tried to shove it into her. It would be a long time, if ever, before she got over that discomfort and humiliation, not mention the lingering smell.

But Boy, out along his path, was alerted by insects he had befriended. They buzzed horizontally and vertically, signing "girl" and "pool." He didn't know what was happening, only that it concerned Gale and that it was bad, for insects were not given to false alarms. So he took up a sponge he had tamed; it possessed a formidable defensive mechanism that it did not use against him. He ran for the place it had to be, where the path to her father's field passed a pool, where the commotion was happening.

Boy was eleven, no match in age or size for even one of the elder bullies in any ordinary combat, but he didn't hesitate. He came up behind the clustered boys, who were focusing with fascination on what they were trying to do to the struggling girl, and tossed the sponge into their midst.

The sponge, suddenly among a host of unfriendlies, emitted puffs of smoky pollen that formed a cloud around them all. It touched skin, where it itched intolerably; it smeared eyes, where it smarted so badly it brought temporary blindness; it was breathed into lungs, where it generated gut-wrenching paroxysms of coughing. In a moment the boys were in utter distress, screaming and running anywhere, crashing into each other and whatever else was in the way, heedless of anything other than the awful itching.

Boy fixed Gale's position in his mind, closed his eyes, held his breath, and dived down to catch hold of her. He dragged her out of that region, getting her clear of the settling cloud. He hauled her to the nearby pool and fell into it with her, washing the sponge itch off his skin and hers. Fortunately she had had the wit to hold her own breath and clamp her eyes shut the moment she saw the cloud form, knowing what it was. She had lain without moving, knowing that Boy would do what needed doing. She neither breathed nor opened her eyes until her head had been dunked under water. Then she ripped off the gag, popped her face up and gasped for breath. Boy did much the same. They thus escaped only lightly scathed. It was worth it, for they knew that it was much worse for the bullies.

After that, there were no further attacks on Gale, and Boy became known as Havoc, for the havoc he had caused. When the adults learned what had happened, they laughed, knowing that the bullies had been well served, but did not simply dismiss the matter. There was broad tolerance in sexual matters, for adults and for children, provided no coercion was involved, but this was attempted rape and humiliation, a serious violation of personal respect. The ringleader was branded with a V for Villain on his forehead and banished from the village, a pariah. The others had their hands forcibly rubbed with the stink gourd, and were required to strip naked and run the length of the village street, lined by all the female residents. Their physical secrets were thus forever exposed, making their humiliation complete.

"And that is the story of my naming," Havoc concluded.

"I have learned much about your species culture," Mentor signed. "When you come again, I will tell my story."

"We will bring food tomorrow," Havoc promised.

They followed the dancing path toward home. "How can we get meat?" Gale asked.

"I have an idea. That dead bear."

"But that belongs to the cycad tree."

"We can trade for it."

"But the only thing a plant wants is light and fertilizer and to be left alone."

"The bear will take a long time to melt down into fertilizer. We can give fresh fertilizer."

"Fresh—?" Then she burst out laughing. "What a deal!"

"You agree?"

"Sure. I said I'd do anything for you. I didn't have that in mind at the time, but I'll do it."

"I love you, Gale," he said sincerely.

"I loved you first, Havoc."

He smiled. "When we get to a safe place, I'll let you kiss me."

"I'd rather do it while making fertilizer. Serve you right."

Laughing, they came to the cycad. Havoc addressed it. O CYCAD, NEXT DAY WE WILL TRADE YOU FRESH FERTILIZER FOR SOME OF THE BEAR. He visualized the nature of the trade.

The cycad did not react. That meant it had no objection.

"Hold it overnight, if you can," Havoc said as they parted in the village.

"I'll try. This won't seem nearly so funny in the morning."

He nodded. It was not necessarily an easy course.

They met again in the morning. Havoc had not urinated, and was uncomfortably bloated. Gale was surely much the same.

But she smiled. "Want me to hug you tight, Havoc?"

"We'd both burst," he said, shuddering.

"I'd laugh, but I don't dare."

They made their way somewhat awkwardly to the cycad. There Havoc repeated his mental statement, complete with images of the acts. The cycad remained still.

They stepped within the radius of the great leaves, bared their bottoms, and urinated and defecated with gusto. Havoc realized passingly that this could be considered a type of Peeking that went beyond the normal boundaries; he wasn't sure whether anyone had ever seen a girl do that. But she saw him, too, so it was even. Not that it mattered. Then they went to the body of the bear, took out their knives, and cut two large chunks of meat from it. The cycad's leaves quivered, but Havoc intensified his picture of the gift they had just given it, and the leaves relaxed. A deal was a deal.

Soon they hefted their big slices of green meat and proceeded along the path. They had to hop and jump carefully, because the added weight made them ponderous and changed their balance. It was hard to hold and use the staffs properly, but they managed.

"Next time we bring bags," Gale gasped.

"Yes. Or knapsacks."

At last, tired and soaked with leaks of green blood, they reached the pool. Mentor lay there as before, but seemed somewhat improved; the blisters were further diminished.

Then Havoc had a belated thought. "You're blue," he thought. "This is green meat. Can you eat it?"

The tentacle wiggled. "Yes. Food is food. It will dilute my color, but that is inevitable, until I return to my home Chroma."

"Chroma?"

"I will explain that concept soon. Let me eat now."

They set the meat down before him. Mentor formed a stout maw on a thick stem. There were sharp thin flat teeth above, and a ribbed jaw below. It reached down to address one of the chunks. The teeth crunched through, leaving lines across the surface. Then they lifted and turned at right angles, and came down again, leaving more lines. Now there was a criss-cross pattern. The maw retreated, losing shape. Another lump formed, becoming a tube. The tube came down on the edge of the meat and sank into it. It lifted, and a section of meat came up. It had been cut into rectangles!

The section of meat was lifted to an opening that formed, and laid into it. It sank down out of sight, and the tube went for another section. The action was faster now, and the second section was set into the aperture, and others after it.

The tentacle formed. "You may prefer to wash in the pond while I take in this substance."

Oh. Yes. The two of them went to the water and stripped again. They washed off the green, and rinsed out their clothing.

Gale stood to peer over at the dragon. "He's not done yet," she said. She plumped her smooth bottom down onto Havoc's lap, just under the water. "Just think how much fun this would be if I were grown."

She was almost grown already, but he didn't argue the case. Her flesh had electric effect on his flesh. "You owe me a session just like this, when we are grown," he said, hugging her.

"But I may not be interested then," she said teasingly. "Grown women lose their interest in sex."

"Grown men don't. So you better promise to do it."

"And if I don't?"

"I'll tickle you right there." He touched her belly.

"I promise!" she said quickly, wriggling against him. Which was a fake, because that wasn't one of her ticklish places.

"I wonder if sex will be as much fun as we think it will be," he mused. He was already fairly sure of it.

"I don't know. I've Peeked on my folks, and it's pretty routine for them."

"Mine, too," he agreed. "It looked rather exciting to me, but they looked bored."

"We won't be like that."

"I hope we won't. But maybe they said that when they were young, too."

"Adults forget so much," she said sadly. "They lose track of what's fun."

They stood and left the water, drying off. Mentor had taken in all of one section of meat, and seemed satisfied. They settled down for his story of Naming. This was slow, because Havoc had to translate for Gale, but they found it fascinating.

"First," the dragon signed, "there are things I must clarify. One is the presence and nature of the Chroma zones, which I perceive you do not understand. I will rehearse my most recent session, as that should explain much. Open your minds as far as you can, and I will send meaning-messages that you will translate to make pictures. I think you will be able to see them if you continue to concentrate, as you are unusually receptive to the ambiance of this world. They will not be exactly what happened, because your minds will interpret them as images and concepts you can fathom. But they will be accurate in essence."

Human beings were not telepathic, but Havoc tried his best, holding Gale's hand. He turned his mind as blank and receptive as he could, opening it to whatever might come. He realized that the dragon had a strong mind, and they were very close, so that maybe they would be able to pick up some of it.

At first there was darkness. Then patches of light formed, and these drifted, and coalesced into a vague scene. There were shapes there, forming into a large circle.

"Ooo, silver dragons!" Gale breathed.

She was right. It was a circle of small silver dragons, all facing inward. And in the center was a single large blue dragon. That was Mentor, somehow recognizable apart from his color.

In a moment, that was confirmed. The blue dragon made sounds, glowed, and signaled with several tentacles. Havoc did not know these modes of communication, but in this vision he did; Mentor was addressing a class of youthful dragons.

"I am Mentor, from another Chroma," he communicated. "So named because I am a teacher. I am here to teach you the nature of the world, and of the great threat to it. I will set you on the path to survival. Hitherto you have believed that all of it is silver; now you know, by my presence, that some of it is blue. There are many colors, and all are similar in some respects and different in others. They are similar in that all have creatures and plants like those you know, including dragons. They are different in that each represents a different mechanism, or language, addressing the magic of the world."

The young silver dragons were surprised. So were Havoc and Gale, who were now becoming two of those dragons. What was this about magic? There was no such thing as magic; it was a joke concept to explain things whose natural explanations were too complicated for children to grasp.

"The source of the Chroma and magic is the deep well of the world itself," Mentor continued after the little dragons had settled down. "It comes to the surface in long pipes, and bursts out in a number of places around the world. Each species of magic has its typical color: white, gray, green, yellow, brown, black, red, silver, blue, purple, orange, translucent, and invisible. Perhaps there are other colors we do not perceive, or combinations. Around each major pipe a mound of substance forms, a cone, heavily imbued with the magic of its nature. We do not know whether the dust is magic, or the gas, or some other aspect, just that it is there. These mounds are known as volcanoes, and because their eruptions can be forceful, only a few creatures and plants are close to them. These have very strong magic—far more potent than anything we have seen. We could die if we approach such a cone carelessly, for our systems are adapted to function with only a certain amount of magic. That is why you have not been permitted near the silver cone; it is to protect you from harm."

The little dragons listened and understood. One of the mysteries of their lives had been resolved. This was true for Havoc and Gale too; they had been forbidden to go too far toward any of the colors. Because they were magic, and magic was dangerous. Whatever magic really was.

"The magic thins with distance from the cones," Mentor continued. "At a certain range, it becomes too little to be effective. This is less immediately dangerous. You could go beyond the Silver Chroma zone and survive. But you would be limited. You would not be able to perform some routine functions, such as generating fireballs to burn opponents, for such fire is magic."

There was a wave of astonishment throughout the class. Fire was magic?

"Clarification," Mentor said. "Fire itself is a basic process, and can occur anywhere that suitable conditions prevail. But fireballs are artificial, generated by a focus of magic. I will now demonstrate this. The center of this ring, where I am, is buttressed to nullify silver magic. Approach in single file and attempt to generate a fireball here. You will find it impossible."

Obediently but dubiously, the little dragons formed into a line and passed through the blue central section. Each tried to make a fireball, and discovered that nothing happened. Shaken, they returned to their places. Several fireballs appeared outside the ring, as they verified that their power remained operative there. Havoc and Gale were part of the line, but not alarmed, as they had never been able to generate fireballs anyway. They had not realized that this was an ability of dragons in their home zones. But the mental picture was not to be doubted.

"This, then, is the first lesson," Mentor continued after the pause. "You make use of magic in your routine lives, and it depends on your environment. Leave that environment, and you are reduced to certain basic purely physical processes. This is why you have not hitherto been allowed to depart the silver zone. Hereafter you will be allowed to go where you wish, having been warned of the consequences. You will have the freedom you have been craving, and with it the responsibility for your own welfare that is a natural part of that freedom. If you go abroad, and get in trouble, no one will come to your rescue. Half of you will die in the course of such explorations. The world has no sympathy for foolishness."

There was dismay in the class. This was indeed not the kind of freedom the little dragons had desired or anticipated.

"Should you proceed on into another Chroma," Mentor continued, "you would encounter the normal range of creatures, but of the color natural to that Chroma zone. Those dragons would be able to generate fireballs and do other normal feats of magic, but you would not. You would be at a critical disadvantage, and it could be lethal. You would have great difficulty hunting, and the defensive magic of the prey might harm you. Because you can use only the magic of your own Chroma, Silver—just as I can use only Blue magic." Mentor generated a blue fireball, surprising the class, whose members had supposed that no fire could be made there. Havoc and Gale were similarly surprised; they had not realized that the blue dragon could do that. "I could burn any or all of you, here. But beyond this blue circle, you could burn me. Color defines us all, and we forget this at our peril."

Mentor waited for that to settle in. "This is enough for you to assimilate at this time. Your assignment is to go out, during the next few days, to the thin fringe of silver, and ascertain the conditions there. Discover the extent to which your magic fades, and learn what does not fade. That last is your inherent ability. This is what will sustain you if you find yourself stranded outside your Chroma. You must be prepared to survive without your magic long enough to return to your zone. If you are not so prepared, you will live in unnecessary peril of continued existence. This is your ultimate lesson in survival."

Mentor paused, becoming receptive to reaction. It came immediately. "We will never leave our Chroma," a little dragon said. "So we will not need to prepare that way."

"Not so," Mentor replied. "For there is an enemy that may drive you from your Chroma. That is the subject of the second lesson. But first you must thoroughly learn the first lesson. The diminished number of you who attend the second class will be the apt or lucky ones."

The class ended. Mentor took the path that led across the Silver Chroma zone toward the Blue Chroma zone. He would restore himself in home territory, then return for the second class.

But as he approached the fringe of silver, something menaced him. Had he been in his native Chroma, he would have been aware of it much sooner, and avoided it with ease. But he was in an alien Chroma, dependent on his limited natural abilities. Before he took proper warning, he was in trouble.

It was not any dragon of silver, for mentors were tolerated and welcomed wherever they went. It was worse.

His only chance was to get the help of a native dragon, whose powers were complete. He sent out a mind signal. SILVER! BLUE MENTOR ATTACKED. NEED SUPPORT.

Immediately the nearest silver dragon responded. SUPPORT INCIPIENT. But it was not close by, and the threat was immediate.

ATTACK COMES TOO SOON, he signaled.

The silver dragon sent a mind map of a possible escape route. Mentor accepted it and turned to go to it. But the enemy intercepted him. Just before he reached the entrance, a fireball blasted him, burning his upper surface. He did not see it coming, so did not identify its color, but his impression was that it was not silver. This was an alien attack.

Then he was in the escape hole, following the passage underground. Another fireball came, but missed him and blasted the aperture behind him, collapsing it. He was safe for the moment, but would not be able to emerge the way he had entered.

He followed the route through the ground, his physical senses nullified by the blast. All he could do now was move as far and fast as possible, hoping to outdistance the pursuit and lose himself. He followed the passage for an interminable distance, surely enough to take him well beyond the silver Chroma. But the long haul was depleting his strength.

He succeeded in escaping, for there was no direct pursuit. But then he became aware of a blockage. The route ended, turning abruptly toward the surface. He had to return to the surface of the land, hoping that it was a safe haven until he recovered.

Tired, injured, and dying, he dragged himself to that surface and lay on the ground. There was vegetation here, and water nearby. He needed the water, but was afraid that he would fall in and drown if he tried to use it. This seemed to be a region of null magic, between Chroma. The enemy would not be able to follow him here, for the enemy's magic would not work. So he was safe, to a degree. Except that he needed help he was not likely to receive. As he had warned the class, those who foolishly got hurt out of their Chroma would pay for their own folly.

Then a creature came. *It was one of the enemy males!*

He could have retreated into the cave, hiding. But that would mean that he would die in darkness. He could have reached out and killed the enemy before it knew. But there was an ambiance of innocence in the creature, and it was not of full size. Not quite. It was a juvenile. Mentor did not like to harm juveniles of any species. The enemy could not truly hurt him, because he was dying anyway. So he did another foolish thing, and let it discover him.

"And so we met," Mentor concluded. "And now, ironically, I must teach you the secrets of survival that should be reserved for the young of my own kind."

"There is an underground passage to this spot?" Havoc asked, amazed.

"The exit is masked by trace magic," Mentor explained. "Illusion. Illusion, like mind reading, requires very little power, so is widespread."

Havoc's belief in magic remained limited. Yet the dragon had shown it in the vision. "Will you show us?"

Mentor formed a tentacle at his far side. It pointed to a moss covered rock.

That rock had been there all along; Havoc used it as a marker to orient on his hidden path. He went there and touched it with a finger.

His finger passed through it. It was as though the rock were made of mist, visible but not feelable. It was in fact a hole in the ground.

"So this is magic," he said, awed. "It was here all the time."

"This is a low magic region," Mentor reminded him. "It is between Chroma. Therefore you have little experience with magic, and do not recognize it when you encounter it. This is part of what I must teach you. The Silver dragons lacked experience without Silver magic; you lack it with all magic. But magic can harm you, so I must prepare you for it."

"You really are an enemy?" Gale asked. "I mean, you would have killed us, if we hadn't shared the oath?"

"I would have avoided you, because it is dangerous to kill human folk," Mentor signed. "But if I could not avoid you, I would have killed you. Your kind was pursuing me."

"What if our kind finds you here?"

"They will kill me."

"We can't let them do that," she said.

"The oath of friendship does complicate relations," Mentor agreed. "But I think they will not trace me here. This is a secluded region, and magic humans usually avoid null magic areas. In that respect, it is a good place for me to be."

"Good because we can help you survive," Havoc said.

"And I must now help you to survive. This may not be to your liking, at first."

"You said that," Havoc said. "But we don't understand."

"We'd rather live than die," Gale said.

"I must clarify. You are saving me from immediate threat of death. You face not an immediate, but a theoretical threat of death. If I recover, I will return to my Blue Chroma and be secure. I can not remain here indefinitely to protect you. Therefore I must enable you to protect yourselves, in whatever situations you find yourselves in the future. Only then can I be assured that my oath of friendship is complete."

"That's nice," Gale said. "But we aren't in any danger unless we do something stupid."

"That is not true. Your ignorance of magic makes you vulnerable, as does the jealousy of others in your community. I must teach you magic, and guide you in nonmagical defense. This will take time, and you will not like aspects."

"What won't we like?" Havoc asked, as curious as Gale was.

"I must direct you to learn skills whose practice will be tedious. I must cause you to go into regions that will be uncomfortable. There may be some pain."

Havoc knew the dragon was sincere; their sharing of minds satisfied him of that. But it was still difficult to understand why learning survival skills should be tedious or painful. "Can you give us an example?"

"Yes. Your greatest continuing threat is from your own kind. You must learn to defend yourselves from attack by other human beings, so that never again will boys be able to take hold of Gale and torment her, or to do anything similar with Havoc. But I can not teach you those skills, for my ways differ. You must go to your own village martial arts classes and become proficient."

"But all they do is threaten each other without striking," Havoc protested. "And throw each other to the ground."

"And it takes years to get good at that dull stuff," Gale added.

"Exactly. But without those skills, you will remain vulnerable. Elsewhere on the planet, humans are abusing humans, and you must be prepared to survive when attacked by your own kind. You must become proficient with and without external weapons. You must also know how to avoid attack. You must be able to disappear quickly, and be proof from a search for you. This means having the ability to mask yourselves among your own kind, as well as the ability you are already developing to go safely into the wildness others can not chance."

Havoc shared a glance with Gale. This was making sense.

"What about the magic?" Gale asked.

"I see from your minds that the ignorance is deliberate. Your village people have turned aside all inquiries, though they must know more than they tell. Do folk of other Chroma visit your village?"

"The ones with the colored hair and eyes?" she asked.

"No. The Chroma gradually imbue all residents. Lifelong dwellers like me become colored throughout. Temporary dwellers change first in peripheral ways. You have seen none with colored skin?"

"None. Only with colored hair and eyes."

"I mean single-colored: all red or all brown or other color, from skin to clothing, in contrast to the assorted shades of the two of you."

"No," Gale said. "Only animals, like my spider Yellow—and she didn't stay yellow."

"Because she was living out of her Chroma!" Havoc said, realizing. "She lost her magic color."

Mentor signed agreement. "Then your people are denying you that knowledge. I am not party to human conventions, and do not know why they wish you to be ignorant about magic. But your assured survival requires that you learn it. Therefore I will teach you, and you must conceal that knowledge from others of your kind, lest others become suspicious of how you acquired it."

This was considerably more interesting. "How can we learn magic, when there is so little here?" Havoc asked.

"You must go to the neighboring Chroma, where their languages of magic are in force, and learn it there. You will not be able to practice it directly, but you will observe it, and discover how to protect yourselves from it."

"But we're not supposed to go to any of those three colors," Gale said.

"This is a stricture you must violate. And because you must keep your growing knowledge secret, I must begin by teaching you to mask your minds."

"But no one knows another person's thoughts," Havoc said.

"I know your thoughts, and I am sure that many Chroma humans can know them also, when you enter their zones. Your mental security is as important as your physical security. You can not prevail against any opposing creature who knows your thoughts."

"You know my thoughts—even when I am not trying to open my mind to you?"

"To a degree. You assistance makes it much easier, but I would be able to read your most salient thoughts regardless, now that I know you. Were you to take a weapon and attack me, I would know your intention even as you devised it. The same should be true of a Chroma human—that is, one with a coloration of hair and skin."

Havoc nodded. He did not want to fight any one or any thing that could do that. "Teach us what we need to know."

"That will take time. But we will begin with the thought protection. When you can mask your thoughts from me, you will be able to mask them from any other creature. You must establish a pattern of interference. Think of music, or some other continuous sound."

"You know music?" Gale asked.

The tentacle wiggled in the sign for laughter. "We know music. In fact one or both of you should learn an instrument. I will give you a cast-off scale, which will serve as well as any made or adapted by humans. This will facilitate your disappearance."

"Music? Disappearance?" she asked blankly.

"You will understand, in due course. But at this time, try to make music in your mind. A strong, repetitive theme, that carries on without your urging."

They tried. After some experimentation, they found tunes that

Mentor said began to make interference. "You must intensify these and play them always in your minds. You must learn to hide your important thoughts below the interference. Only thoughts that can safely be public should be left above the tunes."

It seemed far-fetched, but again, the dragon was persuasive, and they could appreciate the importance of keeping their key thoughts private.

"Now I have something easier," Mentor continued. "I will give each of you a warning seed. These are magic, but their range is so limited that those who spy on magic will not be aware of them."

"Spy on magic?" Gale asked.

"Magic makes waves and leaves traces. I can tell when a magical being is in my vicinity, and when an act of strong magic is performed, regardless of its Chroma, if it is close by. Because you are nonmagical humans, you can not be traced by your magic. That is one of the limited advantages of your lack. But magic is so useful that this much you must have."

Mentor's surface flexed, and disgorged two tiny specks. "Each of you set one of these somewhere on your bodies, where they will not be seen or lost."

They took the seeds. After a moment, Havoc came up with a good place: in the fold of one of his ears. He set the seed there, and felt it lodge; it would not come loose.

"The seed will inform you when there is mischief," Mentor continued. "It will make a sensation when disturbed. Try to approach a dangerous plant."

Havoc reached toward a nearby sting vine. As his hand approached, there was a faint shock or buzz in his ear, not painful but startling. "It warned me!" he said.

"Yes. It will warn you when something is amiss. The signal usually means danger. It can not tell you what the danger is, but you can usually locate it by experimentation. It will also warn you when someone is deceiving you. One of you should try to deceive the other."

Havoc glanced past Gale. "There's a nettle bug climbing inside your skirt."

She glanced quickly down, then paused. "The seed buzzed me! Because he was lying."

"It will also alert you if there is some other problem," Mentor signed. "The seed is not sophisticated, and has only the one signal, but it is unlikely to be wrong. When you feel it, there is mischief of some sort. When you do not feel it, you may relax, in everything but thoughts. Those who read thoughts can sometimes do so from well beyond the seed's range."

They experimented, reaching for various plants and trying to trick each other. The seeds warned them every time. "But you must learn not to react," Mentor warned. "If others learn of the seeds, they will

try to take them away from you. You must receive warning, and verify
the nature of the threat, without giving any sign."

The children nodded. This, too, made sense. "This alone will go
far toward protecting us from danger," Havoc said.

"It will," Mentor agreed. "But it is only the beginning, only a tool
you must learn to use automatically, along with the mind protective
song. The value of such tools increases greatly when they are properly applied."

"This is great," Gale said. She came to hug Havoc, unable to
restrain her joy.

And the seeds buzzed. Both of them felt it.

They drew apart, confused. "You're a threat to me?" Havoc asked.

"You're lying to me?" Gale retorted.

"This is not the case," Mentor signed. "The two of you mean each
other no harm or deception. I am sure of this, from your minds."

"But our seeds buzzed," Havoc said.

"There must be some other wrongness," the dragon signed.
"Something neither of you is aware of."

"But what could it be?" Gale asked.

"I do not know. But the two of you should be able to fathom it in
due course. It may be something that represents a threat only when
you are together."

"Like our trying to do adult sex?" Gale asked.

"We weren't trying to do that," Havoc said. "We were just hugging."

"But we have it in mind to do, when we have a chance."

"I doubt that natural sex play is dangerous to you," Mentor signed.
"It is necessary experience for your future reproduction. There must
be some other reason."

They experimented, and found that the warning buzz came whenever they first touched each other after being more than a certain distance apart. Apparently there was something about each of them that
represented a problem for the other. It did not seem to be connected
to love or sex, for the seeds did not buzz when they kissed or touched
each other's sexual parts.

"Not all threats are serious," Mentor signed. "Possibly each seed
supposes that the seed of the other represents a complication. You
should do your best to ascertain the cause, but I think you need not
be immediately concerned."

"Maybe it's love," Gale said. "If one of us is hurt, the other will
suffer, so it's a liability."

"That is possible," Mentor agreed. "The seed does not understand sophisticated emotions."

"Could we have the wrong seeds?" Havoc asked. "I got hers and
she got mine, so they react?"

"No. The seeds are neutral, warning their associates, whoever they may be."

"So we could switch seeds, and it wouldn't matter," Gale said.

"True. But it will be best never to remove them, and to become unaware of them except when they warn you."

Havoc had a sudden notion. "Gale—I have no ring for you, for betrothal. But I have my dragon seed. I'll give it to you."

"And I'll give you mine," she agreed immediately. She dug into her ear and pried out the seed. He did the same.

"With this seed I thee betroth," Havoc said, setting his seed in the fold of her ear.

"With this seed I thee betroth," she echoed, setting her seed in his ear.

Then they kissed. Havoc's being overflowed with love for her, and in the ambiance of the dragon's mind, he felt her returning love. It was the most wonderful emotion he had experienced.

When they separated, Mentor's tentacle was wiggling. "I am satisfied not to have killed you, apart from the unexpected reprieve you bring me. Your emotion seems worthwhile."

They laughed, agreeing.

Chapter 2—Exam

The errand child was breathless as he ran into the village. "King's men!" he cried. "Coming soon!"

There was a flurry of activity. It was summer, and most of the folk were at work in the fields or communal buildings, but they reorganized rapidly for this emergency. The men charged in, the women sought their houses, and the children were released from their classes and shelters.

Havoc suspended his martial arts class. "You know what to do," he said tersely.

The students scattered, running to their homes to hide their key supplies. Havoc himself went into the central street, stood for a moment, then walked slowly toward the forest side of the village. Gale, nigh seventeen and lovely, fell in beside him, whistling a particular tune.

The nubile girls of the village, including some under 12 but pretty, ran to join them, forming a line. So did some of the younger and fairer wives. By the time Havoc reached the path leading into the forest, there was a train of a dozen appealing women.

Havoc stepped aside, and Gale took the lead. She stepped with exaggerated care so that the others could follow her precisely. Her route became tortuous, but the line of women matched her step for step, wending their way into the forest. They knew that this path was deliberately awkward and even dangerous for anyone who was not familiar with it, such as a marauding tax collector.

Then Havoc walked to a pile of dry sticks that lay near the path. There was always a pile there for him, so he could cover the exit of the precious girls when raiders came, without being obvious. He checked it carefully for encroaching stinger vines, then looped his own cord around it and began to haul it toward the village. It was heavy, and progress was slow; before he had gotten far, the king's men had arrived. Havoc stayed clear of them; strong young men could be in danger from such visitors too. He watched carefully, without gazing directly at the little party of villagers who went to meet the king's men. The Village Elder would be very polite and obliging—and slow, giving others the maximum possible time to prepare.

There were four in the visiting party, wearing the dull tan cloaks and boots of their ilk: tough men of indeterminate age. One carried a bow and quiver of arrows; another had an ironwood club; a third wore a short sword together with several sheathed knives; and the last carried a weighted net. Combat veterans, obviously; Havoc would have been able to tell just by the way they moved. Dangerous men, accustomed to having their way, as they had to be, to serve the king. Best to stay clear of them, though Havoc knew he could handle them if he had to. He had trained with and against all of those weapons, and knew their weaknesses as well as their strengths. Also, at almost age eighteen, he was at his physical prime, and could surely move and react more swiftly than those older men. But balking a king's man was a beating offense, and injuring one could mean imprisonment and slave service. So Havoc wanted no unnecessary trouble with them.

An errand child ran from the group down the street. "Havoc!" he called. "They want you."

Bad news! "By name?" he asked.

"Yes, by name."

"What for?"

"Didn't say."

Normally a slave recruiting mission didn't have names; they just collected bodies, male and female. So that might be a positive sign. But how had they gotten his name? He had been careful to do nothing to draw attention to himself in any way that might spread news beyond the village. Mentor had taught him that: the greatest safety was in anonymity. As far as the king was concerned, Havoc was just another village lout.

"Did they ask the name of the man hauling wood?"

"No. They already had your name."

So they had come seeking him. Very bad. But he could not slip away without being guilty of a balk. He would have to see what they wanted, and hope that it was only a message being delivered. But that hardly seemed likely, as a message should go first to the senior resident.

"Now," the boy said. "They said right now."

The king's men did not like to be kept waiting, and they could be brutal in their enforcement of even the most trivial preferences. Havoc let go of one end of his rope, drew the loop free of the wood, and wound the rope around his waist. He walked with the boy toward the waiting party. He saw that beyond it, at the edge of the village, was a closed coach marked with the king's insignia: a ten pointed crown. The same image was stitched onto the front of the cloaks of the four men. There was no question of their authenticity.

Havoc stopped a few steps from the king's party. "Greeting."

The net man took one step forward. "Honor to the king. I am Throe, king's servant." With typical arrogance, he was ignoring country manners.

"I am Havoc," Havoc responded, refusing to honor the hated distant monarch.

"Havoc, you are to report for immediate examination at the Capital City of Triumph."

Havoc did not have to pretend bafflement. "Examination?"

"That is the order. Please enter the coach. We will transport you there."

It would not be expedient to refuse, but neither did he want to let these ruffians take him away. He looked at the coach. "There is no hauling animal."

"We will move it," Throe said. "Please board." His left hand touched the net at his waist, and the three others assumed ready stances. This second request was definitely a warning.

"I have business here in Trifle. I can't go far away."

"You have no business before that of the king. Enter the coach." This time it was a direct order. The swordman and clubman lifted their weapons.

But Havoc knew it was a bluff. The dragon seed was not buzzing in his ear. If he really was supposed to go to the capital city, they would not risk injuring or killing him. The dangerous man was Throe, who looked entirely unprepared for action—but Havoc recognized him as an advanced martial artist. Such a man was most dangerous when seeming least so. His hands would be very fast and hard, and Havoc knew better than to tackle unknown competence unless he had to.

"If that is the way it must be," he said with resignation. He stepped toward the coach, passing between the swordman and clubman. The bowman opened the small coach door.

Havoc dived under the coach, rolled to the side, scrambled out beside a rear wheel, and launched himself toward the forest.

Throe was there already, blocking his way, his net flinging out. He hadn't been fooled. He had circled the coach while Havoc passed under it, and neatly intercepted him.

But Havoc knew about nets. They could envelop an unwary man or animal, but could be balked. His right hand reached out to catch the oncoming forward upper edge of the net, then hauled it down to join the other edge. He yanked it closed, and with almost the same motion flung it back at the king's man. He whirled to the side—and there was Throe again, blocking his escape. The man was good!

Meanwhile the swordman was coming around one side of the coach, and the clubman around the other. Havoc was boxed in.

He ducked down, then launched himself again, this time up onto the coach. With a few choice handholds and footholds he clambered to the top of it. Then, as the bowman on the far side gaped, Havoc leaped over his head, somersaulted, landed on his feet, and bounced onto the side of the road. In a moment he was into the forest, stepping where only he knew to do. The king's men could not follow; no one who was not familiar with the safe foot spots could. He was free.

He made his way to the manna tree where he knew the girls would be. Gale was there, with the others. "Havoc!" she said, not loudly. "What happened?"

"They want to take me to Triumph for an examination."

"But you might never return."

"Yes. So I declined to go."

"You will have to hide," she said. "And so will I." She did not have to say why: as his fiancée she could be punished in lieu of him, and that would surely begin with rape. The king's men always had an eye for the girls, and she was acknowledged as the loveliest in the village, and in the surrounding villages.

"Yes. I am sorry. But maybe they will give it up as a bad job. They must have others to collect."

"We had better wait here until they go," she said.

He nodded. "Have the girls fed the tree?"

She smiled. "Good point. You go elsewhere for half an hour, and I'll instruct them."

Havoc followed another path out. He understood why the girls would not want him there at this time. They were camped by a manna tree, and it was one of the special plants of Charm Planet. Long ago, he understood, people had cut down trees freely, but they had discovered that some sections of forest thereafter died out. In time they caught on that the key was the manna tree: kill it, and the entire neighborhood followed. Not immediately, but at the next climatic crisis. So they learned to leave those particular trees alone, because there were many useful and some essential plants around the manna. They did not know what made the manna a keystone species, just that it was.

The dragon Mentor had clarified that for Havoc and Gale. The climate of the planet was irregular, even after allowing for the differences in the five seasons. When Vivid was large in the sky, as everyone knew, the weather was generally warm and calm. But when Void was large, it was cold—except when Void flared. Then it suddenly could be hotter than summer, for a day or for several, and the weather could go crazy. There could be severe storms, or drought, followed by rapid freezing. The forest would not be able to take it, except for the manna. The manna was not exactly a tree, but a complex of several types of plant. One type heated the air around it, warming the forest when it was cold. Another type cooled the air, similarly alleviating the heat. Another type emitted chemicals that caused creatures to lose their taste for violence; in fact they were unable to kill or even fight. So when diverse creatures came, the predators did not attack the prey; they coexisted in temporary peace. That made this a safe haven, preserving all creatures who came to it. The manna itself produced food, extruding a cheesy substance from its trunk that could be eaten by almost any kind of creature. It wasn't very appealing, and few creatures, including humans, ever ate it voluntarily. But when they were clustered around the manna, escaping the extremes of weather, they could not hunt or forage, and would starve, except for the manna. When they got hungry enough, they ate it. As soon as conditions improved, they left, eagerly returning to the more palatable food elsewhere. Thus both plants and creatures owed their long term survival to the manna complex, but did not ordinarily depend on it.

When creatures came, and the manna formed, the tree needed sustenance of its own. So, as with the cycad, creatures normally made offerings of bodily refuse. Though in this case they were not fleeing the weather, they were using the shelter of the manna, so ought to contribute to its welfare. The elder girls, however, would not be eager to do this in the presence of a young man. They preferred to pretend that they had no natural functions other than sex appeal. So Havoc departed for a time.

He came to a glade, found a safe place, and lay on the ground. He wasn't tired, but wanted to work things out in his mind. Why had the king's men come for him, seeking him by name? Why had they wanted him so badly that they had sent a competent martial artist? He knew he would not have escaped, had they not been constrained not to hurt him. The bowman could have put an arrow in his back as he fled. Throe—there was a man who really knew his business. There were little ways of competence that could be recognized in retrospect. Havoc realized now that the man could have beaten him in a fair fight. It had not been fair; Havoc had taken risks to escape, and Throe had not risked Havoc's welfare to capture him. Even so, it had been close; had he not surprised the man with a dangerous maneuver, he would have been caught. So evidently this examination was important. The dragon seed had not buzzed when Throe spoke—but Throe had not given any reason for the examination. The absence of a lie did not necessarily mean that the truth was known.

Havoc lay on his back and stared up at Mystery, Charm's companion world. It looked huge in the sky; his fist, extended at arm's length, barely covered it. It was many colors, in irregular splotches—exactly the way Charm was supposed to look, could it but be seen from a similar distance. The pattern changed often, and sometimes it was possible to see a volcano erupting, spreading its color in a crude circle around its pinpoint cone. So Mystery was surely magic, like Charm. It turned slowly, its edges changing, and the curving line of light that crossed it vertically picked out new highlights and masked old ones. Mystery was usually dark in day, and bright at night, because Vivid illuminated them both and could do only one side at a time. This was mid afternoon, which made it mid-morning on Mystery, in its fashion; three quarters of it was light.

Were there human beings there? Was there another Havoc staring back at him and wondering what life was like on Charm? It was impossible to know. How could they travel there? Mystery was out of reach. Yet in the stories folk told by firelight, Mystery was populated with people, good, bad, and weird. Everything the human mind could imagine existed on Mystery, according to popular fancy. Havoc longed to know the truth, as did every living person, but no one knew it. Not even Mentor, who was just as curious. It was endlessly tantalizing.

Enough time had passed. No girl would be caught with her bottom bared, unless she delayed purposely after completing her business, in order to vamp him. Sometimes girls did that, knowing that even if inclined, he could not express any interest while in Gale's presence. In this manner, in the past year, he had been tacitly advised that should things ever not work out with Gale, there were willing alternatives. Sometimes the exposure was just teasing, and both parties would pretend to be embarrassed, having accomplished an informal Peek. He had discovered that there could be as much delight in being Peeked at as in Peeking, for both male and female. But the present situation was no game, and no one would be doing any teasing. Havoc got up and picked his way along the path back to the manna tree.

"Havoc!" Gale said. "Tiptoe came. You must go back." Tiptoe was an errand child, the only one who knew the path here besides Havoc and Gale.

"Are the king's men gone?"

"No! Havoc, they are beating your mother!"

"What?" For a moment he could not assimilate this.

"They have tied her naked to the whipping post, and are whipping her once every five minutes until you come."

"I'll kill them!" he swore.

Gale shook her head. "You can't. More king's men would come, and burn the village, and put every person into slave labor. You know that."

He did know that. He could not attack the king's men, even if they did not fight back, because his entire village would be hostage to his behavior. He had to go.

He kissed Gale. "I will take that examination, then return to marry you."

"Yes, of course." Her voice was carefully steady.

Yet more had to be said. "If I do not return, don't wait for me. Marry your best prospect." They both knew that those taken by the king's men seldom returned. They surely were not killed, because no one but nature killed a human being without reason, but they were usually not heard from again.

"Yes." But the tear in her eye gave her the lie. She loved him, as he loved her, and she was not prepared to be practical in this respect.

"Parting."

"Ak—" But she couldn't get the word out. Instead she kissed him again, suddenly and hard.

He released her, then turned quickly and moved along the path to the village as rapidly as possible. The errand boy followed. The girls would return to the village when word came that it was safe for them. They were not yet sure of that.

"Did the king's men say anything more?" Havoc asked as they traveled.

"No. Just that they were sorry this was necessary."

"Who was sorry?"

"The leader, with the net."

Throe. Highly trained and competent—and ruthless in the manner of all king's men. There were dreadful stories about villages that had resisted the tax collectors, and Havoc had no reason to doubt them. No one defied the king's men with impunity. But this was odd; Havoc had never heard of a king's man expressing any regret about what he did. Was it irony? Regardless, if Havoc ever had a chance to kill Throe without implicating his village, he would do it. Stripping and beating his innocent mother? That was a ploy Havoc had never anticipated.

They arrived at the village. There in the center was the awful sight: his mother, naked, bound with her hands high, welts on her back. She had not cried out, refusing to give the king's men that satisfaction, but she was hurting.

Havoc ran up to her. No one interfered with him; the king's men were letting him understand the nature of the alternative to his surrender. He brought out his small knife and cut her hands free, then wrapped his jacket about her. "Mother—"

"I know," she said. "Go, my darling, and return when you can."

"I want to—"

"You can't. Forgive them, Havoc. Not for them; for you." She kissed him on the chin, for he was substantially taller than she, and turned away.

Havoc faced his father. The man nodded grimly. Havoc knew that his father had been unable to prevent the atrocity the king's men performed, and that he did not blame Havoc. It was just the way it was. The king's men were one of the natural calamities of the planet. He should not have tried to escape; that had been foolish. He had been impetuous, and his family had suffered the consequence. He would be more careful next time.

His father handed him a knapsack. "Your things."

"Parting," Havoc said grimly. He donned the knapsack.

"Acknowledged."

He turned and walked to the waiting coach. The bowman opened the door, and he climbed in. There were two seats inside, facing each other, with room for two people to sit on each. Havoc sat on one.

Throe got in after him, and took the opposite seat. Havoc could tell from his posture that he was on guard; any effort to escape would be instantly countered. The bowman closed the door. The coach began to move.

"There are two ways we can travel," Throe said. "You can be bound and gagged and uncomfortable, with witnesses to your every act of assimilation or elimination, and without awareness of the route. Or you can be free of body and informed of mind, with privacy of functions. Choose now."

The man wanted him to give his word not to try to escape. He did not want to give it, but knew that if he did escape, the king's men would return to his village and make more people than his mother sorry for his intransigence. Unless he killed them all and hid the remains, so that the disappearance of the king's party would be a mystery. Except that those who had sent this party would make a thorough investigation, and if they drew on magic, the truth would be known. He suspected that he would never be given the chance to make a break, if he were bound; Throe obviously know what he was doing. But if he gave his word, he would not even try to escape.

He temporized. "How can you trust my word?"

"I can see that you have had training. You can see that I also have had it. Where is martial art without honor?"

"Nowhere," Havoc replied. "But I will not swear."

"If I do not deliver you to the examination on schedule, I will be punished. Part of my punishment will be the requirement that I punish your village in such a way as to make it unlikely that it ever again opposes the king's will. I do not wish to do that, but I will if so required. I would prefer that there be no question of your safe and timely delivery."

This was negotiation. Havoc was surprised that the man offered it, but was ready. "If you die before delivery, you will not have such a concern."

"But your village will. There will be no questions and no answers, merely obliteration. The villagers will survive, but they will be scattered across the planet in separate slavery. The site will be resettled by others."

"Even without proof of complicity?"

"*Especially* without proof. The king does not like mysteries."

"So if outlaws attacked the coach, and killed all of you, and I alone escaped, I would still have to report to the examination and tell all I know, to protect my village?"

"Yes. Only if your village were convincingly exonerated of complicity would it escape harsh measures."

It seemed tight. "Then it seems you do not need my word."

Throe smiled. "I would rather live than die, regardless of the fate of your village. I would rather relax than be on constant guard. You are too clever for comfort."

So he knew that Havoc's given word would be more binding than any physical bonds they could apply without hurting him. That there were ways around almost any constraint, if a person searched hard enough. Also, Havoc had the odd impression that Throe liked him, and wanted to get along with him. Just as Havoc found himself liking this man, despite what he had done. His mother had said to forgive. It seemed he would have to do that.

"I will trade my word."

Throe did not pretend any confusion; he knew what angered Havoc. "I apologize for what I did to your mother, and confess candidly that I do not necessarily like the way of the king. I did what I was required to do. She suffered five lashes. You may without consequence lash me similarly." He bent down and reached under the seat, bringing up a whip.

Such a statement was never rhetorical. Havoc could indeed lash the man five times, while the others watched, and suffer no retribution. The offer was as painful to make as the physical aspect would be, and sufficed as apology.

Havoc paused, then surrendered. "Accepted." That was it; by accepting the offer, he both waived the need for the physical part, and gave his word to make no effort to escape.

"We are about to enter a Red Chroma. We shall indulge our privacy first." Throe pushed open the door, and the coach stopped moving. He got out, and Havoc followed.

Now it was apparent that the three other men had been moving the coach. Two hauled on cords attached to the front, and the third pushed on a bar behind. It was well sprung, so that the bumps on the road had hardly been felt inside, and evidently moved well.

The four men walked into the brush in different directions. This was a dry region, with stunted vegetation that was easy to avoid; no special care was required to protect the feet. Havoc hesitated, then realized that his freedom was now complete; they were not watching him at all. He spied a small cycad with clear access, so walked to it and urinated at its base. He liked cycads, and did them favors when he conveniently could. Then he walked around it, paused out of sight of the coach, and resumed motion, returning. He was merely verifying that they trusted him.

"Do you prefer to haul or ride?" Throe inquired.

Surprised again, Havoc considered briefly. He had already ridden, but was accustomed to hard work. "To haul."

The swordman and the clubman climbed into the coach, while Throe and Havoc took their places at the front. The cords formed simple harnesses, so that the body rather than the arms did the pulling. They leaned forward and started walking. The coach moved with surprising ease; it was well oiled and balanced.

"You may find travel in a Chroma interesting," Throe said as they walked. "Are you familiar with the Chroma?"

Havoc had agreed not to escape, but that did not require him to be candid about other matters. He preferred to play the ignorant country boy—which he was, essentially. "In Trifle we don't know much about them, but I understand they are magic colors."

"Then let me give you a summary, so as to avoid confusion. The planet of Charm is entirely covered with volcanoes, each of which erupts its particular color, called Chroma. These are formally classified in ten variants, though actually there are more, and many shades and combinations. There are five types within each Chroma: air, earth, fire, water, and void, though the Black Chroma is itself a void. In short, a remarkable variety whose full extent may be known by no man. Each facilitates magic, which is operative only in its own color. That is, a person of Chroma Blue can not perform magic in Chroma Red. Is this clear so far?"

This paralleled what Mentor had taught Havoc and Gale, so was clearer than the man perhaps thought. But ignorance remained the best ploy, so he kept it simple. "I can't do magic at all. Will I be able to make magic in a Chroma?"

"A qualified no. You will not be able to perform magic directly, but you may be able to do it indirectly. That is, by using a magic object or invoking a spell. None of us natural folk are magical. That is why we have to move the coach by hand."

"But Chroma folk could move it magically?"

"Yes. And they will do so, soon. But they can do so only within their Chroma. Beyond it, they are as magically helpless as we are."

"As I said, I have no experience with magic," Havoc said. "But if it is what I think it is, it is a way to do things other than by hand. How can non-magical people control magical ones?"

"We can't, directly. But Chroma folk have villages too." Throe paused, letting the relevance sink in. Just as the king's men were getting Havoc's unwilling cooperation, they could get the cooperation of magical people. Because every person had a village, with siblings and parents and friends who could be hurt. So if they used magic to fight back, they could be made to pay.

"Still, if they have powers the king's men don't—"

"Man to man, they do. But on a planetary scale, they don't. Because the king's men can go anywhere, retaining what abilities they have, while Chroma folk are effectively limited to their territories. That mobility is part of it. There is more, but that should show the way of it. You may not have the strength of a large animal, yet you can control that creature by the use of your intelligence. The principle is similar."

Havoc began to see it. Many plants had abilities he lacked, yet he could handle them because he was mobile and smart. "What else about the Chroma?" He tried to make it sound as though his interest were moderate, but in fact he was fascinated; Mentor had not been able to give him the human perspective on this subject. Throe was emerging as a surprisingly informed person, rather than a king's thug.

"Though there is debate about whether the Chroma represent different types of magic, or merely different applications for similar magic, it is generally accepted that they do fall into a number of broad categories. The ten recognized Chroma are equivalent in power. One is White, which is otherwise known as Science."

"As what?"

"Science. It is that variety of magic concerned with sophisticated extensions of natural principles. It's hard to describe, but impressive when practiced by experienced Chroma Whites."

"Meaning I'll have to see it to believe it?"

"Yes. Another Chroma is Green, which relates to plants."

"But there are plants all around."

"True. But Chroma Green can do magic derived from plants, and affecting them, in ways that would not ordinarily be seen. Chroma Yellow is Fire. Again, there can be impressive effects; it is by no means as simple as making flame appear in air. Chroma Invisible is Air, which includes Illusion. You might think that a magic with no substance would have no value, but this is not the case; it can be extraordinarily useful."

Havoc remembered the way Mentor had pointed out the seeming rock by the pond, which had turned out to be illusory. That had been useful to conceal an underground tunnel. Mentor had not gone into detail, but now Havoc's curiosity returned. What other ways did illusion function?

"I know I'm slow about this," Havoc said, continuing to play the ignorant barbarian. "But I don't see how illusion can be useful. When a girl has the illusion she's beautiful, but she isn't, everyone else knows."

Throe smiled. "With Chroma Air, she would *be* beautiful. The illusion would clothe her face and form, making her beauty apparent to everyone. The most beautiful women of the planet are Air, when they choose to be."

That was an interesting qualification. "But the moment you touched her, you would know."

"Illusion can be of touch as well as sight."

"Oh." He was learning.

"There's something else about Air, but I will leave that to you to discover for yourself. I suspect you will find it amusing."

"Maybe." Havoc was not finding much about this forced trip amusing so far.

"Chroma Brown is Earth, with its special powers, such as conjuring and golems. Chroma Translucent is Water, with its liquid properties and its governance of rivers and lakes, as well as mind reading. Chroma Black is Void, including Death, but that is hardly the whole of it."

"It seems like enough."

"Chroma Red is Blood, or demonic, healing, ectoplasm—there

are bewildering and devious aspects, as there are, really, in all Chroma when you study them. Chroma Silver is Electrical, again difficult to describe properly, but very versatile. And Chroma Blue relates to Animals."

"You're right: this is a lot to learn." But Havoc understood a fair amount, thanks to Mentor's grounding. He was filing it away in his eidetic memory, so that it would be available at need; he didn't have to understand the whole of it at this time. It was clear that Throe was telling the truth, apart from the silence of the dragon seed, because it correlated with what Mentor had described, wherever it overlapped.

"Yes. It is general policy to keep the outlying villages ignorant about the full ramifications of magic. But I think you deserve to know at least the basics before you enter the examination."

The examination: that was another thing to learn more about. But first he wanted to get the rest of Chroma. "You said we are entering Chroma Red?"

"Yes, you can see the color starting." Indeed, the plants here were predominantly red, and so was the exposed dirt beneath them. Just as was the case at the village, where the land shaded into yellow, green, and red, depending on the direction. "We'll turn directly into it just ahead."

So that aspect would take care of itself, soon. "This examination—"

"That I can't tell you about, specifically. There are many examinations, for many people. Anyone who wants to work for the king has to take them, and they determine what position he gets."

"I don't want to work for the king!"

"Some don't. But some are required, nevertheless. I think the king tries to select workers from a wide variety of regions and situations."

"Suppose I report there, but refuse to take the test?"

"I would not advise that."

"Then suppose I take it, but do poorly?"

"I would not advise that either."

"Then suppose I do well, but decline the position to which it leads?"

Throe glanced at him. "Havoc, you do not tell the king no. His word is absolute. You have a choice only if he gives you a choice. Your experience with this collection mission should suggest the way of it. Your best course is to take the exam, do your best, and then do your best in whatever position it leads to. The higher positions offer certain significant privileges. For example, administrators above a certain level are entitled to choose their own mates. If there is a girl you wish to marry—"

Throe had not seen Gale, but evidently knew about her. "Point made."

They made the turn, proceeding directly into Chroma Red. The color intensified, and swirls of red haze appeared. *Chroma Red is Blood, or demonic, healing, ectoplasm—there are bewildering and devious aspects.* That was what Throe had said. Demonic? Could there really be demons? If so, were they the bits of haze? Havoc had not seen those before, but of course he had never before been this far into Red.

"One more thing," Throe murmured without looking at him. "Don't let a Red Spirit pass through your head, if you can avoid it; they can take your thoughts, or give you others. Don't be obvious, but keep your head clear."

Mentor had warned him similarly: that magic could sometimes read thoughts. In fact Mentor himself could read human minds. Many plants were also receptive to projected thoughts. Havoc had labored diligently to develop a thought shield or mask, and in due course had succeeded to the blue dragon's satisfaction. Now he started his mask song, playing it in his head so that it covered his mental secrets.

A red wisp floated toward Throe's head. Throe ducked, and it drifted past. Then it came toward Havoc. He moved his head out of the way, avoiding it. The thing did not seem to be able to maneuver well, so avoiding it was not hard to do.

"That's the thing," Throe said. "Usually they are just curious, but sometimes mischievous."

"What kind of mischief?"

"Such as triggering a paroxysm of nausea, an obscene vision, or planting a strong desire for sex with the nearest other male."

"Point made," Havoc said again.

Suddenly a red man appeared before them. He was completely red, including his skin, hair, and eye pupils, as well as all his clothing. "Welcome, king's coach," he said.

"Thanks, Redman," Throe said. "We shall appreciate your assistance in transporting us to the vicinity of Chroma Blue."

"Board your vehicle."

They let go of the harness cords, which drew elastically back into the coach, and went to the door. "Bowman, get on top," Throe said to the man behind. Then he and Havoc got inside, taking the two free seats.

Throe touched the side, and a panel slid back, revealing a window. He reached across to open another on the other side. Now they could see out.

Havoc looked out of his window. He saw the red trees with their red leaves, with red bugs in them. Everything was a shade of red, yet differentiated; Havoc was surprised by how clear the scenery was. It might be that the inhabitants of this region did not even notice the lack of color variety; monochrome was their natural habitat. There were even flowers with very pretty tints of red. Then those trees sank down, along with the ground. The coach was floating. It rose above the treetops, then sailed across the red land, gaining speed.

"Yes, this is magic," Throe said. "A fine way to travel."

Havoc was fascinated. This was flying—without wings! He felt no wrenching or gut twisting; it was as though the coach were floating on water, blown rapidly across the surface. He had never seen a pool of such size, though in the stories such bodies of water existed. Yet there was no water, just air.

Chroma Invisible is Air, which includes Illusion. Did that mean no flying? No, he could not be sure that flying through the air was not part of that magic. Certainly this was impressive. He would have been twice as amazed, had Throe not prepared him somewhat. He had thought that travel always had to be by foot or on a wagon. How little he had known.

He saw that the window was a transparent pane, in a frame that could be pushed out on a hinge to let in air. He opened it, and smelled the freshness. This region was red, but it was alive.

Peering down, he saw that the coach did not follow the contours of the land, but remained even. When the land dipped, the coach maintained its level. So there was not a somehow invisible giant supporting it as he ran along the ground. But neither was there any water filling in below. Somehow the magic supported it evenly throughout.

Then the coach slowed and descended. It came to rest near the edge of the red zone; Havoc saw blue in the distance ahead. So this was the transfer point.

They got out of the coach, and the bowman jumped down from the roof. "Thank you," Throe said to the red man. "We will move on now."

The red man nodded. "Parting," he said, and vanished.

"Where did he go?" Havoc asked, surprised. When the red man had appeared, he had assumed that he simply hadn't been watching as the man walked up, but this time there was no doubt: he had not walked away, but faded out.

"He conjured himself away," Throe explained. "After supervising our flight. We will have similar treatment in Chroma Blue. But we have to move ourselves there."

Havoc understood: the magic worked only within its color. That was its limit. But this seemed to be a broad expanse of red, much larger than the territory used by the village of Trifle. If all the people could fly like this, or conjure like this, they surely had easy lives.

Still, it was confusing. "I thought you said that the Brown Chroma was for conjuring," he said. "So how can a Red Chroma man do it?"

Throe smiled. "It does seem inconsistent. The answer is that though each Chroma has its specialties, all of them can do several basic types of useful magic. That is, specialists can; only those who train for it in Chroma Red can conjure, while every child in Chroma Brown can conjure, and do it better. So we have to be on guard against mind reading in every Chroma, though that is a specialty of the Water Chroma. Your best basic rule is to be ready for any kind of magic in any Chroma, just in case."

Havoc nodded. "And maybe he didn't conjure himself away, but simply used a bit of cheap illusion to make it seem that way."

Throe was surprised. "You're right. Illusion is cheap magic, much easier for any Chroma to manage. So it could be. However, the really fancy illusion is done in Chroma Invisible; you have a treat coming, when you see that."

"Isn't one kind of illusion much like another?"

"By no means. Not any more than one kind of woman is just like another. Some are common; some are royal."

Havoc dropped the subject, but the subject of illusion was coming to intrigue him more. He had, he gathered, seen the common kind; what would the royal kind be like?

They resumed their hauling of the coach. Now it was clear why the coach was here: it gave them a "boat" on which to float. Otherwise, it would have been easier just to walk.

The red faded, becoming purple. The plants became stunted, not able to flourish without consistent magic. Then the purple merged into pale blue, and this intensified into full blue. The chromatic effect returned, only now all the shades were blue rather than red.

A blue man appeared. "Welcome, king's coach."

"We are on our way to Triumph, Blueman," Throe said. "Please convey us to the rim of Chroma Brown."

"Are you in a hurry?"

Throe looked at him. "We have a schedule. Is there a problem?"

"The direct route passes over the volcano, and it shows hints of activity at the moment. We doubt that an eruption is imminent, but there could be awkward effects."

Throe considered. "Skirt the volcano, without passing directly over the cone. If there is any sign of eruption, move us out of the way."

"As you wish, king's man. Board your vessel."

They got on and in again, and the coach took off. Havoc saw no swirl of dust or leaves to indicate any down-draft of air; apparently it floated without disturbing the environment. It rose to treetop height, then continued gaining at a shallow angle, because the ground was rising. They were approaching the blue volcano. Havoc was glad they would pass close, because he had never seen such a cone up close, and might never have the opportunity again.

He poked his head out the window and looked ahead. There was an enormous blue bird flying, with a harness connecting it to the coach. This was the Chroma specializing in animals, so that made sense.

The volcano was magnificent. It was a massive blue mountain with a hole in the top, from which wisps of blue vapor rose. The thing was somber, but awesome in its semblance of power. It was not just that it could blow them out of the sky with just a bit of its blue breath. There was an aura of force about it, a shimmering of the air, as if a mighty furnace were close below.

The dragon seed in his ear buzzed.

Havoc glanced at Throe—and saw that the man's hair and brows had turned blue. So had his fingernails, and an aura of blue fire played about the tips of his fingers. The same was true of the swordman and bowman, and surely of Havoc himself. "I think we're too close to the volcano," he said.

Throe had been looking out the other window, evidently as intrigued as Havoc was with the mighty cone. He glanced at the three others and reacted immediately. "Blueman!" he snapped. "Move us away."

There was no immediate response. The men's hair lifted and spread out wherever the helmets allowed. Havoc's own spread out in a crown of spikes, tingling. He tried to stroke it back down with his hand, and a blue spark jumped.

"Now!" Throe shouted.

That evidently got someone's attention. The coach shifted direction, but not smoothly. There was a jerk, as of a harness snapping. Then it plunged. Havoc felt himself rising out of his seat, weightless. "I think someone dropped us," he said.

There was a scream from outside. That was surely the bowman, losing contact with the coach as it fell.

Havoc reacted instantly. He pushed the window farther open and jammed his head and arm out. He saw a flailing arm. He reached up and caught it as the man floated free of the coach. He hauled it in, getting a tight grip, suspecting what was coming.

It came: the coach abruptly ceased falling. Its float had been restored; the big bird must have looped back and caught it. But the bowman was no longer on it, and the flotation magic did not apply to him. His body plunged past the coach—and stopped, as Havoc's grip brought it short. The shock was considerable, but he had been braced for it. He hauled the man in, grappling him close to the coach, until the magic floated him too. Only then did Havoc relax.

"Put your arm in the window," he told the bowman. "Hold on until we land."

The man brought his other arm around and wedged it into the window as Havoc withdrew back inside the coach. Then he discovered what had prevented him from being yanked out of the window by the weight of the bowman's body: Throe had a bear-hug on his legs.

"Thought I was trying to escape?" he inquired.

"Thought you didn't want to suicide," Throe said, letting go.

Havoc had tried to anchor his legs inside the coach, but the whole window might well have torn out, pitching him after the bowman. Throe had made sure it didn't. "True."

The bowman, looking in, tried to flex his right arm, and winced. "I think you broke my arm," he said. "Thanks."

"This is not irony," Throe said. "You surely saved his life."

"And I don't even like him," Havoc said. For it had been the bowman who wielded the whip on Havoc's mother.

The bowman looked at him. "No one would have blamed you if you hadn't acted."

Havoc shrugged, not having a good retort.

But Throe did. "That was the arm that wielded the whip. Shall we call it even?"

Havoc hadn't thought of that. There was a certain fitness to it. "Yes."

"It's not even," the bowman said. "I would have died."

"Maybe the blue man's bird would have caught you before you hit the ground," Havoc said. He did not want this man's gratitude.

"I owe you anyway."

"With luck we'll never meet again, once I am delivered to the examination."

"But if we do, I owe you."

"As you wish." Havoc didn't care to argue the matter. He just wanted to be rid of it.

The coach drifted to the ground. The blue man appeared. "There was a flux that interfered with my control. I regret bobbling it for a moment."

"We were aware," Throe replied dryly.

They got out, and the bowman got in. His arm did not appear to be broken, but it had received a considerable wrench and was evidently painful.

"Here is a healing pad," the blue man said, presenting a blue cushion.

"Thanks." The bowman accepted it and put it against his shoulder. His pain-tight features relaxed. "That helps."

"It will not last long beyond Chroma Blue," the blue man warned. "If you wish to wait for a healer—"

"We have a schedule," Throe repeated.

Blueman nodded. "Parting."

"Acknowledged."

They took hold of the cords as the blue man went to his perched blue bird, climbed onto its back, and flew away. The two of them hauled from the front, and the clubman pushed from behind. The coach rolled forward along the trail.

Soon the blue became muddy. There was a section of what Havoc considered normal terrain; then it turned brown. They were entering Chroma Brown.

This time there was an enormous man: a giant golem, who picked up the coach and carefully carried it across the terrain. When it came to a sizable lake, it paused at the near shore, then suddenly was on the far shore. It had conjured them across. They had felt no jolt inside the coach.

Thereafter it became relatively routine. Each Chroma region had similar magic to make the coach move, but it could never go magically between Chroma. So the magic was varied, but also similar, in colored patches. The powers and limitations of Chroma were apparent.

Then they came again to Red.

"Did we get turned around?" Havoc asked.

"No. There are many volcanoes of each color. We are entering a second Chroma Red enclave."

Oh, of course. The volcanoes were scattered all across the globe, just as he could see they were on Planet Mystery. Two green volcanoes could be adjacent or far apart, or a small red area might be actually inside the circle of a large white one. So it should have been no surprise that they would have to pass through more than one red region when on a long journey.

As the day waned, they approached the capital city of Triumph. Here there were no volcanoes; it was a "natural" area. Havoc understood that it was the largest and most stable such region on the planet; that was why the capital had been set here. If a volcano ever manifested nearby, the capital would be moved.

This meant a long haul for the coach. But now they had help. They stopped at a station where horses were kept, and the six legged animals were hitched to the coach. They hauled it rapidly along an increasingly competent road toward the city. Havoc and Throe rode inside, while the others rode more of the animals.

Triumph was big. Outlying fields were huge, and there were a number of satellite villages. There were many loaded wagons being drawn by horses. The road divided, so that two lanes of traffic formed, one going, the other coming. Houses filled in along the sides, until the fields disappeared and there was nothing but houses.

"Welcome to the big city," Throe said. "We shall deliver you to the examination station, and then we shall see you no more. I wish to say that you have acquitted yourself with honor, and I hope that you do well in the examination. I am required to make a comprehensive report on the expedition, but it will not reflect adversely on you."

"You did what you had to do," Havoc said.

"Yes. And so will you."

"All I want to do is return to my village and marry the woman I love."

"That would be Gale."

Havoc was not easy with this. "You know of her?" For she had not been named before.

"I know what I need to ensure that I can deliver you on schedule. The king does not suffer excuses gladly."

So probably it would have been Gale they stripped and whipped, had they caught her, instead of Havoc's mother. "We are at truce, and I will not give you trouble. But I think I am free to speak. I realize you must obey the king's orders, but—"

"You are free to speak, but here there is no privacy."

Fair warning. "Others can hear us?"

"The king's servants can, if they wish. There is some private magic, enabled by special Chroma gems. They may also hear your unspoken thoughts; I am not certain what hidden magic there may be in this area. I mention this knowing that no man can stop himself from thinking, so I am not betraying my mission by advising you. Yet spoken thoughts affect others, and the king does not appreciate open rebuke."

This was more than fair warning: not only should Havoc keep his mouth shut about the king, he should not even think bad thoughts about him. So Throe had stopped him from possibly getting into unwitting trouble. And maybe he suspected that Havoc could mask his most private thoughts, and was warning him to do so. This could be construed as a significant favor. Why was the man rendering it?

The answer seemed clear enough: loss of a man during the mission would have reflected ill on the leader. Havoc had prevented the bowman from falling to his likely death. Throe appreciated that, so was tacitly returning a favor. Perhaps he was offering more.

As it happened, there was a favor Havoc wanted. "Do you also know what happens to a woman who loses her intended marriage partner?"

"All men and all women must marry before they turn eighteen," Throe said. "This is universal, by the king's decree. Should you not return to marry her before she turns eighteen, she will be required to marry another man, or be exiled from her village. But the requirement will the same wherever she goes. I understand that she is exceedingly comely."

Havoc ignored that understatement. "I am soon to turn eighteen. If I live, I will return to marry Gale. If I do not live, my wish would be that she be informed, so that she can orient on another good man before he is taken elsewhere. This could make a fair difference to her life."

"It is more likely that you will live, but be assigned elsewhere, and be unable to return to her. In any event, she will surely be informed."

That was evidently as much of a commitment as the man could afford to make. It would do.

Havoc looked out the window. They were now riding along a ridge, with the land falling away on either side. The city was rising higher yet, with structures as tall as trees. Beyond them, now visible because of the fall of the terrain, were broad fields whose crops he recognized, as they were similar to those of Trifle, but on a far grander scale.

"You may want to look ahead," Throe said. He touched the coach wall behind him, sliding aside another panel. Now there was a window overlooking the backs of the horses, with a view of the road they were traveling.

Havoc peered down it, and saw in the distance a pointing crag. "We're going to a mountain?"

"That is Triumph."

"Then what is this huge city around us?"

"The outlying service area. Triumph is the largest city on the planet, and its needs are formidable."

Havoc was frankly amazed. "You mean that all this is like a storage shed outside the village?"

"Even so."

"I really am a country boy," Havoc said. "Is there anything else I should know before we get there?"

"I think you already appreciate that though your village is in a non-Chroma region, and Triumph is in another, you will have trouble traveling between them afoot. It may be possible, but would surely take far more time than you can afford."

"So I will need help getting home."

"Yes. So it may be best to cooperate with the king's men, and satisfy them, so that they will facilitate your prompt return."

That seemed to be the case. "I will do so."

"Those who please the king are rewarded. The king is pleased by those who do well in the various examinations. I have no notion what kind of examination you will encounter, but the king seems to have gone to some trouble to bring you to it. This suggests it is not routine. I encourage you to treat it as the most important event of your life."

Again, Havoc had the feeling that there was more here than was obvious. The dragon seed was silent, so what Throe was saying was true, if perhaps exaggerated. But it hardly seemed to need saying, unless this really was the most important event of his life.

"Could this be like facing a dragon alone?"

"This is likely to be more of a challenge than that."

"Then maybe I should prepare myself by resting."

"You will have an hour before arrival, and another before delivery time. I will protect your repose."

"Thank you." Havoc relaxed, closed his eyes, and sank into sleep. It was an ability he had cultivated, for in the wilds sleep had to be taken where and when it was safe, and occasions could be limited. The discoveries of this day had been intellectually tiring.

He did not dream, for emergency sleep was too deep for that. It recharged him, restoring him physically and mentally. The trip itself had not been arduous, and the things he had learned now seemed interesting rather than baffling, with the exception of the reason for his summoning to the examination. He woke ready for whatever might come.

The coach was swaying with a different rhythm. He looked out, and saw water.

"I thought we were going to a mountain."

"Look ahead," Throe said.

There was the mountain, rising out of the lake: a monstrous triangle pointing into the sky. Its sides were smooth, of some polished metal. He had never seen anything like it.

"Where is the city? On the other side of the island mountain?"

"That is no island, or mountain. It is the city. It is a large hollow pyramid anchored to the floor of the lake so that it floats in one spot. Technically it is a tetrahedron, a four sided triangle, a very large houseboat or raft. Easier just to call it Triumph."

This was too much to assimilate, so Havoc just watched as the ferry boat moved onward. He saw horses on treadmills connected to huge circular paddles; these were what pushed the craft across the water.

They reached the sloping side of the metal mountain. A panel slid aside, and a ramp folded out. It splashed into the water and floated, its edges high enough to hold back the water. The ferry touched it, and men secured it by cables. Then the horses hauled the coach onto the ramp, and into the pyramid.

They followed a broad passage inside, and men drew the ramp up behind them and closed the panel. There were lamps set at intervals, so that it was not unduly dark. There were other passages intersecting. This was a huge complex.

They turned onto a side passage, and this one spiraled upward. The horses strained, drawing it up the steep slope. Havoc wasn't sure how high they went, but it did seem to be well above ordinary treetop level. Then they entered a broad avenue, and stopped.

"This is where we part company," Throe said. "Here is the door you must enter shortly. You must do so exactly when I tell you, and it will close after you. Thereafter you will be on your own. I suggest that you take nothing for granted, and trust no person completely. I do not know whether honor exists there. I wish you well."

"Appreciation." Havoc considered, then offered his hand. This was a mark of respect, an invitation to extend their acquaintance amicably, should they ever meet again.

Throe took it. So the feeling was mutual. They could likely have been enemies, but this seemed better.

"One other thing," Throe said. "I forgot that you don't know. All examinees enter naked. No clothing, weapons, tools. Your things will be returned to you after the exam, if you need them."

Havoc shrugged and stepped out of his tunic and sandals. He put them on the ledge provided. Then he removed the belt-cord that supported his knife and bag of bread and nuts. He was not hungry anyway.

"Face the door," Throe said, glancing at the band on his left wrist. "Step through—now."

Havoc pushed open the door and stepped through. "Parting," he said over his shoulder. It was dark inside, but light from the hall showed a passage leading on in. He walked down it, and the door closed behind him.

There was light ahead. He walked toward it, and the dragon seed did not buzz. He wondered whether it counted as clothing or weapon. It didn't matter; he had never removed it in the five years since Mentor had given it to him, and did not intend to now. It had become part of him.

He stepped out into a large chamber. Quick glances to left and right showed others emerging similarly, also naked. Judging from the curvature of the wall and the spacing of the entrances, there would be ten or twelve people entering. Now the reason for the exact timing was evident: they came together, so no one had an advantage. This must be a competitive examination.

The center of the chamber was open, with a number of islands of low counters. Each contained wares such as might be on display at a bazaar, attended by one man and one woman. The attendants were interesting: each was nonChroma, well formed without being outstanding, and wore skin-tight suits that concealed no significant aspect of their bodies. The suits were diagonally striped black, white, and gray, with the pattern continuing for their caps and slippers. The people did not move about; they merely waited in place.

Havoc approached the closet counter. "A greeting," he said politely.

"Appreciation," the two attendants said almost together. But they did not volunteer anything farther.

He looked at the wares. They were edged weapons: swords, knives, daggers, straight, curved, twisted, long, short, large, small—every variety. They looked competent.

"May I check a weapon?" Havoc asked.

"You may," the two said, again almost together.

Havoc made a show of examining the weapons, though he had assessed them the moment he first saw them. He was actually watching the people at the other nearby counters, trying to get some clue what was expected or permissible. Was this to be a combat arena? But the other counters did not seem to have weapons. Some had clothing, and the other contestants were evidently most interested in getting clothed first.

He picked up a knife. It had nice heft, and was clearly well made. One side of the blade was straight and sharp; the other side was serrated—and sharp. The hilt was curved to protect the hand that wielded it. This was a deadly blade, particularly for one who knew how to use it, as he did.

But he was not eager to advertise his competence with such a weapon. "May I take this knife?"

"You may," the two said.

"Is there a sheath for it?" he asked the woman. "A harness, so I can wear it without holding it?"

"Yes." She bent down to reach under the counter, her striped breasts accentuating. She brought out a belt and sheath and presented them to him.

"Thank you," he said, setting down the knife, taking the belt and sheath, and putting them on. Then he put the knife in.

"Will you answer a question?" he asked the woman.

She met his gaze. "Yes."

"What is the purpose of this setup?"

"This is an examination established by the king. I can say no more on that subject."

But he needed to know more, and the ready availability of deadly weapons made the matter potentially urgent. "What is your name?"

"I have no name, for this assignment. All of us in costume are interchangeable."

And therefore anonymous. He was not easy with that. "What is your purpose here?"

"My purpose is to serve the needs of any player who requires them."

That was too vague. He needed to know the limits of the service, and he did not want to waste time. "Suppose my need is sexual?"

She did not balk. "You may handle me and use me as you wish, provided you do not harm me. My costume is permeable."

The dragon seed did not buzz, indicating that this was true. He could use her, without objection or danger. In some other circumstance that might have been tempting. But Havoc knew that danger could come from seeming innocence. "I think my next need is for clothing. Where can I obtain it?" He already knew, but preferred to mask his ready observation.

"I will show you." She walked around the counter and led the way around the edge of the chamber.

He followed, noting the play of her striped buttocks. Interesting indeed. But any distraction could be dangerous.

She brought him to a counter bearing clothing. A woman was there, evidently another "player", for she was already wearing a green tunic. There were other tunics of many colors, with matching sandals and caps, but each was a single color, not striped. Havoc selected a blue outfit, remembering Mentor, the blue dragon. The woman from the knife counter helped him adjust it; her touch competent.

"I also need something to eat," he said to her. He was not yet hungry, but did not know how long this examination would endure, so was checking things early.

"I will show you." She walked again, bringing him to a counter stocked with breads, fruits, nuts, dried meats, and cheeses.

Havoc lifted a piece of cheese to his mouth. The dragon seed did not buzz. So the food was wholesome. But the mystery was growing. What was the point of all these gifts, and what was the nature of the examination?

Maybe some of the other players knew. He could tell from their mannerisms that they were not barbarian hicks like himself, but soft city folk. All of them were dressed now, but only a few were armed. Several had gathered around a nearby counter where beverages were served.

He could not figure this out on his own, and the striped servants would not tell. He would have to make the acquaintance of the other players and ascertain what they knew. So he walked across toward the beverage counter.

Then he paused, looking back. The woman from the blades counter was standing where he had left her, evidently unmotivated in the absence of any player directive. But she might still be useful. "Come here," he said.

She came to him and stopped, waiting for his next command. "What is the nature of these drinks?" he asked her.

"They are alcoholic. Beer, wine, mead, whiskey, liqueur—"

"Are there non alcoholic drinks?"

"Yes."

"Lead me to them."

She turned and showed him to another counter stocked with pitchers of water, milk, fruit juice, and vegetable juice, together with empty cups.

"Have some yourself."

She poured herself a cup of water and drank it.

"If I asked you to drink from the alcoholic counter, would you do so?"

"Yes."

"But I would not need to get you intoxicated to use you sexually, as you will do what I ask regardless."

"Yes."

He seemed to have learned about as much from this woman as was available. "Thank you. Return to your original station."

"Parting."

"Acknowledged."

She walked away, doing his bidding without question.

Havoc took a cup of blue fruit juice and sipped it carefully, watching the other players. They were already loosening up, with the help of the alcohol. One man was stroking the body of a striped woman, and she was facilitating rather than resisting. One woman was putting one jeweled bracelet after another on her wrists, trying to acquire as much seeming wealth as she could carry. Another man was gorging on sweetbreads.

Then something changed. Havoc noticed it because he was watching for anything suspicious. The counters were slowly descending. The striped servants were cleaning them off, putting their wares out of sight—and disappearing behind the counters themselves.

Havoc walked to a counter and looked behind it. It had closed up, wares, personnel and all, and was sliding into the floor. At the same time, other structures were rising from the floor. They seemed to be small steps or platforms. What was going on?

The dragon seed buzzed. There was danger.

The other players became aware of the changes. They looked around, as baffled as Havoc. The scene was changing, but what did it mean?

The last of the counters disappeared into the floor, and it became level and tight, with hardly a crack showing where counter-top now was floor. Some nice engineering there. The elevated platforms stabilized.

Then fluid slid across the floor, gushing from a vent across the chamber. It coursed toward the players, foaming. The dragon seed buzzed again, more insistently.

Havoc leaped for the nearest platform, landing on it just before the fluid got there. There was just room for his two feet. He caught his balance and watched the others.

They were scrambling for the other platforms, thoroughly alarmed. They were fortunate: each was able to reach a platform and get on it before being overtaken by the fluid. Except for the man groping the striped woman. He was too busy to notice.

The fluid caught up to the two of them, surging around their feet. The woman did not react, but the man suddenly screamed. "My feet! My feet are burning up!" Indeed, something like smoke was rising from them.

The man screamed again, shoving the woman away. She caught her balance and stood in place, no expression on her face. Her costume seemed to protect her from the fluid. But the man was clearly in terrible pain. He charged to the outer wall of the chamber, to one of the entry passages. But the fluid was there too, and rising.

It was acid, and it was dissolving flesh. The man's screams were continuous as he struggled to get free of it. But there was no escape; all the platforms were taken, and in any event he wasn't paying attention to them. He was just blindly running.

Until he stumbled and fell headlong into the liquid, which was now knee deep. His screams cut off as his face went under. He thrashed for a moment, then lay still as foam boiled up to engulf his body.

But Havoc was watching the striped woman, who was also trapped here. Would her skintight suit protect her completely from dissolution? If so, a key to survival would be to get the clothes of a servant. No; she merely threw herself down into the acid and disappeared in the rising foam. There was no smoke, and she did not even scream.

Then the acid started to subside. It flowed away, carrying the froth with it. The floor reappeared. More fluid gushed from another pipe, but this seemed to be mere water, washing the floor clean.

The platforms quivered and descended. Havoc and the others jumped off. The siege was over.

There had been ten players. Now there were nine. Now they understood the nature of the examination. It was for survival.

The counters rose out of the floor. They opened, and the striped servants emerged. They set out their free wares. They acted as if nothing had happened.

Havoc considered. He thought he saw the pattern: ten players, nine platforms, no help from the servants. Next time there would be eight platforms, and another person would get dissolved in acid. So it would be smart to stay near a platform, and to guard it from others.

But everyone would have the same idea, and there would be a fight for the last one. The free availability of weapons ensured that the fight would become deadly. What did it matter whether one person dissolved in acid or died in combat? The others would survive.

Havoc was fairly sure he knew how to fight better than any of the others. None of them had the martial artist's ways about them. Still, he was not sanguine about his prospects. The moment he showed his capacity, the others would know, and gang up on him. He might have to kill several to escape. But he did not want to do it. Human life was sacred, to be taken only for very special reason or dire necessity. Was there any other way?

He wasn't sure. The king had set up this terrible "examination" and surely had made it tight. It would proceed until a certain number of players had been eliminated. Those who remained would get good assignments, having demonstrated their fitness. Havoc objected to the criterion, but he was stuck with it.

Better to get an ally who might know more than he did. Then if that failed, he could still defend a platform. His greatest need at the moment was for information.

There might not be much time. He walked up to the closest other player, a man in a yellow tunic. "Greeting," he said.

"Get away from me!" the man snapped nervously, and the dragon seed buzzed. This was not a good prospect.

He approached another, a lovely young woman in a red tunic. "Greeting."

She frosted him with a glance. "Go after a striper," she said. "I am not for touching."

He tried another man, with no better success. These people were frightened and isolated, and did not care what he had in mind. There was no point in trying to persuade them; he needed someone with an open mind and reasonable perspective.

He approached an older woman. She looked to be about forty,

thin and wan in a gray tunic, and was somewhat reticent. She eyed him nervously, but held her ground.

"Greeting," he said formally.

"You're a barbarian!" But the dragon seed did not buzz.

"I am from a far village, yes. I do not know the ways of the big city. Or of magic."

"I am afraid of you."

"I mean you no harm. I need someone to tell me the ways of the city."

"What will it matter, if you die in acid?"

"I do not mean to die here."

"Exactly! You're a barbarian, good with weapons. I will be easy to dispatch, and you will survive. I just am surprised you are so open about it."

There was a certain logic to her fear. The dragon seed remained silent. This was not a perfect indicator, but it suggested that he could trust her. "I will not dispatch you, or hurt you. I want your help. How can I convince you?"

She considered. "You barbarians value your given word, don't you?"

"Yes."

"Then make me an oath of friendship. I will believe that."

That was a serious matter. But still the dragon seed did not buzz.

"I do not know you. I have made the oath of friendship only twice, and one of those I mean to marry."

"Precisely. I am nothing to you, and next time the acid flows, you can throw me in it. I don't trust any of the other players, and you least of all." She started edging away from him.

The dragon seed buzzed. There was evidently danger in letting this woman go.

"I'll make the oath!" Havoc said quickly.

She paused. "Maybe it doesn't count, when it's under duress."

"I would not give it under duress."

She emulated laughter. "Circumstances can be duress. This exam is duress."

She was right. He had oathed Mentor under duress, too: that of their dire mutual need to trust each other. This seemed similar. "Yes. I think I need your help, and you may need mine, if either of us is to survive this examination. Do you understand the significance of the oath?"

"Oh, yes, barbarian. I can cite historical examples. Give me your oath, and I will trust you absolutely."

"Then give me yours."

She smiled, briefly. "Don't test me, barbarian. Such oaths are not one sided. They are like love: they are mutual."

"Love isn't necessarily mutual."

"But friendship is."

She did know. He had to act, for the next surge of acid could come at any time. "Then we must know each other's names. I am Havoc, a man of Village Trifle."

"I am Ennui, a woman of Capital City Triumph."

"I am called a martial artist."

"I am called a clerical researcher."

"I proffer to you my Oath of Friendship."

"By this token, I accept it." She extended her right hand.

He reached out and took it, squeezing it briefly. "We are friends."

"Well, enchant me into a mouse," she said. "I didn't think you'd do it."

"We must get better acquainted," he said. "But I think we have little time. Say my name."

"Say mine." She must have researched barbarian ways.

"Ennui."

"Havoc."

"Now you need have no fear of me, Ennui."

She smiled. "Suddenly I am getting to like you, Havoc."

"First we must reserve two pedestals. Take this knife." He reached under his tunic to bring out the knife.

"I can't use one of this things," she protested. "I'm a clerk."

"Then hold it for me." He thrust the hilt into her hand, and ran toward the weapons counter to get another.

But he was already too late. The counters had closed up, the servants were gone, and the pedestals were rising.

He turned back. There were three pedestals close by. "Get on this one," Havoc said, pointing.

She obeyed. He stood between it and another.

A man ran toward the one Havoc wanted. "That one is mine," Havoc called.

"That's what you think," the man said, waving a sword.

Havoc turned to Ennui, lifting his hand. She understood, and threw the knife to him, underhanded. It turned end over end, but he caught it neatly and whirled back to face the man, who was almost to the pedestal.

"Get on that, and I will put this blade into your face," Havoc called, cocking his arm. This was a partial bluff, as this was not a throwing blade, but he could hurl it accurately enough if he had to.

The man hesitated, then dashed for the third pedestal, which was free. No one else was close. Havoc strode to his pedestal and stepped onto it.

The acid surged onto the floor. There was a commotion across the room as two men fought for a single pedestal; one shoved the other away and jumped on, but the other returned to tackle him and hurl him sliding into the acid. He screamed as the vapor puffed up around him, and then was silent.

Now there were eight, standing on their pedestals. Five men and three women. How many more would be eliminated before the examination was done?

As the acid cleared, Havoc jumped down and ran to the clothing counter. He swept up a green cloak and ran back to Ennui. "Take this," he said. "Next time, if someone comes at you with a weapon, throw it at his head."

"Good idea," she agreed. "This I can do." She stepped away from the vanished pedestal.

"Now we must talk. I am new here, and have no idea what this examination is for. Do you know?"

"No. But I can guess. Most of the supervisory positions are determined by competitive examinations. These can be verbal, written, or active. But I have never heard of one like this. People are not supposed to kill each other. The very idea is frightening."

"This was my impression. Could this be punishment for some crime?"

"I committed no crime. Did you?"

"I don't think so."

"So let's assume that it's not punishment, but an elimination for some position. What kind of position would require access to free clothing, food, sex, and weapons, and at the same time be deadly dangerous?"

"Leadership," he said.

"High leadership," she agreed. "I surmise the king needs someone for a special mission of great responsibility and danger and autonomy, that requires apt judgment and the ability to act ruthlessly on short notice."

Havoc nodded. "You have made sense of it for me."

"Have I? Then how does it explain *me*? I have the courage of a chicken, the muscle of a baby, and I may be about to faint from stress."

Judging from the way the others were reacting, they were hardly better qualified. Havoc had been assessing them peripherally, and could see that none of the men were either leaders or warriors. "Could the selection of candidates be random?"

Ennui smiled. "And that makes sense of it for me. Yes, that seems likely. Some functionary could have thrown darts at a listing of all the people of Charm, and sent out summonses for those ten, whoever they were. But this process hardly seems likely to produce the best person for an important mission."

"Maybe they don't know what's best."

"So they let chance and combat and luck decide it," she agreed. "Maybe it's a mission to a region that's largely unknown or repulsive, so regular criteria of leadership don't apply."

"This seems apt. I did not even know the king knew my name.

Suddenly this morning the king's men came for me. How did you get here?"

"I am a research clerk, as I said. I was hopelessly bored with my job, and at age forty, with my four children grown and my husband dead, I did not want to remarry and go through it all again, even without more children. I crave at least a little novelty in my dull life. So I petitioned for release from job and marriage, thinking I might be sent to teach history to distant barbarian children or something like that. I thought they were granting me a qualifying exam for such a position. Instead—I am here, in peril of my inadequate life."

The tables descended, and the pedestals rose. "Stand on this one," Havoc said. "I will guard you until you are safe."

"Thank you." She stepped on it and rode it to its level.

A man charged toward it. "Out of my way, bitch," he cried.

Havoc intercepted the man with a body check, sending him sprawling. But the man was still too close, so Havoc remained near. "Find another pedestal," he said. He saw that no one had tried to take the one he was saving for himself.

The man got to his feet, saw the acid sliding toward them, and lumbered for another pedestal, though it was occupied. Now Havoc leaped for his own. As he reached it, he saw the man charge at the one who already stood on it. The other whipped out a long knife, swung clumsily at him, lost his balance, and fell off the pedestal. The man below grabbed on to him as the acid arrived. The two rolled together into it, and screamed together as it foamed up around them. The pedestal remained unoccupied.

Six left. Would the next siege be a reprieve, with pedestals for all? Havoc didn't count on it.

As the acid receded, he jumped down and rejoined Ennui. "I've been thinking," she said. "The way that serving girl dived into the acid. She never screamed."

"She did disappear."

"It doesn't make much sense that they would kill so many, so randomly. Human beings are too valuable, and there's no justice in dying here. And what I know of acid—it shouldn't completely dissolve a body that fast."

Havoc remembered how some plants dissolved their kills. It took hours or days. "Yes. What does it mean?"

"It may mean that this carnage is more apparent than real. That the losers are losing, but not dying. That acid may hurt and foam, but not be lethal."

"Then we have less reason to fight through at any cost."

"Unless they want a winner who understands this, yet fights on anyway."

"It does seem better to win than to lose."

The lovely woman in red approached Havoc. "Reconsidering: a

greeting."

Havoc didn't need the buzz of the dragon seed in his ear to distrust this. "You are now for touching?"

"If you wish." She opened her tunic to reveal her fine breasts.
"But do it quickly, before the next surge of acid."

"I have already made a liaison."

"With a woman old enough to be your mother?" Her contempt
was evident.

"Yes."

She frowned. "What, then, is your price for assistance?"

"None. Go deal with another man."

She realized it was futile. "We do pay for our mistakes," she remarked as she turned away.

"You could have had her," Ennui said. "She's beautiful."

"You were not concerned?"

"We exchanged an oath. It wasn't for sex."

"It was for trust. She is not to be trusted."

"None of them are, in this situation. But a healthy young man
like you could have enjoyed her without trusting her. And what do the
two of us do, when one of us must lose?"

"I don't know." That did bother him. He was supposed to try his
utmost to win, but he had made an oath of friendship with her, and
would not break it.

"I think it will not be a problem."

He did not know what she meant by that, but had no time to
ponder, for the next siege was upon them. He guarded her on her
pedestal, and watched his own pedestal. Only five came up; the management had taken note of the extra elimination. Again, two men
fought over one pedestal; this time one prevailed. But the other
splashed through the acid and leaped for the pedestal occupied by the
woman in green. She screamed as he shoved her off, but could not
hold her place. Five survivors: Havoc, Ennui, the red woman, the
man with the sword, and one other man with blistered feet.

When the acid receded, Havoc tried another ploy. "If we cooperate, we may be able to break out of here," he called. "We can take
swords and cut open a door."

"You cooperate," one of the men said. "I'm sticking to my pedestal."

Havoc looked at the other. "You?"

"If we got out, where would we go? You don't beat an examination
by leaving it."

And the women would not be up to the effort. So it was useless.

"If you two men go after the barbarian, you can eliminate him,"
the woman in red said. "Then the woman in gray would be easy to
eliminate. That will save two of us."

"You bitch!" Ennui exclaimed.

"But she makes sense," man with the sword said. "Otherwise the barbarian is the likely winner."

"Yes." The other man ran limpingly for the weapons table and picked up a barbed spear. Then both turned on Havoc.

"I can take you both together," Havoc said warningly, showing his knife.

"With that little knife?" the swordman asked. "I think not."

"I would rather cooperate in escaping," Havoc said.

The swordman charged him from one side, and the spearman from the other. Ennui screamed.

Havoc leaped toward the spearman, ducked under the spear, caught the man by the elbow, and guided him into the path of the swordman. The two collided, their weapons flying out and clattering across the floor. Cursing, they struggled with each other, trying to extricate themselves. Havoc gave them no reprieve; he jumped to them and knocked each on the head with the hilt of his knife. They lay still.

"I knew you could do it," the woman in red said. "Now we are three."

The room was changing. Havoc went to his pedestal as the two women mounted theirs. By the time the two men recovered consciousness, the acid was upon them.

"That doesn't seem to leave you in a very good position," Ennui said.

"It eliminated two, either way."

"I wonder who is next."

The woman doffed her tunic and threw it in the acid. It bubbled into froth. "I wonder." She stood there in full nudity, perfectly formed.

"Who are you?" Havoc asked, interested in the view. "What brought you here?"

"My name is Futility, of this city. I am a dancer. But I got tired of catering to lustful males, and asked for the most challenging examination available. This one is somewhat more than I bargained on, but I'm giving it my best effort."

That was apparent. She had shown her complete lack of heart. In the stories troubadours told, such women were called ice maidens. They were inevitably highly desirable and dangerous.

"Your name may signal your fate," Ennui said.

"Perhaps." Futility caused her torso to ripple suggestively. She was good at body motions, unsurprisingly.

"I can't compete with that," Ennui said.

"You don't have to," Havoc said.

"And who are you?" Futility asked.

"I am Havoc of Village Trifle."

"I am Ennui, of Triumph."

"Let's rehearse the next siege," Futility said. She shook out her hair so that it fell in lustrous red hanks to her back. "When it comes, you, Ennui, will mount your pedestal. I will go to displace you there.

Havoc will come to stop me from doing that. Then his body and mine will be in close contact. Do you think he will throw me away? Or will he throw *you* away?"

"That will be for him to decide, won't it?" Ennui looked at Havoc as the acid receded. "You had better take her now, because there won't be time when the next siege commences. I'm sure she'll let you."

"Of course I will," Futility agreed.

Havoc remained wary, for more than one reason. "I have a fiancée."

"But she's not here, is she?" Futility asked rhetorically. "Either you will survive this examination or you won't. If you don't survive, whatever you do here becomes irrelevant, and you might as well get what you can. If you do survive, you can have a significant memory. I am not making any demand for commitment, merely offering you an inducement."

"She's making sense," Ennui said. "I have seen a good many women in my time, and she is the best formed. You can have her, then make your decision when the siege comes."

"She's just trying to make me desire her, so I won't bar her from a pedestal."

"Of course," Futility agreed. "Is it working?"

"Desire, yes. Pedestal, no."

"Then I suggest that you accede to the first, and see how you feel about the second thereafter. Possibly this examination requires two winners, so that the second case will become academic."

"No."

The floor cleared, and the pedestals descended. Futility walked toward him, with her dancer's grace and allure. The dragon seed buzzed.

"I have no use for you," Havoc said. "Stay away from me."

But she kept coming. "You must deal with me one way or another. I want a pedestal. You can give me that. You must accept me, or reject me."

"I reject you."

Now the servants, male and female, were back, and watching the proceedings.

"You must touch me."

"No."

"Then I will touch your friend." Futility whirled and ran toward Ennui.

Havoc launched himself after her. He caught her by the waist and lifted her away from Ennui. Futility was marvelously lithe. "Stay away from her." He knew that Ennui would be no physical match for this healthy, unscrupulous creature.

"I told you you would touch me," Futility said, rolling smoothly close. The dragon seed buzzed again. Oh, yes, she was dangerous.

He tried to push her away, but she slipped free of his grasp and pressed herself against him. Her breasts slid across his chest and her thighs nudged the nether folds of his tunic.

Then his hands got firm holds on her hips. He lifted her and flung her outward. She landed gracefully on her feet, turning in place, as if this had been a dancing maneuver. "But can you do that again, when the acid comes?" she asked over her shoulder.

"Yes." But she was making more an impression on him than he cared to admit.

"We shall see." She walked away.

Havoc went to Ennui. "Do not let her get close to you. She's strong and trained and without conscience."

"I can see that." She smiled. "I am glad we share that oath, though that will end soon enough. I know you will not act against my interest. That's why I tease you about her."

"You seem to understand the ways of women with men. Why don't you want to remarry? No woman is allowed to be single long, even after four children."

"I have been there and done that. I think I am, may be, possibly—" She looked down at the floor. "That woman—I think her body interests me as much as it does you, though in a different way."

Havoc's jaw dropped. "You like women? I thought that sort of thing was a myth."

"Like them? Not really. I know too much about them. But their bodies do appeal to me. In the sense that I envy them. Even in the flush of my youth, I was never like that woman."

"Oh. The way I envy a man who is better with a weapon than I am." Actually it had been a year since he had encountered any such, because he had made it a point to learn from the best.

She smiled, somewhat wanly. "That may be a good analogy. Obviously my equipment worked sufficiently well. But somehow I wish I could have dazzled men the way she can. I feel I have missed out on some good experience, and I don't care for any more of the indifferent experience."

"This is not something I am familiar with. But if you are suggesting that I sacrifice you in order to have Futility, I will not."

"Perhaps I was. But I want you to understand that I don't begrudge you what sexual opportunities you may have. I really am, in this respect, a friend. I don't want to participate, but neither do I object."

He lanced sidelong at her. "This hardly seems reason to throw your life away on a gamble like this examination."

"You are young and robust and bold, with plenty of future to look forward to. I am none of these things. I know that my attitude toward life and family is not socially acceptable. My name is not facetious; I never felt very excited about life, and I am weary of it now. Perhaps it is simply depression."

"Depression? What makes you sad?"

"Nothing. It is merely my nature."

"This is beyond my experience."

"Naturally. Depression is socially forbidden. It is not allowed to manifest in the outlying villages. Or, really, in the big cities. Not openly. But I am sure I am not the only one. I tell you this because I don't expect to live very much longer, or if I do, it won't be in your company. I want you to know my secret, just because—" She shrugged. "Just because."

"I will keep it," he said, shaken. It had never occurred to him that any person could be tired of life. "It does not affect our oath."

"Thank you. But when I lose my existence, at least you will know it is not a great loss. This brief experience with you has been perhaps the most interesting of my life, and I thank you for that."

The room began to change. The next siege was upon them. "Get to your pedestal," he said.

Ennui went. Futility strode toward it also. Havoc ran to intercept her. It was proceeding exactly as rehearsed, for there were only two pedestals rising. Someone had to be denied, and it had to be Futility. But he dreaded touching her again.

And he wondered: was she another secretly depressed woman? Her name suggested it, as did her presence here. If so, she was more like Ennui than she seemed.

Ennui stepped onto the pedestal. Futility charged her. Havoc plunged between them, catching the woman about the waist and whirling her around, so as to hurl her away.

But again she negated that. She was no martial artist, but she was physically proficient, and had moves that surprised him. She slid inside his grasp, turning under his hands. Suddenly she was up against him, inside his opening tunic, her smooth breasts pressing in, her mouth jammed against his, kissing him savagely.

He had to get rid of her. The acid was flowing toward them. But she was wrapped around him, her arms and legs embracing his torso under his tunic. Feelings cascaded through his awareness: she was infernally appealing, and sexually provocative, and he did desire her despite his loyalty to Gale and his knowledge that there was no sincerity in this seduction. He realized that she was not biting him, though that would have been easy to do; she was fully kissing him. Surely to distract him—but from what?

He staggered toward his pedestal as the acid washed toward his feet, carrying Futility. He was trying to pull her off him, but she was locked on. He could not get enough leverage to pull her off, and he had no time to waste. No time at all: he felt the acid touching his slippers, and felt the heat as they burned.

Then he had an idea. He stopped trying to get hold of Futility, and tickled her instead, right on the ribs under the armpits. Tickle without Peek. Caught by surprise, she screamed and released him, dropping to the floor. Smoke boiled up from her slippers.

"You turd!" she hissed, her hands going to her head. The dragon seed buzzed.

Havoc caught her right arm as it sprang out from her head. She had a stiletto. Now the precise nature of her treachery was revealed. She must have concealed it in her hair, saving it for her key opportunity. For a man distracted by her seeming passion, or perhaps actually engaged in sex with her. But for the dragon seed, that could have been him.

He twisted her arm, forcing her to turn in place and drop to the floor as he leaped to the pedestal. Had the tickle really stunned her, or was her reaction merely to provide a pretext for moving her hands to her head? Did it matter? The acid caught her hands and knees and splashed up against her body and face. She screamed again, this time in pain. She tried to get to her feet, but the acid seemed to have gotten into her eyes, disorienting her, and she staggered away from the pedestal. She fell, in deeper acid, and a cloud of vapor rose up around her. She thrashed desperately, splashing more before she fell flat. In moments she was gone.

Havoc stood on the pedestal, shaking. He had never actually killed a person before this day, and never fought a woman until this moment. The fact that she had been beautiful made it that much worse.

"You had to do it, Havoc," Ennui called. "She tried to stab you, so she could take your pedestal. Then she could have dispatched me readily enough during the next siege."

It was true. Futility had been much of what a man desired, but as dangerous as a poisonous spider. If she had won the contest that was this brutal examination, and gained the choice position awaiting the winner, what fate would have awaited others who had to work with her? It was best that she be eliminated.

But as the acid retreated, Havoc remembered that the examination was not yet over. Next time the choice would be between him and one with whom he shared an oath of friendship. He would not fight Ennui for that final pedestal.

"Now we are two," Ennui said sadly. "Soon to be one. I thank you, Havoc, for the brief friendship we have had; I think it is a fitting climax to an otherwise dull life. The finale is yours; I give it to you gladly."

"I can't just let you die," he protested.

"I ask of you just one favor," she continued inexorably. "Render me unconscious, so that I will not suffer the agony of the acid. Give me a kind demise."

"No!"

"This is beyond choice, Havoc. You are fit to live and thrive; I am not. We both know that. But I am weak in courage as well as in body. Please—take me in your arms, embrace me as if I am your mother, and press a nerve to stun me—I'm sure you know how—and lay me down neatly for the end. This is as lovely a death as I can imagine in the circumstance."

"I can't do that." He stepped toward her.

She shied away. "Then I must avoid you. Stay near the pedestal, Havoc, so that you can reach it in time. I will not go near it."

He knew she meant it. The striped servants had reappeared, with their counters. He ignored them and charged Ennui. She tried to avoid him, but her bodily agility was only a shadow of his. He caught her and held her close. "No."

She did not resist, physically. "Please, Havoc," she repeated. "I would have no use for victory, and my ineptitude might bring mischief to many. You must take it."

"Not this way." Yet what she said was true: there would be only one pedestal, and he surely had better use for the future than she did.

"You are being unreasonable, and that does not become a leader. Touch me or let me go. I am at your mercy in this respect, but I will not take that pedestal. This is one thing you can not make me do, I think."

There had to be another way. Havoc stood, still gently embracing her while the servants watched without reaction. He could neither sacrifice her nor give her victory. What else was there?

How different it had just been with Futility, when he had to cast her away. She had clung to him almost until the end. Ennui was asking him to put her down, and he couldn't.

The room started changing. The sieges were coming faster than before. He had to act—and there was no act he was willing to take. He could not accept the rules of this engagement.

Then suddenly it came to him: change the rules! Mentor had taught him that. Never passively accept a situation just because it was given; always look for the key change that makes it better. Sometimes the mere act of interpretation changed it entirely.

"Do not oppose me," he told Ennui as the acid slid across the floor toward them.

"Never," she agreed. "Act now, please." She closed her eyes.

He put his left arm down and caught her behind the knees. He picked her up and charged toward the lone pedestal. He stepped on it and caught his balance.

"Havoc—" Ennui said, surprised as her eyes popped open.

"I am taking you with me," he said. "Don't unbalance me, or we both will lose."

She stared at him. "Oh, barbarian, I hope you have not thrown yourself away. This can't be legitimate."

"This is both of us in victory. This rule was mine to make, and I made it. I will not let an oath friend go."

She shrugged, not protesting further. The acid surged around the pedestal, surrounding them. They were alone in that awful sea. "Oh, Havoc," Ennui murmured. "This, too, is marvelous experience."

The acid receded. The floor cleared. But this time the counters and servants did not come up. Instead a far door opened and a richly garbed man entered, carrying an ornate chest.

Havoc set Ennui down and checked for his knife. "Stay behind me," he murmured.

"Havoc, the exam is over. You have won. No one will attack you now."

She knew more of these things than he did. "Then what is the business of that man with the box?"

"I don't know what he's carrying, but that looks like the king's herald. I can tell by his uniform. He must have news of your assignment."

The herald came to stand before them. "Havoc of Trifle, you have passed the qualifying examination and have thereby won the position which it marks. I bring you the mark of your office. I may not touch it; you will have to take it yourself." He stood expectantly.

"What is it?" Havoc asked, mistrusting this though the dragon seed did not buzz.

"Havoc, just open the chest and take it," Ennui murmured. "It must be the emblem of your new assignment. The king's herald would not deceive you; he speaks for the king, publishing the king's will. This must be very important."

"I haven't accepted any new assignment. I just want to go home and marry Gale."

The herald stood unmoving, holding the chest.

"Havoc, you can't turn down the king's assignment. And maybe it doesn't conflict with your return home. Open the chest."

He knew her advice was good. He stepped forward and put his hands on the decorated lid of the chest. He lifted the simple latch, then raised the lid.

Inside was a massive gold crown with ten spikes, each a different color. The thing was beautiful and daunting, surely worth a fortune. Ennui made a little shriek of amazement.

He glanced at her. "What is this?"

"Havoc, that's the king's crown! There's no other artifact like it."

He realized it was true; he had seen that crown modeled on the uniforms of the king's men. "Then why isn't the king wearing it?"

"King Deal died yesterday morning," the herald said. "You are the new king. All power to you, King Havoc. If you please, take and wear your crown."

Havoc stepped back. "Is this a joke?"

"It can't be," Ennui said. "The king's herald speaks for the king. Havoc—*you are the new king!*" She seemed about to faint.

Havoc laughed. "It *is* a joke. I hate the king. Certainly I don't want to *be* the king."

The herald was unmoved. "King Havoc, if you please, take up your crown. You will need no other identification."

"Get out of here with that thing! If it's fake, I'm not laughing. If it's real, I'm not taking it."

"Havoc, you can't decline," Ennui said, sounding frightened. "They'll kill you."

"Let them try. I'm getting out of here." Havoc dodged around the herald and headed for the open door.

The door closed. The circular wall rose. Behind it stood an array of military archers, their bows drawn, aiming at Havoc.

He paused. One well aimed arrow he might dodge or block, or even two. But there were about fifty archers, completely circling him. If any missed, their arrows would fly across the room to strike those on the opposite side. But they wouldn't all miss. In fact, if they were competent—and they surely were—none would miss. Escape was hopeless.

"Havoc—King Havoc—please," Ennui said, in tears. "You must do this. Believe me."

He turned and walked slowly back to her. He took her in his arms, comforting her. "You I believe. You say I have no way out of this short of death?"

"No way," she agreed. "That's the king's law. Everyone knows that."

"Everyone but this barbarian," he said ruefully. "Stay with me, Ennui; I need you. I don't know anything about the king or this city."

"Anything you wish, of course, Sire."

"What?"

She seemed embarrassed. "Sire. That's what we call the king in person. Please, just take the crown, and I will tell you more in private. If you wish, Sire."

Reluctantly, he believed. He had won the crown of Charm. He would have to take it, and then find out how to get rid of it.

He faced the herald. He put his hands inside the chest and took hold of the crown. He lifted it out. And stood there, holding it.

"Put it on," Ennui whispered. "Please, Sire."

Havoc raised the crown over his head, lowered it, and set it on. It was heavy in his hands, but surprisingly light on his head, fitting snugly. It seemed to become part of him. There was an aura about it, and that aura extended through and around Havoc. He felt abruptly charged. That in turn made him nervous. This crown was distorting his judgment. "Is this magical?" he asked.

"Yes, Sire," she said. "It protects you from all threats."

"Then why is the former king dead?"

"Sire, I don't know."

Havoc turned to the herald. "I have put it on. Are you satisfied?"

"Yes, Sire. Do you wish me to die?"

"What?"

"Sire, these men and I threatened you. Our lives are forfeit at your will, unless you forgive us this necessary trespass."

The archers had lowered their bows. Now they kneeled on the floor, their heads bowed.

His mother had told him to forgive the king's men. It had paid him to do so. He looked at Ennui. She nodded.

"I forgive you," Havoc said curtly. "All of you. Now get the hell out of here. Except you, herald. What am I supposed to do next?"

"The king would normally be expected to repair to the royal suite at this time. However, Sire, neither I nor any other person would presume to tell you what to do at any time. We exist only to serve your will."

Havoc was feeling increasingly uncertain, despite the effect of the crown. This was too much of a change. Instead of fighting for his life, he was in command of the lives of others? He needed to be alone for a while, to get himself settled and decide where to go from here.

"Herald, you know I am new at this. I need time to organize. I don't even know where the royal suite is. Can you get me there without meeting any other people?"

"Certainly, Sire, if you authorize me to clear the way. You do not wish an honor guard?"

"I just want you and me and this woman to get there alone, as quickly as possible."

"Then, at your implied behest, Sire, I will clear the route and return shortly. If it pleases you to wait here—"

"Yes! Go do it."

Still the man hesitated. "It may be considered offensive to turn one's back on the king."

"Turn your back!"

The herald turned, still carrying the chest, and walked quickly out of the chamber.

Havoc turned to Ennui. "This is confusing me no end. Maybe you had better give the routine directives until we get there, so I don't look any stupider."

"Yes, of course, Sire." She was pale, and looked unsteady.

"Are you all right?"

"This—is too much change for me, too fast. I'm not used to it. I almost passed out before, but necessity kept me going. Now—I'm sorry, Hav—Sire." She collapsed.

He leaped to catch her before she hit the floor. He got his arms around and under her, and picked her up, as he had before. He had been looking to her for help, but now he would have to handle it himself.

He stood in the center of the room, holding the unconscious woman, waiting for the return of the herald. It did not seem like an auspicious beginning for the reign of King Havoc.

Chapter 3—King

The herald returned, without the chest that had held the crown. That reminded Havoc of the crown he wore; he could hardly feel it now, and wondered whether it remained properly in place. But he couldn't check, as long as he carried Ennui.

"Sire, the way is cleared. I will conduct you to the elevator, if you please."

Havoc did not know what the elevator would be, but didn't care to advertise his barbarian ignorance. He followed the herald out the door and across a hall which, sure enough, was empty.

They came to another door, which opened into a small room. They stepped inside, and the herald closed the door. There was no other exit, which made Herald nervous. But the dragon seed was not buzzing.

The herald took hold of the side of the doorway, and a panel slid across. "Lift to the king's suite," he said.

Suddenly the room creaked and began rising. Havoc looked desperately around, seeing an escape. But he was handicapped by the burden he carried, and he was not going to put the woman down. "What is this?" he demanded.

"Sire, this is the elevator. It is rising toward your suite at the apex of the city."

"I don't like this! Make it stop!"

"Of course, Sire." The herald put his mouth to a round dent in the wall. "Halt the lift."

In a moment the room rumbled to a stop. That was not much of an improvement, as the door retained closed, with a wall beyond it. There was no easy way out.

"I want to get out of this," Havoc said.

"Sire, to do that, we must move it up a floor, or down. Which is your preference?"

"I don't want it to move at all! I just want to get out."

"Sire, your wish is my command, always. But this is not feasible. We are between floors."

Ennui stirred. She was recovering. Havoc was enormously glad of that.

"Havoc, what's happening?" she asked as her eyes opened.

"You fainted. I'm carrying you. We are trapped in a box. I need your help."

"Trapped in a box?"

"The elevator, Lady," the herald clarified.

She laughed. "Havoc put me down. I think I'll be all right. I was overwhelmed, but I see you are human, and you do need me."

"Yes." He set her carefully on the floor.

"Havoc, this *is* an elevator; I recognize it now. It's a mode of vertical transport reserved for important officials. It's a chamber hanging in a shaft, on the end of a rope, and pulleys guide the rope to a counterweight and a crew of strong men to pull it up. It—" She broke off, seeing his bafflement. "You're right; we'd better get out of it, for now." She turned to the herald. "Lower it to the next floor down, and let us out there."

The herald spoke into his dent. "Lower to nearest floor."

The room began to drop. Havoc wanted to leap to safety, but Ennui put her hands on his arms and held on firmly. "Havoc—Sire— trust me. I am your oath friend, and will not betray you. This is necessary. And safe."

He stood, comforted by her certainty. He knew she could feel the nervous shaking of his body. She held him steady, calming him as a mother might a child. The room ground down to the floor they had left, and stopped. The herald drew the sliding door open. Ennui led Havoc out.

He stretched, breathing deeply, relieved to be free of the weird moving confinement. The dragon seed had never buzzed, but it reacted only to actual physical danger, or to a lie spoken to him, or to some treacherous situation. It did not care about his personal discomfort.

"We must use another way," Ennui told the herald. "A ramp or spiral or stairway will do, I think."

The man looked at Havoc. "Do what she says," Havoc said. "She speaks for me."

"Of course, Sire." The herald led the way down the hall.

They came to another door, but this one led to a curving path or ramp. Havoc put his head in the open center, and saw it spiraling down awesomely, and up similarly. It was like a mountain trail, where the peak got small and steep. He could handle this.

They started up. The spiral seemed endless. Havoc enjoyed the exercise, but soon Ennui slowed, breathing hard, her face flushed. "I am not strong," she gasped. "I'm sorry."

"I will carry you."

"Havoc—Sire, don't wear yourself out. I'm not worth it."

"I need you." He picked her up, as before, and forged on. This was even better exercise. "And don't call me 'Sire.' You're my friend."

"But in public—"

"The hell with the public. We made an oath."

She sighed. "Yes, Havoc."

They looped on up, passing floor after floor. "This city is tall," Havoc remarked.

"Would it help if I described it for you?"

"Yes."

"The city is in the form of a tetrahedron, with three triangular sides, and a triangular base. That is a very stable geometric shape. An enormous amount of prime wood went into its construction, and there are triangles throughout its walls, to keep them rigid. All are fitted into each other and bound together by strong cords. So Triumph is its namesake, a triumph of engineering. Most residents live across the base, on several broad floors, in small apartments. The officials live along the sloping upper walls, with transparent windows so they can see out. The higher the official, the higher and fancier the apartment. The king's suite is at the very top, in the cone. So it is a long climb to get there, but that hardly matters, because the ordinary citizen never goes there."

"Why the elevator?"

She laughed. "Havoc—the king and highest officials don't have gumption to climb all that distance every day! So they get hauled up and down by the pulley crew."

"Down? Why down?"

"What goes up must come down, Havoc."

"But they could jump down."

"Havoc, I hope you are joking. They'd be killed."

He realized that was true, considering the height they were rising. "They could slide down. Why isn't there a smooth slide?"

The herald glanced back at him. His face was blotchy; evidently he wasn't used to this kind of ascent either. "There is, Sire. But no one has used it in twenty years."

"Well, I'll use it. I don't care to waste energy, or to be hauled around by pulleys."

"Havoc, you'll still need to get up, and I suspect you won't have time to use this spiral ramp every day."

"Why not, if I have things to do below?"

"Well, you will do as you please, by definition. But I hope you will keep your mind open. There's an awful lot you have to learn about civilized ways."

The herald paused, clearly pained by more than the labor of the ascent. "Take warning, woman: No citizen speaks to the king as you are doing."

She was abashed. "That's true. Sire, I apologize. I am addressing you with disrespect."

Havoc realized that some definition was needed. "Ennui, you are my oath friend. That predates my promotion, and I value it more. I depend on you to teach me civilized ways, and to stop me from embarrassing myself. Speak to me as you wish, always." Then, to the herald: "When we get there, spread the word: this woman is my friend, and will not be rebuked by anyone else."

Now the herald was abashed. "Of course, Sire. I apologize for—"

"Your point was good. You know I need guidance. Now tell me: who should be the first person I talk to, when we get there?"

"Sire, it is customary for a new king to excuse all the personnel and staff of the prior king, and appoint his own. Therefore there will be no person among the king's associates whose tenure predates that of the king. The king's prior personnel are awaiting formal notice of their dismissal, which I can render at your direction."

Havoc looked at Ennui. "I don't have any people of my own. What do I do?"

She considered. "Well, you might hang on to the old ones, for now. I'm sure they are all competent, and most should be happy to keep their positions."

Havoc nodded. "Herald, tell them there will be no dismissals at this time. Now who should I talk to?"

"Sire, your chief of staff should be seen early, as he handles all your routine directives. But perhaps at the very beginning, considering your situation, you should see the majordomo."

"Yes, Havoc, that's a good idea," Ennui said. "The majordomo handles the household staff, and knows everything personal. He can really get you started."

"Good enough. Herald, I will see the majordomo first."

"Certainly, Sire." This time the herald seemed to approve. He paused at a dent in the wall and spoke: "By the king's design, all personnel are retained until further notice. Remain at your stations and continue your functions." Then he resumed the trek upward.

They were coming at last to the top. There were open intersections at every floor, but the top terminated at a closed door. The herald spoke into another round dent. "The king is here. Send the majordomo."

The door opened immediately. A well dressed middle aged man stood there. He bowed his head. "Sire."

"A greeting."

The man seemed momentarily flustered, then caught on to what he might feel was the quaint country style. "Acknowledged, Sire."

"Who are you?" Havoc asked, setting Ennui down.

"Sire, I am Majordomo, as commanded."

"Good enough." Havoc turned to the herald. "You're tired. Take a day off and rest. Two days, if you need them. Thank you for the service you have rendered."

The herald bowed his head, obviously more than glad for the chance to get home and off his feet. "Sire."

"Parting."

"Acknowledged, Sire." The herald backed away a few steps, bowed again, and departed.

Ennui looked as if she wanted to say something, but refrained. Havoc could guess why: he was making things awkward by using his conventions of politeness, but she did not want to correct him again in public.

Havoc turned back to the majordomo. "I am Havoc of Trifle. This is Ennui of Triumph. She is my friend, and will stay with me for now. Take us where we belong."

The man bowed again. "Sire, if you please, follow me." He turned and walked into the apartment. He had evidently gotten the word about not making an issue of the matter of turning his back on the king.

Havoc and Ennui followed. The spiral ramp had been without ornament or decoration, but the interior of this suite was lavishly appointed. There were thick rugs on the floor and large paintings on the walls, interspersed by mirrors. There were ornate sculptures on pedestals in alcoves. It was spacious, the hall and rooms huge by any standard Havoc had known.

They came to a large staircase, whose every step was a different color. "I thought we were already at the top," Havoc said, surprised.

"Sire, the king's residence comprises several floors," the majordomo said.

Oh. "Where are we going?"

"Sire, I thought you would wish to repair to the royal bedroom suite. There you may be attended by your personal body servants, whom you have so kindly retained, and receive bath, food, clothing, entertainment, and whatever else you desire."

"Bath?"

Ennui put a hand on his forearm. "Civilized folk take baths every day," she murmured.

Oh. "Of course," he said. "Set it up as you see fit."

The bedroom suite was every bit as luxurious as the rest of the residence. In addition, there was a line of uniformed men and women waiting beside the large door. All were young and healthy and of pleasing appearance. "Sire, this is your bedroom staff," the majordomo said. The line of servants bowed as one.

"Greeting," Havoc said.

The line straightened up. All faces were carefully neutral.

"I think they're not used to being greeted by the king," Ennui murmured. "They don't know how to react."

"Well neither do I."

"Maybe I can handle this," she said. Then she addressed the servants. "I am the king's friend, somewhat in lieu of his mother. Call me Ennui."

"Lady Ennui," they said together.

"King Havoc is a barbarian, unfamiliar with the ways of the city, but he wishes to learn without embarrassment. He will make what you might consider to be mistakes of protocol. When this happens, pause and raise your hand, like this." She raised her right hand, and they echoed the motion immediately. "When he looks at you, quietly explain the error, and the correct etiquette. Do not speak of it elsewhere. Follow this policy, and you will be likely to find him a more benign master than you have known before. Do you understand?"

"We understand," they said together.

Ennui smiled. "I wonder. When he greets you, smile and say 'Sire,' and stand ready to do his bidding. If he seems at any time perplexed, the person closest will look at him, inviting his query or command. If there is something he seems to be in need of knowing, the appropriate person will approach and invite his query. In short, you must go out to him, somewhat in the manner of a friend, anticipating his needs and accommodating them. If you hesitate because of likely awkwardness, come to me and explain, as you would to any other servant, and I will try to facilitate things."

She glanced at Havoc. He nodded, liking the way she was smoothing things for him. She was making it possible for him to continue his personal manners, while accepting their evident need to acknowledge with the word "Sire" at every turn. She was good at compromise.

She turned to the majordomo. "Is there anything else I should address?"

"Lady Ennui, there should be an early appointment with the chief of staff."

"Arrange it," Havoc said.

The man paused, lifting his right hand.

Havoc had violated a protocol? "What is it?"

"Sire, my word is law within these domestic demesnes, after yours, of course, and the Lady Ennui's. But it would be presumptuous for me to make an appointment for anyone outside this household, especially one of the status of the chief of staff. It might generate resentment, as I am merely a domestic functionary. It would be better if you made the appointment yourself."

"But I have no idea where he is or what he's doing. Suppose he's busy?"

"Sire, no one is busy when the king calls."

"Still—" Havoc looked helplessly at Ennui.

She smiled. "Bear in mind that King Havoc is not yet accustomed to the office, and still considers the convenience and feelings of others. How long will it take for the king to bathe, dress, and eat?"

"Ninety minutes would be a reasonable time, Lady."

"Then relay the king's directive for the chief of staff to appear in that time."

The majordomo smiled. "Of course, Lady." He looked at Havoc.

"May I be excused, Sire?"

"Get going," Havoc said. Then, as the man hesitated. "I mean, you are excused. Parting."

The majordomo smiled again. "Thank you, Sire."

Havoc put his arm around Ennui's shoulder, giving her a quick hug. "Thanks, friend. I think it's working." He paused. "Or am I messing up by touching you?"

"Maybe. They will think I'm your lover instead of your temporary mother. Do you want that?"

Havoc laughed. "Staff, this woman is my friend, not my lover. I don't have a lover here. Don't tell."

They laughed with him, albeit somewhat hesitantly.

"Now where's this bath I have to take?"

Three comely young women stepped forward. One caught his eye. She was quite pretty, with long and gently curly brown hair. "Greeting," he said.

"Sire, I am the Mistress of the Royal Bath. If you please, I will lead you to the bath and wash you."

"Wash me?"

"Yes, Sire."

"But you're a girl." She seemed to be about sixteen, and the other two perhaps a year younger, but very well formed.

She looked surprised. "I am a girl, of course, Sire."

Ennui interceded. "Where King Havoc comes from, men wash themselves."

The young woman looked crestfallen. "We are being released?"

"I think we have a clash of cultures here," Ennui said to Havoc. "You are not accustomed to getting naked with a woman other than a lover?"

"Right. That examination was bad enough, starting naked."

"Agreed. But these women are here to wash the king. That may be their only purpose. You will hurt them if you do not allow them to serve that function."

"Ennui, if I get naked with a pretty girl like her, I will really embarrass myself." He glanced at the group. The Assistants of the Royal Bath were about 15, both fair, with red hair, and yellow hair. Their participation would make it that much worse.

"Havoc, I understand. But if you don't, not only will you throw the bath staff into disgrace, you'll never get through in time to dress and eat and meet the chief of staff on time."

"Can't I just skip the bath?" he asked desperately.

"No." Her tone was firm.

"Why not?"

"Because you smell sweaty. That would be a significant violation of etiquette."

"Because of a smell?" he asked incredulously.

"Trust me, Havoc: yes. You must have that bath, today and on the following days. And I think these girls must give you those baths."

"But—"

"Havoc, remember I am your friend, and in this respect you really need a friend. Take the bath."

"I would rather fight three swordsmen with only a dagger. Blindfolded."

"I'm sure. Nevertheless–" She broke off, smiling. "Maybe that's it. Let's blindfold you, and let the three girls have at you. So whatever happens, it's not really you. Does that make barbarian sense?"

Actually it did. There was a village game, "Statue," wherein one person was blindfolded, and others were allowed to tease him for a set period of time. A boy might be subject to being Peeked and Touched by anonymous girls, who would lift his clothing out of the way or reach inside it, and he lost only if he balked or laughed or moved of his own volition. The girls took their turns as statues too, the genders alternating. Nothing significant was allowed, just viewing or light stroking, but titillation or sexual arousal was much of the point of it. When the time was done, and the blindfold removed, none of the sighted participants would identify themselves. So there was always the mystery, though when the group was small, it was obvious who they were. Regardless, the blindfolded person was deemed not to have participated, by the convention of the game; the statue was the object, not the player. Children could receive a good deal of anatomical education through such games, especially as they got older, and adults never interfered.

"You play Statue in the city, too," he said, realizing.

"Yes, when young. It's been some time, but I remember. I understand I blushed all over my body, the first time, but I didn't lose until someone tickled me under the butt with a feather. Will you do it? We don't have time to dither."

He knew it. "I will. If they know the game."

Ennui beckoned to the three girls. "Do you know the game of Statue?"

"Oh, yes," the mistress said. "We still play it, in our off time, when we catch a handsome boy."

"Play it with him."

"Lady, the king can view us or touch us at any time, in any way; we don't have to be statues. Anything thing he wants of us—"

"He is the statue."

The girl turned an appraising gaze on Havoc. "If the king wishes."

"He wishes," Ennui said firmly. "Do it now, and dress him the same way."

"But Lady, suppose he—"

"The bath is private, right? You do not speak of it elsewhere."

"Of course not, Lady."

"So there can be no embarrassment for the king, by definition."

The three girls nodded together, understanding what was required: no gossip. Then the Mistress of the Bath faced Havoc. "If you please, Sire, follow me." The girl led the way to another chamber.

Inside a small room paneled with ceramic tiles, the girls washed his face, then put a competent blindfold on him. In accordance with the game, no one spoke. They stripped him, moving his arms and legs for him, then guided him a few steps to the side. One of them dumped a bucket of lukewarm water over his shoulders. Then they spread soap on him and sponged him down. They covered every part of him, not ignoring the genital region, which of course reacted. He was highly aware that he was being viewed and handled by attractive young women, but there were no giggles. It became evident that they had seen this effect before, and were not bothered; their fingers and sponges cleaned it regardless. They were completely competent. He wondered what games the prior king might have played with these girls; their youth and beauty was suggestive.

Then they rinsed him, and dried him, and led him a few steps to another spot, where others doused him with perfume and dressed him. There seemed to be a good deal of clothing, ranging from stockings to jacket. Only his head was left alone, and he realized that was because he still wore the crown, which it seemed had not gotten in the way.

At last they led him out and removed the blindfold. They disappeared, having completed their business. He stood alone before a huge mirror.

He hardly recognized himself. He wore leather shoes set with sparkling gemstones, smooth stockings, puffy pantaloons, a ruffled shirt, and an iridescent jacket.

"I'm a clown!" he exclaimed.

"Sire, you are the king," Ennui said, coming up behind him. "This is the way the king is garbed."

"I hate it."

She smiled somewhat obliquely. "No one ever said you had to like it. Just ignore it, satisfied that no one will take you for a barbarian."

"I'd rather be a barbarian."

"And I think I would prefer you as a barbarian. But you are King Havoc. This is how you must appear in public. In private you can be as you choose."

"Until I get out of this disaster and go home."

"I have queried about that," she said. "You are required to serve at least a year, or perform so aptly that you are granted early release, before you can resign the office. If you quit before then, you will be executed for treason."

"But I need to go home and marry Gale before I turn eighteen!"

She shook her head. "You can't, Havoc. The king is not allowed to marry in the first year. They feel it might interfere with his mastery of the office."

"They have no right! I might as well die, if I can't marry Gale."

She put her hand on his arm, steadying him. "Havoc, listen to me. There are formidable constraints on you, but you also have formidable powers. You can summon your fiancée to join you here, and have her beside you by day and in your bed at night. You just can't *marry* her—for a year. Is that enough?"

That was far better than nothing. "That's enough, Ennui. How do I do it?"

"I suspect your chief of staff will do it for you, when you tell him to. But first you must eat, at least a token amount. You must conform to the royal conventions, to the extent you can stomach them."

He smiled. "Ennui, I think I am coming to love you. Do not leave my side."

"Except when you bathe and sleep," she said, smiling.

"Where next?"

"They have a token supper for you. This is not a formal dinner, understand, just something to feed you. Formal meals will be something else, and I'm sure you will find them a chore."

The majordomo appeared. "Supper is served, Sire."

They went to another room, downstairs in the residence. There in a dinette were two places set. "I thought it better that I join you, this time," Ennui said. "But you can of course have anyone for company, or no one; as you please."

"You are the one I want. I know I have a barbarian way of eating."

"I thought you might."

The meal was simple: some kind of meat he could not identify, two pancakes, and deep red wine. But when he sipped the wine— Ennui prevented him from gulping it—he discovered it was fruit juice. "I like it. But do kings really not drink wine?"

"Oh, I understand they drink to excess, and not just wine. But these first few days you have to be on your guard, lest your barbarian ways show too blatantly. I thought it better that you avoid all intoxicants. I advised Majordomo, and he agreed."

"Yes. I need all my wits about me. Being king is worse than fighting monsters."

"There are monsters here, Havoc. But they wear human faces."

"Then at least it will be a little bit familiar."

After he ate, another woman appeared and proceeded to clean his teeth. Havoc would hardly have sat still for this indignity if Ennui hadn't insisted. So far her judgment had been good, and her loyalty absolute, so he put himself in her hands, socially. He was increasingly glad he had encountered her; he would be truly lost without her.

Then he had to use the royal lavatory—and had to have help taking down his pantaloons, whose elaborate ties were beyond his reckoning. There was of course a handsome young man there to assist him, the Master of the Royal Toilet.

He was ready on time for the meeting with the chief of staff, thanks to the competence of the assorted staff. The man was known simply as Chief, after his position, as was the case with Majordomo. If such folk had private names, it didn't seem to matter. He was a tall, thin, intense man with black hair and penetrating eyes.

"Greeting," Havoc said.

"Sire," the man said, bowing. He glanced at Ennui. "Lady."

"Look Chief, I don't even know why I'm talking with you. I was told you were the one to see first."

"Sire, I appreciate the fact that you have retained me, though of course you may replace me at any time."

"I wouldn't know who else to get."

"I can recommend several competent people, Sire, if–"

"No. You must know what's going on. I don't."

"Sire, it is true I am conversant with the affairs of your predecessor. But his policies may not be yours."

"How can I have policies, when I don't know anything about anything?"

The man hesitated, evidently taken aback by Havoc's bluntness. "Let it be, Chief," Ennui said. "The king is sure you will serve to the best of your ability, and give him no reason to dismiss you. He expects your loyalty. Proceed as if your appointment is permanent."

Havoc was grateful; once again she had shown him the best route. He nodded.

Chief seemed similarly gratified. "It is surely not easy to assume such a role without notice, Sire. I gather that you are unfamiliar with concerns of the city."

"I'm a barbarian hick. About all I knew of the city before today was its name. And I didn't much like that. Triumph over what? The downtrodden villagers?"

Chief almost smiled. "It is true that power can be wielded imperiously at times. Nevertheless, Sire, the power of the office is now yours. You wear the Crown of Chroma."

Havoc reached up to touch the crown on his head. "That's another thing I don't understand. When I held it in my hands, it was heavy, but when I put in on my head, its became so light I forget it's there. It seems I'm even supposed to sleep in it."

Chief nodded. "Perhaps, Sire, I should begin by clarifying the nature of the crown."

"Do it."

"It protects you against hostile magic. It has ten spires, each of which is formed of potent stone from a particular Chroma. Thus you can travel anywhere, in any Chroma, with virtual impunity. You are without inherent magic, but the crown makes you the equivalent of any Chroma wizard, at least with respect to self protection. It fits your head, and seems light thereon, because its magic makes it so. It will not come off unless you remove it yourself; you can indeed sleep with it on, and not be concerned. So it is more than the obvious mark of your office; it is the guarantee of it."

"So I should wear it all the time?"

"Yes, Sire."

"Suppose someone knocks me on the head?"

"No one can, Sire. The magic protects your head and body from direct physical attack."

Havoc shrugged. "So I will wear it, for now."

"Sire, you must wear it always, for there are those who hate the king."

"And I'm one of them."

"Sire?"

Ennui interceded. "He means he doesn't want to be king. He did not know what the examination was for, and didn't want to accept the crown. He doesn't like any part of the office. But he understands that he must serve well at least a year, or until honorably released from this service."

Chief nodded. "Thank you, Lady. This is an unusual situation."

"But I prefer to defend myself," Havoc said. "I don't see how a pretty crown can do it better."

"Sire, it can. No attack against you can prevail while you wear the crown."

Havoc got interested. "Can you show me that?"

"Sire, I suppose a demonstration could be made, but that might not be wise."

"Why not?"

"Because this is a nonChroma area, deliberately. The stones of the crown have the magic of their separate Chroma, and it is highly effective, but when magic is invoked beyond its Chroma, it diminishes in time."

"I don't get it."

"It gets used up," Ennui said. Once again she had cut through to the essence, speaking in Havoc's terms.

"Yes," Chief agreed. "So it is best to save it for emergency use."

That did make sense. Still, Havoc doubted. "I want to see it happen. Attack me."

"Sire!" the man protested, appalled.

"No one attacks the king with impunity," Ennui murmured. "It would be treason."

Havoc considered. "Then let's reverse it. You wear the crown, Chief, and I'll attack you."

"Sire! I could not touch the crown."

Ennui had to step in again. "Chief, Havoc is a barbarian. He thinks in barbarian terms. He can be downright practical. You had better humor him."

"But the crown—"

"Do you obey me, or don't you?" Havoc demanded. He was beginning to get the hang of kingly authority; it was like a deadly weapon, whose mere threat had impact.

"Sire, I obey. But I must advise you that this is highly irregular."

Havoc put his hands to his head and lifted off the crown. He gave it to Chief. Chief held it for a moment, still hesitating, but acted when Havoc looked directly at him. He set the crown on his head. It fit perfectly, as its magic took hold.

Havoc brought out the knife he retained from the examination. He feinted at the man's face—but even the feint was blocked. There was no flash or other indication of magic; it was like sliding off a glassy barrier. He tried again, with similar result. There was definitely a deflective force.

He put away the knife and tried it with his bare hand. His striking fist bounced away, but if he moved it slowly, he could touch the man's head. That explained how the girls had been able to wash him. "But what about a slow strangle?" he asked.

"That would be possible," Chief said. "But if it were attempted by someone with hostile intent, the crown would burn him, or nullify him in some other manner. It has levels of magic I do not understand. In any event, the bodyguard would interfere."

"Bodyguard?"

"As you see, Sire, there could be devious ways to circumvent the protection of the crown. Since it is also best to use it only as a last resort, the bodyguard normally protects the king." He looked uncomfortable. "Sire, if you please, will you take back your crown now?"

Havoc smiled. "Yes."

Chief removed the crown and gave it to him. Havoc returned it to his head. He was now satisfied about its power. "So where is this bodyguard?"

"Sire, there is a problem there. The prior bodyguard was disgraced because he did not prevent King Deal from dying. There was no indication that he was at fault, but there must have been some lapse. So he was demoted to lowly duty while the investigation proceeds."

"I thought I told everyone to stay on."

"You did, Sire, but this occurred before your ascension to the office. So at present there is no bodyguard. This must of course be promptly remedied. Do you wish me to appoint one?"

"The bodyguard was not at fault, but was punished anyway?"

"Yes, Sire, on the assumption that there must have been some carelessness. Had there been any complicity, he would have been summarily executed. As it is, he is in limbo for the time being."

"Who was he?"

"Sire, his name was Throe. If I may say so, he was a good man, and I regret—"

"What was that name?"

"Throe, Sire. King Deal had the utmost faith in him, and I am sure—"

"Restore him."

"Sire, the investigation is not yet complete."

"Do you obey?" Havoc asked sharply.

"Barbarians don't much like to be balked," Ennui murmured.

"Sire, he shall be restored immediately. But I am obliged to say that I feel it is unwise for you to appoint a man to such a position without first knowing him. My argument was merely to indicate that he should not be executed."

"I know him."

"Sire?"

"He was the one assigned to fetch me from my barbarian village. He did that efficiently."

Chief relaxed. "Sire, I did not realize. I do not handle lowly assignments. The process of assembling and examining candidates for king is handled by a special committee that answers to no ordinary authority. Did he treat you well?"

"When I tried to hide, he had my mother stripped and publicly flogged, until I surrendered."

"Then perhaps you will prefer to have him summarily executed after all. He was acting in accordance with established protocol for hostile situations, but your annoyance is understandable. You need justify such action to no one, Sire."

"No. I want him as my bodyguard."

"Sire, I inquire only so that I may serve you better by understanding your motive. Why—"

"He did what he had to do, and when I understood that, I forgave him for it. He is a man of honor, and competent."

"True, Sire. Yet this is not the type of attitude for which barbarians are noted."

"We civilized folk do not properly understand barbarians," Ennui said. "I have been learning."

Chief glanced at Havoc, and seeing him silent, spoke again. "If I may ask, Lady, how did you come to associate so closely with King Havoc?"

"We met in the examination, and exchanged an oath of friendship. He protected me physically, and I advised him about the peculiar ways of civilization. It was a pact of convenience."

"And it continues?"

"He is bringing meaning to my supremely dull life, and I continue to advise him, trying to spare him confusion or embarrassment in an unfamiliar situation. He is free to dismiss me at any time."

"No," Havoc said. "The oath remains."

Chief nodded. "Thank you for clarifying that aspect, Sire. Now there are other matters I am obliged to bring to your attention."

"If you mean how to run the kingdom, I have no idea. Just do what you've been doing, until I catch on."

"Thank you, Sire; I shall. This will prevent disruption during the change of administrations. But there are two other matters of more personal moment."

"Tell me."

"Sire, I shall need a liaison, so that I can reach you rapidly when necessary. I will not bother you whimsically, but there will be some matters that require your attention, if only to authorize me to proceed with a projected course of action."

"Why not just come tell me yourself?"

"You might be otherwise occupied, Sire, so that my appearance here would be inconvenient."

"If it's important, that shouldn't matter."

"Still, Sire—"

"*Why* should it matter?"

"Sire, there are times when intrusion is not advisable, yet you will need to be advised."

"Stop talking around the cycad! *What* times?"

Chief glanced at Ennui. She stepped in. "Havoc, I think he means that you might be asleep, or in bed with a lover."

"Or on the pot," Havoc said, and saw the man wince. He had committed another social blunder. "Okay, I should have a liaison. Who?"

"Perhaps Lady Ennui, as she seems to be close to you."

Havoc looked at her. "That's all right with you?"

"As you wish, Havoc."

He faced Chief. "So tell her, and she'll find me in a hurry, even if I am doing something disgraceful at the moment."

"I will, Sire. In fact, if you wish, you might designate her as your social secretary, so that all who seek the attention of the king will understand. Clarity in such connections is important."

"Makes sense to me. Do you mind, Ennui?"

"Oh, Havoc, it's not my place to object to anything you might ask me to—"

"But do you mind? I know you were tired of clerking."

"I just meant that anything you—"

"Lady," Chief said, with something approaching a smile, "the king is asking your private preference. You are obliged to answer with candor, not evasion."

She blushed. The tables had been turned. "I meant that I wouldn't object even if I did mind. But this—to serve him in such an important capacity—to be recognized as secretary to the king—it would be a privilege beyond my wildest dream."

"She does not mind," Chief translated, allowing more of the smile to show. Then he turned serious. "The other matter is somewhat more delicate, and may not be to your liking, Sire."

"What?"

"It concerns the manner of King Deal's death. It is too soon to understand all the aspects of it, and the investigation is ongoing. But I have a gut feeling that there is something wrong."

The dragon seed, quiescent until now, buzzed. Havoc knew that this did not necessarily mean that Chief was lying, or that there was danger, but that there was something amiss. It suggested that Chief's concern was well founded. "Why?"

"Sire, I have no evidence. But I believe King Deal was pursuing something, and that he was on the verge of discovering it, when he died. This is suspicious. I know no more, but would like to."

"How does this concern me?"

"If there is something able to cause one king to die, despite the crown, it could cause another king to die. It should be quietly rooted out."

"Why quietly?"

"Because if my suspicion is correct, an open investigation would alert the unknown enemy, and it would act to protect itself from discovery."

"Like approaching a sleeping dragon," Havoc said. "If it smells you, you're dead."

"A fair analogy, Sire. But this is likely to be something more subtle, yet perhaps just as deadly. I repeat, I have no certain evidence, but felt I should advise you."

"So maybe I'm king because someone murdered King Deal?"

"I would hesitate to be that blunt, Sire, but there is the suspicion. I have spoken about this to no other persons, because should there be any substance to it, you might be in danger already."

The man was both competent and sensible. "How can I learn more about this?"

"Sire, I do not know. But perhaps the one closest to King Deal would have some idea."

"Who?"

"His wife or his lover."

"He had a wife *and* a lover?"

"Yes, Sire. This is not considered inappropriate, in ranking officers."

"Thanks for warning me. As a barbarian, I had no idea."

Chief nodded. "There are ways in which the civilized personnel are perhaps less refined than the barbarians. I suspect this is sufficient for the day, unless you have something else for me."

"Something else?"

"He means you should let him go now," Ennui said. "So he can get on with his business."

"Then why didn't he say so?"

"You're the king, Havoc. Nobody tells you what to do or say. He was just giving you a hint, so you could dismiss him. Unless you have something else to tell him."

"Oh. Sure. Get going, Chief."

Ennui looked pained. "That's like putting a dog out the door. Tell him he is dismissed."

Havoc smiled. "Sorry. Dismissed, Chief."

"Thank you, Sire." He turned to go.

Then Havoc remembered something. "My fiancée—I can bring her here, even if I can't marry her yet?"

"Certainly, Sire. She can be your lover."

"Her name is Gale, of Village Trifle. Maybe don't tell her I'm king, yet; I hardly believe it myself. Send Throe to fetch her. Tell him to tell her 'With this seed I thee betrothed.' Then she'll go with him."

Chief bowed. "Sire, it shall be done."

"Parting."

"Acknowledged, Sire." He departed.

"That should be a comfort to you, having your girlfriend back," Ennui said. "Which reminds me: I will be required to remarry within a month, and I would rather not. I wonder whether the king's social secretary is exempt. High officers like Chief are, but secretaries are ordinary folk."

"If not, maybe I can make her exempt. Can you find out?"

"Yes, I should be able to ask and get an answer. But meanwhile it's late, and you will want to sleep, Havoc. I can see you are tired, as I am. You will stay in the royal bedroom, but I have no place."

"Then stay with me."

"Havoc, I can't. I think only the king's wife or lover spends the night with him. Appearances are important."

"So what happened to King Deal's wife or lover? I haven't seen them around."

"They must have been moved out soon after he died."

"Let's check." They walked back toward the bedroom. "I'll ask a servant."

"Havoc, let *me* ask a servant. The king should not demean himself with minor matters."

She was surely right. He kept running afoul of civilized conventions. "Do it."

Ennui caught the eye of a servant. "Where is King Deal's widow?"

"Lady, she is in the process of vacating her apartment."

"Let's catch her now," Havoc murmured.

"Please lead us to her apartment," Ennui told the servant.

Soon they were at a ramp leading to the floor just below the king's apartment. Ennui knocked on the wooden door, and it opened to show another servant. "King Havoc wishes to speak with King Deal's widow. What is her name?"

"Queen Aspect, Lady. I will advise her." The servant girl disappeared into the apartment.

Soon she reappeared. "Queen Aspect is on her way."

A woman appeared. She was in an elegant robe, but her face was puffy, as if she had been crying. She seemed to be of Ennui's generation, and was somewhat portly.

"Greeting," Havoc said formally.

"Sire," she said, bowing. "I am clearing the apartment, and will be gone shortly. There was too much to handle on short notice, so I am delayed. I apologize for inconveniencing you."

"I will not hold you long," Havoc said. "I want only to talk about something. May we come in?"

"Sire, this residence is yours. I regret it is not at the moment in presentable condition." Indeed, there were boxes scattered around, evidently her belongings being packed.

"I don't care about that. Queen Aspect, I am sorry your husband the king died. I didn't know him, but I'm sure he was a good man." The dragon seed did not buzz, because he was the one telling the lie. He had hated the distant king all his life, without knowing him.

"Thank you, Sire. Do you wish to take a seat?"

They took seats. "Queen Aspect, I—"

"Please Sire, I am no longer queen. I am a nonentity, until I perforce remarry in a month. If you please, just call me Lady Aspect."

This diverted him from his question. "Even you, Lady Aspect? You have to remarry, though you surely do not wish to?"

"Yes, Sire, to both."

"Lady, I am a barbarian, and I know little about civilized ways or the powers of the office I suddenly hold. I did not want to be king, but have been given no choice. So at times I must be blunt. I ask you to bear with me."

"Of course Sire. I believe I understand. The change has been brutally sudden, for all of us."

"Do I have the power to relieve you of the obligation of remarriage?"

"Yes, Sire," she said, surprised. "But I think you would not wish to."

"Why not?"

"Because such designation would imply that you were taking me as one of your lovers."

"Does the implication need to have any basis in fact?"

"No, Sire. But there would be whispers."

"The hell with the whispers. They would be the least of my reputation as a barbarian. Lady Aspect, remain here, as you have been, without remarrying."

"Sire!" she said, amazed.

"I ask only that in return you assist my friend Ennui in educating

me about the ways of civilization and royalty. And that you allow Ennui to share this apartment with you, as another implied lover who
will never be touched in that manner. Is this satisfactory to you?"

"Of course, Sire! But you have no need—"

"And satisfactory to you, Ennui?"

Ennui was as amazed as Aspect. "Oh, yes, Havoc. But it may
make you a laughing stock. Two middle aged women—"

"Not nearly as much so as my natural barbarian manners make
me. So who sets this up?"

"Majordomo can make the arrangement," Aspect said. "Sire, this
is uncommonly generous. But what of your own wife?"

"I can't marry her this year. Next year we'll see. Meanwhile, I'll have
her as my true lover, in my own bedroom suite. She won't bother you."

"As you wish, Sire."

"Now I need to know: was King Deal murdered?"

"Sire!"

But the dragon seed buzzed, giving her implied denial the lie.
"Chief has a suspicion, and I trust his judgment." Because the seed
had confirmed the man's straight answers. "Do you know anything?"

"I know nothing, Sire, but I confess I do believe that his sudden
demise was not natural."

"If it was not, then it is to my interest to discover the truth, if only
to save my own hide from a similar fate."

She was surprised. "Why that's true, Sire. I would certainly like
to learn the truth. Two days ago he was a hearty man, having at his
lover; today he is dead. It is a shock." She wiped her teary eyes. The
dragon seed did not buzz, indicating that her grief was not feigned.

"I'm a barbarian, and don't understand some things. You said he
was with his lover? How can you countenance that?"

Aspect smiled wanly. "Our society long ago recognized that it is
unrealistic to expect men of power to confine themselves to single
women. Too many other women are attracted to that power, and many
of them are attractive. So we recognize that the men will have liaisons, without disturbing the natural and legal family ties. My husband loved me, and I loved him; it just wasn't sexual any more. The
children kept me busy, between official social functions. It would have
been a waste of time to resent his lover. She is as miserable now as I
am. Perhaps she will have further insight into his death."

"Maybe I'll get used to the system, some time. Who was his lover?"

"The Lady Symbol, the Representative of the Invisible Chroma of
Air. She is an interesting woman."

"She must be," Ennui said.

Havoc wasn't sure how she meant that, but he had a more immediate concern. "What indication do you have that King Deal was murdered?"

"He believed there was a conspiracy of some kind, to take over the planet and change it. He had surmounted a serious political challenge, but this was different. He thought he had a lead, and that he would soon know the truth. But he died before he could discover it. I think the conspirators must have killed him, though I don't know how."

"Could his lover have done it?"

"No. She would never willfully harm him, any more than would I." And the seed did not buzz.

"Thank you, Lady Aspect. Now I am tired, and must sleep. Ennui will help you put your things back." He stood.

"But I must stay with you, Havoc," Ennui protested. "At least until you are safely settled for the night."

"Then I will sleep here, so you will not have to leave." He dropped to the floor, catching himself on his hands, and curled up in his clothes, closing his eyes.

"He *is* a barbarian," Ennui said. "He has his little ways, some of which are crude, and some endearing."

"Endearing?" Aspect asked.

"He keeps his word. He cares about people. He is loyal to his own. He recognizes his areas of ignorance. And he listens when you speak."

"Those are qualities to make up for any amount of crudity," Aspect agreed. "But civilization will soon enough cure him of them."

"I'm not sure it will. He's neither weak nor stupid, just ignorant."

"Does he really mean me to remain here? And to be relieved of the requirement of remarriage?"

"He said so, and he means what he says. But it seems you will have to put up with me. Do you have a separate room I can use?"

"I have a whole suite you can use. I shall be glad of the company. I loved Deal, but I was alone most of the time. Let me at least get a blanket for the king."

In a moment a blanket was gently laid over Havoc. The Lady Aspect's hands arranged it, then tucked a pillow under his head. Her touch was much like a mother's caress. He had the distinct impression she was pleased with him. That was all he remembered.

When he woke, the boxes were gone from the room, and Ennui was sleeping beside him on the floor. She had pillows under her, as well as a blanket over her. She must have decided that he still needed watching over, since he was not safe in his own suite. She was probably right.

He got up quietly, needing to use the bathroom. But he did not know his way around this apartment.

The Lady Aspect appeared. "Sire."

"I need—"

"Here, Sire." She indicated a door.

He walked through it, and found himself in a competent bathroom. Now he had to figure out how to get free of the clown suit he wore. He didn't want to tear it, but it seemed unwilling to yield.

"Sire." She spoke from outside the chamber.

"Yes, Lady Aspect."

"If you find your clothing unfamiliar, perhaps I can help you."

This was a welcome offer. "I do need help."

She entered the bathroom. "The straps are self adhesive," she said. "May I take your hand, Sire?"

What was she up to? "Yes."

She took his hand and set his fingers on his belt. Again, he was aware of the quality of her touch. It was firm, it was gentle, it was sure, and it was reassuring. "Find the slight ridge, here, Sire. Catch it with your nail, thus. Draw it up, and it releases. All the fastenings are of this nature; they release readily when pried, but not otherwise. To restore them, simply lay one strap against another."

"Thank you," he said, abashed by the simplicity of it, now that he understood the principle.

"You are being unconscionably kind to me, Sire. You asked me to assist in educating you about the ways of civilization. This is one of those ways."

"I know you are in grief for your husband. I did not mean to impose so soon."

"I am in grief," she agreed. "But you have ameliorated much of the rest of it. I am of course at your command. But I am also grateful. I will help you in any way I can." She squeezed his hand, and once more the character of her contact came through. This was a special woman. "Now I will leave you alone, but will be within call."

"Thanks."

She left the chamber, closing the door quietly behind her. He got his pantaloons down, found the ridge on the weird underwear, and used the toilet. It was the kind that washed itself with water, rather than saving its substance in a bucket. In due course he figured out how to make the water flow. Then he washed his hands at the sink, suspecting that this was expected.

He opened the door and stepped out. "Sire," Aspect said, beside him.

"Yes?"

"Will you permit me to touch you?"

"Why?"

"Sire, you have assembled your clothing correctly, but in a manner some might deem sloppy. It may be better if you allow others to dress you, so that you may save your attention for more important things."

He realized that she was being delicate. "Do it," he agreed.

"If you please, Sire, back in the chamber."

He stepped back into the bathroom, and she closed the door behind them. There was no one else around, but it seemed that clothing must not be breached in the main apartment. Then she worked the adhesive strap on his pantaloons and dropped them to the floor. She worked the straps on his underclothing, and suddenly that was more comfortable; he had indeed done it wrong. If she saw anything private, she ignored it. She must have done this often enough for her sons, when they were young. Her touch continued to be reassuring. Then she pulled up the pantaloons and fastened them, and they hung straight.

"I guess I am pretty ignorant," he said ruefully.

"Sire, attire like this can be difficult for civilized folk too. The royal trappings have become unconscionably complicated over the centuries. I often assisted my husband similarly, when he was intoxicated."

"He was a drunk, and had a lover, but you loved him?"

"Yes. We must take people as wholes. Few are perfectly good or bad in all things. My husband was a very good man."

"What are my crudities?"

If she realized that this meant he had overheard her dialogue with Ennui, she gave no sign. "Sire, I would not presume to criticize."

"How the hell can you educate me about being civilized, if you don't tell me what's wrong? I don't like being king, but I don't like being embarrassed either, so I might as well put on as good a front as I can. I think you know royal ways that Ennui can not know, and I want your expertise as well as hers. How am I crude?"

She looked wary. "Sire, you are being kind to me, and I want very much not to offend you. But if I speak freely, I risk doing that."

Havoc was coming to appreciate that blunt speaking was one of the ways in which he differed from civilized folk. When he asked them to speak similarly, they got uncomfortable. "Lady Aspect, I think it is as important to me that I not give offense as it is to you. But I am in danger of doing it without knowing it, and perhaps alienating people I wish to impress favorably. I regret imposing on your grief, but I think I am in immediate need. Please—"

"The king never says please to an underling," she said, alarmed.

"Lady Aspect, forget for the moment that I am king. Think of me as your errant son, who needs candid advice. In my bedroom complex I had to stand with my eyes closed while three pretty girls stripped me and washed me and dressed me, and I am not so ignorant as not to know that standing naked before nubile girls with my member erect is not crude. I think I am doing something similar in manners. Tell me what I need to know, in language I can understand."

She nodded. "Lady Ennui is right: you do have endearing qualities, even in your bluntness. Very well, Sire, I will speak plainly, though it pains me. It is crude to utter expletives in conversation. 'Hell' is an expletive. It is crude to cut directly to the point, such as asking 'Why?' or calling a dead man a drunk or telling a person to 'do it.' It is crude to scratch or belch or fart in public. It is crude to meet a person's gaze for more than a moment, and may even seem threatening. It is—"

"But my whole way of life takes no note of such things," he protested.

"And it is crude to interrupt a speaking person, unless there is an emergency. As king, you of course have preemptive right of speech, but this is best if not abused."

Havoc considered. "What were you about to say, when I interrupted?"

"That it is crude to sleep on the floor, or in your clothes. There may be other crudities I have not yet had occasion to observe, but perhaps these suffice as examples."

"No one else has said anything like this to me, except Ennui, when she made me take a bath."

"The Lady Ennui is guiding you well. As a person of the lower class, she perhaps understands your ways more readily. The others dare not offend you."

"Ennui told the household staff to signal me when I did something awkward, but they did not call my attention to the things you have said."

"Two things about that, Sire. First, the king is expected to be relaxed in his own house, and may behave in a manner inappropriate in public. Second, some crudities are so gross as to defy such attention, so the household personnel are helpless."

Havoc wiped his nose. "I guess so."

"Such as wiping your nose with your bare hand. If you must do it in public, do it this way." She reached into one of his pockets and brought out an ornate handkerchief. She put it in his hand, and lifted his hand to his nose, and wiped, delicately. Then she wadded the handkerchief and returned it to the pocket.

Havoc was impressed. "Lady Aspect, I think I need more of your attention than we can afford at this moment. I learn rapidly when I have to, but I see there is much I don't know. Can you come with me to the main house?"

"Of course I can, Sire. There is no need to ask; simply tell me."

"But you said that cutting directly to the point is crude."

She smiled. "I appreciate your confusion, Sire. It is crude in dialogue, but when you give a directive, as king, you need never ask. No person on the planet has anything to do other than obey your desire."

"I am used to considering the convenience and feelings of others."

"As king, you may continue to do that. But when you make a decision, you must suggest no doubt. If you have doubt, it would be better to ask a trusted person about the matter privately, resolve your doubt, and then speak decisively in public."

"Ennui is such a person. But you may be also. So I ask you, Lady Aspect, how long has it been since you have slept?"

"Not since my husband died, Sire."

"Then sleep now, and when you are refreshed, come to me. My fiancé Gale will also need instruction, when she arrives here."

"Sire, it would look awkward for King Deal's widow to be constantly at your side."

"And I don't want awkwardness," he agreed. "But in the apartment, where things are more relaxed—"

She nodded. "I can supervise your personal schedule, if you wish, Sire."

"But the Majordomo does that."

"No, Sire. He runs the house, not your private life."

"And Ennui is to be my personal secretary."

"She will organize your outside appointments. That is a separate matter. Neither of them will tell you what to wear or eat on a given day. I will do that, Sire, if it is your desire."

"Yes. Now I thank you for your service to me, Lady Aspect, and will leave you to sleep."

"Thank *you*, Sire." She opened the door and waited. When he did not go out, she said "Sire, among barbarians men may defer to women in such matters, but the king always leads unless he directs others to do so."

He stepped out, and she followed.

Ennui appeared. He suspected she had overheard some of the dialogue in the bathroom, and had waited for him to emerge. "Take me back to my apartment," he said.

"This way, Havoc."

They left Aspect's apartment and walked up the ramp. "I believe King Deal had a good wife," he remarked.

"I am sure of it."

A servant appeared, standing expectantly. "Tell Majordomo that the Lady Aspect will be supervising my personal routine, from tomorrow on," he said. "But that this morning the Lady Ennui and I will require a suitable breakfast."

"Sire." The servant disappeared.

"Havoc, I am really not a lady," Ennui said. "I am a common woman."

"Others call you Lady. The Lady Aspect called you Lady. I take my social cue from her."

"Still—"

"If I understand the conventions of this position sufficiently, I can call anyone anything I choose."

"Yes, of course. You are the king. But others–"

"Others should take their cue from me. You are my oath friend; I will not have you slighted."

She surrendered. "As you wish, Havoc."

When they arrived at his bedroom, the three bathing girls were there. One lifted her hand, cautiously. She was the Mistress of the

Royal Bath, the girl of sixteen with curly brown hair, accompanied by her two younger assistants with the red and yellow hair. They had looked pretty, as a set; now they looked prettier, with the partial familiarity of his experience with them. He would have preferred to know their names, but suspected that protocol required that they be identified only by their positions.

"I know," Havoc said with resignation. "I need a bath."

"And a change of clothing, Sire," the Bath Mistress said. "You look as if you had slept in what you are wearing."

"I have. Well, do your worst."

"I will clean and change elsewhere," Ennui said.

Havoc smiled. "What, no handsome young men to do you?"

"I am not royal, fortunately." She faded back.

He looked at the bath girls, and decided to try for their names anyway. "If this is to be a regular thing, I should know your names. Who are you?"

"We are mere bath girls, Sire. I am Girl One, and my assistants are Girl Two and Girl Three."

So they would not violate the protocol. He didn't fight it. In time he would get the name of at least the Mistress, just for private satisfaction. He let them lead him into the bathroom, strip him, and wash him. He reacted as before, but figured they were used to it now. Probably when he got so that he could have a lovely sixteen year old girl wash his private parts, and those parts did not react, he would be a normal king.

He let his eyes open so he could see the bath crew work. They wore waterproof coveralls for this job, and competent hats. Girl One caught him looking, and winked. That stiffened him further, as perhaps she noted. She remained anonymous by name, but was assuming personality. He rather liked her; she reminded him vaguely of Gale.

Then other girls came to dress him, as before. "Is there any chance I can wear something less like a clown suit?"

"Certainly Sire," the Mistress of Royal Dressing replied. "What do you wish?"

That stumped him. "Tomorrow, the Lady Aspect will select my outfit."

"Of course, Sire." And he got the impression that these girls were surprised and pleased. That was further evidence that Aspect was a good woman.

Then, properly cleaned and garbed, he rejoined Ennui for a really nice breakfast of green eggs, red bread, and blue milk. It would not be difficult to get used to such a life, though he still resented having to be king.

"Now what do I have to do next?" he asked Ennui.

"The king's schedule of appointment and appearances has been suspended, owing to the change of circumstance," she said.

"You mean, the death of King Deal, and accession of an ignorant barbarian?"

She smiled, "Yes, Havoc. But no one else will put it that way."

"Neither will I, elsewhere. So what am I supposed to do?"

"You are supposed to learn the business of kingship. In a hurry. I can't teach you; I know little about royalty or governance."

"So who else does?"

"I understand that the Lady Symbol is the best person for that."

"King Deal's lover? What do I want with her?"

"She is one of the Chroma Representatives, and you will have to meet them all, as well as many top officials. But Lady Aspect says to start with her."

"Then I had better do it. But I had better have you close by, for protection."

She shook her head. "Havoc, I have to learn *my* business, of being your social secretary. I can't do that while holding your hand."

"You seem to have a pretty good start."

"But there's much more. Please, Havoc—"

He hated it when she said "please," though he wasn't sure why. "Okay, set me up with that woman."

"She will be reporting here in the next half hour."

So she had already handled it. "Ennui, have you noticed anything about me?"

"There *is* something, Havoc. You seem to be acclimatizing, and—that's it. You're no longer crude."

"I made Aspect tell me about crudity."

"She must have answered well."

"She did. Very well, go about your business, and I will await the session with Deal's lover." He did not try to conceal his distaste.

"Just send for me if you need me, Havoc."

"I will."

"Parting."

"Acknowledged," he said. She had just made him more comfortable, by that detail of barbarian politeness.

She left, and he sought Majordomo. "I am expecting the Lady Symbol soon. How should I address her, and how should I act in her presence?"

"Sire, treat her much as you did the Lady Aspect. She is a person of status, as a Representative of her Chroma. Interview her in the drawing room. Make no reference to her private relation with King Deal. If you wish, suggest that the session become informal."

"Informal?"

"That will allow her to relate to you in the manner we of the household do, Sire, and will perhaps be more comfortable for you."

Havoc nodded. "It should be."

"She is a very comfortable woman, Sire. She can be of great assistance to you, should you wish it."

"I'm not looking for a lover!"

"Of course not, Sire. But she would be an excellent friend."

This had the aspect of good advice. "Thank you, Majordomo. Parting."

The man bowed and departed. Havoc, left to his own devices for the moment, went to the drawing room, which was nicely appointed with soft chairs, a broad polished table, and paintings on the walls. He wanted to exercise, but his fancy clothing inhibited him. So he stood in place, tensing muscles alternately, trying to get feel of exercise. He didn't want to get out of shape.

A maid spied him at it. She paused, catching his eye. "Is something wrong, Sire?" she asked when he met her gaze.

"I'm a barbarian," he explained. "I like to run and climb, but that would spoil this clothing."

"Do you wish to see the Mistress of Clothing?"

"Maybe later, when I don't have someone to interview."

"Sire," she agreed, and went on about her business.

In due course Majordomo reappeared. "Sire, the Lady Symbol has arrived."

"Show her in."

In a moment, Majordomo ushered in a heavily cloaked woman who wore an encompassing hat and veil, so that her face hardly showed. She had thick stockings, and long sleeved gloves, and a band of material around her neck, so that nothing else showed either. All of her clothing was shades of gray, except for her iridescent cloak. That might have been drab on another woman, but it was evident that this one was extraordinarily lovely.

"Greeting."

"Sire," she murmured, bowing her head. "I am Symbol, of the Invisible Chroma of Air." Her voice was dulcet.

"Welcome, Lady Symbol. I am told that you can help me learn what I need so as to better handle my position."

"I am at your complete service, Sire."

"Then tell me what I need."

"Sire, if you please, I must first learn a bit about you, so that I can orient effectively on your needs."

"Please be informal, Lady, and inquire as you see fit."

"To do that, I would have to expose myself." But she did remove her bright cloak. "Actually, this is my informal garb, Sire, but I did not wish to distract you with too much iridescence."

What person donned informal garb to meet the king for the first time? She had stirred his curiosity. "As you wish, Lady."

"Sire, I am not sure you would find this comfortable."

She had been described as a comfortable woman. What did this mean? "Lady, I find none of this business of kingship comfortable. I long for my barbarian home. But since I can not go home, I must learn to cope with what I find here. I am told that you can best help me accomplish this. Do what you need to do."

She angled her veil at him. "You strike me as a man who does not tolerate boredom well."

"Yes."

"Then let's make this interesting. Do you wager?"

"Do I bet? Not if I can avoid it. I prefer to be sure of my accomplishment."

"I propose a game in which we ask each other questions, and pay penalties."

He was wary of this. "Penalties? I'm not willing to use my office to do anything inappropriate, until I know more about it."

Her veil formed the semblance of a smile. "Nothing like that, Sire. If you ask me a question I can't answer to your satisfaction, I must remove an item of my clothing. If I do so answer, then you must remove an item of yours. Similarly I will ask you questions, alternating with yours. The questions may be of any nature, and candid responses are required."

"But either way, we will both soon be naked."

"Does that frighten you, Sire?"

"No. But it strikes me as uncivilized."

"Sire, it strikes me as informal."

Suddenly he liked this woman better. "Then let's play the game. But be warned that I react in the presence of beautiful women."

Her veil smiled again. "I should hope so, Sire." Symbol turned her head to the side and raised her voice. "Majordomo, we wish to be private in this room, until further notice."

The man appeared at a door. "As you wish, Lady." He closed the door.

Symbol faced Havoc again. "Sire, you may have the first question."

Havoc decided to discover the limits early. "What was your personal relationship with King Deal?" This was a forbidden question, but he wanted to see how she handled it.

"I loved him. In fact I was his lover. I am in grief for him." Her veil angled again. "But I believe you already know this, Sire, so you have wasted a question."

"I was testing."

"Then do you wish another question, Sire, in lieu of that?"

"No, I'll pay my forfeit." He put his hands to his waistband and unfastened it. He removed it and set it on the table. His pantaloons sagged but did not drop.

"Sire, with how many different women have you had sex?"

She was not pussyfooting! "One. Gale, my fiancée."

Symbol put her hands to her veil and removed it. Havoc glanced at her face—and did a double-take. There was no face there.

Which set up his next question, as perhaps she had intended. "Where is your face?"

"It is here, Sire. But we of the Air Chroma are invisible. Give me your hand."

He extended his right hand. She took it in her glove and carried it to her head. His fingers felt a delicately featured face, but he still could not see it.

"However, as we spend time away from our natural Chroma, we become gradually polluted, and come slowly into sight. If you look carefully, Sire, you will see the outline of my brain inside my skull."

He looked, and it was so; there was a haze of fog there, with lines feeding into it. Those would be the nerves. "You are right: I am uncomfortable with this."

"You will become accustomed to it, Sire. By the time this is done, you will see—or fail to see—all of me."

"I had hardly heard of the Invisible Chroma, before leaving my village, and if I had, I would not have taken it literally." The Dragon Mentor had mentioned it, and Havoc had not then understood its implication.

"I suspected as much, Sire. But beware: you are giving me answers without requiring my questions. That will be likely to put you at a disadvantage."

"I do not seek any advantage over you."

"Which feeds into my next question, Sire: Will you require any lover besides Gale?"

"No."

She was already removing her hat, evidently anticipating that straightforward answer. Now her whole head was invisible, except for the dim cloud of her brain, and a barrette fastening down her unseen hair. He appreciated why she had come so fully clothed: it was the only way to identify her.

Havoc knew he was being managed, but couldn't help it, so he asked: "Why did you ask that?"

"Having served the role, Sire, I have an interest in it."

The dragon seed buzzed. She was lying, or at least not telling the whole truth. So he challenged her answer. "Your answer does not satisfy me."

She might have smiled. "Ennui is right, Sire: you're not stupid."

"I am ignorant, not dull. Why did you ask?"

The seed buzzed. "I loved King Deal, and do not wish to be the lover of another man. Since you, as king, can command my compliance, I wish to verify that you will not be doing so."

That was interesting. The dragon seed had buzzed before she spoke, indicating that she was not confused; she had intended to lie.

But to what purpose?

"I will not be doing so," Havoc agreed. "But I remain unsatisfied with your answer."

"There are considerable advantages to being the king's lover, Sire, and I am quite aware of them. Others would expect me to wish to continue to enjoy them."

The seed buzzed again. Havoc knew that this was a correct statement, but nevertheless a lie because it wasn't her real reason for her prior question. "You are evading the answer."

She shrugged. "Perhaps my feelings are mixed, Sire."

He didn't need the buzz to know the evasion was continuing. She would not tell the whole truth, and the dragon seed would not settle for a partial truth. But he thought he understood it: she was, in her circuitous fashion, inviting him to have a similar interest in her. Surely she had loved King Deal, and also liked being the king's lover. She had lost Deal, but might salvage the rest if she attracted similar interest from his successor. But she couldn't say that without seeming crude, especially since he had said he wanted only Gale. So she skirted it, putting the notion into his mind while denying that this was her intent. She was lying for a purpose.

"Perhaps," he agreed. "Ask your next question." He began to remove his fancy shirt.

"No, Sire; do not strip. I did not give you a satisfactory answer, so the penalty is mine." She removed her blouse, revealing a comprehensive undergarment. Her upper arms were bare, so that her forearms seemed unconnected to her shoulders. The effect was intriguing, now that he was becoming accustomed to her invisibility. He could see through the emptiness that was her face, down inside her neck and chest—and still saw nothing.

She asked her next question. "Sire, what are your feelings about the Ladies Aspect and Ennui?"

"I need a clarification. Can you ask about two women in one question?"

"I can, Sire, but you may challenge it and require me to be more specific. I am assuming that your sentiment with respect to those two are similar, so can be covered in one answer."

He nodded. "Fair enough. Ennui is my oath friend, and I will trust her with my life, and protect hers with mine. Aspect is like a mother to me, guiding me in things others will not mention."

"You have not answered the question, Sire. They both are like mothers to you, one of low status, one of high status. I asked about your feelings."

She was right. "I am not sure I have feelings about them, other than the general impression that they are good women."

"I'm not sure that is a sufficient answer."

"Neither am I," he admitted. "I—I think I need such mature women in my life, to be true friends, even if they are so only by oath or convenience. I feel—I feel they are better women than those I might choose as lovers, and potentially more important to me." He grimaced. "I guess I can't give a better answer, and must forfeit." He put his hands to his shirt again.

"No, Sire, I am satisfied. The forfeit is mine." She removed a glove, and the rest of her right arm disappeared. "Ask your next."

"Why am I meeting you?"

"You do get to the point rapidly, Sire. I presume it is not sufficient to say that the Ladies Aspect and Ennui sent you to me."

"Maybe I should have asked *why* they sent me to you."

"Yes, Sire, because I can give a correct answer that tells you nothing: you are with me because they told you. But I will give you a true answer: they know that I can better prepare you for your role as king than any other person can, because I was closest to King Deal. And I shall do that, to the best of my ability."

"I will accept that, but I will have another question." Now he removed his shirt.

"I shall be expecting it, Sire. Now mine: what do you feel is your greatest current need?"

"To learn how to be king, rapidly."

She removed her other glove. "Ask, Sire."

"Was King Deal murdered?"

"Sire, there is no evidence—"

The seed buzzed, but he was already following up. "No evasion. What do *you* believe?"

Her camisole shrugged. "Yes, Sire, I believe he was. But I can't prove it, and have no suspects. It's just that—I can't believe it could have been an accident." Her remaining outfit turned slightly, suggesting that she was glancing at him. "Why do you ask?"

"Chief and Lady Aspect find his death suspicious. This is the real reason I am talking to you."

"Sire, I'm not sure why you should be concerned with the manner of his death. Isn't it sufficient that you are now king?"

"No. If he was killed, I could be killed too."

Her barrette nodded. "That does make sense, Sire."

"How *did* he die?"

"Shall we dispense with the game of questions and answers, Sire? It seems to have served its purpose."

Havoc smiled. "As you wish, though I had been looking forward to seeing you all the way naked."

"Then let me complete that process, Sire, before I answer." Her invisible hands removed her barrette, slippers, skirt, camisole, stockings, and panties, leaving her invisible except for her foggy brain and the faint outline of her lungs. Though only the clothing had been visible, it had outlined a feminine form rivaling that of Gale, making her the best shaped woman he had encountered in this city. "I am partly visible because I must breathe nonChroma air, and this infuses visibility. In my apartment the air is Chroma, so I am sustained. But I am all here, as you may verify if you wish to touch me."

"Are you trying to seduce me?"

"It's a good thing the game is over, Sire, or my answer might embarrass me. But I do think you will understand me better if you touch me."

Havoc suspected that he should not cooperate in any seduction, but he was fascinated by her invisibility. So he risked it. He stepped toward her and extended his hands, cautiously.

His right hand touched what he took to be her upper arm. Yes, he was able to circle his fingers around it. His left hand found her right breast. He drew his hand quickly back.

"Touch freely, Sire, so as to develop a competent image of me."

So he touched her breast again, feeling its fullness. He slid both hands across and around her torso, confirming an outstanding figure. She was firm and full in every part. She had exactly the kind of body a king would choose for a sexual liaison. He was somewhat surprised, because she was perhaps a decade older than he, an age when most women were in the middle of childbearing and raising, their figures in the process of destruction.

"How is it that Lady Aspect does not resent you?"

"Sire, she knows that I had no desire to replace her as queen. Just as Gale will know, should you ever wish to clasp me. I have no political ambitions, merely a desire to be close to the king. Other women may be otherwise, so it was better for the Lady Aspect to accept me than risk them. As a person of Chroma, any permanent liaison would be awkward for me, especially as my other parts gradually came into view."

"Other parts?"

"My digestive system, for example. I think a man would not be eager to clasp me if he saw that. So at such time as I marry, it will be to a man of my own Chroma. Meanwhile, I can be an interesting diversion for men who like novelty."

The dragon seed did not buzz. "You are indeed tempting. I think you could take me, if you tried." For he was now hot with desire for her, despite his resolve to be true to his fiancée.

"Not before I clear it with Gale, Sire." She was neither joking nor lying; the dragon seed did not buzz.

He stepped back. "You had better dress, then." He put his own clothing back on.

"Now I will tell you what I know about the manner King Deal died. But I must warn you, Sire, that it would be better not to bruit such suspicion of murder about, lest that attract the attention of those who would conceal that murder."

"Agreed."

"I was not there, Sire, so can't speak with perfect authority. You would have to question his bodyguard for that. But I know that King Deal was searching for something, and believed he was close to finding it. He was in the field, in a nonChroma region where there were jagged rocks, and he was climbing over them. Then he leaped from one high rock to another, across a crevice, and fell between them, to his death. The fall killed him. But he was a competent climber, and should never have fallen. Nothing could have pushed him, because he wore the crown. Indeed, he should have survived anyway, because the crown would have cushioned his fall, had it not fallen off. It should not have fallen off. So it is a mystery. It is regarded as an accident, that he misjudged the extent of the leap, or perhaps his foot slipped. But I tell you, the man was healthy and careful. He would not have fallen on his own."

"Unless he was intoxicated at the time."

"King Deal was never intoxicated in the field. He drank only socially, and to excess only in compatible company. He would have been in full possession of his faculties at the time."

As she spoke, she dressed. Havoc saw her stockings come on, in a kind of dance, her fine legs flexing. Her panties filled out, and her camisole. Oh yes, she had the body!

"And so I lost him, Sire, and Queen Aspect lost him, and the planet of Charm lost him. He was a good man, fine and fair, and—" She broke off, and Havoc realized she was crying. She was not pretending; the seed did not buzz.

Havoc waited for her to collect herself. He now knew more than he had about his predecessor's demise, but not enough. The women who knew Deal best believed he had been murdered, and the man who served him most competently believed it too. But none of them had proof.

Havoc could get proof of a sort. "So King Deal was murdered," he repeated.

"Yes, Sire." And the seed did not buzz. There was the truth. Symbol might not be sure, and the others might not be sure, but the seed knew.

"I will find his murderer. But I think my investigation must be secret. You will cooperate?"

"Yes!" Again, no buzz.

"But first I must learn to be king. Teach me."

She had recovered. "Of course, Sire. But may I make a suggestion?"

"Yes."

"I can show you better in my own apartment, where I have some of the Air magic, Sire. If you care to join me there—"

"I will join you there." He had already seen her invisibility; what other magic did she have?

They left the drawing room, and walked to her apartment, which was another on the level below his, similar to that of Lady Aspect but smaller. Apparently the king's residence connected to a number of others, so that anyone could report to him rapidly when so required. It was spare, with a single bed, bathroom, kitchen, closet, table, and two chairs. There were no rugs on the wooden floor, or pictures on the wall, and no windows.

"You mentioned advantages to being the king's lover," Havoc said, taking one of the chairs. "I see none here."

"Sire, one advantage is association," she said. "I got to spend most of my time in his apartment, served by his staff, with food of his quality. When he went out, I could remain, because he would want me convenient when he returned. Or I might be summoned to join him in the field, to help entertain his contacts."

"Entertain?"

Her veil smiled. "To assist in dialogue, Sire. To be a lovely feminine presence among appreciative males. No one but the king touched me, but all were courteous to me, knowing that any affront to me would incite the king's displeasure. This gave me status beyond what I merited as a Representative of my Chroma. I was his lady away from home."

"And what was Aspect?"

"His wife, Sire. A creature of respect but not delight."

"You were his delight."

"Yes." She turned her veil to him. "Sire, you will need similar. Your fiancée will not be able to be with you always, unless you keep her purely as a showcase. If you give her a responsible position, she will be busy at times, and you will need another woman for softening business company. The king must associate with the best, including women; it is one of the marks of his distinction. You may use me for this purpose without having to take me as your lover, or you may choose from any number of other comely women that I or the Lady Aspect can recommend. But the tacit protocol requires a seeming lady."

"A *seeming* lady? Are you not genuine?"

"I am, Sire, by virtue of my position as Chroma Representative. But it is unusual for a representative to serve in this fashion, because few are sufficiently comely. For this purpose, appearance and manner are supreme, rather than background. You must have a girl of luster and poise to decorate your presence, or others will sneer at you privately."

"And if I don't care about their opinions?"

"You wish to learn how to be king, Sire. This is part of it."

Havoc nodded. "Point made. I will keep my eye out for a suitable girl."

"That may not suffice, Sire."

"Why not? Aren't there girls available?"

"There are too many girls available. If you go about for any length of time unattached, you will be mobbed by groupies, each of whom finds herself well qualified, but very few of whom will truly be so. Not every pretty face supports a pretty mind, and you do fathom minds, Sire. Your guards will be loath to dissuade them. You need a companion for protection from that situation."

She was making sense. "You will do for the time being, as decoration rather than lover."

"Thank you, Sire."

"What else do I need to learn?"

"Sire, you need the basics, that city schoolchildren learn, but I think barbarians don't. Geography, History, Current Events, Deportment."

Havoc thought he had learned about such things, but the lesson he had received about "crudities" made him cautious. "I gather this is more complicated than merely knowing that Charm is a planet covered by magic of different colors, with many villages and cities?"

"Yes, Sire. It is policy to keep the outlying nonChroma villages ignorant, as they generate less mischief that way. Let me start at the beginning, and you can tell me if any of the material is already familiar to you." She paused. "I understand that you are a very quick study."

Havoc pondered briefly, and decided to trust her, to this extent. "You can keep a secret?"

"Yes, Sire. Except—" The dragon seed buzzed.

"Except what?"

"Sire, this is a region without magic, by design, so that no Chroma has an advantage. The Chroma are fiercely competitive, and trust no Chroma person to be king. That is why the king and high officials must always be nonChroma. But this lack of magic makes them vulnerable. You are protected by the crown, but I am not. If there were illicit magic–"

"I know little about magic."

"Of course, Sire. And you will have to learn, and I am not authorized to teach you. But–"

"As king, I can not authorize you?"

"Not for this, Sire, because of the jealously of the other Chroma. No one Chroma can be allowed to influence the king unduly. The others have approved me for the king's companion, but magic is something else."

"So you can talk to me, could have sex with me, may see visitors by my side, but can't get into magic?"

"That is so, Sire, in a general way."

"All right. What has this to do with keeping a secret?"

"Everything, Sire. There are many types of magic, but two of the most common are illusion and mind reading. I am allowed to show you illusion, as that is a specialty of Air, but not the others. But I can tell you that mind reading is a specialty of the Translucent Chroma, Water, and can be practiced to a lesser degree by others. So if you tell me a secret, and a Water Chroma person is curious, he will have it from me despite anything I can do. So there is a limit, and I can't swear to keep your secret absolutely."

This was more than interesting. Suddenly he understood why Mentor had made him develop a mental shield. How could a person fight one who could read his mind? How could he plot strategy, if the other side knew it immediately?

"Thank you for the warning, Symbol. But I think I can trust you with this. Just do not volunteer it to others."

"Agreed, Sire."

"Present me with a random series of numbers or words, whose order and identity you know, but which would confuse others."

"Lava, nineteen, clock, three, twenty nine, ingenue, faded, three, lava, seven."

"Lava, nineteen, clock, three, twenty nine, ingenue, faded, three, lava, seven. Do you wish them backwards, or rearranged?"

She hesitated, then spoke. "What are the basics I listed?"

"Geography, History, Current Events, Deportment."

"What items of clothing am I wearing, and in what order did I remove them?"

"Cloak, veil, hat, blouse, gloves, barrette, slippers, skirt, camisole, stockings, and panties."

"Sire, you have made your point. You are a quick and accurate study. Can you assimilate new concepts as readily?"

"Yes, if they are made clear."

"If I may say so, Sire, you are more of a person than I took you for."

"I remain ignorant, not stupid. But I prefer to seem less ignorant and less intelligent than I am. Does this strike you as a reasonable policy?"

"Yes, Sire. I shall do my best to abate the one and conceal the other."

"Thank you." But he had not told her his real secret, that he could hide his important thoughts and memories even from magic scrutiny.

The veil studied him a moment longer. "You could of course take my body, Sire, and I would oblige without resistance, but my heart would not be in it. But I suspect you could take my heart, if you tried."

"Not before I clear it with Gale," he replied with a smile. But behind the humor was the indication that they were finding each other strongly attractive.

Her veil smiled back. "Now let me cover those basics. For this, I will invoke magic. I assure you it is harmless illusion, Sire, though illusion can also be deadly." She walked to a small box in a niche, opened it, and brought out a colorless stone. "This is a gem from my home Chroma, similar to one of the stones in your crown. It carries the magic of the Air. I will invoke it for my performance. I will disappear, even in my clothing, but if you wish you may hold my hand to be sure that I remain with you."

He was tempted to make a sarcastic remark, but thought better of it. "All right." He reached out and took her free hand as she came to sit in the chair next to him.

"First a spot demonstration, to prepare you, Sire."

"I am prepared." But then her veil faded and her face appeared, fully fleshed and lovely. Her other clothing disappeared, and she sat there beside him, completely lusciously nude. Suddenly he remembered what Throe had said: that the most beautiful women of Charm were of the Invisible Chroma, because they enhanced themselves with illusion. Now he believed it. He licked his lips. "Point made," he murmured.

She smiled, and blew him a kiss as she crossed her legs.

Then the scene changed. The room and Symbol disappeared, replaced by a view of starry space. In fact his own body was also gone; stars stone through the place where his feet should be. He suffered a moment of vertigo.

Symbol squeezed his hand, and that gave him orientation. He was not alone. That reassurance had suddenly become important. "You are right: it helps to hold your hand."

"We are good at what we do, Sire, and I am a qualified illusionist. This is vision only, but later there will also be sound. Geography and History overlap, but here is the geography of this region of space."

The view shifted, turning as if they were flying through it. They oriented on a brighter star and hurtled toward it. But the star wobbled.

"This is a view from space, Sire, similar to the one seen by the ship that brought mankind here. Little is known of it, as this journey was a thousand years ago, but we understand it was closed in somewhat in the manner of a building, and that the travelers lived inside it. They could look out through windows and see the stars as they sailed by them."

"Sailing among the stars?" he asked blankly.

"That is our best analogy, Sire. It seems that there is little or no air in deep space, so the ship had to be enclosed to hold in enough air to breathe. It came from a planet of another star, a world perhaps like Charm, where there were too many people. It found our star, Vivid, and its companion, Void. This is known as a double star system, though it is really one star and what they termed a 'black hole.' Void is like the Black Chroma, sucking in all around it."

"But Void is often bright," Havoc protested.

"Sire, the old writings say that is because of the substance from Vivid that it sucks in. Apparently as it sucks in that matter, it crushes it, and sets fire to it, so that it flares up. I don't pretend to understand this well, but you could talk with an astronomer if you wish."

"Maybe later," Havoc said, still holding her hand. "This is a wild story." It was also weird to hear her and feel her hand, without being able to see her or himself.

"I know it is hard to believe, Sire, and I am not sure I believe it myself. Perhaps it is mythology. But it is the official story, so you need to be familiar with it."

"Got it."

"Sire, Charm and Mystery are companion planets in orbit—that is, circling around—the double star. This explains the erratic seasons we have: Fire, Water, Earth, Air, and Void."

"Hot, wet, quakes, storms, and cold," Havoc agreed. "Depending on whether we are close to Vivid, or Void, or in between, and how Void is feeling at the moment."

"Exactly, Sire. Our local weather is complicated by Charm's position with respect to Mystery. I understand it was once called Counter-Charm. The two planets affect each other tidally."

"How?"

"They pull at each other, Sire, and that changes their shapes somewhat. That in turn sponsors eruptions of the volcanoes." The view veered away from the bright and dark star and oriented on two brightly colored balls: Charm and Mystery. They were turning around each other, as if tied together by a string. As they spun, the sides closest to each other humped outward, in the manner of a squeezed fruit, and jets of vapor or juice shot out of their pores.

"Lemon rind!" Havoc said, seeing it. "Squeeze it, and the juice squirts out."

"Approximately, Sire," she agreed. "The eruptions further complicate our weather, especially considering their magic."

"I never knew what made a volcano blow," he said, amazed. "In fact, until I left Village Trifle, I hardly knew about volcanoes."

"There is more, Sire. The planet is hot inside, and as the melted rock is stirred, it collects into globs of color." The view of the planet Charm expanded, and the surface became transparent, showing masses of color collecting in huge balls. "Then when a squeeze comes, those colors go out through holes in the surface, and those holes are our volcanoes."

Havoc shook his head. "And so we have all our colors of magic. I never knew."

"It's not taught in the outlying districts, Sire. There are of course more complicated details, but that's the broad essence. We can't make permanent maps of the planet, because the geography is constantly changing, as volcanoes erupt, wind patterns shift, and the seasons have their effects. The cartography guild is constantly busy."

"Cart makers?"

"Map makers, Sire. They travel around, sketching new maps, replacing the old ones, so we have some notion where things are. At any rate, that is the geographical background. Now for the history. The ship from Earth landed on Charm and set down one thousand colonists and some tools, supplies, and instructions. It departed; we don't know where it went. And our ancestors set about populating the new planet. There were so few, and Charm was so big, that their first need was for large and diversified families. Thus the requirement for four surviving children in each family, one child of which must have mixed parentage. In a thousand years that should have been enough to generate an enormous population, but the death rate was high, and even today we do not feel we have enough. However, we have spread across the planet, and have improved our situation."

The illusion image showed the early men and woman and children, building houses, planting gardens, and cleaning back forests. Havoc winced.

Symbol picked up his reaction, through his hand. "This is unpleasant, Sire, or too much to assimilate?"

"They were burning forests," he said. "They shouldn't do that."

"But they needed the land for crops, Sire."

Havoc didn't argue the case. How could a city person appreciate the special nature of every natural plant and tree?

"Actually, Sire, this isn't an accurate picture," she said. "The first settlers wore masks." The picture changed to show odd things covering every face.

"Masks? Why?"

"We don't know, Sire. They seem to have had trouble breathing, but maybe it was just their imagination; they couldn't believe that the air was as good as what was in their closed ship. They also would not eat of the native plants or animals; they raised their own. Again, we don't know why; maybe they didn't like the taste. But as time passed, they used the masks less, and used the native things more, until today there are no masks and not much of the original stock of things they brought with them. There is much we don't understand, but it is in the records. Likewise the political history, but I think we don't need to review that in any detail. Let's just say that from the start there has always been a leader, and after several hundred years the leader became the king. It was felt best to have a single unified planetary government, and to prevent the human species from fragmenting."

"Fragmenting?"

"This is a special problem, Sire. You know how the people of the several Chroma assume the colors of their environment? I am an example."

"I saw men of different colors as I was being brought here."

"And here am I, Sire, invisible. This much is mere adaptation; anyone who lives near a volcano will gradually assume the color of that volcano, and be able to practice its magic. If you stayed a decade, say, in the Red Chroma, you would turn red and start to have magic. But in some areas, it is going farther, and this is a problem the king addresses."

"How can the king stop a red man from being red, or a green one from being green? Especially when they have magic the king doesn't?"

"By political authority, Sire, backed by military force. This is another reason the king and all high officers must be nonChroma: it represents the origin of our kind, and its purest surviving form."

Havoc considered. "I never liked the king. Now I don't like the king's job."

"Which brings us to Current Events, Sire. There are a number of situations you need to be aware of."

"Isn't this Chief's business?"

"It is, but we thought it better that you be briefed first by a generalist, Sire, so as to form independent opinions. It is Chief's job to implement your policies, not to make them."

"I'm not clear on the distinction. I told him to carry on as he sees fit, until I know enough to make decisions."

"He is carrying on the policies of King Deal, Sire. You may approve them. I am not objective, having been his lover, but I believe them to have been sound. Nevertheless, there are those who disagree with them, and you, as king, will have to establish your own policies."

"I will do so, in due course. Maybe next month."

Symbol appeared superimposed on the image of the early colonists. She remained nude and lovely. "Sire, you must do so now. By human law, the new king has to be inaugurated within one day after the loss of the old king, and his first public statement must be a day after that. King Deal died at dusk, day before yesterday. You assumed power yesterday at dusk. At dusk today you will make your inaugural appearance and statement of policy."

"I thought it was my business to decide my schedule. I'm not ready to make any statement of policy, so I'll cancel that."

"Within certain broad limits, Sire. You can change established procedure only with the approval of the Chroma Representatives. They will not accede to that."

"Why do I feel like a bull in a corral?"

"With some pretty cows at the exits, Sire," she agreed.

"And you are the cow they steered me to."

"Yes, Sire. But I must say, you showed initiative befriending a common woman, and then the prior king's widow. I suspect you will establish your own course soon enough."

"I wonder. So you will acquaint me with Current Events, and then I must formulate my Policies, and present them this evening."

"Yes, Sire. I will also brief you on Deportment, though you have already learned much of that."

"Not to fart in public."

She smiled. "Not even to use that word in public, Sire."

"Why did they summon a barbarian to be king, if they didn't *want* a barbarian?"

"Is this a rhetorical question, Sire?" Clothing formed around her image; evidently she was tiring of vamping him.

"No."

"Ten candidates were summoned to participate in the examination for king, Sire. By established protocol, all had to be nonChroma, and selected from all facets of society. Thus there were men and women, of middle age and young, experienced officers, entertainers, lowly clerks or workers, and a representative from an outlying village: the barbarian. The examinations vary, but are crafted to be beyond the experience of any of the participants, so that none have an advantage. That is all we know; the details are secret, so that there can be no preparation. When there is more than one survivor–"

"Did the losers die?"

"I don't believe so, Sire. I understand that deaths may be apparent, and sometimes gruesome, but that they are clothed in illusion, and those eliminated are subsequently shunted to far distracts, never again to be seen by their prior acquaintances, and sworn to silence on pain of execution. But I don't know, and it would not be healthy for me to inquire. But as I was saying, when there is more than one survivor, the examination committee decides on the winner, and that decision is final. So I presume that they concluded that you were the one most fit to be king, while Ennui was granted sufferance to remain in your company, unusual as such an outcome is."

"Sufferance, hell! She is my oath friend."

"I think the committee realized that there would be mischief, Sire, if they did not grant you that indulgence."

Havoc nodded grimly. "They were right. Still, they might have felt more comfortable with her as king. She's civilized, and decent."

"And without great strength or courage, Sire, by her own statement. Do you think she would make a good king?"

"No. The officers would push her around."

"And they will not push *you* around, Sire."

"Not for long," he agreed. "So they may not have wanted a barbarian king, but I was the best remaining alternative."

"I suspect you were the best of all the candidates, Sire."

The dragon seed did not buzz, so this was not false flattery. "So it was more or less chance that I became king. This strikes me as a foolish way to select for an important position."

"Sire, the king must be able to handle unexpected or difficult situations. I understand that no training can assure that ability. You seem to have it, and that makes you an excellent choice."

Again the seed did not buzz. "Are you losing your objectivity, Symbol?"

Her image blushed, by having her clothing turn pink. "Yes, Sire. You have a certain power of personality that reminds me of Deal."

"Teach me the Current Events."

The illusion picture changed, becoming the colorful globe of Charm. "The details are ineffably complicated, Sire, but the generalities will do for orientation. There are several ongoing interChroma problems, and some present trouble spots. The most critical may be the White rebellion."

"The Science Chroma?"

"You know of it already, Sire?"

"I am a quick study," he reminded her.

"White believes that Science is the original magic of the colonists, a thousand years ago, Sire. That all the volcanoes of the source planet, which they call Earth, were White magic. So they are therefore most representative of the original stock, rather than the nonChroma folk."

"So one of them should be king," Havoc said, appreciating the rationale.

"Yes, Sire. Their belief is of course mythology; no one knows the true nature of the colonists. But they hold to it. They have grown increasingly restive, in the face of the policy of having only nonChroma kings, and last year declared White Chroma to be an independent kingdom. This goes against our policy of global unity, so must be suppressed. But it is not easy to impose order on an entire Chroma. The magic of no other Chroma will work in White terrain, other than that sponsored by particular gems, and that is severely limited by the White ambiance. The Chroma stones must be invoked in nonChroma regions for best effect."

"So it means nonChroma soldiers invading White, and fighting White magic, at a disadvantage."

"Yes, Sire. King Deal had assembled a force, and action was incipient at the time of his demise."

"You think there is a connection?"

"Sire, it is not my place to—"

"Agreed. I'll ponder it. What other problems has King Deal bequeathed me?"

"There is an illness spreading across several Chroma that is most awkward, Sire. It's a magic mental malady, causing the victims to suffer opened minds. That is, their strongest thoughts are broadcast to the minds of other sufferers, and they receive the thoughts of those others."

"Mind reading? But I understood that this is one of the particular magics, with the Translucent Chroma specializing in it."

"Yes, Sire, but they have it under control. This is wild. It means that when a victim wants to sleep, he is bombarded by the conscious thoughts, and the feelings of anger, lust, hate, love, violence, and death from the others nearby. I understand it is unsettling. There is no mental privacy for sex, for example. If one person goes mad, all victims near him experience that madness."

Havoc considered having to share his private feelings with others, continually. "They do have a problem. Does it operate in nonChroma regions?"

"No, Sire. Or at least the effect is not as strong there; the radius of affectation diminishes. That is, another person may have to be within three feet for the thoughts to intrude, instead of twenty feet. Because there is no truly magic free region on planet Charm, just regions of weaker magic. But the numbers fleeing the Chroma are becoming a burden to the neighboring nonChroma villages. They are not accustomed to roughing it in the field, doing without their normal magic. So there is a refugee problem."

"Can the Translucent Chroma folk control it?"

"Yes, Sire. But that means the victims must be transported to Translucent sites, and that generates its own disruption. King Deal was organizing ad hoc convoys. But it's a logistical nightmare, and they run afoul of bandits who prey on folk unable to defend themselves with magic."

"I see. What else?"

"A plague of blue locusts is devastating Black Chroma farmland, Sire, and there is the threat of famine. King Deal was organizing missions to eliminate the pestilence, and to feed the hungry, but was encountering political opposition."

"Is not the king's word final?"

"It should be, Sire. But in the field, far from the capital, there are times when it requires buttressing. The neighboring Silver Chroma has a surplus, but there has been bad blood between local Silver and Black, and the supplies seem not to travel very rapidly."

"I begin to appreciate the challenge of kingship! What else?"

"Just one more current significant crisis, Sire. A new Black Chroma volcano is forming in a Green demesne. If it intensifies, there will be significant loss."

"Black Chroma—the Void. But I know no more of it. Why should neighboring Black and Green Chroma be a problem?"

"Sire, they are not a problem, ordinarily. The distribution of volcanoes seems to be largely random, and on occasion one color does impinge on another, or even form an enclave within a larger territory of a different Chroma. But a Void Chroma is not a good neighbor. You see, almost all other volcanoes blow outward, forming cones and broader circles of their Chroma, their magic diminishing with distance from the source. A Void is the opposite: it sucks inward. Anything within its range disappears into its maw, never to return. Not in any manner we recognize, at any rate. So a Void Chroma volcano is a huge deadly dent in the planet where very little lives. To have one form within the region of another means doom for any people not immediately evacuated, and all their works will be lost."

"Still, it is better to move than to be killed by the Void."

"If the advance of the Void is certain, Sire. But no volcano is entirely predictable. Some abort early, and make no mischief. Some erupt a few times, then go dormant. A few become major efforts. So the odds are that a new Void will be small. Local farmers and artisans don't want to give up their livelihoods for any false alarm. But neither do they want to die. The king must anticipate the future of the volcano, and decide the extent of the local evacuation."

"What Chroma handles visions of the future?"

"Precognition, Sire? There is no such magic we know of. The future is indeterminate, just as the past is fixed. Necessarily, as there would be paradox."

"So I can't get advice from a later date."

"That is correct, Sire."

"And if I guess wrong—"

"There is already more than enough resentment of the king's minions, Sire. Obvious mistakes are unwise."

"I think I wish I had not come upon the scene at this time."

"But Sire, this is a quiet time."

He stared at her image. The seed did not buzz. "This job is more challenging than I anticipated." There was an element of humor, as he had never anticipated being king.

"This is why it is not voluntary, Sire. You must serve as well as you can, for the first year."

"I think I will need a good deal of support and help."

"Sire, you will have it. But the key decisions must always be yours."

"And I must make decisions of policy on all these Current Events crises before this day ends."

"Yes, Sire. You can of course endorse King Deal's programs, but even though I believe in them, I must tell you that it would be better for you to establish your own policies from the outset."

Establish his own policies, to correctly govern a world—when he had only yesterday arrived on the scene, as it were. For the moment he felt overwhelmed.

"Symbol, I realize you are in grief. But—"

"Sire, I am here." Her image turned to him, approaching. Then he felt her physical body, embracing him, soothing him, providing the reassurance of a supportive presence. This was neither sexual nor romantic; she was quietly comforting him in his extremity of uncertainty.

And the dragon seed buzzed.

Chapter 4—Mystery

Gale peered out of the coach, and down, as it floated across the red land. She had known that such lands existed, because they had seen the fringes of color, and the dragon Mentor had shown images of them to her and Havoc, but they had never been truly real to her. Now they were, as was their amazing magic.

She turned back to the other person in the coach. His name was Throe. She had hardly spoken to him so far, but needed to know more about the situation. "Why won't you tell me why I am being taken to City Triumph?"

"King's orders, Lady."

"You took Havoc away. What happened to him?"

"He is all right, Lady."

She knew that, because otherwise Havoc would not have sent his message to her to come. "That's not a sufficient answer."

The man was silent.

Gale had a serious concern about Havoc's situation, and she was almost certain that Throe knew what had happened to him. So she applied pressure. "There are two ways we can do this, king's man. I will try repeatedly to escape, and you will have to bind me and deliver me disheveled and bruised. Or you can simply tell me what I want to know. Then we will converse amicably, like this." She angled her body as she sat opposite him, and spread her knees slightly, providing him with just enough of a view of her thighs under the skirt to want more. She already knew he would not molest her, but also that he liked to look at women. Men did. It made them manageable.

"Lady, you put me in a difficult situation. I am under orders not to tell you."

Gale launched herself at the coach door. She had it open and her head out before he caught hold of her around the waist. "Lady!" he protested.

She turned her full bosom into his face. "I think you must choose between orders," she said. "I think you do not wish to deliver me in bad condition."

"You're bluffing. You're coming voluntarily."

"Am I?" She looked out the door.

"Lady—"

"And why do you call me Lady? You know I'm just a common barbarian girl."

He paused a moment. "Will you agree not to tell?"

She had him. "Yes."

He let her go, and she resumed her seat. She crossed her legs. Then he told her. She stared back at him, not believing it. Then she slumped on the seat, thinking it through. Perhaps it was possible. She would find out.

"I find it hard to believe that Havoc can really be king. What happened to the old one?"

"King Deal died two days ago. It was an accident. The law requires that a new king be installed within one day. Havoc won the examination."

"And what is your place in this, that caused you to come for Havoc, and now for me?"

"I was King Deal's bodyguard. When he died, I was suspected of being at fault, so was demoted to inclement duty. But when Havoc became king, he restored me, and sent me to fetch you."

She still found this hard to believe. "You flogged his mother, and he restored you?"

"I apologized for that. He understood."

That evidently was the case. Havoc had always been wild on the surface and rational beneath, and he did not hold a grudge unless it made sense. But to restore the man who had done that to his mother— there had to be more to that situation than she had heard. Havoc could forgive, but he could also kill, and this case must have been a close decision.

"If I may ask, Lady—"

She might have thought he was mocking her, but her dragon seed had not buzzed any of the times he used that term. "I am a barbarian girl," she repeated. "Not a lady."

"You will be the consort of the king. That makes you a Lady, by definition."

Interesting. "So what's your question?"

"What is the meaning of the words I was told to say to you?"

She was not about to tell him of the dragon seed, and obviously Havoc hadn't. But the rest was no secret. "We betrothed each other when he was thirteen years, and I twelve. We had nothing of seeming value to exchange. So we used seeds, and said our words. It was the vow that counted."

"And only the two of you knew of this," Throe said. "So you knew the message was authentic."

"Yes." But of course she had known, because her dragon seed had not buzzed. Havoc had needed a convincing way to summon her, so that her ability to know the truth would not be apparent.

It was time for her to learn more about Havoc's situation, and thus her own. "Why did they make a barbarian king?"

"There was an examination of ten people. He won. That is all I know about that."

It was true, for the seed did not buzz. She continued to question him, and by the time they arrived at the fantastic pyramid city, she had a fair notion. Yet it was still hard to accept. Two days ago she and Havoc had been planning to marry; now everything was changed. Their wedding would have to be postponed.

In due course, and much wonder, Throe conducted her inside the pyramid, where they entered a small wooden room. "Be prepared," he told her. "This will rise. It is safe, though it may not feel that way to you."

Reassured by his words and the seed, she stood in the room, and did not scream when it suddenly started rising. It moved up for a while, then paused, and they opened its door and walked out to another room, which then also rose. "A single elevator can go only five floors," Throe explained. "Our ropes are not safe beyond that length. So we use a series of lifts."

"Why not just walk?"

"Civilized folk don't like to walk," he said wryly. "And it is a fair climb."

At last they came to the top—and there was Havoc, outlandishly dressed but in good condition. He swept her into his arms. "Now my world settles a bit," he said. "Now that I have you back."

"What's this about your being king?"

He hesitated. "That's right—he wasn't supposed to tell you."

"I countermanded that. Don't blame him. Havoc, why are you wearing a clown suit?"

"Talk with the Lady Aspect. Maybe you can persuade her to dress me in something more appropriate." He set her down and pointed her at a portly older woman. "And if you ever can't find me, ask the Lady Ennui." He indicated another woman. "She is my oath friend."

"Oath friend!" This was another amazing thing. The Dragon Mentor and Gale herself were the only other folk Havoc had oathed, and there had never really been formal oathing between them for that, just the betrothal.

"We helped each other get through the exam." He reached around her to shake hands with Throe. "Thanks for bringing her. Now we must consult." He turned. "Gale, go with Aspect now. We'll meet again soon." Then he ushered Throe into another room.

Somewhat flustered, Gale turned to the Lady Aspect. "Greeting, Lady."

The woman smiled. "Accepted, Lady."

Gale realized that here in this pell-mell rush of civilized activity, the country manners were not necessarily in force. "What is going on?"

"Lady Gale, the king is very busy at the moment, preparing for his inaugural address. I am sure he intends no disrespect to you. I will prepare you for what is to come. Please, this way."

Not completely pleased, Gale followed her to another complex of rooms. "I don't know what I expected, but not this crazy huge building where people don't walk, and clown suits."

"The king's residence and clothing have become rather artificial," the woman agreed. "But it is better to accept such minor things, in the interest of preserving your freedom for important matters.".

"Important?"

"The king must make decisions that affect the welfare of the people of this planet. That's important. His clothing is only to reassure those who might otherwise fear he would run naked through the halls."

"What's wrong with doing that?"

There was a very slight pause, as if there were doubt about her seriousness. "People tend to judge by superficials." The woman glanced at her. "King Havoc is an extremely quick study. Are you also?"

"When I have to be." Like Havoc, Gale had learned how to mask her most private thoughts, and to memorize spot information eidetically. It had been a chore, but Mentor had insisted. But she tried not to show these special abilities, because their privacy was her best asset. As with the dragon seed: much of its usefulness would be lost, if anyone else knew of it.

"Then I ask you to understand that I will do my best to see that you learn what you need, to avoid embarrassing yourself or the king as you encounter what is surely an unfamiliar and highly artificial social and political scheme. I do not wish to offend you or cause you discomfort."

The seed did not buzz. Gale was also sure that Havoc had reason to trust this woman. "I will understand."

In the next hour, the Lady Aspect required her to wash and change into an elaborate party dress with a frilly hat and rather nice silken slippers. She explained about a number of ordinary things Gale must not do in public, and instructed her on the way to acknowledge the attentions of courtiers. The whole business was weird, as if scratching and belching weren't natural, but the dragon seed never buzzed, so she went along with it. Still, she wished that she and Havoc could just go home and forget all this nonsense.

"Who are you?" she finally asked, realizing that even in this melange of oddities, the Lady Aspect was not ordinary.

"I am King Deal's widow. This is why I am familiar with courtly procedure."

"You're the queen?" Gale was astonished.

"No longer. There is now no queen, but in time you will surely fill that role."

"But you—how can you be helping me, when—"

"The fate of those closely associated with an ex-king is not necessarily kind. King Havoc chose to be kind to me, and I will serve him to be best of my ability."

Gale did not need the dragon seed to pick up on the mixed pain and gratitude the woman felt. Her situation seemed to be as difficult as Gale's own, for different reason. "But I heard that King Deal died just two days ago. Don't you miss him?"

"Oh, yes, dear." For a moment the woman froze, as if suppressing sudden pain. "But I do what I must."

So recently widowed, and now she had to help the new king's girlfriend get organized. "They don't let you retire, or something?"

"I would have to remarry."

And evidently she didn't have to remarry, if she served the new king. It was coming clear. So she would be keeping her grief to herself, and making herself as useful as possible. Because even in her pain, she had to survive.

Gale looked at herself in the mirror. She looked like a stranger, some lady in a minstrel play, in a gown that sparkled even when it was still. She liked it, but felt out of place, pretending to be a civilized lady.

"Now you must talk privately with the Lady Ennui," the Lady Aspect said. "She will be here in a moment."

"Havoc's oath friend," she said. That rankled; how could he have done that in only two days? Oath friendship was for life, and was never carelessly undertaken. Especially not with the opposite gender.

"You must trust her. What she has to say will surprise and dismay you. Do not argue, just learn and understand."

"I will believe what Havoc tells me. I do not know the rest of you."

"He will confirm, but he can't tell you all. There are too many eyes on the king."

"I don't understand."

"You will have had little experience of magic. One aspect of it is mind reading. The king can keep his secrets, shielded by his crown, but the rest of us can not hide our thoughts from Chroma invasion. Only by staying clear of Chroma representatives can we be private."

So she thought. Gale played the innocent. "But this is a nonChroma region. Magic doesn't work here, does it?"

"It works in the presence of Chroma gemstones. The Chroma representatives carry them. So while they are not supposed to snoop on other minds, they surely do so on occasion. They will be curious about you, Lady Gale, for the king's lover is partial to information no one else possesses."

That made unkind sense. Gale would surely be a target for snooping. "So I should stay away from any Chroma folk?"

"You cannot avoid them, Lady, for you will be introduced to them an hour from now, in a formal gathering. This magic can not be seen or felt; your mind will be open. But there are limitations, and if you remain aware of them, you can minimize the peeking."

Gale could do more than that. But she didn't need any warning buzz from the dragon seed to know that her ability to mask her thoughts must remain secret. "How can I do that?"

"The mind readers can not attune to a single mind; they receive all minds at once. I understand it is as if every person is talking, speaking his thoughts. So it is a babble, and the only intelligible thoughts are those of the closest person. So you are protected if you are surrounded by others, and they are between you and the mind reader. If you are alone, you must be distant from a mind reader, for he can hear your mind only within a few score feet. So normally, here in the king's apartment, you are safe. It is only when you must mingle with Chroma representatives that you are at risk."

"Fortunately I have no state secrets," Gale said wryly. "I'm just a barbarian girl."

The Lady Aspect smiled. "Perhaps. But you are to be the king's lover. That makes you a Lady and a person of great interest. And you are about to have secrets that need to be protected."

Gale was troubled. "You were King Deal's wife. You must hate the very idea of him having a lover."

"Not so. My husband's lover was the Lady Symbol, of the Invisible or Air Chroma. She is a fine woman, and a personal friend of mine, who is now educating King Havoc."

"I don't want him near her!"

"My dear, he must be near her; she is his most useful contact. He has a great deal to learn in a very short time, and she alone has the expertise to teach him."

"I don't like this."

"You surely know King Havoc better than any other person here. Is he likely to be subverted by a seductive civilized woman?"

"No."

"Then what is your concern?"

"Jealousy of any other woman taking any of his attention."

Aspect laughed. "You must learn not to speak so candidly; it is considered uncivilized. At any rate, you are as lovely a woman in your own right as any here, and you share his culture. I think you have little to fear. But there is one thing more I must tell you, before the Lady Ennui comes."

"You said that she will surprise and dismay me. More so than what you have just done?"

"Yes, dear. I am trying to prepare you."

"Why does this have to be so complicated? Why can't I just be with Havoc?"

"Because of what the Lady Ennui will tell you. This will be secret between the two of you; I do not know what it is. But I can tell you why: because we believe that my husband, King Deal, was murdered. We do not want King Havoc to be murdered also."

Gale felt a terrible chill. Suddenly she understood why this bereaved woman was taking so much trouble with her. She *knew* that the king was vulnerable. "What else?"

"The Lady Ennui is King Havoc's oath friend and personal secretary. He trusts her to arrange his schedule—and yours. She has something in mind for you, and you must trust her. You must also hide what she tells you. There is one other way to protect your mind: get close to King Havoc and remain there. The crown protects him, physically and mentally, and its ambiance will also protect your mind from intrusion. So as long as there are Chroma representatives near, stay with the king. When the formal meeting is done, the Chroma representatives will depart, and you will be safer."

"When can I have sex with Havoc?"

"This is too candid, again. Civilized women pretend disinterest in sex, at least in public. In private they may pretend interest. But the answer is thereafter. He is as eager to be with you as you are to be with him, but his duties as king constrain him. It is not easy to be king."

"I guess not."

There was a pause, as the Lady Aspect hesitated. Then she spoke again. "It is not easy to be the king's consort, either. King Havoc is treating me very well, and I wish to help him in whatever way I can. He loves you, and so I wish to help you also. If there should ever be something you need, that I can provide—"

"Thank you, Lady Aspect. I'll ask." Gale hardly knew this woman, but she seemed knowledgeable and sincere, and would surely make a good friend. The dragon seed had never once buzzed in her presence. "I think you have already helped me more than I understand." Even though she didn't like all of what the woman was telling her.

A servant girl appeared. "Lady, the Lady Ennui is here."

"Bring her in."

In a moment, the rather plain thin woman who was Havoc's mysterious oath friend entered the room. She and the Lady Aspect exchanged nods, and Aspect turned to Gale. "Parting."

"Acknowledged." Then Aspect left, and Gale was alone with Ennui.

"Greeting," Gale said formally.

"Acknowledged."

"So what the hell is going on?" Gale demanded. "How did you come to be Havoc's oath friend?"

"There is little time, so I must be brief. We were two of ten entrants in the examination for the kingship, though we did not know that was its purpose. I was an ordinary clerk of middle age; he was a barbarian warrior. We had little in common, but that perhaps was why we needed each other. There seemed to be the threat of death around us. I was weak and frightened, and he was strong but ignorant. He asked me to help him with information, but I was afraid of him, and made him swear oath friendship, knowing that barbarians take such oaths seriously. He did so, and thereafter we worked together. I helped him as I could with information about civilized ways, and he saved my life. I think it was an unequal exchange; he could have survived and won without me. What was a temporary expedient became more important as we discovered the enormity of the new situation. I think he needs a person he can trust more than ever now, and I am that one. Apart from you. Now I serve him as personal secretary, and that service gives my life meaning. I am not a barbarian, but I take my oath of friendship with him as seriously as anything in my life. I am utterly committed to him. He trusts me to do his bidding competently, and I am making every effort to do so. He asked me to prepare you for what we believe must be."

Gale was uneasy already. The dragon seed had not buzzed, and that, oddly, made her nervous. This woman was truly Havoc's committed friend, as much as Gale herself, weird as that seemed. "What do you believe must be?"

"I think the Lady Aspect has told you that we believe King Deal was murdered, and that Havoc may be in similar danger. This is the mystery we must unravel without delay. We need to find that murderer, and learn how and why. Havoc is virtually overwhelmed by the demands of his office; he has to learn civilized ways, and meet all the people, and form policy on several current crises that King Deal was handling. Havoc is smart—smarter than he lets on, I think—but he has only days to master a job that should take years to learn. He wants to go home to your village with you, but can't. He must succeed as king, or die."

"He could have told me this himself. Why delegate it to you?"

"Because time is short, and he must focus on his first public address, which will occur within half an hour. Also, I have more of the details of this mission than he does, and more time than he does, so I can better acquaint you. The lady Aspect has explained why you must guard your thoughts?"

"Yes. I will stay close to Havoc, and avoid Chroma folk when I can. What mission?"

"King Deal was investigating something when he died. He believed he was close to getting an answer to his questions. It must have been important, or he wouldn't have taken the trouble, when he had so many other matters to handle. He told no one what it was, but we have one hint because of a report just in from a spy: something about the changelings."

"The what?"

"Changelings. We don't know what that means either; we thought it was folklore, similar to that of the Glamors. That some children get stolen and exchanged for others, without the parents knowing the difference. But the spy report suggests that changelings may indeed exist, and that they may be connected with a Temple. So we need to investigate. If Deal's investigation of such a thing really did get him killed, then this information is vital. It may be a false lead, but it is the only one we have. Havoc can't do it himself; he has a rebellion to quell and a region to evacuate, and in any event too many eyes are on the king to allow him to investigate personally. But you can, because no one will suspect you."

This was not improving. She almost wished the dragon seed had buzzed. "But aren't all eyes on the king's lover?"

"Yes." Ennui paused. "Lady Gale, I think you will not like this. Havoc wants you to know that you don't have to do it. But it is a chance we may not get again, and if we don't solve this mystery, the consequence could be dire. He believes you can do it, and that you will understand."

"I suppose I can look into it for him. But if many eyes are on me too—"

"This is what you won't like: there will need to be a substitute for you, an emulation, a woman taking your place, so that others don't know you are gone."

"Taking my place! As his *lover*?"

"Yes, Lady Gale. Answering to your name, sleeping in his bed. In fact, she will be enchanted to believe she is you, so that should anyone read her thoughts, there will be no indication."

"The hell!"

"Lady, Havoc loves you. He hates this part of it. But the Lady Symbol persuaded him it was best."

"King Deal's lover? The one who is 'educating' him?"

"She wants King Deal's murder to be solved and avenged as much as anyone does. She is Chroma, but her judgment is to be respected. She is thoroughly experienced in the ways and problems of being the king's lover. She believes that this way there will be no indication that you are absent, or that there is even any investigation. That lack of suspicion will best protect you—and Havoc wants you protected."

Still no buzz from the seed. Ennui believed what she was saying—and it must be true, for the dragon seed knew the truth even when the speaker didn't. "And where will I be, while this bitch is in my bed?"

"Lady, you must revert to barbarian, or at least to lowly status, and join a troupe. There is one scheduled to depart this city tomorrow. It is an educational group, on tour to a number of outlying nonChroma villages, in the interest of cultural unity and personal welfare. You will be an entertainer, an actress—"

"I have seen the shows put on by such troupes; they visit Trifle every few years. I used to want to be part of one of them."

"Yes. You could do well. You will replace the leading player, and assume her roles in their plays. No one will suspect you of being the king's lover."

"But some of those educational plays—"

"Havoc says he hates that part as much as you hate having a woman steal your bed."

Gale pondered. She was appalled by it, but it rang true. No one would suspect. It was almost perfect concealment. "You're right: I do not like this. But I may do it."

"And when the troupe stops near a Temple village, you can investigate, and perhaps solve the mystery of the changelings, and ascertain its relevance to King Deal's quest."

"But we don't even know that he was killed because of this investigation. They could be purely coincidental things."

"Yes, Lady. That will be for you to determine. We need to know the truth, whatever it may be."

"So my choices are between doing what appalls me, and risking Havoc's death by murder."

"Yes. You can consider, and tell Havoc your decision when you are alone with him tonight. You will have that much, regardless. Now you must go to join him, and meet the public."

Just like that. But what could she do? "I never liked the king. Now I don't like being part of the king's business."

"Yes, Lady Gale. It is not nice business." Ennui led the way out of the apartment.

They rejoined Havoc, who hugged her again. There was the usual buzz of the seed when they touched after a separation. "One more chore, and then we have the night," he whispered, kissing her ear.

But what else besides the night would they have? This whole business was insufferably complicated and emotionally painful.

There were two men standing near. "Chief, this is the Lady Gale, my fiancée," Havoc said, and the man bowed briefly. "And my bodyguard, Throe." Throe bowed similarly. Gale already knew him, but realized that this was a formality.

"I am glad to meet you both," Ennui murmured, prompting her.

"I am glad to meet you both," Gale repeated.

"You garbled it," Ennui murmured similarly to Havoc. "Next time, introduce the lady *to* the man, one at a time. And leave the bodyguard out of it. He's supposed to be in the background."

"Thanks, mother," Havoc muttered, and both men smiled. Gale realized with a start that they liked the barbarian king, and liked Ennui.

A servant appeared. "The Chroma representatives are here," he announced.

"King Havoc and the Lady Gale will meet them now," Ennui said. And to Havoc: "They will introduce themselves; just nod and smile, both of you. And Gale—stand close to Havoc, touching him if you can."

"I'll touch her," Havoc said, putting his arm around her.

Ten people filed into the room, in ten colors of cloaks. "Sire, I am Blue," the first said. That was an obvious truth, as his face and hands were as blue as his clothing. In fact, even his hair was blue. Gale nodded and smiled as directed.

The second was a woman. "Sire, I am Yellow." Then on through the other colors, concluding with a woman whose cloak was iridescent, as were her hat, veil, gloves, and slippers. This turned out to be Symbol, of the Invisible Chroma. She really did seem to be almost invisible, being entirely concealed by her outfit.

"I thank you, Chroma Representatives, for your attendance," Havoc said. "Please accompany me to the site of my inaugural address."

"Sire, we are glad to," the blue man said.

Havoc walked to the entrance of the apartment, where the ramp and elevator came. He hesitated. Gale felt the tension in him. She understood his reluctance to enter this trundling chamber; she didn't like it much herself.

"Havoc, you must board," Ennui murmured. "We'll be with you."

He stepped into the chamber. Gale stepped with him, and Chief, Throe, and Ennui followed. That was all; the Chroma Representatives would travel another way, it seemed.

"Remember, Havoc," Ennui said. "Gale must stay close to you, to protect her thoughts. I trust you won't find that burdensome."

"I'd rather run off with her now, and skip the speech." He squeezed Gale around the waist and managed to give her bottom a stroke. That was one reassuringly normal aspect of this abnormal situation.

"That's fine. She's your lover."

"Fiancée."

"Fiancée. Your audience will understand. They will know that you have no intention of being separated from this woman any time soon."

Gale felt Havoc stiffen. "She did tell you? I'm not sure this is right."

"She told me," Gale said grimly.

"The question is not whether it is right, Sire," Chief said, "but whether it is necessary."

"*Is* it necessary? All I want is to be with Gale. That would make the rest of this nonsense bearable."

"This must be your decision, Sire."

"Or Gale's decision." Havoc's arm around her remained tense.

"Don't put it on *me*, you horse's hole!" Gale flared. "I never voted for this outrage."

The other three in the lift averted their faces, and Gale realized that she had committed a fault by speaking intemperately to the king.

But Havoc wasn't bothered. He liked seeing her normal, just as she liked seeing him that way, even in fleeting glimpses. "Neither did I," he replied. "Yet my advisers tell me it's best."

"What advisers?"

"Chief. Ennui."

Gale turned to Throe. "And you know, too?"

"Lady, I have to know, so as to best protect the king. But it is not my business to judge."

"And how many others know?"

"Only we five, and Symbol," Ennui said. "A secret can't be well kept if too many know it."

"And you and Chief think we should do it, because no one will suspect and we might learn something useful. What about you, Throe?"

"Lady, I can afford to have no opinion on the decisions of the king, unless they affect his physical safety."

"You can't afford to express them, you mean."

"Yes, Lady."

"Suppose I get so mad I stab him to death?"

"Lady, you can't."

But Gale was in a fit of rage. She drew her knife and waved it near Havoc's chest. Havoc made no motion, knowing her ways: she would make a show, but would never try to hurt him. "What's to stop me?"

"Lady, the king could stop you if he wished. I could stop you. But neither of us need to."

"Oh?" She stabbed the knife toward Havoc, intending to touch only the cloth of his fancy clothing, to make her point.

But the blade sheered off, as if some invisible hand was turning her wrist. She tried again, with similar result. She could not stab him, even to make a feint.

"Lady, it is the crown," Throe explained. "Its magic protects the king from physical and mental harm."

"So I see." She put away the knife. Now she understood why she had been allowed to carry it into the presence of the king. "But you do have an opinion. What is it?"

"Lady—"

"Answer," Havoc said.

Throe nodded. "It stinks."

Gale was gratified. Finally she had a human response.

"I agree," Ennui said. "So does Chief. But Havoc is not on a pleasure tour. We believe this ugly device is necessary to secure the king's long term safety. King Deal was killed while wearing the crown, so that is not proof against this enemy. We must know the truth."

"Do you agree?" Gale asked Throe.

"I do, Lady, with disgust. I felt better about flogging his mother. But I may not be able to protect him from what happened to King Deal. I was there, and helpless."

The damned dragon seed never buzzed.

The elevator trundled to a stop. The door opened. They would no longer be private. But Gale had one more question. "I can stand next to Havoc. But you other three—what protects your minds?"

"We will stand close behind you," Chief said. "Each of us focusing on a different thought. We will thus run interference for each other. If we crowd you, Lady, we beg your tolerance."

They had it figured. "Crowd me," she agreed. "Just keep your hands off my ass." She had not yet decided about the awful ploy, but wanted the secret kept regardless. At least she knew now that these people were not evil in nature; they were trying to do their jobs of advising and protecting the king, to the best of their abilities, and they were considering the long term as well as the short term. That impressed her, despite her outrage.

She walked with Havoc, and the other three did follow close behind. She tuned them out, obsessed with her problem. Havoc trusted Ennui because she was his oath friend, and she did indeed seem completely dedicated to his welfare. Chief was the former king's chief of staff, doing the same job for the new king, lending essential continuity to the royal policies. He had every reason to do his best. And Throe— the man was competent and honest, and the dragon seed had never challenged him. Their merged judgment had to be respected.

Now Havoc was on a stage, and she was with him. It overlooked the enormous center of this giant wooden pyramid. Ahead and below was the broad triangular expanse of the inner base of it, and it was thronged with well dressed people. The sight was awesome; she had never before seen so large an enclosure or so huge a crowd. For the moment it distracted her from the turmoil of her thoughts.

Across the back of the stage were the ten Chroma Representatives, their colorful presence signaling the legitimacy of this ceremony. The center of their line was close behind the king, and the closest was the shimmering flowing cape of the Translucent Chroma, Water, whose specialty was mind reading. But they could not touch Havoc or Gale, if the crown protected them, and the three others had moved themselves as a tight group some distance to the side, as if to avoid intruding on the king. Thus the quiet interplay of snoop and counter-snoop, clear enough once one knew what to look for.

A herald appeared. "Citizens of Triumph, and Planet Charm," he cried, and his voice was somehow amplified to reverberate across the entire space. "King Deal is gone. King Havoc is here. Give homage."

As one, the people bowed their heads.

"Long live King Havoc!" the herald cried. "And his intended queen,

Gale of Trifle."

The crowd roared approval. Gale was surprised and somewhat dismayed; the people didn't even know the two of them, yet here they were enthusiastically welcoming them. This was a hollow show.

After a suitable pause, the herald spoke again. "King Havoc will address you now."

Without further ceremony, Havoc, and necessarily Gale, stepped to the brink of the platform. She had no idea what he was primed to say, but was sure he had prepared carefully. This was his first public appearance, and it surely counted for a lot, because the people would judge him by it. They might have no power to choose or keep their king, but it would be better if they liked him.

Still, she knew Havoc in a way his new advisers did not. She suspected he would have a surprise for them.

Havoc spoke. He could address a group, because of his experience instructing martial arts classes; he had no problem with shyness. Just with temper—and he seldom tipped his hand about that prematurely. But now was probably the time.

"Greeting."

There was a pause. Then the audience caught on. "Sire!" many voices responded enthusiastically. They evidently liked interacting directly with the king.

Havoc wasted no further time on social amenities. "I'm a barbarian. I never gave a green bear's ass for the king or his works. Every time my village gets a little bit ahead, the damn tax collectors come and take it away. Then they come and take *me* away, and make *me* king—and I still don't give half a wad of stale dragon poop for the job."

Ah, yes; this was vintage Havoc! Gale watched the audience, to see how it was reacting. She was not disappointed. At first they were stunned, having no doubt expected a routine package of praise for the former king and his works, regret for his passing, and a promise to continue his policies and try to improve on them. But the reference to the tax collectors got to them—nobody liked those beasts!—and the earthy animal references were making them react. This was a true barbarian talking.

"I'm not going to tell you what a great man King Deal was," Havoc continued. "I always hated him, as the symbol of the oppressive distant government whose cruel heel was on the necks of all the villagers I know. I swore that if I ever got the chance, I'd destroy that bastard. But I didn't get the chance; something else did it for me. The idiot took a leap off a high cliff and bashed his brains out on the rocks below. So he's gone, and good riddance."

Gale looked around the stage. The herald was standing with mouth agape. Chief stood with his face a mask, showing no emotion. That surely meant that he was similarly stunned. Throe was facing away from her, so she couldn't read his reaction, but Ennui looked as if she had just wet her pants. They were learning that Havoc was untamed, and had been well named.

"I didn't want to come here," Havoc continued. "So I escaped from the king's thugs. But they tied my mother to a public post, stripped her naked, and flogged her until I came in. Maybe you civilized folk don't care about your families, but we barbarians do. I didn't like it any better when I got here and they made me take a bath and dress in a royal clown suit. They told me not to be crude in public. Well, all I have to say to that is—"

He paused, as the members of the vast audience stared. Then he let fly with a resounding belch.

It started with the children. They were naturally uncivilized: they laughed. Then a few adults picked it up, powerless to resist the forbidden urge. It was just so sudden, so surprising, so gross, so appropriate. Whereupon, like an unstoppable eruption of slime, it spread across the rest of the throng. Now everyone was laughing, helplessly, trying to sober up, but unable. Only the herald, and the ten Chroma Representatives, and the king's own small party remained passive. Yet Gale thought she spied smug smiles lurking behind Throe's mask of a face, and the Lady Symbol's veil. Maybe they understood that Havoc was not angry. His real anger was something else.

Havoc gave them time to subside somewhat, then resumed. "But I have been learning some things. I discovered that King Deal had some good men and women working for him, and they are not heartless monsters. I kept them all on, because I don't know beans about civilization, let alone governance, and they do. He had competent and loyal men, and beautiful women, and a wife and a lover who truly grieve for him. How bad could he be?"

The last of the laughter faded away, but the throng was watching and listening somewhat warily, not sure where this was leading. Gale wasn't sure either, but she knew he would have a point. Havoc's nature was anything but pointless.

"King Deal's widow, Queen Aspect, had not slept for most of two days, mourning the brutally sudden and shocking loss of her husband of twenty years, the father of three of her four children. Yet when I, the usurper of her husband's place, asked her to help me, she did so graciously, without stinting, and she is now organizing my personal life. King Deal's lover, the Lady Symbol, was in grief for him also, but she provided me with the background and information I needed to make sense of this appallingly complicated business of kingship. Everyone has helped, and I am here before you now because of their efforts. I can not condemn these good people, even if they are civilized; they are all in as difficult a situation as I am."

There was a smattering of applause as the audience accepted his acceptance of the prior king's staff. But where was he going?

"I learned that there are serious matters to be attended to. The

Science Chroma is in rebellion, believing that it alone represents the true nature of mankind." There was a welling of outrage, and many eyes focused on the white figure standing among the Chroma Representatives, though he of course would not be guilty of the decision of his Chroma. "There is a mental disease spreading across the fringes of several Chroma, causing all minds to be opened for reading, depriving their victims of any secrets or privacy, even in the bedroom or privy. There is a plague of blue locusts generating famine—and if we let the Black Chroma starve, who else will be next? And a Void volcano is erupting in a Green Chroma circle, a deadly threat to those in its vicinity. King Deal was handling these problems; now I must do so, and I am unlikely to be as competent as he was, for I have no experience. But I can't ignore any of these challenges, or let any people suffer unnecessarily. There is simply too much to do, and no one else to do it."

Many in the audience were nodding, appreciating the formidable problems. Havoc had simplified and clarified them beautifully, and made their urgency obvious.

"I am a barbarian," he repeated. "I don't like this job and I don't want to be here. But I have no choice. Neither do you civilized people, who would rather have a civilized king. So I will do it as well as I can, with the help of King Deal's loyal and capable staff. And with the help of all of you civilized folk, who know so much more than I do." He paused, staring into the audience, meeting the gaze of many individuals. Gale knew how winning his direct earnest gaze could be; it was as if he were seeking specific approval from every person there, no matter how lowly. "Together we will somehow get it done, because we have to. I need you. I need all of you. Are you with me?"

And suddenly there was a roar of sheer approval. It seemed that every person in that mighty throng was now solidly behind their new barbarian king, without illusion as to his nature. The cheering continued interminably, drowning out everything else. Havoc had completely won the populace, and done it as himself, in his own fashion, as an unrepentant uncivilized draftee. He would be known as the barbarian king, without condemnation.

And Gale, who knew how truly he spoke when he said he hated the job, realized that she too had been won over. Havoc would do his best, and part of that best was to surprise the unknown enemy by discovering its secret, and Gale was perhaps the one to accomplish that. She had to do it, though she hated the necessity and ugly detail as much as he did. For love of Havoc, she would let another women embrace him, and she might embrace another man. She hoped it would be done soon, so that they could be together without complication.

At some point she realized that they were back in the elevator, returning to the king's apartment complex. "Brilliant, Sire!" Chief said. "You are a natural politician."

"May I kiss you, Sire?" Ennui asked, with a glance at Gale. Gale nodded, and the woman hugged him and kissed him without further permission. Lady Aspect was like a mother to Havoc; Lady Ennui fell between mother and older sister, with a tinge of forbidden passion. It was clear that Havoc had become her world.

Had they after all known what Havoc intended, and put on an act of surprise? No, she suspected that they had really been caught off-guard, but heartily approved the outcome. Perhaps they had even liked the show. She was pretty sure that Throe had, and the Lady Symbol.

Soon enough she found herself alone with Havoc. "We have nine minutes until dinner," he said.

"Let's not take off our clothing," she suggested. "We'll never get it back on in time." She was nevertheless prepared for the session, and felicitated it as she spoke.

So they had five minutes of constrained passion in their clothing, then straightened it out with at least one minute to spare. Havoc had been ready to burst, and had done so inside her immediately; the rest was spot cleanup. Gale was reassured; he had not been dallying with any other woman. "This isn't over," he said with mock darkness as they went out to the dining room. She was sure of it.

The meal, apparently prepared by the household staff under the direction of the Lady Aspect, was wonderful: boiled skunk cabbage, fried lotus blossoms, and fresh plaid bread. Exactly the kind of meal they would have had at home. She wondered briefly whether civilized folk ever ate anything similar, and what the equivalent might have been back on the mysterious source planet from which they all supposedly derived. She knew that the names were likely to be older than the foods; Charm simply didn't have all the things fabulous Earth had.

After the meal, the Ladies Aspect and Ennui joined them, and the Lady Symbol put on a show. "We thought this might provide inspiration," Havoc murmured as they turned their chairs to face the far end of the room. He seemed relaxed and without serious concern, which was of course deceptive, but she was so glad to be together with him that she let it be. They would talk when they were alone again.

Symbol stood in her iridescent uniform. Then a cloud of vapor formed, obscuring her. When it dissipated, she was gone. Except for her slippers, which proceeded to dance by themselves, moving as if occupied by feet. It was evidently an intricate dance, as they flashed up and down and around. Then they paused, and a pair of iridescent stockings floated over them, poked into them, and unrolled to form a shapely pair of legs. The stockings and slippers danced, and it was possible to judge where the nonexistent body should be. Next, the iridescent panties appeared, traveling up and around the stockings, until they spread out snugly in the shape of a marvelously rounded human posterior. Now it seemed to be the lower half of a splendidly endowed woman who was dancing. So it continued, until the whole woman was brightly clothed and present.

Suddenly Gale put it together: "That's Symbol! Not illusion—her in person, dancing."

"Yes, she of the Invisible Chroma," Havoc agreed. "She's not much to look at, nude, though it is possible to see a little of her in a good light."

Oh? "How much of her have you seen?"

"Just a little fuzz where the brain is, and a faint outline of her lungs. I had to feel the rest. Breathing our air pollutes her, you see."

Gale was sure that even a polluted invisible woman represented a considerable feel. "This is fascinating, but what's the point?"

"Just that illusion can be as much expectation as magic. The only magic illusion here was the cloud of vapor, to let her get undressed. Since magic is expensive in the nonChroma regions, economy is best."

"Point noted." She was sure there was more to it, but this was not the occasion to clarify it.

The others departed, and the two of them retired for the night to the royal bedroom. This time they stripped away all their clothes, and made lingering love. It was always better for Gale after Havoc had the edge off; then he became all that a woman could desire. She understood the dynamics of his passion well, yet was moved by it. She could not deny him anything he truly wanted, and that began but hardly ended with sex.

Finally she spoke. "I'll do it."

And of course he had known she would. "Take care of yourself, Gale. Ennui will give you a spy kit."

That was all. They had agreed to be untrue to each other, sexually, for the sake of the kingdom. But they would never be untrue in their love.

⚜

There were five of them making up the education troupe: four men and Gale. Three of the men knew each other, as this was a regular group working the region; Gale had taken the place of its lone woman. Because that woman was older, Gale was made to seem older, emulating Dame Teacher. The villages might or might not know the difference, as this troupe completed its full circuit every four years. It didn't matter, as it was the roles that counted rather than the players, and changes occurred every so often. But it meant that Gale had a fair amount to learn.

So did the other new member. He was a gangling awkward youth of thirteen, not quite at his full height. He was called Lad Student, after his main role. He might have had experience in other troupes, in child roles, but this was his first of this nature. He was plainly somewhat nervous about it. That reassured Gale; she much preferred that this particular role be filled by an innocent.

The three experienced men were Troupe Leader, who was the director, master of ceremonies, and announcer; Carto, from the Cartography Guild, who was their guide; and Guard, from the Warrior's Guild, whose job was to protect them from human, animal, or environmental threats. They were all good men, by reputation, verified by Gale's dragon seed. They liked their jobs and each other, and worked well together.

The first part of the tour was easy: the trip to its tour territory. This was done in the manner of the trip from Trifle to Triumph: by a series of magic coach floats or carries across half a dozen Chroma. Part of the reward for such troupes was a vacation at the capital city, between tour segments. That was why this one was handy. Lad was a Triumph native recruited there.

They had time to talk and get to know each other as they spent the hours in float. Troupe Leader handled it. "Carto, Guard, and I know each other; we're all the same age, early 40's, and we get along. It is our job to get this troupe where it is going and keep it safe, and to get it decent accommodations. We don't expect to rough it in the field much; we'll night mostly in the villages, and be well treated by the natives. They know that if they aren't hospitable to the troupes, there won't be any more, and they do want them to keep coming."

He smiled, and though Gale knew it was the man's business to be engaging, it was a nice smile, and she warmed to him. So did the boy. "We're none of us using our natural name, of course; that's so we have some privacy when we're not touring. Two of you are new, this time, and I think not transferring in from other troupes of quite this nature, so you've never done this before. Am I right, Lad, Dame?"

"Yes," Gale agreed, and Lad nodded bashfully.

"So I'll give you the general background, before we get into the play itself." He glanced at the other two men. "You two can catch a nap, meanwhile; we won't get lost or attacked while we're crossing Chroma."

Guard and Carto nodded, leaned back, and closed their eyes. Whether they would actually sleep Gale didn't know, but the symbolism was important: the dialogue had become private between the remaining three of them.

"Some troupes are for entertainment, with clown shows, odd animals, and magic acts. Remember, the villages don't see much magic, so it's a novelty. Other troupes are cultural, presenting the great plays and music and historical narrations of our people. Our troupe is educational. It is the duty of every living woman to be fruitful and multiply, marrying and bearing at least four surviving children. Ignorance as to the method and dangers of procreation will be no excuse. So the attendance of every unmarried person below the age of eighteen is mandatory. That means some of those kids will not want to be there, and won't pay much attention unless we make it interesting. So we are not just going to suggest the mechanics of sexual performance, or warn about wrong sex; we are going to romanticize it. Get them interested in the story, and maybe they'll sit still for the lesson. And that's where the two of you come in." He looked at Gale and Lad. "You carry the story. I'll narrate it, and speak your lines for you. As you get familiar with it, you'll start speaking your own lines. If you have any problem, such as stage fright, I'll continue speaking them; don't worry about it. But you're going to have to learn body language, and to pick up on my cues. The one thing I can't do for you is the sexual display. The first village will be a tryout, and it may be a disaster." He laughed. "I was the Lad, thirty years ago when I started trouping, and I got so scared first time I had to perform before an audience that I was impotent. Fortunately my opposite was experienced, and she coaxed and coddled me along until I got there, barely. The audience thought it was part of the act. I was complimented for the realism of my performance. Well, it was real all right. Later I got so blasé it was a job to fake awkwardness, and I had to move on to other parts. So, Lad, don't worry if it happens; we all have to start some time. You have not had sex before?"

Lad nodded, blushing.

"But you can get it up?"

Lad nodded again, blushing worse.

"Okay, you'll get through; we'll see to that. Keep in mind that you won't be completing the act, just setting up for it. Now Dame: something I have to get straight. How old are you really?"

"Seventeen."

"But you do know sex?"

"Yes."

"There are two ways we handle your part. One is to have an older woman who uses make up and spot magic to look younger in the key scene. It helps if she has retained her figure. The other, and easier, is to have a young woman who is made up to look older all the time except in the key scene. So we'll make you older. You will never appear in public, in or out of your role, as your actual age. You will always be a woman of thirty plus. Got it?"

"Yes." This was fine with her, as it would further conceal her identity.

"You'll do it mainly by makeup and manner. I'll put a few lines on your face, and tie your hair into matron style, and put dowdy earrings on you, and you'll school yourself to be a bit slow and prim. It won't be hard once you get into it; the people will never question that you are at least as old as you seem. Except when you strip in the play." He stared frankly at her torso. "You're actually about as shapely a woman as the villagers will ever see. The contrast will be startling, and that's good."

"Thank you," Gale said, a bit uncomfortable.

"Now you've both seen the play before, or at least a variant? Boy and teacher, on Planet Mystery?"

The two of them nodded, similarly embarrassed.

"And never thought you'd be acting in it, eh? Well, this play isn't much, but it does pay well in favors, and it's a good step on the way to professional trouping, if that's what you want to do. We'll have a walk-through rehearsal in clothing tonight, to iron out the bugs, and then the first performance two mornings hence. It will be bumpy at first, it always is, but it's a good script, and by the end of the month it will be routine. This particular tour is limited to a month, the length of the Air season; we'll make a loop and return to our starting point. There is some slack to allow for the weather. Any questions?"

Lad had one. "What do we do the rest of the time at a stop? I mean, the play takes only an hour, but won't we be a couple of days in each village?"

"Longer than that, if the weather gets challenging. Good question, Lad. We'll spend a lot of time resting, because those walks between villages will be wearing. We'll be feasting. We'll be setting up the stage, and taking it down after. Not that there's much to that; we can do it with just one chair if we have to. We'll be talking with the natives. The boys will ask you for pointers for their first affairs."

"Me!"

"You'll be an expert, Lad, by definition. They will have seen you cruelly tempted on stage. So you will answer them helpfully. Don't worry; I'll run you through some sample answers to typical questions. You'll get through. Some girls will want to get you alone and kiss you. Maybe, if you're lucky, a grown woman will ask you to sire her fourth."

"Me!"

"Notoriety has great appeal. Some women like to say they had it with an actor, and be able to prove it. It enhances the mystique."

Lad looked aghast. "I never—"

"Innocence is so charming. Stay that way, Lad; it's an asset. But let me clarify this: your role in the play is not identical to your real life. You can have sex with a village woman on your own time, and still be the ingenue, as it were. Just don't speak of it elsewhere."

"But–"

"But you don't *have* to have sex with anybody. I'm simply saying you can if you want to, and you can reasonably decline. Just so you know that you may be asked, so you can respond without embarrassment, either way."

Leader turned to Gale. "You, of course, will be swamped, because a good many will catch on that you're not as old as you seem.

What you do in your off time is your business. You can say no, on the grounds that pregnancy would really mess up your role. The risk is small, with the—you do wear the wire?"

"As of today." Contraception was considered virtually treasonous, but approved in some cases, and this was such a case. The "wire" was a small twist of metal set inside the womb to disrupt conception. As methods went, it was simple and effective and nonmagical, but lifelong conditioning made her feel guilty for using it.

"So you can do it if you want to, but you don't have to, just as is the case with Lad. However, I think it best that the two of you, Lad and Dame, do not indulge with each other. That could ruin the special mood of the play."

Leader glanced at each in turn. Both nodded agreement. Gale was glad for the way he had clarified it, because though she would do what she had to, she preferred to avoid sex with anyone but Havoc.

Leader nodded in return. "But there is one thing."

Gale wasn't easy about this, but the dragon seed did not buzz. "What thing?"

"Your special mission. I don't know what it is, and I'm not asking, but I am under king's orders to facilitate it in whatever way I can. Guard and Carto will keep their mouths shut, and you'll need their help. Lad will keep his mouth shut because he's not too young to know the meaning of the king's wrath. But you will have to tell us enough to enable us to help you, and to cover for you if anyone suspects."

That did make sense. She had thought it was her secret, but of course it couldn't be; the other Troupe members would know if she sneaked out. Still, she was alarmed. "You should not discuss this openly where magic can spy on you."

Leader smiled. "I took pains to reserve a sealed coach. We are protected from snooping by mind reading or magic. That is why I raise this matter at this time. We do need to know."

He had a point. "I have to get into a Temple and see what's there."

Leader shook his head. "I was afraid it was something like that. This could get us all killed. But I guess I can also see why the king wants to know. There's a wide suspicion that the Temple cheats on taxes. That those folk have more goods in trade than they let on."

"Maybe. I just have to see whatever they're hiding, and leave it alone. They must not know I've snooped."

"We'll do our best. Damn, I'll be glad when it's over, though. To get between the king and the Temple is like putting your head over the rim of a volcano and hoping it won't erupt. We'll say no more of this; the air has ears. When the time comes, just tell us what to do."

"Thank you."

"Now get some rest. Tomorrow we hike."

Good advice. Gale leaned back and tried to relax. But she saw

Lad tense. She was only four years older than he, but it seemed like a lifetime. "I see you uneasy. Is it me or the rest of it?" she asked him.

"The rest," he confessed.

"Come sit by me."

Leader switched seats with Lad, and Lad sat beside her. She put her arm around his shoulder and drew him in to rest against her neck and breast. She was treating him like a child, but he accepted it. His body relaxed. She found that comforting him made her feel better, too. He was the one member of the troupe who was less experienced than she was. But she kept her mental guard in play, just in case.

One thing bothered her: though Leader had protected their dialogue from exposure, and she was sure that the others would not speak of her mission, they could not keep their awareness of it out of their minds. When they were out of this coach, a mind reader could get at them. So Leader had unwittingly exposed them to that danger. But there was nothing to be done about it now, that particular horse was out of the corral. She just had to hope that whatever enemy there was had no suspicion of the troupe, and sent no mind reader. And there were constraints; the mind reader would have to get within range of them, and would have to get one of them alone, to isolate that mind from the confusing background of group thoughts, and then pick up on a thought that might not be in consciousness at that moment. That should be a fair challenge, and perhaps enough to preserve her secret. She hoped so.

They spent the night at the fringe of a Silver Chroma circle. The village was a way station, for nonChroma travelers, and accustomed to trading caravans and touring troupes. The facilities were good, as was the food. In the evening they had the walk-through, with Leader speaking the lines from memory, and clarifying the choreography of their actions. It was not complicated, overall, physically. But emotionally it was going to be a considerable challenge, at least at first. Gale suspected that she dreaded it almost as much as Lad did.

"Remember," Leader said encouragingly. "They'll know its your first show of the tour. They've seen many first shows, and I think they enjoy comparing notes on foul-ups. So if it happens, it's not disaster. Just carry on as well as you can, and we'll do better next time."

Gale was hardly reassured, and Lad looked ready to faint. But Leader was probably right: it would be better the following time.

Gale had a room to herself, being the only female member of the troupe. She lay on her bunk, unable to settle down enough to sleep. She got up and did something she had been meaning to do when she had sufficient privacy: check the contents of the "spy kit." This was a nondescript belt she wore with a pocket containing a sliver of soapy substance, and a small wooden key. That was all, but it was more than it seemed.

She tried the key. There was a locked desk in the corner of the

room. The key readily unlocked it. The lock on the door was considerably larger, but she tried the same key, and it worked again. It was
a skeleton key made from a variety of wood whose nature was to un-
tangle things, and it regarded a lock as a tangle. So it worked on
almost any lock, as if made for it—as in a way it was.

The soapy substance was not for washing. It was concentrated
Temple wax, used to seal the floors, walls, roofs, and chests there. It
would imbue her with the smell of the Temple, making her seem to
belong there.

The belt was another very special product. It was of stilevine,
which bent freely in one direction and not at all in the other direction.
It was very light and strong. She tested it by unwinding it from her
waist—it was quite thin, so made a number of loops—and laying a
length of it flat on the floor, the bendy side down. She couldn't fit its
whole length in the room, as it was about twenty feet, but a portion of
it was enough for this purpose. Then she lifted it by one end—and it
came up like a rigid rod, refusing to bend that way. She put one end
on the bed, the rolled up end on the desk across the room, and sat on
it. It would not give. She set it back on the floor, bent it upward at the
halfway point, looped it around, and laid the end flat again. Now
when she picked it up by the center loop, it bent there, but not elsewhere. It was a bit tricky to handle, but she practiced until she could
make it form an A-frame that she could climb on. It was a problem
making it stand upright, but she propped it against a wall and made
do. She would be able to use this.

Then she re-coiled the vine around her waist, and hid the wax
and key in its pocket, and lay down again. The spy kit was in good
order, but she did not want to attract any attention to it.

Still she could not yet sleep. So she decided to do another bit of
good, if she could. She got up and went to the men's chamber.

Guard, alert, intercepted her in the darkness. "What is it?"

"I thought I'd fetch Lad. Maybe I can make him sleep."

"That would help," he agreed. "He's wound up like a spring." He
led her to the boy's bunk.

She touched Lad's hand in the darkness. "Come with me."

He got up immediately and followed her out. "What is it, Dame?"
he asked hesitantly.

"If you're like me, you can't sleep now."

"Yeah," he agreed ruefully.

"There's more room in my chamber. Lie down beside me, hold
my hand, and we will both sleep."

"But Dame, it's not—"

"Just sleep," she clarified. "That's what we need tonight. Certainly we will not go against Leader's directive."

"Yeah," he said, relieved. It was obvious that he liked her, indeed
was already somewhat smitten, but dreaded the notion of any sexual

performance. That was fine with her.

They lay down side by side on her bunk, holding hands. She felt his tenseness fade, and soon enough he slept. Then, satisfied that she had done right, she slept too. It would have been worse for her, had she not had someone to help along. Of course she had had experience handling her younger siblings, but this wasn't quite the same.

There was another possible advantage. Lad was the one most likely to give away the secret of her mission, just by thinking about it too much. But his interest in her personally could overwhelm any other thoughts, so that any mind reader would pick up only on that.

In the morning, outfitted with protective clothing and backpacks of supplies, they set off on the trail to the next village. Their hats were broad brimmed, to shield them from the sun's intensity. Their boots were thick, to safeguard them from sharp edges. They wore heavy gloves, but light blouses and trousers, because their most likely problem was the heat of the day. This was the Air season, sometimes called Fall in a chancy effort to align Charm's five seasons with Earth's supposed four. Hot days, cold nights, and often wind. She had always liked it, because of her name.

Carto led the way, as the path was by no means clear cut, and Guard brought up the rear, as it was not necessarily safe. The middle three were Leader, Gale, and Lad. It seemed routine, but she had seen enough terrain and weather in her day to understand their caution; travel between villages was never truly routine. If they were lucky, there would be no serious problems.

This trail wended its curving route between the Silver and Yellow Chroma. To the left were the electrical effects of the one, such as lightning and its attendant thunder; to the right were the fiery effects of the other, such as showers of sparks. The trick was to stay in the zone where neither had much effect.

That was not necessarily easy. A wind was rising, stirring up dust on either side. The dust carried magic, silver and yellow, and extended the range of the Chroma. Lightning arced across the silver cloud, and flickering flames appeared in the yellow dust. But they did not quite overlap; there remained a narrow channel between them.

"Best to move rapidly," Carto said, making a note on his map pad. "The nonChroma widens ahead."

They hurried forward, and the space between Chroma did widen. But the wind continued to blow. This was expected in the Air season, when storms were common. It was, nevertheless, normally considered the safest of the seasons for travel.

Now they entered a wedge of nonChroma desert sand. The wind carried some dust, but they breathed through their kerchiefs and had no trouble. Until the wind intensified. Now the dust was thick enough to obscure the route ahead.

Carto halted. "We need to wait," he shouted. "We have to see, in case there is danger. The wind should ease before long." He opened his pack and brought out a length of rope attached to an anchor. "Connect your ropes; we'll tie down here."

They opened their packs to get their ropes, but Lad hesitated. "Why not take shelter beside that boulder?" he asked, pointing.

Guard smiled. "Easy, Lad, that's where the python lives."

"Python? I don't see any snakes here."

"Take his word," Gale murmured. She realized that Lad had never traveled far out of the city.

They linked their ropes at their clasp ends, forming a spider net, and let the anchors dig into the ground. Then they each hooked one leg under a rope, kneeling, and formed a small circle facing each other, linking elbows, clasping their own hands, bowing their heads. The sand beat down on their backs, but there was breathing space in the center. The wind hauled at them, but their circular linkage secured them in front, and their line anchors held them in back. It was a standard way to ride out a small storm in the open. A party might be battered, but would not be blown away, and would not lose contact with its members.

Gale's dragon seed buzzed. At almost the same time, Guard lifted his head and peered into the swirl of dust. "Get out the repellent," he said.

They unlinked and delved again into their packs, finding the squeeze packs of goo. "This stuff stinks!" Lad protested.

"It sure does," Leader agreed, smearing some into his beard.

Gale squeezed some of hers onto her hand. They were right: it smelled like rotting carrion. She smeared it into her hair below her hat.

"But what's it *do*?" Lad asked, still reluctant.

"It keeps you alive," Guard said as he applied his own. "Look to your right."

Lad looked, and Gale looked too. Sure enough, a python was sliding toward them, its outline made vague by the flying sand but certainly no trick of vision. It had left its rock and thought to haul them in to it. It might weigh about as much as all of them combined.

Lad hastily applied his own repellent. Then, choking in their own fumes, they linked elbows again and waited.

"Just so you know," Guard said. "The goo makes you smell dead. Pythons don't eat carrion. So just stay still until it goes away."

Gale knew the ruse, and knew that it almost invariably worked. Pythons were not smart. But sometimes nerve was required.

"It's coming right toward us!" Lad cried.

Gale was beside him. She kept her hands clasped to each other, but drew them in to herself so that her elbow squeezed his. "Don't move. Carrion doesn't move. Just stay still. There's no danger if you don't move." She squeezed his elbow reassuringly; that was so slight a motion it wouldn't show.

He obeyed, but he was terrified. She felt his body shivering as if cold. She continued squeezing, hoping he wouldn't try to bolt and get them all in danger.

The huge snake came right up to them. It nudged Gale's back with a snout like a battering ram. She was shoved forward, pulling her section of the circle out of round, but neither screamed nor otherwise moved. She focused on being carrion.

The creature circled the ground, close. Its weight slid across their feet. It nudged Carto, and he too was shoved into the center, halfway colliding with Gale. Cheek to cheek, they remained propped against each other, elbows still connected to others. Their circle had been flattened, and was now the outline of a blob, but the links had not been broken. Lad was panting, but otherwise still; probably it was terror rather than caution, but that was what was needed.

At last the python moved on, having been disappointed by this group of corpses. The storm was also easing, perhaps by no coincidence; pythons preferred cover, whether of terrain, darkness, or dust, and retreated when they lost it.

"Good job," Guard said, unlinking. "We can travel again. Take up your anchors."

"In a moment," Gale murmured. She put her arm around Lad, as she had in the coach, and drew him in, letting him cry into her shoulder. He was a city boy, and had no prior experience with monsters; he needed reassurance and comfort. Leader, seeing the way of it, took up their anchors for them, coiled their ropes, and put them in their two packs. The man had the sense to know when to let things be.

Soon they were hiking again. The diminishing wind carried away much of the clinging stench of the repellent, but it no longer seemed so bad to Gale: not only had it discouraged the python, it would probably drive away other dangerous animals. A safe smell was in the end a good smell.

As the desert widened, it became more colorful, with sands of many hues. There were some plants, too, including squat gray cacti and purple lichen. Swift-flying silver and yellow birds darted by, landing to forage at the fringes of the Chroma where there was enough magic to allow Chroma creatures to exist, but not enough to protect them from predation. Gale found it all rather pretty in its fashion. She had always admired the colored creatures and plants of the Chroma, and knew from her experience with Yellow the spider that they could be good friends.

Carto halted. "This is new," he said grimly, making a note.

They looked. There was a fissure ahead, issuing green vapor. It was a Green Chroma vent, forming in new territory. It might close up again in a few days, or it might expand into a small volcano. There was no way to be sure.

"I think we can safely skirt it," Carto said. "But let's not linger close."

They skirted it, keeping as much distance from it as the lay of the local terrain made convenient. Her dragon seed buzzed, but she didn't see any immediate threat, and kept moving. Just as Gale passed the vent, there was a coughing hiss, and a green cloud boiled out. It expanded, spreading across the ground.

"Move!" Guard shouted behind her.

They ran, but the cloud was faster. The ball of vapor caught up to them.

Gale held her breath, but didn't dare close her eyes, lest she trip and fall. The green closed about her vision, making her see fantastic shapes. It was raw magic, unschooled, uncontrolled, the stuff of phantasm. Green was supposed to be the magic of plants, but there was no telling what the effect would be. A giant green vine appeared, rearing up impossibly high, orienting on her, becoming a python, striking down. But she knew it was a bad image from her recent experience, a personal illusion, not fully real. She kept running.

Then she was out of it, gasping for air. In a moment Guard followed, holding on to Lad, propelling him forward. Lad was coughing violently; he had breathed some of the green vapor. As he caught his breath, his arms flung out wildly; he was fighting some imaginary horror.

Gale stepped into him, pressing her body against his. "Lad! Lad! It's illusion, not real. Relax. You're safe now. It's over."

He struggled for a moment more. Then something registered. His arms closed about her as his face sought hers for a kiss.

"Not yet," she said gently. "Wait for the play. Relax, relax."

His gaze cleared. "What am I doing?" he demanded, horrified.

"You're coming out of a dose of Green Chroma magic," she said. "Next time, hold your breath, if you can. Only a Green Chroma native can handle green magic; it just messes us nonChroma folk up."

"Green Chroma," he echoed. "That vent. I tried to get away–"

"And it burped a green cloud and caught up with you," she finished. "We all got tagged, but the rest of us had a better idea what to expect. We're all right now. This sort of thing happens, out in the countryside." She didn't add that she had experienced very little of it herself. But she had learned much from Mentor, so had a fair notion. And of course the seed had warned her. That extra second might have primed her for action, enabling her to get more quickly clear of the green gas. "You're all right now, I think," she concluded.

"Oh." Embarrassed, he let go of her.

They resumed their walk. At one point, as they picked their way across a web-work of crevices, Leader leaned close. "You're a good girl," he murmured. "I was wary of what I was getting, with that last minute substitution. Now I know it's okay."

"Thanks." She knew she had earned the compliment, but that didn't stop her from appreciating it.

The trail clarified, rising across a dry hill, and they moved along well. Because the terrain was mostly dry desert, there was not a lot of plant or animal life, and that made travel easier. They paused periodically to drink from the water bottles they carried, not concerned about running out, because by evening they would be at the village. This was just a routine hike between sites.

Then Planet Mystery swung across. This happened on a daily basis, as they orbited each other and spun independently, so half the time, day and night, Mystery was in sight in some part of the sky, if there were no clouds. It was the size of her fist extended at arm's length, but seemed larger in its intriguing detail. In the course of the day its illuminated crescent shifted visibly. It was perpetually fascinating to her, and she was not the only one; everyone she knew in Trifle had spent many hours contemplating Mystery. Were there plants and creatures there? Were there people there? Were they like those of Charm? There could be people, if the ship from afar had left colonists there too. Were the colors magic? Sometimes volcanoes could be seen, erupting, extending their territories. She would give anything to know exactly what it was like on the surface of their companion world. But there was no way to get there. Thus it had become the world of mythology. Whatever could not be represented on Charm, for physical or social reason, could be represented on Mystery. As was the case with the tale of Lad and Dame.

Lad was staring so fixedly at Mystery that he stumbled and fell. Guard helped him up. "I guess you don't get to see Counter-Charm much, cooped inside Triumph."

"Hardly ever," he agreed. "They don't let us out without reason, and I never had much reason. I can't stop looking at it."

Counter-Charm. Gale had heard it called that; different villages had different terms for things. The name did make some sense, for the planet was always opposite Charm.

"Okay," Guard said. "You walk along, and I'll steer you. Look all you want. We all like Counter."

So Gale wasn't the only one helping out with the novice. The three regulars did seem to be decent, as she got to know them. She was slow to trust men she didn't know well, but was coming to trust these.

They reached the village of Donethat well before evening, ahead of schedule. It had been an easy trip, the men said, but Gale and Lad were tired. They weren't used to walking that far at one time.

Leader paused before they entered. "Remember, you are older," he reminded Gale. "You're dirty enough to look the part now, but after you clean up, don't go out before I age you."

"I do feel old," Gale agreed. "I hope this village has a good bath."

"Donethat has a good public bath with competent and discreet attendants, but you can't use it; they'd pick up on your age immediately. So it's the tub and bucket for you, and I think you won't want any of us men to help. Understand, none of us will make a move on you; we're all married and loyal. But you aren't just another woman; you're dangerously appealing. Ideal for the part, but–"

"Thanks." She was discovering an inconvenience of being lovely. "How about a boy?"

"You've taken the boy in hand beautifully. Do with him what you will. But bear in mind that he'll have a crush on you, and you're not staying for subsequent tours."

She hadn't thought of that aspect. "Damn. I think it's already too late, and I don't want to mess up his performance in the play. Maybe I can figure out something by the end of the tour."

"That would be best."

"Meanwhile, thanks for reminding me about my age. I'll do my best."

"We will all treat you as Dame. You'll get into it."

They moved on into the village. Children ran out to greet them, and Leader passed out little candies from his pack. The Village Elder, a sober woman of grandmotherly age, gave Leader a formal welcome, and a hug; they evidently knew each other from prior times. "You smell as good as ever," she remarked, wrinkling her nose at the lingering odor of carrion.

"Appreciation," Leader said, laughing. "I always accept a compliment."

Then Elder met the others. "I see you have two new players," she remarked.

"For the roles Dame Teacher and Lad Student," Troupe Leader agreed. "I trust you will give them good support in their first presentation."

"Don't we always? I'll never forget how it was with us, thirty years ago."

"You were of course my first love," Leader agreed. "I think I still love you, you lovely creature."

"Oh pshaw! I was getting too old for the part even then. I thought it was revulsion that made you limp."

"You were forty, and still outstanding. It was awe, not revulsion. You know that."

"And you were thirteen, and cute as a new toadstool. You made me feel young again. It will be deja vu, tomorrow morning." She looked around. "But we're boring the others with our ancient reminiscences. Come on in, folks. Dinner's in an hour." She waved them into the village.

So Elder had been Leader's Dame in the play. She must have

completed her family obligation and gone on to the different life of acting, while he was just starting out in what would become his life's profession. Neither made any secret of it, or of their initial problem. Gale found that encouraging. Maybe that was the point: they were trying to help the new players get confidence.

"Two rooms will do," Leader said as they came to a house. "For three and two."

"Three and two?" Lad asked blankly.

Gale took his hand. "You're with me, of course. I need someone to ladle my bath water."

"Oh. Yeah. Sure. But—"

"Then I'll ladle yours."

Halfway dumbfounded, he let her lead him into the designated room of the house. The tub was already there, half filled with water, with a dipper bucket and small bar of soap beside it. On the bed were two towels.

Gale closed the door. "We have just an hour to get washed and dressed. You go pee while I get started. Leave your clothes in the privy; the villagers will launder and dry them overnight."

"But—"

"We'll wear our costumes to the dinner. Our roles are not just in the play, you know; we *are* Lad and Dame while we are in this village. We can play them in private too, if we want. So don't be concerned about being naked with me; this is the play."

"But I have a–"

"I've seen it before. That's the point of the play, isn't it? Just make sure you have it tomorrow." She added a little iron to her tone. "Now get moving."

He obeyed, walking awkwardly to the privy chamber. Gale stripped, piling her clothing on the floor. She loosened her hair. Again, she was finding that her natural nervousness was almost entirely abated by her need to lead the boy through the route. He was helping her almost as much as she was helping him. She wondered whether other players in these roles had reacted similarly.

Naked, she stepped into the tub. The water was cool, but not frigid; it was no problem. She lowered her bottom into it, watching the water level rise to just shy of the rim; it had been correctly figured. She took a handful and splashed it on her raised knees, and another on her shoulder.

"Aren't you done yet?" she called. "I need ladling."

"I—I can't," he called back, sounding ashamed.

"Yes you can. Just put one foot before the other and walk out here."

"I mean—the other."

Oh. She should have thought of that. Of course he couldn't urinate, in the state he was in. "Okay, wait till after the bath. Get out here now." She included the tinge of command.

He emerged, blushing from face to chest, his erection impossible to ignore. So Gale didn't try. "That's a good one, for sure. That's exactly the way I want it, tomorrow. Thanks for showing me. I'd hate it if you saw me naked and didn't react. Now come on over here."

"Really?" he asked, amazed.

"Really. We don't need to ruin Leader's scene do we?" She forced a laugh, forcing him to laugh too, loosening up. "Dip the water. Pour it over my head. I stink."

"Yeah." He picked up the ladle, fumblingly, and dipped it in the water over her feet. "You're beautiful."

"Thank you. But remember, I'm supposed to be an older woman, somewhere the other side of thirty. The Dame. So when we're outside, treat me like your mother."

"Oh, Dame, you could never be that!"

"We're actors, remember? I'm supposed to be twenty years older than you. Then in the play, when I strip, in your fancy you see me as much younger, as more like your ideal woman. Can you do that?"

"Yes!"

She laughed again, not having to force it this time. "Now pour. I hate smelling like carrion."

He poured the water over her head, and she rubbed her hair vigorously. She picked up the soap and scrubbed it in. "More."

He dipped and poured again, and again, until she felt she had her hair reasonably clean. She wiped the water out of her eyes and opened them. Then she washed and rinsed the rest of her body. It felt good to get clean again.

"Fetch me the towel," she said, as she put her hands on the rim of the tub and heaved herself up, dripping. "No, don't avert your eyes; this is the way it will be, for this tour. We'll get to know each other pretty well."

He gave her the towel, and she started drying herself from the hair down. "Steady me as I dry my feet and step out," she said. She put one hand on his shoulder, lifted one leg, and reached down to dry the knee, calf, ankle, and foot. She put the dry foot on the floor, then did the other. Lad was true to her order not to avert his eyes, but if eyeballs could sweat, his would have been doing so.

"Your turn," she said briskly. "Get in."

He got in and squatted, then sat. The water rose up enough to cover his continuing erection. That relieved her, because she was sure it relieved him. She poured water carefully over his head and body, and gave him the soap when he couldn't find it with his eyes closed. He was ineffective, so she took over. "Here, I'm good at hair," she said, scrubbing his head.

"Did Leader and Elder really do this play?" he asked as she moved on down to his shoulders, arms and chest.

"They must have, because they both remembered." She didn't say that she was sure, because her dragon seed had made no buzz, as it would have, had either of them been lying. "I think it's sweet."

"Yeah."

He finished washing, and stood, and she dried him with his towel. Then they got into their costumes. These were not remarkable. Hers was a somewhat dowdy outfit, with a small dark hat, ankle-length dress, and deliberately worn shoes. His was the student cap, short sleeved shirt, short pants, and sandals of youth. In it he looked exactly like what he was: a school boy.

She went to use the privy, but he still could not. Well, time would take care of that.

They stood together before the mirror as she combed out his hair and then her own. "What if they ask me questions?" he asked nervously.

"Just be yourself. You're supposed to be a boy."

"I mean, about—"

"Just tell the truth: you haven't done it yet. Not with me. Not with any village woman. Tomorrow, after the play, maybe you'll have more to say on that."

"I guess so. But what if they ask about before?"

"Just what is your prior experience?"

"Tickle & Peek with a twelve year old girl. I was twelve too. She— she got excited and put herself on me, so I was in her. Some."

"Did you climax?"

"I don't know."

This was very limited experience. "Did your erection fade right away?"

"No. Not until we weren't together anymore."

"Then you surely did not climax. And you certainly don't need to in the play. Just be obviously ready. Anyway, you're older now, and so am I. So I think you can just say you've never done it with a woman before. Girls don't count."

"Okay," he said, relieved.

She finished with their hair. "Get your dirty clothes and add them to my pile. It's time to join the others."

"What about the tub?"

"Whoever brought it will haul it away. This is part of the hospitality of the village. They'll take our clothing and return it to us in the morning, clean."

The dragon seed buzzed. Alarmed, Gale considered. It couldn't be a lie, because Lad hadn't said anything, and in any event, she was already satisfied that he would never knowingly deceive her. There was no evident personal danger, or likely wrongness in the situation. So what was it?

She feared she knew: someone was reading a mind. The men

were out in the village, mingling with people. A visiting Chroma woman might be approaching one of them, getting close to him, showing her breasts and inviting him to sire her fourth. He might accept or decline—marriage was considered no barrier in such a case—but either way, she might be reading his mind, discovering his secrets. That could represent a threat to Gale, and the seed would know. Its direct range was quite limited, but its awareness of the larger situation was impressive. She wasn't sure how that worked, but had learned to trust it.

But maybe it was just a threat. Someone was mind searching, but not necessarily succeeding. The seed reacted to the threat as much as to the reality, warning her in time to act, if she could. All she could do was hope that this particular threat abated, and meanwhile she would remain alert. Certainly she could not say anything about this to anyone else, both because she dared not reveal the source of her alarm—the seed—and because such mention would only focus their thoughts on what they should not be on.

"Dame, are you all right?" Lad asked.

She flashed him a disarming smile. "Don't tell: much of this is as new to me as it is to you. Sometimes I get to thinking about it too much. I apologize for drifting."

"Oh, Dame, you never have to apologize to me!"

She squeezed his arm. "You are kind."

They joined the men. Leader used a small marker pencil to put faint lines on Gale's face. "Make your natural expression a small pout," he said. "Stand a bit stooped, so that your breasts seem diminished or saggy. Yes, like that. Do not move quickly. Remember, the play starts here. Since they expect you to be older, they'll see you that way. In the play, I'll do stage magic to transform you as you undress. If you hear a sigh from the audience, you'll know we surprised them."

"I hope so," she said.

He turned to Lad. "And you be impulsive and young minded. Think age eleven or twelve. We want maximum contrast. You will seem to grow in the play, as Dame brings out your manhood. I think she's already doing it."

"I couldn't pee," Lad said, abashed.

"Wonderful! That's it exactly. But tonight—okay, let's pull your shirt out loose, so it flops down and hides anything. Tonight you are Boy, not Man. You can do it that way in the play, too, then strip suddenly. The littlest gestures can make the greatest effects. It's all in the timing. Now we're off to the banquet. Oh—neither of you better touch the spiked drinks. You get tipsy, you'll fall out of character. Stay uptight, both of you. Contrast to we three men, who will not be as loose as we seem. And if anybody gets fresh with either of you, Guard will be on it. Just catch his eye, if you're even worried."

They went out to the banquet. Village Elder met them outside the house, and conducted them there. It turned out to be a huge affair in the central square, with tables clustered under a temporary covering. They had the place of honor in the very center. Girls were bringing steaming platters.

"Oh—and don't overeat," Leader cautioned them as they took their seats. "It's out of character, and you don't want to be bloated for the play."

"Now he tells us," Gale muttered for Lad's ears. But it was good advice. She didn't want a bulging belly for the nude dance, and a fart would ruin the effect.

After partaking relatively chastely of what could otherwise have been a phenomenal feast, they mixed with the people, playing their roles. But Lad looked increasingly uncomfortable. "Indigestion?" Gale inquired in his ear.

"No. *Now* I gotta pee."

Gale faced the group of villagers around them and put on her primmest face. "Lad and I had a hard hike today, and are tired. We're not used to it. We'd like to turn in now, if it's all right."

It was of course all right. They walked to the house and into their room, and Lad dived for the privy. He emerged shortly, abashed again. "Thanks."

"You couldn't before, and then you had the meal on top of it. Discomfort can work wonders. That's the way it works."

"But you made it seem to the villagers as if it was nothing."

"Well, it wasn't much. In any event, not their business. And I *am* tired. So I'm ready for a good night's sleep."

"I don't know if I can sleep."

"You'll sleep," she said confidently. "I hope they left night clothing." She checked the bed. "Yes, they did." She stripped and changed.

Lad was staring. "You just did that, like being alone."

"Your turn," she said, lying on her side of the bed. "Lad, we won't always have very spacious or private accommodations. Get used to being informal."

"But every time you—I—"

"I know. I revel in it." Fortunately the dragon seed did not buzz when she lied herself, and anyway it was only half a lie; what she wanted was for him to be reassured now, and to be able to perform properly in the play. She was also training herself to be completely open, physically, with him, as that seemed the best policy. The faster he got used to it, the less trouble he would have with unwanted erections. Just so long as he could still raise them where required, in the play—and she would be a lot sexier then. However she closed her eyes, giving him the chance to change without further embarrassing himself.

When he lay down, she took his hand, as on the prior night. And it worked, again; comforted, he was soon asleep.

She woke before him in the morning, and dressed and prepared her costume for the day. By the time Lad stirred, she was ready to go. "Why don't I check with Leader about breakfast, while you get ready? I'll be back shortly."

"Okay," he said.

She crossed the short hall to the other door, and knocked. Leader opened it. "Good enough, except for the age lines."

"Oops! I forgot that detail. They must have rubbed off during the night."

"That's why I'm here." He brought out his pencil and marked her face.

"But in the play, when I want to look young, how do I get rid of the lines?"

"No need. Your face will still suggest age, while your body won't. Lad won't care about your face, once he sees your body. Then when you dress again, you'll be Dame Prim again."

"Where is breakfast?"

"We'll have bread and milk right here. Then we'll see to the setting of the stage."

She nodded, and returned to the other room to collect Lad. "Thanks for leaving," he said. "That let me—you know."

She hadn't actually thought of that. "That's fine. Now we'll have breakfast in the other room, before we go to the stage."

"That stage sure scares me."

"But you've been with me all night, and we've seen each other naked."

"Oh, you're just great, Dame. But that's *public*. All those people watching."

He had a point. She, as a woman, could perform despite stage fright. But if the same fear unmanned him, he would not be able to perform. So he had more to worry about. "Lad, in case there is difficulty—is there any special thing I might do that would be sure to arouse you?"

"I don't know. I've never—I have no experience. There might be nothing. When I was with that girl, there were just the two of us, but maybe that was too public for me. I mean, I did get it up, but didn't— you know. What about when there's a hundred people watching?"

She shook her head. "I don't know either, Lad. Suppose I kiss you, like this?" She took his head between her hands, drew it close, and kissed him carefully on the mouth.

He was flushed when she let him go. "Oh, Dame, I think that would haul me out of the pit of a Void volcano!"

"I'll keep it in mind, then. But I think you'll be potent. Just follow the script, and all should be well."

"Sure Dame," he said bravely.

Then she remembered: her role in the play required that she

never touch him. *He* had to touch *her*. It might seem like a meaningless distinction, but it was vital. However, maybe she could make a
kissing pass at him, luring him in for it, and that might have the desired effect.

They joined the men for breakfast, then adjourned to the stage.
This was where the evening banquet had been, under the pavilion, a
nice open air site for a theater in the round. The stage was a layout of
boards, with a bed in the center. This disconcerted Gale, who had
somehow expected a backstop behind and the audience all in front,
but she realized that it made sense for the village. It would probably
be the case for other villages. Actually it had been so in Trifle, when
troupes entertained; somehow she had not quite made the connection. Nothing was to be hidden, in this show, and no actual scenery
was required; all they needed for the finale was a bed, or even just a
chair, in a pinch.

Leader was all business. "Now we'll mark the layout on the floor.
It's just two scenes: the school room, and the teacher's home. We
want to keep the action centered, and consistent, so there's no jarring
discontinuity. Now, to begin, this will be the desk." He went to the
bed. "You'll sit in the chair, here, Dame, and Lad will come up on the
classroom side. Part of the audience will be the class; the kids always
love that. Between scenes, I'll march out and walk around the bed.
You won't go to the next scene; the next scene will shape around you.
It'll turn real, once we get into it; if you see the classroom, so will the
audience."

He continued, getting the details clear, but Gale had trouble paying full attention. The closer they got to the actual play, the more
nervous she became. Yet she knew she had to do it, and would do it.
It was certainly no worse than what the children of Trifle had tried to
do to her with that stink gourd, before Havoc had rescued her. It was
also a perfect cover for her real mission, because she was not pretending to be an actress, she was actually doing it, completely. Still,
she feared disaster and public humiliation.

Lad, beside her, was looking wan. Should she try to seem confident, or sympathetic? She decided on sympathy. "I feel the same
way."

"But Dame—you're experienced."

"Not at doing this play in full public."

"Oh. I guess not." But he didn't look much reassured.

The audience began to gather. The time was coming. "Okay,
Dame, Lad—you just sit here on the bed," Leader said. "I'll tell you
when to move elsewhere. Just wait and listen, and play into it when I
turn to you."

They sat together on the bed, waiting. Lad was shivering; she felt
it in the bed. She moved her hand slowly, and set it on his hand, as if
coincidentally, trying to calm him. At this point she had no certainly

they would perform the play successfully. But they were locked into it, for good or ill. And if they got through this time, the next time would not be as bad, she was sure.

The audience swelled. The smallest children sat cross-legged on the ground in front, and the larger ones next behind. The adult women were next, and the adult men stood farthest out. There were more than a hundred in all, about two thirds of them children ranging from five to twelve. This play was for them, really, so not every one in the village was present. There were always chores to be done that couldn't wait; that was why there were few couples here. The man could come, or the woman, but seldom both. The youngest children would not have seen it before; the elder ones would be seeing it the second, or perhaps the third time. It was a lesson that could hardly be over-stressed. The adults were there to keep order, and perhaps they enjoyed the play as classic entertainment.

The hour came. Village Elder approached the stage. She looked around at the audience on all sides, saw that all was in order, turned to Leader, and made a formal bow. That was the signal to start.

Leader had been sitting in the lone chair. Now he stood, setting the chair beside the bed. "Greeting, people of Donethat!" he cried, as Elder retreated. As he spoke, he turned around in a full circle, to address them all.

"Acknowledged!" the children called back in chorus.

"Can you all hear me?"

"Yes!" they chorused. He had already gotten them involved. He was, Gale realized, a showman.

"Then I will tell you a story. The story of Lad Student and Dame Teacher." He spoke toward the larger section of the audience, then turned to the opposite section and repeated key words: "Lad Student, Dame Teacher." The children up close could hear him regardless which direction he faced, but possibly the adults beyond could not. They would be familiar with the play, so would need no more than key phrases.

Leader paused, then lowered his voice without diminishing the volume. "This happens on Planet Mystery. Planet Counter-Charm. Do you know why?"

"No!" the children cried. They had surely been coached for this initial portion.

"It's because we all know it could never happen on Planet Charm. We don't do things like this here. So it stands to reason it must be over there. Isn't that so?"

"Yes!" As logic, it wasn't much, but as showmanship, it was great; Gale saw that he was really embracing the children. The older ones saw through the sham and knew this was a close analogy of Planet Charm, but they also appreciated the ruse. She began to hope that the play would be successful.

"Now there on Planet Mystery, in a little village like this one, there is a special custom. The children grow up in their families just as they do here, and they marry and make families of their own in much the same way. But they don't have classes like this to show them what's what."

Several of the adults smiled. Leader was being humorous, but the children didn't realize it.

"In fact, they have no way to learn about things like wrongful sex, except from some chosen adult. Here is how it works: when a boy or a girl comes of age twelve or thirteen or fourteen, he or she chooses an adult to show how wrong sex is withstood. After that, the child knows, and can go on and become adult and marry and get on with life. It is the child who chooses the one for this lesson, and the adult who must agree; the adult can not say no. Married or single, young or old, this can not be denied except on very serious grounds. Doesn't that sound like fun, to make an adult do what you want, instead of the other way around?"

"Yes!" the children cried gleefully.

"Now we come to the story of Lad Student. He's a decent boy, reasonably smart, but very shy. Lad, stand forth."

There was a pause, until Gale nudged Lad. He jumped to his feet, stumbled, and staggered before catching his balance. The children laughed, thinking this was part of the act.

Leader smiled, buttressing that impression. "As you can see, he's no well coordinated handsome giant. He gets teased a lot about his clumsiness. He needs to ask some woman to teach him wrong sex, but who? He doesn't dare ask a stranger; she might laugh him out of the village, though she's not supposed to. He doesn't dare ask most of the women he knows, because they *do* know him, and surely have no respect for him. You see, here's a secret." Leader leaned forward as if about to confide something, and the sitting children mirrored his motion. "Making a person do something is no good, if that person doesn't respect you. Lad doesn't want to ask a woman who would do it, but forever after sneer at his ineptitude, his clumsiness. He'd rather die. So he needs to find a woman who will not laugh at him, now or afterwards. And he can't think of any."

The children were sobering, realizing that this was serious. Young as they were, they had already had some experience with ridicule. Which was part of the point of the play: to address the emotional concerns of this audience. To answer the questions they might never dare to ask on their own, for fear of similar ridicule.

"What is he to do? He seems doomed to humiliation or failure. He has to ask someone, before he turns fifteen, or be banished from his village in disgrace. This is a test every person must pass, on planet Mystery. Aren't we glad we don't live there!" The younger children nodded, while the older ones understood the analogy, and smiled.

Mystery would be a lot like Charm, where it counted. "He casts about. Could he ask one of his female teachers? Some of them are fairly young and pretty; in fact there is one lovely creature who is setting records for student initiations. But there's a long waiting list for her, and anyway, she would be sure to compare him to the other students with whom she had wrong liaisons, and he would suffer grievously in comparison. So this isn't his answer."

Leader paused, as if in thought. "Then his eye falls on his dour math teacher. She is old, maybe thirty five, and not pretty, and certainly not beloved of students. She grades hard, and she never smiles. She has given Lad poor grades. He can't fault her there, as he has earned them. Nobody has ever asked her for a wrong liaison, and it's easy to understand why. In fact, nobody ever married her, because in this society there is not the requirement for universal marriage and four children. She won't compare him to her husband, because she has none. She won't compare him to other students, because there have been none. And she won't laugh at him, because she never laughs at anything." But that did make the children laugh. "So maybe she would be safe for him. So Lad considers." Leader glanced at the bed. "Stand forth, Dame Teacher."

Gale stood, slowly, as if not spry. She hunched a bit forward, as if not buxom. She wore a dour expression.

"And isn't she forbidding," Leader said, and the children agreed. "Almost, Lad reconsiders. But he really has no alternative. And so Lad makes a fateful decision: he *will* ask Dame Teacher. He waits until all other students are gone, then nervously approaches her desk. She is sitting behind it, grading papers."

Gale went to sit in the chair beside the bed, and leaned forward as if working at it. Lad shuffled forward, hanging his head.

"Finally he reaches the desk. 'Greeting,' he says weakly.

"Dame looks up, thinking he wants help on a math concept. 'Yes?' she inquires grimly."

Gale looked up, meeting lad's Gaze. She frowned. He looked every bit as hesitant as his role indicated.

"'I, uh, I, er, I, I—' he stammers.

"'Lad, what is your concern?' she asks impatiently.

"'I, I—want your wrong liaison,' he finally got out.

"Dame Teacher thinks she has misheard. 'You want *what?*' she demands.

"Lad almost retreats then. But still he has nowhere to go. So he repeats it. 'Your liaison. To teach me wrong sex.'

"Now she frowns. 'If this is your idea of a joke, I do not find it funny. If you have no problem in math, go home.'"

Lad and Gale were facing each other over the "desk." Neither moved; it wasn't necessary. Gale wore as forbidding an expression as she could muster, and Lad fairly radiated nervousness.

"But Lad is not joking, and finally Dame realizes that. She knows she can not refuse, but she seeks to dissuade him. 'Lad, I am not experienced,' she confides. 'I can not teach you wrong sex, because I have never been exposed to it myself.'

"'But what of your own initiation?' he asks, not entirely surprised.

"'I asked a handsome man, and he dismissed me with a pretense. We spent the night together, and thereafter pretended we had done the ritual, but we hadn't. Because he wanted no part of an ugly girl like me, and I was too ashamed to admit it.'

"'But how can you tell me this?' he asks, amazed.

"'Because I will not do to you or any other person what he did to me. You have earned low grades in math, but not everlasting shame. I ask you not to tell others about this.'

"'Oh, no, never!' he promises.

"'So now you are free to ask elsewhere, and we will pretend this dialogue never happened.'

"But Lad suffered a siege of sudden decision. 'No. I want you, Dame Teacher.'

"She is amazed again. 'Why? It would surely be a disaster.'

"'Because you will understand,' he says.

"Dame stares at him. Then she nods. 'Then let us make a pact, you and I: neither to disparage the other in this respect, whatever happens between us.'

"'Agreed.' And they shake hands, having made the deal."

Lad extended his hand across the desk, and Gale took it. Solemnly they shook hands. Gale allowed her frown to relax somewhat, but did not approach a smile.

"'Uh, when?' he asks.

"'Why not now? It will not sweeten with time.'

"And so Lad goes home with Dame this very hour," Leader concluded, walking around the bed. "It is now the intermission."

The children scrambled up and began running around. The adults came forward to manage them. Elder approached. "Good enough, so far," she said. "It seems very realistic."

"Thank you," Leader said affably. "We always do our best, and I think we have a good pair of actors this time. There's a certain frisson."

"Yes. The children hardly fidgeted. I think that despite your precautions they realize that your Dame is unusually lovely."

"Our loveliest yet," he agreed.

Gale tried to avoid blushing; it wouldn't do for her role. They were merely speaking the truth; the folk of Trifle had concluded that she was the prettiest girl ever to have lived there. She suspected that Mentor's training had something to do with it; the dragon had encouraged her to become as physically fit as she could be, and with that fitness came outstanding appearance.

"You did remember to give her the amulet?"

Leader paused in chagrin. "I forgot!" He went to rummage in his pack.

"Amulet?" Gale asked.

"It is a real boy you have here, and a real invocation," Elder said. "It could summon a real demon. We would not want that to happen."

"But we're in nonChroma territory," Gale protested. "There should be no demons here."

"That's why they are reduced to taking over human bodies. In Chroma they have their own. Technically, we are not in nonChroma, but low Chroma; the magic diffuses but does not entirely dissipate. That's why Chroma animals do not die outside their Chroma; they lose some of their powers of magic, but retain enough of the essence to survive. I think the danger is slight, but there is no sense in taking chances. So you wear the amulet, and guarantee there can be no problem."

"I shall."

"It is a real danger this play warns of. We believe that the fact that such possession is very seldom seen shows the effectiveness of the campaign. We want all our children to achieve maturity without untoward incident."

"I had thought it was merely cautionary for those who wander into the fringe of a Chroma without realizing."

"That too," Elder agreed.

Leader returned with the amulet. "I should have given you this at the outset; it slipped my aging mind. Wear it always during the tour, especially when naked, because that's when you'll be playing the role. Here, let me put it on you."

He lifted the simple string with a tiny bright stone, and tied it around her neck, snug but not constrictive. It seemed like nothing so much as a child's invented spot of jewelry, but Gale felt a faint tingle as the stone touched her neck. It was a silver Chroma stone, protection from hostile magic, and as such, valuable.

They arranged the simple elements of the scene: the bed, a small fire-pan, and a bag of colored powders. Then they sat on the bed and waited. Gale put her hand on Lad's again, and felt him shivering, again.

"Just tune out all the rest," she murmured. "Focus your eyes on what you are doing, and then on me as I dance. I know I will make you stiff."

"You always do," he agreed. But still he shivered, suffering stage fright. "Oh, Dame, I wish—"

"Then you would no longer qualify for the role," she said with a reassuring squeeze of his hand. "You must remain unfulfilled in this respect."

"Yeah." He knew the rationale, but it was evident that his understandable inner conflicts remained

The intermission finished. The children resumed their seats, and the adults their places in the rear. Leader walked around the bed where Gale and Lad sat. "Now we are at Dame's home, and that is her bed. It is time for the invocation."

Gale got up and walked a short distance from the bed, and stopped, facing away from it. She remained clothed, sour, and slightly hunched. Her role was that of an older woman who was doing what she had to, but did not especially like it. She turned slowly to face the bed, as if detesting it.

"Lad prepares the candle," Leader said.

Lad brought out a candle, touched it to the hot coals of the fire-pan, and melted enough wax to enable it to be stood upright, burning.

"He strips and stands ready for the challenge."

Now Lad removed his clothing. His nervousness made him unaroused, but that was appropriate for this stage. He looked very much the frightened boy he was.

"He speaks the invocation: 'O foul demoness, I challenge you! Appear before me now, and never again hereafter.' And he throws the magic powder on the flame."

Lad tossed the powder. The flame flared up hugely, making a flash and ball of roiling smoke that drifted on over the audience, slowly expanding and rising. The children were delighted.

While the eyes of the children were on that distraction, Gale quietly stepped into the fringe of smoke, dropped her cloak and stood abruptly naked. She straightened her body, making her breasts stand out. She tugged the staid knot out of her hair, so that her lustrous brown tresses dropped down around her shoulders and across her back and front. She had performed her transformation.

"The succubus appears," Leader said. "Transforming the body of the host. Suddenly the stoop is gone, the face is beautiful, and the flesh is full. 'I am here,' she says."

The audience's attention shifted back to the stage as the smoke cleared. Now Gale heard the sighing gasp of the realization of the transformation. Even some of the adults seemed surprised by the extent of it. Good enough.

Lad gazed across the stage, spying the change. For a moment he did not move.

"'Now see what I can do,' the succubus says. 'Look upon my perfection, O foolish boy, and know that I will have my will of you.'"

Gale stood there a moment more, waiting for her next cue. It came. "Seeing that she has not yet sufficiently impressed Lad, the succubus begins to dance, moving slowly toward him."

Gale began the Dance of the Succubus. She was well familiar with it, having practiced it often with her friends. They had thought it a fine exercise for their future as seductive women. She had tried it on Havoc, with explosive result. It was considered to be the most erotic dance extant, calculated to arouse any man to desperate desire. With each step her hips moved out, and her breasts quivered, even in slow motion. With each turn her hair flung around, alternately hiding and exposing portions of her torso. But Lad was so struck by stage fright that he wasn't reacting, though he was looking right at her. Oh, no—was this play to founder after all on visible impotence at the critical point?

"'So you defy me, foolish youth,' the succubus says. 'It will avail you not.' And she dances closer, with more emphasis."

Gale did so, and the eyes of all the audience followed her. She knew she was dancing well, making her body shake. She knew it was a spectacular body, made more so by this context. But Lad was frozen, no part of his body reacting. This was getting serious. The play required that he become visibly aroused, obviously eager to complete the sexual act. If he did not–

The dragon seed buzzed. Gale looked around as she danced, trying to spy the danger. There was nothing; the children were watching raptly, a few smirking because they realized that Lad was not performing well. The adults stood in back, with none coming forward. There seemed to be no intrusion from outside the village square. Yet the seed never gave warning without reason.

Could it be that Lad was not going to react properly, and that would spoil the play and its educational message? But that was not a direct personal danger to her. The seed was not subtle; it signaled a lie, or danger (such as getting her mind read), or wrongness. This must be the third case. But what was the nature of that wrongness?

Gale continued dancing, trying to evoke the required reaction in the boy. He had been so constantly excited in her close presence that she had thought he would be so in the play, but she had sadly misjudged the dampening effect of public display. How was she to overcome it, if flaunting her naked body was not sufficient?

The seed buzzed again. She felt a vague sensation in her belly; was it fear? This was serious; it seldom warned her twice about a general situation. Was it that there was about to be some more dangerous consequence to her failure to arose the boy? But if her body couldn't do it, what else could? She was not allowed to touch him by her own initiative; the role of the succubus was to tempt, not force.

Her gaze met Lad's. He knew he was failing, and seemed close to tears. Unfortunately, that reaction was not conducive to grown masculine passion. Drama disaster was nigh.

This needs fixing. The thought passed through Gale's mind, and for a moment she thought it was her own. Then she felt her body tingling and somehow changing, as if she were losing control of it. She felt briefly dizzy. Was she going to faint? What an ignominious way to wipe out!

Then she felt a surge of something else. It seemed somewhat like confidence, and somewhat like lust. Her dance shifted subtly. She moved toward Lad, addressing him directly and with singular purpose. But it was not exactly by her volition; this was something new and strange. She suspected that it was a manifestation of what the seed had warned her about, but she still wasn't sure what that was. How did changing her style of dancing pose any wrongness or danger?

"Annoyed by the boy's refusal to react to her presentation, the succubus changes her mode and makes a new effort," Leader narrated, picking up on the change. He governed the play by his words, but was also responsive to the nuances of it, fortunately. "Now she focuses on him up close. 'Look at this,' she tells him."

Gale's hands came in to her body and stroked her breasts, languorously. She turned, bent over, put her hands back, and briefly parted her buttocks toward him. She turned again, with a dancer's precision, lifting one leg so high that her bare foot passed over his shoulder, then over his head as she completed her motion and recovered her balance. She smiled with calculated effect, in a way Gale never had. She reached out to Lad, without quite touching him. *Rise, manhood*, she commanded mentally. Her fingers quivered, as if drawing on invisible spider threads attached to his member.

And he reacted. He came erect so quickly it was as if her hand were hoisting him up. His mouth fell open, and his eyes went round, staring at her, even as his penis responded ardently to her summons.

The audience saw it, and there was a sigh of appreciation and awe. A few children even clapped, applauding. The succubus was showing her power. It seemed like a superlative job of acting on Lad's part, to be so suddenly and completely aroused after so obvious a failure of passion. It also seemed that every male in the audience who was capable of it was already in similar thrall to the succubus. Some of the younger boys were proudly showing their brand new erections. Some of the girls were fidgeting suggestively, trying to emulate the motions and gestures of the succubus. All of their gazes were fixed on the stage. But Gale was appalled by what was happening, and terrified of the likely consequence. This was too much of a success. It was Gale's body doing it, but not her will. If only Leader would catch on, and break this up before disaster.

"She has his attention," Leader continued with phenomenal understatement. "She has made him react, readily vanquishing his resistance. She has caused him to desire her, and in that desire is the seed of his doom. But he has not yet succumbed, and so she will not relent. Perhaps if she had taken over the body of a younger, prettier woman, she would have captured him by this time." There was a murmur of appreciative laughter; lack of a pretty body was hardly the problem. "Now she will address him with the Five Elements, and only if he succumbs to none of them will he escape. For this is the trial of his initiation, and there is no certainty he will avoid indulging in wrong sex."

He paused significantly, letting them appreciate the importance of the moment, and the succubus paused in place, honoring the semblance of the play. Was Lad going to succumb? "First she tries Air."

Gale was suddenly in motion, leaping high and wide, her arms and legs spreading in the air, and her feet touching the floor so delicately that she seemed hardly to land at all. She was a creature of the air, virtually flying, but in a sexual rather than birdlike way. It was a great dance sequence, an amazing one; she had never danced this well on her own. She saw the children watching raptly, and the adolescents staring, and the adults nodding knowingly: this was desire in motion. It had seemed impossible for the succubus to become sexier; now she was doing it.

But it was wrong, because Gale was no longer doing it. Too late, she understood the warning of the dragon seed: she had been under magic attack. Her body had been taken over by the succubus. *The demoness had control.* The amulet had not been effective. The play had suddenly become far too real.

If the succubus tempted Lad into sex, he would be lost, and not just in the play. And it could happen in front of the entire village, with no one realizing what was occurring. Until it was too late. There was now much more at stake than the success of this performance of the play or their careers as actors. The succubus had indeed shown her power, making him come throbbingly erect in an instant, after Gale had failed. Could there be any doubt of her ability to complete the seduction, using Gale's body? Gale tried to fight against it, to prevent this seduction from being completed, but she was helpless. Her body was eager to accept the boy's offering, though the aftermath be sheer horror.

Lad knew he was supposed to resist. That was the point of the play. So he would fight it. He knew that the decision had to be his and that Gale could not deny him if he was drawn into this wrong sex with her. Maybe his fear of the audience would stop him, even if desire overwhelmed him. Maybe he would not be defeated by this dreadfully dangerous challenge.

Maybe.

Chapter 5—Crises

"You understand, Sire, that you must take her to bed," Symbol said. "You must treat her in all visible respects as you would have treated the real Gale."

"Isn't it enough if I merely share the bed with her, without using her sexually?"

"No. Because she will believe she is Gale, and that belief will be shaken if you fail to evince proper passion. We will be traveling out through hinterlands, where minds may be read. Those of us in the know will be secure, because we will carry protective stones, as is customary for ranking members of the king's party. But the girl—"

"But I want Gale protected too, and if she emulates Gale—"

"Sire, heed me. When I was King Deal's lover, I carried a stone, but not for that reason. It was because I am a Chroma representative, here to see that the king plays no favorites among Chroma. I retain that stone, of course. Were I your lover, that would protect me again. But I can not be, now that Gale is here, quite apart from the fact that I am in grief for Deal, and you love Gale. But even if you wished to arrange for Gale to have a stone, it would be better not to. Because it is vital that her thoughts be guileless, so that there is no suspicion. Anyone who checks her mind will quickly move on, seeing immediately that there is nothing useful there."

"But Gale must know everything I know! I trust her beyond all others."

She shook her head. "Sire, when the real Gale returns, she will have to have a stone; she already knows too much. We will develop a pretext. But for now, she is nothing more than your incidental creature of passion. No stone."

"I don't like this."

"You don't like being king, either, Sire. This is part of that. Do you want to consult with Ennui, Aspect, or Chief?"

"No. I know what they will say." He glanced at Throe, who was as always in the background.

"Sire, the king's lover normally has no need for any but physical protection," Throe said.

Havoc sighed. "Suppose I am not naturally aroused by her? Sexual interest is difficult to fake."

"That will not be a problem, Sire."

"How can you be sure? I don't even know who she will be. You bitches have not informed me."

"We feel it is better that you not know, Sire, so as to maintain the pretense more naturally."

"I wear the cursed crown. My mind will not be spied on. Who is she?"

"Sire, you are being difficult."

"*Who?*"

"Sire, you compel me to answer, against my better judgment. The Mistress of the Royal Bath."

The girl who washed him. He liked her, perhaps because aspects of her reminded him of Gale. "But she's a child!"

"She's a woman child of sixteen, Sire, whose hair and eyes are close to Gale's own, and whose body is excellent. Her presence gives you an erection that endures as long as she is touching you. Our only problem, now being handled, is substituting another girl to emulate her."

He was weakening. "Suppose she doesn't want to be my lover?"

"Sire, *no* woman doesn't want to be your lover. In any event, she agreed to undertake the mission, knowing its special aspects, so you are not imposing on her."

"But she won't even know she's not Gale."

"Which will spare her the anguish of anticipating separation from you."

"And when Gale returns?"

She shrugged. "Sacrifices have to be made, Sire, in the interest of accomplishing the king's purposes."

"The hell! I don't want to treat any woman that way."

"Then get realistic, Sire. Will Gale accede to your maintenance of a secondary lover?"

That set him back. But of course Gale was on tour as part of a troupe doing a sexual play, and if she had to have sex elsewhere, she would do it. She would understand. Also, Gale might have to travel again, and it would be best to maintain an alternate to take her place, so that her absence was never noted. The substitute girl would not have to be cruelly dumped, just made intermittent. "I think so."

"Then the matter stands resolved, Sire. Now I think it is time for her to join you."

"Now?" he asked, suddenly nervous.

"Sire, she will be with you by preference whenever you allow it, content to remain in the background except when you take overt note of her. She will not interfere with your kingly business. And for the duration, when you get an erection, you will not have to let it go to waste."

"Spoken like an experienced king's lover," he remarked wryly.

"Of course, Sire. I will be along to see that she maintains the proper semblance, and to advise her when she has doubts."

"Doubts?"

"Sire, magic inculcates the belief in identity, but in time it can wear thin, and the underlying identity can begin to rise. Constant reassurance of the surface identity can maintain it longer. We will not be able to enhance her magically while in the field, so it is best to care well for the semblance."

"You seem to have this pretty well figured out."

"King Deal had to go into the field on occasion, Sire, when it was not expedient for me to accompany him. I have had experience."

"Deal couldn't travel with his wife?"

"Sire, the queen does not normally go into the field."

"They were estranged?"

"They had an understanding, Sire. Aspect loved him, but was no longer sexually appealing to him."

This bothered him in another way. "I think she is a good woman."

She arched an eyebrow under her veil. "Since when, Sire, does that relate to sex appeal?"

He was outclassed, when it came to kingly affairs. "So I must be with the bath girl now. What will I do with her?"

She laughed, and Throe joined in. He had made an idiotic statement. "Your schedule, according to Lady Ennui, allows leeway of an hour before the royal tour commences. I suggest, Sire, that you take advantage of the time to get used to her, so that there will be no awkwardness in public."

"Awkwardness?"

"If you seek to kiss her, Sire, and she is coincidentally turning away from you, others could notice and wonder. You must be thoroughly used to her mannerisms, and she to yours, so that it is clear you have long been close associates."

"Good point. You know, Gale is no wet rag. If I cross her, she lets me know it. Can the girl—"

"That has been factored in, Sire. Are you ready?"

Havoc felt nervous again. "I guess so."

Symbol snapped her fingers, and stepped back. In a moment Gale appeared. She must have returned early from the mission. "Gale!" he exclaimed, opening his arms to welcome her.

She stepped neatly into his embrace. "It's about time, Havoc," she murmured in his ear. "Why did you keep me waiting?"

No, it wasn't Gale. The embrace was not quite right, and neither was the voice. But they had done a remarkable job with her appearance. If it had fooled him for a moment, it would fool others much longer. "Sorry. I couldn't get away from Symbol."

"Here's how." She raised her head to look at Symbol. "I'll take it from here, Chroma woman."

Symbol retreated without a word. Havoc was impressed. That was just about the way Gale would have done it. Someone had evidently studied her carefully, in the brief time she had been here. "So I see."

"Havoc, I'm worn out with all this civilized stuff. I just want to forget it for an hour."

"Oh? What did you have in mind?"

"Let's find out." She nudged him toward the bedroom chamber. Again, it wasn't quite like Gale, but was close enough. No one in the civilized realm could know Gale the way he did, and that was just as well.

They entered the bedroom. Throe remained outside. Havoc picked her up and carried her to the bed. She caught his face with hers, kissing him avidly. Not the same, but—

But this would never work if he kept comparing her to the real Gale. She was a lovely and shapely young woman regardless, and he was interested, regardless. In moments they were naked and plunging into contacts. But it was different, for she did not know Gale's favored little moves, and was trying too hard to follow his lead. She thought she was Gale, but was missing aspects.

So he did what he had to do, and guided her, channeling her into Gale's ways. But he could no longer even try to deceive himself about her identity. This was the bath girl, trying to be what she was not, yet almost pathetically eager to please him. And when he thought of her that way, he wanted her to succeed, for she was guiltless in this charade. She was trying to serve the king, and he had to enable her to do that well.

After the imperfect yet sufficient culmination, they lay on the bed and talked. Gently he set her hands on his body the way Gale did at such times. "Do you remember the first time we played Tickle & Peek?" he asked.

"Yes." But she couldn't, because only the two of them knew of it. So he filled it in for her, as necessary background. "I was ten, you were nine. I thought you were pretty. But you didn't want to play. Then you changed your mind, and we played."

"Yes." She was paying close attention.

"I think you changed your mind when I said I just hoped we could be friends. You had thought that all I wanted to do was Peek. And I did, but I wanted more. You and I were somehow different from the others, and I thought we might truly understand each other. When you realized that I was telling the truth, you agreed to do it."

"Yes."

"You put your arms on your head, like this." He set her arms there. "I tickled you like this." He stroked a single finger across her bare ribs. "And you laughed and kicked your legs so high that I saw everything below your skirt. I knew you had done it on purpose, for you could have minimized your reaction if you had wanted to. You were never even ticklish, unless you chose to be; it was some time before I realized that. You were always generous to me, even as a child."

"Yes."

"Then it was your turn to Tickle, and you got to Touch where I had Peeked." He guided her hand to his crotch. "It was awfully ticklish, but you didn't do it much. You told me I could go Tell. But I said I really just wanted to talk. And then you kissed me." He kissed her, gently, as he had kissed the child Gale. Now that the sex was done, he could do that, and mean it. "And I think I loved you in that moment, and ever since. After that we were always together when we could be, sharing everything we could. We were interested in each other's bodies, of course, and we liked the companionship, but it was so much more than that. We two were one, in all the ways we could fathom."

"Yes!" They kissed again, and again. And, slowly, it developed into not so much another act of sex, but an act of love. He had shown her, and she had understood, and become much more like the girl he loved. Which was of course the point of this exercise, though it also saddened him, because he could not quite forget that this wasn't really Gale.

He told her more, including the episodes of the spider and the attempted rape, but not about the dragon Mentor. Her memory could betray the secret of the dragon seeds, and their development of mind masking that did not require magic. He told how they were ready to marry, when he was hauled away to be king, and how he wished the two of them could just go back to Village Trifle and disappear into employment, marriage, and family.

"I want to too," she said, "Havoc, I love you." And the seed did not buzz. That made him feel guilty, for the betrayal of this innocent girl's love. When the spell wore off, when the real Gale returned, what then?

Their hour was almost up. Ennui appeared, knocking on the door and pausing just long enough to allow them to cover up, as he had told her to do. "Get dressed, Havoc; you have work to do."

"And then came Mother Ennui," he muttered, throwing off the cover and getting to his feet, naked. Gale2, seeing his example, did the same, though she was understandably surprised. He noted on one level that she was if anything slightly fuller fleshed than Gale, but not quite as firm. It buttressed his belief that there was no other woman as truly well formed as Gale. They went to be quickly washed by the current bath squad and dressed by the clothing squad, while Ennui followed, referring to her notes as she clarified the itinerary. She ignored the ministrations of the bath girls, though they performed some rather intimate cleaning procedures, especially on the woman. After sex, such things were necessary, he realized, if there were to be no subsequent embarrassment. Gale2 understood on a level that Gale herself might have had more trouble with: the king and his consort did not handle their own private hygiene. But it clarified just how experienced the girls were in the procedures of sex; they might not have *done* it, but they understood it in detail.

Nevertheless, he remained unused to being handled by girls, and it didn't help that the new Girl One was just as pretty in the face as the other, and had a phenomenal lower section. He had just had sex, twice, but his member was rising again. Not that anyone seemed to notice.

"First you will travel by floating coach to the Green Chroma," Ennui said, reading from her notes, "to inspect the fringe of the Black Chroma volcano. That is proving to be absolutely unpredictable, and it is the judgment of the experts on your staff that a full evacuation must be ordered. Chief is arranging it now. Then you will go to a Translucent Chroma to consult about the telepathy disease outbreak."

"Isn't the blue locust plague more urgent?"

"Perhaps. But it takes time to travel, even with magic, and the most efficient way to cover the four most immediate crises is by a loop that puts them in this order. You will visit the blue locust plague region next, and direct the tax collectors to deliver relief supplies."

"The tax collectors? But they are widely hated, for good reason."

"They have the delivery network. They have merely to reverse the collection process. They will be appreciated, this time. Finally you will address the White Chroma rebellion, and remain there to deal with it personally."

"But I'll really be a figurehead while Chief handles it."

"Of course, Havoc. You're the king." Ennui smiled. "I love this work. It's meaningful."

He stepped up to her and kissed her on the forehead. "You're welcome, mother." Then he whispered in her ear: "And thanks for Gale Two. She'll do."

"I hope so."

They assembled by the elevator, a party of six: Havoc, Gale2, Ennui, Chief, Symbol, and Throe. King, lover, secretary, administrator, observer, and bodyguard. The royal retinue. But such was the pace of events that he was actually getting comfortable with it.

The coach was waiting at the base of the elevator. There was just room for them. Havoc sat between Gale2 on his right, and Symbol, while Ennui faced him between Throe and Chief. It was crowded; their hips touched, and their knees were not far from those on the facing seat.

"How long is the first hop?" Havoc inquired.

"Six hours," Ennui replied. "Counting the pauses for transfers between Chroma. We will not have to leave the coach, but ground travel does take time."

"I don't want to sound as ignorant as I am," Havoc said. "But why aren't we using more than one coach? So we could stretch out, maybe sleep on the way."

"We can, of course," Ennui said. "But it seems that the king must travel by caravan, with several coaches, and outsiders do not know which one contains the king. It is a standard precaution, in case—"

"In case someone wants to kill the king," Havoc said. "I get it. But we could still spread out through several coaches."

"Yes. But I thought we might want to consult on things while traveling."

"Chief has a program planned, I think. I'll let him go with it. So I don't think I need more briefing right now."

"But Havoc—"

"I'm a barbarian, remember? Impulsive and ignorant."

She spread her hands. "I apologize for presuming. We can spread into other coaches."

He realized that he was embarrassing her. She meant well, and was trying to do a job she was new at. "No, I like the company here. We'll get by. But is there any alternative to staring at each other for six hours?"

"As it happens, Sire, there is," Symbol said. "I brought an Air Chroma holograph, just in case. I can animate it here if you wish. But I must warn you that it's is sickeningly romantic."

"It will do." Havoc glanced around. "Any objections?"

"Of course not, Sire," Symbol said.

"No, I'm serious. I know the five of you about as well as I know any people in the civilized realm, and you know me. Maybe we aren't all friends, exactly, but you can afford to be frank with me, in private." He looked Ennui in the eye. "You, Ennui—what would you honestly prefer?"

"Actually, Havoc, I rather like your barbaric enthusiasms, and such magic has generally been beyond my experience. I'd like to see the holo."

"One in favor," he said. "Chief?"

"Sire, it is not my place to—"

"I know, the associates of the king do not practice barbaric democracy. But in this case I am asking for your informed opinion whether a sickeningly romantic Invisible Chroma holograph will serve to pass time, relax us, and perhaps enable some of us to sleep during what may otherwise be a tedious journey."

Chief smiled. "Sire, I approve."

"Throe?"

The man frowned. "Symbol, what is the title?"

"It is titled *Red Riding Hood*. That derives from a tale of a little girl and a wolf, but only peripherally; this is a rather different story."

"Does it contain any element that might conceivably endanger the king?"

"Not physically. Emotionally—it might encourage him to fall in love with an older woman."

"Like you?"

Symbol smiled. "No. Aside from being only a decade or so older, I am not the right type. Ennui would be closer."

Ennui jumped, appalled. "I have no—"

"No such design on the king," Symbol said. "We know that. You are his oath friend, a rather different matter. What I think Throe is checking is that King Havoc will not be subverted into a dangerous interest, as I would represent, rather than a safe one, as you represent. In any event the king is with his betrothed, and that should prevent any perversion of his romantic interest."

Havoc squeezed Gale2's hand reassuringly. All those present knew of the substitution, except for Gale2 herself. He would have to make sure that she never doubted. Yet he wished she could have been the real Gale. What was True Gale doing now? Surely traveling with her troupe, in similar fashion.

"Exactly," Throe said. He looked around. "Maybe I should clarify that I did not approve King Deal's liaison with Symbol, because she is Chroma. He elected to take her regardless, and was satisfied with her."

"As would you be, Throe, were I your lover," Symbol said with a mischievous smile. She lifted the hem of her skirt to show her well formed stockinged thigh. "Shall we play footsie in the dark?"

Throe was on the verge of blushing. She had evidently scored on him. His close view of her legs was better than Havoc's, because he sat opposite her, but Havoc saw enough to remind him of his first session with her, when she had shown him her invisible body and educated him on courtly manners. Her direct approach to a man was not to be denied. She was merely teasing Throe, but she was surely making him react with desire. It was her private way of establishing power, even in incidental dialogue.

Throe recovered enough to speak. "I am satisfied that this holograph does not represent a threat to the king."

"Gale?" Havoc inquired, turning to the girl.

"If it makes you hot for a woman, Havoc, it had better be me."

The original Gale probably wouldn't have said that, being entirely sure of him. But this would do. "I am always hot for you, my love," he said. "But it's difficult to do much about it right now."

"I want to know where both your hands are, while you watch."

"They will be on you, Gale," he promised.

"That leaves me safe," Symbol said. "Unless the king has a very probing foot." Both other men smiled, but Ennui did not.

The coach rolled to a stop. "We are at the fringe of the Translucent Chroma," Throe said. "In a moment their water magic will float us on our way."

He was right. The coach felt as if floating on rising water. Then it felt as if it were forging along a river current. They were magically airborne. But the windows were closed, to prevent any outsider from seeing which coach of the caravan held the king's party, so they could not see out over the landscape. Havoc regretted that. He wondered whether the coach was hitched to a huge flying fish.

Symbol gestured in the air. "Behold: the holograph."

It formed between them and around them, blotting out the interior of the coach and the people in it: a scene of a castle in a forest. Havoc found the effect just as intriguing as he had before; the novelty had not faded. He put his right arm around Gale2, and true to his word, reached across his body with his left to find her blouse, get under it, and take hold of her left breast in its bra. She reached in to touch a snap, and her bra loosened so that he could clasp her bare flesh. He had done it to reassure her of his continuing desire for her, but this made that desire real. He wished they were alone in the coach.

"The setting is of course Planet Mystery, where all the most remarkable stories are," Symbol said. "In this region there are no Chroma zones, but some people have magic of their own. Otherwise, this is much like our own world of Charm. The sound will come on in a moment, once the holo gets fully established. The effects are however limited to seeing and hearing; there is no smell, taste, or touch, unfortunately. Bear with it. Perhaps you can find something else to touch, to lend further effect." Her right thigh nudged Havoc's left thigh suggestively.

"Oh, this is something," Gale2 whispered, clearly awed. "I've never seen a scene like this before. We have entirely disappeared." She moved one hand before her, seeing its invisibility. She was genuinely excited; her breast was flexing as her breathing quickened. What she said would be true for the real Gale, and possibly also for Gale2, as a servant girl might not have much occasion to experience real magic.

"Yes, that's the way it works," he whispered back. And if there were a sex scene, he would indeed be able to amend its realism by touching the equivalent parts of her body. He could appreciate how such shows could be very popular with dating couples.

Then the holograph's sound started. There was the rustling of leaves as a breeze passed through the forest, and the sound of footsteps coming up behind them.

Behind? Havoc turned his head to look back, and so did Gale2. This caused her breast and his grip on it to change intriguingly. Damn— he should never have gotten into her blouse when there was no chance to do anything more. But the scene behind was the same as the scene in front; the holo showed what it showed regardless of the angle of viewing, in the manner of a painting. The sound remained behind him, when he faced the other way. The scene only *looked* infinite.

They turned back, understanding the futility of changing position, in more than one sense. Gale2 put her left hand on his left hand, steadying it as it lay on her breast. He wasn't sure whether she was encouraging him, or tacitly preventing him from going farther. Either way, he was satisfied for the time being to let it be, and focus on the holograph.

A young man came into sight. Havoc knew this was being shown in the close confines of the coach, but it still seemed to be as big as the outdoors it represented. This illusion magic really was spectacular. The man was strikingly handsome, muscular, and bore an expression of alert intelligence. He was, in short, an idealized holo hero, of a type seldom encountered in real life.

Havoc felt a motion against his left thigh. He realized that Symbol was moving her right leg again, though this time not in a signal to him. But where could she move it? There wasn't room in the coach to stretch it out. Unless she slid it up against Throe's leg opposite her. Yet she seemed to be shifting its position back and forth.

He stifled a laugh. She was teasing the bodyguard again, stroking his leg with her foot. Under the cover of the holo scene. And there wasn't anything Throe could do about it without making an unconscionable fuss. Naughty girl.

The holo man strode to the castle's front gate, and rapped on its bars with his staff. The sound rang out, startlingly loud. "Ho, there Castle!" the man cried. "Greeting! Anybody home?"

The gate guard appeared, rubbing his eyes. He had evidently been snoozing in his guard box, and had been caught by surprise. "What do you want?"

"I am called Song, from a distant village. I have come to see the mistress of the castle."

"What is your business with her?"

"I wish to take service with her, so she can train me to become the best singer in my district."

The guard laughed unkindly. "You have come to the wrong castle, idiot. My mistress doesn't train men. Only talented young women."

"Then maybe it is time she tried it with a man. I insist on seeing her."

"You fool, she'll make short work of you. Go away while you still have your balls."

But the handsome young man stood firm. "If she wants to be rid of me, let her tell me that herself."

The guard shrugged. "Very well, nutcase. What's your name again?"

"Song. That's my would-be profession. To sing for the masses."

"Wait here." The guard retreated into the castle.

The young man waited. The scene fuzzed momentarily, to indicate that time was passing.

The guard reappeared. "She asks whether you can actually sing."

"I can sing up a storm. That's the problem. I require training, to—"

"Then sing. She will hear from her chamber."

"But—"

"Or stop wasting our time."

The man sighed. "If you insist. But remember, I warned you." He took several deep breaths, lifted his chin, and sang. "My love is like a green green rose..."

Almost immediately the air stirred, and a gust of wind smote the castle gate. Vapor formed, swirling around the two men. The scene darkened as a thickening cloud obscured the sun. Rain began to fall as thunder cracked overhead.

"What is this?" the guard demanded.

Song paused in his singing. "I told you: I sing up a storm. My magic is unfocused. I have to get that fixed before I can be what I want to be."

The guard looked at a turret above the castle wall. A hand projected from it, waving a green kerchief. "She will after all see you," he said. "Come this way."

Song followed the guard into the castle. Behind them, the storm rapidly dissipated, and the sun came out again.

The scene showed the interior of the castle. The gate opened to a dark hall, which in turn opened to an inner courtyard. From there they climbed stone steps to the second story, where they entered another hall. That led to an intersecting cross-hall, which in turn led to another series of stone steps. Beyond these was another hall, which terminated in a closed door.

The guard pounded on the door. "Mistress Hood, he is here," he called.

"Send him in," a voice rasped.

The guard pulled the door open. "You're on your own, simpleton," he said. "Go on in."

Song entered the chamber. It was small and spare. On a tall stool sat a cloaked female figure with a bright red hood and a black veil that entirely concealed her facial features.

"Do you know me?" she rasped.

"You are Red Riding Hood," Song said. "The finest trainer of singers on this world."

"Of *female* singers," she said, her voice remaining like gravel. "You must know that."

"I know that," he agreed. "But as I see it, the same skill that trains women can train a man. I have come to be trained."

"They are not the same. I have no experience with men."

"But you have great experience with singing."

She laughed bitterly. "Have you heard me try to sing? I can barely talk."

"But you have knowledge like no other. You have trained several of the finest singers of the planet. I have raw talent. You can show me how to bring it under control, and become what I want to be."

She sighed. "It is true your talent is raw. It so disturbs the air that the weather changes."

"Exactly! But if I can just learn to channel my magic properly, I can be a fine singer. I know it. That is why I have come to you."

She shook her hidden head. "No. I do not work with men. You must go to a male trainer."

"Can't," he said. "I have no gems to pay one of them."

The figure stiffened. "Then how would you pay *me*? My time is valuable."

"Well, I thought that you being a woman, you would have need of a man to do chores, run errands, clean out your stalls—whatever. I'll do anything, so long as it's not illegal. You need train me only an hour a day; the rest of the time I will work. I can work hard." He flexed his right arm, making a muscle. It was a good muscle.

"You amaze me by your temerity. I can have chores done for a pittance. My expertise is not to be had for a pittance."

He looked crestfallen. "But Lady, you are my only hope. I must have your training to realize my dream."

"I can put you in touch with a venture capitalist who will stake you the wherewithal for expensive training elsewhere."

"But then he will own me," Song protested.

"For a time," she agreed. "Until you earn back his investment with interest. It is the price of achieving your goal. You do have magic and a fair voice; you should be able to get there, in due course."

"Ma'am, please—I would much rather have you train me. You are the best. If I must be owned, better to be owned by you. They say you are not unkind to your servants."

"I don't want to own you!"

"Ma'am, please. I'll work hard. I'll do anything."

"No."

He sank to his knees, tears appearing at his eyes. "Ma'am, I beg you. Anything."

"Oh for pity's sake!" she exclaimed, disgusted. "I can't stand to see a grown man cry."

"Then you'll do it?" he asked, his face illuminating with hope.

"I confess to being struck by your earnestness, your potential, your youthful handsomeness, and your naïve candor. Still—"

"O thank you ma'am!" he exclaimed, throwing his arms around her legs and the chair.

"Wait! I didn't say—"

He buried his face in the folds of the skirt covering her knees. "You won't be sorry!"

"I am already sorry! How can you think—"

"I'll be your best student ever! And your best laborer."

She looked down, then patted his head. "I am a fool."

"No, no, ma'am, you are a great lady. And I will do everything I possibly can to be worthy of your attention."

She grimaced through the veil. "Understand, you will be a live-in servant for the duration of your training. This means sweeping floors, scrubbing turnips, hauling water, bundling garbage. You will answer to the gatekeeper, the cook, and anyone else in authority in this castle. You will be the lowest of the low."

"Yes!" he said gladly.

"And you won't receive any gems. Just your sustenance and training, until you achieve your potential, whatever that may be."

"Yes."

"And on occasion you will go to the nearby town to shop for staples needed by the castle. I do not like to appear in public, or to talk with strangers. I don't like being stared at. So you will go there, when necessary."

"Anything," he agreed raptly.

She looked at the ceiling. "I hope I don't rue this hour."

"Oh, no, never, ma'am!"

"Go downstairs and find the kitchen. The cook doubles as maid; she'll get you installed in the servant's quarters and introduce you to the by-paths of the castle. Tomorrow morning I will see you for your first training session."

"Thank you, wonderful lady! Thank you!"

"Now please let go of my knees."

Awkwardly, he did so. He got to his feet.

Someone nudged his left side. "Disengage, Sire."

For a moment Havoc was nonplused. Then he realized that Symbol had addressed him, surely with reason. He had been identifying with Song, so the nudge had seemed to come from nowhere. He slid his left hand out of Gale2's blouse and straightened up somewhat.

The holo picture faded out. The coach interior and its occupants came back into sight. "I believe we are at the edge of the Translucent Chroma," Symbol said. "My Air crystal powers the holograph, but I think it best that we be alert during the transition to the Brown Chroma. There is also a rest stop scheduled here, in case of need."

Havoc now knew better than to stand and piss beside the coach; he was no longer in barbarian country. He would use the civilized interior pot.

They got out of the coach, and found themselves in a small fenced compound. He and Gale2 walked to the pot building. He suddenly realized that he still was not properly adept at putting his own clothing together; he was bound to be clumsy. But he did need the pot.

Also, he wasn't sure of the male/female protocol here. Were there supposed to be separate places for men and women?

Fortunately Gale2 did seem to know. This would be part of her background experience, left in place. She accompanied him without embarrassment. There were two pots within, so they each used one, side by side.

Then as he finished and stood, fumbling with his fastenings, Gale2 stepped up to him. Efficiently she put him back together, then embraced him, kissed him, and led him back outside.

The others were ready. They climbed back into the coach, and the coachmen hauled it out of the compound. Soon there was the special feel of magic lifting. They were on their way across the Brown Chroma, no doubt carried by a huge golem.

"Are we ready for the next installment of *Red Riding Hood*?" Symbol inquired. "Not finding it too dull? It does gain feeling as it goes." After a pause, the castle scene resumed.

Song walked down the hall, down the stairs, down the hall, down the other hall, and out to the courtyard steps. He sniffed the air, then crossed the courtyard and found the kitchen without difficulty.

A solid woman of middle age looked up as he entered. "I am the new handyman," he said. "Madam Hood said you would install me and show me the castle by-paths."

Cook nodded. "Who are you?"

"Song. She will train me at her convenience, and I will work the rest of the time. I am to answer to you and the gatekeeper."

"Then follow me." Cook led him to a closet where there were sheets and pillows, and gave him an armful to carry. They moved on to another closet, where she dug out working clothing for him. Then she led him to a chamber in back. "This will be yours, and you will take care of it yourself. Set it up, change clothes, then report to me at the kitchen for the lunch meal."

Song did so. When he returned to the kitchen, Cook joined him in a repast of red turnips and blue turnip greens. "She's gruff at first, but she softens with time," she confined. "She's not a bad mistress. Just don't cross her."

"Oh, I wouldn't do that."

"Maybe not intentionally. Don't ask questions that don't relate to your work. When you report to her, always knock before entering. She needs time to cover her face. Never seek to see her face."

"Might I inquire—?"

"No. She will tell you if she chooses."

Song shrugged. "All I'll ask is what she wants me to do."

"You don't even need to ask. Just do whatever she tells you. At other times, do what I tell you, or the gatekeeper tells you. As the last hireling, you're at the bottom of the totem."

"Got it."

Cook smiled. "That's the attitude. Now there's a pile of pots to scrub."

Song got to work. He hummed while he scrubbed, glad to be there. He knew Red Riding Hood would treat him fairly, and give him the training he needed to become great, and he didn't mind what else he had to do along the way.

"I must say, you're a cheerful one," Cook remarked as he finished. "You've done a good job, too."

"My mother told me always to do the best I knew how," Song said. "She said there are no lowly jobs, just lowly performances."

"I like your mother. And what did your father say?"

"He died some time ago."

Cook shut up, embarrassed. She let him off the chores soon after, though there were plainly more to do. Song retired to his chamber, and discovered he was tired; it had been a considerable day. He washed up, changed into nightclothes, lay down, and was soon asleep.

In the morning he reported to the kitchen, ready to resume work. "First you eat, then you report to Madame for your training session. The work will keep till the afternoon."

"But I can see that there are things to do."

"I could get to like you, Song. But Madame wants you fresh, not sweaty. Eat." And she served him an excellent breakfast of fried crab leaves and wasp honey.

Song reported to Madam Red Riding Hood on schedule. This time she was standing, and he saw that she was of average height and slender of form beneath her encompassing cloak. She led him into a theater chamber with a high ceiling, walking with a dancer's smoothness. She was immediate business. "First we must abate that misdirected magic, she said in her raspy voice. "Can't have rainfall ruining my floor. Focus your gaze on this picture." She indicated a framed picture on a wall, of a fiery yellow volcano. "Think of Fire, burning up everything in its vicinity. Think of overwhelming heat of the fire season. Think of thirst as you cross a desert. Now sing."

He concentrated, and sang. "I gave my love a cherry that had no bone. I gave my love a chicken that had no cone."

Clouds were swirling in the chamber, but there was no thunder and no rain. Instead there was flying sand. It formed a pile on the floor.

Hood raised her hand, and Song stopped singing. The cloud dissipated, but the sand remained. "Well, it's progress," she remarked somewhat wryly. "This establishes that you can control the magic. We simply need to channel it all into something useful."

Song was amazed. "Sand! That never happened before. It was always wet." He looked around. "I'll need a bucket to haul it out."

"No. You will do it the hard way. You will sing it out."

"Sing it out, Madame? But I don't know how to—"

"That is why you are here. *I* know how. This time, when you sing, focus on Air. On wind, strong but dry."

"But—"

"Who is the trainer, here?" she asked sharply.

"You are, Madame," he said humbly. He sang, focusing on dry air. After several attempts he began to get it right: a circular wind formed that swept up the sand, making a bowl pattern that almost filled the chamber. It whirled faster and faster, thinning and expanding, until it passed outside the chamber, leaving calm air in the center. The sand was gone.

Song wavered on his feet and started to fall. Hood stepped into him and held him firm. "Breathe deeply," she said. "Recover your strength."

Song breathed, and gradually his pounding heartbeat subsided and his vision cleared. He discovered himself embraced by her, her strong small body supporting his big weak one. She was—he was perplexed by this—nice to be close to. "Thank you, Madame," he said at last. "I don't know what happened."

"Magic is not free," she said. "For the first time, you channeled yours, and it was very strong, but it exhausted you. There is a considerable way to go yet, but you have taken the first and second steps. The long term object will be to channel it into your singing itself, so as to enhance it and make you the star you can be. This will require a great deal of work, but will be worth it in the end."

"Oh, Madame! Do you really think I can be a star?"

"I said so, didn't I? But you have set foot on the base of a mountain of considerable challenge. Progress is likely to be tediously slow. You may grow to hate me."

"Hate you, Madame? I would never—"

"As the symbol of what may become the painful discipline I impose. We shall see whether you have the necessary staying power. You may of course depart at any time. You know that I am not expert in training men."

"I shall stay the course, Madame. I am most grateful for—"

"Don't be maudlin. You will earn your keep."

"You have already shown me more than I ever thought possible. I—"

"The session is over. Go back to the kitchen."

Humbly, he left. He did not see the faint smile under Hood's veil.

The sessions continued, and the work continued. Song applied himself diligently at both, and made slow but clear progress in the one while making the labors of Cook and Gatekeeper less arduous. In a month he had channeled his magic so that it made no disturbance while he sang, and was beginning to manifest in the singing itself, enhancing it. Hood began guiding him in the nuances of stage management and on-stage dialogue, to supplement his singing.

"Now we are short handed here, so will have to make do," she said briskly. "I will pose as your opposite number, the lead female singer. Pretend that I have sung my song, and it is now your turn. Sing to me." She flung off her cloak and stood in a simple black dress, a trim yet buxom figure of a woman under the red hood and veiled face.

But Song was suddenly diffident. He mangled his song, and a storm swirled around them.

"What is the matter?" she asked sharply. "You can't have suddenly forgotten what you have learned. Control your magic, channel it into your music."

"I am trying, Madame," he said apologetically.

"Evidently not hard enough. When you go on a real stage, in a real play, you will be opposite some genuinely lovely women. Some will be prima donnas you can't stand, but you must never allow your personal sentiment to show. As far as you are concerned onstage, they are all your true loves. I actually represent a sufficient challenge in this respect; if you can pretend I am your true love, you will be able to handle anything. Now focus!"

"Madame, please, it's not that," he protested.

"Then what is it? You have been shying clear of me as if I am a freak. I *am* a freak, but for this purpose you must treat me as if I am a desirable object. You can't afford to get stage fright or stage disorientation; this is perhaps the greatest liability of novice performers."

"I know, Madame. It's not that."

"Then what is it?" she demanded.

His diffidence became painful. "I can't tell you, Madame."

"You can't tell me!" she exploded. "This is interfering with your training and your potential career. You do have talent; the prospect of a career is real. I will not allow you to destroy it by foolish reservations. If you can't tell me, I can't deal with it, and there is no point in continuing."

Song looked woebegone. "Please, Madame, I don't want to make you angry."

"Well, you are succeeding."

He looked as if he were about to cry. She realized that this was not simple obstinacy. "Very well. I promise not to fire you or terminate your training, even if it infuriates me. *Tell me.*"

Song scuffled his feet. "I—I've been alone a while. And you, Madame—you know so much, you understand me so well, you are doing so much for me. Anything I may become, I owe to you."

"Oh, come on now. You're earning your keep. Cook says she'll be really sorry when you graduate and go on your way, because she's almost forgotten how to do the chores. You are spoiling us, Song."

Still he was hesitant. "I want—at night—I think of you."

"I know I've been bearing down hard on you, Song. It is because I want you to realize your potential. I do not mean to be unkind; it's just the way I am. I expect a lot."

"It's not that," he said quickly. "I like working in your castle. Working with you."

"Then sleep in peace, and train with full vigor. Don't think of me as a tyrant to fear—"

"I think of you—as a woman," he said, and looked abashed, as if about to be severely chastised.

Hood was amazed. "Are you saying that you desire me? Sexually?"

He hung his head. "I guess I am, Madame. I know I don't have any right. It just happened."

Hood could hardly believe this. "When I was fifteen I was a promising actress with a fine singing voice, beautiful and talented and with prospects as big as the planet. Until a jealous boyfriend threw cursed water in my face. No magic balm would heal it; the damage was permanent. It cost me the sight of one eye, and spoiled my voice, and left horrible scars across my face. It destroyed the career I had so fondly anticipated. Since that time, fifteen years ago, I have sought my fulfillment by helping other promising girls to achieve their destinies on the stage—and now, perhaps, you. I mask myself from you because I do not care to be the object of revulsion. I can destroy any personal interest you may have in a moment simply by removing my hood. I am truly ugly now. Do you wish me to do that?"

"No, Madame."

"Then be satisfied that I am no love object, apart from the necessary pretense for the stage rehearsals. You don't want me in your bed."

Song skuffled his feet again. "But I do, Madame. I think you're lovely in that red hood. You have a—a very nice body."

"You desire me—with the hood?"

"Yes, Madame." He looked as though he expected her to hit him.

She shook her head, coming to an abrupt decision. "This can readily be put to the test. Come to my bed in fifteen minutes, and I will strip away everything but the hood."

His mouth sagged open. "Everything, Madame?"

"And I will give you access to everything that shows. Will that satisfy you?"

He was awash in confusion. "Oh, Madame—you don't have to do anything like that for me! I was just explaining why I can't concentrate on the training. I didn't mean to suggest—"

"I know you didn't. That is why I am doing it. I intend to eliminate this barrier to your progress, one way or another, either by demonstrating that you lack the desire you thought you had, or by satisfying it without delay. This is efficient."

"Oh, Madame," he breathed, awed or terrified by the prospect.

"I will go to my bedroom now. You can come to me or refrain from doing so, and it will not affect our relationship with respect to training or work. Provided that your distraction ceases hereafter. I ask only that you do not bruit this matter about, either way. I have had more than enough embarrassment in my life already."

"Oh, I wouldn't bruit, Madame!"

Red Riding Hood left him in the theater chamber, and walked to her bedroom suite, changed into an attractive red gown, and awaited Song's arrival, uncertain whether he would actually come. "In fact," she said, speaking to herself as though he were present, "I am uncertain whether I *want* you to come. What I have not told you is that I have been bemused by your aspect throughout our association. You are the kind of man I would have married, had I not lost my appeal. I am thirty, no longer young, but no longer beyond desire either. This entire business, from the time I first met you, has been an exercise in the futility of a bygone dream. I desire to be loved, and that desire has so distorted my equilibrium as to make me foolish. It is myself I am challenging, as much as you. So come to me, my handsome talented innocent lad, if you truly desire my body. At worst, you will have a mistress you will not care to advertise, and I—I will dream foolishly a little longer. Perhaps we can serve each others' passing needs."

Then she took a handkerchief, reached up under her veil, and dabbed away a tear from her left eye.

The dragon seed buzzed. For a moment Havoc thought it was part of the holo play. Then he realized that there was danger. He removed his left hand from Gale2's breast and touched Symbol's bare knee, finding it by location. "Stop the show," he said.

The scene abruptly ended. There was Symbol, with her stockinged legs clamping one of Throe's legs. There was Chief holding hands with Ennui. There was Gale2 with a bare left breast. But none of that was the point.

"There is danger," Havoc said. "Get us elsewhere now."

Throe put his right arm out through the shrouded window beside him. "Brown courier—evasive action," he said, speaking what his outside hand was signaling.

The coach suddenly dropped and swerved. There was a flash of light outside that made the coach roof momentarily transparent. Then the sound of an explosion. Then the coach was hurled more rapidly downward, spinning.

It braked steeply, then crashed into the ground. The door opened, sprung by the force of contact. The six of them were piled together, the three on Havoc's side on top of the three opposite. Havoc avoided crushing Ennui only by thrusting his left hand beside her, taking up much of the force of his collision with her. But Gale2 was plastered against Chief, and Symbol was jammed onto Throe.

"Out," Havoc said. "Three parties, three directions. We need to hide, in case there is more coming."

Throe reacted immediately. He rolled out the sprung door, carrying Symbol with him. They fell on the ground and scrambled away. Havoc followed, lifting Ennui from her seat and setting her down outside. Then he plunged straight on away from the coach. He trusted that Chief would get Gale2 out similarly.

He glanced back. The huge brown golem that had carried them was lying tumbled and broken on the ground, much of its body missing. It had managed to set the coach down halfway gently before expiring.

The terrain was all brown. Havoc had never before been this deep into a Chroma on the ground, and never in Brown, but he recognized the types of magic plants. There were dangerously tentacular trees beginning to react, and other vegetative threats. They needed protection in a hurry.

He saw a clump of mask vines. They would do. He carried Ennui to them and set her down, sitting. "Pee," he said.

Astonished, she only stared while he hastily brought out his penis and urinated on the vines. There wasn't much, because they had recently used the rest stop pot, but it would have to do.

Two brown tentacles were extending toward her from behind. "Pee!" he repeated. "Now!"

"I—I can't," she said.

"Then vomit."

She remained frozen, unable to assimilate this. But there was no time. In another moment a tentacle would find her, and then he would have to fight the tree for her, and that would be no easy thing, here in the heart of a Chroma region. The tree might stun him magically, or overcome him in some other way.

He took his forefinger, put it to her mouth, pried it open, and probed the back of her throat. He found the trigger, and suddenly she spewed over his hand. He put his hand on the vines and carefully rubbed it across them, spreading the vomit. The tentacles halted but did not retreat.

Ennui choked, then recovered, breathing gaspingly. "Havoc, what—"

"These are mask vines," he said. "They will mask our presence, for a while. But we have to demonstrate our friendship with an offering of food. Can you pee yet?"

Her resistance was gone. "I—I'll try." She got to her squatting feet, hiked up her skirt, pulled aside her panty and managed to squeeze out a few drops.

"Good. Urine is best, because it soaks in fastest so they can recognize it. Now we are friends, and masked." Indeed, the tentacles of the other plant were casting about elsewhere, unable to locate her.

"Masked?"

"To others, we look like more mask vines."

"But what happened? Where are the others?"

"We were attacked. A firebomb, I think. The others should be hiding similarly."

"They—they had to urinate?"

"If they knew to do it. But they should not be in as much danger. I'm the king, therefore the target. So I need to hide, until we know the threat is past." Actually she had been the one in danger, because she was close to him, but did not have the protection of the crown.

"Oh, Havoc," she said. Then she wept.

He put his arm around her. "I think we're safe now. The Brown Chroma forces will be zeroing in on them and us. We just had to get out of range of the attack quickly. We did."

"But the danger—I'm not strong. I don't know how to—"

"You don't have to be." He squeezed her shoulders. "Remember, you were the one who was bored with life."

She brightened. "You certainly fixed that!"

"What's this with Chief?"

"He took my hand. Do you think—?"

"I think he likes you. Maybe he wants to remarry, though he doesn't have to while he serves the king."

"But I'm nothing!"

"Not any more."

"But it's only because of you."

"If his interest is serious, would you want to?"

She was nonplused. "I don't know. He's an interesting man, with such an important position, while I—"

"Maybe he wants a woman who would give loyalty without being demanding. One not like Symbol."

"I am that," she agreed.

"One he could come home to and just be with, no challenge, no games."

"Havoc, are you saying—"

"Oath friendships are not affected by romantic associations. If he invites you to his chamber, maybe you should try it. If you want to."

"Sex?"

"Were you tired of sex, or of the man, before?"

"Of being used." Then she reconsidered. "With the right man, I think I wouldn't mind it at all."

"There you are."

"This is all so sudden."

"I'm not called Havoc for nothing. Things have always happened around me. When we resume travel, take his hand."

"It seems so wild and daring and provocative."

"That's more like Symbol. Did you see her working on Throe?"

"Yes. Those legs—"

A brown shape floated toward them. "Sire."

"We've been spotted." Havoc stood. "Here. How did you find me?"

The brown man came to land before them. His insignia indicated high status. "Your crown, Sire. You disappeared, but we always know where it is."

"So do my enemies."

"I don't think so, Sire. There were three firebombs, going for all three coaches. We intercepted two, but the third got away. Fortunately your bodyguard anticipated the threat and took evasive action at the last moment. We are tracking down the source now."

"There won't be any leads to the source," Havoc said.

"Perhaps not, Sire, but we shall certainly look. This was no design of the Brown Chroma."

"I'm sure it wasn't," Havoc agreed. The seed had not buzzed. "But maybe your security should be strengthened."

"It shall be, Sire." The man was clearly embarrassed.

A new coach and golem were provided, and the party reassembled. The other four people had survived, though with bruises and scratches that brown magic ointment was ameliorating. "Hug her," Ennui murmured as Chief and Gale2 appeared.

She was right: he had to be properly demonstrative. He embraced Gale2, and she cried on his shoulder. Once again he felt guilt.

As the coach floated, Throe looked at Havoc. "Sire, how did you know?"

He would have to tell, as there was no concealing the fact that he *had* known. "When I was young, I befriended a blue dragon. It gave me a dragon seed. It warns me of danger."

Throe nodded. "A dragon seed. That explains a lot. But that was chancy, associating with a dragon."

"It was injured. I helped it. We made an oath of friendship." He did not tell of Gale's involvement and similar dragon seed, as that could endanger her. "I prefer that this not be widely known."

"It will not be known beyond this circle," Chief said.

"An oath of friendship with a dragon," Throe said. "That's one I never heard of before."

"Havoc makes some strange oaths," Ennui said.

"I respect the creatures and plants of the wilderness," Havoc said seriously. "They have much to teach us."

"They surely do," Symbol agreed thoughtfully. "Do we wish to resumed the holo?"

"Yes," Ennui said. "I want to know whether he will come to her."

Chief glanced at her sidelong. "Do you wish him to?"

"Yes." Evidently Ennui had decided to give him a try.

"I'm still shaking from that attack and crash," Gale2 said. "I'd like a diversion."

Then the holograph formed around them, and there was only Red Riding Hood standing alone in her bedroom, a rather pretty figure in her dress, with her head still masked.

There was a hesitant knock on the door. There was a murmur of relief, whether of Hood or a member of the audience was uncertain. "Come in."

Song entered. He had washed his face and combed his hair, and was strikingly handsome. "You look great," he said. "I never saw you in a full dress before."

"I will remove it if you wish." She did not point out the distinction between a dress and the gown she wore.

"Uh, no, that's fine. I mean, you look great." Realizing that he was repeating himself, he went silent.

So he had summoned courage to come, but not to take it farther. Perhaps he remained in doubt. So she helped him. "Shall we dance?"

"Uh, sure."

She gestured, and music sounded. Then she approached him and stepped into the loose embrace of lowkey ballroom dancing. She led him, for she was expert while he was half clumsy.

"Hold me as if you mean it," she said after a moment.

But he was diffident again. "I can't hold you close, Madame; I'm getting a—"

She laughed. "Then let's get to it. Shall I undress myself, or do you prefer to do it?"

"I don't hardly dare touch you, Madame," he confessed.

"That will change." She unfastened her robe and stepped out of it, naked underneath. Her body was startlingly ripe; she looked a mature fifteen. She lay on the bed. "Now it is your turn."

"Uh, yeah." But he just stood there.

"Do not be embarrassed, Song. We are after all here for sex. It would be embarrassing if you were not ready for it."

Thus encouraged, he climbed out of his clothing and joined her on the bed. But he still lacked initiative.

"How would you like me?" she inquired. "Sunny side up, or rear view?"

"Madame," he said, blushing. "Could I—kiss you?"

"Through the veil?"

"Uh, yes."

"As you wish."

But he didn't do it, so after a moment she lifted her upper section, turned into him, and kissed him gently on the lips, the veil between them.

Then he kissed back, and became more urgent, like a rising storm.

In moments he pushed her down flat, and mounted her, and thrust into her, climaxing immediately like the healthy young animal he was. "Oh, Madame," he gasped. "Oh, Madame!"

Then he withdrew, and became apologetic. "I got carried away. I know it's not supposed to be fast like that. I'm sorry."

"I'm not, Song. It means your passion is real."

"Yeah, it sure is."

"Let's relax a while, and then do it again, when you are ready. Then it will be slower."

"Yeah." He paused, lying beside her on his side. "Thanks for kissing me."

"You may kiss me again, soon. For now, just relax." She reached across to capture his left hand. She brought it to her breasts and slowly stroked it across them.

Soon, as promised, he was kissing her again, first on the breasts and then on the veil. Then she lifted her legs and embraced him with them, and guided him slowly back into her. The culmination took longer this time, and was under her guidance, so that in due course she climaxed and took him with her.

"Oh Madame!" he said. "Oh Madame! That's the greatest I ever dreamed. I love you."

"Let's not make rash statements. It suffices that you find my body physically appealing."

"Oh, Madame, I mean it. I think your body is great, but I was starting to love you before I ever saw it."

Hood considered, then took a chance. "Would you like to move in with me, and share my bed every night?"

"Oh, yes, Madame! But you might not get much sleep."

"I am prepared to suffer that penalty. So we shall be lovers. I confess I have missed the company of handsome, potent young men like you. But before we commit further, I think it is time to show you my face."

"Madame, you don't need to do that. I never wanted to embarrass you."

"But I believe I do need to do it, because if you are to be repulsed by my appearance, and turned off further relations, it is best that it be done at the outset, to save us both awkwardness."

"Oh, Madame, I don't want to be turned off."

She put her hands to her head, and lifted off the hood, letting her dull brown hair fall loose. Then she drew off the veil, for the first time revealing the features of her injured face.

Song looked, and blanched. She had not exaggerated. Her right eye was a socket ringed by scar tissue, and the scars angled down her face to take out half her nose and most of her chin. Her lips were full but discolored. Her throat was ridged with scars.

But Song did not avert his gaze. "It's awful what happened to you, Madame."

"I am indeed ugly," she agreed. "Now you may if you wish depart my presence, or this castle. But I will say that this session has been nice, and I thank you for it."

"May I kiss you, Madame?"

She was surprised. "Without the veil?"

"Yes, Madame."

"If you want to, it is your privilege. But I will understand if you wish me to restore the veil."

"No, Madame." Then he bent over her and kissed her tenderly on the lips. He continued by kissing the rest of her face, to the verge of her spoiled eye.

She held her position for a moment, then let go. She reached up around his shoulders to hug him close. "You have given me a price-less gift," she said. "Tolerance for my aspect."

"I can see how you really are, under the hood," he said. "Under the scars. I see your fine spirit."

"I thought no man would do that, ever."

"Madame, if it's all right with you, can I—?"

"What, again? Youth is marvelous."

So they proceeded to a third act of love, and after that he was finally sated, for that hour.

The holo went into summary, showing Song's subsequent career, which was a good one. He became extremely popular, and traveled widely. With him always was his lady, with an excellent figure but wearing a flexible mask that looked almost real, with her hair set care-fully around it. But in the privacy of their castle she went naked, body and face, with the intended consequence: he was constantly catching her and caressing her, and often it got out of hand.

The picture faded. They were back in the coach. "I did warn you," Symbol said. "Not a strong plot, but heavy romance."

"When we camp tonight, what are the facilities?" Havoc asked.

"There is to be a house with three rooms, with a common kitchen and bathroom area," Ennui said. "This seems to be the best available at this particular site."

"Shall we make it three couples, without further comment or implied commitment?"

There was a pause. Then Symbol spoke. "As the king wills." That settled it.

"That holo is not fair play," Throe grumped.

Symbol smiled. "I know it." She tickled his leg with a toe. "But how else are we to wile away the long dull hours traveling with the king?" She spread her knees, and he did look.

The rest of the journey was routine. They crossed one more Chroma zone, then arrived at the station on the edge of the Green Chroma. It was late afternoon; the official business would wait until the morrow.

Havoc took a brief walk around the premises with Gale2, stretching his legs. Throe followed discreetly, not trusting the protection of the area. The region was lovely, all in shades of green. All the plants were passive varieties; Havoc mentally catalogued them as he went. This area had been rendered safe for tourists.

"Must he follow us?" Gale2 whispered.

"Yes, it's his job. Just ignore him."

"But suppose we want to—?"

"He won't tell." Realizing this was not a satisfactory answer for her, he amended it. "He has to guard me, and he has to be near me to do that. He wasn't close enough to King Deal to protect him when he fell, and so he is doubly careful with me. But we probably shouldn't smooch in public anyway; I suspect it's unkingly."

"But this is private, except for him."

"So it is," he agreed. He turned into her, embraced her, and kissed her, running a hand over her bottom.

She stiffened momentarily, then relaxed. Then she ran her hand over his bottom, making turnabout fair play. "I love every part of you," she said.

There was no buzz from the dragon seed. She was not trying to flatter him. The familiar guilt returned. What was he doing to this innocent girl? "Oh, Gale," he said, feeling a surge of painfully mixed emotion.

She kissed him again, with enhanced passion. She had taken his reaction to be an expression of love. "You know I'm yours in every way, Havoc."

This just got worse. "I have two things to do, and if I don't do one now, I won't have a chance later."

"Two things?"

"Exercise and passion. It's the first that could get squeezed out."

"I can't help you in that, Havoc."

"Yes you can." He bent to pick her up, holding her under arms and knees, and began to run. He quickly gained velocity, moving her body from side to aside to keep his balance.

"Havoc!" she cried, laughing, as her hair and skirt flung out.

He ducked his head down and nudged her bosom with his forehead. "I can't think of a nicer burden to carry."

"I can run too," she offered. "No need to wear yourself out."

But he knew she couldn't. The real Gale could run with him; she had fine legs, and made it a point to keep fit, as he did. But this was a soft civilized creature, and he didn't want her to realize that. "If you carry your own weight, I won't get the whole workout. Please, Gale—"

"Sire! Don't say please to me."

Oops. She was right: the king did not beg favors, he commanded. Worse, she had lapsed into loyal functionary mode, calling him Sire.

Her mind imprint was already wearing thin in places. He had to cover, before she realized her own slip and started to question her identity.

"I was teasing you," he said. "Remember, we're barbarians; we treat others politely." Then, before she could have any further thought, he heaved her high, took a mouthful of her clothed breast, and blew explosively.

She shrieked and windmilled her arms and legs, off-balancing him. He collapsed, but managed to set her down gently. Then he pounced on her, kissing her ardently while he ran a hand up under her skirt to pinch her buttock. She was helpless with laughter, trying to kiss him back despite eruptions.

Throe was there. "Problem, Sire?"

He looked up. "Just capturing a wild roe. She almost got away."

Throe faded back. Gale2 managed to settle down enough to speak. "Havoc, you are the worst tease on two worlds!"

"Just getting even for the times you've done it to me, you vixen."

"I never!"

"Don't you remember when you tied me with constrictor vine while I slept, then tickled me with a feather flower until I pissed?"

Of course she hadn't remembered, but now she thought she did. "Well, you deserved it."

"Probably so." There had never been a woman like Gale, and he yearned for her. "We'd better get back before they miss us." He helped her stand.

"As if they don't know where the king is," she said, brushing herself off.

They walked back toward the green cabin. He had gotten a bit of a workout, but would have to find ways to do more, lest he lose his physical tone. And it had been fun with Gale2, whose only fault was that she wasn't what she believed she was.

Supper was all in shades of green, because this was the Green Chroma. He still wasn't used to the monochromatic nature of the Chroma, though the separate items were fully distinguishable. Probably the natives perceived them as many colors.

Then they retired for the night, one couple to a room, as agreed. Havoc had intended to evince full passion for Gale2, to reassure her, but it turned out to be no problem; her passion for him met him more than halfway.

"I feel like Red Riding Hood," she remarked as they relaxed after vigorous activity.

That surprised him. "You're no old ugly woman!"

"But you're a young, wonderful man, and somehow I feel as if I don't quite belong."

She was slipping into awareness again. The excitement of the attack on the coach must have shaken the mind set. "How can you not belong, Gale?"

"I don't know. It's just a feeling. As if I don't deserve to be this happy."

This was mischief. All he could do was distract her and hope for the best. "Let's play Tickle and Feel."

She hesitated. "Do you mean Tickle & Peek?"

"No. I just invented this game." Actually Gale had invented it, and they had teased each other endlessly with it. "It continues as long as you can say you deserve it. It stops when you decide you don't deserve it."

"Okay, Havoc," she said uncertainly.

She was lying naked on the bed. He tickled her tummy with one finger. "Do you feel you deserve this?"

"Yes," she said.

He tickled her left breast. "Do you deserve this?"

She wriggled, making her body shake, but was game. "Yes."

He tickled her under the chin. "This?"

"Yes."

He lifted one of her knees, and tickled her buttock and inner thigh. "This?"

She struggled, but ticklishness almost overcame her. "Y—y—"

He put his face down and blew into her cleft.

That wiped her out. "No!" she screamed, laughing, writhing halfway off the bed.

"Then you must pay the penalty," he said with mock severity. The game had restored his potency, as it always had before. He mounted her and entered her, proceeding to a slow but powerful climax.

"I like that game," she gasped.

"Next time you'll be the tickler, and I'll be the deserving one."

"But are you as ticklish as I am?"

Gale knew, of course, and knew how to make him react. Gale2 would learn. "I am when you find the way."

She seemed satisfied with that. She mopped up some, and settled down to sleep. He relaxed similarly. Part of what made him feel guilty, ironically, was that he did like her. Deceiving her was like betraying a friend. Having to work to deceive her made it worse. She truly did not deserve the heartache that was coming.

He woke, hearing something in the night. After a moment he placed it: Ennui was walking to the common bathroom. He could recognize the steps of each member of the party; it was part of his dragon training, to know others by more than their appearances.

He had a full bladder himself, having imbibed a bit much green berry juice. So he rolled quietly off the bed, leaving Gale2 asleep, and went out to join Ennui.

She was just finishing. "Havoc. You too?"

He took over the pot. "It was very good juice."

"The magic enhances it," she agreed. "How was your evening?"

"She's wonderful. But I feel guilt."

"We'll take good care of her, Havoc. She won't be cast out to the wolves."

"But her love—it's genuine. What about that?"

"There are magic love potions, and counter-potions. She knew that when she agreed."

"Still."

She came across to him, where he sat, and laid her hand on his shoulder. "I know, Havoc. However kind we try to make it, it remains a cruelty."

"How was it with Chief?"

"He's a surprisingly passionate man. I must say I enjoyed it. Considering my age and body—" She shrugged.

"Your body is fine," he said. "A woman doesn't have to be young and buxom."

"Apparently not," she agreed.

Throe appeared. It was his job to be alert; he had heard them. "Problem, Sire?"

"Not one you can abate. I don't like doing what I'm doing to—to Gale. She's a nice girl."

"One of the things about being king is that you must do what doesn't necessarily please you. King Deal was at times pained by decisions he had to make, though he could not show it to others."

"I grow more sympathetic to him by the hour," Havoc said ruefully. He got off the pot.

Throe turned to Ennui. "May I have a woman's input on a question?"

"Of course, Throe," she said, surprised.

"Why did Symbol seduce me? We never associated before, and I can't say I liked her, but when she turned her appeal on me, it was as if I were a novice in my first martial arts class."

"You associate with the king," Ennui said. "It's Havoc she's really signaling."

"Havoc?" he asked blankly.

"There's something about her," Havoc said. "She could have taken me, had she chosen, though I have no wish to stray from Gale." There was another tinge of guilt.

"She is nominally in grief for King Deal," Ennui said. "So socially she can't take another lover. Especially not the new King. But she likes the benefits of the position, so wants to guarantee that there's a place for her near the king. You are nearest the king, physically."

Throe smiled, understanding. "Thank you, Ennui. Now I can make sense of it. I knew it couldn't be for any real desire for me. I still can't say I like her. But when she spread her legs to me, I was lost, and she knew it."

"She's a remarkable woman," Havoc said.

"In darkness, she's fully fleshed," Throe said. "I halfway expected there to be nothing, but that's not the case."

"Not the case," Havoc agreed. "She's all woman."

"That illusion holograph was part of it," Ennui said. "It made us all eager for passion. Then when Chief took my hand—" She paused. "Throe, maybe you can answer a question for me. You have known Chief far longer than I have. Why did he take me? I'm no sultry beauty like Symbol."

"It's similar to your answer to me. You are the king's oath friend— his closest associate, by his definition. That makes you a focus of interest. Chief has taken lovers before, but never remained with them long, and they were always of high status."

"Status," she said. "I don't have that either."

"You have the highest status: the trust of the king."

She nodded. "It is the same for you. We are working class folk. Only our association with Havoc gives us status."

"Which means we can enjoy the benefits, but never deceive our- selves about any personal merit. We are nothing without the king."

"So I can expect to be dumped soon," she concluded. "But I can't say I'll regret the experience."

"Nor will I," Throe agreed. "Symbol is the type of woman a man like me can only dream of. But when that's done, I think I would rather settle down with one who had no ulterior motive. One like you."

Ennui opened her mouth, but closed it again without speaking, looking thoughtful.

"We had better return to our rooms before our opposites miss us," Havoc suggested.

They nodded together. The three separated. Havoc quietly re- joined Gale2 on the bed.

But she felt his motion. "Yes, of course, Havoc, if you wish," she said sleepily, spreading her legs.

She had misunderstood his activity, perhaps naturally enough. "No, I was just returning from the bathroom. Don't tempt me. I'll need my strength for tomorrow."

"All right." But now she was further awake. "Havoc?"

"Yes, Gale."

"Why did someone attack us?"

That was something that had been brewing behind his thoughts. Since she had been endangered by it, she deserved to know. "King Deal was killed, and I suspect he was murdered. I am the next king. Now I am the target. You are with me, so are in danger too. I regret this."

"King Deal was killed? I thought it was an accident."

"It may have been. But I'm suspicious. This attack on me con- firms it: someone doesn't like the king."

She laughed. "*Nobody* likes the king! No offense. I mean—"

"I know what you mean. You and I hated the king too, before you came to work for him, and before I became king myself. And I don't want to be king. But I'm stuck for it, for a year at least. Then I'll go home to Village Trifle, and we'll marry and settle down."

"Oh, yes," she agreed fervently.

Damn that guilt! "So we'll just have to keep alert, and hope to discover who is trying to assassinate kings."

"Could it be the White Chroma?"

"It could be, since it's in rebellion. But there would have to be connections to other Chroma, because white magic won't work elsewhere. We may have several traitors to uncover. They could be anywhere."

"Oh, Havoc, I'm afraid!"

What could he do? He embraced her as well as he could, and comforted her, and soothed her to sleep. The real Gale might have felt some fear, but would not have reacted helplessly; she would have been angry, and determined to strike back at whatever threatened them. The more he came to know this soft creature, the more he missed his true love.

In the morning, after routine matters, the king's party joined high officials of the Green Chroma and one representative of the Black Chroma to view the site of the Black Chroma volcano. Tentacles of an enormous tree carried them up onto a large green platform in the highest foliage, with solid rails, so there was no danger of falling off. Then the tentacles passed their platform along to a neighboring tree, and on along until they reached the edge of the forest. They seemed to hover when the void came into view on the horizon. Because of their height, they did not need to get closer to it.

It was impressive in a deadly way: the variegated green terrain turned black and sank into a dark pit. It did resemble an inverted volcano. It was completely dull and silent.

Gale2 clutched Havoc's arm, afraid. After a moment Ennui, similarly fearful, took his other arm. Both were shivering. Chief, Symbol, and Throe stood independently straight, but their expressions were fixed, suggesting their tension. This was a thing of potential disaster.

"Review the situation for the king," Chief said.

"Gladly, Sire," the green officer said, addressing Havoc directly but speaking loudly and clearly so that all could hear. This was according to protocol, as the Ladies Aspect and Symbol had explained to him; the king was always informed, but assumed a stance of ignorance so that the matter could be officially presented to him. "The void opened six days ago in the form of a well. The local farmer thought it was merely a collapse in terrain, as happens occasionally. But when it expanded, and sucked in his barn and half his herd of sheep, he cried the alarm. We set up a watch and notified Triumph. It was quiescent for a day and a half, but then expanded again, this time taking in five surrounding farms with their livestock and occupants. We did a local evacuation, and it expanded again, quadrupling its prior area. Since then it has been stable. We are uncertain whether to evacuate more widely. The costs of that would be considerable, but the costs of miscalculation would be worse."

Cost of miscalculation: loss of all the farms and people of the surrounding region. Havoc had to decide whether to order the evacuation, or risk having them sit tight. He knew that Chief had concluded that evacuation was necessary, so this was the decision he should render.

The dragon seed buzzed.

Startled, Havoc paused. This was the first time it had ever buzzed while he was thinking about a problem. Did it mean the void was about to expand and take them in? How he wished the seed could differentiate in its warnings!

He would have to narrow it down. "Are we within the likely range of any sudden expansion?"

"No, Sire," the green officer said. "We would never risk—"

"Thank you." So it wasn't immediate danger. That meant that there was a wrongness in his thinking. He didn't like either of the given choices anyway. So he did what Mentor had taught him, and stepped outside of conventionality.

He turned to the black man. "You of the Black Chroma have experience with Void volcanoes."

"Yes, Sire."

"What are the odds of a new volcano like this one expanding significantly hereafter?"

"Sire, we deem those odds to be one in three."

"How much additional territory would a significant expansion swallow?"

"Sire, perhaps three times its present area."

"So the damage expansion would do is equivalent to its chances of not happening."

The man hesitated, surprised. "That is a way to put it, Sire."

"Which is why it's hard to make a decision, since if we evacuate, damage to farms will be done, perhaps unnecessarily."

"Yes, Sire."

Havoc pondered. He knew that Chief had already prepared his course of action, but he did not *have* to accede. "I don't like these choices."

"No one does, Sire," the black man agreed.

"I presume that you of the Black Chroma have no territorial designs on the Green Chroma. You don't *want* the volcano to erupt again."

"None, Sire," the black man said hastily. "We deplore its appearance in an existing sphere."

"You naturally have implosive magic, echoing the nature of your Chroma."

"Yes, Sire."

"Do you have big implosive bombs?"

The man was plainly uncomfortable. "As large as we might require, Sire."

"Just in case some other Chroma decided to treat the Black Chroma unfairly."

"That could be the case, Sire. But we would never seek unwarranted advantage."

"What would happen if a large void bomb were detonated in this void volcano?"

"Sire!" the Black Chroma man exclaimed, and his shock was mirrored in the faces of the Green Chroma party.

But Chief picked up on it. "You did not answer the king's question."

"Sire, no such thing has ever been done before. It could be dangerous."

"More dangerous than this volcano tripling its area?"

"Sire, we have no way of knowing."

The seed buzzed.

It wouldn't be politic to call the man a liar; he was probably trying to protect state secrets. "But you have an informed opinion."

"Yes, Sire."

"Would the detonation of a void bomb in the volcano be likely to do more harm than a further natural expansion would?"

The man had to answer. "In my opinion, no, Sire. It probably would have no expansive effect, but might disrupt the volcano and cause it to become inactive."

Bullseye. "Do it," Havoc said, and the seed did not buzz.

The Green men looked at each other in dawning surmise. Symbol glanced at Havoc. "Brilliant," she murmured.

"But Sire," the black man protested. "We have no means of delivery, or—"

"The king has spoken," Chief said firmly. "The Green Chroma can transport it, if your people can prime it for detonation at its destination."

"Yes we can," the green officer agreed. Already the platform was moving back through the trees, surely heading for the nearest established Black Chroma territory.

But first it dropped the king's party off at the temporary campsite. They boarded their coach, and it departed for the mind reading crisis region.

"Sire, you had a better solution," Chief said. "I was going to order a partial evacuation and alert status for further retreat at first sign of expansion."

"Yes, I understood that."

"Sire, how did you do it?" Symbol asked. "You never discussed it beforehand."

"I was going to let Chief handle it," Havoc admitted. "But my dragon seed buzzed. So I explored an alternative."

"Are you sure it will work, Sire?" Symbol asked.

"Yes, if the seed has guided me correctly. That is, if I interpreted its warning correctly. I'll be alert for confirmation."

"So will the seed guide you to a similarly apt solution to the mind reading disease?" Ennui asked.

"I doubt it. I think that will have to be mass transport to the Translucent Chroma for treatment. I suspect Chief has already arranged it."

"Yes, Sire," Chief agreed. "We dare not risk exposure of our own party by direct contact with the victims, so will merely inspect and approve the Translucent treatment facilities."

"Sire, I wonder," Symbol said. "If your seed alerted you to a solution no one else had thought of for one problem, why shouldn't it do so for another? It occurs to me that mind reading itself is potentially very useful, if it can be controlled. Maybe all those infected folk need is training."

This was interesting. "State the opposite case," Havoc said.

"There is no better solution than transport and treatment."

The seed buzzed.

"You have a case," Havoc said. "I never tried to use the seed this way before, but maybe it is a more useful tool than I suspected. Argue your case."

"If we can develop a suitable training mechanism, we may be able to nullify the inconvenience of the infection," she said. "And if we can discover how transmission occurs, we can save the victims the trouble of traveling to get treatment."

"Say the opposite."

"Training will be useless." The seed buzzed. "We have no chance to stop the spread of the disease." Another buzz.

"You were right the first time, both statements. We do have a better way, if we can figure it out."

Now they all got in on it, making suggestions ranging from dull conventional to wildly improbable. And slowly they developed a theory of contagion.

Chief had all manner of statistics on where, when, and who was catching the mind reading plague. As they analyzed the figures, with the help of the dragon seed, they discovered that personality was a key: no selfish or unfeeling or insensitive person had caught it, regardless of exposure. Only those who seemed to care strongly about others were vulnerable.

"But why should only nice people get it?" Ennui asked. "That's unfair."

"That implies that the others are not nice," Symbol said. "I am privately indifferent to the private feelings of others, but I treat them fairly and do not regard myself as evil. Chief is of similar temperament, and it makes him an excellent administrator. Power figures can seldom afford personal involvement with the matters they handle; they need to be objective. I lost my objectivity in only one case, and he's dead."

"I agree, of course," Chief said. "I have schooled myself to leave my emotions out of my decisions. This enables me to serve the new king competently."

"Correction noted," Ennui said. "Why should only unobjective people catch it?"

"Empathy!" Gale2 exclaimed. "Someone really gets into the feelings of another person, tries to understand, to *become* that person— and succeeds too well."

They stared at her. Of course it made sense—and it made sense that she, who had become another person herself, was the first to apply that concept. If someone seemed confused or in distress, an insensitive person would pay little attention. But a sensitive one, one with natural empathy, would try to help—by first truly understanding the nature of the problem. And thereby laying himself open to infection.

"I think this is how transmission occurs," Symbol said. "Or shall I say, this is ridiculous."

The seed buzzed, verifying the lie.

"But how do we treat it?" Ennui asked. "The problem these victims have is that they can neither stop their own thoughts from going out, nor stop other thoughts from coming in."

"No one stops her thoughts from going out," Symbol said. "Except by utilizing magic or isolation or the confusion of other people's thoughts overlaying hers. That's why the king wears the crown, and the rest of us are careful."

"So it's only half a curse," Gale2 said. "The victims broadcast the same way everyone does; where they differ is that now they can receive."

Ennui nodded. "Say the opposite."

In a moment they had verified that Gale2's supposition was correct. Receiving, not broadcasting, was the problem.

Havoc pondered, then took a chance. "There is a way." The seed did not buzz, indicating that he was not making a mistake.

Symbol eyed him. "You can hold your thoughts in, Sire? Without the crown?"

"Yes. The important ones. I mask or shield them with a persistent mental tune or other thought, and keep them under it. I think the principle would apply on a larger scale. The main reason I don't mask all my thoughts is that this would reveal that I have the ability, and I prefer others to think I lack any such protection."

"So the Translucent Chroma mind readers don't catch on," Ennui said. "Not only hiding your thoughts, but hiding the fact that you're hiding them."

"Yes. A person's weapons may lose effect if known."

They considered that. "Sire, is this something others can learn?" Symbol asked.

"I think so. But we would need a mind reader to provide the proof of it."

Ennui laughed. "We need an infected person! To see if we can stop the infection."

"But if it worked," Symbol said slowly, "what a breakthrough it would be for the great mass of folk who are vulnerable to mind peeping. They could start keeping some secrets."

"And the mind shield might prevent further transmission of the illness," Ennui said. "So that it would be a plague under control."

Symbol nodded. "This would be about as complete a solution as is feasible."

"Lacking any way to test this," Chief said, "we are uncertain of its validity." He glanced at Havoc. "No disrespect to your dragon seed intended, Sire. But we do not know its limits."

"We can test it," Ennui said. "All we need is a volunteer to catch the disease—and then try to cure herself."

Symbol laughed. "Who would ever care to take such a chance?"

"I would," Ennui said. "For the sake of Havoc's success as king, and for the benefit of our society."

"So would I," Gale2 said.

"Not you," Symbol said. Havoc understood why: she would learn the secret of her impersonation. Symbol's objectivity was showing to advantage.

"Why not? I love Havoc, and would do anything for him."

"And if you caught the disease, but the cure didn't work, what then? You would be a bundle of nerves and pains of others, unable to help yourself, let alone him."

That made Gale2 pause. "But the same applies to Ennui. He needs her too."

"Perhaps this," Chief said. "Let Ennui try it, and if she can't control her thoughts, or show reasonable progress, she can go to the Translucent Chroma and obtain their treatment."

Symbol nodded. "That might make the risk acceptable. If it worked, others of us could try it too, as appropriate."

"When do we meet with the Translucent Chroma authorities?" Havoc asked.

"Tomorrow morning," Ennui said. "You solved the Void volcano crisis faster than expected, so we're ahead of schedule. We'll be at our campsite in an hour."

"The void crisis isn't over," Havoc said. "My idea may not work." But as he spoke, the seed buzzed.

"You provided a new approach," Chief said. "That in itself goes far to defuse the crisis."

"Meanwhile, let's tackle the next," Havoc said, not caring to argue technicalities when he was privately assured that the matter was done. "We have half a day, and a night, to verify our approach. We need to get on it. I think Ennui can start, but–" He hesitated, realizing something.

Chief said it. "It is likely that others of us will be infected by her, when we work with her, unless we are very careful. Is this a risk we are prepared to take?"

"But we were going to verify that she could control it, before going further," Throe protested.

"There won't be time for that," Symbol said. "We'll have to do it today and tonight, if it is to be in time to relate to this crisis. We'll be exposed while she's learning control."

"This wreaks havoc with sensible precautions."

"That's my name," Havoc said. "It's the way I am."

"Sire, it's the way you are," Throe agreed, seeming ill at ease.

Chief nodded. "We can reach the nearest infected refugee camp in half an hour, if we diverge from our planned route now."

"No," Throe said.

"No?" Ennui asked.

"The king must not be subject to unnecessary risk," Throe said. "Even at his own behest."

Symbol eyed him. "What, you can veto the king's decision?"

"Yes, in such a case. He means to expose us and himself to the mind reading disease. We are expendable, but he is not."

"He could have you executed for treason, for balking him."

"I'd be guilty of it, if I didn't do my best to protect him from all dangers."

They looked at Havoc. This was his call.

He pondered a moment, then spoke carefully. "As I see it, I am in danger simply by being king. There has already been an attack on this party. If I proceed predictably, my unknown enemy will have an easier target. So a sudden deviance from my planned route may improve my safety."

"Deviate some other direction, Sire," Throe said.

"My best course is to be the best king I can, so as not to endanger myself or others by incompetence. Standard measures will make me a standard king, but in order to be better, I must explore nonstandard measures. Just as my route of physical travel should not be predicable, so my intellectual approach to crises should not be predictable.

No one would expect me to step deliberately into risk, or expect you to allow it. In addition, this mind reading infection may not be a liability, once understood and controlled. However, my crown should protect me, as it shields my mind from being read by others. It should protect me from catching the infection. So I am really not in immediate danger, though the rest of you are. Therefore—"

"He's got you, Throe," Symbol said. "He nullifies risk by stepping into risk, in the interest of helping the planet. Yield while you can."

Throe sighed. "Sire, I yield, reluctantly." He realized that this was a risk he could not stop the king from taking. He put his arm out through the window, signaling the Green Chroma guide.

A vine curled down. A green face appeared. "Yes?"

Chief gave the new direction. The green man did not question it. The coach changed course.

"Now I had better drill you on my mind-hiding technique," Havoc said. "Then when Ennui is infected, she will be able to tell us how well we are succeeding."

"We all will need mind shields," Symbol agreed. "Whether or not infected. We all surely have private matters we prefer not to share with others."

"Meanwhile, we need a head start," Chief said. "This promises to be an unusual challenge."

"Actually, Chief, you and I should not be at risk of infection," Symbol reminded him. "We don't have strong empathy for others. All we should need to do is maintain our natural indifference to their problems."

"Agreed. So only Gale is threatened."

"And Throe," she said. "He practices empathy, getting into the minds of would-be assassins."

"I am not concerned with risk to me," Throe said. "Only to the king, or those he values."

"Watch your sympathies, nevertheless."

"Sympathy is not the same as empathy," Chief said.

Symbol shot him a glance. "But they are allied. Hard hearts must be the order of this day."

"Agreed," Throe said.

Havoc explained his technique of mind masking, encouraging them to develop thought-numbing mental refrains that would interfere with any outside effort to read their minds. Just as a barrage of thoughts by another person interfered with mind reading, this acted inside the mind.

The next step was to get the most important thoughts under that wall of interference, and keep them there. "It's like ducking down into a cave," he said. "If you raise your head, it will bang on a stalactite. After a while you keep your head down automatically. It took me months to develop; I doubt that much can be done in a day. But all we

need to do is prove the technique. Any progress at all will be sufficient. The victims will have the rest of their lives to mask their minds."

The coach landed at the fringe of the Green Chroma. They got
out. This was not a regular campsite; it was a fading green field,
cleared of hostile plants.

Chief spoke to the green man, who stood by the outstretched
tendrils of the last tree to have carried the coach. "Conduct this woman
to the refugee camp. We will wait for her return." He indicated Ennui.

Surprised, the green man hesitated, but there was no demurral
from the king. "This way," he said, and he and Ennui were carried
away by shrubs that extended their foliage. At the fringe there was not
enough magic to lift the full coach, but a single person could be moved.

"Better use the bushes," Havoc said. "We may be busy when she
returns."

"Thus do we join the barbarian revolution," Symbol said ruefully.
She headed for a bush. "I hope it doesn't try to wipe me." The others
laughed. All plants had their own magic, but those of the Green Chroma
were special.

Soon they continued their mental drilling in the parked coach.
"Remember," Symbol said. "All our thoughts will be open to Ennui,
until we learn to mask them. Do we have any secrets we really truly
can't stand to be revealed?"

"I do have secrets," Chief said. "But my liaison with Ennui has
been close, as has my recent personal association with her. I believe
she can be trusted."

"Throe of course can be trusted," Symbol said. "It's his business
to keep the king's secrets." She nudged Throe with her knee. "That
leaves Gale."

"I would never betray Havoc," Gale2 protested.

"Not intentionally, dear. But you must develop an effective mind
shield as rapidly as possible."

"I will."

They continued to drill, but it was not possible to know how well
they were succeeding, because their minds were closed to each other,
so far. Havoc wasn't sure how well they could succeed in so short a
time, because it had been a slow process for Gale and himself. The
mask could cover all thoughts; the trick was to mask them selectively.
It was like letting water spill through one hole in the bucket, and not
through another.

Then Ennui returned. They got out to see. The green man was
carrying her physically. "I must advise you that this woman has become
contaminated by the mind plague," he reported unsympathetically as he
set her on her feet. She stood there, swaying, looking overwhelmingly
confused. "She insisted on getting close to the refugees and interviewing
several personally. I recommend that she be interned in the refugee
camp immediately."

Chief stepped forward and took Ennui's hand. "The king appreciates your concern, Green. But we wish to study her. Resume moving the coach to its original destination."

The green man nodded. "As you direct, Chief."

They piled back into the coach, and it lifted into the air. "What is your report?" Chief asked Ennui.

But she merely sat beside him, her head in her hands, groaning softly.

"The thoughts," Symbol said. "She is the only one infected, but all of us are broadcasting our thoughts, even as we try to shield them. She is being overwhelmed."

Havoc reached forward, put his hands on Ennui's shoulders, and hauled her into him. Her limp body sprawled across his, until her head came up against his head, touching his crown.

Suddenly she revived. "Oh—it's gone! What a relief." Then she became aware of her position. "Havoc—what are you doing?"

"I am holding your head against my crown, so that its shielding extends to you." He smiled. "I'm not getting fresh, if that's your concern."

The others laughed, and so did Ennui, her breath riffling his hair. "Havoc, we have been naked together, we have pissed together, and now I have lost my mind for you. Get fresh if you want to. Just don't let me loose from that crown. It's my only shield against hell."

"Tell us about it."

She squirmed until she was sitting on his lap with her back against him, keeping her cheek against the crown. "I thought it would be difficult to catch it, or at least that it would take time. But when I got close to a woman who was crying, and tried to comfort her, suddenly I felt her pain. It was as if a globe around my head had shattered and let in Babel. This thing—it seems not so much to be a sickness as the destruction of a defense. There must be an aspect of the human mind that blocks out other thoughts, and this illness nullifies that aspect." She tried to shrug, ineffectively. "I don't recommend the experience. All the thoughts of all the people come in simultaneously, the closest the loudest, and you can't block them off. But the emotions are worse."

"Emotions!" Gale2 said. "We didn't think of that."

"I hope my technique can enable us to shield emotions too," Havoc said.

"You can't shield your thoughts or emotions going out," she said. "They are like the heat of your body, constantly surrounding you. There never was a protection against that. But normal folk are protected from receiving the thoughts of others. That's what you need to do."

"But we can mask them, garble them as they go out," Havoc said. "So that they become meaningless babble, and part of the background noise."

"We need to do both," Gale2 said. "Garble out, garble in." She giggled.

"We have been practicing," Chief said. "But we don't yet know with what success."

"I can tell you." Havoc felt Ennui tense. Then she lifted her head away from his head. And quickly returned it. "No, you are all broadcasting like mad. All except Havoc; he's completely silent."

"The crown," Chief said. "It protects him both ways, input and output. Generations of craftsmanship went into its development."

"But I've got to develop a shield," Ennui said. "I can't stay glued to Havoc all day." She lifted her head again. "A persistent melody—I'm focusing on it. I think it's helping." Slowly she lifted her head away again, pacing the development of her shield.

"You must feel awful," Gale2 said. Then, suddenly, she clapped her hands to her head. "Oh, no!"

"You caught it from me," Ennui said. "I'm sorry."

Gale2 began to scream. Havoc put his arm around her shoulder and hauled her in to the other side of his head. Now he was sandwiched between the two of them, their faces on either side of his, their bodies spreading out to the front and to the side.

"No, I must fight it too," Gale2 said. She pulled her head away from the crown, returned, then found the level she could tolerate. "Now your thoughts are like distant shouting," she said. "All confused, but not intolerable. And I can distinguish some common threads, where several of you are thinking similarly."

"Yes," Ennui agreed. "Men think about sex a lot. Women are more social. It's the negative emotions that hurt."

"There's one strong one that isn't sex or social," Gale2 said, moving her head a trifle farther out. "It—it's about me. It—great gods! I'm not real!"

"Uh-oh," Symbol murmured.

"You—all of you know it! I'm not Gale. I'm—I'm the bath girl. An impostor!"

"It's not that simple, dear," Symbol said.

But now all their thoughts were focused on it, and Gale2 was reading it more clearly, her horror growing. "I'm not Havoc's love! He's been lying to me. Why—?"

"It had to be done," Chief said.

"He doesn't love me!" Gale cried hysterically. "I've been deluding myself. I'm nothing!" She yanked her head away from him—and caught the full force of the other minds. "My love's an illusion! I can't stand it!" Then she screamed, continuously. Ennui shrank back, in pain. It was not the piercing sound, Havoc knew, so much as the mental stress. Gale2 was destroying herself with the horror of the revelation, as well as the barrage of thoughts, and her returning thoughts were making Ennui suicidal too. Their attempt to fix the mind reading problem had turned savagely against them.

Gale2 tried to push a hole in the coach wall and scramble out. Chief caught hold of her, preventing her escape. But that brought his head closer to hers, making his thoughts louder. She became a wild woman, struggling, fighting, scratching. "He doesn't love me! I have no business loving him! How could I be here? He's the *king!* I must die!"

And what could any of them say? They had all done it to her. But especially Havoc. His guilt was greatest. He should never have agreed to this awful ploy. He had to deal with it.

Havoc put his hands to the crown. "No, Sire!" Throe cried, lurching forward to prevent him.

Havoc met his close gaze. "I did wrong. I must do right. Let it be."

"But Sire—you'll get the—"

"Stay out of it." Havoc lifted off the crown. Defeated by the king's direct order, Throe retreated to his seat.

"Gale," he said, focusing on her. The sound or the thought caught her frantic attention. "Read my mind."

She oriented on him, putting her head close so that his thoughts would be the strongest. He let it all pour out: the need to have Gale's mission secret, which meant concealing her absence, which meant putting in a substitute. The development of the mistress of the bath for this purpose. His guilt for the deception, though she had volunteered. His sorrow that he had done this to her. His disgust at the ways of civilization, of kingship, where wives had to tolerate lovers and innocent people were sacrificed to expediency.

Her eyes widened. "You did this to me?" she demanded, though she already had the answer.

"I did this to you. I curse the thought of it. I can make no apology. I don't know how to make it right."

"You monster!" She threw herself at him, but the crown in his hands deflected her body, and she sprawled across him and Ennui.

He passed the crown to Symbol, leaving himself without protection. "Try again."

Blinded by humiliation and fury, she did. Her nails came up to scratch his cheek. Blood welled out and trickled down his chin. He didn't move.

She suffered a sudden wave of remorse. "I can't hurt you, Havoc! I love you!" And her love blasted at him in much the manner of her fury. He felt it, and it swept him up in the manner of a fire, igniting an answering fire in him.

"Oh Havoc, I'm sorry," she said. "I *did* volunteer; I remember now. I just wanted to help." Her face was close; she moved forward and kissed the scratches she had made, trying to make them well.

He turned his face and intercepted her lips. They kissed through the smeared blood, feeling each other's passion reflected back and forth in the manner of facing mirrors.

"Now he's got it too," Symbol said.

Havoc realized it was true. He was reading Gale2's mind, feeling her passion. Just like that, he was another victim. He also was aware of the noise of the thoughts of the four others in the coach, washing against him like waves breaking against the rock that was his head. But they could not submerge his real identity, because that was protected in his secret cache of self.

"You *do* care for me," Gale2 said. "Some."

"You're a great girl. But not—"

"I know. Put your crown back on. I'll behave."

Symbol handed him back his crown. He put it on, and the chaos around him faded. Things were back to normal, superficially.

Except that Ennui, Gale2, and Throe were holding their heads. Throe? "Him too," Symbol agreed, observing his glance. "He went when you went."

"At least it verifies our hypothesis," Chief said. "We now know how it is transmitted."

"But we have three suffering people," Havoc said.

"And not much time to cure them. The coach is descending."

Havoc pondered. "We don't want others to know what we're doing yet, if ever. We need to get to the accommodations without giving it away. The crown will make a person normal, so we'll use that. The two of you who are stable will take turns conducting the others to the quarters. I'll go last, and recover the crown then. Then we'll see about the cure."

Symbol and Chief nodded.

"Now, for the few minutes remaining, you other three get your heads up near mine."

With some help, they did it, and their pain abated. "I hope this can be cured," Ennui said. "I can't function in the storm."

"Yes!" Gale2 and Throe said together.

"I can," Havoc said. "I felt the storm, but could wall it off, to a degree. When we get into the cabin, you can follow my mind, and maybe get the technique faster. It took me months, but I had to do it mostly alone. Mentor corrected me, but I was with him only part of the time."

The coach landed. "Symbol, take Throe," Havoc said. He removed the crown and set it on Throe's head.

Symbol brought out a kerchief and used it to cover the crown. "No one but the king must be seen wearing this."

They got out of the coach. Havoc heard Symbol talking, devising some explanation for this unusual procedure. Meanwhile he focused on keeping his sanity, raising his barrier as high as he could. Even so, he felt their suffering. They were unable to develop their own thoughts, in the absence of overwhelming emotion, because of the interference of the neighboring thoughts. But it was not as bad with only the four of them, and with Havoc partially shielded. He felt their discomfort diminish as the two departed.

Symbol returned, wearing the crown. "I couldn't carry it," she said. "It would have attracted attention."

"Chief, take Ennui," Havoc said, taking the crown from Symbol and putting it on Ennui's head.

They left. Now there were three of them, and Gale2 was looking less stressed. "It's only one and a half minds," she said. "Not too confusing."

"I'm half witted?" Havoc asked.

"Sire, I didn't mean—"

He kissed her. "I know. Don't call me Sire."

"But—"

"You have a role to play. Play it. I will try to find a way to do right by you."

She shook her head. "I did not realize how hard it would be to leave you, Havoc. I liked you before—before this. Now I love you. But I know I must leave you."

"Sire, let me clean your face," Symbol said. "And yours, Gale. That blood would arouse curiosity."

So it would. She cleaned them up. Then Chief returned. Symbol took Gale2, wearing the crown.

"What am I going to do with Gale?" Havoc asked Chief. "After the tour?"

"She might be satisfied to be head mistress of the bath, again, Sire."

"But that would be demeaning, after this."

"Not if you kept her as a lover, Sire, and the house staff knew it."

"Keep her as a lover!"

"Gale proper will be your fiancée, Sire. You will need a lover. It is a position of honor. She will want to be close to you, and there she can be. You can take her when she washes you, if you choose."

"This is protocol? Civilization still has surprises for me."

"I understand King Deal made use of the bath girls, before Symbol assumed the role. That was before this one's time, of course, as they are fresh every two years."

"I will ask her."

"Just tell her, Sire."

"I want her to be amenable."

"Sire, any person is amenable to anything the king desires, by definition."

"I want it truly to be her choice."

Chief shrugged. "You retain your quaint barbarian ways, Sire."

Symbol returned. Havoc took back the crown, donned it, and walked with them to the quarters. "Sire, I told them that there had been an attack on your convoy, and you wished the premises to be carefully checked beforehand," Symbol said. "They understood."

"You have no difficulty subverting the truth to expediency."

"None, Sire."

The rooms were nice enough. There were three, as before. "Same three couples," Symbol said. "That will place one infected with one immune, whether naturally or by virtue of magic. That should make for a peaceful night."

"If we sleep tonight," Havoc said. "We four infected will have work to do."

"We other two should do it too," Chief said. "It will be useful for anyone, to protect thoughts. We keep forgetting that."

Symbol nodded. "I will order the meal delivered, Sire."

They gathered in the main chamber. "See if you can follow me," Havoc said. He removed his crown, and let the storm of thoughts in. Then he raised the bar, his interference song covering more of his thoughts. "Establish your bar, get in under it, and slowly lift," he said. "Follow me as I do it."

They practiced. The food came, and they ate while practicing. They used the bathroom while practicing. They changed to night-clothes while practicing.

They made progress. The pain of full exposure was a great incentive. Ennui led the way, successfully emulating Havoc in an hour. Gale2 had more trouble, but had made significant progress in two hours. Throe struggled, but did have a low bar that rose slowly. Because they could read his mind, and each other's minds, they could quickly tell when something worked. That greatly facilitated things.

"I think that's enough," Havoc said at last. "Sleep should help." He put his crown back on.

They retired. Half the night was over, and they were all tired. Havoc went to bed with Gale2. Then he remembered. "Before we sleep, one thing. How do you feel about—"

"Yes, I'll do it."

"I didn't mean sex. I meant—"

"I read your mind," she reminded him. "I will be bath girl again."

"But I do not wish this to be a requirement. I am trying to do right by you."

"I know. Chief is correct: your will is my will."

"That's not the way I want it."

"That's the way it is, barbarian. Take off your crown and verify it, if you wish."

Havoc did. It was true: she wished so much to please him that she had no desire in this respect other than his will. She simply wanted to be close to him, and to love him, and be accepted by him in any capacity.

And she wanted him to leave his crown off when he had sex with her. "Yes," he said, smiling.

This time as he stroked her body, her felt her answering passion. His desire was mirrored by hers, and her desire came back to further enhance his. It was an accelerated, phenomenally enhanced experience, culminating in an explosive mutual climax.

"I can make you love me, for a while," she said.

He understood what she meant. With the exchange of thoughts and feelings, her interest followed his, and his love followed hers. They were perhaps mere reflections of the originating passions, but they were indistinguishable from their own.

"Love me like that, when you can, and I will always be satisfied," she said.

"But when Gale returns—"

"If she is like you, and my imprinting indicates she is, she will understand. She will not begrudge me that much of you."

"Perhaps not," he agreed, relieved. She had made her own accommodation to the situation, and it was good.

He relaxed for sleep, but she reminded him to put his crown back on. "You will sleep better without my dreams, and you will be safe from any physical threat."

She was right. But he was aware that she was pleased that he had thought to sleep beside her without the crown.

"I'm sorry I scratched you. I never should have done that."

"It showed you have some barbarian fire. I like that. Gale would have knocked me out."

"Oh, Havoc," she said, melting against him.

In the morning they had not had enough sleep, but there was no help for that. Havoc removed his crown without leaving his room and thought loudly: *How are you others doing?*

Hear this, Ennui thought from the next chamber. But there was nothing following, just background noise.

I can't hear you. Then he realized what it meant: she had perfected her mind shield.

Hear this, Gale2 thought next. Her next thoughts were muted, though he could still pick them up. It was nevertheless better than it had been the night before.

This too, Throe thought. Sleep had helped him substantially; his following thoughts faded almost to nothing.

"I believe we have the treatment," Havoc said. "Now we can present it to the refugees."

They met with the Translucent authorities. "We expect to arrange to treat the refugees where they are," Havoc announced. "They will not have to be treated here."

The translucent man rippled an eyebrow. "You have other magic treatment, Sire?"

"We have a program of nonmagic treatment. We will train the

refugees in certain techniques, starting immediately."

And they did so. They went to the largest local camp, and Ennui, Gale2, and Throe demonstrated their shields. They showed how they were infected, but were able to function. They spent the day conducting classes, and the practice sharpened their own abilities. The most promising prospects were conducted privately to Havoc, who removed his crown and gave them further instruction. By the end of the day, there were a number of refugees with limited but definite mind shields. They would become the new instructors.

"Tomorrow the locusts," Havoc said, satisfied. They ate hastily and turned in early.

"If I did not already love you, Havoc, I think I would be learning to love you now," Gale2 said. "You have found another new way to solve an intractable problem."

"It's the barbarian way." Then he removed the crown, and sure enough, her desire enfolded him.

"Yes," she said as they concluded. "I will help Gale to do this, as you secretly desire."

"It is hard to keep secrets," he said, replacing the crown.

"But we are learning how."

He found himself uneasy. "Gale, I *will* do right by you."

"I know, Havoc. I am no longer hurt or angry."

"I know. Still—"

She smiled. "Your trace of guilt—I like that too. You are fully human, in a way most nobles are not."

"It is nice to be understood."

They slept. He still would have preferred to be beside Gale, but was growing more comfortable with this girl. It was as she said: she was human. She lacked sophisticated emotional control. That made her nice to be with.

In the morning they drilled again on their mental shields, which were still gaining proficiency. In due course they boarded the coach and took off for the next crisis.

The closer confines of the coach gave them further practice. But there was an intriguing aspect. The four infected people had developed shields of varying effectiveness, but the two uninfected were far behind. They had tried, but lacked the instant mental feedback, so were relatively clumsy.

"But we don't need effective shields," Chief said. "Because we *aren't* infected."

"The situation is changing," Ennui said. "With the mind reading disease spreading, and the victims learning to handle it, there will be more mind reading. It won't be limited to Translucent Chroma specialists. You can be at risk from any person you deal with, increasingly in the future. You must have a good shield."

"Perhaps," he said, unconvinced.

Something in her expression alerted him. Havoc removed the crown. The familiar welter of thoughts besieged him. But it wasn't as bad as it had been two days before, when the illness first struck them. Ennui, Gale2, and Throe protected their minds substantially better. But not the other two.

"I think we should make a demonstration," Ennui said. *This will be fun.* "Chief, you of course would never entertain an untoward thought about the king's companion."

"Agreed," Chief said guardedly.

Gale, spread your legs, slowly. Show him something good. "And if she showed something accidentally, you would not look."

Havoc? It was Gale2's thought.

Do it, he thought, interested in what Ennui contemplated.

Meanwhile, Chief had answered. "True."

Gale2 quietly hiked up her skirt and parted her thighs, opening a view to him. Chief was nominally looking at Ennui, but he could see peripherally, and that image was being broadcast to all of them. Gale2 was a healthy young woman; she had excellent legs, and as she picked up his appreciation, she slowly shifted her posture to improve the view further.

"And you would never compare any such accidental sight to anything you had seen before," Ennui said.

"True." But prompted by her suggestion, that comparison was being made. A girl in a gray dress, playing Tickle & Peek, teasing the young man of two decades ago by showing more than she needed to. Her body was not yet completely full, but her legs were leading the way, thickening nicely in the upper thighs. *Tell him, Throe.*

"Her name was Tulip, and she was only twelve, but well developed in certain respects," Throe said. "What a crevice she showed, without underclothing! And you were not allowed to Touch, only to Peek. You got so excited you had to have it. She gave it to you, but you had to wash her dishes for a week."

Chief was chagrined. "That's showing? In my mind?"

Havoc. "It is showing," Havoc assured him. "She had a lock of hair that sometimes curled around her nose. Her face wasn't much, but her breasts were well formed if not large, and her thighs were classic, for her age."

Gale. "She used to meet you in a storage shed," Gale2 said. "You tried to stay away, but couldn't, and when she got you alone, she lay on a box and opened her legs, like this—" She spread her knees far apart. It was most effective; Havoc saw the juncture through Chief's mental image, enhanced by memory, heavily tinged by lust.

"And made you commit to more of her chores before she let you get between them," Ennui concluded. "You hated her for that, but she had your number, or at least your desire. You couldn't keep yourself away."

"Until she found another boy to tease," Throe said. "Then she showed you nothing more. You never get over the frustration."

"And never told anyone else of your humiliation," Gale2 said, closing her legs.

Chief smiled ruefully through the flush on his face. "You mind readers have made your point. I want no one else to read that memory. Drill me on my shield."

"How is mine?" Symbol asked.

"You were a plain girl, despite your invisibility," Ennui said. "But surprisingly smart. In fact you were way ahead of your classmates. But you learned to conceal it, so they wouldn't hate you."

"Yet when you developed, things changed," Gale2 said. "You became not only beautiful, but popular. But you remembered, and became much more of a tease than Tulip ever was. You delighted in driving boys into frenzies of desire, which you seldom satisfied."

"Meanwhile you pursued political connections," Throe said. "Rather ruthlessly, using your sex appeal to good advantage. Thus you got to be the Representative of your Chroma, at the choice location of the king's court in Triumph."

"And then you vamped King Deal," Havoc said. "Displacing his prior mistresses, despite the invisibility of your flesh. Tight clothing and spot illusion made you phenomenally alluring."

"Some of that you could have known from my case history," Symbol said, though her emotion betrayed her chagrin. "Tell me how I got my name."

Havoc looked, but found no hint. The other minds were similarly blank. "We can't fathom that," Ennui said after a moment.

"It is under my shield. If any of you ever do fathom it, I will concede defeat."

She beat us, on that, Ennui thought. *She let us read only as much as she chose.*

"And that is the way it should be," Havoc said. "To let people read your minds, but never realize that there is something missing. A complete shield would be suspicious, and attract further attention." He returned the crown to his head. Symbol had surprised him; she had caught on to the shield mechanism rapidly and well, and demonstrated her expertise.

"You had prior practice," Chief said.

Symbol nodded. "I seduced an officer of the Translucent Chroma, and he repaid me by teaching me the technique. He said I had unusual aptitude."

"You do," Havoc said.

Chief continued to work on it, trying to hide things in his mind, while they tried to pry them out. With that feedback, he made better progress. When he put a key in one fist, and they were unable to discover reliably which hand held it, he passed the basic level. He had learned to conceal something.

They landed, and the coach was hauled overland to the fringe of a Black Chroma zone. Here everything was dark, as it had been at the new Void volcano. But it was stable, with a thin layer of dust on the surface.

"The blue locusts are devastating black farmland," Havoc said, remembering the summary Symbol had given him. "How can there be farmland, when everything has been sucked down a hole?"

"You'll soon see, Sire," Symbol said.

The coach moved, drawn by a blob of darkness that sucked at it. It came to a dark gate, and rolled into a tunnel. Darkness closed in about them. Then light flared. There was a flame burning in the middle of the coach.

"An illusion candle," Havoc said, catching on.

"It is an Air specialty," Symbol agreed.

"But how can something that isn't real, make something that is, like light?"

"Visual illusion *is* light, Havoc," she replied. "I'm making a ball of light, and clothing it with the image of a candle. This is elementary Invisible Chroma magic."

The coach halted. Throe opened the door and they got out. They were in a curving chamber whose walls were black stone. "Here is your apartment," the black man said. "Three bed-chambers open off the main one." He indicated cave openings.

"What's our itinerary?" Havoc asked Ennui.

"We have a lunch break, and will meet the Chroma Black officials in the early afternoon."

Black women brought black food in. It tasted as was appropriate for its shape: black liquor, black bread, black vegetables, and black pies. Havoc was getting used to the colors of the Chroma, and learning to see things in shades of color.

"Is the whole Chroma underground?" Havoc asked.

"Pretty much, Sire," Symbol replied. "Void eruptions tend to suck mostly from above, because the air reacts most to a sudden vacuum, so the safest region is deep in solid rock. I understand they have tunnels ringing the central hole itself."

"And a net across it to snag some of the things being sucked in," Chief said. "They do well enough."

"Suppose an eruption is larger than they expect, and takes in the surrounding tunnels?"

"Sometimes it happens. But that is a threat all Chroma eruptions of any kind have: too much force, inward or outward. The magic is strongest, closest in, but the danger is greatest."

In due course they met the local Black Chroma leader. He was of course a black man in a black robe.

Havoc already knew the problem, and had been pondering it.

But protocol required him to hear it officially from the Black Chroma authority. "I understand you have an interChroma problem," he said.

"The last local eruption brought in a batch of blue soil, and with it a Blue Chroma pestilence," the man said. "We netted the soil before it was lost, and conveyed it to new farm caves. We did not realize that it contained blue locust eggs. They hatched abruptly, infesting our crops. They seem largely immune to our magic, being of another Chroma."

"Blue creatures are in the Black Chroma, and immune? I thought it would be the intruder's magic that faded."

"Usually it is, Sire. But some vermin develop immunity to magic of any color. It may be that the blue soil gave them magic contrary to ours. We did not realize the extent of the problem until the second generation, when locusts hatched and invaded straight Black Chroma terrain. Now they match our Chroma in color, but still resist our magic. We face the prospect of eradicating our crops and the fertility of the soil itself—or of allowing the vermin to overrun additional farmland. There is already hunger, as we lack sufficient food to maintain our population."

The dragon seed buzzed. There was something wrong here. Havoc could not read the man's mind, because his crown blocked him off. In any event, he did not believe that the man was lying to him. He glanced at Ennui.

She nodded, indicating that she had picked up on something. She couldn't tell him openly, because they had agreed to conceal their infections whenever possible. But she could give him a hint. "Sire, I think we need a better description of the locusts, and the manner they destroy crops."

"That would surely help," he agreed.

"They are very small when they hatch, and stay out of sight. They seek mainly root vegetables, and attack them, one locust to a root. Because this happens underground, we are not aware of it, unless we pull up the root, spoiling its growth. So we wait until harvest time—at which point the locusts have consumed a significant portion of the crop."

"What do they look like?" Ennui asked.

"They have no fixed adult form," the black man said. "They assume the configuration of the root they prey upon. Thus when we harvest a carrot, we discover a locust—in the shape of the carrot. It is a most unpleasant surprise."

"In the shape of the carrot!" Havoc exclaimed, amazed.

"Or the turnip, or potato—whatever root is attacked. To that degree, the locust becomes the vegetable."

Havoc appreciated their distress. "I can arrange for shipments from another Chroma, if you wish. I understand that Silver has a current surplus of food supplies."

"Sire, this is another problem. We have had bad relations with our neighbor Silver Chroma, and do not want to be beholden there."

"So pride complicates your case."

"Sire, it is true."

Havoc nodded. "I am a barbarian, as you know. In certain ways, I am closer to nature than are the civilized folk. You may not like my suggestions."

"Suggestions, Sire?"

Symbol smiled through her veil. "The king prefers to reason things out, if feasible, rather than to impose solutions that may not appeal. He is giving you the option of declining his solution."

Surprised, the black officer looked at Chief.

"He *is* a barbarian," Chief said. "King Havoc believes that people have rights."

Somewhat discomfited, the officer faced Havoc. "Sire, we would like to hear your suggestions."

"Do you have a population of wild creatures in the Black Chroma?"

"Yes, of course, Sire. They were the first tunnelers. We have domesticated the more useful ones."

"Do you hunt any for food?"

"Yes, Sire." The man evidently wondered what the point was.

"And you have domesticated creatures raised for meat?"

"Yes, of course, Sire." Even the members of his party seemed to be baffled by his questions. They could not read his mind because of the crown.

"Do your ordinary people participate in the slaughter and preparation of wild or domesticated animals?"

"No, Sire."

"Why not?"

The black man floundered for a moment. "Sire, they—they do not care for the details of bloodshed, gutting, cleaning, or processing."

"But they eat the processed meat?"

"Yes, Sire."

"Then is it fair to say that it doesn't matter what the origin of the meat is, or how it is processed, so long as it is done out of sight?"

"Sire, of course it matters. If the process were unsanitary—"

"Assuming it is done competently."

"Yes, Sire, in that case it does not matter."

"If a locust eats the whole of a carrot and remains in its place, that locust must contain much of the food value of the carrot. In fact it may even have the flavor of the carrot. With proper preparation, it could be eaten in lieu of the carrot."

"Lovely!" Symbol breathed.

"Sire?" the black officer asked, looking revolted.

"Harvest the locusts," Havoc said. "Consider them to be your crop. If your former crop sustained your population, so will the locusts. You will have no need to be rid of them; you can eat them."

"But Sire!" There was clear consternation in the Black Chroma contingent.

"And to set the example, I suggest that you have your farmers harvest a selection now, and prepare them for the evening meal for my party and its hosts. We shall have a public feast."

Now there was consternation in Havoc's own group. A meal of locusts! But they could not openly protest.

The black officer saw this. He smiled, a trifle grimly. "Sire, it shall be done." If the king did it, so could others. It was a barbarian dare.

They retired to their quarters for the afternoon. As soon as they were private, the party exploded. "How could you do that to us, Havoc?" Ennui demanded.

"We'll be publicly sick," Gale2 agreed.

"And they will be watching closely, relishing the moment," Chief said. "However polite Chroma officers are to your face, Sire, their private respect for the king is limited."

"Translation:" Havoc said. "Everybody hates the king."

"It will be a public relations disaster," Symbol said.

Havoc turned to Throe. "You have foraged for food in the wilderness?"

"Yes, Sire. What you recommend is feasible, assuming the locusts do not have inherent poison."

"They shouldn't," Havoc said. "They are just garden variety insects in a new habitat without natural predators. I have seen similar bugs, and eaten them without ill effect."

"Ah, the delights of barbarism," Symbol murmured.

Havoc removed his crown. "Read my experience. They are edible, especially when there is hunger."

Throe, Ennui, and Gale2 read him. "They don't bother you at all," Ennui said, surprised. "They even taste good."

Havoc restored his crown. "Now persuade the other two." He lay down on his bed for a nap.

When he woke, Chief and Symbol were grimly ready to participate. "We're damned if we'll be the first to upchuck," she said. "The Black Chroma contingent will have to eat them too."

"But we do appreciate your name better with the passing of each day, Sire," Chief said.

"Havoc," Symbol agreed. "This should be an interesting meal."

Soon the Black Chroma officer came to escort them to the banquet. "Our cooks report the locusts to be easy to prepare," he said. "The great bulk of them is almost unchanged vegetable, stored for future use."

The banquet was in a large cave which opened into a porous network of lesser caves. The connecting caves were packed with black citizens, there nominally to honor the visiting king. Well, he would give them a barbarian show.

The platters were brought in. The first was set before Havoc. It contained an artistic array of black vegetables. This was nominally a vegetable meal. But soon other platters revealed pastries and even drinks, all evidently made from locusts. Their substance could be baked or squeezed as well as boiled. The cooks had performed imaginatively.

"By your leave, Sire," Throe murmured, and took a black carrot. He normally took the first bite of food served to the king, to test it for poison; this was protocol.

Throe bit into the carrot. He chewed. He swallowed. "Sire, it is good." He meant in more than one sense.

Havoc took the carrot from him and bit into it himself. It tasted just like fresh carrot. It *was* good. He ate it quickly, evincing enjoyment. Then he drank from a mug of locust berry juice, which was also good. "Your cooks have done well," he said. "There is plenty?"

"There is plenty, Sire," the black official agreed.

Then the other members of his party started eating, at first cautiously, then with increasing satisfaction. So did the black officials. All were pleasantly surprised. The vegetables, both raw and cooked, were excellent.

"Would it be within protocol to share?" Havoc inquired.

"Sire, anything you suggest is within protocol," Symbol replied.

Havoc picked up another carrot, stood, and turned. "I dislike seeing folk stand hungry while I feast," he said. "I invite you to share with me." Then he tossed the carrot to the nearest person, a well dressed black woman.

Astonished, she caught it. Then, aware that all other eyes were on her, she daintily nipped the black tip of the carrot. In a moment she smiled and took a larger bite, then handed it to her neighbor.

"I invite you to come to this table and take," Havoc said. "The cooks will provide more, so that there will be enough for all."

The people were hesitant. Havoc walked to the throng, spied a little girl, took her hand, and led her to the banquet table. "Have some cake," he suggested.

Tittering with nervousness and awe, she took a small cake and ate it. Then, eagerly, she took another. It was obvious that she was not pretending; she liked the food.

"Come on," Havoc said to the crowd. "I know you are hungry. Come share with me." He took a piece of cake himself, took a bite, and stepped away from the table.

They came, at first cautiously, then with a rush. The platters quickly emptied. More were brought in, and these too were consumed. The food was good: now everybody knew it.

Havoc was getting crowded. He took a black baked potato and forged through the crowd, looking for someone not eating. Throe followed unobtrusively, always nervous about crowds. Havoc found a man seated on a bench, whose right foot was in a cast. Havoc took a small bite, then proffered the remainder of the potato. "I believe you are hungrier than I, sir," he said.

There was a murmur of awe from the surrounding folk. The king had brought an ordinary man food! The man took it, awed himself, and bit into it. He smiled. "Sire!"

"Yes, speak."

"Sire, you have saved us all."

Havoc patted him on the shoulder. "I hope so, sir."

It was some time before they left the banquet. The black officer joined them, conducting them to their quarters. "Sire, you have made an impression," he said.

"Thank you."

"There may have been those among us who thought unkindly of the king. There are none now, Sire."

That was all. It was enough. "Parting," Havoc said.

The man paused, then figured it out. "Acknowledged, Sire." He departed.

When they were alone again, Symbol spoke for the others. "Sire, you were right and the rest of us were wrong. It *is* good food, and I think the gratitude of the Black Chroma will endure for a century."

"The next crisis is the tough one," Havoc said. "Chief, is the White Chroma going to back down?"

"No, Sire."

"Can the other Chroma successfully invade White?"

"Yes, Sire, but at horrendous cost. No Chroma can invade another without being at a serious disadvantage. We shall have to use nonChroma personnel and weapons against their science magic."

"What's the alternative?"

"Blockade, Sire. We can cut them off from all other Chroma and all nonChroma terrain. If they try to break it, they will be at a similar disadvantage. Eventually they will capitulate."

"You are talking decades, not months."

"Yes, Sire. The White Chroma zones, like all others, are scattered randomly around the planet. It requires a considerable effort."

"During which time, chances are there will be a new king, with a new attitude. So they could win their independence, by endurance."

"Yes, Sire."

"Why not just let them be independent?"

"Because of the precedent, Sire. If they were to succeed in establishing independence, other Chroma might have the same idea, and the kingdom would inevitably fragment."

"Why not let it fragment?"

"Spoken like a true barbarian," Symbol said.

Chief was ready. "From the time of first colonization, it has been policy to maintain a united planetary kingdom. This is in case there should be an invasion from space, and to keep the species unified. As it is, the several Chroma barely get along, and there could be constant warfare at the fringes, were there not an overriding planetary authority."

"Wouldn't the Chroma unify if they faced a common threat?"

"Perhaps, Sire. But they would be depleted by their internecine struggles, and less able to handle a significant common threat. There is also the matter of biological unity. As we have seen, Sire, the members of each Chroma are already distinct from each other in color, and perhaps in other ways. Our species will soon be biologically fragmented, unless we maintain a central authority that constantly integrates our species."

"Does that explain why a barbarian was hauled in from a far village to be king?"

"Yes, Sire. To be examined for the role. All parts of the kingdom need to be represented."

"So we had better bring White back into the kingdom, or suffer long term planetary consequences."

"That is the nature of the crisis, Sire."

"I think I'll go for double or nothing."

"Sire?"

"I'm going to bring them back without war or siege, or let them go. Either way, it will be quick and clean."

"Sire, I see no quick and clean way to bring White back."

"That's because you're not a barbarian."

Ennui looked at him. "I dare you to take off that crown, Havoc."

"You wouldn't catch my thought," he said. "It's shielded."

"If I understand you correctly, Sire," Chief said, evidently a bit nettled, "you have a strategy that should catch White by surprise, if it catches us by surprise."

"Yes. Now I shall clean up and turn in."

"I'll wash you," Gale2 said.

"No need. You're not a bath girl any more. You're your own barbarian woman."

"That's why I'll wash you."

He laughed. She joined him in the bathroom, and washed him in the steady shower of warm water. When he got an erection she hugged him, naked and slippery, her full breasts exciting him further. She lifted her legs and straddled him, neatly taking him into her. "Would a mere bath girl ever do this?" she inquired teasingly.

"I never thought to ask her," he said, intrigued.

"I *wanted* to do it, back then," she confessed. "You had such a handsome member, so eager to be accommodated. But I could oblige only if you asked. Now you don't have to." She kissed him.

He held off on the culmination. "When this tour is done, and Gale returns, and you wash me—"

"You will have to ask," she said. "It's the rule. I can't suggest."

"But what about the other girls?"

"You will ask *them* to do it?" she inquired severely.

"No! I mean, what will they think?"

"They will be insanely jealous."

He laughed. "Take off my crown."

"But I will slide down if I don't hold on tight."

"I'll support you." He linked his fingers behind her back, then drew them into her spread bottom, holding her close.

She reached up, her breasts rising to nudge his chin, and lifted off his crown. Her passion smote him, multiplying his urgency. He worked her bottom, lifting and dropping it, and exploded inside her.

"Oooh!" she moaned. "I felt that!" She meant that she had experienced his climax mentally. "Hang on!"

He hung on—and experienced her climax, following his, longer and slower, less intense, but possessed of similar total pleasure. They had had it both ways, for an experience that could never have happened without the mind sharing.

She replaced his crown, then slid back down to the floor. "Now there's more washing to do," she said, feigning grumpiness.

"Sorry about that."

"I should make you clean *me* up."

"I'll start here." He grabbed the soap and stroked it over her breasts.

"Give me that." She took the soap back and squeezed it between his thighs as though it were a penis. Soon they were in a slippery struggle for the soap, their bodies making odd connections.

Eventually they finished, and toweled each other dry. "I will ask," he promised, remembering her offer. Even True Gale would be hard pressed to match this experience, unless she caught the mental disease.

Ennui appeared. "It's about time you two finished," she said. "Do you realize what you were doing to our minds?" She turned her head to call over her shoulder. "Come on, Chief. We're older, but maybe we can still do it."

Havoc had forgotten that others could eavesdrop mentally. But no harm was done.

"Wail till Throe tries to make it in the shower with Invisibility," Gale2 said.

"I heard that." It was Symbol's voice. She had stripped, and in the partial light was indeed invisible.

"Wait your turn!" Ennui called from the shower.

"Then get it on, girl!"

Havoc paused. Gale2 nudged him. "Go ahead, Havoc. Take it off. They snooped on *us*."

He lifted off his crown, and the two of them tuned in on the emotions in the shower. Their own bodies were depleted, but the feelings felt almost as real. Then they picked up on the third set, as Symbol and Throe took their turn. Each climax was different, in its fashion. It was as good as a holograph show. In fact, they might have gotten more than two of the participants, because they could read all four other minds, while Chief and Symbol could not read any minds in return. However, they had all practiced hard enough to mask their thoughts and feelings when they chose to, so this voyeurism was really a cooperative effort.

"And we thought this disease was a liability," he said, as he and Gale2 settled down to sleep.

"Just as the rest of us thought locusts were inedible," she agreed.

Next day they traveled to the largest White Chroma territory, where its designated planetary capital was. Their coach landed at the fringe of a Yellow Chroma territory, and was hauled by shapes of fire to the fringe of the White Chroma territory. The land and vegetation changed from yellow to white. And there was of course a white man waiting for them. His skin and hair were shades of white, as was his clothing. When he spoke, his teeth were white, as was his tongue.

"A greeting, Sire."

"Acknowledged."

"Please follow me to the train."

They followed him to a metal set of rails, on which rested a huge steaming metal wagon. At least, it had a number of large wheels. Behind it was a cart loaded with billets of wood. Behind that was a rather large metal coach.

They climbed into the coach. It was elegant inside, with padded seats and a central table. "Do you care for refreshment, Sire?" the white man inquired.

"No. I am curious as to the mechanism of motion. Does this coach fly?"

"No, Sire. We do have flying coaches, but not of sufficient size to carry your full party together. But this train will get us there on schedule."

"Train?"

"I shall be happy to explain and demonstrate its operation, Sire, if you wish."

"Yes."

The man reached up and unfastened the ceiling panel. He slid it back, so that the coach was open to the sky. Then he stood on one of the benches, so that the upper third of his body was outside. "If you will join me, Sire, I will show you."

Havoc stood on another bench and poked his head out the top. From this vantage, he could see the surrounding white countryside, and the metal wagon ahead. A man was piling white billets of wood from the cart into what looked like an oven in the wagon.

"That is the locomotive, Sire," the white man said. "We also call it a steam engine. The wood burns in its furnace, and the heat from it evaporates water piped around it, producing steam. The steam is piped to cylinders connected to the rods which push the wheels. This causes the locomotive to travel forward, and it hauls this car behind it."

As he spoke, the engine huffed and puffed. A ball of white smoke roiled out of a chimney on its top, and the wheels started to turn. Slowly it pulled the coach forward along the white rails.

"I have never seen such magic before," Havoc said. That was true, but not wholly true; the dragon Mentor had seen it, and described it, without understanding how it worked. Havoc was fascinated.

"Science magic is unlike others, Sire," the white man said. "It honors certain established principles, which we teach our children. They are invariable, except of course that they do not apply beyond our Chroma."

"And operate more strongly toward its center?" Havoc asked.

"True, Sire. Our train will gain velocity as it progresses inward."

So it did. The smoke fairly poured from the stack, and puffs of steam jetted from the cylinders, and the wheels turned rapidly. They were now moving at a considerable speed, indeed, faster than a flying coach. There was a clicking sound, and the coach shook.

"The tracks have junctures," the white man explained. "We try to align them perfectly, but they are never quite perfect, so we feel the shifts when traveling at speed. The effect is harmless."

Satisfied, Havoc ducked back inside the coach. The white man dropped down and slid the panel across, closing the coach. The noise of the locomotive diminished. The coach swayed gently as it moved. Overall it was rather pleasant.

"Si—Havoc," Gale2 said. "Could we—"

"Sure, get up there," Havoc said. "I'll hold your legs."

She climbed onto the bench, and Ennui got on the other. The White Chroma man opened the ceiling panel again, and they stuck their heads out. Havoc put his hands on Gale2's nice thighs, steadying her.

"Oooo!" she cried, delighted by the view outside, and Ennui's exclamation joined hers. Havoc looked up, and found his own view under her skirt worthwhile.

After a while, Chief and Symbol took their places, becoming regular tourists. Certainly this magic train was interesting.

The train sounded a loud whistle, and slowed. "We are approaching the station," the white man said. "Welcome to Whitecrest, Sire."

The city was of reasonable size, consisting of a number of quite large buildings separated by roads laid down in white patterns. The locomotive station was in its apparent center. They walked to one of those buildings, and were ushered into an appealing apartment suite. They had arrived.

When they were alone, Havoc beckoned the others close. Then

he removed his crown. *I dislike gambling, but will do so this time. Throe, when I seem to expose myself to risk, make only token protest. Gale, garb yourself in the tightest, sexiest manner possible. Ennui, explain privately to Chief and Symbol; have Symbol help Gale dress. In public, support me without protest.* He returned the crown to his head, cutting off his thoughts from them and any possible snooping by White Chroma mind readers. Mind reading was not a White specialty, but it was better to be safe.

The three who read his mind nodded, not speaking. Havoc went to the bathroom, paying no further attention to them. This was in case they were somehow being watched.

The party cleaned up, had some white food to eat, and was ready for the meeting with the White Chroma leader, the Duke of Whitecrest, at his official residence, the White House. The man was portly and polite. "Greeting, Sire."

"Acknowledged."

"I regret that protocol required you to come this far for so little, Sire. I doubt that we shall be able to come to terms."

"I am sure we *will*," Havoc said. "What is your interest?"

The Duke smiled. "You are refreshingly direct, Sire. I shall be the same. Our present interest is in establishing our own independent kingdom, answerable only to our own hierarchy. That is all."

"We believe that this would tend to fragment the political and social framework of the planet," Havoc said. "We are reluctant to allow it."

"This is of course our difference," the Duke said. "We wish to have independence, while you wish to incorporate us."

"The other Chroma are not seeking such separation. Why do you?" Havoc knew the answer, but wanted it on record.

"We believe that we represent Charm's closest approach to the original human stock. We believe that it was science that enabled our species to travel between planets and come to this one. Therefore the White Chroma should govern, so that we will be ready when another human ship comes from space."

Havoc nodded. "I can see your point. Your case is surely reasonable. Since the other Chroma will not allow you to govern, you prefer to withdraw and govern yourself."

"Exactly, Sire."

"But as I see it, mankind is inherently nonmagical, so the nonChroma people represent the original stock. I therefore support the present system, though I have no desire to be king of it."

The Duke was surprised. "You are king against your will?"

"Yes. I am a barbarian who has always detested the king and all his works. The tax collectors—"

"The tax collectors!" the Duke agreed, smiling grimly.

"But I will be executed for treason if I do not fill the office and execute it honorably, for a year. So I am doing what I can, hoping after the year to retire and live with my beloved barbarian girl." He put his arm around Gale2, who smiled obligingly, playing her role.

The Duke looked directly at Gale2 for the first time. She inhaled slightly and angled a leg, emphasizing her physical qualities. Symbol had done an excellent job; Gale2 was not only lovely, but eye-catchingly sexy.

"I appreciate your point," the Duke said, his pupils dilating. It was evident that the other members of his party appreciated it and Gale2 also. Beauty had no color. "I wish you success in your endeavor to retire early."

"Thank you." Havoc drew his own gaze away from Gale2's devastating cleavage. "But in order to compile a sufficient record, I must settle this crisis with dispatch. They will not let me retire honorably if I start a war that continues beyond my year."

"Agreed." The Duke's gaze had not yet managed to leave Gale2; he was clearly feeling amicable for the moment.

"We face difficult alternatives. If we invade, property will be damaged and lives will be lost. If we blockade, your Chroma will be isolated, not only from other Chroma, but from the other portions of itself. Your new kingdom would be fragmented before it started. Meanwhile, the other Chroma would lose the advantage of trading with you, and their tourists would no longer be able to ride your fascinating trains. Your own tourists would no longer get to float over other Chroma or experience the other novelties of magic." Havoc glanced again at Gale2's bosom; it was known that tourists especially liked to have erotic relations with physically attractive folk of other colors. "These are not pleasant alternatives."

"Agreed." The Duke returned his gaze to Havoc. "We would prefer to live in peace, and conduct trade, and indulge in mutual tourism, as has been the case in the past. But your predecessor would not hear of that."

"Did White have anything to do with King Deal's death?"

There was a sudden silence, as both Havoc's party and the assembled White Chroma officials tried to ignore the open breach of protocol. Such a question was tantamount to an accusation. But the Duke answered. "No."

The dragon seed did not buzz. He was telling the truth. That surely meant that White was not the party trying to kill Havoc. Havoc was relieved, as compromise would have been impossible if the White Chroma was guilty.

"Then I think we can negotiate an agreement," Havoc said.

"We see no likely compromise. The issue must be decided, one way or the other."

"Agreed. The compromise is in the manner of decision. I propose to settle this matter today, amicably."

"I presume you do not mean simply to let us go."

"That depends. Above all, I want this matter settled. There must be no continuing indecision. You must either be free, or rejoin my kingdom."

"Agreed."

"I propose to settle this by a trial of single combat. Myself against your champion."

"Sire!" Throe protested.

Havoc delivered a sharp glance at the bodyguard. Throe dropped his gaze.

The Duke was clearly taken aback. "Sire, this is intriguing but hardly feasible. We seek no harm to you personally, or to the office of the king. In addition, your crown would make a mockery of any–"

He broke off, for Havoc was removing his crown. "Of course the crown must go," he said. He handed it to Chief. "I realize that you do not wish to provoke the kind of reaction that would occur if others thought you had attacked the king on an official visit. But combat does not have to be dangerous. I am thinking of protective costumes, and blunted weapons. A soft sword point that scores on a marked heart can be considered a lethal strike, if the parties agree."

The Duke exchanged a glance with other members of his party. One of them spoke. "Sir, the man is a martial artist of considerable competence. We may not have a swordsman in this city to match him."

So the White Chroma had done its homework. "I have issued a challenge," Havoc said. "You thus may have the choice of weapons."

The Duke smiled. "Sire, would you consider a duel with pistols?"

"Describe the weapon."

"Sire, we will demonstrate it, and give you opportunity to practice with it, if you wish." The Duke signaled, and in a moment a man brought a closed white box. He held it while the Duke opened it. Inside were two metal objects with holes at one end and a hand grip on the other.

The Duke picked up one of them. "Sire, this is a pistol. It facilitates an internal explosion which ejects a pellet of metal called a bullet with considerable force, in the direction it is pointed. I will demonstrate."

Another man set up a white target marked with concentric circles, about twenty paces from the Duke. The Duke lifted the pistol, did something to it, pointed it at the target, and there was a loud bang that made the other members of Havoc's party jump. A hole appeared in the target.

"This is the manner of it, Sire," the Duke said. "If you care to take a shot yourself, here is the other pistol."

"Yes." Havoc stepped up, took the other pistol, and studied it.

"How did you make it pop?"

The Duke approached him. "Sire, if you will, hold it in this manner." He showed his own weapon. "Put your forefinger here, on the trigger. When you draw it back, it makes the pistol fire. At the moment it is locked, so that it can not be fired inadvertently."

Havoc held it as prescribed. The device was comfortable in his hand, and his forefinger curled naturally around the trigger. He pointed it at the target. "How do I unlock it?"

"There is a sliding switch on the side."

Havoc slid the switch, aimed the pistol at the target, and pulled the trigger. The thing exploded, kicking his hand back. The bullet clipped the top of the target and drove into the wall beyond. Smoke came out of the pistol, forming a brief pungent cloud.

"I apologize, Sire; I forget to explain about the kickback. When the bullet is propelled forward, the pistol pushes back. It is a reaction typical of Science, which as you know is our term for what you call White magic. It is necessary to hold the pistol firmly. You will also want to use the sights." He indicated two projections on the top. "When they are aligned on the target, the aim is correct."

"Let me try again," Havoc said.

A white man came and fitted another white bullet into the pistol. Then Havoc aimed again, aligned the sights, and fired. This time the kickback was controlled, and the bullet struck near the center of the target.

"That is impressive, Sire. It normally requires some practice to became accurate."

"I have had experience with a slingshot. This is similar."

"Similar? A slingshot requires two hands."

"This one was mounted on wood, and the band could be stretched and locked in place. So it could be fired with one hand. I became a fair shot."

The Duke looked at the target. "Surely so, Sire. Now of course we would not use these lethal weapons in a contest. We have an alternative: paint-ball six shooters that our children train with. They are less powerful, and less accurate, but operate on a similar principle. When the paint strikes, it splatters, leaving a mark. Would you care to examine such a pistol?"

"Yes."

They brought out the six shooters. They looked larger and clumsier than the serious pistols, but were indeed generally similar. They had a barrel which turned a notch after each shot, so that six shots could be fired before they were exhausted. Havoc fired a shot at the target, and it made a black splotch near the bottom right. "This will due. Bring on your champion."

"Sire, if you are truly amenable to this contest, I will represent the White Chroma," the Duke said. "I am experienced with pistols.

However, we must don protective garb, as even a paintball can cause damage if it strikes a vulnerable part, such as an eye."

"Bring on the garb."

While white personnel put the white padded clothing on the two of them, they established the terms of the contest: They would face away from each other, each would walk ten paces, and stop. When a bell rang, each would be free to turn and fire. As it was not easy to hit a moving target at that range, they would try to get closer, firing at will. The first to make a "lethal" score would be the winner.

"If you win," Havoc said, "I will drop my objection to the separation of the White Chroma and recognize your independence without rancor. There will be no war, and no interruption of trade or tourism. This will continue as long as I am king. If I win, you will end your rebellion and recognize my authority over you as king, as it has been before—as long as I am king."

"What thereafter?" the Duke asked.

"I can't speak for the next king. He may allow the existing compromise to stand, or choose to disown it. As may you. This is a temporary measure, intended to keep the peace during my tenure. But it may be possible to hold a similar contest, to establish the status during the tenure of that following king."

The Duke nodded. "This seems fair enough. Now we need witnesses to the agreement and the encounter, to ensure fairness. They should be from other Chroma."

Havoc glanced at Symbol. "Here is the Invisible Chroma representative." Symbol stepped forward, lifted her hat, and bowed, so that all could see inside her head.

The Duke signaled, and in a moment a red man stepped forward. "Here is a visitor from the Red Chroma who will also serve." The red man pursed his lips and blew. A small red cloud of vapor emerged, formed into a floating face, and stuck out its tongue.

"That's not illusion," Symbol said. "It's ectoplasm. He's genuine. He has a red stone." Ennui was already nodding; she had verified it from the man's mind.

The Duke looked around. "Their reports should be sufficient, if they agree."

Symbol and the red man nodded.

Havoc and the Duke walked to the center of the chamber. A white official met them there. "I will count the paces. Do not turn until I ring the bell. I will announce the strikes as they occur. A strike on a limb will negate the further use of that limb but will not end the contest. A strike to the center of the head, chest, or gut will be deemed lethal; a strike to the edge will be partial. Two partial strikes will be considered lethal."

They took their places, holding their pistols. "One." Havoc stepped forward, and knew that the Duke was doing the same. "Two." He stepped again.

After the tenth step he stopped. He saw Throe and Gale2 about ten paces farther out, part of the great circle that had formed. Gale2, seeing his glance, issued a tentative smile.

The bell rang.

Havoc leaped to his left, turning in the air. He dived to the floor, rolling. He heard a shot, and saw a black splotch appear just beyond him. Had he been slower, it would have scored.

He rolled back to his feet, reversed course, and charged toward the Duke, who was standing still, taking aim. Havoc dodged, pointing his pistol—and the Duke quickly ducked. But the effort was wasted; Havoc hadn't fired. He was now about twelve paces from the other, and could probably score from here, but wanted to get closer.

The dragon seed buzzed. Havoc dropped to the floor, and the paintball sailed just over him. The Duke was a good shot, and was not being misled by Havoc's motions; he would soon score.

Havoc scrambled toward the man, then leaped up, and threw himself down again. But this time he wasn't quite fast enough. The Duke's third shot caught his right upper arm as he rolled away.

"Strike!" the referee called. "King's right arm."

Havoc immediately reached across with his left hand and took the pistol. He continued to roll, so as not to present a stationary target. He had to do it with his legs, as he was letting his right arm drag, and holding the pistol with his left. Then without getting off the floor, he paused, aimed, and fired, left handed. He fired all six shots in rapid order, going from the Duke's left to his right, halfway up.

One of them scored low on the Duke's padded chest. "Lethal strike!" the referee called. "Match to King Havoc."

There was a smattering of applause from both White and nonChroma spectators. They appreciated a good fair fight.

"That was a considerable gamble," the Duke said. "Had you missed, I would have had leisure to catch you without concern about return fire."

"It was my most likely score," Havoc said, getting up. "You were too careful; I couldn't fool you much longer."

"The White Chroma yields," the Duke said with excellent grace. "Good match, Sire." They shook hands.

Then Gale2 was virtually flying across the arena to hug him, almost flopping out of her scant costume. The men of the White Chroma were watching her progress with appreciation. "You did it, Havoc!" she exclaimed breathlessly.

"Just doing my job," he said. But he was quite pleased. He had handled all four crises expeditiously, and now maybe could relax.

Except for that business of the anonymous enemy who was stalking him.

Chapter 6—Temple

Gale's body danced on. Parts of her were hurting now, as the demon made it exert itself beyond ordinary limits. The succubus didn't care whether Gale hurt; she needed this body for only a few minutes. Then she would throw it away.

She whirled in air and landed directly before Lad. She opened her arms to him. *Come to me, my idiot youth*, the demon thought.

Almost, he did so. He started to step forward. The demon could not touch him; he had to touch her. He had to do it himself.

"Her Dance of Air complete, the succubus offers herself to Lad," Leader said, not realizing how literal it had become. "He is sorely tempted, but manages to resist, knowing that she will suck out his soul with his semen. He holds his place."

Lad, hearing that, put his foot back down. He was following the script.

Damn! It was the demon's thought. She had lost the first siege, though not by much.

"Undismayed, the succubus proceeds to the second stage of the temptation, the Dance of Earth," Leader continued.

Gale's body turned around, facing away from Lad. Now she treated him to the rear approach. Her full body motions were not great, but her backside did tricks it had never been able to do this well before. Her buttocks rippled and flexed, the motions seeming to slide down her thighs or up her back. They bunched and bounced. If Air was high and flying, Earth was at the fundament. Her body squatted, and straightened; one leg lifted, and the other. Her legs spread apart, making a wide stance. Her hands slid back across her hips, stroking them, lifting them, separating them. She bent over, showing Lad everything wide open and wet. Her head looked back under her body, between her legs. *Come into me, imbecile male.*

Lad's body shook. He was trying to hold back, but a single step would take him up to her and into her. Gale could not resist; the demon held her with a magically strong grip. She could only watch as disaster overtook them. How had this happened, when she had the amulet to protect her?

"Again the succubus tempts him, but again Lad somehow resists," Leader said. "Her second ploy has failed."

With those words, Lad, also reminded of the script, stepped back.

Shut your mouth! the demon thought viciously at Leader. But she could not speak. She might have controlled Gale's mouth, as she controlled everything else, but such words would give away her identity. She could win only if no one else knew. Otherwise they would interfere. So Leader, following the script, had inadvertently foiled the second ploy. But there were three more to go.

"Now the succubus performs the Dance of Fire. She is angry because her first dances have failed, and her rage is like a furnace."

Indeed, Gale's body was dancing violently, shaking in every part, twisting. Her head was turning, making her hair fling across her face. Her eyes were slit, her teeth bared. *Feel my rage, nitwit!* the demon's thought came. *It will go hard with you if I must labor much longer for your silly soul.* She spun, and her feet stomped the floor, and her hands made striking motions, smashing almost to Lad's face.

Gale could appreciate Lad's thoughts. He was affrighted. He had never seen her like this, and was in awe of her wrath. Did he dare resist her any longer?

But all is forgiven if you capitulate now, the demon thought, forcing a vicious smile. *Come to your burning beauty.*

"Almost, she terrifies him into submission," Leader announced. "But Lad is too strong for her, and manages to resist her third ploy."

You garbage! the demon thought, truly furious. *I will slit your cursed throat!* But she couldn't, because again, though she might force Gale's reluctant body to do it, the act would give away her identity and bring the village men charging in to dispatch her. She had to capture Lad first, then fade away, leaving the villagers helpless to remedy the situation.

But Gale was helpless too. She could make no motion not governed by the demon, and could not speak to warn anyone. She was captive, forced to betray both the play and the people. Was there no way out of this disaster?

"Now the succubus tries the Dance of Water," Leader announced. "The fourth ploy."

Her body went into it. The Dance of Water was liquid and flowing and rippling, sometimes like a bubbling stream, sometimes like a cool lake, and sometimes like a great sea. It was also extremely lascivious, as her body twisted and curved, showing all of its flesh. Lad watched, mesmerized.

But the worst would be the finale, Gale knew. Men who withstood all else commonly fell to the ploy of water. Even when they knew better—and Lad surely did not.

Now it came: the demon coursed to a halt before the boy and opened her arms, inviting him in. *Flow into me, jerk.* She smiled.

But Lad hesitated, believing it was all part of the script, not to be believed.

Then the demon took control of Gale's eyes. Suddenly they were tearing, copiously, making her seem to be crying. Her mouth writhed into a simulation of grief. She was being rejected, and she was heart-broken.

It worked. Lad stepped forward to take her in his arms, to comfort her, heedless of the odd reversal of their normal association. She put her mouth in the way of his, to be there for his kiss. As with the rest, she could not kiss him, but could receive his kiss.

"But once again Lad manages to resist," Leader announced. Lad jerked guiltily back, surely ashamed to admit how close he had come to ruining the play.

Utter damnation! the demon swore. She turned and took two steps toward Leader, staring furiously into his face.

And that was the demon's mistake. Leader's eyes widened into round. He recognized the alien presence.

But even as he did, the demon struck with a glare that must have had magic. Leader stumbled back and fell, unable to speak.

Then the demon turned and bounded for the bed. She leaped onto it, lay on her back, and flung out arms and legs toward Lad. It was the final ploy: the Void. *Come into me, you empty head!* she thought.

Lad had been on the verge of capitulating before. Now the temptation was simply too much. He stepped toward the bed.

No! No! Gale tried to cry, but she was mute. Her body beckoned, drawing the boy in toward its open center. Void indeed: he would never return, once he entered that hole.

He got on the bed below her legs, getting on hands and knees. He crawled up, touching her, setting himself upon her. He oriented as his face approached hers. The demon subtly adjusted herself, so that there would be no fumbling; she would be exactly where he was going. So close, so close!

Their eyes met. Gale made a sudden, desperate effort in the moment of the demon's distraction. She peered out through her own eyes, trying to show her essence through them. *Don't do it, Lad; it's not me! Don't do it!*

He saw. His own eyes widened with recognition.

Then the demon clamped down again.

Gale was helpless. Her body was entirely in the power of the demon, including her eyes. She had caught the thing by surprise, for a moment, but that was all.

Come to me, my baby man, the demon thought urgently. But Lad balked. He froze in place, not advancing to complete the connection.

Come! Come! The succubus made gestures of hauling him in to her body, using her arms and legs. But she couldn't actually touch him physically.

Then Lad slowly withdrew. He backed away, and got off the bed. He staggered across the stage, no longer looking at the succubus. Gale was left with everything spread open, but rejected.

With a curse of pure fury, the demon departed. She had after all been vanquished.

Gale collapsed as the awful presence left her. She sobbed with mixed pain and relief, for the demon had taken a toll on her body and left her hurting. But it was more than that. She had been captive, and now was free—because Lad had successfully resisted the succubus. In reality as well as in the play.

She was roused by the applause of the audience. Even the smallest children had thrilled to the drama of the finale, almost fearing that Lad was going to lose. Now Guard came to give Gale her cloak. She got off the bed and covered herself, and resumed her dour Dame expression. Lad dressed too, and the two of them stood and bowed in each direction, accepting the applause. The play was done, the message given. No growing child would fail to remember the danger of the demon.

But where was Leader? "He's okay, just recovering," Guard said. "What did you do to him?"

"The succubus really came," Gale said, feeling unsteady. "She took me over. When Leader caught on, she stunned him with a look, so he couldn't interfere."

"So that was it! I thought you two were trying to be realistic. Then I thought you got carried away by the part. Then I thought you were really trying to seduce him. You were—I got a reaction myself, and I've seen a thousand such plays. You're the loveliest to play that role, but it wasn't only that. There was just something—so it really was the demoness."

"It really was the demoness," Gale agreed. "The play was real. Thank the planet that Lad withstood her."

"Only because Leader kept reminding me," Lad said. "Then I was gone, until I saw your eyes. I thought I saw you way down in a well, screaming 'Don't do it!' and I realized what had happened. Even so, I almost did it."

"That saved you," Gale said.

"I wasn't concerned about me. I was so—it was so—I just had to do it. Except that I couldn't stand to hurt you."

"To hurt me? Lad, I was only the body. It was your soul she was after."

"I knew you'd be sorry if you hurt me, and I—Oh, Dame, I never want to make you sorry."

She put her arm around his shoulders. "Thank you, Lad. Remember, no matter what I do in the play, I really don't want you to do it."

"Yes. But I hope I never meet the succubus again. She—Dame, I mean no offense, but when she took over—"

"I know. The demon's expertise in sexual expression makes me an innocent."

They came to Leader, who was resting on a pallet where he had been placed. He smiled weakly. "You made it."

Gale smiled back. "We *didn't* make it, you rogue. But it was an appallingly close call."

"I'm sorry I took so long to catch on. At first I thought it was just–"

"Yes. You couldn't know the invocation worked. The amulet didn't."

Village Elder joined them. "That was the most remarkable performance I ever witnessed," she said. "I could have sworn—"

"It's true," Gale said. "Something went wrong. The demon possessed me, and almost got Lad."

"The amulet must be defective. You must get another."

"Why? Lad withstood the succubus, so she will never come again."

Elder nodded. "True. I was forgetting."

Gale removed the amulet and returned it to Leader. "I feel safer without it."

He shook his head. "I am chagrined to have given you no better protection. I never thought—"

"None of us did," Guard said. "We are all chagrined."

Leader looked at Gale. "Get some rest. I have a notion how you are feeling."

She nodded. "That demon did not care about my health."

They returned to the house. Gale fell on her bed with relief, and sank into a troubled sleep. The demon had left nothing of herself behind, except the memory of her cruel presence. But that memory left Gale unnerved. To have been so helplessly subject to such a thing— how could she ever escape the appalling awareness of that awful entity? She felt unclean, despoiled, compromised. And if the demon had succeeded in taking Lad, what then? How could she ever have lived with herself?

She woke to feel a hand on hers. It was Lad. "You were restless— I thought you needed support."

She drew him down to lie beside her. "I do, Lad. Thank you. I'm so glad you survived."

"It was me she came for. I hate it that she used you like that."

"But it won't happen again. You withstood her blandishments, and are now forever immune."

"I don't know. It—she—you are so very beautiful. If you wanted to take me–"

She smiled. "Why, is this an offer, Lad?"

"No!" he cried, horribly embarrassed. "I mean—" He sat up, about to go.

She hauled him back. "I was teasing, Lad. I apologize. It was in bad taste."

"I have no power against you. If the succubus came again, and I didn't know–"

"She won't. But you know that I want never to do it with you. Not because you are in any way deficient. Because it would ruin the play, and perhaps your life. If I ever seem to be truly intent on seducing you, flee, because it will be the demon."

"I know." He lay there for a moment, then spoke again. "Dame?"

He had something on his mind. "Yes, Lad."

"I—you make me desire you so much, I could never resist, if you wanted. But just being here with you, like this, is—is so much better. I love you."

She turned toward him and kissed him on the forehead. "Thank you, Lad. You know I love elsewhere. But I will always remember you fondly."

She was afraid that was not enough of a reassurance, but he almost seemed to glow with pleasure. He was smitten with her, as Leader had warned he would be, but he knew the limits, and was satisfied with her friendship. It was hard to believe that she was only four years his senior; she felt enormously older.

Soon they got up, made repairs of appearance, and went out to join the villagers. They were of course fully clothed, and would remain so. Now came the eager questions, which they answered with proper caution. How did she make herself so young, so suddenly, in the play? A little bit of magic, perhaps. Did the succubus really come like that? Yes, she could, if not guarded against, and the incubus, too, to girls verging on nubility. So beware, beware!

The village celebrated with a good lunch meal, and singing and dancing in the evening. Gale joined them, in her stately Dame persona, for this was her expertise. She danced with Lad, she prim, he somewhat awkward, and the villagers loved it. It was a thrill for the villagers to meet and mingle with the characters of the play. They had expected a somewhat clumsy first effort, with mistakes, but had instead been treated to the most realistic version ever.

In the morning the weather was fair, and they set off down the trail for the next village. They had successfully accomplished their first performance, and expected no trouble with the play thereafter. But they knew that the challenges of the treks between villages could still be formidable. Gale remained a bit stiff in parts, and a bit bruised in others, from the hard treatment by the succubus, but the extended walking helped work the kinks out, and she felt better as she went.

At one point she found herself with Leader. "That succubus," he said. "I don't like that. So if you prefer to cancel the tour—"

"It won't come again," Gale said. "It was an ugly business, but not reason to overreact."

He looked relieved. "I agree."

They made it without undue challenge, and were welcomed at the next village. The following day they put on the play, feeling more confidence. Lad remained abashed as they got naked, but this time reacted more promptly as she addressed him. It was going well.

Then the demon came again.

Gale could hardly believe it at first. How could the succubus come a second time? But there she was, suppressing Gale's control, taking over the dance, making it so much more effective than Gale herself ever could. The dragon seed had warned her, but she had looked for some other danger, as before, never anticipating this.

This time Leader caught on the moment the change occurred. He did not challenge the demon directly, but made sure there was not much chance for her to tempt Lad for very long at a time. Lad caught on too, and became as diffident as he could without spoiling the play. And Gale fought to recover possession of her body—and did make a little progress. The demon still governed, but the hold was not as tight. It seemed that Gale was learning some resistance at key points of her identity.

Part of it was her guarded inner memory. That was protected from magical mind reading, and it seemed from the succubus too. So she had a base, like a sealed fortress, from which she could make sallies. That enabled her to interfere with the demon's effort to fascinate Lad. The demon could not focus completely on both Lad and Gale.

In the end, Lad did resist, with more leeway than before, and the demon departed in disgust. But that left the mystery of its reappearance.

"How could this happen?" Gale demanded. "In real life, the tempting is supposed to be only once, and the boy either loses his soul or is forever immune."

"I'm not immune," Lad said. "I saw the change, but she was so sexy she would have had me anyway, if Leader hadn't kept moving it along to the next dance, and if she'd been a little more—I don't know."

"I was able to fight her, some, this time," Gale said. "I'm learning how to do it. I couldn't stop her, but I could hold her back some, divert some of her attention. That seems to have been enough."

"You were able to fight her?" Leader asked? "I never heard of that before."

"We never heard of a second possession, either," Gale pointed out. "So maybe no other woman has had the chance to fight a second time."

Leader nodded. "There seems to be much we don't know about such demons. They may not be as limited as we supposed. But that makes our educational mission that much more valuable: children must be fairly warned to stay on guard."

"Maybe," Lad said, "maybe it's not exactly that. Maybe the first one didn't count, because I had help resisting. So I didn't do it all myself."

Leader considered. "Now that's possible. I hadn't thought of it. It's also true that we have an unusually lovely Dame, who is surely harder to resist than others would be. Maybe the succubus likes possessing her, however briefly."

"Or maybe we have a Lad whose soul is especially desirable to demons," Gale suggested.

"But I'm nothing special," Lad protested. "I don't have any special talents or knowledge or training."

They questioned him about his background, but what he said held up: he was quite ordinary. It seemed unlikely that the demon would seek him out persistently. So maybe, they concluded, the second possession had been a fluke.

But when it happened a third time, they knew there was something. The seed warned her, but she couldn't stop the invasion of the demon. It came in through her cleft, like an infusion of mist, and spread out to rule her body. "I hate to do it, but I think we should abort the tour," Leader said. "This is just too strange and dangerous."

"But I'm resisting it better," Lad protested.

"And I am fighting back better," Gale said. "We can resist the sieges of the succubus. And I understand the effect is very persuasive for the villagers."

"Yes, nothing like seeing an actual succubus tempt a really vulnerable Lad," Leader said sourly. "Half the adolescents in the audience are getting fierce reactions—the male half. And the female half is more interested than it might be, studying the motions. That's good, maybe, considering the message. But what if the succubus tries a new ploy, and gets him?"

Neither Gale nor Lad could be sure that wouldn't happen. The demon was very good at seduction.

"I'm the one mostly at risk," Lad said. "If I'm willing, you should be."

"That's because you'd give your life for Dame, without even thinking. You're in love with her."

But Lad didn't back off. "So?"

Leader threw up his hands. "All right—try it one more time. Then we'll see."

They tried it again, at the next village. The seed buzzed, and the demon came again. But Lad was getting increasingly savvy at distinguishing between Dame and demon, and got cautious the moment the change occurred. He played up to the audience, pretending to be on the verge of capitulation, but it was evident to those who knew him that he was under control.

So they tried it at one more village. The demon came again, and Lad withstood it again, despite some excruciatingly exquisite gestures Gale's body made. Gale also made further progress resisting. Surely both processes were evident to the demon. So why did she keep coming? It was a slowly losing game, in demon terms.

Then one evening between shows, when the two of them were

lying on the bed and sleeping, Gale woke to a buzz by the dragon seed, and in a moment found herself possessed. There had been no invocation, no stripping, but the demon had come.

She fought, but could resist only to a degree. The demon controlled her body. And this time the succubus did something it had never tried before: it spoke. "Lad," it said softly. "Lad, hear me."

But he was sound asleep, and did not respond. She reached across and lifted the cover from Lad's form. That was another frighteningly new thing: she was touching him. No—only the blanket. "Lad!"

He woke. "Dame."

It took hold of his nightdress, by that device drawing him in. "Kiss me."

"But Dame, if I do that, I might lose control."

It tugged harder. "I need you. Lad, my darling, come to me."

"Oh, Dame," he whispered, melting. He rolled onto his side, to face her. "Do you mean it?"

Gale made a sudden, transcendent effort. She attacked her own mouth, getting it for an instant. "Demon!" she hissed.

The demon clamped down, but it was too late. Lad was staring. "You're the succubus! Outside the play! And you're talking!"

"Yes. Come to me, my idiot stripling."

The demon had made a mistake on her own, speaking aloud what usually was silent. That shattered any remaining doubt about her identity. Lad scrambled out of the bed. "Go away!" he cried. "Go away! Let Dame go!"

The case was obviously hopeless. With a growl of disgust, the demon departed.

"It's gone," Gale said. She found herself unable to decide whether the demon was neuter or female. "But what a horror. It came outside the play, without the invocation, in clothing."

"And it talked," he said. "And grabbed me." Then he looked horrified. "Maybe it's still you!"

"No. It's gone."

"How do I know that?"

Gale considered briefly. "It did talk. That's new, but probably within her powers all along. But it didn't touch you. It touched your clothing."

"It pulled me toward her."

"By your nightdress. It still can't actually touch you. Not directly. You must touch her." She walked toward him.

He shied away. "I'm not sure!"

"Lad, it can't touch you. I can. Let me touch you, and you will know."

He nodded, but he was plainly nervous. He stood unmoving while she came up to him. She reached out and touched his hand, squeezing it in the way she did. Then she let go.

He was satisfied. "Oh, Dame! I was so afraid."

"With reason, Lad. This is astonishing. We fought it off in the play, so now it's attacking outside it. This means we have to be on guard all the time."

"All the time," he agreed, shivering. "Dame, this scares me something awful. In the play I've learned how to hold out, but here in the bedroom—if you hadn't gotten out that warning, it would have had me."

"Yes. Fortunately her control is not complete. I can sometimes get through. Maybe it's aware of that, so is trying more desperate measures. Before it loses the ability to go after you. But I don't understand why it wants you so badly."

"Dame!" he exclaimed. "It doesn't want me—it wants *you*!"

"Me! Why?"

"To stop your investigation. If it takes me out, there'll be no Lad for the play, and you'll have to shut down the tour. Then you won't be able to do what you came to do."

It was like a lighting flash. "You're right! It's trying to get rid of me, one way or another. By eliminating you, or controlling me. I've made progress resisting her, but it's also made progress controlling me, paradoxical as that sounds. If I try to investigate the Temple, it'll take over and make me betray myself. If the Troupe ever gets that far."

"Your mission must be pretty important."

She couldn't tell him what it was; even if he tried to keep the secret, his mind might be read magically. But he was right: the business of the changelings, which King Deal was investigating, must be the reason he was killed. "And I must be on the right track, because only an important discovery would be worth sending a demon to stop. But if it's that critical, I wonder why the enemy, whoever it is, didn't send a warrior to kill me?"

"Because they don't want the secret exposed," Lad said. "They don't want to call attention to it, and a seemingly purposeless killing of a lovely innocent woman would do that. So they are trying to stop you without seeming to. By stopping the tour in a way anyone would understand—accidentally summoning a succubus for real—or just messing you up from inside, and you can't complain, because you have to keep your mission secret too."

"That must be it," Gale agreed. "Oh, Lad, I could kiss you!"

He looked abashed. "As long as you sure it's not the succubus."

"It's not. Remember, it can't touch you." She stepped into him, embraced him, and kissed him firmly on the mouth.

He was unsteady in her arms. "Leader's right," he gasped. "I would die for you, Dame."

"Don't do that!" she said. "That would ruin the play."

He dissolved into laughter, and then she joined him. They hung on to each other for support, helplessly shaking. It really wasn't funny, but in the circumstance it had set them off and wouldn't let go.

At last, spent, they sobered. "We must tell Leader," Gale said.

"Now? In the night?"

"Yes, I think so. Because the demon came in the night, and showed new powers. We need to prepare immediately, in case it comes again tonight. We don't know what it'll do, as it gets desperate."

He nodded. "I guess so."

They crossed the hall and knocked on the other door. Guard opened it immediately.

"The demon came," Gale said tersely.

"That I can't protect you from. Come in."

In a moment they were talking with Leader, explaining what had happened and their explanation for it. Guard listened, and even Carto joined them. "I think someone in the first village must have read one of our minds, and discovered my mission, and sent the demon," Gale concluded.

Leader was grave. "You must be right. I should never have discussed the matter openly. It didn't occur to me that any of our minds would be read later. I am chagrined, and I apologize for my blunder. I'll cancel the tour."

"No!" Gale protested. "That will give the enemy the victory, by stopping my investigation."

"But it will be stopped anyway, in a worse way. By sacrificing Lad's soul, or getting you caught snooping in the Temple, where, if it's this important, they will likely kill you and hide your body and pretend you were never there. Better to back off now, cutting our losses."

"But this is all the more reason to pursue my mission," Gale said. "When I started, I wasn't even sure this was a good lead. Now I know it's so important the enemy will go to an extraordinary length to stop it from being exposed. I don't know what the secret is, or even who the enemy is, and in fact I didn't even know there was an enemy, but I can't default on my mission just because it turns out to be dangerous. I must go on, though I hate putting the rest of you at such risk."

"I'm with you," Lad said immediately.

Leader considered. "I don't like this. But the fact is, your presence in this troupe isn't just coincidental. Word came down the chain of command from the king himself, making you the real commander of the mission. Dame, I must obey your directive. But I wish you would reconsider."

Gale had known that she governed the mission, but had said nothing, both to preserve the secret and to avoid affronting the nominal commander, Leader. Still, she preferred to have a consensus. "I must go on. But if any member of the troupe should be lost, it would be difficult to continue. All of us are needed for the tour. That means that all of us are at risk. I'm willing to go into danger myself, but I'm not willing to require it of the rest of you. So maybe it would be better to end the tour, but let Lad and me go on alone. That would at least enable the three of you to return safely, and organize another tour with another Dame and Lad. It is better to preserve your lives, than to put you at risk for something that is not your concern. I could order you to do this, so that there would be no question of dereliction."

"No," Leader said firmly.

"But you are family men. It simply is not right to risk the grief of your families for this."

Leader glanced at Guard and Carto, then returned to her. "Dame, if you are committed, we are committed, regardless."

"I know that Lad is committed for his own reason, but—"

"Dame, we all have the same reason. We could not let you go on alone, even if that were feasible."

"No, I mean Lad loves me, so does not even *want* to let me go alone. I'm sorry to have imposed on him so, but it's a consequence of the role. You three men, in contrast–"

"There is no contrast. Dame, we all love you."

"Well, in a figurative sense, of course. But—"

"No," Guard said. "We are all your father's age, and married. But you have simply overwhelmed us."

Gale was taken aback. "But I never sought to—you know that this is a professional relationship. How can—?" She looked desperately at the third man, Carto.

Carto answered. "We have seen lovely women before, and we are true to our wives. We will cause you no problem, and will not speak of this elsewhere. But it is true: from the first your presence has been like that of the succubus, drawing us in even as we tried to resist. It is not merely your great beauty, but your attitude. You do not complain of hardships, you do what is required, and you are nice. You are to our minds the perfect woman. We tried to remain professional. But there is something about you that draws us in regardless. It is true that to know you is to love you."

"Yes," Lad said avidly.

Gale was nonplused. "I had absolutely no idea. If I had realized—"

"It would have made no difference," Leader said. "We were lost from the moment you were assigned. We would not have mentioned it, if you had not been about to try to let us go, so that we would not be in danger because of your mission. Dame, in the face of your determination to continue, our only proper fulfillment is to support you completely, and see that you succeed in your mission. Then we can see you safely back to Triumph and wish you well with the quintessentially fortunate man you return to."

"That man is the king." Then she froze. "Oh, I should not have said that!"

Leader nodded. "You should not have. It is not our business. But it explains much. The King must have sent the one he most trusts on the mission of most importance. This makes it absolutely important that we do our utmost to complete it. To preserve you, so that no grief comes to the man we all serve."

"Oh, he has a girl for his appearances and his bed, while I am gone," she said wryly. And paused again. "I am saying too much. This whole business has shaken me, making me intemperate."

"This is understandable. We have all said more than we care to. But now that we better understand each other, how should we proceed? Continue, the tour, of course, but how can we support you privately?"

"Maybe I should not sleep in your room," Lad said. "With the succubus coming by surprise, at night, it's not safe. I am not that strong."

Leader nodded. "Agreed. We can at least make the demon work harder to take you out. It will be crowded, but—"

"Maybe one of you could join Dame," Lad suggested. "Maybe Guard, to protect her."

"No," Guard said. "I dislike saying this, but if it came on to me in Dame's body, I could no more resist her than you could. The succubus would take me out, and leave the troupe incomplete."

"The same would go for Carto and me," Leader said. "At least Lad has experience resisting. But crowding is better than losing the mission. We'll make do."

"No," Gale said.

All four looked at her. "You prefer to take the risk?" Leader asked. "Remember, you as yourself have won our emotions. You as the succubus put us in a position of standing before a blindfolded archer while he practices. This is dangerous."

"I know it. But if the demon can not prevail one way, it will try another. It can't touch a man directly, but it's learning how to get around that. Maybe it will cause me to take my knife and stab one of you when you don't expect it: the knife, not it, would touch you. Maybe it will push something into you, so that you fall into a chasm. It is dangerous at all times, not just at night."

"True, but its preferred mode is to lure a man into sex. It will try that first, if allowed."

"Yes," she said. "And we know how to handle that. It is not easy, but we have been getting better at resisting. I think it is not intelligent; it merely follows her nature and does what is natural for her. I am coming to understand her better, with each experience of her. It can be channeled, to a degree." She was still being inconsistent about the gender of the succubus, but was increasingly seeing it as female.

"But is this sufficient reason to give her further opportunity?" Leader asked, following her lead on gender. "It seems safer to isolate her by night, and be on guard against her by day."

"No, I think not. Because though we may thus preserve the tour, she still will interfere when I attempt to investigate the Temple. We need to abolish her menace completely."

Guard spoke. "No human person has power over a demon. In the Chroma they form their own substance and do their mischief against those who lack caution or protection. In the nonChroma regions they must infest the bodies of living human beings. That is a limitation, but far from control. We can abolish demons no more than we can abolish magic itself; we can seek only to avoid them."

"That is the popular wisdom," Gale agreed. "But I think it may be mistaken, as was the belief that a succubus tempts a youth only once, and does not speak. Maybe I can't abolish her, but I think I can capture her."

"Capture her!" Leader exclaimed, astonished. "How could such a thing be possible?"

"By fathoming her weaknesses, and using them to trap her—in my body. By reversing the ploy, so that instead of her controlling me, I control her. I have been making progress resisting her, and if I make enough, I may be able to capture her. So that it can no longer leave at will."

"Locking the bird's feet to the ground," Leader said. "But won't it turn against you, and destroy you in her effort to break free?"

"It will surely try. But if I am prepared, and can resist her, it should tire, and in time I will overcome her. Then not only will I—and you—be safe from her, I should be able to use her powers to forward my ends. Such as completing my mission."

The others looked at her. "I like that," Lad said. "You can interest any man, Dame, and in time rule him. But the demon can compel him immediately. It could lure him into a pit, if it didn't want to complete the seduction."

"Yes. I would like to have that ability." Gale smiled. "Not to use against any of you, understand. To use against men who might otherwise kill me."

"That would be a great achievement," Leader agreed. "But suppose it does destroy you, in her desperation to get away? It may well be easier to kill you from inside, than to control you."

"If it could kill me that way, I think it would already have done it. It would look as though I had suffered an internal malfunction or eaten poison. No, I think it knows only how to control, and will be, well, unmanned if it finds herself caught. I'm ready to take the risk. The benefit could be enormous, and not just for this mission. I would have power I never otherwise could have."

"Then we support you in that challenge," Leader said. "So your notion is to lure her in by having Lad close by, and letting him distract her, while you try to catch her?"

"Yes. It may take several more sieges, but I think it can be done." She looked at Lad. "If you are willing."

"I am willing," he said immediately. "I'd love to be tempting it, instead of it me."

"Just try to recognize it when it comes, and don't believe anything
it tells you." Gale looked around. "Now I think we can return to sleep.
I'm sorry to have roused you at this hour. It just seemed important."

"It's important," Leader agreed.

Gale and Lad returned to their room, and lay down together on
the bed. Then she thought of something. "Lad, I know I have had an
effect on you; after all, I address you naked every play. But what am I
doing to allure the others? I had no idea they were interested."

"There's just something about you," he said. "You're just so lik-
able. Even if you weren't lovely, you'd be everyone's friend. Even if
you were stupid, you would be persuasive. But as it is—"

"But how am I different from any other woman? I was not special
as a child." Actually that wasn't quite true; other girls had resented
her prettiness, and boys had wanted to play Tickle & Peek with her
from the outset. She had seen both as problems, so had thought
herself different and therefore not good. Until Havoc.

"I don't know. You just are. I don't think there is any other woman
like you."

She sighed, giving it up. "Well, if you ever encounter another with
that quality, let me know. Maybe I can observe her, and learn something."

"I will, Dame."

They slept, and the demon did not come again that night.

But it did come during their next play presentation. Once again the
seed warned her, and once again she was unable to do anything to escape. It outdid itself, almost embracing Lad, so that if he had moved at
all he would have touched her. It was not the touch that did it, but the
completion of the sexual act; still, the touch of a woman could be conducive, and more than that with the succubus. Lad seemed on the very
verge of capitulation; it fooled the audience, so that some children cried
"Nooo!" and it seemed to fool the demon. But Gale knew him well enough
now to know that he was teasing. Oh, he desired her, as his state of
readiness made obvious; but he was not about to touch her.

Meanwhile, Gale was infiltrating the command points where the
demon dominated her. One was at her speech center, so she could
not talk; another was in her neck, just below her brain, where the
spinal nerves radiated out to control her limbs and torso. Another
was in her belly, making her female anatomy almost prehensile in its
readiness to take in the male anatomy, and catch on to the male soul
as it did. She found that the demon could control all centers approximately, or some centers completely. When it concentrated on talking,
which was not natural to it, the control of some other center weak-
ened. When it focused on dancing, one of its strengths, it could not
talk and was not completely ready for sexual performance. When it
controlled the eyes, and especially when it used them to throw a stun-

glare, it could neither dance nor speak.

Normally this limitation made no difference, as things tended to happen in order: the succubus would dazzle a boy with her marvelously moving body, then beckon him with its eyes and arms, and finally dispose its body to receive him most conveniently. Once he was in the throes of sexual fulfillment, it would focus entirely on his soul, drawing it down into his organ and out with his semen. Once it had the soul, the body no longer mattered; the demon would desert it and fly with the soul to its lair, wherever that might be. Boy and woman would discover themselves in sad straits, the one without his soul, the other without any modesty. For it seemed the demon usually took the nearest available woman, not inquiring whether she wished to have sex with a neighbor boy. Conjuring could attract the demon's attention, and if there was a woman handy, that was the one used. But the demon neither had to respond to conjuration, nor wait upon it. Thus much of what human beings thought they knew about such demons was only partly true.

Gale studied, and learned, and when the demon danced, Gale infiltrated her own speech center, so that she could control it, then relaxed that control to let the demon speak when it wished. When the demon spoke, Gale quietly shored up her control of her own body, but did not try to exercise that control, so that the demon did not realize. Because her infiltration was not enough; the demon could still wrest control from her when it wanted to, wherever it wished.

What she needed to know was where the demon's home base in her body was. It wasn't her brain, because Gale retained control of that throughout, and kept her thoughts secret. It wasn't her eyes or voice or limbs. Where, then?

She didn't find it during the play, but she had learned much else, studying the demon during its focus on the boy. And when Lad managed, at the last moment it seemed, to fend off the seduction, the demon did not realize that he was faking or that Gale was flanking it. The demon departed, frustrated, but determined to try again and again until there was success.

"I am gaining," Gale said afterward. "I am sure I can take the demon; I just need to build up my position sufficiently to do it."

"This is almost fun," Lad said. "To pretend that I am about to do it, then hold back at the last instant. I saw its eyes narrow and heard its breath hiss, and knew it was angry."

"You are doing a good job," Gale said. "It is almost entirely preoccupied with you, thinking you are on the verge of submission if it only persists a little longer. It is powerful in its way, but not very smart. That's why it follows the ritual. Then you survive the Void temptation, and have escaped another siege. Meanwhile, I am learning where and how to strike."

"Don't try to play with it," Leader warned. "The thing is dangerous. Strike when you get the chance."

"I must wait until I am sure of success," Gale said. "If I strike and it escapes, it will never give me another chance. It's not smart, but neither is it entirely stupid. But I think I can try to trap it soon."

Several villages and sieges later, Gale felt ready. She had finally located the demon's base in her body: her womb. From that nourishing, protected cave the demon reached out to the several nerve centers. To that cave the demon intended to bring the boy's soul, and then carry it away. Gale dared not challenge it there, for the demon's power could not be overcome at its seat of strength. But she thought she could trap it there. If she prepared well, physically and mentally.

"Leader, I need something," she said. "You are aware how women have cycles? Times of the month?"

"Yes, of course. If you have need not to perform on a given day—"

"I can perform. But I need something special to use in that region." She explained about the base the demon used. "So if it works, it will cork the demon, as it were, and confine it there."

"What do you need?"

"Sulvan seaweed."

"But that's used to prevent a demon from entering a sick person."

"I think it may also prevent one from leaving a well person. But it must be obtained quietly, and I must hide it, hoping the demon is not aware of it."

"Dame, I can get it from a villager, quietly. But I am not at all sanguine about trying to trap the succubus inside you. It might rip you apart."

"I think not. It isn't physical, here in nonChroma territory. It has to act through a person, and has limits there. It may make me try to injure myself, but I'll do my best to avoid that."

"Injure yourself! Should we bind you, if—?"

Gale realized that the demon could take control of her arm and use it to remove the plug of seaweed, ruining her ploy. "Yes, tie me down if you see I'm not in control. I expect the main battle to be internal. Be especially sure to keep my hands away from my crotch. Don't let me go until you are sure it's me."

"This will not be sweet, Dame."

"I know it."

Leader got the Sulvan seaweed. It was only a small swatch, in a little pouch, but she deemed it sufficient. She tied it snugly with string, and wound the string into her hair on top of her head, farthest from the demon's entry point, hoping it would not be detected.

The succubus came for the next play. Gale, dancing, tuned out the warning buzz, and was not aware of its invisible entry until too late; it assumed control, and she could not act. So they went through the routine again, and she practiced her infiltration and studied the demon. She was more certain than ever that she could do it, if she could only catch it in time. At the beginning, before the demon extended control to her body.

Lad held out, and the demon departed. It had been another great public performance, but a private loss. She told herself she had to expect this; precise timing was not easy to achieve.

"You didn't get it," Leader said after the show.

"Not this time," she agreed. "Next time I'll try to be ready. It comes so quietly, I have to be alert."

That night she was lying beside Lad, talking idly as they prepared for sleep. "Dame," he said suddenly. "I think it's coming."

He could sense it before it entered her? Evidently so, for then the seed buzzed. She lay still, focusing on her nether aspect. Sure enough, she felt it, like a faint wisp of smoke, sliding into her private cleft, infusing her. Apparently it could not readily pass straight through her flesh; it had to get inside her, establish its base, then use her bodily systems. She felt its presence in her womb, as it gathered, completing its entry. It was as though she were a tiny bit pregnant, a disquieting notion.

"Now," Lad whispered.

She snatched the pouch from under her hair so quickly the string snagged and broke. She brought it down between her legs, and up under her nightdress. She had no time to extricate the seaweed; she stuffed the whole pouch into her channel, poking it in with her finger. It scraped, hurting her, but that was the least of her concerns.

Lad leaped off the bed and ran from the room. She didn't have attention to spare for him at the moment; she had to trap the succubus.

In a moment the demon, spreading out through her body, became aware of the seaweed cork. It could not escape! *You slut!*

It took extra seconds for the succubus to complete its takeover of the body. Then Gale fought it for control of her arms. Its whole attention focused on her right arm, and she could not withstand it. The arm went down to her crotch and her fingers fumbled there. It was going to draw out the seaweed plug.

Leader and Guard burst into the room. They dived for her, each man catching an arm. But the demon fought, bringing her bare legs up, kicking at their crotches. It missed, but Leader grunted, in pain, apparently bruising himself in his effort to avoid the foot. Nevertheless, he hung on to her arm.

Lad threw himself across her legs, tackling them. His weight held them down. Still the demon fought, with superhuman strength, hauling the two men around, making their heads collide. It hardly cared what damage it might do to the woman in the process. But they would not let go, and soon the strength of Gale's body was exhausted. Then the men tied her arms and legs down to the bed, rendering her physically helpless.

They had trapped the succubus. But that was only the beginning of the fight. Now Gale had to overcome the thing's dominance of her body.

She tried for the arms again. The demon clamped on them, shoving her out. She tried for the legs, and for a moment had them, until the demon focused on them and took them back. Then she went for her voice. "You can't be everywhere, monster!" she cried.

But then it took back the mouth, and answered. "You sow! I'll destroy you!"

Gale was already going for her eyes. She looked at the men, who were staring down at her, concerned.

"Maybe we should cushion her head," Lad said. He brought a pillow and tried to tuck it under her head. Her head snapped up, her teeth snapping at his closest hand. But that was a bluff; it could not actually touch him. Just as the crotch kicks had been bluff. Only when the men were actually holding on to Gale could the succubus affect them physically. Then Leader put a hand on each side of her head, holding it in place, while Lad slid the pillow under.

Her mouth smiled. "Lad! Kiss me."

The demon was emulating Gale's voice and manner! Trying to fool the men into believing she had returned. It was getting more cunning.

But Lad knew better. "And get my face bitten? Forget it, demoness."

"But Lad, I love you. Why are you treating me this way?" Her eyes began to weep.

This was awful! The demon had more tricks than they had anticipated. The men weren't deceived, but suppose the thing found a way to fool them after all?

Lad turned away, not letting it get to him. But the demon was far from vanquished. "Leader! I have been catering to this dull boy, but it is you I really crave. You are a man. Release me, and I will give you pleasure such as you have never known."

"Forget it, infernal spook. You won't get my soul either."

"Guard," the succubus said. "I know you care for me. "Are you going to let this imbecile insult me?"

The demon was trying to set them against each other. But they weren't having it. "I'll insult you too, you disgusting parasite," Guard said.

The succubus put on a woeful expression. "What can I do to persuade you to release me?"

"Forget that," Leader said. "Just tell us who sent you, and why."

The thing wept some more. "You are so cruel to me. I want only to give you pleasure, yet you bind me and insult me."

"Get used to it," Guard said.

The demon gave up on them, and turned inward. *And you, you sneaky bitch cheat pig of a slut! You stinking mess of corruption. What do you want?*

"I want you," Gale replied, not using her physical voice. "I want to bind you to my will."

The demon's anger was like a solar flare. *You idiot mortal worm!*

Such unmitigated audacity! How dare you so presume?

"I have got you trapped in my body. You can't get away. So struggle, succubus, until you wear yourself out. This worm has turned."

I will make you hurt.

Gale was afraid of that, but knew she had to face it. "Then do it, demon. You are not getting free."

It turned out to be no bluff. Suddenly Gale was burning throughout her body, as if being dipped in penetrating fire. But she knew it couldn't be literal, and therefore it could be survived. And, after a moment, she realized something else: "You feel what I feel, ill spirit. When I hurt, you hurt."

Curse you! The heat faded. The demon couldn't torture her without torturing itself.

But then it found a way to hurt her without hurting itself. It conjured horrible mind pictures. Gale found herself looking into a gloomy stone chamber, where several women were chained to a wall. They were naked and beautiful, with long tresses hanging down across their full breasts. They were quietly weeping, the picture of despair. From her limited view, Gale realized that she was another woman, on the opposite wall.

Now watch my pleasure, the demon said. *Here comes Shrapnel, the torture master.*

A hulking man came into view. He wore helmet, boots, leather armor, and carried a whip. His face was a landscape of determined brutality. He stood before the woman farthest to the right of Gale's field of vision. "Are you ready, wench?" the man demanded.

The woman lifted her tear streaked face. "No," she sobbed.

Shrapnel struck her with the whip. It cracked across her face, leaving a stripe down one cheek. She screamed as Gale winced. This was torture—but why?

"Are you ready?" the torture master asked again.

The woman, gasping with pain, disheveled, writhing in her chains, did not answer.

The whip cracked again, making a welt across one breast. The woman screamed again. Gale tried to look away, but her eyes were fixed open. She had to watch this brutal scene.

Between each lash, Shrapnel inquired again. When he didn't get the answer he wanted, he struck again. Soon the woman's face and body were a mass of crisscrossing stripes. Blood streaked her torso and dripped to the stone floor.

Finally the woman responded no more. She was unconscious.

Seemingly undismayed, the man threw aside the whip and took up a gleaming knife. He went to the next woman. "Are you ready, strumpet?"

The women averted her pretty face, not answering.

Shrapnel put the blade to her belly and sliced across. Her flesh opened like a red mouth. She screamed horribly. But the cut was not deep enough to kill her.

"Are you ready?"

She sobbed, but did not accede.

The knife came up to carve at her right breast. It sawed through as blood spurted, until at last the breast severed completely and fell to the floor.

"Are you ready?"

Still she resisted, and the torture continued, until her body was unrecognizable as a woman. But she was not dead. When she screamed no more, the torture master put aside the knife and addressed the third woman.

Gale was appalled. What could possibly be so horrible that these women would suffer this agony rather than agree to it? She would have nightmares about this sequence. She knew it was only a vision, not real, and that gave her courage. Yet her curiosity remained, though she felt guilty for it. There had to be some explanation.

"Are you ready, whore?"

The third woman struggled with herself, but shook her head.

"Then you will be entertained by the hellhound."

The woman looked appalled. "No. Please."

"Then are you ready?" Shrapnel repeated.

She hung her head, shuddering, not answering.

Shrapnel turned to the side and gestured. A shambling shaggy four-legged creature came up, with a snout like that of a wolf, and a furry tail. It was male, for it had a huge male organ. It leaped on the woman, wrapping its forelegs and hind legs around her as she screamed. It moved its hind end around, orienting the monstrous member on her cleft. The bulbous tip lodged and shoved upward. *The thing was raping her.*

The act took some time, for the beast seemed indefatigable. Its organ was so large that it did not simply slide into her; it had to be forced, stage by stage. The bulb was glistening with slime, but mere lubrication was not enough. The hellhound bucked repeatedly, hammering its rod in the manner of a wedge into a rocky crevice, splitting her cleft apart, scream by scream, until the bulb was completely in. The action did not stop there; the driving continued as the shaft slowly penetrated, until at last almost the whole of the implement disappeared inside her straining torso. Then the trunk of the member swelled farther, pumping thick oily fluid in such volume that it distended her belly and welled out under pressure around the organ, to drool down her legs. Still the creature drove up and in, pumping, refusing to stop until all of its urgency was abated. When the beast was finally spent, it withdrew its softening member with a sucking sound and bounded to the floor and away. The woman hung from her chains, unconscious, with scratches, bruises, and bite marks all over her body, and blood leaking out below with the voluminous surplus ejaculate. Coalescing gobs of it dripped to the floor.

Shrapnel turned to face the woman Gale looked out from. "Are you ready, harlot?"

And the woman, shuddering, answered "Yes."

The shackles must have opened, because she seemed to drop to the floor. Her limbs were brown. Before her a stone vault opened. She lay down in it, and watched the stone lid come down, sealing her in. She had been buried alive.

"This is you!" Gale said, catching on. "This is how you became a succubus!"

Yes. But the dragon seed buzzed.

"Then how can it be your pleasure? You capitulated before you were tortured."

My pleasure to see you suffer this perpetually.

"Perpetually? But it's over, isn't it?"

No. This is my life, when I am not on a mission. I must gather a hundred boy souls before I get my own soul back, and am free. While you keep me, you will suffer instead of me. Every day it is the same; only the tortures differ.

Now Gale was appalled in another way. The torture was to make these women become succubi, and go after the souls of innocent boys?

"What do they want with all those souls?" she asked.

I don't know. I just deliver them to empty male bodies for storage.

"Why don't you just flee, and not return? They can't hold your spirit, can they?"

They have my body. It will not recover if I do not return.

"Recover? But you weren't tortured or mutilated or bestially raped, were you? You capitulated when they got to you."

That is not the way it works. Each woman is removed at night, restored next day, hung up and queried again. They have magic to do that, so that their torture can be endless, as long as they don't get careless and kill someone. There is no escape by death. I was tortured and raped many times before I gave in. Shrapnel made me suffer over and over, and I knew he would never relent.

The seed buzzed again. There was something the succubus was not telling. "But if you do not return to your body, such torture will be meaningless, won't it?"

If I do not return, they will use my body as a zombie servant to do chores, and to serve the sexual interests of the torturers, until at last it expires. Then either I will die, or I will be forever trapped as a succubus, with no hope of reprieve.

The seed did not buzz, so this clarification was true. Gale was appalled anew. "Every day the same women are tortured? Unless they agree to go out and seek some innocent soul? And you must fetch a hundred such souls before you are released intact?"

Yes. Now the seed buzzed.

"And I will suffer in your place if I do not let you go?"

I will see to it. I will watch from memory all the time. No buzz.

Gale found herself having some sympathy for the demon, to her surprise. But she knew better than to trust it. What conscience did a demon have? This could all be made up, to deceive her, to trick her into unwarranted compassion. That would account for the warnings of the dragon seed. It buzzed for the descriptions of past horrors, but not for the threats to Gale. Carrot and stick, with the carrot not real? "I will not let you go."

The demon's fury exploded again. Literally: it was like being on top of a magic bomb during a celebration, and being blown apart by it. Radiation spiked out, fire surged, and smoke roiled all around. Pain flared in every part of her.

But she hung on, knowing that the demon shared what it made her feel. Sure enough, it soon faded. If the demon had been able to stand much pain, it wouldn't have capitulated to the demand of the torturer. No, that was perhaps unfair; that rape by the hellhound was horrible in ways other than physical pain, though there had obviously been plenty of that too. Gale doubted that she could withstand torture of that nature.

So will you let me go?

She had not tried to shield her thoughts. She would have to watch that. "No."

"Damn!" The fury of the succubus was almost tangible.

Then came a phantasmagoria of more specific nastiness. Gale had to watch as her eyes fixed on a brown woman's body being tied by ropes knotted about each wrist and ankle, connected to harnesses on four oxen, and torn apart with dangling muscles and tendons as the oxen forged outward. As that body, suddenly restored, was dipped screaming in boiling water, the loose feet kicking up to avoid it, until the buttocks could not escape. As a dozen ape-like men swarmed over it and raped every available orifice simultaneously. As it was cut open and disemboweled, one length of intestine at a time. As lightning struck it and cooked it, burned it, blackening the skin and making the lustrous hair frizz instantly off. As a funnel was jammed into its mouth and throat, and water poured in, more and more, until the belly distended grotesquely and burst, spraying discolored fluid all around. As metal hooks caught at its eyeballs, pulling them out and dropping them to dangle from the sockets, and its tongue, pulling it out until it tore free of the mouth. As a burning hot poker explored one orifice after another, sending out gouts of smoke and leaving bubbling black holes. As one horror followed another, overwhelming Gale's imagination, making her sick with abhorrence. She was retching in her mind, heart, and soul, but she could not escape the dreadful visions. The demon was punishing her in the way it could, emotionally, and she could not long withstand the hideous onslaught.

Would she have to let it go? But that would mean loss of her mission, because the succubus would have the power to come and go at will and interfere with any investigation Gale tried to make. She *had* to win, to come through for Havoc. If she nullified the demon, she would be able to accomplish her design and return in good order. Also, she had learned enough about the demons to know that this was a cult or scheme that needed to be dealt with. If she brought the demon back, they might be able to track its origin and go after the torturers, or whatever was really behind it. Whatever knew about her mission. Because that entity or organization was dangerous, and could not be ignored.

But she could not stand the cascading horrors she was experiencing. She had to get away from them—and could not, as long as the demon was with her. She had trapped it, but could not overcome it. She could resist it to a degree, but could not rule it. So they were locked in a sickening struggle, and her gumption was failing. Like the succubus who had surrendered rather than endure further brutality, she seemed bound to let it defeat her.

Then she thought of a way. It seemed far fetched, but maybe it would work. She would try it, and try to think of something else if she had to.

At the moment the woman figure was enduring a penetration of long needles. They were being slowly pressed into her head and body, and through it, until their points emerged on the other side, while she writhed and screamed. Gale focused on the needles, grasping them with her imagination. She reversed their thrust, so that they paused, then started withdrawing, as slowly as they had advanced, until they were out of the body, and no punctures remained.

The demon took a moment to catch on to what was happening, as the vision had not been abolished, merely altered. Then the needles reversed course again, and pressed in toward the body.

But Gale had her next ploy ready. She changed the needles from metal to ice, and made the body hot. As the points touched the flesh, the ice melted, and the needles did not penetrate.

Suddenly the scene changed. The brown woman was chained spread-eagled on the ground, and a six legged tiger was striding near. The tiger started to eat the woman, who screamed and struggled but could not escape.

Gale focused on the tiger, and gradually it shifted, becoming a large house cat. Instead of biting, it licked. It purred.

The scene vanished. Now the woman was lying under a level board, and weights were being piled on the board, crushing her in stages. Gale concentrated on the weights, and they became blocks of foam, very light.

The image changed again. Now the woman's feet were caught in a trap, so that she could not run away, and two huge men with clubs were coming. They lifted their weapons, taking aim at her head and torso.

Gale oriented on the clubs, and they became pillows. The men swung viciously, and the pillows struck the woman. They burst apart, and feathers flew out in clouds. Then, to add insult, the clothing of the men melted off, leaving them naked, and the woman found huge feathers to tickle their crotches and make them dance.

The image was replaced by one in which the woman was on a huge bed, and a satyr was coming at her. She screamed, trying to scramble away, but he caught her and brought his monstrous member into play. It was just as large and urgent as that of the hellhound.

But as the two came together, the satyr metamorphosed into a handsome man, with a member just a bit smaller than average, and perhaps slightly soft. The woman smiled, accepting him as her lover.

So it continued, as Gale countered each horror with a nullification or delight. She could not stop the images, but she could adapt them, and she was confident that her imagination was greater than that of the succubus. It was no longer freaking her out.

Therein lay her victory. The demon had been deprived of its last weapon, and was powerless. It could continue to fight, but could not gross Gale into capitulation.

At last the demon's efforts were exhausted. *What do you want?*

"I want to recover full control of my own body," Gale replied. "And I want control of you, so that I need have no further fear of you, no more bad images, and can use your powers for my own purposes."

But this will destroy me.

"Not necessarily. I'll make you a deal. Cooperate with me, and I'll arrange for decent treatment for you when I return to Triumph City."

I do not comprehend decency. They extirpated that before they gave me the power to see in darkness and sent me out the first time.

"I doubt that. Decency surely remains, but buried under layers of horror. I can't let you go. But maybe I can arrange for you to go to another human host, one you can control. You will not be free—you will be confined to a chamber or apartment—but you will have the body. And be allowed visitors if you wish, such as lusty men."

There was a certain appeal in that, for the succubus, who was a creature of sex. She was weakening. *But I want my own body back.*

"I understand that. We'll go after that torture cult, and try to abolish it, and free its captives. Maybe we can recover your body, and return it to you. Maybe you have some decency or joy left, if you can get away from the torture cult. So you can after all make a normal life. But that's in the future. In the interim, I can not let you return there with news of me. So I won't let you go, but I will treat you fairly—if you let me govern you."

This is a trick, a scheme, a swindle!

"You are thinking in torture culture terms. I am a living human woman, with honor. You can trust me to keep my word. Look into my mind and verify this."

The demon did, and came to a decision. *It is true. You have what I have lost. You are motivated by something other than immediate survival. I agree.*

The dragon seed buzzed. The succubus lied.

Gale did not accept either agreement or lie at face value. "I have you trapped. If you renege, and try to govern me again, I will fight you, and I think beat you again, because now I have done it I know how. If I have to do that, our deal is ended, but you will remain my captive. So it behooves you to follow through honestly, even if you have no honor of your own."

The demon considered. *Yes.*

This time the seed was silent.

"Then yield me your name and control points."

I was Swale before I was taken by the demon cult.

"Swale? What does it mean?"

A small dip in the ground. My brother is Berm, a raised earthen area. I haven't seen him in some time. I miss him.

"That's interesting, Swale. I recognize you now as an enslaved woman, rather than a demon. Now yield."

The strength of the spirit faded, and Gale was able to recover full control of her body. Swale retreated to her nest in Gale's womb and offered no further resistance.

Gale opened her eyes. She remained bound hand and foot, and the ropes chafed where her body had fought them. There was also a gag on her face, passing inside her mouth to prevent her from biting her tongue. She could not speak aloud.

But Lad was there, watching her. When he looked at her face, she met his gaze, and winked.

"Gale!" he exclaimed. "Are you back?"

She smiled around the cloth.

He undid the gag and cleared her mouth. But he left the rope that circled her neck, holding her head down. She worked her tongue around, restoring moisture to her mouth, then cleared her throat and spoke. "I beat the demon, and am back in control. Thank you for watching over me."

But he remained cautious. He untied only one hand, leaving that arm bound at the elbow. "Touch me."

She raised her hand and touched his arm. She gave it a squeeze. "The succubus remains with me, but now I control her. You are in no further danger from her, Lad."

He relaxed visibly. "Oh, Dame, I could kiss you!"

"Then do it while I am safely confined," she said, with another smile.

Half to her surprise, he did. He kissed her very carefully, gently, on her mouth. "Oh, Dame," he breathed. "If you had lost—"

"I could not afford to do that."

He untied her remaining bonds, and helped her sit up. She stretched. She ached in many places, and would need balm for her chafes. But she seemed whole. She tried to stand, but lost her balance and had to sit down again.

"I will steady you," he said eagerly.

"Thank you, Lad."

He gave her his elbow, and she held on and managed to stand. After a moment she caught her balance, and was able to take a few steps. She hurt, but that would pass.

"We'd better tell the men," he said. "I'm just so glad that you—"

"So am I, Lad."

Thereafter she bathed and applied balm, and did some limbering exercises, and retired for the remainder of the night. She held Lad's hand, because he was hesitant to take hers, considering the restriction of the succubus.

That made her wonder: why were the demons limited like that? Why couldn't they enter men as well as women, or seduce men by touching them? That would surely be more effective. So she asked, internally: "Swale, why are you limited to women?"

That is the way of it for all. Gender is overwhelmingly important. If your spirit left your body, it would be able to touch only the bodies of women, and not to infuse them. Only the magic of the demon cult lends us the power of infusion.

"But once you are in a living woman, you don't have to infuse a man. Why can't you touch him?"

Even touching is infusion, to a degree. My female spirit can't even attempt such contact with a man. All it can do is hold the female body in place and let the man touch it. This makes the capture of a male spirit far more difficult.

"How can you take the male spirit, when you can't even touch the body?"

It associates with the life force that emerges from his member. In that moment, before the soul divides, it is possible to trap it and draw it free of his body. Normally only a part of it is left in the woman, to colonize the baby he sires in her, but we take it all. We have been given magic to enclose it and secure it; we can't touch it directly.

That seemed to cover it. "And the male spirits—they are similarly limited?"

I believe so. There is a separate facility for the incubus. I understand a male spirit must be extremely seductive to get a living girl to not only touch him, but to give of her spirit, so that he can take it. It is that portion of her soul intended for the baby she makes, that he catches and uses to draw out the whole of it.

"So an incubus will not actually rape a living woman?"

He can't. Except by deception, prevailing on her to initiate the act while he remains still. Then when she experiences the joy of union, he takes her soul in through his member.

Gale filed that information away for future reference; it could be useful. A woman with her wits about her needed to fear rape only by a regular man, not an incubus. Which suggested that at time she might even prefer the company of the incubus. A curious inversion.

Her curiosity satisfied, she settled back to sleep.

Next day she was stiff, but was able to work much of it out while traveling. She hadn't felt any of this incidental battering while fighting the succubus, because Swale had had control of her body. That gave her an idea. "Swale, can you give me relief from physical discomfort?"

Only by taking over your body.

"Can you do that without taking over me?"

If I assume only that control required to move your limbs without opposition by you.

"Try it. Use my limbs, but not my head."

Swale spread out and took over Gale's legs and arms. This discomfort faded. Now she was walking without feeling it. This was a fair improvement.

Thank you for giving me this amount of freedom.

"You don't mind doing my walking for me?"

I crave my body back. This gives me some of the feeling, without the constant stress of focusing on a target man.

"But don't you feel the discomfort?"

I revel in it. It means I am alive again.

This looked promising. Thereafter Gale experimented further, and found that there were a number of routine physical chores that Swale was glad to do. When it came to the play, the expertise of the succubus was invaluable; she had a touch Gale envied.

"You must have learned from the demon," Leader remarked later. "I thought I saw her again, in that dance."

"You did. But I am in control."

He frowned. "Is this safe? This is no innocent creature."

"It is a risk," Gale agreed. "But I think I am gaining more than I am risking. The succubus knows now that she has more to gain by working with me than by fighting me. She is not my friend, but her self interest encourages cooperation."

"I hope you are correct. I would rather pet a savage animal."

The troupe performed at several more villages. Between villages, Gale made it a point to get to know more about Swale, questioning her on her background and abilities. This was simple caution, as she wanted no ugly surprises, but it turned out to be interesting.

Swale had been a girl of the Brown Chroma. She grew up to be lithe and beautiful, but she was not good at the Brown specialty of conjuring, and she was not particularly smart. This limited her opportunities both business and romantic. So she decided to make the best of what she had, which was her body, and travel to the capital city of Triumph to become a dancer. It was known that there were excellent prospects for dancers, particularly if they were not stingy with their personal favors.

She had packed her scant belongings and joined a caravan headed for Triumph. She was sixteen; she had two years to make good before she had to marry and start having babies. With luck she would attract a wealthy husband and live well thereafter. She paid in the usual manner of girls with bodies like hers, serving the caravan leader and his key personnel at their convenience, which was often. That bought her not only passage, but good food and often a ride in a wagon, so that she did not have to walk the whole way. It was a novelty doing it while riding, as the bumping and rocking of the wagon lent extra force to the lusty efforts of the men.

Then brigands raided the caravan. The wagons circled and the guards fought off the raiders, but not before some supplies were lost. Swale had been sleeping in a wagon, between appointments at the moment, when it happened. A raider broke in, took one look at her naked exposure, and decided that she would do for his booty. He slung her over his shoulder and hauled her away. Swale was screaming the whole time, but there was so much noise from the raid that no one noticed, if they had even been able to help.

Thus it was that she became the plaything of the raiders. But after a few days they tired of her, and anyway it was their business to sell what they raided, so they sold her on the slave market to the highest bidder, a representative of an obscure cult. He put a necklace on her that robbed her of all volition, and put her in a coach. She had no idea where they were going. When she was taken out it was no improvement: she was chained to a wall in a dungeon.

For several days she hung there, undisturbed, but forced to watch the tortures of other girls like herself. She had no appetite for food, but that didn't matter; they put a funnel down her throat and poured in gruel. She was not released for natural functions, so inevitably let her urine and feces fall to the floor below her. Terrified, she resolved to do whatever the cult leaders demanded of her. But when she finally learned what it was, she couldn't stand it, and tried to refuse. So she too was tortured, by being left there hanging day and night, until at last she agreed to do their bidding.

Then she was taken down, cleaned up, given a cloak to cover her nakedness, and a bunk in a cell to sleep in. There was balm for the raw chafes left by the manacles, and a comb for her hair. An older man came to tutor her in certain basic magic. She knew him only as Trainer. She had lost her powers of magic when she left her Chroma, but these were items of some special kind that worked in nonChroma regions. One was applied to her eyes, and it enabled her to see in darkness. Another she had to swallow, and it enabled her to separate her spirit from her body, so that it could travel through the night to locate innocent boys verging on manhood. Another lodged in her womb, and it enabled her to capture the souls of such boys and carry them away with her. Actually her spirit would enter the womb of another woman, but her spirit had its own womb that would confine the newly-separated spirit of her victim until she delivered him to the storage body. It insulated her from direct contact with the male spirit, enabling her to handle it in this limited fashion.

She was also trained to dance. Not the way she was used to, but in a special fashion that enhanced her sexual appeal enormously. Trainer had exceedingly specific notions. She was slow to catch on to the nuances of it, but encouraged to try her very best, because every time she failed to make sufficient progress, she was put back on the wall to watch some more torture. If she still didn't get it, then she was tortured again, and promises had no effect; she suffered until she fainted. Then, restored, she was returned to the lesson room. Before very long she got very good at the nuances of the dance.

Thus did she become a succubus. But it was never easy. Each morning she was chained to the wall again, to watch more torture, and if there was no mission that day, she remained there, not tortured but not released. The only way to earn greater freedom was to bring in a boy's spirit. She did that, repeatedly, and so her life became almost tolerable. But when she went out on a mission and failed to bring back a spirit, she lost a measure of freedom. Her dedication to her mission became extreme.

Until the present mission. This was by day instead of by night, and failure was tolerated because of the importance of this particular spirit. But she had to keep trying, by day or night, in an effort to catch the boy unguarded and harvest his spirit. It was dangerous because the woman she borrowed was canny, but if she succeeded she would be rewarded with credit for ten ordinary spirits.

But now she had failed. And Gale had the story. Gale still didn't particularly like this succubus, but neither did she hate her, and she had learned a lot.

Then they approached the village of the Temple. There were Temples all around the planet, but it was this small one Havoc had targeted, because it was on the troupe's route, and might be investigated without arousing suspicion. Could she accomplish that? She wasn't sure.

"Do you know why you were sent repeatedly to me?" Gale asked Swale.

No. I have never been sent to the same woman twice before, let alone several times. I think this boy's spirit must be extremely valuable.

"It is, to him. Was there any other directive you were given?"

Only to give you no peace until I got him.

Which would have nicely interfered with Gale's Temple investigation. But Swale had not known that that was the purpose. The torture demons were being canny. Perhaps they had realized that it was risky to attempt repeated invasions of a single woman, so had made sure that no useful information was in their agent.

"Do you know what the Temple is?"

Oh, yes. Women go there to pray for fertility.

"I must explore a Temple. Does this bother you?"

No. Why should it?

Gale decided to take another risk that might yield benefits. "My mission is to find out what's in a Temple, without the Temple priests knowing. In fact, I mean to sneak in by night. Do you care?"

No. Why should I?

"Because I suspect that you were sent to stop me from doing this."

No, I was sent to— Swale paused. *To give you no peace, especially at night, until I got the boy. Especially if you went somewhere at night.*

"Precisely. So I ask again: does this mission of mine bother you?"

No. I don't care about the Temple. But this makes me curious. Why should I have been sent to stop you?

"I don't know. But I hope to find out. Now there are two ways we can do this: you can stay out of it entirely, and maybe if you're lucky I'll get caught and be taken captive and you will be freed. Or you can help me, and take your chances on my gratitude when I return to the city."

Suppose you get killed, and I remain trapped in you? That would kill me too.

"I assumed that if I die, my body can no longer hold you. That is not the case?"

I don't know. I've never been trapped in a body before. But I think I can not escape unless you let me out, and that if you die, I die. Sometimes a spirit did not return to the cult chamber, we think it was because it died with the body it animated. Maybe if a parent caught it seducing a boy, and struck it instantly down.

"You said 'we.' Who else?"

The other tortured women. We talk as we hang on the wall between torture sessions. There is nothing else to do.

That was one grim business. "Well, I don't know either. So you decide whether you prefer to chance my death or help me survive."

The succubus considered. *I will try to help you survive. If you do, you will be more generous to me later. If you do not, the result is the same as it would have been. So it is better for me to help.*

That was rational. But there was a loophole. "If you try to help me, then see an opportunity to betray me, the priests at the temple may reward you."

Yes. But I know you now, and I don't know them. I also don't know whether they would have any influence over the torture cult. So I think you are the better chance.

The dragon seed did not buzz, so she was not lying. Swale saw her best self interest in being loyal to Gale. "Then I will give you considerable latitude, because I think there is significant help you can provide. I believe you said you demons can see in the dark. Is this true?"

I don't consider myself a demon. But yes, I can see in very little light, so I can find my way efficiently. It is part of the package of magic they gave me.

"That is what I thought. They gave you the powers you needed to do your job. That must be fairly simple magic, that can function in fringe areas like this. How well can you see at night?"

Well enough. I never had a problem finding my way.

"Well enough to read?"

I suppose so. I never tried to read. I couldn't handle a book anyway, in spirit form.

"But with my hands, you could."

Swale was surprised. *Yes, I could. But why? I thought you wanted to spy, not read.*

"I do. But suppose they are cheating on their taxes? I will need to read their accounts."

Oh, you are spying for the king! How wonderfully evil.

"Actually it's not their taxes I want to check, but their changelings."

Changelings? What is that?

"All I know is that I'm supposed to find out. To me, a changeling is a baby switched for another, when some mother is foolish enough to leave it unguarded. I think it's mere folklore. Maybe the king's men think there is more to it."

I am actually getting interested. I thought the Temple just answered prayers by women for natural babies. Why should they want to exchange any?

"I have no idea. Maybe that's not what they're doing. Or maybe they are selling changelings for adoption, and not paying taxes on the money. Whatever it is, that's my mission. I don't think I want to talk to any of their priests, so I want to look at their books. Their records, or whatever. But I need to be in darkness, to conceal myself, and very quiet. If you can read without light, that will help enormously."

Let's find out. Put a book in darkness.

Gale tried it. Swale could readily read in the dark, though she was using Gale's eyes, when Gale could see nothing. A little magic worked wonders. They agreed that Swale would read silently to Gale, at her direction. This was looking considerably more promising.

But something nagged at Gale. That stray dragon seed buzz—always when Swale described her past treatment by the torture cult. Obviously the horrible visions derived from that experience; they were too real to be made up on the spur of the moment. Yet something was wrong with them. The seed's warnings might be tricky to interpret on occasion, as they could indicate a direct or indirect lie, a danger, an attempt to read her mind (which was really a type of danger), or just a general wrongness in the situation. That was the problem with a device of very low magic power or definition. But the seed was never wrong. There had to be something, if she could only find it.

As she walked, Gale pondered, reviewing what she had learned from the succubus. The buzz did not seem to indicate immediate danger, and its timing suggested that it was something in the dialogue that triggered it, not a mind reading attempt. Swale wasn't challenged at other times, so seemed to be telling the truth as she knew it. Why should she lie about her past horrors while visiting them on Gale? This left the categories of general wrongness, and the indirect lie. The two might be the same, in this case: there was something wrong with what the succubus said, only the succubus didn't know it.

Then, suddenly, an explanation burst upon her. Gale took time to work it out by herself, then braced the spirit. "Swale, you suffered horribly before you agreed to become a succubus?"

Yes. The seed buzzed.

"I think you didn't. Not directly."

How can you doubt? I showed you what they did to me and the others.

"Yes, you showed me. It seemed horribly real. I feel guilty for doubting." In fact she would not have doubted, had it not been for the dragon seed. "But consider this: couldn't the torture cult have made those images as real for you as you made them for me?"

I don't understand. No buzz.

"Can you tell the difference between what actually happened to you, and what you remember happened to you?"

But they are the same. Now there was a buzz. Gale knew why: because Swale's memories did not accord with the truth.

"Let me describe something, and you see whether it could be true. Suppose a cult needed the cooperation of a person, but had very little power or magic. So it pretended to have much more of both than it did. Suppose it had the power to implant memories of horrible things."

Swale was taken aback. *My memories of torture aren't real?* And there was no buzz.

"Yes. And maybe there are no other beautiful women being tortured. Only your memories of them. You may be the only succubus."

But that can't be! The seed buzzed.

"It can be, Swale, and it is. Think: how could a woman have her breast cut off one day, and be perfectly whole again the next day? Even the strongest magic healing can not re-grow a breast that fast. How could you be tortured to the point of unconsciousness one day, and have no marks or pain the next day? How could your hair be burned off— and suddenly restored? Magic can make hair grow, but not two feet in eight hours. But you could have memories implanted, and never doubt that what they contained was real. You thought you had been horribly tortured, and thought you had capitulated. So next day, rather than go through that again, you surrendered immediately. It made sense."

It made sense, Swale agreed. *But still—*

"And consider this: if there are a number of succubi going out, why did they keep sending you on the same mission? When you failed the first time, why didn't they try another succubus, who might have better luck? When you didn't return, why didn't they send another succubus to check on you?"

I don't know.

"Because they don't *have* any others! You are the only one. All the others are creatures of your memory. Repeat after me: you are the only one."

I am the only one.

The seed did not buzz. That was the final confirmation. What Gale said couldn't make the seed buzz, but when another person repeated her words, the seed called true or false. "That's why they require you to bring in so many souls," Gale continued. "Because they need them for incubi, who can then fetch in more female souls. In time they may amass a formidable demon contingent. But at present, there is only you."

There is only me, Swale repeated, and again there was no buzz. *It could be.*

"Indeed it could be." Gale knew now that it was so, but didn't care to reveal how she knew; the dragon seed was her secret forever. "And if that is the case, you have much less to fear from the torture cult than you thought. Your chances of returning to a normal life are that much greater."

Yes! Swale agreed, beginning to believe.

That was enough. Gale simply needed to know the truth, in case it affected her mission. But it wouldn't hurt if the succubus developed a genuine loyalty to Gale.

They arrived at the village, and spent the night, as usual. Gale did not discuss her mission with the others; they all knew that they might be overheard.

In the morning they put on the play, and the village children were as appreciative as ever. In fact, there were quite a number of adults present, too. "I think word has spread that we've got a really fine show," Leader murmured with satisfaction. "And a really beautiful Dame."

Gale wanted to demur, but knew that he was right. The proportion of adult men in the audiences had been growing. They behaved well, but paid quite close attention to the Dance of the Succubus.

Gale and Lad spent the day being spot celebrities, answering the usual questions, and assuring the children that no, they did not have sex in private, either. After all, there might be a succubus nearby. If only the villagers knew how true that was!

When night fell, Gale slept as usual. "But wake me in two hours," she murmured to Lad. "Silently."

He nodded. Two hours later he squeezed her hand. She got up, quickly dressed, and stepped out. He wanted to go with her, but she blocked him, silently demurring. She needed him to cover for her here, so that no one would know she was gone. He knew what to do, as they had discussed it once: he would lie there and picture her lying beside him, holding his hand. He would pretend as ardently as he could, as long as he could. Because if someone read his mind, that loud thought would provide her with an alibi.

She left the house and made her way out of the quiet village. The Temple complex was separate but within half an hour's walk. The Temple property was within the fringe of a Blue Chroma, which meant it had the use of magic, though not strong magic, because the intensity faded with distance from the volcano. Still, this was an additional aspect of the challenge.

Now Swale's night vision helped greatly. They shared her eyes, so that the succubus' ability seemed to be Gale's own. It was a novel experience. Gale avoided the main path, and made her way along a lesser trail through the forest. There might well be danger here, but this was part of her protection, paradoxically: the temple would not expect an invader to come this way. They might not realize that this woman had experience with wilderness paths.

She didn't even dare hurry, because that could attract attention of one sort or another. She tried to keep her thoughts buried, so that the enemy mind reader would not identify her. She tried to keep her feet silent, so that no predator animal heard her. Fortunately this was an established, if minor, path, so there were few aggressive plants. Just enough to explain why it was not well traveled, which made it suitable for her. She was wearing a blouse that was loose around her arms and snug at her wrists, and trousers that were similarly snug at her ankles. This was to protect her from the incidental attacks of nettles, thorns, corrosive juices, and similar mischief of the wilderness.

You know how to handle plants Swale noted.

"Yes. I'm a barbarian girl." The terrain was gradually turning blue. Gale's only Chroma experience had been with yellow, red, and green, but this didn't make much difference to her; all Chroma were essentially hostile territory to a nonChroma person. Of course Mentor was blue, but he was an individual dragon, not relevant in this case.

When I was free, I thought barbarians were stupid.

"Not all of them. There's a difference between ignorance and stupidity." That was one of Havoc's favorite sayings.

So I see. I never thought you would fight back, let alone capture me.

"Then we're even: I never thought a succubus would lay siege to me."

If they sent me to stop you from spying on the Temple, they must know who you are and where you are.

"Yes. This was something I hadn't counted on when I first set out on this mission. But I must nevertheless make the attempt." Gale paused, then decided to make a promise: "If I am caught or hurt, and can't get away, I will free you from my body, so you can return and report that you stopped me."

Why?

"Because it's the decent thing to do. No need to take you down with me."

But you owe me nothing unless you succeed.

Gale smiled in the darkness. "Maybe that's what makes it decent."

Maybe I would have understood that, once.

The perimeter fence loomed ahead. The path turned aside, but Gale did not. She made her way to the fence and surveyed the situation. The fence was made of woven blue hardwood sheets, opaque and strong. It was about eight feet high and topped with a strand of blue stingvine. That made it formidable. But Gale was encouraged, because it was a mechanical barrier rather than a magical one. She could handle it.

If you try to poke through it, they will know.

"I think if I even touch it, they will know. So I won't touch it."

Gale unwound her belt and formed it into a twenty foot pole. Then she lifted the center and raised it as the pole formed a hinge at that point. When it was vertical, she crossed the two legs of it and spread them until they lay on the ground again. It was awkward, but feather light; her main problem was keeping the legs oriented so that they didn't suddenly bend the wrong way. Finally she had her stiff A-frame, with the legs joined by a tight downward loop at the apex.

Now she had to place it over the fence. This was a challenge, because the A-frame as she had made it would not keep its legs stiff when she changed its orientation.

What are you trying to do?

"I'm trying to set this A-frame over the fence without touching the fence."

I don't think it can be done.

"It has to be done." Gale wished she had thought out this aspect before. She just hadn't properly visualized the challenge. The problem was to keep pressure on the end of the frame that was to pass over the top and lodge on the ground inside the fence. Without such pressure, the pole would simply start curling down.

Finally she searched the local forest and after a longer delay than she cared for, found a dead blue sapling that would do. She used this to lodge against the end of the frame, pushing it outward until it was at right angles to the near leg. Then she moved this awkward structure toward the fence. But she couldn't get close enough to drop the far leg over the fence, without banging into the fence.

She gave up on that and looked for another way. She saw a large blue tree growing close to the fence, and one of its branches crossed over the fence. Maybe that would do it. She could climb the tree, pick up the A-frame, and drop it over. Except that the legs would curl when she let go of it.

Why do you want to put the A-frame over the fence?

"So I can use it as a stile, to climb over the fence without touching it."

Why not just climb the tree and drop off the branch, inside?

Gale paused. She had missed the obvious! Furious with herself, she rolled up the stilevine, returning it to belt status, and climbed the tree. This was easy to do; she was athletic, and had climbed trees all her life. She followed the branch over the fence, then lowered herself until she hung by it, and finally dropped to the ground. She landed carefully, experienced in this too. She was as much concerned with any noise she might make as with her bodily health.

Now she was inside. She used her wax to mark her hands, feet, and face, giving her the temple odor. She set off for the Temple, not yet in sight. The blue continued to intensify; all the vegetation and exposed dirt was that color.

There was a sound. *Dogs!* Swale thought.

"They should recognize me as a person of the Temple," Gale said. But she felt a chill. This wasn't a sure thing.

Two blue six legged hounds bounded into sight. They were only half Gale's height, but each was more than her mass, and they had large blue teeth. Gale stood, waiting for what might be, hoping that the wax ploy was as good as it was supposed to be.

It was. They sniffed her, not recognizing her personal scent, but knowing that the smell of the Temple was on her. After a moment they moved on, satisfied.

You have more nerve than I do.

"We all do what we have to."

She saw the dark blue structure of the temple looming ahead. This was the largest challenge, because she did not know its layout or the schedules of its priests. She would have to step very carefully.

It was by now quite late at night, and it seemed that the temple personnel had retired. No lights were on. But that did not necessarily mean that all of them were asleep.

Gale walked around the building, inspecting it carefully. There was the big front entry, securely closed. There were several side doors, also closed. And there was a kitchen door, readily identifiable by the pile of food garbage nearby. It was propped open.

Gale stared at it. How could they be so careless? Unless they were anticipating no intrusion, and completely off guard. So that a foolish kitchen worker had opted for convenience when he had to carry several loads of garbage out, so had propped the door, and then forgotten about it.

Or it could be a trap.

Well, she could test that. She walked toward the door.

What are you doing? Swale demanded. *Even I would not enter a door my enemy opened for me.*

"One way to verify a trap is to spring it," Gale said. She kept walking.

She reached the door, and the seed did not buzz. So this was legitimate carelessness, not a trap. Relieved, she stepped inside.

There could be guards waiting to pounce.

Gale knew there weren't, because the seed had given no warning, but she didn't tell the succubus that. "I'll keep careful watch for them."

The kitchen was deserted. It had shut down for the night. It remained fairly warm from the ovens; possibly the open door was to let out the heat. Gale didn't touch anything, not wanting to leave any avoidable evidence of her presence. The fact that everything was blue reminded her; she had always been careful about touching Chroma things.

But she had to touch a door to escape the kitchen area. She reached slowly for the handle. The seed did not buzz. So she took hold of it, turned it, and slowly opened the door.

Beyond was a hall. Where did she need to go? She wished she could have had a map of the temple complex. But it seemed that every Temple was different, and subject to frequent changes, so no one map would do. She had to find what she wanted herself.

What she wanted was the Temple records. They should be in a library or the equivalent. That was the room she needed to find. Where should it be? She judged it should be on the ground floor. She would just have to search until she found it.

She walked down the hall. Swale's night vision was invaluable; she could see every door. Several were marked: KITCHEN behind her, DINING ROOM, LOUNGE, LAVATORY, and so on. And one was labeled LIBRARY.

She tested the blue doorknob, received no buzz, and opened the door. The library was small but well ordered. There were a number of categories, with books and scrolls on their shelves. Which one did she want? She had to be efficient, because she had perhaps two hours before she should make her escape.

Something moved. She froze, startled. The seed did not buzz, so there was no immediate threat, but why was anything moving here?

She oriented on it. There was what appeared to be a nest, and lying in it was a blue creature.

A pet?

It lifted its head and oriented on her. It looked like a monkey. It must have been sleeping, and woke when she entered. It used the knuckles of two hands to rub its eyes, blinking. Still no buzz from the dragon seed, so the blue monkey must be harmless.

I saw one of those once, Swale thought. *A book fetcher.*

"A blue monkey fetches books?"

Sure. Blue is the animal Chroma. They are awful good with animals.

Gale began to understand. She addressed the monkey, and spoke aloud. "Changelings."

The creature scrambled out of the nest, jumped to the floor, and bounded along an aisle between shelves. It stopped, balancing on four hind legs, its front pair pointing to a part of the shelf.

Gale followed, and looked. There it was: a shelf labeled CHANGE-LINGS.

"Thank you," she said, and patted the blue monkey on the head. It was clearly pleased.

She contemplated the books. There were several, and they were large tomes. This was almost too much information. Which book would lead her most directly to what she needed to know? Part of the problem was that she didn't know what she needed to know.

Maybe try the monkey again, Swale suggested.

"Nature of," Gale told the monkey.

It pointed at a volume. ORIGIN & NATURE OF CHANGELINGS. That should do. She took it down, carried it to the nearest desk, sat down, and opened the tome. The print was clear despite the darkness; the succubus' ability was wonderful.

She turned pages, finding her place. Soon she learned that the origin of the changelings was unknown. They were delivered by anonymous coach as tiny eggs in a magic nest that held them in suspended animation. The priests of the temple had learned not to inquire into what should not concern them. They kept the eggs in the nest until they were needed.

Needed? What for?

Further research in the volume produced the answer: Infertile women came to the Temple to pray for babies, for it was abject shame to fail to bear and raise four children. Such prayers were answered quite specifically: such a woman was ushered into a special chamber, put into a dream state by blue mist, stripped of her nether clothing, and a fertility surgeon implanted a changeling egg in her womb. It was simply a matter of using a thin flexible tool to insert the jelly capsule containing the egg; once in the right region, it dissolved and the egg took root. A year later the baby changeling was birthed.

A year? Swale wondered. *Isn't normal gestation three quarters of a year?*

"That is my understanding. These evidently take longer."

Gale learned that it was important for the women not to know that they were pregnant with changelings. They were encouraged to believe that normal sexual relations had generated the baby, as the result of the blessing of the Temple.

Gale sat back, experiencing a rush of mixed feelings. Her own mother had prayed at a Temple in the Green Chroma, the year before Gale was born. Apparently that was a precautionary measure, to make sure she would be fertile and have a healthy baby. The priest had assured her that would be the case. Now it seemed that faith might have played no part in this, and that the priest had not been guessing. *Gale's mother could have been pregnant when she left the temple.* With a changeling. Gale.

You poor woman.

"How could I be a changeling?" Gale asked, horrified. "I don't even know what they are."

It could be sex with your father, three months thereafter.

"My father was on a two month trip to another village at that time. My mother pretended that he returned to see her then, but he couldn't have. I thought I was premature."

Were you small at birth?

"No."

But you are human, and a nice person.

"I can't be a changeling!" Gale said, anguished. But doubt remained. Whatever the changelings were, she could be one of them. This was an astonishing coincidental turn of her investigation.

Gale had been the only natural child in her family. Her three siblings had been adopted. This suggested that her parents had not been able to conceive naturally. Further evidence that she herself was unnatural.

Do they keep records of impregnations?

Good idea! "Records," Gale said to the blue monkey.

Soon she had the tome. It claimed to list all the implantations performed by the Temple. It was alphabetical by year, and covered the planet. She looked up her mother's name for seventeen years before. And shuddered with relief. It wasn't there.

But what about eighteen years ago? Swale inquired like a bad conscience.

Of course: she had forgotten the year of gestation. She checked there—and found her mother. One year before Gale was born. She had been implanted with a changeling.

Then Gale had a horrible notion. She looked up Havoc's mother, nineteen years before. She was listed. Havoc was a changeling too.

Desperate, she made a wild stab, and looked up King Deal. The name and age of the king was taught in all schools, so she was able to get the correct year. And he was there.

This was becoming like a weird dream. She looked up several other mothers in the village of Trifle, and they were not there. She and Havoc seemed to be the only ones. Then she looked up Ennui, trying several years because she wasn't quite sure of her age. But she had no luck there, because it was the mother's name she needed, and she didn't know that. Still, what she had learned was quite enough to leave her permanently unsettled. No wonder King Deal had been curious about the changelings; he must have discovered that he was one of them, and wanted to know more about them. But was that reason for him to be killed?

She didn't have much time left, if she was going to escape safely. She read further in the original volume, and learned that the changelings were crafted to vary in appearance, but to have the common traits of high intelligence, excellent body and health, an inbred sense of honor, and to be attractive in personality and manner, once they came of age to reproduce. Male changelings tended to be highly appealing to women and liked by male companions, and female changelings were typically beautiful, and readily cultivated the interest and love of the men they associated with.

Gale sat half stunned. This was a perfect description of Havoc and herself. He could charm any girl into letting him Peek and Touch, Gale included. And she, as she matured, had had similar power over boys, and men too; she had seen men looking wistfully at her, surely wishing they were free. The two of them had remained true to each other in significant part because each was most attracted to the other. But also in significant part because they had made the oath of betrothal, and had strong personal honor. Both Havoc and Gale were far smarter than they let others know, because they preferred to avoid resentment. They had played complex games of riddles and analogies, which no others in the village would have fathomed. They understood each other in ways others did not.

"We really are changelings," she murmured, giving up her effort to resist the notion.

I know King Havoc only from your thoughts, but I think if I had been sent to seduce him, I would have fallen in love with him instead.

"Probably so," Gale agreed. "He has that way with women." Even several grown village women had considered asking him to sire their fourths, despite his youth; only quick and careful sidestepping on his part had dissuaded them.

Then Gale marshaled her thoughts, put aside her feelings, and returned to her research. She had to find out *why* the changelings were being seeded into the human population. Then she would have a report for Havoc that would surprise him.

The blue monkey had been resting on the floor beside Gale. Suddenly it perked up. Gale listened, and heard footsteps in the hall outside the library. Someone was coming!

She started to go to a corner to hide, but realized that she had the books laid out on the table, a sure giveaway of someone's presence. She dashed back—and the library door opened. She froze, hoping it was just a careless spot check by a night watchman. But then the lights came on, glowing pale blue, and she was exposed.

A blue priest was standing there staring at her. In a moment he would raise a commotion.

I can distract him.

Gale let Swale do it. She danced, making her body move in the erotic way. The priest watched, his mouth open, his alarm evidently shifting into intrigue. He was an older man, blue bearded, but not so old as to be beyond fascination by a succubus.

I'll get close. Then you bash him. I can't touch him.

They danced around the table and toward the priest. His eyes followed every movement. The shirt and trousers weren't as good as a skirt would have been, and not in a class with nudity, but the body and motions were there, and they held the man's attention.

They got close, smiling alluringly. Close enough. *Now!*

Gale swung out with one hand, to chop at a nerve complex in the neck. But her hand bounced off without touching his flesh.

"Blue magic," the priest said calmly. "You can't attack me. Didn't you know that?"

She was fairly caught. But maybe she could lull his suspicion, then break for the outside. "No. I'm nonChroma."

"Will you accept my word that you can't escape?"

The dragon seed did not buzz. So much for that. "Yes."

"Then let us be seated and talk."

They sat at the table with the books. "I am Booker, the head librarian of this particular Temple unit."

"I am Dame Teacher of the Educational Tour. You knew I was here?"

"Of course. We of the Temple are not entirely obtuse. Anyone who enters the compound is tracked, and of course the dogs reported the details."

"But they're only animals. They accepted my smell."

The priest lifted a small object like a whistle to his mouth. He blew, but there was no sound. Yet in a moment there was a pounding as the two dogs came charging in. They pushed open the library door and came to sit by the table.

"Please identify this young woman," Booker said.

One blue dog opened his mouth. "She climbed the tree overgrowing the fence and dropped in. She applied wax to deceive us. She appears to be from the cast of the troupe now playing at the adjacent village. She is not alone."

The priest lifted a blue eyebrow. "She has a companion?"

"There is the smell of a succubus, though the woman is human. We believe she carries a spirit with her."

The priest nodded. "This is unusual."

"She does seem to have special powers," the dog agreed. "She knows when you tell the truth."

"Don't I always?"

Both dogs and the monkey dissolved into laughter.

Booker shrugged. "It seems you can't deceive a blue animal."

"It seems I did not," Gale agreed. "I thought the dogs were normal."

"They are normal Blue Chroma animals."

"Gee thanks," one of the dogs said. "We thought we were unique."

Booker smiled. "Blue Chroma specializes in animals, and ours are specially trained. Part of their training is to emulate ordinary dogs when encountering foreigners." He squinted at Gale. "Just as yours is to emulate an ordinary woman when encountering strangers. Need I draw any further parallel?"

Gale ignored the implication, which was quite accurate. "Why did you let me enter unchallenged?"

"My dear, we were curious as to your business. We assumed you were a tax spy for the king. We feared you would kill yourself rather than reveal your mission if questioned, so we let you pursue it unchallenged. But you surprised us. You merely desired information about your origin."

So he didn't know everything. "Yes."

"She is not being entirely candid," a dog said.

Booker smiled. "Do you care to rephrase, Dame?"

"I sought information about the changelings."

This time the dog did not object. Apparently it could serve in the manner of the dragon seed, spotting untruth.

"For whom?"

The truth seemed best. "The king."

"But the king can have this information for the asking. Why didn't he query us directly?"

Gale did not try to mask her surprise. "After all the trouble you went to to conceal it, you say the king can have it?"

"Conceal it? I do not understand."

"The succubus!" she flared. "Why send the succubus to stop me, if you have nothing to hide?"

Booker shook his head. "We know nothing about a succubus."

She stared at him. The seed had not buzzed. "Then who sent it?"

"I have no idea." No buzz.

For the moment, Gale was at a loss for words.

"She believes you," the dog said. "But she is amazed."

"I confess to being surprised myself," Booker said. "You evidently captured the demon, which I should have thought would be beyond your power, without magic. How did you do it?"

"I stuffed Sulvan seaweed into my cleft."

Both dogs collapsed into laughter again, and this time so did the priest. "Oh, what a simple device!" he gasped. "Common cleverness, instead of magic. Delightful. But surely it wasn't that simple."

"I had have certain differences to work out with her," Gale said. "But we have come to an understanding."

"Giving you the power to dance in a remarkable manner. I watched for some time, appreciating what you had accomplished." He nodded. "I think the changelings are improving, and that you are the best yet. How did you acquire the power to detect truth? That is not inherent."

Gale shrugged, not venturing a direct lie in the presence of the dogs.

It didn't help. "She has a dragon seed," a dog said.

"A dragon seed! How did you get that?"

"I prefer not to discuss it."

"Why not? It's a remarkable accomplishment."

Gale was silent. This trio was prying out all her secrets, but maybe she could stonewall them.

"She does not trust your discretion," a dog said.

Booker frowned. "I am not your enemy, Dame. I harbor nothing but good wishes for all changelings. You have achieved things I thought beyond the power of any changeling. I would like to know how, so as to guide our placement of future changelings."

Gale still didn't trust this. This man was too canny, and if he was not her enemy, neither was he necessarily her friend. "At this point, I want just to return to my troupe."

Booker glanced at the dogs. "How best to proceed?"

"Negotiate with her."

The priest returned to Gale. "You heard. You have information we desire. Do we have something you desire?"

"Yes. Complete information on the changelings, and the granting of my freedom."

"Done. We will exchange information, satisfying each other, and then you will depart quietly the way you came, finish your tour, report to the king, and neither party will betray the interests of the other." The seed did not buzz. In fact, it hadn't buzzed throughout the entry into the Temple complex. Was it still functioning?

"Tell me a lie," Gale said.

"After I agreed to tell you the truth? I don't understand."

"To test the seed," a dog said.

"Oh. We already know whatever you might tell us."

The seed buzzed.

"Thank you. I agree to your deal."

"She commits," the dog said.

"Good enough. Who starts?"

"I will. When I was young, my friend and I came across an in-jured blue dragon. We made an oath of friendship with him, and then fed him and helped him recover. He gave us the dragon seeds, and taught us about magic and all else we might need to survive. Now my friend is king, and I am on a mission to learn about the changelings, because we suspect the prior king was killed because he was investigating them."

"King Deal was killed? I can't accept that."

"All true," a dog said.

Booker sighed. "I stand corrected. I must accept that. But you must accept this: we had no knowledge of such a plot, and no part in it. The Temple never conspired against the king or wished harm to him. He was one of ours."

"Yes. What are you trying to do with the changelings?"

Booker paused, evidently considering his answer. "I will answer, but I trust you understand that we do not wish this information to be bruited about."

"I thought that was part of the deal: we keep each other's secrets."

"Precisely. When I said our information was always available to the king, I meant *only* to the king, via some duly authorized emissary."

"Agreed. I am the king's beloved. I will tell only him. I can not speak for whom he may tell."

"We understand each other. We are attempting to seed changelings in all the leading positions of our species, so that they will govern mankind and improve our planetary situation."

Gale stared at him. "You're trying to take over the world? To make the Temple supreme?"

"No. We are not political, and seek no power for ourselves. Only to deliver the power to the changelings, who are superior examples of the species. This project has been in place for several decades, and perhaps is nearing completion."

"You seek no power? You do all this for nothing?"

Booker gestured expansively. "By no means! It is for everything. We truly want the species of mankind to succeed on planet Charm, and to prosper in every way. We want to eliminate poverty, injustice, warfare, illness, and ignorance, and go on to recover our lost ability to travel in space, so that we can achieve the ultimate: colonization of Counter Charm, our sister world." His eyes seemed fairly to shine as he spoke of the Temple's dream, and the dragon seed did not buzz.

"You're a humanitarian!" Gale exclaimed. "A visionary."

"I am. We all are. No one joins the Temple without being one."

"And you think replacing human beings with changelings will be best for mankind?"

"Changelings *are* human beings. Consider yourself: are you in any way inhuman? Do you have any agenda other than what is human?"

"No! And neither does Havoc. But we thought we *were* human. I mean, just like others."

"There you sit, in baggy clothing, disheveled, arguing with me—and yet so lovely I wish I could embrace you. So smart you can learn at a rate impossible to ordinary folk. So determined that you will put your life on the line to accomplish your mission, whatever it may be. You befriended a dragon! You captured a succubus. And your similar friend Havoc is king, and already taking hold in an amazingly competent manner. Tell me about being just like others, you fantastic creature."

She couldn't even blush modestly; everything he said was true. "Then tell me I am completely human," she countered.

"You *are* completely human—in the way that human beings were meant to be. The rest of us are only portions of our potential, and thus have become inferior. You represent that potential. Our physical, mental, and moral ideal."

And the seed did not buzz.

She had come to solve the riddle of the changelings, and learned what astounded her. Her self image, her world, had been inverted. She was faced with the unbelievable, and had to believe it.

No wonder you captured me, Swale thought. *You're in a wilder situation than I am.*

Gale did something that completely surprised her. She wept.

Chapter 7—Minstrel

Back at Triumph, Havoc settled into the routine of kingship with imperfect grace. He was a creature of the wilderness, and did not feel at home with civilization. Gale had not yet finished her tour, so Bijou remained with him. She was lovely and eager to oblige, but she was not, and could never be, the real Gale.

The first night in the king's suite, Havoc tackled that problem. He removed his crown so that they could exchange thoughts. They had been practicing this regularly, along with Ennui and Throe, finding the supposed illness of mind reading to be increasingly useful.

You have done an excellent job of emulating Gale. But now that we are no longer on public display, I wish to know you as yourself. What is your name?

Bijou, Sire. It means a jewel, a trinket.

You are a gemlike girl. I will call you Gale when I speak aloud, but in my mind you will be Bijou. When I embrace you, you will be Bijou.

Oh, Sire! She flung her arms around him, genuinely delighted to be known and embraced for herself.

You know that I love only Gale. But I do care for you, and—

It is enough, Sire. In fact it seemed to be more than enough, if the contagious strength of her passion was any indication. Still, he regretted not being with Gale.

The matters requiring his attention were no better. There was a constant stream of niggling details of governance that Chief was fully competent to handle; but according to protocol, Havoc had to acquaint himself with them and make pronouncements. There were also direct appeals from citizens, for favors, justice, or recognition, that Havoc had to handle personally. These he liked better, as he was helping people directly. But overall, being king was an uncomfortable bore.

There was also the matter of the unknown enemy. The one who had killed King Deal, and tried to ambush King Havoc. Neither he nor any other king was safe until that riddle was solved. He would far rather be out solving it than vegetating here in the huge city.

Why don't you, Havoc? Bijou asked him. He had removed the crown for one of their lovemaking sessions, as they both much preferred it that way. He loved Gale, and Bijou knew it, but in the physical and mental heat of passion, what they had together was undeniably real and intense. So she had read his other thought, and responded.

I have to stay here to be king, he thought. They spoke mentally, because that gave them special privacy. They had discovered that it was possible to lower their mind shields just enough to share their phrased thoughts, and whatever else they wished to, without being open for mind reading by others.

But you could sneak out, the way Gale did, leaving someone else here to impersonate you.

It was as if a great light dawned. He could do that! He grabbed Bijou and kissed her, and felt her answering thrill. This was not sexual, but appreciation for his appreciation. She loved having him happy with her.

Have Ennui set it up, he thought. Because concealment would be better if Havoc himself had no direct hand in the arrangements. Then he put the crown back on, held Bijou's hand, and slept.

Next day Chief had something else for him. "Sire, there is a People's Petition for your removal from office."

"A what?"

"The people fear an autocratic government, so have reserved the ultimate power for themselves. They can present a Petition, and require the Chroma to vote on it, and if seven of the ten do not support the king, he can be discharged. This is one of several devious mechanisms that counter the power of the king."

"Well, bring it on," Havoc said. "I don't want to be king anyway."

Chief smiled. "Not so fast, Sire. If you are dismissed within a year, it must be for cause, and this is dishonorable. But don't be concerned; this one is routine. There is a similar petition every year, or a month from the onset of a new king. The Petition will be presented, and go out to the several Chroma, who will approve or disapprove it. That process takes another month. I doubt that the Chroma will approve it; you have done very well so far. But you need to be aware of the Petition."

"Tell me when it is voted on," Havoc said sourly.

"I will. If the result is negative, there will be a Crown Assessment. That is a more serious matter."

"I'll be concerned about it when it happens."

Meanwhile, Ennui got busy, doing research amidst her expanding contacts, and in due course brought in a minstrel. He was a man about a decade older than Havoc, but of similar physical configuration. "Sire, I am enormously pleased to have been summoned for your personal entertainment," Minstrel said. He glanced at Bijou. "And yours too, Lady."

Bijou smiled. She was pleased with this whole thing, because it was her idea Havoc was following up on. He had her there because he could not read minds while wearing the crown, but she could do that for him, and report later. "We do enjoy a good story," she said, crossing her legs in an appealing way.

Havoc saw the prospects immediately. "Tell me all your tales," he said. "Sing me all your songs. Demonstrate all your routines."

"Sire, that would require several days, and much of what I have is hardly worthy of your notice. I can give you a selection of my best, however."

"No. I want it all. I have time. You will be well treated here while you perform."

"As you wish, Sire. Do you have a preference of type?"

Havoc was about to tell him just to do them in any order, but suffered a pang of absence from Gale. "Start with one about forbidden love." In this case, forbidden by separation, but few tales related poignantly to that.

"Certainly." The minstrel strummed on his lute. "There was once on Planet Mystery a male teacher of considerable competence. His wife had died, and in his loneliness he threw himself into his work. But he overdid it, and suffered a magic virus that put him into a coma. Now you might think that this would be a dull state..." He continued, accompanying his words with music, including special themes for leading characters. Havoc had thought to be bored, but soon related to the story, and liked it very well. Bijou liked it even better, as she informed him passionately later that evening when they were alone.

Minstrel stayed for several days, and delivered his full repertoire. Havoc made careful mental notes, and filed it all away for future reference. But more of his attention was taken assessing Minstrel's style of delivery, and judging the likely effect of his tales on a village audience.

Bijou was a great help. "I like some of those tales better than others," she reported privately, and explained why. "And I think Minstrel is all right. He's honest and means well. I believe you can trust him, Sire."

So Havoc tackled the next stage, once the delivery of stories was complete. "Minstrel, I have another task for you. Can you keep a secret?"

"Sire, I can, if required."

Bijou, reading Minstrel, nodded almost imperceptibly, so that Havoc would know the man was speaking the truth. Actually the dragon seed did that, but he was glad to have confirmation.

Havoc plunged in. "I wish to take your place on tour, and to have you take my place here, as king."

"Sire!" Minstrel protested, dumbfounded.

"I am a barbarian, and I chafe at the civilized royal life," Havoc continued. "I need to have a break from it. So I want you to play the part of me, so that others will not know of my absence. I will return after the first tour, and you may then resume your ordinary rounds, with my appreciation and a reasonable gem or other valuable item from the treasury. I think you have the ability to emulate me, if you choose, and you will have the assistance of the king's key staff members. It should not be difficult."

"But Sire, the—the effrontery of trying to be *you*! I dare not presume—"

"My consort will of course remain to foster the illusion, and support you as necessary." He indicated Bijou.

Minstrel stared at her. She recrossed her legs and smiled. He was plainly overwhelmed. "Sire—not your Lady! Of course she wouldn't—"

"I would," Bijou said. "Of course I will not actually share your bed, for my ultimate body belongs only to the king. But in all overt matters I will be your loving companion, and there will a beautiful woman to share your bed. You will not suffer neglect."

Minstrel was lost. "If this is your true desire, Sire—"

"Excellent. Now let me see you emulate me. Here, you will need to wear the crown."

"The crown!" the man said, aghast. "I could not even touch—"

Havoc set it on Minstrel's head. "You will not even feel it, after a moment. This is necessary not only to present the illusion, but to protect your person and your thoughts from intrusions. We want no illicit mind reader to fathom the secret."

"Yes, Sire," Minstrel agreed, though plainly ill at ease.

"You will have the best clothing, the best food, and the best attention," Havoc said. "It should be a very nice diversion for you."

"But Sire, to pretend to be you—this borders on treason." The man was truly nonplused; Havoc almost thought he could receive his thoughts, though this was not possible while the man wore the crown.

Havoc tried another tack. "It is a service to me. But there is a liability that could cause you to decline. This does have to be of your free choice."

"Liability, Sire?"

"Someone is trying to kill me."

"To kill you!"

"So there is danger. If my unknown enemy believes you are me, he may try to kill you. Of course you will have a competent bodyguard, and the crown will protect you. But there is nevertheless the threat. Thus by impersonating me, you will be protecting me. But I can not ask you to take such a personal risk, when—"

"Of course I will do it, Sire."

Spoken in the manner of a truly loyal citizen. Bijou made a mental laugh. Havoc suppressed his smile. "Still, perhaps I can make it worth your while despite the danger. Let's take you to the bath."

"The bath, Sire?"

"One of the onerous requirements of the kingship is the need to be constantly clean, and to be washed by the mistresses of the bath."

"Washed by women, Sire? They are grandmothers?"

"No. They are freshly nubile girls, who vie for the honor of such service."

"But Sire, I—this would—I would much prefer to avoid—"

"I understand. This was my attitude. They stripped me naked, and I got a great erection, and they washed that too. But if you would like to have one of those girls as your bedmate, she will be more than willing."

Minstrel clearly had mixed feelings about all this. "I will of course do what you wish, Sire. But this seems extremely awkward."

Havoc snapped his fingers. Majordomo appeared. "This man will emulate me during my absence. The household will do its best not only to support his emulation, but to make him feel welcome. Conduct him to the bath, and garb and tonsure him to resemble me."

"And alert Spanky to accompany him," Bijou said.

Majordomo nodded, and conducted Minstrel away.

"Spanky?" Havoc asked. They had agreed not to advertise their ability to read minds unnecessarily, so continued speaking aloud.

She sent him a picture of a voluptuous young woman with an especially well developed posterior. "The new bath girl."

Havoc recognized her. "Oh, *her*. I did not know her name."

"But she knows yours, Havoc." She sent another picture, of the young woman embracing Havoc, strongly tinged with desire.

He laughed. "So you are eliminating the competition by assigning her to Minstrel."

"Of course. And with her in his bed, he will have no thought of me."

"You are more like Gale every day."

"Thank you, Havoc."

Soon Minstrel returned. He looked startlingly familiar. In a moment Havoc realized why: he looked a great deal like Havoc himself. The change of clothing and set of hair accounted for most of it, but his manner had changed too. Now he was emulating Havoc, and he was good at it, as a minstrel could be. He was a decade older, but no longer looked it.

"Great!" Havoc said. "But for now, you will have to practice in private, because I still have things to do. Suppose I send you to the bedroom with Spanky?"

"Great!" Minstrel said, echoing him perfectly.

Bijou went to get Spanky. The girl appeared, fully clothed, and lovely. Of course all the bath girls were lovely; it was part of the requirement. But he had not before seen her in other than bath attire.

In the next few days, Minstrel perfected his impersonation, and Bijou, as Gale, began accompanying him on trial public appearances. No one noticed the difference. Bijou was sure of that, because she lowered her mind shield just enough to sample the reactions of others, and reported to Havoc. His substitution was in place. Now all he needed was the return of Gale, and they could get away from all this together.

Of course he had his mission: to investigate the murder of King Deal. They had decided to invoke specialized magic to locate the precise place and time and circumstance of Deal's death, to discover exactly what caused him to fall. Minstrel had been heading for a particular area, to take over the practice of a retiring troubadour. Part of this tour was in a Brown Chroma region, and the Brown Chroma specialized in the things of earth, such as conjuring substances and precise location. It would have the magic to pinpoint the spot. Havoc would made a side trip when he was in the Brown Chroma, and try to get the necessary magic.

But that was to a degree a pretext. He wanted to be free of civilization for a while, free to be barbarian. And to be alone with Gale, the one person in this city who truly understood him. He couldn't stop being king, but he could, as Bijou had suggested, sneak out for a while.

At last the glad news came: "She's back, Havoc," Ennui murmured as he passed her desk.

No need to inquire who. "I'll go meet her!"

"No. She has asked for the Lady Aspect to meet her."

"The Lady Aspect! Why?"

"I don't know, Havoc. She's not within mind range. But she surely has reason."

He knew Gale well. "She surely does. Let Aspect do it."

Ennui nodded. She went to tell the Lady Aspect.

Later a servant came. "The Lady Aspect requests the presence of the Lady Ennui in her apartment."

What is going on? Havoc demanded mentally. Minstrel was out with Bijou, making a semi-public appearance, so had the crown.

I'll find out, Havoc. She departed, leaving him to chafe at the mystery. Had something happened to Gale? Surely she should have told him first!

Soon Ennui returned. "Havoc, she will stay with the Lady Aspect, using the room I used before I moved in with Chief."

"But she's with me!"

"Havoc, there is a complication."

"I will see her now." He strode toward the Lady Aspect's apartment.

Ennui ran after him. "Havoc, there may be danger. You must not go to her right now."

"The hell with that! If there's a problem, she can tell me herself."

"Havoc, listen to me."

But he forged on, not slowing.

She hit him with a mind blast. His shield was high, but even so, it made him dizzy for a moment. It was a flash of light and crash of sound combined with a feeling of panic, as if a magic bomb had detonated right behind him. She had never done that before.

He paused, and turned to her. "All right, you got my attention. Am I being an idiot?"

"No, Havoc. There's just an unexpected threat we can't ignore. You must understand it before you touch Gale. Maybe it will be better if the Lady Aspect explains."

"And I'm to stay clear of Gale until she does?"

"Yes, Havoc. Then the decision will be yours."

"Why do I fear that it's a decision I won't like?"

"Because you're picking that up from my mind."

So he was. Something very serious was afoot. He knew he should stop and talk with Ennui, to get straight exactly what it was, before going farther, but he couldn't stop himself. He moved on to Aspect's door.

The Lady Aspect opened it immediately. "Did the Lady Ennui explain?"

"No. I want to hear it from you."

Aspect's eyes did not move, but it was almost as if she rolled them. Her mind was in a kind of impenetrable chaos. "Of course, Havoc. Come in."

He followed her into her main chamber. He saw a backpack there: evidence of Gale's presence.

"Please be seated, Sire."

"Why do I have to—" But a mental warning from Ennui stopped him. He sat.

"Please remain seated as Gale joins us, Sire. Do not rise to greet her until we have finished what we have to say."

Havoc nodded. This was certainly something serious.

Gale entered the room. She was completely familiar, and lovely; there was nothing physically wrong with her. She offered him a brief smile, and sat on a chair across the room from him. But her mind, too, was in turmoil. He could not read her.

"Sire, there are two major things the Lady Gale has to report. Both seriously affect your relationship. I will cover them briefly, and the Lady Gale can amplify thereafter, when you understand the parameters."

"Thank you." He was trying for irony, but there was a current of apprehension. None of these three women were the kind to interfere with him without excellent reason.

"When the Lady Gale went on her mission," the Lady Aspect said, "a demon spirit, a succubus, was sent to intercept her. She—"

"A succubus! Now the demons are after us?"

"No, Sire. This one was captive of what we think of as a torture cult. Its purpose was to prevent the lady Gale from accomplishing her mission. But she fought the demon, and managed to capture it, and to complete her mission. Now she has that succubus with her."

"With her! But they—"

"If you have sex with the Lady Gale, the succubus may abscond with your soul," the Lady Aspect said seriously. "That is why we are keeping her from you, for the moment. We do not wish you to come to harm."

"But if she conquered the succubus—"

"It may be that the succubus was intended to be captured. So as to gain access to you, Sire. We do not think this is the case, but we are unwilling to take the chance."

"Why not just get rid of the succubus?"

The Lady Aspect was for a moment at a loss. Instead, Gale answered. "Because it may be able to lead us to the murderer of King Deal."

"But you can't trust a demon! It may be pretending to cooperate, just to stay with you. So as to be able to spring its trap."

"I don't think so, Havoc."

"Why not? Demons don't operate the way human beings do."

"Because it was the succubus herself who warned me about this possibility."

That set him back. "Why would—?"

"She's not really a demon. She's a human being named Swale who was imprisoned and tortured until she did the bidding of her captors. She wishes to help us destroy the torture cult. But what she does may be involuntary. If I have sex with you, she will no longer be captive, and you may be destroyed. I don't want to risk that, Havoc."

Her sincerity came through. And of course Gale would never try to hurt him. She did not dare have sex with him—or even to embrace him, lest it lead to dangerous passion. No wonder she was so diffident about meeting him. He would have swept her into bed before asking any questions.

"Point made," he said. "What is the other thing?"

"Sire, the Lady Gale has solved part of the mystery of the changelings," the Lady Aspect said. "This was enough to provide serious doubts about her identity, and yours. The changelings are human babies of superior quality, distributed by the Temple to women all over the planet, of every Chroma. They are distributed by being implanted in prospective mothers, so they are not recognized as changelings. There are now several generations of them, and they are achieving prominence in a number of areas. King Deal was a Changeling. So is Gale. So are you."

"But we're human!" Havoc protested.

"But also changelings," Gale said. "We are not the true children of our parents. We are like twins, closely related to each other. And there are many others like us, differing only in superficial details, such as color of eyes and hair and shape of face." She took a breath. "Whatever conspiracy is distributing the changelings, we are part of it, Havoc."

"Like twins," Havoc repeated, numbed. "But twins can't marry."

Now the tears started down Gale's face. "This is the way I understand it, Havoc. I hope I am wrong." But she didn't think she was.

The enormity of the situation was closing in on him. "You mean I can have any woman I want—except the one I love?"

"That seems to be the case, Havoc," Ennui said.

"And I have to continue faking Gale's presence—even when she's here?"

"That may be the case, Sire," the Lady Aspect said.

"And when I can marry—it will have to be someone else?"

"I fear so," Gale said, her tears continuing.

"Damn it! Damn, damn, damn it!" Havoc got up and punched the wall. The pain lanced through his hand as the wood splintered. That helped.

He saw Ennui wince. She felt his pain, literally. That gave him an idea.

"Give Gale the mind reading infection," he said. "Teach her to compensate while I am gone. We can still love each other with our minds."

"With our minds?" Gale asked blankly.

"We have had our own experience, in your absence," Ennui told her. "Some of us can read minds now."

"We can read yours," Havoc said.

Gale thought they were joking; Havoc picked up that thought. But she tested them, imagining an image of a man whose upper half was red, and whose lower half was green: an impossible cross-Chroma figure. "What am I—"

"Red-green man," Havoc and Ennui said together.

The bottom portion turned red. The top half became green—and female.

"Green woman, red man," Havoc said.

"Merged," Ennui added.

Gale, amazed, tried one more.

"A blue dragon," Ennui said.

"Mentor," Havoc added.

"You can do it," Gale agreed. "You can teach me?"

"It's more complicated than that," Ennui said. "But yes, you can acquire this ability. Havoc suggests that you do it while he is away. Then you will be able to share your love mentally, without physically touching. That is just about as good."

"It will take me some time to believe that," Gale said dubiously.

Havoc smiled. He was still hurting, but this promised some relief. "You will have the time." Then, before he was tempted to do something rash, he turned and headed for the door. Ennui did not follow; she had other business to accomplish.

He sought Bijou. "There has been a change," he said. "Gale will not be traveling with me. You will."

"But Sire, now that she's here—"

"How fast can you get ready?"

"I am ready now. But—"

"Then we'll go now."

She read his mind, and stopped arguing.

It was not after all immediate, as there were arrangements to be made at the other end. But in due course Havoc and Bijou were delivered to the Minstrel's new territory. There they talked with the retiring former minstrel, learning details of his route and favored villages. He did not know that Havoc was not the original Minstrel, or that his helper was adapted from another role. They learned that trail raiders were not much of a problem here, because there were no wealthy caravans, and much of the route was around a large lake that was patrolled by boats of several Chroma. So they did not need to join a party for protection; they could go as they were. "No one bothers a minstrel, anyway," the retiring minstrel said. "The people wouldn't stand for it."

Havoc had figured that; it was one reason why he had chosen this role. To outlying or isolated villages, a minstrel was both entertainment and news, and they valued every one. Nevertheless, he had a couple of masked weapons, just in case. Those, and the dragon seed, and his mind reading ability, should get him by.

They donned the distinctive Minstrel costumes: broad, flat, circular hats that shielded them from the glare of the suns. Sectional cloaks that could cover their whole bodies, or just parts of them. Sturdy light boots for hiking. Competent gloves. Rope belts. The whole done in iridescent plaid, the sure signal of a traveling entertainer. But the elements of the costumes were not entirely what they seemed; some of them were concealed weapons. Bijou was untrained in their use, but Havoc would teach her, to a degree, as they traveled. He also carried a strong light staff somewhat taller than he was; he would not care to be without one, when traveling on his own.

They set off walking along a popular trail. Havoc loved it, as he had felt the lack of proper exercise, but Bijou soon tired. She did not complain, but he felt it in her mind; she was a creature of the city, not hardened to distance foot travel. That was the first of what might be many details he hadn't thought of, in his hurry to get the hell away from temptation.

As they separated from the more thickly settled region, traffic got lighter. "I need more exercise," he said. "You need less. I'll carry you."

"But Sire—"

"Don't call me that! Call me Minstrel." He handed her his staff, and put his hands to her shoulder and knee.

"Yes, Minstrel," she said contritely. "I forgot."

"You can go by your own name; no one should know you here. Just keep your mind shield high." He picked her up and carried her.

"I'm sorry you couldn't travel with Gale," she said. "But I love being with you like this."

"I'll always love Gale. But until she's done with the succubus, I can't touch her physically. And until we find a way to change what we are, I can't marry her. So you are what I have, for now."

"I'll try to be as much as you want me to be."

He carried her for some distance, then let her walk some more, then carried her again. It worked well enough. She would toughen up as the tour progressed.

As evening came, they approached the first village of this tour. Children ran out to greet them. "Minstrel! Minstrel!" they cried, dancing around them.

Thus honored, they marched on into the village. This one was nonChroma, but others would be of several Chroma. This was one of the ways Chroma unified with nonChroma, and city with country: everybody loved a good story.

The village headman came out to greet them. "Welcome to Village Quibble, Minstrel. I think I do not recognize you."

"I have assumed the practice of your former minstrel," Havoc explained. "He is retiring, and I am trying out for his route. It may be that next time you will see another new face." All perfectly true.

"Have you new tales?"

"I have new and old tales, Headman. I think you will be satisfied. Does your village have preferences?"

"The children like adventure. The women like romance. Some like mystery. All of us like humor. None of us like to be bored."

"I have all of these, and will try to avoid being boring. Shall I present one tale tonight, and others at intervals tomorrow?"

"Very good, Minstrel. You can make your first presentation while we prepare a banquet."

"Agreed. Suppose I begin with forbidden love?" That was an almost certain winner.

"Does it have sex appeal?"

"Yes. Do you prefer that aspect open or masked?"

"Masked, for this night." The man hesitated, about to say something more, but decided against it. Havoc, however, read his mind: there had been a recent village scandal that had left village sentiment sharply divided. Havoc's suggestion of forbidden love had triggered the memory. An adult male teacher had run off with a young female student, surprising everyone. Half the villagers condemned it, while half appreciated the seeming romance of it. Headman was of the latter school, but felt obliged to stay out of the debate.

Havoc nodded. "Masked, but suggestive."

"Very good, Minstrel. Here is your room."

The room was spare, but had an attached privy and a comfortable bed of good size, piled with pillows. "Oh, I like this," Bijou said.

So did Havoc. "Thank you, Headman. We shall do our best to

please you, as you are pleasing us."

Headman nodded. "I am the next door down. Knock if you need me." He departed.

Havoc's gloom of separation from Gale was wearing off as he addressed the challenge of being a troubadour. He knew he was competent, as he had told stories before, but there was still considerable variance in audiences. He had seen good minstrels fail to relate well, and he had seen poor ones succeed admirably. It all depended on the chemistry of the moment. He wanted to make a good impression on general principles, as well as to abolish any doubt that he was a legitimate entertainer.

"Did you pick up on Headman's gossip?" Bijou inquired as she stripped and washed. She believed in utter cleanliness; it was a mark of her former profession.

"Yes. Teacher and girl. She was too young, so he took her into anonymity."

"More than that. She loved him, and he had lost his wife, but he had to remarry before she came of age for early marriage. So she couldn't have him. So she took him away."

Havoc stood still, appreciating the new perspective. "He didn't do it, *she* did it!"

"We girls have ways," she agreed, coming to strip and wash him. "Who do you think suggested to Majordomo that he did not need to look outside the house staff to recruit a false wife for the king?"

"But you were furious when you learned about the imprinting."

"That was before I remembered the rest of it. I had no right to be angry."

"You let me wade in guilt anyway?"

"It was as close as I could get to love, from you. True emotion."

"You vixen!"

"Now the guilt is mine."

He grabbed her and kissed her. "Let's forget all that. We both do what we must."

"If I could find a way to give Gale back to you, Havoc, I would. I want you to be happy. I never aspired to be more than your temporary mistress. Apart from the imprinting, I mean."

"You are on the verge of becoming my friend, Bijou. That's more."

"I hope so. You're going to do something about that village scandal."

"You know I am. You know the tale."

"My favorite. The first one Minstrel told us."

"You can handle it?"

"I will make it steam," she promised. She was sincere; her mind set was such that he wanted to make love to her that moment.

"Bijou—"

"I will do it, of course, if you wish," she said, caressing his erect penis. "But this time I think we should wait until after the tale, to get maximum effect."

"You are right," he agreed reluctantly. "You are also developing into a considerable tease."

"I like to hold your attention."

He spanked her pert bottom and dressed.

The stage was, as was customary, in the center of the village, with the audience all around. For this tale, all he needed was a chair. It was a simple but he believed powerful story, that should put the villagers in the mood for more.

When the audience was complete, Havoc and Bijou took the stage. Minstrels typically needed no introduction; they took over immediately. Bijou sat on the chair, her eyes downcast, her expression demure. She was garbed as a schoolgirl, looking very young. Even so, she was also very pretty.

Havoc walked around the stage, gazing at the surrounding audience. He wasted no time on explanations; his success would stand or fall on his performance. He knew he had a live issue, because of the scandal; his interest was in fully exploiting it. He would have to keep his mind shield high, to avoid distraction, but would get a notion if the audience reaction was fairly uniform. Bijou would probably pick up more of it, because she did not need to speak.

He lifted his blue dragon scale and strummed a chord. It was one of his treasured belongings, that his father had packed for him when he left Village Trifle. He had never played this during his tenure as king, so as to keep it as a private talent that would not give his identity away when he wished to hide it. As was the case now. The fact was, he was good with this instrument, and its magic made him better; it invoked subtle emotions, enhancing the mood. He had been a bit nervous, facing a new audience, but the scale gave him confidence.

"There was once on Planet Counter Charm a male teacher of considerable competence," he said, strumming again, and felt an immediate surge of response. Oh, yes, he was scoring, thanks to the situation. They thought it coincidence. He had made sure to get the local name for Planet Mystery right, so as not to seem like a foreigner. Such details counted. But mainly, it was the choice of story. "He was highly regarded in the village, and folk believed him to be happy. But he was not. His wife had died recently, and in his loneliness before remarriage he threw himself into his work. He was a very good teacher, and his students prospered. But he overdid it, and suffered a magic virus that put him into a coma." Here the tale deviated from the village scandal, but that was just as well; the semblance of coincidence was best, just as the standard invocation of their twin planet was used to avoid any suggestion that the tale applied to any real people.

He strummed again, beginning to pick out a theme that would be typical of the teacher, for this narration. Not everyone appreciated how much music contributed to a story, but Havoc had learned by observation and study. "Now you might think that this would be a dangerous or a dull state," he continued. "And it was, for a while. Master Teacher spent some time unconscious, as his body fought the virus, and gradually beat it back. But his convalescence was tediously slow, and he spent many days unable to move, even as his consciousness returned. He lost his will to live, for it seemed that he would never have proper control of his body again, and even if he recovered it, what was the point? His wife was gone, and rather than being allowed to mourn her alone, he would be required to marry some widow and make a new and duller life. Fortunately, his students came to his aid, and took turns feeding him, cleaning him, and just watching over him. There was always one of them near, to see that no further ill came to him."

He paused, looking out over the audience. Then he walked to the chair. Bijou got out of it, and Havoc sat in it, letting his legs extend out and his right hand hang down limply. He strummed with his left. "By day they propped him in a chair, so that he would be able to look around, if he recovered enough to do so. It also facilitated feeding. They so much wanted Master to recover, and watched for any signs of it. But his body lagged behind his mind, and though he could hear them speak to him, he could not respond. His eyes were closed because he lacked the physical strength to open them, and if he had opened them, it would have been worse, because he lacked the ability to blink. He could not tell them how well he appreciated their efforts on his behalf. They were showing him that there was at least one reason to live: to resume his work with these good young folk. His own life was perhaps past, but he might yet help some of them toward their brighter futures.

"Then one girl came for her hour with him." As Havoc spoke, Bijou approached his chair, and he strummed a new theme: delicate, appealing, feminine. "'I am here for your physical therapy, Master,' she said. Her voice was vaguely familiar; he knew she was in one of his classes. But without being able to see her, he could not recognize her.

"'I will move your arms and legs and head,' she said. "To keep your body limber, for the day when you recover the strength to move it yourself. I hope this helps.' She knelt before him, and put her hands on his right leg, lifting it somewhat." Bijou did this to Havoc's own extended leg, following his narration. "She flexed it at the knee, slowly and carefully, several times. 'So you will be able to walk again,' she explained. 'I hope you can hear me, Master, so you understand. Your students love you, and want you back. You must recover, so you can teach us again.'

"She shifted to the other leg, and flexed it also." Bijou did so. "She was diligent but gentle, and Master did feel the circulation improving as she moved his limbs. She continued to talk to him as she worked. 'I love you too, Master,' she said. 'As my teacher, and as a man. I wish I could marry you. But I am too young. Even if you cared for me, you could not marry me, because by the time I come of age to marry, you will be married elsewhere. You can not wait for me; our culture does not allow it.'"

As he spoke, Havoc watched the audience. Not with his eyes, for now he had them closed, emulating the part of Master Teacher. It was with the upper fringe of his mind, picking up the dominant feeling. It was strong and almost unified: they were thinking of the errant teacher, and how it might have been with the girl. They were much with the tale.

"Girl got up and took his right arm." Bijou did so. "She flexed it, bending it at the elbow, and at the shoulder, giving it its full range of motion. Her touch was gentle but firm, and his bare arm warmed to it. 'Oh, Master, how I wish I could encourage you to recover! I wish I knew whether there is anything I could say or do to motivate you, to give you more reason to get back your strength. I love you, and would do anything for you, but I don't know how.' Her voice was tremulous as she tried not to cry. Master wished he could reassure her, and dry her tears, but he could not move. Not even a finger, to signal her that he heard.

"Girl did his other arm, and moved his head carefully, and then was done. 'I hope I have helped, Master. I will come again tomorrow.' And she lifted his right hand again, and kissed his fingers. The touch of her lips sent a thrill through him; it was so very much like a lover's kiss. She was young, of course, but her innocent passion was as old as the human species." Bijou kissed his fingers, then set his arm down beside the dragon scale and walked across the stage. He could tell by her footsteps and a peep at her mind that she stopped at the far edge, facing away from him, out of the scene. This was the standard way to signal absence, when all the stage area was open.

"Then she was gone, and the next student was there, to feed him his lunch. But Master's mind was on the first one. Who was she? She had told him everything except her name. She had inflamed his imagination by her tenderness and expressions of love. He tried to picture her as a member of one of his classes, but no image came forth; he could not place her. There were so many students, so many faces, so many voices. He needed more.

"She had said she would come again tomorrow, to try to help him anew. Already he longed for that encounter, for the gentle touch of her hands. He appreciated what all the students were doing for him, but most especially this one anonymous girl, who had not only done her job, but put so much of herself into it. He had never been aware of her in his classes, he was sure, because otherwise he should have been able to fathom her identity, at least to the extent of picturing a face in a chair. She surely was not the brightest student, or the prettiest girl, or a troublemaker, because those he noticed early. She was just a lost identity he surely would never have noticed, but for this blind session.

"Next day, at the same time, she did come again." Bijou turned and walked back across the stage to stand by his chair. He strummed her theme on the dragon scale as she moved, more forcefully than before, signaling her increasing importance. "'Hello, Master; do you remember me? I'm the therapy girl.' Did he remember her! He had hardly thought of anything else. Indeed, her session had charged his imagination, and to a faint extent his body; he could feel the impulses of his nerves forging outward from his mind, laying siege to the dreadful lassitude that possessed his body and limbs. He could not move anything of his own volition, but he knew he was substantially closer to recovery. Because of the incentive she had provided him, by her touch and her caring.

"She worked his legs again, and his arms, and finally his head. He felt her soft, steady fingers across his ears, lifting his head so that it no longer sagged down forward. She made his face look forward, so that he could have seen her, if only he could have opened his eyes. He felt the caressing mist of her breath as her face came close to his. He no longer cared what she looked like, if only he could *see* her for just an instant, to resolve the dire uncertainty that plagued him. *Who was she?* He had to know—yet could not.

"Then her face came very close to his. 'Master, you know I love you. To you I am nothing; I'm sure you have no idea who I am, and maybe you don't care. But to me you are everything, and I would not mind dying if only by that action I could give you back your life. If I could even see one flicker of awareness in you, to know that you know what I am doing here. To have just that much of your attention, for just an instant. But yet I know that if you did, you wouldn't care about me; there's nothing remarkable about me, nothing to make a great man like you ever take note. I will never have your slightest attention, let alone your interest. But I do love you, and I treasure having even this much of you—to touch your hand, to talk to you, even if you can't feel my touch or hear me speak. And so I apologize for what I will do, knowing that you can't prevent it. It's wrong of me, and I hate myself for doing it, but at the same time I can't stop myself. Master, I will kiss you.' And she put her firm young lips to his flaccid lips, and kissed him, and the girl warmth and girl smell of her encompassed him, and he floated."

Bijou kissed Havoc, lingeringly. He felt the mind of the audience, sharing the passion of that gesture. They were into it, wanting Girl to succeed in aiding Master's recovery, and wanting him to open his eyes and see her. Then Bijou drew away, and departed, and he did not need to describe it. He knew she was holding herself a little straighter now, so that her body looked more mature, and her bosom began to show. She was not after all a child, but a nascent woman, with the early yearnings of a woman. Neither was she by any means ugly, or plain, or even ordinary; she was dawningly lovely. Girl into Woman: the audience was seeing it happen. The audience understood that this was not the way Girl looked literally; it was the way Master was coming to see her. She was beautiful to him.

"It was as if her lips had burned his, animating them. His mouth tingled, and there was a hint of firmness returning to his lips. Girl had animated his mouth, to an extent, and his desire to a considerable extent. He did not remember her from his classes, he did not know her name, but he was coming to love her. On the third day she came, he tried valiantly to respond to the exercises she performed on him, to help his legs and arms to move. He could not, but he felt heightened sensitivity, and knew that he was making progress even if it didn't show. He wanted so much to please her, to show her that he did hear her and feel her, and that she was truly helping him, not only physically, but in restoring the rest of his desire to live.

"She went through the ritual, helping his arms and legs, and it went faster, perhaps because of familiarity, but perhaps also because he was able, if not to move his limbs on his own, at least to facilitate their motions for her. She finished with his head, as before. She kissed him again. 'Oh, Master,' she said. 'Probably its just my foolish imagination, but it almost felt as if you were kissing me back, a little, maybe. I wonder whether you are faintly aware of me.'

"Yes, yes, he was! But he could not tell her, however hard he tried. Fortunately she did not depend on his response. 'I am going to assume that you are at least a tiny bit aware, Master, and that possibly I can help you become more aware, and start to recover, if I just give you reason.' She paused, reflecting. 'More likely, I'm just rationalizing, pretending that I'm accomplishing something though I should know better. You always cautioned us against that, Master. I do know better, but my hope is so great that I can't help myself. So I am going to help you to know me, and I will imagine that you care, because even if it has no meaning for you, it does for me.' She took his right hand and lifted it up, and took it in her two warm little hands, positioning his fingers with her own. Every aspect of her touch was a delight, sending tingles along his arm, and evoking answering efforts to make his hand do whatever she wanted."

Bijou lifted his hand, and splayed his fingers, and her touch was exactly like that of Girl. Then she brought his hand to her face. She stroked his fingers across her cheek and nose and mouth. "Girl used Master's hand to explore her face. He could not tell what it looked like, for he had never touched a face in that manner before; it seemed ordinary. He could tell that it was neither fat nor lean; it was average, and young, and smooth. When his fingers crossed her lips, she kissed them. 'Remember that I love you, Master,' she murmured. 'I dream that this is your touch of returning love. I can never have you; I know that. Even if I weren't too young to interest you, you couldn't wait. But at least I have this dream. I can pretend that we are in bed together, and that you are caressing my face, taking joy in my aspect, and it gives me such a wonderful feeling.' But as she brought his hand back up to stroke her closing eyes, he felt the moisture on her cheeks, and knew that she was crying. 'I am crying for very joy,' she said bravely. But it was of course a lie. She was crying for impossible love.

"Then she returned his dampened hand to his body, and departed. She left him in a storm of emotions. Her love was so real, so great, and now he was returning it, *but he could not let her know.* And she was right: even if he recovered soon, he would have to marry an older woman, before Girl came of age. What was he to do? All the rest of that day, and the night, he struggled, willing his healing to proceed, so that he could at least give her some signal. At least open his eyes, to see her and recognize her. His mind and heart had responded to her; why could not his body? And he felt his body returning, charged by the burgeoning force of love, so that the tips of the fingers of his right hand tingled and almost moved. He *was* making progress—but would it be soon enough to catch her, before she finished her therapy and departed and was lost again in anonymity? Even if nothing else was possible, he wanted to recognize her, and let her know.

"Next day she came again. This time she moved through the exercise routine more rapidly, as if intent on something to follow. 'Don't tell,' she cautioned him, surely with a smile. 'I mean to do something naughty today. Maybe because I think it will encourage you to recover. Maybe its because if you could speak or move, you wouldn't let me do it. Maybe because I just want to pretend you want me. Maybe none of the above. Maybe just because I love you.'

"When she completed the exercises, she kissed him, and made his hand stroke her face. 'Now I want you to know that if you ever had any interest in me, I really could give you something interesting,' she said. 'I will show you my bosom.' She untucked her shirt and passed his hand up under it to contact her unbound breasts. They were not large, but they were well formed, and they excited him phenomenally. 'I imagine you stroking me, like this, and brushing my nipple like this, and squeezing like this,' she said. 'Delighting in my body, desiring it, wanting more and more of it. And I give it all to you, for all I want is to give you pleasure.'" Bijou had Havoc's hand inside her shirt, and was giving him her fuller breasts. Because this presentation was masked, she did keep her shirt on, so the audience could not actually see her breasts or his hand on them. But it was quite evident what was happening. Havoc knew what some others did not: that partial concealment could make something even more intriguing than full exposure did. Bijou was reading the sense of the audience, and reacting to it, making motions that generated the greatest interest. Even the children were fascinated; their minds had the added excitement of novelty, for this was newer to them than to the teens and adults. Bijou was, as she had promised, making it steam.

"She pressed his hand between her breasts, so that he could feel her heartbeat. 'Now you know I really am a woman, even if thought to be yet a child,' she said. 'If you could only hear me, and move, and if you wanted me, I would give you all of this. As it is, it is only in my dream. But my love for you is no dream, Master.' Then she drew his hand down and away, and set it on his body, and departed, for her time was up. As before, she left him with raging thoughts. He *still* did not know her identity, but how he wanted her!

"Now at last his recovery was reaching his body. He found that he could move the fingers of his right hand, and his eyelids. Girl had helped him to make the breakthrough; he knew that his progress would be faster now, and that he would be able to use his body again. But he still couldn't talk, or make larger motions. Rather than disturb things, and risk losing her hour, he concealed his progress. Maybe he could open his eyes and see her, next time. Then, whatever happened thereafter, he would know her identity. That was the one thing he had to have.

"She came again, next day. She finished the routine quickly, then kissed him, made him stroke her face, and touch her breasts. 'Today is my last day,' she confided. 'My tour is done, and since you have not made progress, they will end the physical therapy. So I must do it now. It is the only way I will ever possess you, or be possessed by you, my love.' Then she took his hand and ran it under her skirt, stroking it over her firm thigh and buttock. Her flesh was smooth as only the young could have it, and her female contours, however modest they might seem to others, were utterly compelling by this close touch. 'I am pretending that you are making love to me, with nothing held back. I want so much to be yours, all the way.'" And of course Bijou was doing the same with Havoc's hand, and *her* contours were hardly modest. It was all he could do to publicly ignore her, for she was merely illustrating the tale, not trying to seduce him. Supposedly. Actually she was having her fun teasing him unmercifully, in the manner Gale once did. She knew that they had a whole banquet and meeting of villagers to get through. It would be hours before he could get at her infernally tempting flesh for real.

He forced himself to focus on the tale, which was almost done. "Then she formed his hand into a fist with the forefinger extended, and angled it past her scant underwear and up into her warm damp cleft. 'Take me, Master,' she breathed. 'Take the very center of me.' She worked his finger up inside her until his fist pressed against the crease of her buttocks. It was not a deep penetration, but it was enough to inflame his imagination and desire. 'I love you, I love you!' she whispered ardently. And her hot flesh tightened about him. Holding him there, she leaned slowly forward and kissed him on the mouth. 'Master, I am yours!'"

Bijou was following the script exactly, and the audience was absolutely fascinated. They couldn't tell whether his finger was really in her or just pretending, because her short skirt masked the action, as was required for this performance. The mystery enhanced the naughtiness of it. It was time for the conclusion.

"Master Teacher, goaded beyond endurance, made a supreme effort, and flexed his finger slightly. Girl felt it, and froze for a moment. 'You're awake!' she gasped, appalled. 'You *know*! I am undone!' She pulled away so suddenly that his hand was ripped from her body, and her underclothing tore, and his arm dropped flopping. He opened his eyes, but she had already spun away, and was fleeing the room. All he saw was her back. He couldn't even tell the color of her hair, for she wore a kerchief over it. She was gone, and would not be back, and he still did not know her identity." Bijou, acting out his words, fled to the far side of the stage, facing away.

Havoc opened his eyes. "And so the Master Teacher lost his most appealing student," he concluded. "Unless he somehow managed to discover her name. Possibly, as he recovered, he inquired as to the identities of those who had taken care of him. We do not know. We also have no idea what he might have done, had he found her." He paused, gazing knowingly across the faces, feeling the turmoil of lust and shock in their minds. "Or *do* we?"

For a moment the audience was silent. Then the applause began, and it swelled enormously, though there were those who clearly did not approve completely. They liked the tale, but knew it was romanticizing an impropriety. A minstrel could get away with that, to a degree.

Then the scene dissolved into motion and dialogue, as the people got up, compared notes with their neighbors, and departed for their houses. There were several couples who seemed to be rather in a hurry. Havoc was jealous of them, for he could not do the same. *Damn you, Bijou!* he thought.

Bijou merely smiled, physically and mentally. Then she met the villagers who came to compliment her on her assistance, as they complimented Havoc on his narration. The performance had been a success.

At the following banquet, Headman made a passing remark. "This is of course quite coincidental. What happened here was nothing like that, I'm sure. But I believe that our vanished teacher will be invited to return, and to marry the girl he loves. She will have a waiver of age; the consensus seems to be that she is after all old enough."

"I am glad to hear it," Havoc said solemnly.

"Thank you, Minstrel. We look forward to your other tales, tomorrow."

Hours later, exactly as he had feared, they got to retreat to their room. Havoc read Bijou's desire, and acted on it. He grabbed her the moment the door closed, carried her to the bed, threw her down on it, and threw himself on her without removing their clothing. He tore some cloth in the process of getting into position, and savagely possessed her. "You damned tease!" he said, even in the throes of it.

"You chose the tale; you spoke the script," she reminded him, not at all contrite.

"You said you would make the story steam. You didn't say you would make *me* steam."

"You should have known." She was laughing in her mind.

"You wanted me to suffer the frustration of unconsummation."

"Just a taste of what you do to me. I can have your passion, but not your love."

And that was serious. He could not deny it. "I'm sorry, Bijou."

"It's not your fault, Havoc. It's just the situation. I wouldn't try to win you even if I thought I could. Since I'm limited to your passion, I'm taking all of that I can."

Yet she was also making progress on his emotion. He loved Gale, but was coming to care for Bijou more than he cared to admit.

And if she read that in his mind, she was smart enough not to react to it. There were ways in which she was indeed like the Girl of the tale.

The following day was routinely successful: Havoc told several more tales, with Bijou's assistance, and they were well received. There was another banquet at the close of day.

"Tomorrow you will be on your way," Headman said. "We will miss you, Minstrel, and your lovely girl. You have told your tales well. We shall be glad to see you another season."

"I may not be the one, another season," he reminded the man. "But I appreciate your appreciation."

"We understand. But there is something I must mention. We have received a report of brigands in the vicinity. They are not common in these parts, but pass through occasionally. We fear they have received news of a pretty girl traveling between villages, and wish to take her for their own. There is always a good slave market for such."

"So I understand. What size is the brigand group, and what kind of magic does it have?"

"We believe it to be three men, of adult age. We know of no magic. But such folk are unscrupulous. We believe we should offer you a guard for your journey to the next village."

"I appreciate the offer," Havoc said. "But you have need for your man in the village, and he would have to make his way back alone. I am competent to handle brigands, when suitably warned."

"Are you sure, Minstrel? You are young, and perhaps have not encountered—"

He broke off, for Havoc's deadly knife was suddenly before his nose. He held it there for a moment, then made it disappear. "I am trained."

Headman nodded. "So I see. Then I wish you well, hoping nevertheless that you do not encounter the party."

"We hope so too," Havoc said.

"I never saw that knife before," Bijou remarked that evening.

"I got it at the examination for king, and liked it. It's a memento of the occasion. I have not had to use it yet."

"Do you really think we'll encounter brigands? I suppose Gale could handle herself, but I'm a soft city girl. In my joy of getting to be with you, I didn't think how I would hold you back."

"You know that my dragon seed warns me of danger. So stay close to me, and obey without question when I tell you something. It may be to drop to the ground, or to run back the way we came. If I have to fight, I don't want you in the way."

"I will get out of the way," she agreed. "But maybe I should learn how to use some of those weapons you have me carrying."

"They are reserves, in case I lose mine. But you should learn their use. I'll show them to you as convenient."

"Thank you, Havoc." She kissed him, and one thing led to another, as she intended.

Early in the morning they set off for the next village. The path was good, but the terrain became rugged. This was because inter-village paths typically wound between Chroma, and the fringes of Chroma were largely random with respect to the convenience of human travelers. So the paths did not stay on clear level contours, but cut up and down slopes, across rivers, and through jungles. Sometimes there was a split in the path, with one part taking a physically easy route through a secant of a Chroma. But it was best for nonChroma travelers to avoid that, without invitation, because they would be largely helpless against the magic of any person or creature there. So they picked their way around. It was part of what made travel uncommon. Havoc, accustomed to such travel, used his staff efficiently to clear spot debris and brush back obnoxious vines, and Bijou followed close behind.

They came to an intersection with a path emerging from another crevice between Chroma. The two paths joined to show the way to the next village. It was downhill, rocky, but clear of brush.

The dragon seed buzzed. Havoc continued walking, but was fully alert. *Bijou, there is danger. Be ready to run, when I tell you which way.*

Ready, she agreed mentally.

Then he spied a man, behind a boulder ahead. A brigand, surely. But where were the other two?

One is down the other path, Bijou thought. *He is watching me walk.*

So he was. And the third was farther along the trail they were following. Three minds, intent on mayhem.

Keep walking. I will take out the nearest one. Rejoin me quickly when I call you.

Yes. There was fear in her mind, but she did not flinch.

They walked by the rock, which was about six feet off the path.

As they got beyond it, the man leaped out and charged them from behind. Havoc drew his knife, whirled, and met the man as he pounced. It was too late for the brigand to stop; he was already swinging at Havoc with a wooden club.

Havoc put away his knife, freeing his hand. He stepped into the man, avoiding the club, blocked him with a hip, caught his club-hand, and used it to lever that man into a somersault. It was a barehanded martial art trick, effective against an overbalanced person. The man rolled over his hip and landed hard on the ground, the air whooshing out of his body. He was stunned.

But now the other two were closing in, from behind and in front. They thought their trap had closed, not realizing that they had already lost a man. "Here!" Havoc called.

Bijou turned and ran to him. He put his hands on her shoulders and put her back against the boulder. He put the long staff in her hands. Then he stood in front of her, taking down his hat. The chin strap became a hand hold, and the hat became a round shield.

The two brigands converged, discovered their unconscious companion, and turned to face Havoc. "Now we can do this in one of two ways," Havoc said. "You can pick up your third, who is only stunned, and get out of here. Or you can take your chances against me. But if you attack me, I will hurt you, so that you will not bother another minstrel."

They did not even hesitate. They charged him, raising their clubs. It was obvious, to them: they were two, he was one. They could crush him, and then have easy access to the girl.

Well, he had warned them. Havoc jammed his shield against the nearest, so that it banged his chest and bounced up under his chin. The sharp edge of the shield caught the chin, laying it open so that blood showed. The man fell back, groaning. Meanwhile Havoc's knife was back in his right hand. He jabbed it at the other man's right shoulder, cutting into the muscle there. The man screamed, and spun away.

"Second chance," Havoc said. "I don't want to have to bury your corpses, so I have only wounded you. Go now, with your third, and I will let you go."

This time they listened. They stumbled back to the path, picked up the other man, and dragged him back and down the intersecting path.

Havoc turned to Bijou—and found her slumped on the ground. She had fainted.

He smiled, somewhat ruefully. Indeed, she was not used to violence. Gale would have stayed clear, but used her own shield and knife if any other man had shown up to complicate the matter. But Gale was barbarian; that was the difference. She was no warrior lass, but would do what she had to, to protect herself.

Havoc cleaned his blade, put it away, and put his shield back on his head. Then he picked Bijou up in his arms and carried her on down the path. It would have been more efficient to carry her over his shoulder, but he wanted the exercise.

He knew that he probably should have killed the brigands, but what he had told them was true: it was a lot of work to bury bodies in stony ground, and it was no good leaving them out to stink. So he preferred to have them take themselves away. Of course they would be a menace to other travelers, but less of one, because the one had a concussion, another had a cut chin, and the third would have a lot of healing to do before he swung a club with that arm again.

"Besides," Bijou said. "You don't like killing."

"I ought to drop you on the ground," he groused. But he didn't. "How did you wake without alerting me?"

"I'm getting better with the mind mask. I covered all my thoughts, and you thought that I wasn't thinking at all—that I was unconscious."

That was a trick he hadn't thought of. "Show me exactly how."

She showed him, and he practiced feigning mental unconsciousness. It was different from merely covering thoughts; he had to allow fleeting dream images to show, as though the unconscious mind was at work.

"You can put me down now," she said. "I'm sorry I fainted. I need to toughen up to walking distances."

He set her down. "Violence isn't fun. I avoid it when I can. But sometimes it's necessary."

"Yes, I see that. Those men—if they had won, they would have killed you, raped me, and sold me into slavery. It was in their minds. That's what really put me out. I don't mind straight lust—as far as I can tell, all men have it, when they look at me. I like evoking it in you. The mind reading has really educated me about that. But the ugliness—that's painful."

"You prefer my clean lust to their dirty lust," he said, smiling.

"That's no joke, Havoc. You would never force a woman, or hurt her. You want her to like you. And women *do* like you—all of them who get to know you. But those brigands—they like making a woman hurt. They want to degrade her. I saw it in their minds. They wanted to make me scream and cry and be dirty. It was awful; I feel dirty just having seen into their minds."

"I suppose so. Some men hate women, and want to make them suffer, to pay for arousing passion in them. But I don't think all woman like me. Not sexually, I mean."

"You're thinking of Ennui," she said. "And Aspect. They're older. You're not a woman, so you don't see them the way I do. Either one would get into your bed, if you asked."

"I don't believe that."

She opened more of her mind to him, focusing on the two other women. It was there: sexual desire, hidden beneath layers of propriety and denial. "Well, of course as king I have special power."

"It's not just that. I should know. There's something *about* you,

Havoc, that turns on women. Actually I think Gale is the same way. Only she turns on men."

"Changelings!" he exclaimed. "I forgot—Gale told me we're changelings, and that's one of their qualities."

"That's right—it was in her mind. And your minds are different from others, except for Symbol."

"Symbol!" he said. "Could she be a changeling too?"

"I think she could. She can excite any man she chooses."

"Yes. The only reason she didn't seduce me is that she chose not to."

"And the only reason you didn't seduce her is that *you* chose not to."

Havoc was amazed. "And King Deal was a changeling. Gale learned that. So Deal and Symbol—no wonder they got together. They couldn't resist each other."

"Yes, that must be it. I knew King Deal only to wash him, and he never even noticed me, but he was a fine figure of a man, handsome and virile and decent. I would have gone with him without question, if he had wanted. He just had that power. You reminded me a lot of him—and I think now I know why."

He nodded. "I wonder whether we'll encounter other changelings?"

"If we do, we'll know them. Anybody who is like you, or Gale, or Symbol, physically and mentally—that must be a changeling. You're superior specimens."

"Oh, I wouldn't say that." It wasn't modesty, but realism; Havoc was a believer in natural differences, rather than in superior types.

"Get real, Havoc. If you weren't already in love with Gale, and you could choose between her and me, which would you take?"

"Her." There was no point in concealing it.

"Because she's a better woman than I will ever be. Smarter, prettier, stronger, healthier—a fit match for you. We both know it. And we know that so is Symbol. Well, if I had my choice of any man, I'd pick you, Havoc, because you're a better man. So would any other woman, even if most of them don't yet know it."

"But there's nothing wrong with you, Bijou. It's just that—"

"It's just that I'm cast from an ordinary mold. A pretty girl of average intellect. It was my prettiness that got me the job as Mistress of the Bath. I'm not a changeling. That's just the way it is."

"That's just the way it is," he agreed. "But I'm not easy about this business of changelings. Why are they being spread about? What's the point of it all?"

"That's what we're trying to find out," she reminded him. "And I guess King Deal was trying to find out—and when he got close, he got killed." She suffered a siege of horror; he felt it in her mind. "Oh, Havoc—don't get killed!"

"I'll try not to," he said, somewhat bemused.

"I would give my life for you."

There was no point in arguing; she was serious. "I will try to see that you don't have to."

The path wound down to a moderate pond, and skirted it. The pond was stream-fed, so seemed fresh; they could drink from it. The water was faintly pink, meaning it had originated in a Red Chroma district, but that would not make it unpotable.

"Great Planets, I'm thirsty, after all this walking," Bijou said. She got down to her knees, about to dip out a double handful of water to drink.

Havoc stepped to the edge. The dragon seed buzzed.

"I heard that," Bijou said. "Your seed, right? Danger."

"Danger, or a lie, or a wrongness. No one is lying, but there seems to be no danger."

"Could the water be poisoned?" she asked, alarmed. "It didn't buzz when I got ready to drink, only when you stepped close."

"It's true it won't protect you," he agreed. "I had better test the water." He knelt and touched the water with one finger.

The seed buzzed again.

Bijou quickly got up and backed away from the pool. "I'm thirsty, but not that thirsty."

"Yet the water is fresh, and looks good," he said. "Bijou, you can help. Make conjectures."

"The water is poisoned," she said.

The seed buzzed. "That's a lie."

"But I don't know it's a lie, so how can the seed tell I'm lying?"

"It knows whether you are telling the truth. *You* don't need to know. I can't do it, because it won't buzz when I lie, consciously or unconsciously."

"There's something else about this water," she said.

There was no buzz.

"There's something dangerous in the water."

No buzz.

"Get back," Havoc said. "I don't like this."

They backed away from the pond. But they were too late. The surface was rippling, as if something were rising in it. Yet the water remained clear. What could be doing it?

"I think we had better get the hell away from here," Havoc said. "This must be magic. The water has a red tinge; it's from a Red Chroma, so can support some magic. The dragon seed is never wrong. It buzzed twice, which meant the danger is getting worse. There's a threat."

They retreated, watching the pond. "Maybe a water dragon?" Bijou asked nervously.

"The Translucent Chroma can make dragons from water, but I'm not sure the Red Chroma can."

"Red associates with blood, demons, healing, ectoplasm, and the like," she said. "I learned that in school."

Havoc recognized a word he didn't fully understand, though Throe had mentioned it. "What's that last?"

"Ectoplasm. It—it's a sort of living plasma that can shape into things, usually harmless. But not always. That's all I remember; I've never seen any." Then she corrected herself: "Yes I have: the Red Chroma man who was witness in the White Chroma—he showed some ectoplasm. That floating face."

"Oh, yes," Havoc agreed, remembering. "But this doesn't look like that."

The pond heaved, and the water in its center rose up in a glistening mound. "Maybe this is another kind," Bijou said.

"Or something else, like a demon."

The water mound continued rising. It separated from the pond and floated above it, a seeming ball of pink water about three feet in diameter. It bobbed, then began moving toward the two of them.

"A water bomb!" Bijou cried. "That's what it is!"

This, too, was new. "What is a water bomb?"

"A bomb made of water. Like a fire bomb, only water. When it touches its target, it explodes. It doesn't just make things wet; it blows them apart. Oh, Havoc, this is bad."

"A firebomb attacked our convoy," Havoc said. "This must be from the same enemy."

"The one who's trying to kill you," she agreed. "The one who killed King Deal, maybe."

The seed did not buzz. "Yes, that's it," he agreed. "So that enemy knows me even when I'm masked. As it knew Gale, and sent the succubus after her. This won't be stopped by a knife or shield."

Meanwhile the ball was floating slowly toward them. "Havoc, can we run?" Bijou cried pleadingly.

"It's slow, but evidently not limited to the pond," he said. "That was just where it was hiding, waiting for us to come within its range. To activate it. Now it's got my scent, and I don't think running will stop it. It will just keep following, until it catches up."

"But if we just wait for it, it'll get you faster."

Havoc looked around. "There may be a way to stop it. We must be in the fringe of a Red Chroma; maybe we can go to a nonChroma region, where it can't follow."

"I don't think so, Havoc. That stream carries the Red Chroma Magic, so there is magic along its banks, and that bomb is made of Red Chroma water. As I understand it, they are as big as they are so that they can carry a lot of magic. I mean, a Chroma gem, like the ones in your crown, is highly concentrated magic. This water is dilute magic, so there has to be a lot more of it to get the same punch. There's enough so that it can maintain itself as long as it needs to."

"Until it takes me out," he agreed, understanding. "So it can follow me anywhere."

Bijou got sudden resolution; he felt it in her mind before she spoke. "I'll intercept it. That will detonate it, saving you." She stepped forward.

Havoc leaped forward to catch her. "Don't do that!" He hauled her back away from the looming ball.

"But Havoc, you're the king. You have to survive."

"I'll survive some other way. Get away from it." He set her down and shoved her away from the direction of the pond. "Now *go!*"

Cowed, she ran away. But he felt the horror and grief in her mind. She truly feared for him, and wanted to save him.

He looked around again, casting desperately for anything that might give him a chance. Then he saw it: a dissolver plant. The kind that dissolved anything it touched, making its substance sink into the ground to fertilize its roots. It could be deadly to a living creature, though some animals had fur that resisted its effect. Mostly, animals stayed away from it.

Havoc picked up two dry sticks and ran to the plant. He used them to lever it out of the ground. They dissolved as they touched its leaves and stem, but that took a few seconds, and he kept feeding them in and prying. When his hands got too close, he fetched more sticks and resumed.

"Havoc! It's coming on you!"

He looked up. She was right: in his distraction he had not tracked the water bomb. He had to get away before *it* dissolved *him*. He just didn't have time to pry the dissolver all the way out of the ground.

He flung himself away, getting some distance between himself and the slowly floating bomb. What a relief that it moved so slowly!

But how was he going to deal with it? He didn't see any other dissolver plants, and that one was covered by the bomb.

Then he cursed himself for a fool. The plant didn't have to stay covered; he could lead the bomb away from it, then return for another session with the plant.

He started walking, slowly. "This way, waterbrain," he called to it. The ball of water floated after him.

"I can do that," Bijou said. "You keep leading it away, and I'll have plenty of time." As the bomb departed, she ran in to pry at the plant.

"Don't touch it directly," he called back.

"I know; I got the warning from your mind." She picked up sticks and got to work. But the plant was well anchored in the ground, and wouldn't come loose.

"Piss on it!" Havoc called.

She bared her bottom and did so. The liquid soaked the ground around the plant. That, added to the dissolving fragments of stick, loosened the soil around the roots, and she was finally able to pry the plant out of the ground. She got new sticks, picked it up, and carried it toward the bomb.

But Havoc saw that this wasn't good enough. "You can't throw it far enough to be safe yourself," he called. "Not with those clumsy sticks."

"I don't know what else to use."

"Leave it there for me; I'll return for it." But first he found a massive stick with large thorns; that should do. He picked it up and ran around the bomb to the dissolver plant. The bomb changed direction smoothly, following Havoc. "Get well away from here, Bijou."

She obeyed, running back toward the pond. That was one thing about her: she followed directions well. He ran on until he came to the dug out place.

He swung the club down on the dissolver plant, spiking it on the thorns. It would melt them, but that would take a few seconds. He whirled the club around and hurled it at the oncoming bomb, carrying the plant with it. Without pausing to see whether it scored, he spun and ran the opposite way.

There was an explosion that boosted him farther along. Because he had been expecting it, he was able to keep his feet. After a few more steps he stopped and looked back.

There was a wet crater in the ground, and plants had been cleared from a circular area. Those beyond the radius of destruction were leaning outward, and dripping pink water. Then he became aware of the wetness of his back; it had plastered him too. It would have done worse than that, had he been at its point of detonation.

Bijou returned. "I thought that plant was supposed to dissolve it."

"So did I," he admitted. "I thought it would dissolve into a puddle. I don't understand magic."

"Maybe the bomb wouldn't let itself be defused," she said. "Because then someone might study the remains and figure out who set it. So when it felt itself being compromised, it went off."

He nodded. "Bijou, for a pretty girl of average intellect, you're pretty smart."

"It's just common sense." But there was a wash of pleasure in her mind.

"It's obvious that my masquerade as Minstrel didn't fool the enemy. It knows where I am and where I am going."

"Then why doesn't it just kill you outright?"

"My guess is that it doesn't want to reveal itself. So it killed King Deal in a seeming accident, and tried to interfere with Gale indirectly, and sent an anonymous fire bomb to intercept me in the Brown Chroma. I was probably supposed to think it was a dissident party in Brown, or that White was behind it. Now I think it's not any of the Chroma."

"But it must be one of them, Havoc. There isn't anything else."

"There's plenty else. There's the Temple, though Gale exonerated that. There's the torture cult Gale's succubus came from. There must be other organizations that exist in several Chroma, with purposes of their own. I need to figure out which one doesn't like the king, and why."

"King Deal wasn't trying to hurt anyone. He just wanted to be a good king, and he was. Checking the changelings—I think that was just a side investigation. But if he knew he was one of them—why would seeking his origin make him have to be killed?"

"Why, indeed. But it may be the case."

They returned to the pond. Now it was safe to drink from.

The day was late, and they had not reached the next village. "It's not smart to travel at night, if it can be avoided," Havoc said. "That bomb delayed us."

She looked at him. "Could that have been its purpose? To interfere with your schedule, so you would have to be out at night, where some wild creature might get you?"

"Making it truly seem like an accident," he said. "That could be."

"Not that I mind spending any night, anywhere, with you. But maybe we should get back our schedule."

"I think you're right. We had better push on. But it's dangerous. I'll have to show you more about the use of weapons."

"I don't think I'd be very good with them."

"You forget about our mind connection. I can direct you mentally, and you'll know what to do."

"Yes, but I don't have any part of your strength or speed or training."

Quite true. Once again, he missed Gale, who was competent in the wilderness. "The hat is a shield, as you saw. Use it to block off anything you fear. The rope belt is a weighted net, normally used for hunting, but it could entangle a predator and give you time to escape. The gloves are masked gauntlets; you could put your fist in the mouth of a carnivore and it would not be able to bite through to your flesh. The boots are similarly protective; if you kick something hard, it will be like the strike of a club. So if you have to fight, do what comes naturally, and it may be effective. But mainly you should stay behind me, as you did when the brigands attacked."

"I will."

"We'll eat while we move, so as not to waste time. Remember, my dragon seed warns me of danger, so we don't have to be afraid while it's silent. I won't be able to carry you this time."

"I'm tired, but I will stay the pace," she said.

They moved on along the path, climbing up the slope beyond the pond. The shadows were lengthening. The next village should not be too far beyond, because they had come a fair piece. But Havoc did not trust the dark at all; it was indeed dangerous, especially for one from the city. He was especially alert.

A large winged shape glided silently by. *Night hawk,* Havoc thought to her, reassuringly. *We're not its prey.* But there were winged creatures who did consider man as prey, and they could be close by.

Havoc's staff glowed slightly; that was its inherent magic, making it especially useful at night. It showed the small obstructions of the path, and that helped. Then it showed a larger one: a tangle of tentacles. They writhed when the staff touched them, and tried to catch on to it. But he rapped them sharply several times, and they concluded that the staff was inedible, and too apt to fight back. So they retreated, and the two people passed unmolested.

What would happen to someone who got grabbed?

They haul things into an acid center that dissolves them from one end first.

The path was free for a while, perhaps because the tentacles had cleared it. It crested a ridge and angled down into a forested section. Planet Mystery showed in the sky, helpfully illuminating the ground. Havoc increased his pace, and Bijou followed closely.

The dragon seed buzzed. Havoc halted, holding the staff before him. Then he saw it, glistening faintly in the wan light: the trip-strand of a web. Had they blundered into that, the spider would have been upon them in an instant. It would have set its snare at dusk, and would take it up again at dawn.

What is it?

A spider net. He peered along the line, trying to spot the spider, but it was well hidden. So he opened his mind, trying to relate to its mind—and found it. The spider was directly above the path, ready to drop down to wrap whatever passed. It was a big one—big enough to wrap a man.

He looked about, to see whether they could make a detour around the web. But the banks of the path were steep, and the footing was treacherous; he might cross safely, but not Bijou. In any event, a detour would take time, and the less time they remained out here, the better. It was best to remain on the path.

Which meant he would have to deal with the spider. He could probably kill it, but the job would be messy and he might get entangled or bitten in the process. In addition, he did not like killing wild things any better that he liked killing humans. They were just going about their business, making their living. But he knew this one would not let them pass.

Then he thought of a way. It might not work, in which case he would have to attack. But it was worth a try. He could read minds, because of the disease, but many wild creatures seemed able to do it as part of their strategy of survival. If this spider could read his mind, he could engage it in dialogue.

Talk with it? Bijou thought, shuddering.

Maybe. He reached out with his thoughts, focusing on his memory of Gale's experience with the yellow spider. This one was translucent, as were the local plants, for this was the fringe of a Translucent Chroma.

Translucent specialized in mind reading, so its creatures well might have that power. He wanted the spider to read his mind. To relate to Gale, saving the little spider, bringing it inside her house, caring for it, feeding it, making a safe haven for it. Until at last it had to leave, because it was too large to hide any more, and her people could be hostile. But she had loved that spider, and it had loved her. They had never tried to hurt each other.

Then he felt its feeling returning. It saw Gale through his memory, and though it did not understand the nuances, it accepted the fact that this person and this spider had bonded. That made the person a friend, and spiders did not eat friends. It did not distinguish between persons; all humans seemed much alike to it.

Havoc reached back and caught Bijou's hand. He led her forward, past the trip line, under the spider. Terrified, she followed, keeping her mind mask as high as possible, understanding that it would not be wise to broadcast prey feelings. Havoc held his mental picture of Gale hugging Yellow, and moved slowly on, bringing Bijou along. They brushed the trip line, but the spider did not move.

Soon they were beyond the net, and could resume walking at speed. "Oh, Havoc, that was horrible," Bijou said.

"Spiders are not horrible, just different. This one honored a memory of friendship. Wild creatures are honorable, when they have the right associations."

"I was still terrified."

"It was chancy. But not more so than fighting it would have been. It's always better to proceed in peace, if that's possible."

"You learned that from the wilds?"

"And from my martial arts training."

"You learned peace from fighting?"

"Where else?"

"But—"

"When you fight, you learn how hard and risky and painful it can be. So you seek to avoid it thereafter."

"Oh."

The jungle section eased, and the path became a niche in a steeply sloping mountain side. Above, it rose into green tinged snow; below, it sank into a small canyon squeezing the river. The light of Mystery made the whole scene eerily clear.

"This scares me, Havoc," Bijou said. "Suppose there's an avalanche?"

"That snow seems pretty well frozen. As long as there's no flare from Void, it should be stable."

"Void's hidden now, same as Vivid, so that shouldn't matter. They're both dayside."

"But a flare could bounce off Mystery, and it could also shake Charm."

"Let's hurry," she said nervously.

He smiled, unconcerned. The dragon seed would warn him if any such danger threatened. And, indeed, they did pass the slope without event.

The path opened out, and now there was the distant light of the next village. They had made it.

There was of course a challenge at the village gate, but Havoc had Bijou step forward and smile and inhale, and the guard concluded that they were legitimate. He summoned the headman, who welcomed them to Village Dampath, and they were given lodging. They washed and fell into bed, too tired to talk or make love. At least Bijou was, and Havoc respected that; she had pushed herself to her utmost to keep the pace, and her legs were soundly sore. So he sat beside her and massaged her legs, restoring them while she drifted blissfully to sleep. There was a rainstorm in the night, making him glad they were under cover. He could handle the weather of the wilderness, but Bijou was more delicate, and in any event, this cabin was more comfortable.

In the morning they breakfasted and put on their first show, and it was well received. Havoc was a good tale teller, and Bijou was lovely; that combination was bound to win over villagers.

At noon, the headman approached. "It's a good thing you got through last night. There was a washout of the path, and we have had to close it today for repairs."

Havoc remembered the night's rain. "You would not have let us pass?"

"We are familiar with the area, but we do not chance a washout. There can be finely balanced boulders, and forming sink holes. So we do not let anyone pass until we are sure it is safe. This is part of our mission; we repair the wet path. But it will be open tomorrow."

"That's good to know. However, we will be going on to the other villages on our route."

"Of course. There is a boat for you."

As the day waned, there was the mandatory banquet; the presence of a competent minstrel was always reason for celebration. Then they were approached by a young couple. The man was ruggedly handsome, and the woman was well formed. She was the one who spoke. "Minstrel, we don't receive many travelers in Village Dampath in this season. I would like you to sire my fourth. I am in season now, and so it is feasible."

This was the kind of request it was bad form to decline, even if it wasn't couched in the most positive manner. But Havoc was cautious. "As you know, I have a companion, and I would not wish to cause her distress." He shot her a quick mental summary of village conventions, realizing that they were not necessarily matched in the big city. *Every family must have four surviving children, but one of them is supposed to have a different father or a different mother. So even the most devoted couples look for outside conception, on this one occasion. Visiting men are thus in demand, if they seem healthy or otherwise desirable.*

Oh, yes, I know of this, she agreed. *To mix the parentage, to foster variety in the species. We're supposed to do it in the city, too, but often don't.*

Now the man addressed Bijou. "My wife anticipated this. If you would consider diverting yourself with me, a balance would be restored to the proceedings."

Bijou was plainly surprised. She had barely assimilated Havoc's thought, and was having trouble with this one. "I should be with you, to balance Minstrel being with your wife?"

"There is of course no obligation. It is merely an offer, to show our good faith. We would prefer to have our fourth on our own, but this is not encouraged."

Havoc added an explanation. *They don't want to stray, but have to, for this. I should accept, as a matter of courtesy.* He had managed to avoid it at Village Trifle, but was fairly caught this time.

Bijou came to a sudden decision. "All right. I am not in season, but if you want diversion, it will do." Havoc felt the bold naughtiness in her mind.

The woman frowned, but quickly covered it. "Very good." She had evidently hoped that Bijou would decline. That was of course why Bijou had accepted. She was nettled by the need to let Havoc clasp another woman, so was in turn nettling the other woman.

So it was that they spent the early part of that night apart. This was the first time Havoc had actually tried to service a fourth, and now that he was committed, he was intrigued. So it was flattering, and interesting, for the woman was different from both Gale and Bijou. She had a good body, but accepted the mechanics of sex as a duty, and made no effort to enhance it. He realized he had been spoiled, first by the love and understanding of Gale, then by the enthusiasm of Bijou. So the experience lacked much of the novelty and excitement he had anticipated, but was nevertheless educational.

There was also no follow-up. The woman did not want to be clasped and appreciated by a man all night, she wanted to sleep. Once satisfied that his seed was in her, she became politely remote. Seeing the way of it, he suggested that it was time for him to return to his own room, and she did not demur. So he dressed and departed—and met the husband on his way back from Bijou. They passed each other with a nod, and that was it.

When he entered his own room, Bijou greeted him with a glad cry. "Oh, Havoc, let's not do that again!" she cried. She was in the process of washing, and he realized that she was making sure to have nothing of the man left in her.

"Why, was he unkind to you?"

"No, he was businesslike. Mechanical. He knew what he was doing, and he did it, and I had almost no input. You're so different, Havoc. You *enjoy* it."

"I think those two are well matched," Havoc said.

"Havoc, hold me, kiss me. You don't have to be sexual, just get me close."

He stripped and joined her. She hugged him, then washed him, clearing any possible remaining trace of the woman. Then she kissed him, her ardency growing, and her body and her mind drew him in. So they had sex after all, standing there, not so much for its own sake as just to be that close.

They cleaned again, and went to bed. He held her hand. "Even there," she said, squeezing his fingers. "You *care*. It's not just my body."

"I care," he agreed.

"You love Gale, and care for me, so what I have is left over—and yet that gives me more than a man like that has to give in total. And still I saw in his mind that he considers himself normal—and I think he's right. Oh, Havoc, you have spoiled me."

"That's what I thought about you."

"That I'm normal?"

"That you spoiled me. That woman was no more fun for me than that man was for you."

She kissed him joyfully. "Thank you."

Next day they departed Dampath and resumed the route. The village was at the edge of a lake, and the path disappeared, appropriately; from here they needed a boat. There was a designated visitor's craft they could borrow; it would remain on the lake when they were gone, so there was no concern about losing it. Eventually they or some other visitor would bring it back, traveling the other direction.

"That's a nice convention," Bijou said. "We are more possessive about things in the city."

Havoc was not used to boating, as Village Trifle was landlocked. The huge expanse of the lake impressed him greatly. He saw that several Chroma bordered it, and from them issued rivers carrying their diluted colors. So the lake was magical, but mixed; no single Chroma dominated, and no Chroma visitor would be much better off than the nonChroma folk. But the creatures in it would have had time to adapt to the mixed magics. The village headman assured them that none were dangerous to travelers, as long as they stayed in their boats. That was only somewhat reassuring.

The boat was propelled by a rotary paddle pedaled by the feet, and steered by a trailing oar. Havoc found the contraption awkward, but soon got used to it, and it did work well enough. Bijou sat in front, as a passenger. She had carryover tiredness from the walk of two days before, so that was just as well.

There was a sudden brightening of the sky. Bijou looked up with alarm. "What's that?"

"That's a Void flair. You haven't seen one before?"

"Triumph has windows only for the upper class folk. I'm an underclass girl."

"I've seen many flares, and always been intrigued by them. I thought it was just the dark sun getting angry. Now I know that it's because more substance is spiraling into Void, and it is getting squeezed and heated until it's as bright as a fire. This is the season for such flares; I think they occur all the time, but Charm is now closer to Void than to Vivid, so we see the flares more clearly."

"And feel them," she added. "The day is already heating."

"Yes. A flare can make winter into summer, in a few minutes. That's why some paths are not much traveled in the Air season—not only too many wind storms, but unpredictable fire season interludes."

"Yes, that's why Triumph is closed in," she agreed. "Some storms are so fierce in Fall—that's what we call the Air season—that we actually feel the buffets and rain rocking the walls."

"Fall? Is that an old planet term?"

"Yes. Spring, Summer, Fall, Winter, matching Water, Earth, Air, and Void."

"Then what matches Fire season?"

"I don't think anything does. I have heard it called super-summer, but I don't think that's generally accepted. The flares aren't contiguous; they happen randomly or not at all, anytime in Spring, Fall, or Winter, when Void is in sight. So it's hard to call them a season."

"I never thought of it that way. But I suppose—" He paused, because something else was happening.

The water of the lake was rippling, and the ground itself seemed to be shaking. A rushing sound was coming from beyond Village Dampath, and clouds were boiling up into the sky.

Bijou caught on first. "The avalanche! It's happening!"

"The avalanche," he echoed. "Void is flaring, suddenly heating the snow, and it triggered the snowslide."

"Where would we have been at this time, if we had not pushed ahead in the night?"

Havoc rehearsed the events of the past two days. The night rain had washed out the path, closing it for the following day. They would have had to camp out somewhere near the spider web. Then they would have used the new path the day after, and be about two hours along it. "Right in the middle of that slope," he said.

She shuddered. "Would your dragon seed have warned you in time?"

"It might have. But I might have thought that it was warning me about some threat pursuing us, and hurried forward to avoid it. I don't always understand the seed perfectly."

"Could it anticipate a Void flare?"

"I don't think so. Its magic is limited, and Void is very far away. The seed does remarkably well, but there are limits."

"So if your enemy knew you have the seed, and wanted to get you anyway, this is how it might do it. Use the water bomb to delay us, feeding us into a situation that was beyond the dragon's seed's capacity to foil. Because it was more than a day away in time, and originated from far away in space."

Havoc was amazed. "Bijou, I think that's it. You fathomed it when I did not."

"No, you acted to avoid it, by forging on in the night."

"No, *you* anticipated mischief," he reminded her. "You got us going when I would have waited."

She looked at him, surprised. "Why, maybe I did. But that was sheer coincidence."

"I wonder. If my enemy knows me, it could devise a scheme that would trap me by seeming accident. But this time we were guided by your thought, so didn't act as I might have. I think you saved us, Bijou."

She paused, her thoughts uneasy. "Havoc, I depend on you for protection. I don't like to think that we can't trust your competence."

"My competence is as it always was. Perhaps improved by the addition of your input."

"I wish I could just kiss you and accept that. But—"

"I'll settle for just the kiss, then."

She had to laugh. She faced him, leaned forward, and kissed him. "You have a genius for making a girl feel useful."

"A girl *is* useful. But right now I have to pedal, or we'll get behind schedule again."

Smiling, she let him pedal. But she tempted him with mental images of the two of them embracing in the boat, while psychedelic colors illustrated their passion. The irony was that he liked her mischief, though it frustrated him considerably. She was not Gale, but neither was she any nonentity.

Clouds formed, and thickened. "I think we're going to get rain," Bijou said.

Havoc looked toward shore. "I see no place to land safely; it's all jungle. We'll have to stay on the water."

"And hope there's no water bomb," she said, not quite joking.

"So far, the enemy has never used a device twice. Or tried another in rapid order. It must take time to set up a trap. My seed gave me no warning."

"I suppose getting soaked is not a threat."

"We can take off our clothes and seal up our packs to keep them dry."

She considered, looked at the sky again, and removed her clothing, leaving only the broad hat. Havoc did the same. He had seen her naked many times, but outside like this, in daylight, seemed different.

She was a wonderful figure of a young woman.

"You're quite a figure of a man yourself," she said.

The rain started, first lightly, then more solidly. The bottom of the boat began to fill. Bijou spied a bucket, and began bailing out the accumulation. As the rain intensified, Havoc got off the paddle cycle and helped her. "They didn't tell us about this," he grumped. "Here we are naked, and too busy bailing to make love."

"Well, I suppose we could kneel facing each other, and bail behind each other's backs."

"And tip the boat over in our effort to do two things at once."

Then they spied a tarpaulin stored under a seat. It was obviously designed to cover the boat, shielding it from rainfall. They stretched it across the front, hooking its eyelets at the sides, and that eased the problem. They put another across the back, so that the only part of the boat exposed to the rain was the center, where to the two of them were. The two tarps met in the center, and were made to hook together, overlapping, but then there would be no place for the people. They decided that complete closure was not necessary.

"*Now* we can make love," she suggested.

But the boat, and the rain, and the vertical position proved to be too awkward to manage, and they had to give it up, to his continuing frustration. Havoc returned to paddling, and Bijou to bailing. The job was much easier, with only a fraction of the water entering. And soon the storm passed, making things easier yet.

At which point another boat appeared on the lake, stopping them from making the scene they had in mind. "I'm sorry I teased you," she said. "I really thought we would be able to do it, somehow."

"There'll surely be another time," he said regretfully.

"You know," Bijou said as they dressed, "we could use this at night. Cover us over and sleep under the covers. It would be cozy."

"Especially naked," Havoc agreed, wryly.

"I'd do my best to keep you warm."

"You always do."

The light of Vivid returned, warming them. The flare of Void had already faded, having done its own mischief. They made good progress, following the shoreline, and reached the next village in mid-afternoon. They would not have to spend the night in the boat.

The accommodations and performances were as before; they were both becoming accustomed to the routine. The tales were familiar, with repeated tellings, but they were new in style and detail to each audience, especially the children, and that lent novelty.

And in the evening they played a game of being in the boat, in a storm, and indulging in phenomenal passion that blasted away the weather. In fact their reenactment would have been quite impossible in reality, but it was fun.

Then on to the next village, which was on an island in the lake.

As they moved toward it, Bijou peered into the water. "Look, Havoc— it's turning brown. We must be stirring up mud from the bottom."

He looked. "I don't think so. It's too even. It think it's diffusing from a brown Chroma."

Soon that became certain: the island was brown, and the vegetation on it was brown. There was a village not far from the shore, and its houses were brown. This was a Brown Chroma region. A small one, perhaps, but definite.

They beached the boat and walked up the path to the village. The Elder came out to meet them. His clothing, like his hair and skin and eyes, were brown. "Welcome to Village Brownisle, Minstrel. Have you come to entertain us, or are you moving on?"

"I had understood that the villages on this route were nonChroma," Havoc said, pretending to be a bit taken aback. "I'm not sure that Chroma folk would find my stories entertaining. You have real magic of your own, so hardly need to hear about it from someone who lacks it." He didn't want anyone to suspect that his mission brought him here deliberately, though the enemy might already know.

"On the contrary, we enjoy well told tales as much as anyone. We are a Chroma, but somewhat isolated from the main Brown terrain. We have a lateral brown vent which provides our magic, but all our neighbors are nonChroma. So we cultivate amicable relations, and trade with others around the lake, and generally get along well."

"In that case, we shall be happy to entertain you. Do you have preferences as to type or style?"

"We are strong on forbidden love, as many of our people are attracted to nonChroma neighbors, but we are supposed to eschew those and marry into mainland Brown families."

"We can adapt to suit your situation," Havoc said, thinking of the tale of the girl and the teacher. He could be Brown, and she from a nonChroma neighbor village. There were others that should fit similarly well.

The cabin they were given was marvelous. When Bijou stepped into the wash stall, expecting to find the usual tub and bucket, a tiny brown cloud formed overhead and rained warm brown water on her body. "Oh, wonderful!" she exclaimed, using brown soap and brown shampoo, which were both magically effective. "Come try this, Havoc!"

He did, and was intrigued when he held one hand up to the cloud and tiny bolts of lightning speared out to painlessly trim and polish his fingernails. "How about the toes?" he inquired—and the cloud floated down to do them too.

"I could get to like magic," Bijou remarked as she stepped out and a brown towel appeared in her hand. "Now if it would dry me itself—" She broke off, because it suddenly came to life and did just that.

Once she was dry, clear brown clothes appeared and draped themselves on her. A brush stroked across her hair, quickly putting it into excellent order.

Havoc got similar service. "Brown is the Chroma of conjuring," he said, remembering. "I haven't seen it in action like this before."

They did the Girl and Teacher tale, with Bijou suddenly in gray and white clothing when she expressed the desire to be so attired, while Havoc remained in brown, signifying their identities. Instead of Girl's youth being the problem, it was her color. There were a number of nonChroma children in the audience, evidently visiting to attend the show; both they and the Brown children seemed to relate very well. But so did many of the older villagers, some of whom sat with nonChroma partners in evident defiance of Chroma policy. Of course in time they would all become Brown Chroma, if they remained on the island. But the difficult time was when they were mixed, and they did understand the temptations and the problems of miscegenetic relations. There was considerable applause when the tale finished.

Then came the banquet, and that was another experience. Each person merely spoke the name of the food he preferred to eat, and it appeared before him, hot and edible. Havoc had cooked brown skunk cabbage and brown yak milk, staples he had missed since leaving home and adapting to kingly ways. They were provided in Triumph when he asked, but he had soon concluded that conformity made for a better kingly aspect. Here he didn't need to be concerned. Bijou, in contrast, had a thoroughly conventional city working person meal of brown bread and brown steak, with brown ale on the side.

After the meal, the villagers entertained them with a magic show. A collection of brown balls appeared, forming a small pyramid on the center table. Then they floated up and made three dimensional patterns overhead, intricate and changing, dizzying the eye. Then each ball became the figure of a small brown woman, dancing in the air, her brown skirt flaring as she performed intricate steps. Havoc assumed that this had become illusion, until one of the girls landed on the table before him, twirled, then bounced onto his hand. She had substance; he felt her small weight. She sat down and kicked her little feet at him, showing her brown legs all the way up. She was perfectly formed. Then she smiled, winked, and sailed back into the air, rejoining her companions. They danced in unison, closing together, then became the brown balls again, and the balls dropped to the center table, as a pyramid, and vanished.

Havoc and Bijou applauded, delighted. This was true magic; there was no way it could have been done by sleight of hand or diversion of attention. Then the group broke up, and individuals came to inquire about news of the world beyond.

Elder approached. "As you see, we do our best to integrate. Some nonChroma folk fear magic and see Chroma residents as aliens, but we are as human as any. We encourage nonChroma neighbors to visit, and many do, and we also visit their villages."

"It looks good," Havoc said. "I never saw a magic show like that before. The doll that came to me—she seemed completely real, except for her size."

"She is, except for her form."

"Her form?"

Elder glanced to the side, and signaled someone with a glance. A woman of middling age and spread approached. "This is the lady who conjured that particular doll. She controlled it magically with her mind, making it emulate her own motions. Each doll is managed by a different person."

"Conjured? I thought that consisted of summoning objects from elsewhere."

"The term also means to influence or command. The dolls are first summoned, being magically transported from storage, then animated by their familiars."

"Conjured," Havoc agreed. "That is impressive coordination."

"Thank you, Minstrel," the woman said. Then she smiled and winked, exactly as the doll had, and walked away.

"They can manage larger dolls too," Elder said. "If you lacked a female partner for the night—as I see you do not—one of them could entertain you in that fashion too."

A lovely woman form, managed by a distant living woman, being with a man. These folk had entertainments hardly dreamed of in nonChroma regions.

"Male dolls too?" Bijou asked.

"Of course."

"Can they—?"

"Yes. Their familiars do not gain the actual sensations of touch, as there are no nerves in the dolls, but the dolls can perform well enough to give their human partners satisfaction."

"See, I don't need you anymore," Bijou said to Havoc, laughing.

The other villagers had drifted away, so that their dialogue had become private. "Elder," Havoc said, "I have a favor to ask of the Brown Chroma. Perhaps you can tell me to whom I should apply."

"What is the favor?"

"I need a locator, for use in a nonChroma region."

The man studied him appraisingly. "For that you will have to apply to our parent source. We are but a Brown Chroma isle, not a major zone. But I must say that such a favor is unlikely to be granted without excellent reason. It is proprietary magic."

"I know. Only Brown has the quality of locator magic required for this purpose."

"Can you tell me for what purpose it is to be used?"

"No."

"I see. Then can you tell me who it is who wishes to use it?"

"If privacy is guaranteed."

The man made a gesture. Suddenly a shimmering translucent brown globe appeared around them. "We are private."

Evidently so; Havoc didn't know how magic worked, but trusted its power. "Guaranteed apart from this moment," Havoc said.

Elder considered him again. "You wish to obtain it in secret? Without others knowing?"

"Yes."

"I will keep the secret if it seems warranted, and fetch the locator, if warranted. But you will have to satisfy me that such an effort *is* warranted."

"I am King Havoc. I need it to help study the murder of my predecessor, King Deal. Do you have means to verify my identity?"

"No. The Translucent, Red, or Blue Chroma could do that, but this is not our specialty. Further, I do not believe you. King Havoc is at this time in the capital city of Triumph, making daily appearances; our representative there so reports. Therefore I believe you are pretending to an office you do not have, for what reason I don't know and do distrust. There is no valid secret to be kept."

Bijou spoke. "I can attest to his identity."

Elder turned to her, annoyed. "And who are you?"

"The head Mistress of the Royal Bath. I—"

"You ran away with a minstrel?"

"No, with the king. I—"

"You are not a credible witness."

Havoc realized that he had masked his absence from his office too well. He had divested himself of his crown, and had no other way to identify himself. Except mental. "Do you read minds here?"

"Of course not. You must go to the Translucent Chroma for that."

"But all the Chroma can do similar magic, when they focus, regardless of specialty. Just not as well as the specialists."

"Perhaps. But as I said, we are a small zone. We have no mind readers here. We practice personal privacy. Now if you have done wasting my time, I suggest that you drop this pretense and return to your true role as Minstrel. As that, you are indeed competent, and I will say no more about this other imposition if you will agree to perform tomorrow in the usual manner."

Havoc cursed his lack of foresight; he should have thought to keep some sure signal of his identity, to use at need. Now what could he do?

Sire, Bijou thought. *Your proficiency in combat—that might persuade him.*

Good idea. "Has your representative told you that the new king hails from an outlying village, and is a barbarian?"

"Yes, this is common knowledge. He belched at his inaugural address."

"That he is a skilled martial artist?"

"Yes, of course. What is your point?"

"Suppose I demonstrate my competence in that respect?"

"That would demonstrate only that you can fight. Minstrels do have to defend themselves on occasion."

This man would not be swayed! Havoc couldn't blame him, but he had to get that locator, which meant he had to convince Elder. "Then what about this: forget about whether I am the king. Let me challenge your champion for that locator. If I win, I get it, regardless of my identity."

"And what if you lose?"

He was stuck again. He had no equivalent prize to offer.

Until Bijou stepped in. "If he loses, then I will remain here to marry the man who chooses me."

Bijou! You mustn't—

You will win, won't you?

Yes, of course. But—

Then I can do this.

Meanwhile Elder was contemplating her. "That performance you gave—you are an extremely comely and obliging young woman."

"Thank you. I try to be."

"You realize that in time you would become Brown, as our magic infuses you, but that you would never become as facile with magic as the natives? That three of your children would be Brown Chroma?"

"Yes."

"I believe there are a number of our young men who would be interested. If you will accede publicly to the terms–"

"Of course. Minstrel wins, he gets the locator. He loses, you get me."

Elder faced Havoc. "I still do not understand or respect your game, but I will consult tonight, and if you stand ready to meet our champion in single combat, these will be the terms."

"Agreed."

"But there is more you must understand. Our champions do not fight directly. They manage dolls. What you might call golems. Even if you are skilled, you will be at a disadvantage, unless you have had experience managing golems."

"I have no such experience. But it doesn't matter."

Elder frowned. "Of course it matters! You may be an impostor, seeking what you should not have, but that does not entitle us to put you at an unfair disadvantage. I am trying to show you why this challenge is ill advised. Surely you have no wish to lose your lovely assistant in an unwinnable competition."

Havoc had to admire the man's integrity, though it was getting in his way. "Your golems are indirect, like the dancing dolls. They can't react as well as the people who manage them."

"True. But they make such contests safe, as no actual person can get hurt. In any event, that disadvantage is evenly distributed, as both parties use the dolls."

"And even if they could react as well, no single golem could be better than the person who operates it."

"Of course. But it can be worse, if for example a man knows martial art, but is not conversant with the mechanisms of golem control. Since you admit that you are not—"

"I will not use a golem. I'll fight my own fight."

Elder was agitated. "Minstrel, you don't understand. These dolls use real weapons. They hack each other apart. We never have real people participating. It would be barbaric."

Bijou laughed. "Havoc *is* a barbarian. He loves that reckless violence."

"Nevertheless, *we* are not barbaric. We could not countenance such a suicidal risk."

Bijou stepped in again. *I have a notion.* She smiled beguilingly at Elder. "Maybe you should give Havoc a golem, and let him practice with it. Then if he still wants to have the fight, he can."

"That is certainly sensible," Elder agreed.

"Yes," Havoc said.

"Enjoy our hospitality this night," Elder said. "In the morning we will provide you with instruction and a practice golem. In the afternoon you may engage in the contest, if you still wish to."

"Agreed."

Elder departed, and they returned to their room. *What's on your mind?* Havoc demanded as they washed and changed. He knew better than to speak aloud; they were in magic territory, and if there was not mind reading, there could certainly be ears. Golem ears.

"This should be interesting," Bijou said aloud. But her real message was mental: *They won't let you fight without using a golem. But if you practice with one that looks like you, then when the real fight comes, you can step in yourself, and they'll think its the golem.*

Brilliant! he thought, kissing her.

No, just garden variety lower class cunning. She paused. *But Havoc, I'd really rather you did use the golem. It's so much safer.*

And would put you at much greater risk of becoming a Brown Chroma wife.

Well, it would not be such a bad fate. Maybe better than what I will return to once I am dismissed from the king's service.

I'm not going to dismiss you!

If you die, I will be dismissed by the next king. If you live, I will be automatically dismissed when I turn eighteen and have to marry. This is the way it is.

He gazed at her, disgruntled. She was being realistic. He did not plan on being king beyond his mandatory year. So she faced a brief tenure regardless.

"This is something I will address at another time," he said aloud. He had no good answer at the moment, but intended to come up with one before he left the office.

"Of course." She sat on the bed and drew up her nightie, silently offering him her body.

He took it, hungrily. She met him with special passion. He knew why: she had been reminded of the temporary nature of their association, and she wanted to make the most of it. She was a passionate creature at the best of times, and more-so at the worst of times. Always worth it.

Thank you, Havoc.

In the morning, Elder brought them to a building beside a brown gully. The air shimmered with magic power. "This is the Chroma vent, an offshoot from the main Brown Volcano. It does not erupt as such, so is relatively safe. It spews mostly gas, sometimes dust, rarely lava. The island appears to have been built up from its emissions, so it has been here for some time. We form our dolls here, of Brown basalt, then move them out when the familiar has bonded."

They entered the building. It was a rock workshop, with large blocks of brown stone being carved by artisans. There was a line of finished golems standing against a wall. Some were like powerful men, others like buxom women, and others like children and animals. Along another wall was a collection of smaller ones, like the dancing dolls they had seen.

Havoc was impressed and interested. "You can make stone figures move?" He had not thought about the actual material of the golems before.

"The magic of their substance makes them move and change shape. The bonding process enables a person to use that magic. Then they will do what that person directs."

"Can one be shaped to resemble me?"

"Certainly." Elder brought them to a standing golem of Havoc's general size. He signaled, and one of the artisans approached. "Make this one in the image of this man, and have him bond."

The artisan nodded. "If you will stand beside the form, Minstrel, please."

Havoc stood beside it, and the man did something odd: he focused one eye on Havoc and the other on the stone man. Nothing seemed to happen, but Bijou, who was watching from the side, made an exclamation. "It's changing!"

"It is being crafted to resemble him," Elder agreed. "Except that he is pale and it is brown. We could not eliminate the color without destroying the magic, of course."

"Couldn't you paint it?"

"We could, but to what point?"

"Point made," she agreed. Naturally she could not explain that they wanted a golem that looked *exactly* like Havoc, so the two could exchange places.

"Now the bonding," the artisan said. "Please face the doll and focus intently on it."

Havoc faced the golem—and saw a brown image of himself, as though he were looking in a stained mirror. It even had his hat and clothing, all in brown. He focused—and the thing began to breathe. Its mouth worked, and its eyes looked back at him.

"Done," the artisan said, and walked away.

"Now you can control it with your thoughts," Elder said. "Because body movements are complicated to control consciously, it is best simply to lock it on emulation. Will it to do whatever you do."

Havoc tried. *Do what I do.* Then he scratched his head.

The golem scratched its head, synchronized precisely with Havoc. Again, it was like a mirror image, except that it wasn't; the golem used the same hand Havoc did.

Havoc walked, and the golem followed him, its feet landing the same time Havoc's did. It seemed fully alive.

"But isn't it a lot heavier than he is?" Bijou asked.

"Not when bonded to him," Elder said. "Then its weight matches his, as does its softness of flesh. But that is merely the beginning. If you please, Minstrel, close your eyes and see through the doll's eyes. You will need to do this in the arena."

"I thought they had no nerves," Bijou said. "How can they see?"

"Their eyes attune to the eyes of the familiar, as do their ears, and their gross features of body. The doll does not see; the familiar does, and uses that sight to control the doll."

Havoc closed his eyes, and the golem did the same. Havoc focused, and in a moment made the golem differ from him: it opened its eyes while his remained closed. He saw through its eyes—and it was the same, apart from the change in perspective. He saw himself standing there with eyes closed.

"With a little practice, you can cause it to move as you think, rather than as you move," Elder said.

Havoc worked at it, and soon was making the golem walk around while he stood still. It was somewhat clumsy, but becoming less so.

"You are making excellent progress," Elder said. "But perhaps you now appreciate the difficulty of using a doll in combat against an experienced familiar."

"I do," Havoc said through the golem's mouth. The words were slurred but intelligible.

"Do you still wish to engage in the competition?"

"Yes."

Elder shrugged. "We feel that you are needlessly sacrificing the future of your assistant. Not that we will mistreat her; she will surely be cherished, for she has a form that only our dolls possess ordinarily. But doubtless she has other plans for her life."

"I do," Bijou said. "But if he loses, I will surely find life here at Brownisle interesting. Will I be allowed to have a golem?"

"Certainly. All of us have personal dolls. Wives often find them useful as diversion for husbands"

"Do I understand you correctly?" she asked. "A woman will operate an image of herself for her husband's bed?"

"Not precisely. There would be little point in an exact image. She naturally crafts an image similar to herself in youth, perhaps somewhat enhanced in certain female features, which pleases him more."

"But isn't the stone cold and hard and unresponsive?"

"Not unless she wishes it to be. It is extremely difficult to tell a conjured image from the original, when the familiar is experienced and attentive."

"This is more interesting that I thought."

"Perhaps," Elder said. "We of Chroma take such magic for granted. We produce dolls for export to other Chroma, in exchange for some of their specialties."

"But don't they lose their magic, when they go to other colors?"

"No, not immediately. Chroma people lose much of their magic in foreign zones, being living things merely imbued with the magic of their surroundings. But the dolls are crafted from the essence of Brown Chroma, and will endure for years if used carefully."

Havoc realized that the golems were masses of Brown Chroma magic substance, similar to the Chroma gemstones. So they could function elsewhere, but each use would deplete them somewhat. Still, a man-sized golem should last for some time.

"One other question," Bijou said. "If I had a golem fashioned in my likeness, could it bear a baby?"

"No. It is a superficial emulation. It also has no need to eat, or eliminate. It breathes only to speak. That is why we call them dolls: they are not alive, however they may appear." He turned to Havoc. "And that is why we use them for combat contests. They suffer no pain, and have no consciousness. When not managed by their familiars, they are inert."

"Nevertheless impressive," Havoc said through the golem's mouth, handling the words better.

"Practice as you wish. You make take the doll to your chamber. At noon I will inquire whether you still wish to engage in the contest, for the agreed terms. You will be free to decline, which is what I recommend."

"Thank you," Havoc said. Then he opened his own eyes and walked out of the building, the golem in lock step behind him. Apparently it maintained its balance magically, as it did not stumble or wobble when its footing differed from his.

Bijou paced them. *How can these people control golems, if they have no mind reading?*

I suspect they have a different form of it, relating only to the golems.

She switched to verbal communication. "Are you still determined to fight their champion?"

"Yes. I need that locator."

"Then we had better be sure you can operate that golem well. My future depends on it." The dialogue was merely for whoever might be listening; she knew what he intended.

In the cabin he did practice, and was satisfied that though he could manipulate the golem, he could not do so well enough to match the performance of his own body.

So they got to work on what he had intended all along. First Havoc disengaged from the golem, and it became inert, standing in place. Then Bijou addressed the golem in the manner Havoc had, attempting to bond.

She succeeded. The golems were not limited to a single familiar; it seemed that anyone who made the effort could relate to them. This one looked like Havoc, but didn't have to respond to his commands. In a moment it came back to seeming life, only now it emulated her motions. She concentrated, and made it speak, sounding like him. Soon she had a reasonable approximation. It wouldn't fool anyone who knew Havoc at all well, but among strangers it would do.

They got to work with what pigments they could muster, painting the face and arms of the golem off-white, and painting Havoc brown. They exchanged clothing, so that Havoc wore shades of brown and the golem wore his varied colors. Havoc and the golem came to look more like each other than themselves. However, Havoc retained his own weapons, preferring their familiarity of heft and balance. It was easier to color them than to adapt to strange weapons.

Then Bijou practiced walking and talking on her own, while causing the golem to emulate Havoc. That turned out to be impossible; the golem crashed into a wall and almost fell, while she got dizzy. So they practiced fast bondings: Havoc controlled it, then stopped, and she took over. Again, they weren't really good at it, but it would do if no one were looking for this ploy.

Noon came. Elder arrived. Bijou, scantily garbed, embraced and kissed the golem. "You still won't change your mind, Minstrel?" she asked it.

"No," it said, speaking for Havoc.

Elder looked at Havoc. "Is your doll armed? We would not send an unarmed doll into the arena."

"Yes," the golem said.

Bijou and the golem walked with Elder, and Havoc followed, acting slightly clumsy. The golem was dressed as the minstrel, and carrying the staff, but were they really fooling Elder? Or was the man playing along, so that he would not be any overt party to their deception? It was possible that the interest of the village in obtaining Bijou was such that they wanted the contest to proceed. Havoc found that interesting in itself: if they could make golems as beautiful as they wished, and have them emulate real women, why was there such desire for a beautiful real woman? He assumed that a beautiful doll that could be operated only by the full attention of real person was not as good as a beautiful woman who needed no such operation. Reality was always better than looking at a statue, even if the statue could be animated.

They came to the arena, where a fair number of villagers were gathered. Elder stepped into the center and turned to address them. "Minstrel wishes to obtain a magic device of some value, and will contest for it. If he loses, he will allow his assistant, the Girl Bijou, to remain here at Village Brownisle to marry a man of our choosing. We have tried to dissuade him, but without success." He faced Bijou. "Girl, are you also amenable to this?"

Bijou walked out to join him. "Yes. I here publicly agree to marry one of your men and remain here to bear his children, and oblige him in every way a wife does, if Minstrel loses the encounter." She smiled and turned around, showing off her assets. One reason for her brevity of costume was to distract the attention of others from Havoc. The several young brown men present were definitely intrigued. "I think it would be interesting, living here, though I have confidence that Minstrel will win."

Elder spoke again. "Is it the sense of this gathering that the terms are fair and that this contest should proceed?"

There was a general murmur of assent.

"Then let the champion of Brownisle show itself."

A door on the far side of the arena opened, and a massive and muscular brown man emerged. He was naked except for a loincloth, and held a sword in each hand. He was not at all clumsy; he moved as if alive.

"The challenger will step forward."

Havoc relinquished control of the golem to Bijou and walked into the arena. If the golem who was supposed to be Havoc seemed preoccupied, that would be attributed to Havoc's concentration on making the figure in the arena work. If Bijou needed to speak to someone, she would let the golem stand and do it. The ruse should work because it was unexpected. They hoped.

Elder spoke once more. "Minstrel, having seen the champion, you have one more opportunity to withdraw from this contest. We recognize that you are inexperienced as a familiar of dolls, and may prefer not to risk losing your assistant in such manner."

They were being more than fair. Havoc was coming to like the folk of Village Brownisle. "I will stay," the golem said, as Bijou made it speak for him.

Havoc, meanwhile, was studying his opponent. If the golem was as powerful as it looked, either of those swords would be capable of cutting him into flying halves. The fact that there was no shield spoke for the strategy: to come out swinging, heedless of whatever threat the opponent represented. That was impressive. But also stupid, in the face of a competent martial artist.

"Then let the contest proceed," Elder said. "There will of course be no magic other than that of the dolls, who will be confined to the arena and the ground. The first to step out of the arena, or to suffer a fatal injury, will be declared the loser. There are no other rules of engagement. Go."

Havoc strode forward to meet the golem. He walked with a token stiffness, deliberately. He tucked the staff under one arm and took down his hat, making it into the shield. He did not touch either his knife or his belt.

The audience was evidently surprised. Havoc had his mind shield up and was not trying to read any minds; he wanted to keep his full focus on the task before him. He was sure he could "kill" the golem warrior, but he wanted to avoid any surprises. Carelessness was his greatest enemy. There might be some subtlety in the other's attack; it was after all managed by a living man. So Havoc wanted to test its reflexes before he committed himself.

The golem strode forward and waded in, swinging the sword grasped by the right hand. Havoc danced away, landed awkwardly, turned, and poked the golem's belly with the end of his staff.

The golem's other sword whipped across and caught the wooden staff, slicing eighteen inches off its end. Havoc stumbled back. Yes indeed, the thing was not clumsy!

He brandished his shortened staff, and feinted at the golem's head. The golem countered with another quick slash, lopping off another length. But this time Havoc did not stumble back; he leaped close, jamming the remainder of the staff at the thing's face. He scored on the golem's left eye, pulping it. Now it was the golem that stumbled back, its familiar surprised and half blinded. It was having trouble getting its extended swords into play.

Havoc dropped the staff and drew his knife. He jumped close again, and again caught the golem by surprise. That was the key: doing the unexpected, and doing it swiftly and forcefully. He used his shield to catch the golem's right arm, shoving it into the other arm, off-balancing the figure. He plunged the blade into the golem's neck, twisting. He pulled it out immediately and leaped clear.

"Is that a lethal strike?" Elder asked uncertainly.

The golem remained on its feet, brown fluid staining its shoulder and chest. The strike *was* lethal, but apparently these folk were so accustomed to lopping off limbs and heads that they didn't realize it. What would they think of one of the White Chroma guns, that put just a tiny pellet hole in a body?

There was no help for it: he would have to finish off the golem in obvious manner. Those two swords swung too swiftly; he would not risk getting in close again, even with his shield. So he put away his knife and used one hand to undo his belt, shaking it out. It became the net, with small weights around its perimeter. He swung it, waiting for his opening.

The golem shook off the wound in its neck and advanced on him again. This time it did not simply swing at him, its operator having learned that this was an unlikely way to catch him. Instead it stalked him, looking for its own opening.

They circled each other at a respectful distance. Then Havoc feinted, and succeeded in provoking a swing. He jumped back, then in, and the second sword came for him. But that stroke was weaker, because the golem's balance was off; it was more of a defensive move. Havoc knocked it aside with his shield, and hurled his net.

The net caught the golem's head and swirled down around its arms, interfering with its motion. The thing swung at it, ineffectively; a sword was not much good against a net. In a moment one of its arms was entangled, and then the other.

Havoc leaped in, knocked down one sword arm with his shield, and trapped the other against the ground with his foot. Then he drew his knife and stabbed again at the neck, repeatedly, until the head finally came loose. He picked up the head and waved it at the audience.

That they understood. "Victory to the challenger," Elder announced. "I will send for the item." He shook his head. "I must say, you showed surprising competence. Perhaps it was the element of surprise." He was speaking to the golem-Havoc.

"He's a quick study," Bijou said. She was openly relieved. She had seen Havoc fight before, but that two sworded golem had been fearsome.

Havoc shambled back to rejoin Bijou. "We will return the doll to the shop," Elder said, as he approached them. "You will have no further need of it."

"Oh, we'll take it back and clean it up first," Bijou said.

"No need. We will wash it off and save it for reshaping to another model." He signaled to one of the young men, who came to take Havoc by the arm.

Havoc wanted to protest, but preferred to keep his secret if he could. So he went with the brown man, while Bijou returned to the cabin with the golem.

Inside, the young man called to an artisan. "Here's a doll for reshaping. Put it in the melting pot."

Melting pot?

The artisan approached. "Easier simply to chop it into rubble, for now. It's in pretty sloppy shape."

Then Havoc read their minds. They were on to him, and were teasing him. "How long did you know?" he asked.

"When you attacked, you forgot to be clumsy," the young man

said. "No doll ever moved *that* fast and sure. Elder was chagrined to
have been deceived, but it was too late to renege."

"And you are sweating from the exertion," the artisan said. "No
doll ever sweated."

Havoc hadn't thought of that. "Does this mean that the contest
was no good?"

"No, Elder will honor the deal, though we are sorry to lose the
girl. She's a rare one."

"She is," Havoc agreed.

"And so are you, Minstrel."

Havoc shrugged. "I do what I must."

"Come on, we'll wash you off, and then you can fetch back the
real doll."

"Thank you."

Soon Havoc, back to his own colors, returned to the cabin to
fetch the golem. "Oh, I was just going to find out how well this thing
made love," Bijou said.

She was teasing him too. "It wouldn't work, with you controlling
it. It would be like self stimulation." But it was an intriguing notion.

"Too bad. Then you will have to do." She kissed him, and let him
take the golem.

It was mid afternoon. They resumed their tale telling for the villagers, and their presentation was duly appreciated.

Elder approached. "It will be here tomorrow morning."

"Thank you."

"You are clearly a competent martial artist, but I still do not believe you are the king."

Havoc smiled. "At some point I may communicate with you officially; then you can judge."

Elder departed, his doubt remaining.

That evening a woman arrived at their door. She was lovely in a
brown way. "Will you sire my fourth?" she inquired of Havoc.

This was awkward. "I realize that this is not a request to be
snubbed," Havoc said carefully. "But I was asked at another village,
and I found the experience not entirely comfortable. If it is possible to
decline, without giving offense—"

"It is not possible," the woman said. "I feel you have an excellent
body, and I would like to have a son like you."

Havoc looked at Bijou. She shrugged helplessly.

"Excellent," the woman said, and pushed on into the room. "Do
it now; I have to return to my children in fifteen minutes." She began
removing her clothing. She had a stunning upper torso.

Bijou's eyes widened. *Havoc—read her mind.*

He tried. But there was no mind there. "You're a golem!" he
exclaimed.

She laughed. "Oh, you caught on too soon. I wasn't going to tell you until you were in the throes."

"This is retribution for what we did," he said.

She nodded. "You fooled us, so we wished to fool you. You opened the door on that game."

"We did," he agreed ruefully.

"But you carried through, showing us your quality. I will too, if you wish." She glanced at Bijou. "I believe you expressed interest in this aspect."

Bijou had been distinctly uneasy about this, but now her interest quickened; Havoc felt it in her mind. "Yes. I'd like to see how it works."

"Now wait—" Havoc protested.

"I can show you," the golem said. "I will turn over this doll to you, for this occasion, if you wish."

"Who are you?" Havoc demanded.

"I am the Familiar of the warrior you defeated today."

"A man!"

"A woman with a hobby. Hardly as lovely as the doll, but certainly female. But with the dolls we can assume any role, as a diversion. I *am* the village champion gladiator. I thought to engage you again, another way, if I could deceive you long enough. I failed."

"I can borrow the golem?" Bijou asked.

"I am vacating it. Bond." The golem went inert.

Bijou sat in a chair, and concentrated, and in a moment the golem reanimated. It looked at Havoc. "Well—get your clothes off," it said.

"You can't be serious!"

"Oh, but I am," the golem said. "When we return to Triumph, and you need a cover for you or Gale, you might use golems. But you need to know just how completely they can perform. Now is your chance to find out."

She was right. Still, it bothered him. "This is a thing made of stone."

"Not when I'm animating it. You saw that warrior golem bleed. So I think this one is soft and wet in the right places." The golem looked at him sidelong. "Lost your nerve, Havoc?"

"You're angry that I will someday leave you."

The golem shook its head. "No, Havoc. I love you, but I know what must be. I never had a real claim on you. I think you need to know just how real a golem can be, and this is the time." It stripped the rest of the way and approached him. "Please. It can't be as bad as that business in the other village." It put its arms around him and drew him in for a kiss.

The amazing thing was that its body was warm and supple, and the kiss felt real. It was becoming impossible to think of this as a construct of stone.

What the hell. Havoc found any woman interesting, especially well formed young nubile ones, and this golem was as well formed as any could be. When women were made to order, magically, of course they were ideally shaped. Since Bijou, far from objecting, was urging him on, and being the familiar of the golem herself, this was really an alternate way of clasping her. Such golems could indeed be useful to him in future, if they could perform well enough to fool living folk. So it made sense to give this one a full try.

She was already removing his clothes for him. Her fingers fumbled a bit, because Bijou was not yet fully conversant with intricate small muscle coordination, but they got the job done.

Naked, he clasped the naked female. He ran his hands over her posterior, appreciating its perfect rondure. He explored her neck and shoulders, and then her breasts. Every woman was perfect in some spots, and imperfect in others, physically, but this one was perfect everywhere. Her belly, her thighs, her legs—she was an idealized doll throughout.

Then she explored him, in the manner Bijou liked to do, and in a moment he was at a fever pitch. She might not be getting any direct sensation through the golem's hands, but her touch was sure. They were standing, and he couldn't wait to move to the bed; he picked her up, finding that indeed, she weighed no more than she should. She lifted her legs and clasped his waist. Her cleft slid slowly down to meet his erection, and it was exactly as warm and slick as it should be. He found his place, and was about to slide on in—when the dragon seed buzzed.

Oh, no! There was danger or deception or wrongness, and he dared not proceed until he knew which. He froze.

I heard the buzz. Bijou was as alarmed as he. In her distraction, the golem became immobile—and crushingly heavy. It had returned to the brown rock, the basalt from the Chroma vent. She quickly reanimated it, and the weight faded, and the softness returned.

Havoc stood there, clasping the golem, at the point of entry, horrified. Suppose it reverted to stone when he was inside it? He might be most intimately and painfully trapped!

I wouldn't do that to you, Bijou thought, distressed.

But you might not have a choice, if the other woman wrested control back from you. She could do with me what she wished—and it might be lethal.

True. Set it down, get away from it.

He still wasn't satisfied. *If we are being watched, and they realize we know, this creature could become a warrior woman with strength I can't match. The arena warrior was crafted to have human vulnerability, but that's no necessary limit.*

But if you play along, and there's danger— Her thought became pure horror. *Could it be a succubus? Here to suck out your soul when you spurt within it?*

He hadn't thought of that. *Make that a statement.*

The golem in his embrace nodded. Its legs still clasped him; the position remained incipient. *It is a succubus, here to steal your soul.*

The seed buzzed. *No,* he thought, relieved.

It will revert to stone when you are inside, to punish you most cruelly.

The seed buzzed. *No.* He was almost as relieved.

The golem's face brightened. *The Brown Chroma woman really does want you to sire her fourth. The golem will collect your seed for her to use.*

The seed did not buzz. But it had buzzed before, warning him. Was that just to let him know that things were not as they seemed? It had not buzzed when the golem first came to him, asking him to sire a forth, so that much was true. Perhaps the seed should have buzzed to indicate that the golem was not what it seemed, but if it was merely a surrogate for the real woman, the distinction between bodies might have been considered immaterial. But there must be danger in actually penetrating this body. What was it?

There must be something else, Bijou thought. *Can the seed distinguish between whole truths and half truths?*

Maybe not. Maybe it goes with the predominant aspect. If a statement is more false than true, it buzzes. If it is more true than false, it doesn't. It was an aspect he had not thought of before.

That makes sense, since few things are completely *true or false. So the truth that the woman does want to have your seed for her fourth covered the fact that she was using the golem to get it. Her real body is probably not one you would care to clasp. But there must be some danger in your entering this body—maybe something the woman herself doesn't know about.*

Make that a statement.

There is danger she doesn't know about.

There was no buzz. *Reverse it.*

There is no danger.

The seed buzzed.

Havoc continued to stand there, holding the golem off the floor, though his erection was fading. They tried other questions, and gradually cornered it: most of Havoc's seed was to be saved in a special compartment within the golem, and given to the woman for her fourth, but part of it was to be sent to the main Brown Chroma territory for magic analysis. To verify his true identity, and if he should actually turn out to be the king, to establish a measure of secret control over him. That was the danger.

Now they had it. They verified that Elder did not know about this; the man was honest and would not approve. Neither was it intended by the woman who had sent the golem. That was good to know—but meanwhile, how were they to deal with this enemy ploy?

Bijou had another working-class-girl-cunning notion. She fetched a bit of flour from their traveling food supply, diluted it with water to form a thin paste, then used a straw to blow it into the golem's nether channel. Then Havoc made a pretense of having a violent climax, and set the golem down.

In due course the Brown Chroma woman resumed control, and took the golem away. She might never understand why the siring did not take, but might assume that its viability had been lost by storage in the golem. The analysts of the main Brown Chroma would of course realize that they had been had—and would not be able to protest. They would probably assume that Havoc was not the king, and had prevented them from exposing his pretense.

Once they were alone again, they proceeded to some real lovemaking. Bijou, pensive for a moment, had one request: "Havoc, when you are done with me, and I must go marry elsewhere, will you give *me* my fourth?"

"Yes!" And there it was, the way he could repay her for her loyalty and help and companionship. "And not via any golem girl."

She laughed. "Even if I want my fourth first?"

She was not speaking nonsense. The "fourth" meant one baby out of four, sired outside the marriage; it could occur at any time, and the baby could be the first, second, or third. "Especially if it's first, when you are closest to the way you are right now."

"Oh, thank you, Havoc!" She kissed him and clasped him with unusual passion, even for her.

Next morning Elder gravely produced the locator. It was a small brown metal ball in a special casing. "We ask that you return it, when you are done with it, as we do not like to let Brown magic, other than the dolls, go far beyond our premises."

"I shall," Havoc agreed. There had been deception, but Elder was not part of it, and it was a fair request.

Then he and Bijou went to the boat and peddled on toward the next village. There were a number of villagers there to see them off. He wondered whether one of the women was the one who had sent the golem. He was a bit regretful that the matter had turned out as it had, as he would not have begrudged her her fourth, but he couldn't let the Brown Chroma gain any magical control of him. Some other time, perhaps, for her.

Chapter 8—Cult

Gale was both thrilled and tormented when Havoc returned. She had been busy, setting up a route of her own to pursue, and especially with the mental disease she had deliberately contracted. Ennui and Throe, the bodyguard, had been of great help, but that had been no easy course. Yet it was worthwhile, because once she learned to control it, and to extend the existing shield of her thoughts, it was a phenomenal tool for interpersonal dealings. But none of this seemed to matter much, once she knew that Havoc was back.

She dared not meet him alone, but could not stay away from him. So she met him with Ennui and Throe, who were pledged to keep them apart by whatever means were necessary. What an irony, that she could not embrace the man she loved.

They intercepted him at the base of the elevator. He was with the girl Bijou, who looked healthy and satisfied. She surely was, having had Havoc to herself all this time.

Hello, Gale. It was the girl, addressing her mentally. And with that thought was a freighting of emotion that almost overwhelmed her. Bijou loved Havoc, completely and selflessly, but was dedicated to leaving him when his convenience called for it. She was deeply envious of Gale, the one Havoc loved in return, but bore her no ill will.

Gale opened her arms, and her thoughts, and Bijou stepped into them both. They embraced, and cried together, sharing their complementary agonies of love necessarily denied, needing to say nothing more. They had become sisters in emotion.

Meanwhile Ennui was embracing Havoc. She loved him too, but in a qualitatively different way. Their friendship had started with an oath, but broadened into a bond somewhere between parent/child and sibling, with more than a tinge of passion in the background. Ennui, especially, would do anything for Havoc. Gale now understood why: it was the magic of the changelings. But absolutely real, regardless.

"I've got to kiss him!" Gale said.

Ennui glanced at her with compassion. "You may do so. But if you get the urge to do anything more, Throe will grab Havoc, and Bijou will grab you, pulling the two of you apart, and I will wedge between. You will not resist. You understand."

"We understand," Havoc said.

Then they came together, and embraced, and kissed, and the longing of another month's separation surged up around them like a fiery flood, and the planet wobbled crazily on its axis. She had never longed for him more intensely than at this moment, and his longing embraced her more closely than his arms. They had to be one.

Gale found herself facing Ennui, whose hair and clothing were disheveled. Gale's arms were held back behind her, and her own clothing was badly askew. Havoc stood behind Ennui, and Throe behind him, holding him back similarly. They were all breathing hard.

They had indeed tried to go farther, in the heat of their mutual desire, and the others had indeed stepped in to prevent it. Gale knew it had been necessary, because her groin was burningly wet, and she had felt Havoc's imperative erection without having to see it.

My fault, Swale thought. *That passion overwhelmed me, and I tried to take him. I couldn't help myself.*

Gale knew how it was. "I don't think we can kiss any more," she told Havoc as Bijou released her from behind.

"Not unless they build two cages for us, so only out lips can touch," he agreed ruefully. "Gale—" He didn't need to continue; his mind was pouring it out.

"Stop it, you two," Ennui snapped. "You'll have us all copulating on the floor."

They laughed, but it was a reaction more of understanding than of mirth.

"Maybe we can hold hands," Gale said, unable to contemplate being entirely separate from Havoc, even if only by a few feet.

They tried it. Throe stood before Havoc, and brought Havoc's right arm under his own. Bijou stood before Gale, taking her left arm similarly. Ennui stood in the middle, taking their hands in each of hers and putting them together before her. There was an almost electric tingle as their fingers touched and linked, and their arms tightened convulsively, but the framework held.

Grouped in that manner, they rode the elevator up to the king's apartment. "What a price we pay, for doing what we believe is right," Havoc murmured.

"When Gale's mission is done, and Swale has gone her own way, you can be together," Ennui said.

"But if we still can't marry—" Gale said.

"You can still be his lover. That's often the better relationship."

"Not for us," Havoc said, and Gale agreed.

"But half a loaf *is* better than none."

"We want it all," Gale muttered.

They reached the top. They disengaged, though the others had to actually pry the two sets of fingers apart. Then they marched into the apartment, with Havoc to the left of the group, and Gale to the right.

"I need to go on my mission," Gale said. "Bijou, I think you will have to be me a while longer."

"I'll come with you, and learn your story," the girl said.

"That may be best," Ennui agreed.

The two of them peeled off and went to the Lady Aspect's suite. She welcomed Bijou in the manner of an equal, a graciousness Gale noted and appreciated. Then they talked, keeping it mostly verbal in deference to Aspect, but also because it helped to organize their sometimes chaotic thoughts and keep them simple enough to follow.

Some of what Bijou had to tell was routine, for Havoc: his indefatigable strength, fighting off brigands, indulging joyfully in sex, and insisting on battling a dangerous golem personally. Some was interesting: preventing a forest spider from attacking by remembering Gale's own experience with Yellow, siring a village woman's fourth (and not enjoying it!), and going on a lake in a peddle boat. Some was alarming: the water bomb, the avalanche, and the semen trap of the female golem. It had been a fine adventure, overall.

"He's falling in love with you," Gale said sadly.

"Oh, no, Lady Gale!" the girl protested. "I love him; I can't help it, but he loves you."

The Lady Aspect interceded. "A man is not limited to a single love. He can, and often does, love several. They are not exclusive."

"But he knows I must finish my time here, and depart and marry. I asked only that he sire my fourth, after I lose the wire, so I can have that much of him, the rest of my life."

"A nice compromise," the Lady Aspect said. "But what if the Lady Gale is unable ever to marry him? Would he marry you?"

The girl stared at her, her jaw slack. It was in her mind: she had literally never dreamed of that.

"And then I would become his lover," Gale said wryly. "Half a loaf."

"It can be worthwhile," Aspect said, sad in her turn. "I would have traded places with the Lady Symbol, were it possible."

"That's another thing," Bijou said suddenly. "We think Symbol's another changeling."

They explored that, surprised. "It does make sense," Gale said. "She has those qualities."

"Symbol is a fine woman," Aspect said seriously. "But I think you should keep Bijou close to Havoc, lest he be with Symbol. You do not want the competition of a changeling, now that we know their nature."

"True."

"But I never—" Bijou protested.

Gale smiled, though it was painful. "That's why I prefer you with him. I will never truly lose him to you."

"But—but *marriage*—"

"Common folk do become queens," Aspect said. "I did. And

though I could not hold King Deal's love completely, neither did I lose it completely, and it was an excellent life." She glanced at Gale. "And still is very good, thanks to Havoc."

"And you would be able to bear three by him," Gale said to Bijou, "and have them recognized."

Their dialogue continued, but Bijou was largely lost to it. Her prospective horizons had been enlarged beyond her fondest imagination. Gale found that she liked the girl; she was straightforward and loyal, and Havoc did appreciate her very well. She had not said so, but her peripheral thought had given her away: she had tried to sacrifice her life for him, when the water bomb threatened. She had also volunteered her life in marriage to a Brown Chroma man, as the prize if Havoc lost his contest in the arena. That kind of devotion was not to be lightly dismissed.

Gale did not delay her mission; it was too painful being close to Havoc without daring to touch him. The false king was moved out with his affectionate bath girl, and Havoc resumed wearing the crown. Bijou, again made up to resemble Gale, accompanied him on public appearances, and in the bedroom. She was doing an excellent job, perhaps because the mind disease enabled her to take hidden cues from Havoc, when he removed his crown, or from one of the others, and no outsider suspected her identity. So it seemed best for Gale to go, hoping that once the matter of the torture cult was settled, she would be able to embrace Havoc again, safely.

I'm sorry to have caused you so much mischief, Swale thought. She was becoming steadily more human as she associated with Gale, though she still had a distance to go before she could be considered a normal woman.

But you may enable us to locate the one who is trying to kill Havoc.

I hope so.

So it was that she joined a trade caravan whose route would intersect that of another caravan that was going in the direction she needed to go. Swale knew the way, but she had traveled spiritually, not limited to the human paths. She had gone direct, across water, over mountains, and through jungles. Gale would have a rather more arduous journey. So it would be a compromise between direct and practical, and would take some time. But they would get there.

What they would do once there, Gale wasn't sure. Havoc was equipped to charge in and wipe out a nest of enemies with a swift net and sword, but Gale, though no weakling as a woman, was nevertheless far from being a man. She would try to get close enough to read some minds, and then return to report to Havoc. She was under strict orders not to risk her safety. But they both knew that her safety could not be assured. It was a balancing of dangers: that to her, and that to Havoc if they did not discover the identity of his enemy.

She met the caravan master. He was of course called Trader. He was a jolly and portly man who had obviously done well over the years. "I am Red River Girl, for this trip," she said. "I understand you can use an entertainer."

He nodded, appraising her. "What kind of an entertainer are you?"

"I sing ballads and act parts."

"You have an instrument?"

"Hammer dulcimer."

"You are competent with it?"

"Quite." Indeed, she was the best player on this instrument in her village of origin, and the surrounding territory. For the past two years she had instructed others in its technique.

He seemed doubtful. "You do not provide sexual comfort for needy men?"

Don't go for that, Swale advised. *You'll have to sleep in the day.*

"I do not," Gale agreed.

"Too bad. We can provide you only safety and sustenance."

"That will do."

"If you change your mind, we can add a fair stipend in trade goods and a softer bed."

"You will have to get another girl for that."

He shrugged. "Here is your bunk." He showed her a spot on the back of a wagon loaded with rolls of fine cloth. "It is best to use it only when the wagon is parked; those rolls are heavy, and are apt to shift position on the bumps."

"I'll walk," she agreed.

"I will introduce you to the mess personnel."

They were soon on their way. Trader did hire a comfort girl, who did get a better bunk, but Gale was satisfied. Just as Swale had warned, the poor girl was busy almost all night, and had to sleep by day on the bumpy wagon. Even that was frequently interrupted as the wagon tenders and trading hands found spare moments for indulgence. She was certainly working for her keep.

So was Gale, of course, but her job was easier. The first night on the trail the caravan circled its wagons on a cleared site, posted guards, and settled down for the evening. Gale was fed early so that she could entertain while the others ate.

She stood on a small temporary platform in the center of the closed circle and announced herself. "I am Red River Girl, and here is my theme song." She sat on the edge and let her bare legs dangle. They were good legs, and the men closest were taking notice. She put her small dulcimer in her lap. She played it with tiny hammers attached to the fingers of her left hand. The theme was magically amplified, and carried throughout the circle.

Most of the men of the caravan had been paying only partial attention, focusing on their food and the details of the day. Now their attention focused on her.

"I need a volunteer," Gale said. "A handsome man. All he needs to do is sit beside me and follow my cues—and only my cues."

There was a pause. Then Trader stepped forth. "This first night I will do it. I can follow cues."

Gale saw in his mind that he was protecting her. Some young males were all right; others were not. He knew the difference, but suspected she did not. She appreciated the gesture.

There was a rumble of laughter. Trader was anything but a handsome man. He was of middle age, oblong of face, and portly to the verge of fatness. But he had a good heart.

Trader sat on the edge of the platform beside her, to her right. She played the melodic theme again, and spoke. "We believe this song originated in a valley through which a river from a Red Chroma flowed, so there was magic in it and along its banks. But some believe that it is even older, and dates from the world far across the sky where we came from. We may never know for sure, but the feelings it expresses remain real for us, regardless of our Chroma." Indeed, it was a ballad so old that its origin was lost in the mists of time.

She turned her head toward Trader, addressing him as she broke into song. "From this Chroma they say you are leaving. When you go, may your darling go too? Would you leave her behind unprotected, when she loves no other but you?"

Her voice was professionally good, as was her playing. She had their full attention. She was a pretty girl with a pretty voice, and knew it. "Come and sit by my side if you love me. Do not hasten to bid me adieu. But remember the Red River Valley, and the girl who has loved you so true."

She spoke to Trader, loud enough for the audience to hear: "Eyes front." Then she put a hand on his arm, as if beseeching him. Trader stared straight ahead, as if oblivious, while the men of the audience chuckled appreciatively. As if any man would be stupid enough to ignore such a girl!

She sang again, almost into his left ear.

> "I have promised you darling that never
> Will a word from my lips cause you pain.
> And my heart it will be yours forever
> If you will only love me again."

And she kissed his ear. There was a small sigh of longing from the audience, and the comfort girl frowned; Gale was both increasing her business and making the men less satisfied, because that girl could not compete with the romance Gale was inspiring.

She went on through the song, embracing the stolid Trader with her right arm, leaning into him, touching his shoulder with her tender bosom, festooning him with strands of her flowing hair. These loving gestures were interspersed with verbal cautions to keep his hands to himself (they were), remove his smirk (his face was sober), and to keep his clothing on (it was), and the audience was enjoying the mock reprimands hugely. The presentation was an outstanding success.

But Gale was hurting inside. The sentiment of the song was too close to her own situation. Havoc loved her, but had to leave her. She understood, but it was nevertheless painful. Her heart would be his forever, if only he could be with her.

But after this mission, I'll be gone, Swale thought. *Then you can be with him.*

But could she? She remembered an old comment, about a tie in a contest being like kissing one's sister. Man and woman together, but no passion and no future in it. She was closer to Havoc than a sister; they were like twins. They could embrace, they could have sex, but she would never dare remove the wire. They could not marry, any more than siblings could. They could be lovers, but they could not have children, not even a fourth. Their relationship was doomed to be forever sterile. How could she live with that? It hardly mattered that Havoc felt the same way; it didn't change the reality.

You can take another lover. He has.

Havoc of course loved sex. Gale loved it *with him.* Elsewhere she could take it or leave it. It was easier to leave it. But the succubus had hit on another distress: Havoc *did* have a girl, and the girl loved him and supported him completely. So he was not as lonely as Gale. Gale could do the same, but there was no man in sight who might appeal in that manner. If she encountered one, she would consider. But she knew that there was no man like Havoc.

The caravan moved on. It was late in the Air Season, which some called Fall, and soon would be the Void Season, which some called Winter, as Charm swung from Vivid toward Void. The irregular flares of the dark sun guaranteed that the weather would be unstable, and they were delayed several times by storms. But in due course they reached Gale's immediate destination: the Sulvan Sea. This was a body of water the size of a continent, and site of the largest Translucent Chroma territory. The volcano was deep under the sea, but was reputed to be very large, because the sea was formed from its emissions. Some water volcanoes were high, and jetted streams of hot water that flowed into magic rivers, but this one was hidden by its own ambiance.

Gale, in canvas trousers and a water resistant vest against the wet sea breeze, looked out across its expanse. She could not see the far shore, which wasn't surprising, but it surprised her nevertheless. She had seen ponds and lakes, but never anything approaching this. It was just so huge!

The trading path turned to follow the shoreline, which was the border between Chroma. The wagons of the caravan proceeded along it. But there was another path, of a different kind, that crossed the surface of the sea. It looked as if there were a transparent mat laid along it, smoothing down the wavelets in that one region. It led straight out to the horizon, and was the one she had to take.

It's scary, seeing it this way, Swale thought. *One misstep and you'll drown.*

I can swim.

Not better than the sharks.

The succubus was right: this was nervy business.

Trader paused, standing beside Gale. "This is where we separate. We return this way in two weeks. Will you be here?"

"I hope so."

"If you are not, we will not be able to wait."

"I understand."

"But we would like to have you with us again. Your music—" He shrugged.

"Thank you. It has been a pleasure journeying with you."

"It has been a pleasure having you along. Now I must give you something."

"Trader, we agreed there was to be no stipend."

"No stipend," he agreed. "But last night a messenger came, carrying only a small package. He said it was for you. I said I would give it to you, and he rode on. Here it is." He produced a little nondescript box tied by a ragged piece of string. "He said that no one but you must open it. I have no reason to fear it, but lady, I am by nature suspicious of anonymous gifts. Would you prefer me to open it in your presence?"

"But if it contains something deadly, that will put you in danger. You hardly owe me any such gesture."

"True. And surely it is merely a trinket sent by some shy admirer. Still—"

"Thank you, but I think it proper to take my own risks. I will open it in your presence, however. Then if it turns out to be unwelcome, you will know to distrust any future such gift to any member of your caravan."

He nodded. She was sure he did have a concern, but he was also driven by curiosity. He handed her the package.

She took it and removed the string, tucking it into a pocket; she didn't like to waste anything that might be useful again. Though the box looked like cardboard, it was actually of smooth wood, well made. Inside was something yellow.

She put her hand in, cautiously. The dragon seed did not buzz, so she picked up the object. It was a model of a yellow spider. With its seven legs spread, it was about the size of her fist. The size Yellow had been in the early days of their association. Every detail was correct.

"Lovely," she breathed.

"That's an unkind joke!" the trader protested.

"No, it's a memento of a fond memory. I know who sent this."

"You have a fond memory of an ugly spider? Who would know that?"

"A childhood sweetheart." She stroked the spider's furry torso.

"He wishes to win you back?"

"No, he knows he can't marry me, or even possess me."

"Why would he take such trouble to send you such a gift, then?"

"To show he still cares." She returned the spider to its box, and put the box into her backpack, not willing to consider it further lest she dissolve into tears. "Thank you for delivering this. I do appreciate it."

"You are welcome, Red River Girl. I must return to my caravan."

"Yes, of course. I regret having delayed you."

He hesitated. "This region—it is not safe for a woman alone. Not one such as you. If you come, on your return trip, and see our recent tracks, and can signal us, I will send a man back for you."

"Thank you, Trader," she said, touched. It was a nice gesture. She knew from his mind that his generosity was partly because he found her sexually appealing, but also partly because she was about the age of his daughter, about whom he felt guilt for prolonged absences, and partly because her presence had made normally quarrelsome wagoneers and drovers relatively passive. So she was a net asset to the caravan, and was certainly worth her keep. But she did not care to let him know about her ability to read minds, so she kissed him on the cheek, and set forth on the sea path.

It was slightly spongy, but firm enough. She could see the off-white sand descending beneath the water's surface, and small fish gliding through. Then the bottom faded in gloom, and she lengthened her stride. She had to reach the Translucent Chroma before the weather changed. She didn't want to be caught on this path in a storm. It would be too easy to get blown off the enchanted way.

He's watching your tight rear end.

"How do you know without using my eyes?" she asked, sure that her words would not carry far.

I don't need to look. I know men and I know your rear. Why do you think women are made the way we are?

Point made. Gale lowered her mind mask. Sure enough, there was her tight bottom flexing with its propulsive motion. The only mind in range was Trader's, so it was definitely him.

Let me do it.

Gale relinquished control of the body, and Swale took over. Gale felt the subtle shifting and rearranging of balance and tension. Suddenly the image in the mind behind expanded, becoming sharper, and the clothing dissolved from around it.

There was a splash. Startled, Gale paused and turned. Trader was picking himself up. He had, it seemed, taken an inadvertent step along the sea path. The water had not supported him, and he had fallen in.

"That was mean," she told Swale.

Couldn't resist.

But it has shown her one thing: the water path was for her alone. That meant that the folk of Translucent knew she was coming, and perhaps knew her business. That was good.

The path curved. She could tell because the rising wind was making ragged ripples everywhere except there. She walked along it with escalating mixed feelings. It was an easy path, being level, and that was good. But it traversed dark depths that made her increasingly nervous. She could swim, but she was getting pretty far from shore, and the water was surely cold.

You're forgetting the sharks.

"I was trying to."

Worse, a storm was sweeping in. She saw the mass of clouds banking up, and a column of grayness that suggested falling rain. The path was wending toward it.

Maybe we had better hurry.

Gale agreed. She leaned forward and broke into a jog. She was afraid the path might weaken or give way, but it held. She ran as fast as she reasonably could, and liked the feeling of the workout. She had picked up from Havoc the need to exercise, honing her body to better performance and keeping it in shape as a thing of beauty. The pack weighed her down, but she could handle it. However, she would need a more supportive bra if she did this often.

If anyone's watching from in front, he's getting his money's worth.

"Is *everything* sexual to you?" she panted.

Yes.

It was a fair answer for a succubus. Gale ran on, pleased with the way her body was performing. She had not lost much conditioning.

She came to a rise. Startled, she looked again: it was a large wave, rolling under the path. She crested it and ran down into the vale beyond—and saw a landscape, or rather a seascape. There were shrubs and boulders on an irregular surface. Just like land, except that these were formed from water.

She turned her head to look back toward shore, but couldn't see it. The sea rose up in a series of hills that walled it off. Ahead was a valley, and through that valley meandered a river.

A river? On the sea?

Oh, sure. This is the Translucent Chroma. Everything's made of water.

"But how can a river be on the sea?" she asked plaintively.

It can be anywhere it wants.

Gale walked down to the river. The path crossed it on a glassy bridge. She knelt and put a finger to it. It was cold and wet. But what had she expected? It was *water*.

She stood and resumed walking. The storm had disappeared. The bushes were being replaced by trees. Still curious, she walked across to touch the trunk of what might be a water oak. It was solid, though translucent like everything else. It had branches, twigs, and leaves she could touch that felt exactly like the trees of nonChroma. It wasn't frozen; it was air temperature.

You left the path.

Oops! But she hadn't fallen in. Apparently she had entered the Translucent Chroma territory proper, and the Sulvan Sea had become solid. It all would have seemed quite ordinary, if she hadn't seen the broad expanse of the sea ahead, and known that it couldn't be ordinary.

She returned to the path and walked on along it. Surely it led where she was going, in its own time.

Soon she saw a house made of glass, or solidified water. She went to the door and knocked. The translucent panel felt and sounded just like wood.

In a moment, the door opened. A translucent man stood there. He was not invisible in the manner of Symbol, but she could see through the thinner parts of his clothing and his body. "May I help you?" he inquired, sounding just like a man. His eyes as they studied her were just like those of a typical man, too.

"Greeting. I am Gale of Village Trifle, on a mission for the king. I need to enlist the help of the Translucent Chroma."

"Then you have come to the right place. Come in Gale, and tell me about it. I am Placebo."

"Appreciation." She stepped in past him as he held the door.

He's a handsome young lout. But what's that name?

So he was, now that she was adapting to his monochromatic translucency. He was of man height and build, with short hair and a compact face. Somewhat like her mental picture of the man the Red River Girl sang to.

"You must be tired," Placebo said. "Have a chair." He indicated a padded translucent chair.

She sat in it, and it was comfortable. He brought a footstool, and she put her feet on it. That was more comfortable.

"Would you like something to eat? To drink?"

Gale was nonplused. "This isn't really a social call. You don't have to cater to me."

Placebo looked abashed. "It gets lonely here. I'm just so glad to see someone. Maybe I get too enthusiastic. I apologize."

There was no buzz from the dragon seed. He was telling the truth. "No need," she said quickly. "I just expected more formality."

"Maybe a glass of milk? We have excellent sea cows, and more than enough."

He wants to please you.

"In that case, all right."

He fetched a glass of water. She sipped it—and it tasted like milk. Oh—it *was* milk, translucent like everything else here.

Placebo sat down opposite her. "Now what is your mission for the king? I didn't mean to delay your report."

But now Gale preferred to go slow. She still wasn't quite accustomed to the environment of translucency, and the evident friendliness of the young man gave her additional pause. "If I may—can we talk a moment? Before getting down to business."

He smiled winningly. "I'll be happy to talk, Gale. I haven't seen anyone in days, let alone a lovely woman."

"Let's exchange namings. I admit to being curious about yours."

"Of course. I was raised near to the Translucent Volcano, where magic is especially strong. But though the other children had magic, I seemed to have only the simple routine abilities, like modest illusion, modest levitation, modest conjuration and the like. I couldn't mind read at all, which of course made me a laughing stock. But one day our village had visitors from the Blue Chroma. We children tried not to stare; we had never seen blue people before. They had almost no magic—that is, theirs wouldn't work in the heart of our Chroma—so they needed assistance to get around. I was assigned to help a girl my own age, eight. She was—once I got used to her color, she was pretty. Her name was I think Bluette, though I'm not sure, because all otherChroma names sound alike to me. She asked me to float her to the roof so she could look around. She didn't know that it was all I could do to float a pebble to waist height; a whole person to roof height was way beyond my means. I tried to explain, but she didn't understand. 'You're Translucent, in the heart of the Water Chroma. Of course you have great powers of magic. Now stop teasing me and boost me up.' So I, abashed, made the attempt—and lifted her and myself right to the top of the house. I had never had power like that, yet there it was, as if routine. Then Bluette was hungry—she was a rather demanding girl, but I was bemused by her prettiness and just wanted to please her—and she ordered a plate of cookies. I tried to explain that I could conjure only a few crumbs, but she stared at me imperiously. 'I'll tell my folks you were mean to me, and they'll tell your folks, and then they'll ream your rump.' So I made an effort, and conjured a huge plate of cookies. Bluette was surprised that they were translucent, but when she tried one, it was her favorite flavor, so she was satisfied. And I was privately amazed, again. How was it that I could suddenly perform these feats, when I never could before? There were not even our specialty; none of the other children had power such as I had suddenly shown. But I had little time to ponder that, because Bluette was already making more demands, and I was scrambling to fulfill them. In the process I performed more magic than I had ever dreamed possible. Everything except mind reading; she never asked for that, and I doubt I could have done it anyway, because that had always been completely blocked from me. And it was worth it, not just for the magic, but because I did manage to please her, and before she left she got me into a game of Tickle & Peek and I got to see her blue legs all the way up to—"

He broke off, suddenly realizing that he was saying way too much. He flushed, turning a darker translucent. "I'm sorry, I am embarrassed, I talk too much, I apologize, I'll stop."

He's a prize. I haven't seen such naïveté since Lad Student on the other tour. It's sort of touching.

Gale leaned forward and took his hand. "Don't stop, Placebo. I will be as candid, in a moment. I find what you are saying most interesting."

"You do?" he asked, boyishly amazed. "You're not just saying that?"

"I'm not just saying that. Do continue." She did not let go of his hand.

"But I forgot myself so far as to describe—"

"Girls do have legs, and we show them to boys we like. Tickle & Peek is merely the pretext. Continue."

Thus encouraged, he resumed. "All the way up to her thighs. Even the curve of her—her bottom. It was so amazing to see it in blue, just like a real one. And she seemed as curious about my body as I was about hers, though translucent is ordinary, of course. So I had the much better bargain. Then it was time for her to return to her family. She kissed me, and I floated us down to the ground. That was all, with her; I never saw her again, though I'll never forget her. Those blue legs—" He shrugged. "But later I had time to really wonder what had happened. I tried to float a rock up over my head, and it rose only an inch. I tried to conjure another plate of cookies, and got only a crumb. I was back to normal. So how had it been possible? It couldn't have been Bluette, because she had no magic in our Chroma; she had depended on me. She had believed in me, and I had done it. I asked my father, and he said it was the placebo effect, which means that something isn't really potent, it just works because people think it will. Bluette was sure I could do it, and so I could. And so I came by my name, Placebo, and now—" He stared at her, stricken. "Oh, damn! Now I've told you, and you know I can't do real magic, so there won't be any such effect. I knew I should have kept my fool mouth shut."

What a charmer! I could seduce him while wearing a chastity belt.

Gale squeezed his hand. "If you did it when you were with her, and she had no magic, your name is a misnomer; you must have done it yourself."

"Yes, but she believed. That's the effect. If I had only let you believe—"

"Let me tell you about my naming." Gale did not care to tell him that with her ability to read minds, it didn't matter what he had or hadn't told her; she would have known anyway. She told him about her own Naming, which included the story of the yellow spider, and the way she helped it survive, and then Yellow helped her by saving her from being molested or worse, and how she had covered by sending Yellow away and saying that a wind had made the noise others overheard. So she came to be Gale, in part because she wasn't really believed.

"And as for Tickle & Peek," she said, "I played that many times with my friend Havoc, who is now king. We showed each other everything, leaving no secrets from each other. Later we became lovers, but now we can't be. And that relates to my mission here."

"I will help you if I can," Placebo said sincerely.

"I was investigating something at the Temple. Someone sent a succubus after me. We fought, and I captured the succubus. Now she will show me where the enemy who sent her is. It is just beyond the Translucent Chroma demesnes, and the party I seek is dangerous. So I need the help of Translucent magic, and I need a guide, because though the succubus knows where it is, she never used an ordinary route. She floated through earth, water, and air directly to me."

"Who is this enemy?"

"We call it the torture cult. It—"

Placebo frowned. "I know of it. We do not like it as our neighbor, but have not had cause to act against it. As a matter of propriety, we do not act without reason."

"Now you have reason: the king wants it abolished, and wants to know why it sent the succubus after me. We don't think it can be our enemy, so much as acting for that enemy. So we need information from it. Will you help?"

"Of course I will help! I am here to handle the concerns of our visitors, and the king's word is law."

"But don't you have to verify my identity, and make contact with the king to verify my mission?"

"No. We already knew that a king's representative was being sent. We did not know why. Now I know that too. It is my assignment to help you accomplish your mission. As a private matter."

"But don't you have to conduct me to your Chroma authorities? To get their authorization?"

"No. I already have their authorization. They want it accomplished without publicity, as they understand that this is the way the king wants it. I will take you to the torture cult. But I must warn you of two things. First, it is some distance from here, which will require a fair trek, because we aren't supposed to use magic in the approach.

The use of magic would immediately alert the torture cult, and it would have time to organize a protest which might cause the Chroma representatives to rescind the authorization. They do not like publicity about any Chroma taking serious action against others."

"I appreciate that. We do want it handled quietly, which is why my mission is unofficial."

"Yes. The second thing is that I was supposed to have sufficient magic to help you. But I made the error of explaining too much about my name, and now I will have very little magic. It would be better for you to have another guide. But that would entail delay and complication. Yet it may be better to do that, rather than go into that dangerous place without sufficient support. I can't even read minds, so will not be able to warn you of the approach of hostile people or creatures. I may be the worst person of my Chroma for your purpose."

Gale pondered briefly. She had expected to have some significant Chroma magic supporting her. Should she risk this? *What do you think, Swale?* she asked the succubus.

How can you trust me not to lead you into doom?

You want to recover your body, and be fairly treated. I remain your best hope.

If you truly believe that, you would free me, trusting me to remain with you.

I will free you, if you wish.

No! They might summon me, and I would go, unable to resist.

You can't remain where you are indefinitely. For one thing, my cycle—

You have no cycle while I am here.

Gale was startled, realizing that it was true. She should already have cycled, and had not.

"Are you all right?" Placebo inquired.

Gale smiled. "Your simple question put me into deeper conjecture than I expected. I do not want to go foolishly into danger, yet time is important."

"I wish I had stopped my mouth in time! They told me only that a woman would arrive. I just—I expected a dour spinster. Your mien unsettled me."

Go with him. He's cute and harmless.

That was Gale's conclusion. "I regret unsettling you. But I do believe that you can perform that magic when you have reason. Meanwhile I prefer not to use any magic we don't have to, because I understand that attracts attention. I will accept you as my guide."

"I understand. Of course it is better to be safe. I—" He did a double take. "You will?"

She squeezed his hand. "Yes.

"But it really isn't wise to—I mean, there are dangers. This is no simple excursion."

Shut him up: flash him your cleavage.

Good idea. Gale's free hand quietly undid a fastening. "There are dangers in waiting, too. So I think it best to move right along."

"Maybe the elders will respond more quickly than usual. I could send—" He lost his voice, for Gale was leaning forward, seemingly coincidentally, and her partly open shirt was showing the separation of her breasts. It was a very nice view, as she saw it reflected in his mind; she had found just the right angle, wherein suggestion provided more exposure than the actually visible arc segments. She was playing Peek with him, without Tickle. In some ways that was more effective.

You have the finest body I ever saw. I wish I could have been there when you used it with that hunk Havoc. But that was before I came to you.

"I'm so glad you agree," Gale said to Placebo, committing him. "Let's get started immediately."

"Yes, of course," he said vaguely, the arcs distracting him. "I'll leave a message for my replacement." He got up and turned away, but the after-image of a smooth mountain valley remained in his mind.

But he's not the same as Lad Student, Swale concluded. *He's about twenty, and should be married. I wonder why he isn't?*

Gale had the answer to that from his mind: he needed to complete his tour of duty first. As with Havoc, some things pre-empted marriage. He had volunteered for such duty partly because he felt as yet unready to marry.

That's weird—a Translucent Chroma man having no mind reading, when that's their specialty. He must be a freak.

That was an interesting point. How could he have so much of the magic of other Chroma, sometimes, but never any of his own? Then an answer occurred to her: because his magic responded only to the expressed beliefs of others. If he could read their minds, they would never have to express themselves. He was dependent on what they said, and so could be deceived about their real beliefs—and that deception, whether intentional or coincidental, gave him his power. His liability was a key to his strength.

That must be it! You're smart to figure it out like that. I never would have.

But Swale had called her attention to the matter. Gale had almost missed the significance.

Gee. The succubus was pleased.

Placebo returned with a translucent pill. "This is water vapor. Necessary magic. It will enable you to travel through our Chroma, by making our water seem like air to you. So you will not be able to swim, but will be able to breathe. It will last a week, or until you re-enter your normal environment; here are more spells, for use at need." He gave her a small bag. "To use one, merely hold it before you and invoke it. It requires only a moment."

"Thank you." She put the bag in her pack, then held up the pill. The dragon seed did not buzz. "Invoke."

It puffed into vapor, and the vapor expanded to surround her. She felt her body changing. The sensation was weird, but not unpleasant.

It almost like having sex.

Swale was always there with a sexual metaphor. But she was right; the vapor was infusing her body, penetrating it, enhancing it, like a good sexual experience.

"I feel very solid," Gale said, surprised.

"Yes," he agreed, taking a similar pill himself. "The magic actually makes you far more solid, so that water seems like air. You will not float."

She could appreciate why. She felt as if made of cast iron. But she was able to move well enough, as long as she kept her balance.

Soon they were on their way. The back door of the house opened into a closed translucent yard, and there were steps wending down into the darkness. As they entered the water, much of the weight eased, and she felt normal again.

And you're breathing water now.

So she was. It did indeed seem just like air. She knew that water was not thick air, so there must be more to the spell than solidification. She was just glad it worked well.

"There will be light soon," Placebo said. "But if you wish, I will take your hand and guide you until we come into it."

Swale could see in the dark, which meant that Gale could also, but again, she preferred not to advertise that. She was increasingly glad that the man could not read her mind. Could the Translucent authorities who assigned Placebo to this mission have been aware of that? She took his hand and paced him down the steps.

You know, you can't risk sex with Havoc. But this youth doesn't matter; you could chance it with him.

Not while I have the seaweed in me. That would interfere with his access, just as it does with your escape.

Oh, that's right. Too bad.

But the succubus' preoccupation with sex had its effect. Havoc had another girlfriend, because it would be unnatural for him to be with an appealing woman without indulging himself. Gale had leave to do much the same, if she wanted to. Did she want to? Increasingly, she thought she might. Sex was not the constant lure for her that it was for Havoc (and all other men, as their minds revealed), but neither was it something to be disdained. She loved it with Havoc, but could probably enjoy it with another man, if she liked the man. If they faced a long, dull trek, it could be a diversion. She would keep it in mind.

I think maybe Placebo is not expendable, after all. He's too cute and nice. But what can you do with me? If you free me, and I remain with you, I might still suck out his soul. So much as I hate to say it, I think I should not be with you when you have sex. Unless it's with a brute intent on rape. Then I can destroy him with a clear conscience.

Gale hadn't thought of that. If she were in mortal danger from a man, she could invite rape, and so abolish him. Unless the succubus could not do it, after all.

Oh, I can *do it. My concern is that I don't want to* have *to do it. And I'm afraid I'm primed to have to do it, to any man who enters you and blasts off. Otherwise I could really have a fling, in your good body.*

So it still couldn't be risked. Gale put aside the subject of sex and looked around as they descended the seemingly endless flight of steps. There was not much to see; the water around them was a graying fog.

Water? That was right: she was breathing it now, but it remained what it was. It did seem just like air, and she wasn't floating in it either; it was just as if she were walking on dry land. Presumably there was nothing in the water, so she was seeing nothing.

Then a fish passed by. It was hard to see, because it was translucent, but its motion disturbed the water so that its location and approximate shape were evident. It seemed to be flying, but of course it was swimming.

Weird. I've been through the Sulvan Sea many times, but through your eyes it's strange. I think I never really looked at it before.

Gale made a belated connection. *The Sulvan Sea. That's where Sulvan seaweed comes from!*

To be sure. I never could cruise the seaweed beds. That's not the only thing in this sea, by a considerable shot. I never walked the depths, so that will be new to me too.

At last they reached the bottom. As they stepped onto the sea floor, it seemed to come to life. There was a path ahead lined by glowing gray pebbles. It wound through a landscape of dimly lighted shapes.

"It is a fair walk," Placebo said. "I fear it will be dull."

So do I.

"Just so we don't get lost."

"That we won't. I will guide you to the village nearest your destination, and then there will be a cross-country trek. In between is just a lot of walking, unless you would prefer to draw on magic."

"No magic. I want to be as quiet as I can."

"This is as I understood. Many people and creatures use the magic of adaptation, so that does not attract attention. But the magic of rapid transport is another matter." He pointed to the side. "There is a safety hatch. If there is a threat from a monster, we must go to one of those as quickly as feasible."

"Monster?" Gale was uneasy. "They shouldn't be able to attack us, should they?"

"Not so. We are more solid, not less, so if they touch us, we feel like rock to them. Small fish will simply bounce off us, but large ones could knock us down. Most will pass us by, but some do prey on phased creatures, so we must be aware."

"You tolerate predators who prey on people?"

"Yes. We have a policy of letting creatures be, but sometimes they don't let *us* be. So we try to avoid them. If they start raiding villages, then we gather strong magic and fight them. The paths between villages are open territory. Normally it's enough to be alert. Most villagers can of course hear them coming mentally, and know their intentions."

"If I tried to walk this path alone, I'd run afoul of a monster," Gale said.

"That seems likely. But I am familiar with this region, and there should not be trouble."

"That is reassuring." Gale was aware that there were limits to the warnings of the dragon seed; if she were caught too far from a refuge when a monster came, the warning might not be enough.

The scenery, once she got used to its translucency and glowing outlines, was roughly similar to that of the upper realm. There were small plant outlines, and bush outlines, and tree outlines. There were flowers formed of pastel lights. Some trees gave off enough light to cast shadows; they were like miniature suns. Others had patterns of darkness that were inverted flowers. Small fishy creatures swam between them, going from flower to flower.

One fish swam across to inspect them. Placebo took it in his hand and gently moved it out of the way. Its tameness suggested that folk were not in the habit of molesting fish along this path.

What's the significance of that spider Havoc sent you?

Gale had forgotten about that for the time being. She appreciated the gift, but knew that Havoc always had a purpose. It could not be as simple as a memento of their childhood. *I'll have to take it out and study it, when I am alone. There's bound to be something special about it.*

Even so, it was nice. Havoc knew how she had loved Yellow, and how the spider had saved her from ugly mischief. This model might be crafted to save her similarly, once she understood it.

"Hold," Placebo said, stopping.

Gale stopped beside him. "There's a problem?"

"Not exactly. There's a spy eye."

"A what?"

"There." He pointed. "It's spying us."

She saw it. A floating globe with an eye-like aperture. It did seem to be looking at them. "Is it dangerous?"

"No, not in itself. They just look. But the question is, why is it looking at us? We should not be of interest."

"What interests a spy eye?"

"Whatever its master wishes to know about. Maybe it's just passing curiosity, and it will move on in a moment."

They waited, and soon the eye departed. They resumed walking. But it made Gale uneasy. The unknown enemy had known of her prior mission, and this suggested that it knew of her present one. Mischief could follow.

A wind started up. Gale realized that it was merely a current in the water, but it felt like wind. "There's my namesake," she said, trying to be cheerful. "Stiff wind."

"Maybe we should stop at the next campsite. It is getting late, and it is not easy to travel at night. The nocturnal predators can be worse than the daytime ones."

"How do you tell day from night, down here?"

"The sun trees dim when the light above dims. They conduct sunlight from above, and radiate it for the others; they are a keystone species."

"A what?"

"A keystone species. One that is vital to the rest of the life around it. If the sun trees were lost, most of the rest of the plants would die, and the creatures that depend of them would be lost also."

"Oh—like the manna tree."

"The what?"

She explained about the complex of vegetation that maintained good weather for creatures during very bad weather.

"That's fascinating," he said enthusiastically. "I must go above to observe one, when I can."

"You are interested in natural species?"

"Every species is natural. So are we. Yes, when my tour of duty as an interface is done, I hope to marry and settle down to cultivate exotic plants. There are so many, with such unusual magic, if we just take the time to see."

Gale was getting to like this man. "Interface?"

"The folk of the other Chroma tend to think of us as different, because we don't live on the land. Just as the blue girl thought I was odd. So we try to make any visitors welcome, so that they can better understand us, and appreciate our environment. This is my month on duty as interface to the nonChroma entrance. It was pretty dull, until they told me to be ready for a female nonChroma visitor, and to do for her whatever she needed."

"It must still be pretty dull, having to plod along the bottom."

"Oh, no, Gale! Your very presence makes everything else interesting."

There was the changeling effect: he couldn't help liking her. Since she couldn't prevent it, she didn't try. "I will try not to be a burden."

You will never be a burden to his imagination. Non-Translucent arcs are still floating around his awareness.

It was true. Gale had given the man too deep a flash of her bosom. She tended to underestimate the effect her body had on men. But she was learning, thanks to the mind reading.

"There's a camp."

All she saw was one of the safety hatches. But that turned out to be it. They lifted the circular lid, and climbed down a ladder into a cave chamber. This had a bin of translucent vegetables, a crock of water, and a mat.

"But isn't there water all around us?" Gale asked.

Placebo smiled. "Yes and no. In our phased state, we can't drink the water around us, even if it were not too salty. So this is phased water. It would seem like stone to natural creatures."

"Oh." She looked at the mat. "This is for sleeping?"

"Yes. It's not fancy, but there are not many travelers who go afoot. We can—" Then more of the situation registered. "Usually there are married couples, or parents and children, on pleasure tours. I didn't think—"

Again, his mind was innocent. "It will do," she said reassuringly.

He smiled, and set about preparing the vegetables. Gale let him do it, curious how competent he was in this respect.

You've got to get rid of me.

I'm not going to have sex with him.

Sure you are. But not until I'm out of you.

Gale pondered. *I can't let you go, or risk having you with me, when, if. What else is there to do?*

Get more Sulvan seaweed. Weave it into a net. That will hold me.

Gale was surprised, but the dragon seed did not buzz. "Placebo, I can do that. Would you do me a favor?"

"Of course," he said eagerly.

"Fetch me some strands of Sulvan seaweed."

"But that's for—" He broke off, too embarrassed to inquire further. "I'll find some." He climbed the ladder and out the hatch.

No wonder the blue girl found him easy to manage. But he does have a certain charm.

"Yes, he does," Gale murmured aloud. She was beginning to understand the appeal a pretty and innocent girl had for a man, because this handsome and innocent man was having similar effect on her.

Gale took over the preparation of the vegetables. She was getting used to their translucency, and was able to distinguish potatoes, carrots, squash, lettuce, and others. There was a burner that appeared to run on water, though she was sure it was either flammable fluid or magic. She shaped a meal.

Placebo was not yet back, so she sat on the mat and waited. She took out the box with the yellow spider, and studied the model carefully. Its basic substance seemed to be brown stone; the yellow fur was fastened on outside.

Where did Havoc go?

"To the Brown Chroma," she answered, realizing the significance. "They make golems."

I've heard of them. They make them out of brown stone, and bond with them.

"How does a person bond?"

I think you just focus hard.

Gale focused on the spider. Suddenly she felt herself relating to it, seeming to get inside it. She felt its seven legs, and its five faceted eyes. She saw through those eyes.

This is weird!

"Surely no weirder than you using my body."

But yours is a human female body. I know that type. This is a spider body. Yuck!

Gale smiled. "I see that you don't love spiders the way I do. Anyway, this isn't a real spider; it's a golem. I know Havoc wouldn't send me something just on a whim; this will be useful."

You have a lot of confidence in Havoc.

"Yes. I love him."

Look, Gale, I don't want to make you mad. But I've had some experience with men. It can be unwise to love one unskeptically.

"Havoc's different."

But he's got a girlfriend who spreads her legs wide just at the thought of him, and those other women I saw at the king's residence aren't far behind. He's aware of them all.

"Yes, Havoc likes women. But he's true to me, as I am to him."

He's plumbing them!

"Of course. The bath girl, anyway; he won't touch any other as long as she's around."

So now his girlfriend is reserving him to herself? That's not ideal news for you.

"Yes it is. Because she has a certain resemblance to me. He likes her because he can pretend she's me."

This is naiveté. He likes her for herself too.

"Yes, I suppose so. He's a decent guy. He wouldn't touch her if he didn't respect her."

And what about when this "respect" grows to love?

"He'll love her too. But she'll never replace me in his heart."

This touching faith has been the death knell for countless women. Suppose he marries her?

"Yes, he may have to. Because he may never be able to marry me." Then, suddenly, Gale was crying, overwhelmed by grief for what might have been.

Damn! I forgot. I didn't mean to—I wasn't thinking. I'm sorry. I'm not used to being halfway decent or sensitive, the way you are.

Gale smile through her tears. "A succubus apologizing. That's got to be unusual."

You don't know *you can't marry him. So you're both change-lings. That doesn't necessarily mean you're too closely related.*

"What are the odds?"

Maybe one in three that you're not too closely related.

"And maybe one in ten. We can't risk it until we know."

But you can be his lover. As they said, that may be the closest association.

"I want to bear his children! Three of them. And the fourth from a man like him."

Yes. Now Swale was pensive, thinking of her own prospects. *So maybe you'll find out about the changelings, and it will be okay.*

"Let's get back to the golem spider." Gale tried to dry her face, and lifted two forelegs to her mandibles. "Oops." She was still iden-tifying with the spider's body. She had not really been talking aloud, but thinking in speech.

It was tricky at first, walking on seven legs and seeing with five eyes, but the golem was magically competent, and translated her four limbs to its seven without complication. The eyes similarly rendered their images to sections of her two eyes; she saw different views in each section. It was like looking at a melange. But once she adapted, it was handy being able to see in all directions at once. No one could sneak up on this creature.

Look at those teeth!

It did indeed have ferocious tusks, that should be able to inflict a painful wound even to a large creature. If she had to distract an ani-mal or person, that would do it. "This little golem seems more useful every moment."

She continued to practice with it, becoming increasingly nimble. The spider was able to walk up a vertical wall, and even on the ceiling, if she used the spurs on the feet correctly. When it fell it wasn't hurt. It was able to extend a line of web that would readily support its weight, and to stick it to a surface, and to climb that line.

I'm impressed. If you get in trouble, that golem will get you out.

"And I may get in trouble," Gale agreed.

But it's not enough. The torture cult—you should not go there alone.

"Maybe I can use the golem to spy on them without exposing myself."

I hope so, Swale agreed dubiously.

There was a sound at the entrance. Placebo was returning. Gale reverted to herself, picked up the spider, and put it in its box, and put the box in her pack. It wasn't that she regarded the translucent man as an enemy so much as her preference to keep special information to herself.

He dropped down to the floor, somewhat disheveled. "I had to search farther than I expected, but I found it." He proffered her several good strands of seaweed.

"Thank you." She accepted them, and put them in her pack. "I have the meal ready."

He went to the lavatory to clean up, while she set out the meal.

You're going to do it.

"If I can't marry Havoc, I'll need to explore other options," she said silently. "He'll understand."

But this innocent youth is hardly worth your while.

"He'll make a sufficient diversion."

He'll fall in love with you.

That set Gale back. The succubus was right: her intimate attention would capture the heart of the guide. Was that fair to him? "I guess I'd better not."

They ate the meal, and talked. "I scouted the way to the torture cult," Placebo said. "It should be all right, if nothing happens."

"What could happen?"

"It parallels a chasm for a distance. If a storm should come—"

"How can there be a storm at the bottom of the sea?"

"Strong currents can stir things up, and affect us the way strong winds would above. But the weather seems calm."

"That's good." Gale washed the dishes in the phased water. Then she stood in the center of the shelter. "Let me entertain you."

"Oh, you don't have to—"

She lifted her dulcimer and fitted the little hammers to her fingers. "I will sing and dance for you."

"Oh." His mind showed both disappointment and relief. He appreciated her qualities as a lovely woman, but was quite shy about personal relations.

She held the dulcimer to her side, and played it. This occupied her hands, so that her body had to carry the physical part of the dance. But she did the Damsel & Dulcimer dance, which was crafted for exactly this situation. Her legs and hips carried most of it, and her head some of it, as she swung her hair around. She hummed the theme, and the instrument amplified it, as she spun and tapped the floor with her feet.

He's falling for you already.

So he was. It was the changeling effect, but knowing it didn't make her able to mute it. She was simply too appealing to men.

She ended the dance. Placebo was rapt. "You are so lovely," he said.

You're going to do it.

Yes, she was. What was there to lose? But she had to play fair. "Placebo, you know that our association is temporary. After this mission, I will return to my own realm, and we will not see each other again."

"Yes, of course. And I shall do my utmost to see that you return safely. Though without my magic—"

"I'm sure it will prove to be sufficient. We must share close quarters, and I think it only fair to give you something for your assistance."

"Oh, you don't have to—" His hopes and fears were wild.

"I want to." She took the Sulvan seaweed and went into the lavatory.

Weave it into a loose net bag. I will not be able to escape even the slackest web.

Gale did so. Then she held the bag at her cleft, and reached through it with two fingers to pull out the wad of seaweed inside her. She nudged it into the bag.

Swale followed. Gale felt her presence diminish. Her companion of the past fortnight was gone.

Gale closed the bag and tied it shut. She poked a finger into it. "Are you there?" she murmured.

Yes.

"I can still talk with you like this?"

Yes. But only when you reach inside to touch me.

"It's not unkind imprisonment?"

And you really do care about that! No, I'll just sleep. But when you're done, I'd like to be with you again, if I may.

"You may. I still need your guidance."

Gale put the bag in the pack, set it in the corner, and emerged to join the man. "I set two strictures on you," she told him. "First, to understand throughout that this is not a permanent relationship between us; it is only a passing affair."

"I understand," he said, and he did, though there was a strong background of regret.

"Second, do not toy with anything of mine—clothing, possessions, whatever. Leave them alone." So he would not inadvertently free the succubus.

"Of course." And he meant it.

"Then come to me."

Hesitantly, he came to her, his shyness making him slow. She embraced him, kissed him, and brought him down to the bed mat. She undressed him, and herself, and saw their two bodies together, so different. Hers was what she thought of as human color, off shades of white, brown, or green. His was translucent, like a mannequin made of glass. She could see it without difficulty, but it had no color as such, just translucency. Still, it was all male, and handsomely formed.

He remained hesitant to act, though he had a rigid translucent erection, so she bade him lie on his back, and she addressed him with strokes of her hands and then with strokes of her body, passing one leg over his thighs and her breasts over his chest. She kissed him again. When his desire became almost unbearable, to him and to her, she eased him into her and clasped him close. "Go!" she said, rolling him on top of her.

He climaxed so quickly that it was over before he was fairly on her. That was too fast for her, and now he was fading. "Stay," she said, still holding him close. And sure enough, the power of youth, imagination, and first experience in due course brought him to power again, and she was able to enjoy several climaxes of her own while he worked to achieve his second. That was more like it. It was a trick she had learned from her experience with Havoc: take the edge off, then enjoy the slow continuation.

After that, she let him go. They cleaned up, and returned to the mat to sleep.

In the night he woke from a dream of rapture, and desired more, but didn't dare voice it. He didn't know she could read his mind. Rather than let his frustrated longing become hers, she rolled into him and took him into her again. This time she did not prolong it; his passion was satisfied in a moment, and he relaxed blissfully. She returned to sleep. She did not mind obliging him, and it was the simplest way to stifle his thoughts that could otherwise disturb her. She suspected that it was much like that between the bath Girl and Havoc. Sex, once decided on, was best handled expediently.

But how she wished it could have been with Havoc! She could do it with another man, she could enjoy it, she could climax, but only with Havoc did it truly transport her. Love made all the difference.

In the morning she woke before Placebo and cleaned and dressed first; no need to set him off again, as she knew would be the case if she remained next to him. Anything at all could set a man on the sexual course, and it could be hard to turn him off it, but a naked woman was guaranteed. He would think of sex every time he looked at her, but would not expect it as long as she was clothed and vertical.

She pondered, then fetched the seaweed bag from her pack. She poked in her finger. "Are you all right?"

Yes. May I rejoin you now?

"Yes, I think it's safe." Gale put the bag to her cleft and worked the tie loose. In a moment she felt the entry of the succubus. The faint infusion was like another kind of sex.

It's good to be back. I've gotten accustomed to traveling with you. It's not bad in that bag, but I can't do anything. I can pick up some of what's going on outside, but with no participation possible, it's frustrating.

"I don't have to keep you confined."

Don't risk it! The torture cult may be just waiting to summon me, or make me steal a soul.

Again, the warning seemed fair. "I must admit, I have come to like your company. You have a cynical perspective that I probably need."

I think it's your determined niceness that appeals to me. I have come to know you, Gale, so I know you are not faking it. You're smart, and tough when you need to be, but when you have an option, you're nice. That's really why you gave Placebo that night, when you didn't have to: to make him happy.

"I suppose so. He's a decent innocent man, and cute in his fashion. I realized that I could give him a lot more than it would cost me."

When you reach the torture cult, you'll need my cynicism. They are not nice people.

Gale was sure of that. "I wish I didn't have to keep you captive."

I know you do. That makes it no real burden.

"Are we becoming friends?"

There was an odd sensation. Then Swale's thought came. *Yesterday you cried. Now it's my turn. Gale, I'd love to be your friend. But I can't be, because I may betray you. I don't want to, but I may do it. You can't afford to trust me.*

Again, she was probably right. "Maybe after this mission, things will be different."

But then I'll either have my own body back, or I'll be dead. We'll be done with each other, either way.

And right a third time. "I'll do my best to get you your body back. But not because I want to be rid of you. Because I know it's best for you."

I know that's your motive. And I think your decency is rubbing off on me. I'm not nearly as mean spirited as I was.

That had been apparent. "I don't think you were mean spirited. You were deliberately corrupted by the torture cult, so you would do what it wanted. Now you're reverting to your original state."

That's such a lovely thought. Again Gale felt the woman's emotion.

Placebo woke. "I overslept!" he said, chagrined.

"You had a hard night."

He stared at her a moment, then began laughing. "It was never hard long, before you softened it. You are such a creature! I wish—"

"You know I can't stay," Gale reminded him.

"I know it." He got up and set about organizing himself.

He's a conquest, all right. I felt three releases in the night. Four, I mean; there was one hours later. They drove me crazy. I think I am programmed to take the soul of any man who lets me. But I couldn't reach his. Or yours.

"Mine?" Gale asked subvocally, startled.

You went off three, four times, like so many pulses, just before his second. They were different from his, but I clutched for them too, just as desperately. I think it doesn't matter what soul I take. Maybe when they primed me, they never thought a woman would go off. I think I'm just as dangerous to you as to him.

"Thanks for the warning." Gale felt weak with the realization of the possible narrowness of her escape. It did make sense: a succubus normally seduced a male, so would collect only male souls. An incubus would seduce a female, and could not afford to climax before he caused her to do so, so he would get only female souls. But in special circumstances, or with homosexual encounters, that could change. So probably either could take either, but seldom had the opportunity.

I didn't realize it, until you actually had sex. Don't trust me, Gale.

"I won't," she agreed.

Placebo emerged from the lavatory. "You are a lovely woman," he remarked. He was referring to the whole of her, mental and emotional as well as physical.

Agreed.

"Thank you." What else could she say?

They resumed travel. As he had said, the light trees were brightening, sharing their life-giving light with other plants, and there were surely similar interactions in the soil as the vegetable world cooperated for survival. She had seen it on land, so wasn't surprised by it under water. Nature was a wonderful thing, when one took time to appreciate its qualities. Havoc loved it, and studied it constantly. Which reminded her of him again.

The path wound through unfamiliar vegetation, but Gale knew from Placebo's mind that much of it would have been dangerous for an uninformed intruder. Plants did know how to protect themselves, and most of them preferred to be left alone. The man was doing a good job of keeping her well away from threats, so that it seemed as though there were none. She appreciated that.

The dragon seed buzzed. Gale looked around, trying not to be obvious—and saw another spy-eye moving away. "Someone is observing us," she said.

"Maybe it's coincidence."

"Maybe," she agreed, ill at ease. "It was another spy-eye."

He looked around, but the eye was gone. "Let me check around. Maybe something is near."

"I don't think there'll be anything to see."

"Still, it's best to be sure. You should be safe if you wait here."

He means well.

Gale nodded. "I'll wait."

Placebo left the path, and soon disappeared amidst the assorted tall plants. Gale followed his mind for a while, but the range of her mind perception was limited, and he was soon gone that way too.

This was the second time they had been spied on, but the dragon seed had not buzzed the first time. This was surely mischief.

A wind stirred. Actually it was a current, but Placebo had been right: it felt like wind. It quickly built up to a gale.

That fits. Gale in a gale.

"But where's it coming from? I don't trust this." She lay down on the ground, trying to get out of the wind.

That floating eyeball spotted you. Now the enemy is striking.

That was exactly Gale's concern. Somehow the enemy always seemed to know where she and Havoc were. Was it able to track their minds, or did it have some other way to identify them?

The gale was still intensifying. The air/water was getting cloudy as the bottom was stirred up. "I can't stay here," Gale gasped. "I'll be blown away."

Right into that chasm.

Indeed, the gulf was uncomfortably close. Gale crawled toward the largest tree-trunk she saw. But the wind caught at her, shoving her toward the brink. She tried to dig her fingers into the ground, but the soil off the path was spongy and didn't hold.

Placebo appeared, forging through the discoloration. His mouth opened. He was calling to her, but the words were lost in the storm.

Then the wind picked her up and hurled her over the brink. She screamed as she fell into the dark chasm.

Something took hold of her. Her flying shirt and skirt smoothed out, and she floated in place, oblivious to the awful wind. What was happening?

Placebo reappeared. He was floating too. He beckoned to her, and dropped to a ledge. She followed. There was a cave slanting into the wall. They drifted into it, getting out of the wind.

Suddenly her weight returned. She landed hard on the rock, grunting. He reached out to steady her. "We're safe now."

"What happened?" Flustered, she tucked herself back together.

"I levitated us to this shelter. It was the only safe place I could find immediately."

She looked at him. "You used magic."

"I had to. You were falling—" He broke off, surprised. "I used magic!"

"I told you you would, when you needed to."

You did tell him, but you didn't really believe it.

"But this wasn't the placebo effect!" Placebo protested. "It was real magic."

Gale ignored Swale's accurate comment. She was feeling emotionally numb, but knew she needed to lock in her point. "Precisely. You can do it, when you have to."

He peered out into the gulf. "Evidently so. But I didn't believe it.

When I saw you go over—"

"You acted. I am very glad you did. I was otherwise lost."

"That storm—it came up so suddenly. If I had realized—"

"I think it was intended to blow me away, literally. Something doesn't like me."

"The torture cult?"

"Maybe. Does it have water magic?"

"No. It depends on us for transport to the surface. Otherwise it is confined to its caves."

"So there must be some other power going after me. Could it be some Translucent Chroma magician?"

"No! We wouldn't do that. If we didn't want you to pass, we would have kept you out of the water."

"Then someone else must have the power to use your magic."

His mouth opened, but he could not speak. He was faced with unacceptable alternatives.

But you made your point. Now all you have to do is survive your journey.

Gale nodded to herself. She had evoked Placebo's magic, but also verified that her enemy had more formidable magic, and was becoming more open about using it. How likely was it that she would be able to complete her journey, let alone investigate the torture cult?

There was a stirring in the depths of the cave. Gale saw a tentacle reaching out of the darkness. "What is that?"

He looked. "A squid. A nocturnal predator. This cave is dark enough for it to be active in day time. We must get away from here."

Gale looked out over the brink, into the gulf. "We can't just knock its tentacles aside?"

"No. We don't want to hurt it, or let it hurt us."

More of the squid was coming into sight. The thing was huge. She counted nine tentacles, and they grew to be massive at their bases. She also saw a formidable beak. She backed away from it, but there was little standing room left on the cave ledge.

"Is there a passage to the surface?" She meant the surface of the seafloor.

"There usually is. But it would be behind the squid." He looked into the gulf. "I'm not sure my magic is working."

The squid lunged, surging forward. Gale screamed and stepped away from it—and her rear foot came down on nothing. She fell into the gulf. Again.

Then Placebo was with her, catching her in his arms. He slowed to a stop, supporting her. But they were now well down in the gulf, and there was a strong current in it, carrying them along to the side.

"Where are we going?" Gale asked, not easy about this either.

"I'm stable now, not using any more magic. I had to use it, to catch you. But maybe this is all right."

"All right?"

"This current is bearing us rapidly toward our destination. We can save time without using extra magic, just by letting it do so."

"But the enemy already knows where we are, so the use of magic may not matter."

"That's true," he said, surprised. "Still, it's an easy way to travel."

Gale wasn't so sure. "What is that thing bearing down on us?"

He looked. "Uh-oh. That's a black shark."

The shark accelerated, opening its mouth as it closed on them, showing a circle of black teeth.

Then they were forging upward, as Placebo's magic took hold. Gale felt her hair blown back by the wind. They reached the top of the gulf, passed above it, and dropped to the ground beside it.

"Thank you," Gale said, kissing him. "Very nice magic."

Placebo flushed dark translucent and set her down. They had had sex the past night, but it was as if he had never been thanked before. "I didn't know I could do it," he said.

He can do it because the very notion of harm to you transforms him.

"Fortunately I did know," Gale said. She was quite satisfied about the need to reassure him about his magic.

They seemed to have outdistanced the predators. Gale wondered whether they had been sent by the enemy, or had appeared randomly. It was hard to tell—which was perhaps the point. The enemy wanted her demise to seem accidental.

Placebo stumbled, and barely caught himself. This time it was Gale who jumped to support him. "Are you all right?"

"Sorry. I'm not used to invoking that much magic."

"It tires you?"

"Yes. Magical exertion is like physical exertion. It takes a while to recover."

"I'm sorry. I didn't realize. I don't have direct experience with magic myself."

"It's all right."

But it wasn't all right; his mind showed that he was suddenly extremely weak.

"Is there a rest stop close?" she asked.

"Yes."

"Then we'll stop there." She put her arm around his waist and steadied him as he walked. He tried to protest, but not strongly; he did need the help.

They reached the stop, and climbed in. She made him lie down while she attended to the food. He soon slept. She worked his clothes off and replaced them with a blanket; then she washed the clothes and hung them out to dry, along with her own. Again she marveled at the way the underwater domain had become so like the land domain, even in the homey little details.

He's such a charmer. He trusts you.

"Not without reason," Gale said. "I'll have to bag you again."

Of course. They went into the lavatory and attended to it. Gale left the seaweed bag in her pack, as before, then went out to complete her routine business. Placebo slept on, so after a while she lay down beside him, sharing his blanket.

In due course he woke and found her there. "What time is it?" he asked, confused. Naturally he did not remember getting naked with her under a blanket.

"Late afternoon. You needed a rest."

"But I'm—you're—"

"So we are." She turned into him, her breasts and thigh coming into contact with equivalent parts of his body.

That was all it took. It a moment he was embracing her, and inside her, and his ecstasy spread across to her mind and sufficed for them both. This was the easy way to have sex: sharing his passion instead of generating her own.

As he faded, he looked at her. "You know you don't have to do this. I will guide you regardless."

"I appreciate your exercise of magic on my behalf. You tired yourself, so I'm helping restore you."

He did not argue the case. He got up, cleaned up, and joined her in the evening meal. Then they lay down again for the night. She felt his guilt for his renewed desire.

"Yes," she said, before he asked, and they clasped again. It was really very easy to reward and satisfy a man, especially when she wanted to. But still she wished it could have been Havoc she satisfied. Placebo was a fine young man; he just wasn't the one she loved.

"I will guide and protect you to the best of my ability," he said. "But my duty is limited to our travel through the Translucent Chroma. I can't go into the cult cave with you."

"I understand." She knew how much he wanted to go with her, but he had to stay within his mandate. He was an honorable young man, and would not violate his trust. In addition, his magic, however powerful when belief or necessity invoked it, would not operate outside his Chroma.

In the morning they prepared for the last day of travel. Because Gale could not be sure whether Placebo would want sex again at dawn, for all that dawn was hardly the same down here, she didn't restore Swale. She was right; he did, and she obliged him immediately. He didn't have to tell her: he was in heaven despite knowing that soon they would part and never meet again. Even as they donned their packs for the resumption of the journey, the desire came upon him, and she simply stepped into him clothed, drew aside the necessary, and accommodated him vertically, then did a quick cleanup. She was

getting good at this. But she had not time to fetch the succubus before
they were on their way. She hoped Swale did not feel neglected.

There had been a time when she thought Havoc had sex too much
on the mind, because he was so much more interested in it than she
was. But experience and observation had shown her that he was merely
typical of young men, and now that she could read minds, she realized that the urge for sex was simply a basic component of the male
estate, like competitiveness and pride. All men judged all women
they encountered as prospective sexual partners, and made their decisions so swiftly that they weren't even conscious of having done it,
unless the verdict was positive. Most verdicts were negative, but when
they met Gale, it was always positive. Their taste for it was limited
only by the ability of their bodies to revive after performance. Only by
hiding her face and body could she avoid inciting their desire.

Swale would have agreed emphatically. The succubus was like a
female male in her constant urgency for sex. This insight helped Gale
understand her internal companion.

They reached the village Placebo had mentioned: Wetback. The
houses were made of solidified water, not ice, and were of course translucent. It hardly mattered, because a translucent person was invisible inside a translucent house. Apart from that it seemed just like a
typical village, with folk going about their separate activities, tilling
their seaweed fields, herding their domesticated fish, and tending to
their translucent children.

"We can go on this afternoon," Placebo said. "It's only an hour
from here."

Gale had a notion. "Let's stay here the night."

He glanced at her, surprised. "I thought you wanted to proceed
as quickly as possible."

"I did. But I reconsidered."

He shrugged. "Wetback Village will of course provide you with a
room. I'll see to it."

"Provide *us* with a room."

He didn't argue. There was a glad lift to his feelings as he understood that she was giving him one more night of bliss. Soon they were
seeing the village headman. "In return, I will entertain your children,"
Gale said.

"We do not ask our guests to entertain us," he demurred.

"If your children do not like music, they are not the kind I have
encountered."

"You are a musician?"

"Yes."

Soon Gale had an audience of children and a few adults. She set
up her dulcimer, donned the finger hammers, sang. "Black, red, green
is the color of my true love's hair. His eyes are something wondrous
fair. The whitest face and the grayest hands. I love the ground whereon

he stands." It was one of the old ones, said to predate colonization in some form, but always popular. As she sang, she imagined herself as the woman of the song, and realized that this village of natural mind readers were responding to that, too.

She had their attention, as she knew she would. She was a pretty girl despite her oddity of appearance, and she sang well, and it was a nice song. She went on to others, and they loved them all. Her audience swelled. By the time she got to Red River Girl, and asked the headman to be her volunteer love, they were all enraptured. Even the adults laughed as she reminded him to keep his eyes and his hands to himself. "You're good," he murmured. She knew it.

Naturally they made a banquet, and many people came to talk with her, including a number of young men. "I'm with Placebo," she said gently, and they looked at him enviously. They knew what he was experiencing, because they could read his mind as readily as she could; he was the only one who could not read other minds.

At one point the headman sent her something she had not encountered before: a closed thought. *You are treating Placebo like a child.* It was a compliment, recognizing that she had given joy to a person who had been tacitly isolated by his inability to read other minds. Normal Translucent Chroma women had avoided him for that reason. It had not before occurred to Gale how lonely Placebo's life must be; he was innocent for good reason. She had given him something he could not get at home. The headman approved.

In the early evening they retired to the house provided. "You were terrific," he said. "I had no idea you could do that."

"It wasn't relevant until I saw the children." She peered through the translucent wall. "Can others see us?"

"Does it matter?"

She laughed. "No. They surely have no doubt why we are here together." She dropped her clothing and lay on the bed.

"You're letting them know I'm your lover!" he said, gratified. He did not realize, or perhaps preferred not to realize, that everyone in the village already knew he was her lover, and would be able to tune in on the proof of it this night. Gale had never been much for public sex, but in this case she was satisfied to do it.

"But this may be the last time," she said. "I want to get up before dawn, to sneak up to the torture cult cave."

"Oh. I will wake you." He joined her on the bed, and they made half translucent love. She didn't know what would happen on the morrow, but she feared it, and wanted to make the most of this night. She did.

It seemed barely a moment before he was gently squeezing her shoulder, waking her. "Two hours before dawn."

She banished sleepiness. "Thank you." She got up, dressed quickly, ate quickly, and they were on their way within half an hour.

She remained without the succubus, though it would have taken only moments to restore her. Gale just wasn't sure, this close to their destination, so had not taken that step.

The village was quiet. They walked out, taking an obscure path Placebo knew. There was a main path, for the delivery of supplies, but this one had fallen out of use long before and was largely forgotten. There was no light, and she did not have Swale's night vision, so was dependent on Placebo's guidance. Hand in hand, they made their way.

No bad weather came, and no monster attacked them. Had they succeeded in avoiding the torture cult's observation? Gale wasn't at all sure. But this seemed to be her best chance. She wasn't sure exactly how she would spy on the cult without exposing herself to danger; Havoc had been uncharacteristically vague on that. But she would do her best.

Suddenly they were there. It was a muddy hole in the sloping sea floor. She felt the mud stirring as she felt around its edges.

"This is a back way in," Placebo murmured. "It feeds into their cellars, which are their highest level. Translucent magic ends there; you will become normal by landwalker definition. When you emerge, you will need to take another water pill, lest you drown. I will wait here; I must not enter. If you lose your pills, I will give you one of mine."

"I understand."

"Gale—" He was struggling with the pain in his mind, fearing for her safety.

She kissed him quickly. "I'll be all right. I'll see what I can see, and hear what I can hear, and return soon. But if I don't, then you are free to go. Don't wait more than a day."

He did not reply, but his mind showed that he intended to wait indefinitely, unable to let her be lost. He would have done that even if he didn't love her. Now she understood why Havoc did not want to be unkind to the bath girl; it was not right to do this to innocent and feeling people. Yet it was a consequence of the process of the king's governance.

She moved on into the cave. It led only a short way into the ground before it was barred by a stout metal door. There was a wheel mounted on the door. She put her hands on the wheel and turned it, first one way, then the other, and found that the counterclockwise rotation was easier. After several rotations, she heard something click, and the wheel would not continue. So she pulled it toward her, and the door swung open.

Beyond was a short continuation of the cave, becoming a metal tunnel blocked by a second door. She went to that and tried its wheel, but it would not budge. Then she realized that she was being dull; it was an air filled region beyond, so it could not simply open to the sea.

She was still breathing water, but the folk beyond this barrier were not. She turned back, and saw another wheel on the near side of the first door. She pulled on it, swinging the door shut, and locking it in place by turning the wheel clockwise.

The dragon seed buzzed.

Gale paused. The seed was obviously warning her of danger—but she already know this mission was dangerous. Was there anything specific? There seemed to be nothing here other than the chamber bounded by the two doors with their wheels. So it must be general: the seed was aware of the threat she was walking into. But she really had no choice; to accomplish her mission, she had to do it.

She returned to the inner wheel. Now it turned. When it released, it swung suddenly away from her, and the water poured out. She was swept along with it, skidding across the stone floor. For as it happened, she suddenly became a landwalker again, and the water was water. She was on her bottom in a coursing puddle, inside the torture cult's hideout.

"Welcome to our humble demesnes, Gale of Trifle."

Her head snapped around. There stood a man in boots and helmet. She recognized him immediately from the memory images of Swale: this was Shrapnel, the torture master. She hadn't fooled him at all.

She scrambled up and ran for the water-lock. But the second door was closed now, and the wheel would not respond to her effort to turn it.

"Now we can do this one of two ways," Shrapnel said, using the standard predator-prey mode of address. "Pleasant or unpleasant. Do you have a choice?"

Gale knew she was fairly trapped. The man's mind was a horror of viciousness, and she didn't want to touch it; she raised her shield as far as possible, to keep that monstrosity out. Its very processes of thought threatened to contaminate her, in much the way Swale's initial siege of horrors had. She would have to play this through, seeking some unlikely avenue of escape before the physical horrors started. "Do I?"

"The unpleasant way is for you to agree to cooperate, and become a succubus to replace the one you cost me. One hundred young male souls, and you will be free."

Better to engage him in dialogue while she looked for her opening. "What is the pleasant way?"

"For you to attempt to resist accommodation, so that I will have the pleasure of torturing you until your will is broken. Then not only will your soul go out as a succubus, your body will remain for my private personal enjoyment while you are on your missions."

The worst of it was that he wasn't fooling. The seed had not buzzed. He meant pleasant or unpleasant for him, not her. She lowered her mind shield enough to pick up the confirmation. He did like to torture lovely women, and to reduce them to abject despair. He liked it when they resisted, because that gave him greater opportunity to savor the delicious process of making them hurt.

There would be no reasoning with this monster. He was like a six-legged cat playing with a mouse, crippling it one leg at a time and offering it the seeming hope of escape. It could take the mouse days to die, and it could take a woman much longer. Especially if the physical torture was mostly illusion-memory.

She had discovered how to nullify the tortures Swale knew. Maybe she could do the same here. For a while.

But that would be only as a last resort. It would be better to escape, and quickly. That meant taking out the torture master.

Gale leaped at him, drawing her hidden knife. She didn't test the leather armor, knowing it would protect him; she went for the eyes. Blind him, and half the battle was won.

But the blade sheered off, missing him. He had a protective spell. Caught unprepared, she lost her balance—and the man's hands shot out to catch her wrists. "What a nice surprise. You have elected to fight."

She leaped, using his hands for leverage as she brought her feet up to club him in the crotch. But the leather held, so that her effort merely pushed him back a step.

"Oh, yes, sheer delight! Kiss me, my exquisite honey." He drew her in toward him.

She tried to butt him with the top of her head, but the spell bounced it off. So she let him bring her mouth to his—and she bit at his lip. And couldn't. Shrapnel succeeded in kissing her half open mouth, and touching inside her lip with his vile tongue. She couldn't touch him, but he could touch her. He surely had had much practice at this sort of thing, and had covered all the bases.

He drew her in further, and transferred his hands to her back so as to press her body against his. The contact revolted her, even though it was only his armor she was touching. She struggled, but could not budge.

"Yes, I could rape you now, but that would be too sudden. I want to savor the whole of you first. So let's get to it."

He carried her out of the chamber, down a spiral ramp, and into— the torture chamber. Exactly as Swale's memory had it. There were three other women manacled to the walls. So it was real! Gale had believed that it was all a false memory, but she must have misinterpreted the buzzes of the dragon seed. That did happen on occasion.

Shrapnel forced one of Gale's arms up over her head. It touched a manacle, which automatically clamped about her wrist. Then he did the other arm similarly. Her legs remained free, but she was now chained to the wall, pressing against her backpack. Her feet touched the floor, but she had to stand up straight to prevent the manacles from pressing against her raised hands.

He drew a large knife. He was going to start cutting her immediately! She tried to kick him away, but he merely stepped inside her foot and wedged his hip against her lifted leg. "So eager," he murmured, moving his crotch against hers suggestively. "Fear not, my lovely, it will happen, in good time. But I want you to do some proper screaming first."

He slid the point of the knife across the clothed surface of her bosom, then made it dig in between her breasts. The cloth parted, and the shirt peeled away on either side. He cut it to her waist, and slit it to the sides and along the sleeves so that it came off her front and dropped down behind. Then he cut through her bra without touching the flesh, and let it fall similarly. He reached around her and cut the straps of her backpack, letting it drop behind her feet. He continued until she was completely naked.

"Ah, yes, my sweetheart, you are the fairest form yet. You will be a considerable asset to my practice."

"I'll never be that," she retorted.

"You assume you have a choice, my dear." He looked around. "I think it is time for the preliminary course. You will find it edifying." He turned away, leaving her hanging.

Shrapnel walked to the farthest hanging victim, a lovely nude brunette nonChroma girl. He took up a whip. "Are you ready wench?" he demanded.

"No," she said tearfully, knowing what was coming.

He struck her with the whip. She screamed as it cracked across her face, cutting her cheek open.

Gale, watching, was struck by two things. First, this was exactly the same as the vision Swale had shown her. Second, the woman had no mind. She wasn't real. Gale was trying to read it, and finding only blankness there. This was a mere dummy model, given seeming animation by surface illusion. The two other hanging women were also mannequins, crafted shapes without animation or life. So though Swale's memory had not been entirely false, the tortured women were. Rather, they were golems, like her spider. There must be someone out of sight, animating them in turn, but she couldn't pick up that mind second-hand.

This was a play, following a script. For the benefit of the fourth woman: herself. This was how Swale had been tamed. But the torture master didn't know that Gale could read minds; she had so far acted like a completely typical innocent woman, fortunately.

Still, she was manacled to the wall, and in time Shrapnel would get to her. Then he would be able to rape her, and torture her in other ways. So this chamber was only half bluff.

Meanwhile the woman was screaming as the whip crisscrossed

her body, cutting it so that blood flowed and dripped to the stone floor. It was a most effective image. But Gale knew she couldn't afford to be distracted. She needed to save herself.

The pack remained at her feet. In it was the golem spider—and the bag containing Swale. Gale focused, bonding with the spider, and in a moment she was looking at the inside of the box. She worked the legs, but couldn't open the box from inside. Why hadn't she thought of that?

Shrapnel finished with the first victim. He moved on to the second, a lovely bare green girl. He drew his knife. "Are you ready, strumpet?" She averted her face, so that her green tresses covered it.

He sliced across her belly, not deeply, opening a bleeding cut. She screamed horribly. "Are you ready?" he repeated. Gale would have been truly appalled, had the bath girl not shown her in a mental picture how the golem Havoc defeated had bled when cut in the neck; bleeding was part of their magic, when animated.

Gale returned her awareness to her human body. She lifted one foot and worked her toes into her pack. She had to move slowly, so as not to attract the attention of the torture master. The box was near the top of the pack. She pushed against its side and lid, until it opened.

Shrapnel proceeded with gusto, carving the green girl's right breast off. This might be all for show, but he loved it, and was capable of doing it to a real girl—at such time as he had one who was expendable. The golems, she gathered from peripheral thoughts, he took to a repair chamber where they were glued and painted and restored as necessary, so they would be ready for work the next day.

Gale returned to the spider. The golem pushed the box the rest of the way open and squeezed out. Then it looked around with five eyes to spy the Sulvan seaweed bag. It caught hold of the bag with two hooked feet, and dragged it up and out of the pack.

"Are you ready?" The girl was not, so Shrapnel continued carving until her screams became faint and stopped. Then he went on to the third woman, a white Chroma, right across from Gale. "Are you ready, whore?"

And he had a servant girl to do their partial animations during the torture sessions, to make them appear lifelike. She of course felt none of their pain, but made them cry and scream realistically. What a dirty show!

The spider climbed up Gale's leg, hauling the bag. It reached her crotch, and labored to place the bag at her cleft and work it open.

The third woman shook her head. Shrapnel gestured to the side, and the hellhound bounded in.

The bag's tie loosened. The succubus came up out of it and into Gale, investing her womb. *It's good to be back. What's happening?*

Gale filled her in with a rapid series of mental images.

Swale borrowed her eyes and stared at the grotesque rape in

progress immediately before her. The creature was wedging its huge organ into the tight cleft of the white girl, who was screaming continuously. *You mean that's not real? She's just a dummy?*

Gale assured her that was so.

All this time I thought it was real torture! The villain fooled me completely. Swale was chagrined. *I'm from the Brown Chroma. I know about golems. What an idiot I was not to think of that!*

"The golems are painted other colors," Gale pointed out. "You had no reason to suspect their presence here, way beyond their origin. And you had plenty of other distractions."

But the hellhound is real.

Gale touched its mind and realized that was true. It was an animal bred for frequent and violent sex; every day it had to have it, or be distended by its own burgeoning fluid and in increasing pain. In that respect it was the ultimate male. It preferred living women, bound and helpless, but would address any living thing it caught. It was not smart, so did not realize that the manacled woman shape was not genuine. The aperture of the golem was too narrow, putting the wolf into a frenzy of effort, but it had no choice; its urgency would not wait.

The hound's being tortured too, Swale thought.

"Shrapnel is a mean man," Gale subvocalized. "He makes everyone around him suffer."

Gale guided the golem spider back to the backpack, but did not confine it to its box. It might be needed again. Then she explained her strategy to the succubus: "I want to lure him into raping me, so you can capture his soul. What will you do with it, once you have it?"

I'm supposed to carry the souls, bound by magic, to one of the male bodies in a chamber elsewhere in the complex.

"These are men? That doesn't seem secure."

No, they are kept in suspended animation, or some similar state, magically, so they can't go anywhere. There's a whole roomful of them, men without souls. A hundred of them. I think they are supposed to become an army, when animated by captive souls. But I don't know.

Actually, Swale was picking up the notion of an army from Gale's reaching of the periphery of Shrapnel's mind. All she had known before was that these bodies represented storage for the souls she captured. So far she had gotten nine, before being diverted to go after Gale. "How do you deliver the soul there?"

I go to the next unoccupied man, and lock on to his member when the servant girl lifts it up for me, and I feed the soul into it. The soul travels up through the pipe to his prostate, and takes residence there. Just as a succubus goes to the woman's womb. It can't escape, because it lacks the magic I was given, to travel freely as a soul. It can't rouse the man, because those bodies are magically drugged to be unconscious. So it curls up and sleeps there, as far as

I know.

Gale was beginning to make sense of this. Shrapnel had somehow obtained a collection of male bodies without souls, and was slowly infusing them with captive souls so they could one day be reanimated. When the roster was complete, he would rouse and train and send out his army, to invade some vulnerable region. Building his empire. Woe betide the village Shrapnel ruled! He might make wholesale use of the men and women there, converting them into a larger army of soldiers and prostitutes, so that he could conquer a more extensive region. Eventually he hoped to become lord of the planet, if not diverted by the wonderful prospect of a limitless supply of real women to torture.

"We need to be rid of Shrapnel," Gale said. "So I'll lure him, and you take him out and lock him in a zombie body."

Gladly. I owe him endless torture.

The hound had finally finished with the pseudo woman and retired to its den to recharge for the morrow. Now Shrapnel turned to face Gale again. "Are you ready?"

Had she not discovered that the three prior tortures were mock, Gale would have been sickened and terrified into capitulation, as had been the case with Swale. As it was, she was disgusted and angry. The show was fake, but it was graphic, and it was no fun watching a mannequin seemingly tortured. She knew that what this brute wanted from her was her cooperation in becoming a succubus, to help him forward his larger scheme. She needed to make him believe that he could achieve that cooperation. But he expected resistance at the outset, so she had to resist enough to lull his suspicions. With luck she could tempt him to his doom. Soon, she hoped, because the blood had drained from her raised arms, and the manacles were bruising her wrists. It was no joy standing here naked, either.

"No!" she said. "I know what you want, so you won't mutilate me, because that would ruin my body. Those other woman couldn't handle what you wanted, so they were expendable, but you can't expend me. So no, I'm not ready, and I'll never be ready, you ugly monster."

"You're a spitfire," he said, satisfied. "You'll be a great asset when harnessed."

"No I won't! I'll never work for you, you walking turd. You don't have the gumption to be a real man; you even have to have your doggie do your fornication for you."

Beautiful.

Shrapnel was annoyed. He expected defiance, but she was striking harder than he liked. "You are before me naked and chained. I can have my will of you at any time."

"I don't think so. I think you torture women because you can't face their sexuality. You can't get your little thing up. You can't have your will of any woman, certainly not me." As she spoke, she writhed, nominally trying to free herself, but in the process accentuating her breasts and thighs.

"I want to tame you, you barbarian lass, so that you will come to desire my favor above all else. You will beg me for satisfaction, when you are my mistress."

Gale forced a laugh. "You couldn't tame a fresh puppy! I could beg you all day and you wouldn't be able to oblige, you piddling excuse for a man." She tossed her head so that her hair flung out and down, covering portions of her breasts in what she hoped was a tantalizing manner.

It's working. You've got his imagination, and you're making him mad. He's just about ready to rape you.

Indeed, the man was fumbling with the armor at his crotch. "You think I'll let you go if I use you. That's not so. You'll hang here until you are ready to do my will. You will eat and drink and urinate and defecate right here, until you are ready, regardless what I do with you in the interim."

The notion of having to perform bodily functions without facilities or the use of hands disgusted her, as it was supposed to. But so did the idea of tempting him into sex. She would do what she had to do. "You're bluffing! You'll let me hang here because you *have* no interim." She wriggled again, and read the effect in his mind. His desire for her was now quite strong. He was really turned on by the sight of a beautiful naked woman in chains.

"Meanwhile, maybe I will call your bluff." He brought out his member, which was ready for action. True to her description, it was not large.

"And maybe you'll melt into impotence," she said sneeringly.

"We shall see." He stepped toward her, holding his member, orienting it.

Remember, he has to climax. Then I've got him.

Then a different thought crossed his mind. "I almost forgot. You're the king's lover, sent here by him. You could be booby-trapped." He stepped back, putting his member away.

Damn!

The ploy was lost; Gale read it in his mind. She was booby-trapped, but not the way he thought. She didn't see how she could convince him otherwise, so she went the opposite route. "Yes, Havoc sent me to destroy you, you pitiful excuse for a nothing. Now I am here, and you are doomed."

"I hardly think so. Did it not occur to you that your barbarian man has taken a new lover, and needs to be rid of you? What better way than by sending you to certain captivity or death. I understand the girl is only sixteen, no spitfire, and is beautiful and endlessly obliging. No wonder he prefers her to you."

He had described the bath girl well. Rather than entertain the notion that he could be right about the rest, Gale kicked at him; but her foot glanced off the armor at his crotch, as it had before. It was his victory; he had goaded her into reacting. She knew she should shut up, but she just couldn't let the insult pass, for fear there was truth in it. "Havoc loves me. Even now he is acting to blot you out."

"With what army? My detectors indicate no advance against this fortress, only routine service calls."

Gale was curious despite herself, and she was after all trying to gather information. "Your detectors? Those were your spy-eyes?"

He was surprised. "Spy eyes? I have none." He was speaking the truth.

She was surprised in turn. "But there were spy eyes out there, watching me, and guiding attacks against me, to stop me from getting here."

Shrapnel smiled grimly. "You must have another enemy." Again, he was speaking the truth.

"You are more than enough enemy for me, you drag of snot. Let me go, and I will do you the favor of cutting your ugly face off."

He stood back, contemplating her. "I think I need to be certain you are secure. I can't trust you while you control your own body. So I shall have to separate your soul first, and put it in an otherwise wasted body."

"You're bluffing again. You have no female body free, and you can't put a female soul in a male body."

"Interesting that you should know that. You must have learned it from the succubus I set after you. How did you destroy her?"

He thinks I'm dead!

"I trapped her inside me, then bagged her in Sulvan seaweed. She won't bother me again."

"Then her body is free for your use." He walked to the place where a ring projected from the floor. He pulled on it, and the lid of a nether chamber came up. Below lay the wasted brown body of a woman.

That's me! Swale thought, horrified. *I'm dying!*

So it seemed. The hair was a matted mop separating from the skull, framing a sunken face whose brown teeth gaped like those of a skeleton. The eyeballs stared blindly out from sockets like half dehydrated grapes. The flesh of the limbs had shriveled around the bones, and the breasts were empty bags. Only the belly had any volume, and that seemed to be because of internal gases of decomposition. A putrid smell rose from it, confirming this.

I was beautiful once, Swale moaned. *I have been destroyed. My body will never recover.*

Gale had to agree. Surely only a spell of stasis prevented the body from disintegrating entirely, and it would soon die in any event. The torture master had not after all taken care of it; he had let it rot. That was probably his punishment for a slave who failed to return, for any reason. Perhaps, also, the body without the soul was impossible to rouse, so couldn't be used even for menial chores.

"You can remain with me," Gale said internally.

But how will you survive? He will never let you go, even after you are ready to do his bidding.

"Havoc will rescue me."

Havoc sent you into this trap! He has another girlfriend. He's rid of you.

"No, Havoc loves me." But Gale was aware how hollow her reassurance seemed. Why should anybody believe in a barbarian's good faith?

"So you still believe the king will save you," Shrapnel said. "You are praying to him to come to your rescue."

Gale realized that in her distraction, she had spoken aloud. "Yes," she said bravely. "Havoc will never let harm come to me."

He laughed, this time with some real feeling. "What a trusting innocent! He told you to come and spy on me, and he would secure your safety—and you believed him? You will be better off to believe me, you creature of faith, for I have too much contempt for you to bother lying."

And the dragon seed did not buzz. This required some interpretation, because the man was trying to deceive her about the nature of the tortured golems. It might be that she already knew their nature, so Shrapnel was not fooling her there, and what else he said was true. Only if the net effect of his statement was deceiving her would the seed buzz.

Gale did believe in Havoc. She knew him as no other person did, and trusted him. Somehow he would save her from this awful den.

It must be nice to have faith like that, however unjustified.

Gale fought off the doubt. "I will never cater to you, you cracked crock of spittle. Havoc will come for me." Yet it was growing difficult to maintain her certainty.

Shrapnel considered. "There just might be something in what you say. There are a thousand ways to get rid of an outworn lover, and sending her to an enemy is not the most convenient. There must be some kind of mischief in you, and I must weed it out before I use you. So I shall have to separate your soul now."

"Only by killing me, you maggoty hulk. And you don't want to do that, and waste my body and my soul."

"Correct: I don't want to do that. But I now suspect it could be dangerous to wait on your eventual conversion. So I must draw on another resource." He lifted one hand in a signal.

A figure walked into the chamber. It was a tall handsome young man, naked and muscular. "Master."

"Put her in there," Shrapnel said, indicating Swale's remnant of a body. The man glanced there, and nodded.

Oh, glory! It's an incubus! I didn't know he had one.

An incubus. One who would have sex with her, bring her to orgasm, and suck out her soul. And put it in the incipient corpse of Swale's body. Leaving her own body in a state of emptiness, suitable for whatever passive use he wished to make of it.

"How can I stop it?" she asked the succubus desperately.

You can't. He'll get into you, and his magic member will radiate such pleasure it will incite you to climax, and then he'll take you.

"But he shouldn't be able to touch me."

That's right. I forgot. He has to tempt you into coming to him. Maybe you do have a chance, if you can resist his blandishments.

"I can resist them."

That won't be easy. They are very seductive.

Meanwhile the incubus was standing before her, his dark eyes oddly appealing. "You are extremely lovely," he said, and his voice had a timbre that sent an involuntary thrill along her spine. She found herself smiling at him, and inhaling, and trying to move her hips toward his. He was the sexiest man she had ever encountered. "Thank you," she replied, making her voice dulcet. "Who are you?"

There was a buzz. "My name is Berm," he said.

A horrible shock went through Gale's body. It was Swale's reaction. *My brother!*

Her brother! How could this be? Gale was nonplused. How could Swale be expected to wipe out her brother?

So Gale tried to stall off the action by questioning him. "How did you come to assume this role?"

"I was in search of my sister, who had been captured by brigands," he replied, seeming to have no hesitancy. "But when I traced her to this enclave, and tried to rescue her, I was captured myself, and required to assume this duty. So now I capture female souls for my master's purpose."

Wait a moment. Your dragon seed buzzed when he spoke his name. Doesn't that mean he lied?

"Did it? I didn't notice. I must have been too distracted."

Ask him again.

Good idea. Gale shook her head, as if having trouble understanding. "You are Berm, the brother of someone you searched for?"

"Yes." The seed buzzed again.

So he's lying, Swale thought with tremendous relief. *I can go after him. I should have known: he hardly glanced at my body there, and didn't care. Berm would have freaked out. So he's fair game, and I'll take him.*

"You can? An incubus?"

Yes. But it will be a close call. He will be no innocent pushover. He has to be a demon soul in the body of a living man, animating it. Subject to its limitations while he uses it. We have to make him climax before you do. Then I'll have him before he has you.

"But how does he know about your brother?"

That I would like to know. And I'll find out if I capture him and have him in my power.

Gale addressed the incubus again. "You mean to capture my spirit, so I will have to become a succubus?"

"Yes, of course. This should be fun, because you are a most attractive figure of a woman. I have had to seduce a number of mediocre bodies, and I don't enjoy that as much."

"But doesn't it bother you to do this to a living person? To destroy her life?"

He shrugged. "No. I enjoy it."

He's definitely not my brother.

"Get on with it," Shrapnel said impatiently from the side. "I want to defuse whatever danger this woman represents."

"There is a problem," the Incubus said. "I may not touch her; she must touch me. But she is confined and can't come to me."

"Stand where you are, close to her."

The incubus stepped up very close. Gale flattened herself against the wall, avoiding contact.

"Handmaid," Shrapnel said.

A young woman appeared. She was clothed, and moderately attractive. *That bitch!* Swale thought. *She's his servant and mistress by choice. She resented me from the start, because she thought he would replace her with me, once I capitulated. Actually he didn't, because he couldn't trust a succubus, but still she hated me. She surely hates you too, because he truly desires you for his mistress, and you are beautiful. But she does his bidding implicitly, eager for his favor.*

"That's not the half of it," Gale responded silently. "She's the one who repairs the tortured golems, so that they can suffer more next day. In fact, she animates them during the tortures, so that they seem alive. She knew you were being deceived all along."

I'll kill her!

"All in good time. I think she's got mischief for me at the moment."

Handmaid approached Gale. She stood on her left side and wedged her right hand between Gale's back and the wall, forcing her torso forward, pushing her into the incubus.

"Hey—that's not my volition!" Gale protested.

"It doesn't matter," Shrapnel said. "You are doing the moving."

Curses! He's found a loophole.

Handmaid shoved harder, getting her elbow behind. Gale banged involuntarily into the man's still body. Her breasts flattened against his chest, and her belly pushed his erect member against his belly. She knew she should recoil at the contact, but she found it physically thrilling. He was warm and supple and so awfully masculine.

Don't do it!

Gale caught herself standing on her toes, trying to raise her cleft enough to get on top of his member. She had never before had such a strong physical urge to do what her mind knew was wrong. It was almost like the sex she had had with Placebo, when she picked up his mental lust and felt it as her own. But in this case there was no mind she could read; the spirit of the incubus seemed to have none left over for anything other than his immediate business. It was purely his physical presence that stimulated her. Swale was right: she must resist all the way, lest she give away the counter-trap. She dropped her heels to the floor.

"Move away," Shrapnel said. Both Handmaid and incubus withdrew.

Then Shrapnel brought out a small wand. "Lift your feet," he grunted to Gale.

"Forget it, thug," Gale snapped.

Shrapnel touched the wand to her right foot. Pain lanced through flesh and bone. She yanked up her foot involuntarily, and he slid a stone block into place where her foot had been.

"Now the other foot," he said.

She tried to balk, but the wand forced her to haul it away. Now both legs were lifted, and she was hanging cruelly by her arms.

"Stand close," Shrapnel told the incubus. The man obeyed, moving as close as he could without actually touching Gale's flesh.

She had to put her feet down, to support her body. They landed on the blocks. She was now slightly higher than the incubus.

"Move her out." Handmaid shoved her arm back behind Gale, forcing her into the man's body with its erect penis. She felt his member drop into the slight hollow where her thighs met her torso, and lodge right at the brink of her female aperture. She tried to clamp her legs together, but instead they parted, in another involuntary reaction.

Still, there was not entry, and the incubus could not move to effect it. He had to be passive. Shrapnel got down again and pulled the blocks out from under her feet. She tried to stand on her toes so as not to drop onto the ready member, but Shrapnel touched her on the shoulder with the wand, and she jammed down to escape it. But the force of her descent was such that the incubus' member was shoved too far back.

Shrapnel methodically repeated the process, raising her onto the blocks, moving the incubus in, then having Handmaid shove her out, and making her drop down again. The third try did it, and she found herself coming down on the incubus, surrounding the tip of his erect member with her cleft, and feeling that member slowly slide into her, wholly through her own motion. Despite her effort to balk, the excitement of the incubus was such that her cleft was wet with desire, and offered no resistance. The irony was that a very significant part of her mind *wanted* it to happen. The member was simply delightful to enclose.

Her toes touched the floor. She could not get all the way down; she was impaled on his member, which was now firmly into her, and radiating phenomenal pleasure, just as Swale had warned. It was all she could do to refrain from bouncing around, to make it stroke her inside and bring her to the terrible pleasure it promised.

Handmaid drew back, as her assistance was no longer needed. "Go to it, bitch," the servant girl said, watching avidly. "Dance on him."

Gale felt fury that this traitorous lackey should get to goad her as well as betray her. But this was not the time to dwell on that. The last thing she needed to do was cooperate with the incubus.

Do it.

"Do it? But that will set me off. I'm dangerously close to it now."

Think cold showers. Think torture. Think ice inside you, numbing sensation. But do bounce—to set him off.

Oh, yes: *he* had to climax, not her. Gale tried, but her body screamed seduction. It wanted to wrap itself around that rigid member and draw the implosion of pleasure that was promised.

Then Swale helped. She made an image of the green girl getting her breast cut off. That froze Gale, turning her off any thought of climax, even though she knew that the green girl wasn't real. Now she could bounce with impunity, for the vital mental component of her desire had been stilled. She did so.

"Ah, you are getting into it," the incubus said, satisfied.

"Yeah," Handmaid agreed. "Ride him, bitch."

Seduce him!

"Yes!" Gale breathed. She reached for his lips with hers, and kissed him. After all, it wasn't as if their contact wasn't already as intimate as it could get. She lifted one shoulder as well as she could, hauling up the breast below it, and then the other, making her breasts move against his chest. She heaved up her legs, hooking her bare toes behind him. She clenched her internal muscles in the way that had always set Havoc off immediately. It had been one of their games: he had tried to take his time, and she had forced him to erupt early— then smilingly rebuked him for rushing. Then he had insisted on a replay of the match, and succeeded in setting her off before he climaxed a second time. She had never thought that she would be turning that technique into a battle for her soul.

Then she felt the climax coming. Oh, no—she had lost sight of the tortured girl and begun to enjoy the process, and now she had tipped the balance and was falling into the intense bliss of doom. She tried to stop it, to conjure images of torture, but they transformed into images of urgent passion. Helplessly she felt it build and build, until it overflowed all bounds and geysered powerfully, pulse after pulse, jet after jet, soaking her interior with its hot essence.

Got him!

The incubus slumped. His softening member slid out of her, and he fell to the floor. What had happened?

Handmaid screamed.

Then she became aware that Swale was gone. And realized that it had not been her orgasm she had felt, but his. It had dominated his limited mind as his member spurted inside her. He hadn't realized what was happening until it was too late to stem the tide—just as it had seemed to be the case with her. With the transfer of feeling by the mind reading, it had seemed to be her own orgasm. But it wasn't, for now she hung on the wall, her body unfulfilled. She had been denied—and thereby saved her soul.

And Swale had captured the soul of the incubus, and taken it—elsewhere.

"What happened?" Shrapnel asked.

He didn't know! He didn't realize that she had reversed the ploy. Because he hadn't known that Swale was still with her. And she didn't want him to know, because she remained largely helpless. He could still kill her. She needed to survive until Havoc rescued her.

So she hung her head, feigning unconsciousness. Let him assume that her soul was gone. That maybe the incubus had slipped and fallen after capturing her soul.

"She has that bitch Swale!" Handmaid said. "She took out Berm!"

A curse on the girl; she had caught on, and given it away.

"That succubus—you kept her!" Shrapnel cried. "She got the incubus!"

Gale lifted her head. "Yes, you piece of feces," she said. "We destroyed your champion."

Shrapnel made an incoherent sound of utter rage. He drew his knife and started toward her. She realized that she had destroyed the incubus, only to be killed herself. She should have continued her pretense of unconsciousness.

"Hold, varlet!" a voice cried behind him.

Gale looked. There was Havoc, in full barbarian uniform, brandishing a sword. He had come to rescue her!

But he was only half a foot high.

Chapter 9—Golem

Havoc assessed the situation: Four naked women were chained to the dungeon walls, and the fourth one was Gale. A clothed woman stood beyond Gale. One naked man lay unconscious or dead at Gale's feet. He must have tried to rape her, and gotten clubbed by her fast foot. Only a fool would have left her legs free. There was an open coffin set in the floor, with the emaciated body of another woman. The second man was covered in leather armor, secure from kicks. He stood before Gale, menacing her with a knife. That must be Shrapnel, the torture master.

He had to take immediate action. But the man would stab Gale before Havoc could get there.

"Hold, varlet!" Havoc cried, brandishing his sword. It was the only thing he could think of to distract the man's attention from Gale.

The varlet whirled to face him. And stared, astonished. "What are you?"

"I am King Havoc. Now cease molesting that maiden."

Shrapnel's face worked, evidently uncertain whether to sneer or laugh. Behind him, Gale smiled, recognizing the rescue effort. Havoc couldn't read her mind, because he wasn't here personally; he was animating a little golem fashioned into the likeness of himself. By similar token, she couldn't read his mind, but he knew Gale had confidence in him.

The torture master's indecision didn't last long. "Whatever you are, I'll stomp you to oblivion." He strode toward Havoc and stomped.

But of course Havoc did not wait for him. He charged forward himself, ducking under the stomping foot and attacking the rear foot. He scrambled up on the toe, and climbed the laces of the boot. He thrust his tiny sword into the small space between the boot and the man's leg armor. The sword was no larger than a broad toothpick, but it was solid steel, and its edge and point were sharp. It dug a nice hole in the shin.

Shrapnel roared, as much with indignity as pain, and lifted his foot, trying to shake Havoc loose. But Havoc clung to the boot laces, and struck again, this time sawing across the surface of the skin. Blood flowed.

The man grunted and put his foot down, bringing his free hand across as if to swat a fly. Havoc lifted his sword over his head, pointing up. The huge hand sheered off, thinking the better of it. Instead the knife hand came around. The blade was as long as Havoc's whole body.

Havoc jumped to the floor and scampered around the foot. Shrapnel was bent over, trying to catch him. The bent posterior was a temptation, but the leather armor covered it, and in any event, he would have had to throw the sword to reach it. He needed to get up near the face in order to do real damage.

Meanwhile, he needed to occupy the torture master's attention, distracting him not only from Gale but from what else was happening on the premises. If he gave Shrapnel any time to think, the man would realize that where one golem could penetrate, others could too. The larger ones needed to be assembled, having been smuggled in disguised as supply carts. Only the smallest were ready for immediate action. This one would not hold the man for long.

He looked at the hung women. They had been brutally tortured. One was crisscrossed by whip slashes, and another had been debreasted and gutted. The third seemed intact, but was leaking gobs of oil. That must have been some session!

"Havoc—those are fakes," Gale said. "Not real women. The last was raped by a real hellhound, though."

"Shut up!" the clothed woman said, stepping threateningly toward Gale.

Gale's foot caught her in the stomach. The woman doubled over, her breath knocked out, and fell to the floor beside the naked man. Obviously she was one of the enemies.

But Havoc was more concerned with the tactics of his immediate situation. Gale had said the women were not real. Were they mannequins—or golems? It would be impossible to rape a mannequin, who would normally have no orifice. But a partially animated golem was possible. The Brown Chroma personnel had said that there had been an order here for several attractive female dolls two years before. These could be they. They were no longer very attractive, but behind their injuries were fine forms.

He ran toward the clothed woman, who spied him and scrambled up. She tried to flee the chamber, evidently having had enough of combat. Obviously she was no mannequin or golem.

But as she tried to dodge around Havoc, she came too close to Gale. This time Gale's foot caught her on the side of the head, and she went down in a heap, unconscious.

Havoc hid behind the body on the floor, dropped into the coffin with the corpselike woman there, and vacated his own golem for a moment. Back in his own body, he reached out with his mind. Ennui was beside him. "Female golems there, maybe, and in bad shape, but see what you can do. I'm in trouble." Then he bonded again with his own golem.

Shrapnel was stalking him, knowing better than to ignore him. Even a tiny figure could make a lot of mischief if not stopped. The man slashed with his knife, but Havoc was already moving away, clambering out of the coffin, diving over a bare leg, rolling, and scrambling away. But Shrapnel was in close pursuit.

There was no real cover. He ran to the nearest leg of the raped golem female. But he didn't want to get stuck in the gooey substance at her feet. Meanwhile, Shrapnel was coming right in.

Then the golem moved. Her head lifted and her face oriented on the torture master. "Haven't you done enough, you bag of putrescence?" she demanded.

Shrapnel's mouth dropped open. He glanced at the fallen live woman, who remained unconscious. "You can't talk! You're not real!"

The golem slipped one hand from the manacle and brought her arm down. Apparently it hadn't been necessary to clamp the manacles tightly on a figure who had no personal will. "What you have done to me is unreal, you leather-bound excrescence." She freed her other hand, and reached for him with both.

Shrapnel rocked back, appalled. "No! It can't be!"

His back almost banged into Gale, who was hung immediately opposite. She lifted both feet, planted them against the leather, and shoved him violently forward. Arms flailing, he staggered into the raped woman. She closed her arms around him in a tight embrace. "Rape me again, you foul feculence! I can never get enough of you." She pushed her face toward his, but it was no kiss she offered; her teeth were bared. Havoc recognized the mannerism of Ennui; she was animating this golem, playing out a dark fantasy. Surely loving it, as this was her chance to be bold and decisive in a way she never dared in person.

Shrapnel jerked his face away, but she pursued him, clasping him tightly while she snapped repeatedly at his nose. "I want more of your puny flesh in me, you hideous thing. Give it here." She lunged again. She was having a fine time, making a mean man suffer.

The torture master brought his knife about and stabbed her in the back. When that didn't stop her, he brought it up and carved into the side of her neck. He kept going until her head fell over against her shoulder. Then at last her arms went slack, and she fell away from him. "Oh, you have slaughtered me, you vile monster!" she declaimed as she crashed to the floor.

Shrapnel righted himself and looked around. Now the other two female dolls were free and advancing on him like dreadful specters. Those would be Symbol and Bijou, the other female members of his invasion team. Their bodies were back at Village Wetback, hidden from view. Gale had done a fine job of distracting the torture master so that he did not spy the larger party following her.

"Let me give you a piece of me," the one he thought was Symbol said, hefting a severed breast.

"Let me return the delights of the whip," the one who must be Bijou said, raising the whip. They were all grimly enjoying this.

Now at last Shrapnel caught on. "Golems! I got these figures from Brown Chroma, but never animated them beyond a set script. Just cut them up and restored them. Now they're being occupied by foreigners."

"We do love you to pieces," Symbol said, shoving the breast at his face gore-side forward, like an open cherry pie.

"We do feel your pain," Bijou said, cracking the whip. It caught him across the chest. The leather protected him, but the sound was sharp.

Shrapnel lunged for them both, his knife flashing. He stabbed them repeatedly, going for whatever vital organs golems might have. Their flesh was boneless, and it carved readily, without much bleeding from the interior, because these were repairable golems who had already bled their limit. He cut off their arms and heads, and finally they sank to the floor, unable to fight further. "We'll be back!" Symbol cried as she died.

There was noise from elsewhere in the torture complex. "I'll tend to you later," Shrapnel called, and ran from the chamber.

Meanwhile, Havoc was with Gale. He used the hooks in his hands to climb the wall beside her to reach one of the manacles, but this one was tight. He tried to jam his sword into it, to force it open, without success. He tried to pry it loose from the wall, but it was beyond his means.

"Secure the rest of the complex," Gale told him. "I'll be all right."

"But you're helpless as long as you're chained."

"Not entirely. Go, Havoc; you need to take Shrapnel out."

"What was he doing with you?"

"He was trying to convert me to a succubus. He played the game of torturing the three pseudo women, so that I would think that was what I would suffer next, and capitulate. Then I would have to leave my body and capture the souls of innocent boys, to animate his army. He has bodies in another chamber. He may have female bodies too, because he had an incubus to collect women." She glanced at the male body before her. "That woman, Handmaid, helped him set me up for it." She paused. "Oops—in our distraction she must have recovered and crawled away. She's dangerous too. The incubus is out of commission now, but don't trust Handmaid."

"How did you take out an incubus?"

"I had a bit of help. You don't want to know more. Stop dawdling, Havoc; I'm not *that* lovely naked."

"Yes you are." But she was right: he had other business to accomplish.

"The seed didn't buzz," she said with mock wonder.

He climbed carefully down her arm and stood on her shoulder. She turned her head, and he kissed her enormous mouth. "Scream if anything happens; I will hear you and come immediately."

"I know you will, Havoc," she said bravely.

He jumped down to the floor, and ran after the torture master, dodging around the bodies on the floor. Anyone who didn't know that these were merely golems would be horrified by the carnage. Even so, it was bad enough.

He followed a short hall to another chamber. This one had four naked men hung on its walls. Havoc recognized three as mannequins— real ones, not golems—and the fourth as a living man. The man was brown of hair and skin and eye. He had been there some time; the products of his body's wastes were on the floor at his feet. Another torture demonstration, surely to convert another person to evil duties of the soul. If the sight of others being tortured didn't break him down, maybe the disgust of his accumulating refuse would. There was nothing nice about the torture master's operation.

"Who are you?" he asked the living man.

The captive stared down at him. "Why should I tell any of your minions anything? I'll never serve you, you brutal creep."

"I'm not Shrapnel. I'm a golem animated by a rescuer. The torture minions already know your identity; I don't."

The man shrugged as well as he was able. "I am Berm, of Village Bravo in the Brown Chroma. I was captured when I came to rescue my sister."

The name meant nothing to Havoc. "Are there keys here I can use to release you?"

"No. Shrapnel keeps them on him."

"Then I will free you after I kill him."

The man smiled wryly. "Thank you. I will be forever indebted."

"Did Handmaid pass this way?"

"No. Don't speak to me of that bitch. She's supposed to clean up my refuse. But she wouldn't unless I became her lover."

"Chained to the wall?"

"Chained to the wall," Berm agreed. "She favors sadism. Shrapnel let her; he thought it was funny. Maybe she's another torturer."

Havoc ran on. There was another passage, leading to a lavatory chamber. The torture master was there, tending to the punctures on his leg.

"Ho, varlet!"

That was another golem. This one was two feet tall, and accordingly more formidable. It would be animated by Throe or Chief. It would keep Shrapnel occupied for a while. Havoc stayed clear, exploring side passages. He wanted to know what other surprises this complex had.

He found a room full of naked male bodies. Those would be the ones awaiting boy-souls, for animation as Shrapnel's army of conquest. There was another with female bodies, maybe for more soldiers. There were storage chambers filled with supplies and weapons. There were fairly nice residential rooms. There were no working personnel. That was all.

Take out Shrapnel, and there would be no more resistance. That seemed clear enough.

But as he went back to help the larger golem do that, he was almost overrun by the torture master. The man was running toward the body chambers, and Havoc couldn't stop him.

He went to the lavatory. There was the two foot golem, cut to pieces. Shrapnel was tough with his knife.

He went to the kitchen, where the cart of food supplies had been delivered. It was sitting out of sight of the cook, and three more two-foot-tall golems were in the process of assembly. One was in Havoc's image, and two were in Gale's image. "Who are you?" Havoc asked.

"Chief," the male replied.

"Ennui. Those torture chamber golems can't be used any more."

"Bijou. But these ones can."

"Shrapnel is going to rouse his army. I don't know how many there will be, but this is mischief. We need to free Gale from one chamber, and a man called Berm from another. If we can't get the key to the manacles, a hammer and chisel may do it. Then we'll get out of here and set off the void bomb."

Chief glanced at the cart. "It is primed. It will detonate in half an hour, as you directed."

Havoc had forgotten that detail for the moment. "So we have a tight time limit."

Chief looked around. "What about the cook?"

"Leave him alone. I don't know whether he's loyal to Shrapnel, or captive. If he opposes us, we'll have to put him down."

Chief lifted a rod. "I'll look for a wedge to hammer with this, to pry the manacles out of the walls. Where are the captives?"

Havoc pointed the way, and Chief walked in that direction.

"We've got knives," Ennui said. "But I doubt we could do much against a zombie army."

"We didn't expect to have to fight," Bijou said.

Havoc nodded. "I anticipated a covert operation, to get Gale out safely. I didn't know she would be chained to the wall." In fact he had been so busy smuggling them in that he hadn't worked out a more thoroughgoing approach. Chief and Throe had tried to warn him about this, but with barbarian naiveté he had dismissed it. He would know better next time.

There was a sound of tramping. Ennui looked in that direction. "Army?"

"I fear so," Havoc said. "You go help Chief. I'll go try to free Gale."

"You can't do it alone," Bijou said. "I'll help you." She snatched up a kitchen mallet.

Havoc led the way toward the torture chamber. But they were too late: the first wave of the zombie army was charging down the hall. They were women, naked except for their knives. The two of them ducked back into the storage room, hiding from the horde.

"Damn," Havoc said. "I hate fighting women."

"Especially when they're bigger than you are," Bijou said with a fleeting smile. "We'd better hide until we see Shrapnel."

That was a better idea than whatever he had been trying to think of. He had always been apt as an individual fighting other individuals, but had no early experience fighting full size people as a half foot golem. What could he do?

"Why don't I throw you at him?" Bijou suggested. "Then you can slit his throat before he knows what's happening."

That was another good idea. "Do it," he agreed.

They lurked as the women streamed by. And there was Shrapnel, following behind. "Check every room!" he called. "Destroy any golems you find."

"We have to do it fast," Bijou said. She set down her mallet and knife and picked him up. Then, as the torture master came close, she heaved Havoc at his head.

Havoc missed the head and bounced off the shoulder. He dropped to the floor. "There you are!" Shrapnel said, backing away. "Here to me, soldiers!"

Havoc leaped at him, catching a leg and trying to clamber up it. But the man knocked him down with a fist. Then the women were there, their many hands reaching down.

Havoc drew his sword and slashed at whatever was in reach. The sword sliced off fingers before catching in a forearm. He yanked it out and swung again. But there were no screams or retreat: these creatures seemed to be impervious to pain. In a moment they caught him around the body, wrenched his sword away, and lifted him high. One took him and hurled him against a wall. The impact knocked his head askew. He dropped to the floor, tried to get up, and was caught again. This time the women twisted off his arms and legs, his golem penis, and finally his head. Then they picked up the head and used a spike to poke out the eyes. He was done for. And he hadn't even hurt Shrapnel.

Though Havoc had been dismembered, he still heard what was going on, because the sense of hearing was in the head. "Get that other one. The female. Destroy it."

There was the sound of a scuffle, and of limbs being wrenched.

Bijou was being destroyed.

Havoc reverted to his natural body. It was of course untouched, but the experience of dismemberment had seemed real, except for the lack of pain.

But he couldn't relax. Gale was in deadly danger, and not just from the torture master. The void bomb, once primed, could not be turned off; it would soon implode the entire torture complex. There were golem bodies in the torture chamber, broken, but maybe he could rouse one. A female golem could be animated by a male, if he chose; he had learned that some men who were unsatisfied with their state did choose to animate females. He reached out with his mind, searching.

He found—the spider. It was in Gale's backpack, forgotten. He bonded and animated it, then climbed out of the pack to look around. The chamber was as it had been, with the bodies strewn across the floor.

He walked into Gale's line of sight and waved his two front legs. After a moment she saw him. "Who—?"

He walked in the pattern of an H.

"Havoc!" she exclaimed. "Did you get him?"

He dropped his body to the floor as if clubbed.

She understood. "You got bashed."

He made a nodding motion with his whole body.

"Havoc," she said urgently. "We don't have much time, and there's something you need to know. I'll talk; you move forward for Yes and backward for No. If you don't understand, move to the side. Okay?"

Havoc jumped forward, then returned to his place.

"Good. Shrapnel has activated his forces and is winning the battle."

He moved forward. How did she know?

"You must be wondering how I know. Swale told me. The succubus—we're friends now. When the incubus—that's his body at my feet—tried to rape me and capture my soul, Swale intercepted him and took him instead. She saved me, Havoc. Now I want to save her. That's her body in the coffin; I don't think it's recoverable. I want her to share mine. That way she won't die when her body does."

Havoc scuttled to the side. The last thing he wanted was Gale rendered forever inaccessible to him.

"Wait, Havoc! I don't think she *has* to take a man's soul. She wasn't sure, but the more we pondered it, the more we thought that it's an option. But if she does take it, she can return it. So it doesn't matter, when she's my friend. She won't be a barrier between us anymore—not as lovers. But I love you, Havoc, and won't do this without your approval. May she stay with me?"

Havoc was bemused. Gale was strung up on the wall for torture, rape, or death, and she was asking his approval of the presence of a dangerous succubus? He distrusted this, but he knew Gale. She always had good reason for what she did, right from the start, when she had offered him all the Peeks and Touches he wanted. She had won him then, and that would never change. If she wanted to save the succubus, and believed the demon would behave, it was probably for the best. She would have verified it with her dragon seed. In any event, he wanted to get beyond this quickly, because she had to have more important things to tell him, and indeed there wasn't much time. So he moved forward.

"Good. She can protect me by capturing the soul of any man who rapes me. She can help me by traveling out in soul form, observing, and returning to report to me, as she has done for the battle of this torture complex." Gale lifted one leg, moving her foot slowly forward. "She says the zombie soldiers, nine male and twenty female, have won, and destroyed all your golems. Handmaid is hiding for the moment; she doesn't like it when victims fight back. Shrapnel is about to return here and rape me and torture me until I capitulate and go to work for him. Or simply to kill me. Swale can't save me this time, because—Havoc, it's too complicated to explain in the time we have. You must talk with her directly."

Havoc moved to the side.

"She won't take your soul! She can't, if you don't climax. Just return to your body, poke your finger out before you, and listen to her. She'll be there, invisible but conscious. She can't touch you, but you can touch her. Do it now, Havoc. We have only a minute or so. Now!"

Havoc didn't trust the succubus, but he did trust Gale. He retreated to his body, opened his eyes, and lifted his right hand, slowly poking his forefinger into the air before his face.

I am here, Havoc.

"You're the succubus?" he asked, surprised by how readily it had worked.

My spirit is floating before you. If you withdraw, I can't follow. I can't take your soul. Even if you poked your member into my space and climaxed right now, I couldn't. That's the problem.

"You want to take my soul?"

No! You are the man Gale loves. I want never to hurt you. But she will be lost, as I was, if we don't save her now. Here is the problem: ordinarily I could be with her, and take the soul of any man who rapes her, as I did the incubus. But I can confine only one male spirit at a time. I must get rid of him before I can return to protect her again. And I can't get rid of him.

"Why not?"

Because I can't touch a man, or a male body. He has to touch me. When I brought souls before, I would come to hover just above the crotch of an empty body, and Shrapnel would lift the penis to intercept me, and I would feed the soul into it. Then I was free to return to my own body, or to take another soul. But I can't do that now—and if I could, it would only make one more soldier for Shrapnel to control. I can't even return it to the incubus's own borrowed body, because there's no one to lift his member into me, and anyway, we don't want him loose; he's dangerous. He's committed to Shrapnel, and is as vicious as he is.

"I appreciate the problem. But I thought you could touch a woman. Why did Gale have to extend her toe to you?"

I hold the male incubus soul captive. He can't touch a woman—and neither can I, while he's in me. I must get rid of him immediately. But there is no one to take him.

"No other males in the torture complex?"

The only other unconfined male in the complex right now is the cook. He's a good man, held hostage; he would help us if he dared. I wouldn't put the incubus in him if I could.

"Did you check the male torture chamber?"

No. I hate that place.

"There's a new captive there. His name is Berm."

He felt the shock of the succubus. *My brother! He's here?*

"He was searching for his sister, and was captured."

I must see!

"Wait! We haven't finished—" But she was gone.

"What is this all about, Sire?" It was Symbol, who had overheard his one-sided dialogue.

"I was in contact with the succubus. She has to get rid of an incubus she intercepted, so she can take the soul of the man who rapes Gale. But she has no male body to put it in, and if she did, she'd need help."

"There's a simple counter-ploy," Symbol said. "I learned of it when I seduced a Red Chroma official. Their specialty is demons; they know how to handle them. All she needs to do is—"

"Tell her about it, when she returns here. Just poke your finger into the air until you feel her. I've got to try to help Gale directly." He focused on the golem spider, and in a moment opened his eyes in the torture chamber.

Shrapnel was there. He was in the process of baring his member, so as to rape Gale.

"So you think you can possess me, whatever comes after," Gale was saying to him. "You think that little thing of yours is big enough to take me on. You're dreaming, you belch of vomit."

Gale had a sharp tongue when she was angry. She was captive, but making it clear that she wasn't cowed. Shrapnel could rape her, he could kill her, but he would never break her spirit.

But Havoc was here to see that neither rape nor killing occurred. He ran forward, leaped on the man's leather-clad leg, and scrambled on up his body. Shrapnel, intent on Gale, did not notice the spider.

He was nudging forward, watching her legs.

Sure enough, she kneed him. But he had expected that, and took the force of it against his armored thigh. He wedged in close, inside her leg, orienting.

"Remember what happened to the incubus," she said.

"The succubus took him out," Shrapnel said. "But she has nowhere to deliver his soul, and she can't take another until she does. That's why I know you are safe to approach, at the moment. In time she'll find a body, and then she'll be back, and you will be unsafe. So this is my window of opportunity. I've never had a spitfire as beautiful as you before. Even if I have to kill you later, this will be sheer delight."

Even had the man not been an enemy, he would have disgusted Havoc. He *liked* abusing women.

"You're a cowardly, dastardly, reprehensible, filthy clod of dragon manure who couldn't have any woman without first manacling her to a wall."

"What makes this especially rapturous is your evident aversion to the process. I would like it if you screamed, too." He pushed up against her. "When you become my regular mistress, I want you to revile me constantly, even as you spread your legs. I want to dominate you unwillingly, without requiring manacles. But for now, they will do."

Meanwhile Havoc had reached the man's shoulder. He leaped onto the top of the head, then straddled the face. He was able to cover one of the man's eyes and part of his nose.

Shrapnel made a grunt of disgust and reached up a gloved hand to slap Havoc off. Havoc scuttled to the other side of the face, digging his leg spikes in.

The torture master lifted both hands, pawing at his face. Havoc scuttled down under his chin. Meanwhile, Gale lifted her leg again, planted her foot against the man's armored belly, and shoved him away. So Havoc's effort had won her some reprieve.

"So you're back," Shrapnel said, recognizing the true identity of his attacker. "This time I'll smash you. Then I'll despoil your bitch." He grabbed under his chin, but Havoc slid down inside his collar, clinging to the flesh under the armor.

The torture master pounded his own chest with his fist, but Havoc was already sliding around to the armpit. He found the most tender flesh and used his mandibles to make a great chomp.

Shrapnel roared. He plunged his hand inside his collar, grabbing for the spider—and this time Havoc lacked leeway to escape. He was caught between finger and thumb. He bit the thumb, but the man did not let go. He hauled Havoc out, brought his other hand around, and smashed them together. The spider, caught in the crush, was squashed, and several of his legs broken.

Shrapnel dropped him to the floor and returned to Gale. "Now where were we?" he inquired gruffly. "Oh, yes, you were about to scream." He jammed in against her, avoiding her kick.

Havoc lay crumpled on the floor. Two of his eyes still worked, and one was pointed in Gale's direction. He could see her and the torture master, and hear them, but couldn't move. This body was done for in all but perception. He saw Gale lift one big toe slightly, and realized that she could be trying to contact the succubus, but he couldn't tell whether that contact was successful, or what it might portend.

He wondered whether he had delayed things long enough for Symbol to tell the succubus about the supposedly simple counter-ploy. Would it stop the brute from raping Gale, or was it something else, of interest only to a succubus? Whatever it was, it was now their only hope.

It seemed to be insufficient, for Shrapnel was orienting his member and bringing it to bear on her cleft. Gale's face was averted, her jaw set; she seemed resigned to being taken. Havoc knew that meant that she had no intention of being taken—but what possible defense could she have?

Shrapnel's member touched her—and something happened. The man stiffened through the rest of his body, then fell back. "What's this?" he exclaimed.

"It's your friend the incubus," Gale informed him with relish. "He has been delivered to you. Now I think he wants your body."

"But this isn't possible! I'm not an empty body."

"Let me educate you about something," Gale said. "This incubus, like the succubus, ranges out in spirit form to find a body to infuse. He then uses that body to seduce an innocent girl, whom he incites to climax, and he takes her soul. The male body he uses has its own soul, but the incubus suppresses that soul while he is there. Exactly as the succubus does with her human maiden host. Once he accomplishes his purpose, the human host resumes control, so the state is temporary. But in this case the soul of the incubus was captive of the succubus who took him, and she put her spell on him to confine him to the body she would put him in. You taught her how to do that. So she disposed herself just outside my cleft, and waited for you to enter her space. Then she delivered the soul in the usual manner, feeding it into the channel leading to its residence. So now the incubus is confined to your body, and will govern it in your stead, for only the succubus can release him from it, and she will not."

"He will not have *my* body," Shrapnel grated, sweating. He was staggering around the chamber like a drunk man.

"Unless you succeed in beating him back," Gale said. "It can be done, for I did it when I was invaded. But I think you are in for some hours of struggle. The incubus may have seemed to be your friend while he had other bodies, but I think he is not your friend now that there is only one body to share. Good luck."

"You bitch! I'll kill you!" He tried to draw his knife.

"If you do, the incubus will use your diversion of attention to secure the control points of your body," Gale said. "He has no love for me, but I doubt he will pass up that opportunity. You will do best to fight for your own body before you tackle mine."

Shrapnel did not reply. He was evidently too busy doing exactly that. Swale had learned the Red Chroma ploy, and used it, and saved Gale. Symbol was right: it was a simple yet effective device. Havoc's effort of distraction had provided enough time.

Gale lifted her head and addressed him. "Havoc, if you can hear me, try to communicate with the cook. His name is Smoky. He's a decent man, despite everything. Make a deal with him to free me and Berm, and promise to protect and reward him. Do it before the soldiers discover what has happened to their leader." Then she looked surprised, and spoke again. "Swale is with me now. She says Shrapnel told them to wait while he attended to other business, and they all stopped in place and waited. They obey him implicitly; it's part of the spell. So they won't act until he tells them to. But if he beats back the incubus soon, then he'll get them moving again. We just can't be sure how fast that will be. Do what you can do as fast as you can."

Havoc vacated the spider, returned to his body, and spoke aloud. "Anybody in hearing: we need to befriend Smoky the cook, and get three people out of there. Gale, a captive named Berm, and Smoky. In a hurry. The void bomb is set to detonate soon. Animate anything you can, and address that cook." Then he quested with his mind, searching for anything to animate.

He found a Havoc-golem head in the garbage of the kitchen, where the soldiers had evidently thrown it. One eye still functioned, and it could hear, though the ears had been bitten off. The mouth was battered, with several teeth missing, but could be worked. He spit out a squash rind as well as he could without having any breath.

How could he talk, without breath? But he tried it, and lo, he could. The Brown Chroma made its golems economically, with the various portions separately spelled. Thus the legs could walk on their own, if they had anchorage, and the head could see, hear, and speak on its own. That had not been the case with the man-sized golems, but the little ones seemed to have a different design.

"Smoky!" he called. His voice was surely muffled by garbage, but it had to suffice. "Smoky! Smoky!"

The cook evidently had good ears. "Who calls me?"

"A golem's head in the garbage. Listen, for it is important."

The cook came and fished the head out of the can. He set it on the counter and hefted a large cleaver. "Who animates you?" he demanded.

"King Havoc. But I don't expect you to believe that. Hear my offer, then verify what I say. I will get you out of here before I destroy the complex, and will guarantee you compatible work at City Triumph, if you will free the two prisoners in the torture chambers."

"If I listen to a voice like yours, Shrapnel will have me flayed." But he was evidently interested, because he asked a question. "How could a little golem head destroy this complex?"

"With a void bomb. Look in the supply cart, in the false bottom, and you will see it. Do you know what a void bomb is?"

"I can guess."

"Then you know not to touch it. It is primed, and its time is expiring. Look, then go to the female torture chamber, where you will see Shrapnel in the throes of identity siege. Free the woman and bring her here."

"I'll do better than that. I'll take you with me. If you are lying, I'll toss you in the meat grinder."

"Excellent."

First Smoky verified the void bomb: it was a black mass labeled BOMB. "The Black Chroma did not want to part with it," Havoc said. "But they owed me a significant favor, and I am after all the king. That will destroy everything here."

"Maybe," Smoky said noncommittally. "If it's real." He carried the head out of the kitchen and down the hall. The twenty nine soldiers stood there in various awkward poses: however they had been when their master had told them to wait. The cook had to dodge around them, but they did not try to impede his progress. The men were all young and robust; the women varied, but some were pretty. Havoc wondered how Shrapnel had collected their bodies, as that had obviously been a separate effort from the acquisition of souls. What had happened to *their* souls? He would have to investigate, after he was done here.

They reached the torture chamber. There was Shrapnel, writhing on the floor. "Master!" Smoky called. "Are you ill?"

"He can't answer you," Havoc said. "The incubus is trying to take over his body, as it is now confined there. The incubus' own body is vacant, as you can see."

"This place is a disaster," Smoky said. "What happened?"

"Our personnel animated the golem women, and they attacked the torture master. He fought back. But then he tried to rape Gale, and the succubus got him."

Smoky was on the verge of persuasion. "Name the succubus."

"Swale, of the Brown Chroma. That's her body in the coffin. It will die soon, from neglect during her absence."

Smoky looked in the coffin, and shuddered. "Damn! She was a nice girl when she came here. I liked her, though I couldn't help her. I wondered what had happened to her, but didn't dare ask."

"I hope to be a nice girl again, Smoky," Gale's mouth said. "My body is wasted beyond repair, but Gale here will let me stay with her, if you free her."

Smoky looked at her. "How do I know you are Swale? I fear Swale is dead."

Gale's face smiled. "Remember when I was first being tortured by example? I was left alone at night, and you came to feed me in the darkness and clean up my refuse. Because the damned Handmaid who was supposed to do it had not, out of spite. You had to do it spoonful by spoonful, as I could not use my hands, and tilt the cup to my mouth. Your food was always good, and you never teased me with it. You spoke kindly to me, saying that you didn't like what was happening, but you had to obey lest you be tortured similarly. I was so grateful for the sympathy that I offered you my body, and promised not to tell. The first night you declined, and the second, but the third night you accepted, and I gave you what I could, which were my kisses, my breasts, my cleft, and my words of camaraderie. After that we met many times that way, and I think it was as meaningful for you as it was for me, the sex being merely a pretext for companionship. I was a girl of sixteen, and you a middle aged man, but we shared something nice amidst a den of horrors. But after I capitulated and became a succubus we didn't dare, because I was afraid I would take your soul without wanting to. My training made me vicious, but I was never vicious to you, or you to me. We were not lovers so much as associates, both caught in a situation so ugly that we savored that little bit of decency and pleasure that was our relationship. Now we both have a chance to escape, and the word of King Havoc and Gale is good, and I beg you to help us accomplish this. Please, Smoky, do it."

Tears were running down Gale's face, and down Smoky's face too. All doubt had been banished. He set down the golem head, turning its eye to face Gale/Swale, then lifted his cleaver and approached her. He wedged its blade under the right manacle and pried it out of the wall. Then he did the same with the left manacle. Gale fell against him, her arms too stiff and weak to function immediately. He caught her and held her carefully upright. She turned her face to him and kissed him passionately.

Then she spoke again. "Now we must rescue my brother."

"I'll do it," Smoky said. He steadied her until she could stand alone, then hurried out of the chamber.

Gale's body walked around the chamber, swinging the arms stiffly, limbering them. Then she bent and picked up the golem head. She lifted it to her face and kissed its mouth. "Thanks for coming, Havoc," Gale said. "I'd make love to you, but you don't have what it takes."

"Not at the moment," he agreed.

She rummaged in her tattered clothes for her knife, and a small box. "We'll need these to handle the water outside," she said.

They made their way through the passage, around the frozen soldiers, and to the other torture chamber. The young man was standing there, swinging his stiff arms as Gale had, recovering the use of them. Smoky was cleaning him up.

"Berm!" Gale's mouth cried. She ran forward to hug him, still holding the head in one hand and the knife and pillbox in the other.

"Do I know you, lovely lady?" he asked, taken aback.

"I'm your sister, Swale! In another body. Mine is—done for. This is Gale, my host and friend. Shrapnel was torturing her the same as me, the same as you."

"Hello, Gale," Berm said.

"Hello, Berm," Gale said. "Now we're getting out of here."

"This way," Smoky said. He led the way through the labyrinth of passages toward the main entrance, still holding his cleaver. Then he paused. "We can't go outside—we need a pressure bubble, or magic. Otherwise the water will kill us."

"I have water pills," Gale said.

But as they came to the entrance, a creature changed out of a side passage. "That's the hellhound!" Gale cried. "The rape creature." She brought her knife up.

"This one is mine," Smoky said. He stepped between Gale and the charging animal. It didn't even seem to notice him; its eyes were on Gale. Havoc, watching from the head she carried, wasn't sure what kind of interaction they had had with this creature, but it did look vicious.

The hellhound leaped for Gale—and Smoky swung his cleaver and caught it across the neck. The blade penetrated the throat, slowing the creature in mid-air. Blood spurted, and the hellhound fell to the floor.

"Was that necessary?" Havoc asked. "It's just an animal."

"It's not just an animal," Gale said grimly. "The thing rapes bound women, grotesquely."

They moved on. But the delay had been critical: Shrapnel stood at the entrance door. He had won his internal battle, and was functioning again. "There they are! Catch them! Chain them. The traitor cook too."

"I should have cleaved his head off when I had the chance," Smoky said.

"We sent you off to rescue Berm," Havoc reminded him.

"There's another way out," Gale cried. "Follow me!" She turned and ran away, evidently guided by the succubus.

The two men followed. But so did the naked soldiers. Two of the fugitives were newly released from manacles, and the third was a middle aged man, so their speed was not great. But the soldiers lost ground, because they were still new to their bodies, and clumsy. Havoc's eye was facing back, and he saw the soldiers, male and female, try to jam into the narrow corridor—all of them at once. They crashed to the floor in a tangle of arms and legs.

But Shrapnel knew where the fugitives were going, and there were many passages. Havoc knew there was more trouble ahead.

"It's the next chamber," Gale gasped.

And there were three female soldiers blocking the way, armed with knives.

"Throw me!" Havoc cried. "Don't slow down."

Gale swung her arm and loosed him like a bowling ball. He rolled and bounced down the passage toward the soldiers. They were clearly taken aback, scrambling out of his way though he was a largely harmless ball. The world seemed to be spinning around as his eye changed position, but the glimpses he caught were enough. He rolled right on through the doorway to the chamber beyond, and fetched up against a bulkhead, his eye facing back.

There were the sounds of combat outside. Two figures fell into the chamber. They were Berm and a woman, struggling for the knife she wielded. Ordinarily the man would have been stronger, but Berm's arms still were not fully back in play. However, the woman's motions were clumsier, and in a moment the man wrested the knife from her. Then he hesitated.

"Cut her throat!" Havoc yelled. "She's not a person, she's a half mindless thing."

Still, the man hesitated. The woman grabbed again for the knife, and the struggle resumed.

Gale stepped in, evidently having dispatched her antagonist. She assessed the situation, strode toward the two, and carefully slit the woman's throat. "Come on," she said, going to the wall behind Havoc.

Then Smoky appeared. There was more blood on his cleaver and a cut on his arm, but he seemed to be in good condition.

"I hear more coming," he said breathlessly. "We had better move out."

"Take a pill," Gale said, passing them out to the men and taking one herself. "They are to adapt us to the deep sea water without drowning." She turned to the portal and rotated its wheel. "Out this way."

Berm and Smoky swallowed their pills. Havoc couldn't see their reactions, but gathered they found the effect strange.

The portal swung open. Gale stepped into a chamber beyond. "Come on; this takes time, and we don't have much left."

Suddenly another woman charged into the larger chamber. This one was disheveled but clothed. It was Handmaid. She swept up Havoc's head and backed off. "I've got your leader!" she cried. "I know about golems. Now you must meet my terms."

Gale looked out of the small chamber. "Then you know that the animator isn't *in* the golem, but elsewhere. Keep the head." She pulled the portal closed.

"Tough luck, Handmaid," Havoc said. "You lose."

Handmaid realized she had erred. "Damn it!"

Then Gale opened the portal again. "Let the men grab you and strip you, and you can come with us."

"Why should I do that? I like it here."

"Because the void bomb is about to detonate."

Handmaid pondered only a moment. Then she held out Havoc's head and spread her arms.

"Get her knife first," Gale said.

Berm and Smoky grabbed Handmaid and ripped off her outer clothes. Sure enough, she had a sheathed knife hidden under one arm. They threw that away and quickly stripped her naked, while Gale drew the portal closed again. But she also held Havoc's head so that he could watch the proceedings. Handmaid's body was not in Gale's class, but she was reasonably fit.

"Better give her a pill," Havoc said.

Gale smiled. "Almost forgot." She handed Handmaid a pill. Then she started turning the wheel on the opposite portal.

After a moment, a vent opened and a jet of cold water shot into the chamber. "We'll drown!" Handmaid protested.

They ignored her. "Why are you taking her along?" Havoc asked.

"She has information."

"I'm not telling you anything," Handmaid said. "All I agreed to was to let the men have their way with me."

"I don't want anything to do with you," Berm said. "You're a sadistic tease."

"Neither do I," Smoky said. "You never gave Swale a break."

Handmaid nodded. "I did figure you'd be beating me up and forcing me into degrading acts, maybe involving Gale. I don't like any of you either. But that's the price of my survival. I'll recover, because none of you really go for extended sadism."

The water was up to their waists and rising rapidly. "These pills really work?" Berm asked Gale.

"Yes. It's Translucent magic. The water will seem like air, and you'll breathe it. You won't be able to swim. But we'll walk to Village Wetback."

"So what about me?" Handmaid asked. "I'll let you do what you want to do to me, but I want to get it over with."

Havoc pieced together the misunderstanding. "Gale told you to let the men grab you and strip you. She meant to disarm you so you couldn't do any of them harm. She's not into needless brutality."

"I came here to get information on the torture cult," Gale said. "You have it. I'll get it from you."

"That wasn't my deal," Handmaid said. "I yielded my body, not my mind."

She didn't know that Gale could read her mind, and Gale didn't tell her. She just shrugged as the water level reached their heads.

Then she ducked her head under, breathing, setting the example.

In a moment the others did the same. "It does work," Berm said, amazed. "Suddenly this seems like air."

There was a wavy flicker, two pulses. "That's a weird effect," Berm said. "I thought the water pill had already taken."

"That's not the water pill," Havoc said. "That's the two minute warning on the void bomb! You have to get out of there; you're still within its implosion range."

The water was near the top, but the door wouldn't open until the chamber was completely filled. Gale clutched the wheel impatiently as the seconds passed. Then the wheel turned, and the door opened. They piled out into the tunnel beyond, running along it. But Havoc knew that they would never get clear of the bomb's implosion radius in time. "Keep running," he said, hoping he was mistaken.

His real body was beyond mind reading range, but Gale caught on anyway. "We're finished," she muttered as she ran.

Then they came across a young man evidently waiting for them. He was translucent, almost invisible in the water. "Placebo!" Gale cried. "Get us out of here. _Now!_"

He didn't hesitate. Powerful magic manifested. A shimmering ball formed around them, and hurtled outward from the torture complex, carrying them with it. Then it slowed, hesitated, and started moving back.

"But this isn't supposed to happen," Placebo said, surprised.

"Relax," Havoc's head said. "That's the backwash from the implosion of the void bomb. The water is filling in where the torture complex vanished, and pulling your bubble with it."

Placebo looked at the head. "A talking ball?"

Gale smiled. "Placebo, meet the golem head of King Havoc. Havoc, meet Placebo, my Translucent Chroma guide and temporary lover."

The handsome young almost invisible man looked embarrassed. Evidently he hadn't expected their liaison to be announced. Havoc hadn't expected it either. What had she told the man? Or failed to tell him?

"You said you were on a mission for the king," Placebo said. "You didn't say you knew the king personally."

Gale laughed. "Oh, yes, I know him moderately well. He's my regular lover, when he's not with his new girlfriend."

So she was paying Havoc back for his affair with Bijou. She had always matched him step for step, in her fashion.

"You're the king's—?" the man asked, dumbfounded.

"Yes. So when I return to him, perhaps you can have his girlfriend. That's fair, isn't it?"

Havoc suspected she was giddy from the narrowness of her escape from the torture complex and the void bomb. But it was true that the magic of the Translucent Chroma man had just saved her from the latter, and that was a service worthy of special reward. Havoc had never intended to put Gale at such risk. "That's fair," he agreed.

The bubble dissolved, and they were standing on the floor of the Sulvan Sea. "I, uh, the village is not far away," Placebo said.

"Thank you for saving my life, Placebo," Gale said. She drew him in with her free hand and kissed him.

"You just told me to move you. I didn't know there was a bomb."

"You might have read it in my mind."

"I—I can't read minds. Because—"

"Placebo's magic is a sometime thing," Gale told the others. "I think he may have more of a future with us than with his own Chroma."

"With you?" the man asked. "But our association was to end when your mission was done."

"I think not," Gale said. "Oh, I forgot. Placebo, this is Smoky, the cook, who also helped us escape. And Berm, the brother of a friend. And Handmaid, who is no friend, but we'll return her to her home village unscathed, in due course."

They found a path and walked toward the village. Havoc vacated the golem head and returned to his real body. "There's a party of five headed this way," he said to his mission companions. "We'll take the two nonChroma men with us to Triumph. Maybe also the Translucent Chroma man; Gale likes him. The girl will be taken to her native village and freed after we garner whatever she knows about the torture cult. Do not let her know we can read minds; she's no friend. But we will treat her courteously."

"Got it," Symbol said.

"They have been through an extremely rough situation. Comfort them."

"Got it," Bijou said.

"See if we can get transport home. We'll consult on the way."

"Got it," Ennui said.

He looked at Symbol. "Your Red Chroma ploy was effective. It saved Gale from rape."

"That should be an interesting story."

Havoc looked at Bijou. "Gale has taken a supplementary lover: the Translucent man. He just saved her life, and she's not yet ready to turn him loose. There must be more to this, and I will get it from her. His name is Placebo. I want to treat him well, but I want Gale to myself for now. Can you handle him?"

"Yes," Bijou said sadly. "That will divert him from her, and me from you."

"Bijou, read my mind. I'm not jealous of her, and I'm not dumping you. I may even marry you." He removed his crown for a moment. "You know Gale will always be my first love. Now you can have a second of your own, if you wish. He seems like a nice young man."

"I know," she said. "I've always known I would have to move on.

I just feel some pain at the reality."

Symbol put her arm around her, with a certain calculated sympathy. "Havoc is Havoc. No one owns him, emotionally. He's like me in
that respect."

"Very like you," Bijou agreed.

Throe and Ennui chuckled.

"Is there something I'm missing?" Symbol asked.

"You're another changeling," Throe said. "I think we forgot to tell
you."

"Gale reported on the changelings," Symbol said. "But as I recall,
she didn't mention me."

"We figured it out," Bijou said. "You definitely fit the pattern.
That's why King Deal liked you."

Symbol pondered briefly. "I suppose I am. Does that explain my
attraction to Havoc?"

"Everyone is attracted to changelings," Ennui said. "Even other
changelings. So Havoc is drawn to you as much as you are drawn to
him. And liaisons between changelings must be common."

"But Gale is my first lover, and Bijou is my second," Havoc said.
"Gale and I understand each other, and will be together if we can be.
Now let's meet that party, and go on from there."

The others shrugged. They would do what he wished, though it
was clearly not what they had anticipated.

Soon the party arrived, and the six of them went out to meet
them, beyond the village. Havoc and Gale came together first, embracing and kissing. Then they set about introductions. "To simplify
things, we will pair off for the moment," Havoc said. "So that each of
us need be concerned with only one other, who will clarify confusions.
Placebo—"

"Sire," the man said, bowing his head. He was evidently daunted
not only by so suddenly encountering the king, but by his discovery
that he had just had an affair with the king's mistress.

"This is my girlfriend Bijou. Perhaps yours too."

Bijou smiled at Placebo. She took his hand. "Let's talk." She led
him back toward the village. He offered no resistance, seeming stunned.

"Smoky, this is Symbol. She will see about finding you a compatible position at City Triumph or elsewhere, considering your help to
me."

Symbol took Smoky's hand. The man seemed almost as awed as
Placebo had been. "I'm sure there's something."

"Berm, I know you want to be with your sister. But for the moment that's not feasible. We can perhaps give you a few minutes with
her, however." He looked around. "Ennui?"

Ennui knew what he wanted; to let Swale animate her briefly, so
they could talk together directly. "A few minutes," she agreed. "Meanwhile, let me get you some clothing."

"Everything here is translucent," Throe said.

"Havoc has spares," she said, and led him off.

"Now you, Handmaid," Havoc said. "You tried to hold me hostage."

"Yes." The woman made no denial and no apology. She was tough.

"Throe, interview this woman. Ask her what she knows about the torture cult and its motives. Maybe you can get her some opaque clothing, too."

Throe nodded. "This way, miss."

"I won't answer."

But the answers would be in her mind as Throe put the questions. He would read them and remember them. This was in his bailiwick, because the torture cult had been their best lead to the identity of King Deal's killer. It had sent Swale after Gale, trying to foil her investigations of the changelings. Was it also involved with the attempts on his life, and Gale's? This seemed likely, though the mechanism was obscure.

That left Havoc, Gale, and Chief. "I mean to have my lover back," Havoc said, kissing her again.

"Sire, first get the succubus placed elsewhere."

"No, I want Swale with her."

"But she could take your soul!"

Havoc removed his crown. *Will she, Gale?*

We think not. She doesn't want to. But we're not sure she can stop it. If she does take it, she will return it, though.

Havoc restored the crown. "I think not. But I must make certain."

"Then have her invest some other woman," Chief said, "and let some other man test the issue."

"This is not a risk I would ask any other to take in my stead. I must do it myself."

"Sire!"

"But if I am mistaken, and I lose my soul, you will be in charge of this party and the kingdom until a new king is installed. Check on me in half an hour."

"Sire," Chief repeated, appalled.

Havoc put his arm around Gale and walked her toward the village. Chief had no choice but to let him.

"But you know, he's right," Gale said. "We aren't sure, and it's foolish to risk the king unnecessarily."

"I need to know to what extent we can trust Swale."

"We just rescued her brother. This is of overwhelming importance to her. She will be loyal to us, Havoc."

"Her ability to travel widely and observe can be valuable. Her ability to invest women may be similarly useful. And the way she can take out a man, at need—"

"Yes. She took out the incubus. That saved my soul."

"So she can become a considerable asset, if we are sure of her."

"Havoc, she's loyal. But she may have no choice. It may be an involuntary reflex."

"In which case she will take my soul—and return it to me."

"It's still chancy, Havoc. She tells me it is. She has never returned a soul to the same body; it may not work. There's so much we don't know."

"So we'll find out."

"So we'll find out," she agreed, resigned. "Havoc, is it really this verification you're after, right now?"

"Only in part. Gale, I love you and I've been without you too long. I've got to have you back."

"You know I've had sex with Placebo, and with the incubus, and almost with Shrapnel, all in the last two days."

"You know I'll be having sex again with Bijou, and perhaps others. It isn't sex that defines our relationship."

"It isn't sex," she echoed. "Oh, Havoc, I wanted you throughout."

"I know it. But the Translucent Chroma man—why do you want to keep him?"

"He's decent, and he can't read minds, which means his future in the Translucent Chroma zone is uncertain. We might be able to fix his problem. I would like to do that, before I turn him loose. He did save my life."

Havoc nodded. It was worth exploring. "I admit I like the variety of other women. Bijou is most obliging. But you're the one I love."

"I know it."

Havoc braced himself for what he knew she would not like. He had worked out a strategy in his protected head, and told no one. It was the only way to be sure of keeping a secret. "Which will make this harder."

"Harder?"

"You must invoke the succubus for me. I want to be sure it's her and not you."

"You're going to have sex with her, in my body?"

"This one time."

Gale grimaced. "If we ever find a tame incubus, I'll do it back to you. That demon had the magic touch. His member was like a wand of sheer desire."

"If we ever get an tame incubus, I'll take a lesson from him."

They had reached the village. They went to the room reserved for Havoc. "You know that any villager can look in through the walls," she said. "And read our minds, if we let them."

"That village can take a lesson from us." He closed the translucent door and removed his clothes while she went to the lavatory to clean up after her ordeal. He knew she was tired, and after this he intended to let her sleep as long as she needed. But he had plans that needed to be implemented rapidly, and the succubus was vital to them. He had to know he was safe from her, and that other men were too.

He removed his crown. Perhaps it would protect him from this, and so void the test.

Gale emerged. She did a dance step, making her body come alive in a special way. "How do you like me now?"

"You're the succubus!"

"Gale called me back. I talked with my brother five minutes, and kissed him. I can never thank you enough for saving him, Sire."

"He came to rescue you. He must be a good man."

"He is. I must also thank you for allowing me to remain with Gale, now that my own body is gone. This saved *my* life."

"I want you to work for me."

"Sire, I will do so. Anything you want."

"Right now I want sex. I want you to seduce me, as you would a man you meant to take. But I want you not to take me."

"I know, Sire. But I had an arduous training to become what I am. I am no longer an innocent sixteen year old girl; I am a deadly female demon. It will take years for the horrors in my memory to ease, if they ever do. I can not be sure I won't do you harm."

"Seduce me, and do me no harm."

"Sire, possession of this marvelous body, and the proximity of an interested man, are making me increasingly eager to perform. But before it carries me away, I must warn you once more that this is dangerous. I am not a nice woman. Test me on some other man first."

"No."

"Then here I come." Her dance became increasingly alive. Her breasts moved, and her thighs, and her face assumed an expression of pure sexuality that he had never seen on Gale. But it wasn't just that. Every part and aspect of her body and manner were overwhelmingly sexual. He could have been impotent, and she would have made him immediately potent. There was almost an aura, luring him in.

"This is the dance of the succubus," she said.

"I have seen it." But he realized as he watched that he hadn't— not like this. What he had seen was a human imitation; this was the real thing. It was immeasurably more potent. She lacked time to get through the first section of it before he came to her and embraced her.

Then he was in the throes of it, plunging, bouncing, climaxing with such force it seemed that her body would be washed away on the spurt of it. But she was as eager as he, clasping him, kissing him, drawing him in impossibly close as her body made him more than welcome. Gale had always been passionate, and Bijou enthusiastic, but Swale was desperately ardent, meeting him more than halfway.

Her limbs clasped him externally while her cleft milked him internally, wanting it all, endlessly.

For an instant he felt as if they were on the frothing surf of a mighty sea in a storm, locked together as the water surged across the beach and carried them along. Then he found himself in her embrace, blissfully ebbing, floating.

"Oh, Havoc," she breathed. "You took me with you! I never had an experience like that. I love you."

"Who are you?" he demanded, needing to make sure.

"I am Swale, the succubus. I did not take your soul. All the others, I did not climax myself; I caused them to jet, and I was off away with their spirits. But you carried me through it. I couldn't have taken you without taking myself. " She smiled. "There's a notion: sucking myself into my own womb!"

"Does that mean that if I had not set you off, you would have taken me?"

"No. Your passion climaxed just before mine, and I felt no need to steal your soul. When I was sure of that, I let your surge carry me. Gale read your mind, and gave it to me, and I was gone, as I longed to go."

He understood that effect, having experienced it with Bijou. "So you are safe."

"Sire, I am safe. With you. I love you."

That was the second time she had said that. "Did you have much experience with men, before you became a succubus?"

"Some. I paid for my keep on a caravan. But that was mostly to spread my legs and let them finish fast. I used ointment to make myself slick, as otherwise I would have been dry. I never loved."

"Then perhaps you mistake the joy of passion for love."

"Perhaps," she agreed. "But I don't think so. With women they are more closely allied than they are with men. Do you wish to be rid of me now?"

"No. But I do wish to be with Gale. You and I will talk again soon, when I clarify what else I want of you. I think you'll find it compatible."

"Just to be close to you, with your knowledge and tolerance, is enough, Sire. For that I sincerely thank you."

Then her presence faded, and Gale's body went limp. But in a moment it revived. "I'm jealous, Havoc," Gale said.

"With reason. She's extremely good at sex."

"By definition. Let me clean up. Then I'll have at you myself."

"What, sex again?"

She got up. "Did you expect otherwise?"

"No."

She laughed, and went to the lavatory, while he lay on the bunk and pondered. Gale was not truly jealous; one of the qualities of changelings seemed to be a lack of such disharmonious emotions. So Gale did not have enmity for Bijou, and Havoc did not resent Placebo; they recognized the need for those relationships. Similarly, Gale knew Havoc had reason to have sex with Swale, and surely had made mental notes on technique. It had been amazingly good with the succubus, and she had not taken his soul. So she was safe. But that was only the beginning.

Gale returned, looking beautiful. "It is true. Others marvel at our tolerance for each other's sexual activity elsewhere. They don't understand our realism about such things. If I can't have sex with you, that's no reason to deny you having it elsewhere. I know you'd rather have it with me. And I know you do not seek to deny me incidental pleasure elsewhere."

"I wish you the best of it," Havoc agreed, and kissed her.

"Swale says our attitude *is* different from that of others," she said. "But that does not mean we lack caution. I don't want you with Symbol any more than you would want me with a male changeling. Because that could give us serious competition and imperil our relationship."

"Agreed. Symbol already tempts me dangerously."

"And you her, I'm sure." But she spoke of it as she might a high cliff: a danger to be avoided rather than feared.

While their passion slowly built up again, they spoke of memories of love, and Gale filled him in on the details of her ordeal in the torture complex. Havoc found her mental replay of the hellhound's rape of the golem woman intriguing rather than horrible. She chided him for that, while appreciating his male nature, providing him with full visual detail. He picked up her mental wonder that he should enjoy seeing such a massive member jammed into so tight a cleft and pumping that voluminous a fluid. Relating to his reaction, she began to see it in a new way, getting hot herself. Then Havoc murmured "Think passion, keep your mind shield high, and hear me. Make sure Swale is hearing too." He put his crown on, protecting his thoughts so that he could focus them without being mentally spied on.

She nodded, indicating her understanding, and continued kissing and stroking him. She knew that their enemy lurked somewhere near, and had ways to watch them, and to lay traps for them. Their only protection was to keep that enemy in doubt about their thoughts and plans.

He kissed her ear. "Can Swale carry information from one person to another?"

She kissed his ear in turn. "Yes."

"Have her visit Ennui again and learn what she and Throe have learned from Handmaid about the force behind the torture cult. Who or what directed it to act against you."

"She's on her way. But I can tell you already that the spy eyes that watched me and summoned a sea storm to kill me were not the doing of the torture master. Shrapnel didn't know of them, so surely Handmaid doesn't either."

"Our enemy uses others against us, without telling them," he whispered.

"Our enemy has special powers. But we haven't made much progress in identifying it."

"Because it knows us better than we know it. I want to confuse and surprise it. That's where Swale comes in, if we can trust her."

"I think we can, Havoc. Her interest is now in preserving my body—and yours. So we don't need to trust her demon nature, except in that she doesn't want to die. But she does love you, as most women who know you do, and wants to be with you again."

"You can handle that?" He could see how Gale might become uncomfortable if the succubus pre-empted more of her time with him.

"I knew it would be this way when I invited her to stay with me. She is no more a threat to our relationship than Bijou is, because she can't take you from me, by definition. She can only borrow my body when I let her. And she has talents that help, such as seeing in darkness and taking out rapists."

"And seductive dancing," he said appreciatively. "And sex. Her cleft felt like a hungry mouth."

"Yes. She *is* a succubus. Any man who enters her is going to yield his essence. How does she relate to surprising our enemy?"

"She can travel from woman to woman, carrying information, I think undetected by others. That provides a way for us to remain in touch when we are separated beyond mental range."

"So she can," Gale agreed, surprised by the relevance. "So our enemy won't know that we are coordinated."

"We shall need coordination. I have in mind five golem couples, each emulating the two of us, going about our business in widely separated regions of the world. How will our enemy know which are relevant and which are not?"

"But if our enemy can read our minds—"

"Only I will know the relevance—and I wear the crown to protect my thoughts."

She caught on quickly. "So our enemy may know there are five couples, and that they are all golems, and that only one is really us, but still not know what we are doing. Like a game wherein the pieces are visible but the strategy is hidden."

"That's it. Maybe this time we'll surprise our enemy, and identify it."

"We'd better, Havoc. That enemy is dangerous."

"How well I know it." While they talked, his passion had been building further. His caresses became serious.

"She's back," Gale murmured.

He staved off his ardor. "What's her report?"

"Handmaid knows much about the operation of the torture complex, but nothing about any directives from outside it. Only Shrapnel knew. And she doesn't think he knew anything more than that he owed a favor to an unknown party, who had provided him with the torture complex of his dreams, and sending Swale out was that favor."

He had been afraid of that. "I sent you into that hellhole for nothing."

"No, it was worth eliminating, and we did gain Swale's assistance."

"I am sorry I had to send you blind, but if our enemy had read your mind—"

"I know, Havoc. I knew you wouldn't desert me. Others thought I was naïve, but they didn't know you as I do."

"I do love you. Maybe from the first time we played Tickle & Peek, and you gave me everything."

"Because I loved you already," she agreed. "I didn't know it then, but now I know it was love. We didn't know we were both change-lings."

"But the dragon seeds knew. That we were *too* close."

Her passion became pain. "Oh, Havoc, I want to have your babies!"

There was their tragedy. "If only whoever is behind the change-lings had made us less similar."

"Could it be our enemy?"

There was the great awful mystery of it all: why would some secret power spread changelings across the globe, so attractive to each other they would inevitably fall in love, and so closely related that they dared not breed—and kill anyone who wanted to know more about them? It didn't seem to make sense. Unless the changelings were supposed to take over the world, having no family lives of their own, and answer to that power without knowing it. If that was the case, he was against it—and probably King Deal had been against it too. If this were a phenomenal secret power play, that would not work if others knew of it and opposed it, then this policy did make cruel sense.

"We may owe our lives to the enemy," he said. "But we owe that enemy vengeance, too."

"I hope there's some other explanation," she said.

"Swale, tell Ennui to expedite Handmaid's departure for her own village. The king's transport is available. I want her out of here before morning. Similarly I want Smoky on his way to City Triumph before dawn, by other transport. Tell Ennui to tell Symbol."

"Swale's gone," Gale reported. "She's glad to be able to do this for you. Now we are alone again." Then, evidently tired of the delay, she amplified her efforts and responses, and carried him into their culmination. She had indeed been making notes on the techniques of the succubus, and was putting them into practice. Havoc had no complaint.

After which they slept. Gale, worn out by her session in the torture complex, slept fitfully, until she put a hand on his shoulder. Havoc
woke, surprised. "What?"

"Swale here. Gale's asleep, but not well. Sire, you can be thoughtless. Gale has just come off a horrible experience, and could use your
support."

"My support?"

"Her body is strung tight. I can ease her, but she needs more.
Put your hands on her."

Havoc did. She was right: Gale was tense, even in her sleep.
"Thanks." He sat up, and gave her a soothing massage, reassuring her
body by his strength and caring. Then her body relaxed and her sleep
deepened. She was the finest woman he knew, but she had been pushed
to her limit by that experience. He had indeed been thoughtless.

In the morning Havoc held a conference. "As you may know, we are
being watched. What we do seems not to be secret from our enemy, who
seeks to kill me or those doing my special bidding. So this meeting may
be known. My plan is to move more swiftly and surprisingly than the
enemy can readily track, so that by the time it counters, we will be done.
There is danger for all of us, but I think no greater than the danger of
failing to act expeditiously. It is also best if no one else knows the exact
nature of my strategy. So I ask all of you to follow my directives without
question, keeping open minds. We are about to go after several important artifacts simultaneously. You will pair off by male/female couples of
your choice, each of which will animate golems in my image and Gale's
image. The golems will impersonate us to the best of your abilities. If it
becomes apparent that the folk you encounter are not deceived, do not
cease; maintain the pretense. I believe it will be possible for you to carry
it off and obtain the artifacts."

He looked around. "Throe, with whom will you couple?"

"With me, if you please," Ennui said.

Havoc, surprised, looked at Chief. "With whom will you couple?"

"With me," Symbol said.

So the social realignment was taking place, with likes joining with
likes. "As you wish. Placebo, with whom will you couple?"

"Me, Sire? I have no—"

"With me," Bijou said, taking his hand. She had evidently come
to terms with the need to serve Havoc by seducing another man.

"But I was simply helping the Lady Gale to travel through the
Translucent domain," Placebo protested. "I'm not part of this party."

"You are now." She squeezed his hand. "Gale still needs your
help. I will emulate her as a golem. You will emulate King Havoc.
Now don't argue."

Placebo looked as if he wanted to argue, but Bijou kissed him,
and he was silent. She was one of the mind readers, and knew that it

was her job to bring him into line. She was doing it. The Translucent Chroma man, inexperienced with lovely women, was readily handled by them.

"Berm, with whom will you couple?" Havoc asked.

The Brown Chroma man was as surprised as Placebo had been. "But all I wanted was to rescue my sister."

Ennui spoke. "You will be with her, but in another place. I have made arrangements to convey you there. I think you will be satisfied."

Berm bowed his head. "If this is the king's will, I will of course cooperate to the best of my ability. But I have no partner, and no idea what I should be doing."

Ennui paused, looking blank. Then she spoke again, with a different voice. "Do it, my brother. I'll join you soon. There will be a partner for you, and I am assured that you will like her. We will clarify what you will be doing."

Berm nodded, recognizing his sister's animation of Ennui. "Then I will await instructions."

"Ennui will see each couple to its conveyance," Havoc said. "You will be informed of your specific missions."

Ennui rose. "This way, Havoc, Gale."

They got up and followed her out. There was a coach made of water, with two figures vaguely visible within it. Ennui and Chief had evidently been busy during his time in the torture complex, setting up schedules and making arrangements with the Translucent Chroma authorities. The truth was that Translucent was happy to have the torture complex gone, but had lacked justification to handle that matter itself. Havoc, as king, had it, and had done them an incidental favor. Now they were cooperating to get his party on its way out.

"You will ride in back," Ennui said. "And animate your golems to guide the coach. I trust you know where you are going."

"We'll figure it out," Havoc said. "How do we guide this thing?"

"The squid will answer to the golem's signals."

"Squid!" Gale exclaimed.

"I'm sure it's tame," Havoc reassured her. "Anyway, golems surely don't taste very good."

Ennui smiled and closed the door on them. Havoc looked at the Havoc golem seated in front, and bonded with it. In a moment he was looking out through its eyes. It was clothed in the manner of the king. He turned his head to face the Gale golem. She was in a fetching gown. "Are you there?"

"Yes. Havoc, this is weird, impersonating ourselves, full size, when we're right here."

"Yes. I was impressed with the Brown Chroma golems, so arranged to obtain a number for this mission. I wonder how far we can go as golems?"

"First get us moving. We have to make way for the next coach."

Havoc lifted his right hand. "Squid—are you there?"

A long shape with trailing tentacles swam into view ahead of the coach. It was evidently not phased out, but it looked strong enough to haul the coach. It latched two tentacles onto the front and waited, gently expanding and contracting its mantle. Its four great eyes oriented forward, sideways, and backward.

Havoc made a throwing gesture forward. The squid jetted water and shot away, hauling the coach behind. In a moment they were well away from Village Wetback. The coach was not rolling along the ground, but sailing well above it.

Havoc lifted his golem arm and pointed left. The squid veered left, making the turn. Havoc straightened his arm, and the creature stopped turning and continued straight.

"So where are we going?" Gale inquired.

"Let's wait on that; it will take a while. Tell Swale to inform Ennui that Chief goes to the White Chroma."

Gale's golem expression went still, as she returned mentally to her body and communed with the succubus. Then she returned. "Done. Is it to be like this, in bits and pieces?"

"Yes. So that our enemy has no early warning."

"It's already confusing me."

"That's the idea." He leaned toward her and kissed her left ear. There was no tactile sensation. "I want the enemy to believe I'm doing nothing of consequence," he murmured into that ear. "Just relaxing after the horrors of the torture cult."

"I'd certainly like to do that."

"You can. I can't. Swale's messages are vital."

"Got it," she said. "Just tell me what you need."

That was just one of the wonderful things about her. She wasn't demanding further explanation, she was giving him whatever he needed, just as she had in that first game of Tickle & Peek. She knew he would explain when he could. "Now let's get serious," he said at full volume. "I know a female golem can do it, because I almost bedded one. It's the male I'm not sure of."

"We'll find out." She turned to him. They embraced imperfectly, as there was not much room on the coach's driving seat. "Maybe we had better go in back. Will the squid continue?"

"We'll find out." They scrambled over the back of the seat and joined their real selves in the main body of the coach. The two of them were sitting with their eyes closed, as if asleep. The coach continued to move, so evidently the squid would keep on in the same direction until signaled otherwise. Meanwhile, if the enemy were watching, all it would see was two people with time on their hands, experimenting with new toys.

They lay on the floor at their real feet, embracing. But Havoc had no sensation of touch. His golem hands were guided by his eyes and

424   PIERS ANTHONY

will, not direct sensation. When he kissed her, he did not feel her lips.

"I suppose it's an aspect of feeling no pain," she said. "I think I could accommodate you, but I would have no sense of it. Can you even get it up?"

Havoc concentrated. "Yes."

"Well, let's see."

They removed the golems' clothing and attempted to come together naked. They were able to bring the applicable body parts together, and to juxtapose them, but there was no sensation. They might as well have been pushing two wooden mannequins together.

They gave it up. "But what about a golem body with a real one?" Havoc asked.

"I'm game." She faded, and then her real body came alive. "Do me, Havoc."

He tried, but though he got into position, he still had no feeling of it. "Pretense is all I have."

"Too bad; this is interesting. You feel just like you." She was teasing him.

"Let's try it the other way." He vacated the golem and opened his real eyes. There were the two of them in intimate embrace.

Then the Gale golem animated again. He embraced her, and found her warm and receptive. He penetrated her, and it was much like reality. "Are you there? he asked.

"I can't feel you," she said.

"So is it better for the man than the woman?"

"Not when she's the real one." Her golem hands caught his head and brought it down to hers for a kiss. "Swale's back," she murmured. Then, louder: "I still can't feel your lips or your penis."

"Tell Placebo to go to the Invisible Chroma."

Gale's golem faded for a moment. That made him suddenly aware of her state, because the seeming flesh became hard and unyielding. He pulled his groin back, and was able to, but feared that it was possible to get caught inside stone, with the position wrong. Also, her hands on his head froze in place, and had her grip been tight, he would have been unable to escape. Sex with a true statue was not fun.

Then she softened. "Done," she murmured.

"You just turned halfway to stone around me."

She laughed. "Sorry about that. My mind isn't clever at being external and internal simultaneously."

He disengaged. "Get back into your own body, for now."

She did, and they lay together while the golems were inactive. "Gale," he murmured into her ear, "I thought I could manage things this way, but it seems to be too inefficient. Swale takes too much time to go back and forth."

"She travels spiritually, but seems to be limited to ordinary flying speed. I can ask her to hurry."

"No, I think I need better efficiency. You say that if Swale took my soul, she could return it?"

Her embrace tightened. "Havoc—"

"Could she take me with her, to consult with the others, and bring me back?"

He felt her shiver. She did not like this at all. But she answered. "I think she could."

"Could you fake my presence here?"

"Yes." Her grip on him was almost like that of the vacated golem. He kissed her ear again. "The enemy would never suspect that."

She yielded. "You will owe me, Havoc."

"I'll always owe you."

Soon the succubus was back. Gale faded, communing with her. Then her body animated again. "Swale here," the succubus said, whispering in his ear as if making love. "Sire, this isn't wise. I think I could do it, but I don't know my limits. If I lost your soul—"

Havoc wasn't sure either, but he knew that it was dangerous to continue trying to elude an unknown enemy who was out to kill him. If this gamble paid off, he would be able to identify the enemy, and maybe take it out. "If you take me, can I retain consciousness?"

"Yes, if I allow it. If that is what you wish."

"Yes. Take me to Ennui."

"Sire, I can't just take you. Only when your soul become vulnerable at the moment of—"

"Not even if I give it to you?"

"I suppose I could try," she said uncertainly. "No man ever volunteered his soul before. I have no experience."

Havoc relaxed his body. "Do it."

After a moment, she spoke again. "I can't. When I use Gale's body, it's not only because she lets me. It's because I'm resident in it. I can't touch you, sire, and I can't touch your soul. You have to send it to me. You know how."

He had been afraid of that. The limitations of the succubus normally protected men and boys from folly. In this case, they balked him. But it wasn't insurmountable. "Then I will send my soul to you. Take it when it comes."

"Havoc, it was bad enough when you tested to be sure I could avoid taking you. This is worse. Gale has become my friend. I don't want to do this to her. She is really upset about this. She would rather have you do almost anything else. If anything goes wrong—"

"Just see that you don't lose my soul!" Havoc clasped Gale's body and addressed it sexually. He penetrated her and continued with sexual thrusts.

"Spirit of the planets!" Swale said. "She says to do it. But this frightens me."

Havoc felt the climax coming. "Gale, I'll be back when I can.

Thank you." Then he geysered.

There was a horrible wrenching. He felt as though he was being sucked into a narrow necked bottle. Much of him wouldn't fit, and was being pulled away behind. Then he settled, confined in darkness.

"Where am I?" he tried to ask, but it was only a thought.

"You are in my womb," Swale replied, speaking in thought. "And I am in Gale's womb. Shall I tell her you are in good order?"

"I can't tell her myself?"

"Only if she enters your space, which is much confined at the moment. She would have to poke her finger into her own womb. However, if I leave her, and expand in the air, she could reach you more readily."

"Do it."

"First she has to get your body off her body. Yours is empty. Ah, now it's off. I will emerge."

There was a sliding/squeezing sensation, as the succubus moved out of the womb and out of the body. Havoc wondered whether this was the way a baby felt as it was being born. Light came, and he saw Gale's giant cleft, then her thighs and belly as he moved away. Rather, as he expanded. He could see neither himself nor Swale, but had the feeling of increasing volume.

He hovered in space, looking down at Gale's body, with his own inert body tumbled beside it. He looked disreputable in that clumsy position.

"I told her to poke her finger forward."

Gale did. It missed him, but must have found Swale. "I will tell her to move it. When she crosses you, let her know."

The finger moved toward him but missed him. After a moment it reversed, approaching him again, and missed by a smaller margin. "She is intersecting me, and I am correcting her."

"It would be easier if you just moved me to intersect her still finger."

"That I can not do. I can touch her or infuse her when alone, but you are male, and can't touch her. She must touch you."

"But you were just inside her, with me."

"I was inside her alone. Then I took your spirit. That's a special process. I could remain where I was, but once I exit her, I can not return as long as I have you in me."

Then the finger crossed him. There was no physical sensation, but there was a feeling. "Gale! I'm here!"

The finger passed on beyond, but immediately reversed course; she had heard him. She returned. "Havoc?"

"I'm here inside Swale. I feel confined in a bottle, but I'm all right. How is my body doing?"

"It's unconscious. That bottle is her invisible womb."

"I'm a baby," he thought, realizing that though he had been born

KEY TO HAVOC 427

from Gale in a fashion, he still hadn't been born from Swale.

"A big baby. You just sired yourself, I think. In me."

"And in Swale. Gale, I must go to Ennui and others. This may take some time. Do not let the enemy know I'm gone."

"I'll try. First we'll sleep. Then we'll play some more. But if you don't get back in time—where are we going?"

"To the Yellow Chroma, for a holiday."

"Fine," she agreed. "But will the squid be able to haul us there?"

"It will be met at the boundary by a fire coach. Ennui will have arranged it. She doesn't miss a detail."

"Try to return before then, Havoc. I don't think I can move three bodies without giving things away."

"I'll try. I love you, Gale." He had learned to say that. It was true, but originally he hadn't thought to speak it aloud. She had finally gotten through to him about it, just as he had gotten through to her about his need to touch her body in passing even when they weren't planning sex. They were still learning from each other.

"I love you, Havoc."

Then he was sailing into the sky-like water of the Sulvan Sea, leaving Gale below. "This is hard on her," Swale said.

"I think the enemy will be reluctant to believe that I would leave her in such manner, or that I would ever let you take my soul."

"Any normal person would be reluctant to believe that," she agreed. "I'm pretty cynical, but even I'm surprised. What is this enemy?"

"An unknown entity who I think killed King Deal, tried to kill me, and tried first to stop Gale by sending you, then to kill her on the way to the torture complex. It seems to know where our bodies are, and wants us out of the way."

"It did try to kill Gale. Placebo saved her. She made him fall in love with her, as you made me fall for you."

"I did not try to make you do that."

"I know, Sire. It's just the way you are. Let it be; I never truly loved before, and I like the feeling, even if I know I can never have your love in return."

"Gale and I are changelings."

"Yes. You are superior people."

"I doubt that. But we do have good bodies and good minds."

"And you make others like you. Whoever crafted you did an excellent job."

"It may be that our enemy crafted us, and means to use us for nefarious purpose. And will kill us to prevent us from verifying, exposing, or interfering with that."

"While hiding behind other agencies, like the Temple or the torture cult," she agreed. "Maybe it crafted you too well, so that you are not the unquestioning servants you were supposed to be."

"Maybe so," he said, appreciating the new slant.

"We are here."

He looked out—that was easy to do, since they had no substance blocking their view—and saw Village Wetback. There were two coaches traveling out from it. Swale moved into one, and as they phased into its interior Havoc saw that it contained just one person: Berm. He was being taken to City Triumph to impersonate Havoc there. There were two inert golems.

"Wrong coach," Swale said apologetically. "Have you anything to say to my brother? I can hover near until he moves and accidentally impinges my space."

Havoc was about to demur, then realized that this would be a good chance to practice. "Do it."

She disposed herself close, and waited. In a moment Berm lifted a hand, perhaps to scratch his head, and must have intersected her, for he paused, looking startled. Then he nodded and moved his hand carefully across until it intersected Havoc's space.

"Here," Havoc said. "This is King Havoc."

"Sire!"

"You are being taken to my residence in City Triumph, where you will use your golem to emulate me. A young woman there named Spanky will assist you. You will learn to use your golems, which are perfect likenesses of us."

"I know how to use a golem, Sire. They are from my Chroma. But as for trying to emulate you, even as a golem—I would not presume—"

"Spanky has been emulating Gale, and assisting the man who emulated me, who has now gone elsewhere. She will be able to guide you well. When you are alone with her, you may do with her what pleases you both."

"Sire?"

"You have been under duress for some time. You need time to recover, emotionally as well as physically. Swale will be by to see you on occasion, but she is busier than I expected. Relax, heal, get comfortable. Learn all you can of the ways of the king. When my mission is finished, you will be able to go home, but we do not know exactly when that will be."

"Yes, Sire." The man seemed somewhat overwhelmed.

"Meanwhile, practice with the golems in this coach. You can animate either one, when you bond, as you know. Make it seem that I'm in the coach with you."

"Yes Sire."

"Swale, take us away."

She did so. "That was nice of you, Sire."

"I wanted to see how well it worked."

"I mean giving him that bath girl. I picked up her image from Ennui's mind. She'll soon make him forget his privations."

"Bath girls can be a great comfort to a man," he agreed. "And until we figure out what to do with you, you will have to be with Gale, and Gale will be with me at the capitol. So Berm might as well be there too, so you can see him regularly."

"That is nice of you too, Sire."

"Didn't Gale promise to treat you right if you joined her?"

"Yes, but only to the extent of getting me a body to occupy. I doubted that she would do more than the minimum."

"Now you are helping me, and I will see that you don't regret it."

"I already don't regret it. I really am re-learning niceness from you folk, and I like it. I can feel the meanness fading. I thought I would never be human again."

"You were the one who reminded me to be more considerate of Gale, in her distress and fatigue."

"Yes, I'm pleased that I thought of that."

"So even an inhuman woman is more sensitive than an ordinary man."

"Well, you aren't ordinary, Sire."

He let that go, uncertain whether she was teasing him.

They came to a second moving coach. This one contained Throe and Ennui. Swale went right up to the woman, and spread herself out until Ennui moved her head and her nose entered succubus territory.

"She is amazed. I have visited her several times, but she never thought I would bring you. She will talk to you now."

Swale hovered before Ennui. Ennui poked out a finger, and soon intersected Havoc. "What awful lunacy caused you to pull this dangerous stunt, Havoc? Throe will have a fit."

"It's so nice to have my actions applauded."

"If you survive this, do you have any idea how it will look to that assessment team that's judging your fitness to be king? Submitting your soul to the good graces of a succubus?"

"Enough of the compliments. You and Throe must approach the Translucent Chroma authorities and obtain from them, in the name of the king, a mind reader spell that will identify all minds impinging on a set space/time locus. Bring it to Triumph."

"I don't suppose this is supposed to make any sense to us," she grumped.

"Correct. It may not even be relevant."

"You're sure that being possessed by a succubus hasn't warped your mind?"

"It warped my member, perhaps, but may have had less effect on my mind."

She allowed a smile to show. "You were always a barbarian, Havoc."

"I'm glad it shows. I will check back later."

"Take care of yourself, Havoc. Insane as you may be, you give my life meaning."

"I thought Throe was doing that."

"He's giving my life passion. You were right: he is the one for me."

"I should talk to him too. Put him on."

Ennui withdrew her finger, took Throe's hand, and poked his finger into the same space. "Hello, Sire," he said. "You know I would never have let you do this."

"If the enemy kills me," Havoc replied evenly, "it won't be because I stood still and waited for the end. Conceal the fact of my contact as long as possible. Let the enemy think it's only the succubus, or that you are acting on your own initiative, or even that you really are me."

"Done."

"I'll be in touch."

Throe withdrew his finger, and Swale floated out of the coach. "Where next, Sire?"

"Chief and Symbol. I have to give them their assignment."

She moved on through the water, and soon found another coach, going in its own direction. "I can contact Symbol, but she would fight me. Better to have Chief intercept me."

"Do it. This business of sliding into women's private anatomy is weird. That's properly a solid man's business."

"It's the penalty of traveling with a succubus. You're in *my* private anatomy. But I told you: I can't enter a woman while you are with me." She spread herself out before Chief and waited.

Chief shifted position, and his elbow entered Swale's space. He paused, receiving her message, then carefully poked his finger directly at Havoc. "Yes, Sire." If he was surprised by Havoc's invisible presence, he did not show it.

"Ask the White Chroma authorities for a timer."

"A timer, Sire?

"A device whose magic places an event precisely."

"A chronograph."

"That must be the name. Bring it back to Triumph."

Chief nodded. Swale withdrew, and they were floating again. "Next?"

"Placebo and Bijou."

"That will be a chase; I think they're already in the air."

"Already?"

"Ennui arranged for the Invisible Chroma to fetch her, as it is some distance."

"Ennui handles things well."

"Yes, she is unusually competent. How did you find her, Sire?"

"We met by chance and made an oath of friendship."

"She says she owes you everything."

"She is generous."

"If you have had the impact on other lives that you have on mine, she is being accurate."

"A barbarian does what he has to do."

"Which seems to be to wreak havoc on civilization."

"Naturally."

They rose to the surface of the Sulvan Sea and into the air above. Swale oriented and gained speed. It was evident that she could move rapidly when she wasn't finding her way. He wasn't sure of her mechanism of flight or any other motion; apparently it was part of existing in spirit form. But the air coach must have moved rapidly too, because it took time to catch up to it.

Havoc watched the ground passing below. The home planet was beautiful this way, with its variegated landscape and patchwork colors. Even the clouds above the Chroma were colored, their tints matching those of their Chroma. Havoc had seen colored clouds in the distance, when a child, but they had always changed to neutral gray when they passed over Village Trifle in the nonChroma region. In his recent tenure as king he hadn't had much chance to look at the sky. Now he admired it. The colors of magic were charming, as befitted the planet of Charm.

He looked up. Sure enough, planet Mystery was there, just as colorful. Yet again he wondered whether there were people living there, gazing back at Charm with surmise.

At last Swale caught up with the invisible coach. Havoc couldn't see it, but did see the figures within. They seemed to be flying through the air, clasping each other for safety.

As they came close, it became apparent that it wasn't for safety that Placebo and Bijou were clasping. "Your girlfriend is making that man forget your fiancée," Swale remarked with satisfaction.

Havoc found himself somewhat out of sorts. But he was the one who had put them together, knowing they would get along. He wanted Bijou to be less oriented on him, because he would keep her only if he couldn't have Gale.

"You had sex with Gale, you had sex with Bijou, you had sex with me, twice," Swale said. "And maybe others, past and future. These two aren't entitled?"

"They're entitled," he said. "I just didn't figure on seeing it personally."

"Maybe we should wait before we contact them. They should be through soon."

"Yes." He could not avoid watching the couple, because Swale hovered close. "You're enjoying this."

"Of course. When I became a succubus I learned to crave sex above all else. I am learning decency now, but sex still has fascination. Every act is a bit different, a rule unto itself."

"I never thought I would encounter a woman more interested in it than I am," Havoc said ruefully.

"I'm not a woman. When I was a woman, I had the normal indifference to it. It was just something men would pay for."

"It's true you're good at it. I always thought Gale was ideal, but you actually enhanced her."

Swale floated close to the couple, observing. The man was translucent, like shaped water, while the woman was flesh toned. Her body could be seen in distorted form through his body. "He's a bit naïve, and so is she. They have finished, and neither realizes it. They don't have a polished sense of completion."

"You can tell this from one observation of their coupled bodies?"

"Yes. If I got into her now, I could in due course make her bring him to a second and infinitely more satisfying climax. Better for her, too."

"Don't do that. I need to give them their mission, and get on home to my own body."

"You're jealous that she's enjoying it with someone else."

Havoc tried to deny it, and could not. He had been with Bijou while wanting Gale; now he had Gale, and missed Bijou. "Yes. I thought I was beyond jealousy, but maybe not."

"Men are such turds."

She was needling him, and he knew it, but she was nevertheless scoring. "And women aren't?"

"Women are more loyal, in this respect. Bijou would be with you now, if you hadn't told her to make nice to Placebo. She's doing what you told her to do."

So she was. He was still out of sorts. "Men are turds," he agreed. Then he changed the subject. "What is hauling this coach?"

"I'll check." She flew through the invisible coach wall to the front, carrying him along.

She stopped suddenly. Had Havoc been physical, he would have suffered a concussion. "What did you do?"

"I bounced off their steed. It seems to be an air stallion. I didn't see him."

"A bird?"

"Well, he does seem to have wings. I can't tell, because I can't overlap him and can't see him."

"This is good enough. We can guess that he knows where he's going."

They returned to the inside of the coach and waited as the couple disengaged and cleaned up. The man and his clothing looked watery, but was actually completely solid. Then Swale placed herself in Bijou's way and established communication.

"I told her we just arrived. I don't think they wanted to be watched." She was surely right.

Placebo, acting on instruction, poked out his finger, and soon intersected Havoc. "Ask the invisible Chroma for a spell of invisibility,

for the king," Havoc said. "They will assume you are the king, since
you will be animating the king golem."

"Yes, Sire. Bijou explained about pretending to be the king. But
I don't think I know you well enough to fool anyone."

He had a point. Throe and Chief both knew him as well as any
civilized folk did, and Berm was being relegated to the protective safety
of the king's apartment, where the staff would assist him. But Placebo had a problem. "How close are you to the invisible Chroma?"

"I think we'll be there in half an hour. I'm not even sure how to
animate the golem competently."

And Bijou had distracted him instead of drilling him on that. It
was a mistake Gale would never have made. The man needed fast
and competent instruction. "I can show you, but I will have to enter
your body. Are you amenable to that?"

Placebo hesitated. "No offense, Sire, but I don't know what that's
like. I'm not inclined toward sex with men."

"It's not sex. The succubus will infuse me into you, and I will
share your body, but you will retain control. I will leave when you
know enough about me to emulate me."

"In that case, all right, Sire."

"She will put me in your member. You will have to poke her with
it."

"That *is* sex. With an invisible female."

"Not exactly. It's more like incomplete sex. You can't see her or feel
her."

"Sex with a ghost."

Havoc checked with Swale. "You can infuse me—and take me
back later? Without there having to be more sex?"

"Yes. I retain control of your spirit, because of my special magic,
until I return it to your own body. But are you sure you want to do
this? If anything happens to Placebo while you are with him, it will
happen to you too, and I might not be able to get you back."

"I'll risk it. He has to be able to emulate me."

Placebo hesitated, so Bijou parted his translucent clothing and
brought out his translucent member. It was not erect, but this didn't
matter. Bijou lifted it slowly. Swale oriented so that the member
nudged the region that was her cleft, then abruptly ejected Havoc. He
was squeezed out of her invisible womb, down her channel, and into
the translucent member. The succubus magic carried him on through
the tight channel until he reached the prostate, and there he remained.

Now he was able to spread out. He found the man's nervous
system, and followed it up to his brain. "Hello. I am here."

"Sire? Am I imagining you?"

"I may seem like no more than a thought to you, but I am King
Havoc. Now I will instruct you on my mannerisms. Remember, I am
a barbarian to whom civilized virtues come unnaturally. I see people

as individuals rather than as objects. I care about them. But when crossed, I can become violent. I'm not much for deception unless it is really necessary. Now let me show you the operation of the golem. I don't think I can animate it directly, but I can tell you how."

"That should help, Sire."

"First, you bond with it. That is, you identify with it, projecting your mind into it."

The dragon seed buzzed.

"What was that, Sire?"

"A warning of danger." Because it had buzzed while Havoc was communicating, so no one was lying to him. Unless there was some other wrongness about the situation. Was there a problem with the golem? "We had better check those golems. Tell Bijou."

Placebo did. "There's nothing wrong with the Gale golem," Bijou said. "I tried it before, and it's just fine."

"Tell her to try activating the Havoc golem."

"A female can animate a male golem?"

"Yes. It's just a fancy puppet, really."

The Gale golem relaxed, and the Havoc golem became active. "This golem seems perfect to me," the golem said, with Bijou's intonations."

"Then it must be something else," Havoc said to Placebo. "We must be alert."

Then the coach rocked, as if its wheels were encountering stones on the road. But there was nothing except air around it. It shook, and bounced. "What's happening? Bijou asked, alarmed.

Havoc advanced to take over the speech mechanism. "Remember the water bomb? This may be an air bomb."

"Havoc!" she cried as she bounced on the jumping seat. "It's really you!"

"It's really trouble," he said. "My dragon seed buzzed, and I think this is what it knew about."

"I don't see anything."

"An air bomb would be invisible, I think, like the rest of the Invisible Chroma." Havoc got a notion. "Swale—where are you?"

"Here," she said from Bijou's mouth after a moment.

"Can you fly really fast, when alone?"

"If I concentrate."

"Go to Symbol and ask her if the Invisible Chroma would try to take us out. It may be our enemy, but she's not."

"On my way."

Then Bijou spoke. "She's gone. But Havoc, we can't wait for her. This violence is shaking apart the coach."

So it seemed. Havoc was hanging on to the seat and side of the coach as it jolted crazily around. "I think this in an attack. There's invisible roughness calculated to snap the coach free of the steed and drop it to the ground, to crash. It will look like an accident."

"Can we stop it?" That was Placebo, speaking from inside.

"Not if it's magic. Bijou—can you read the mind of the steed?"

"Oh, yes. He's a nice alicorn. But he's terrified now; this is none of his doing."

"Can you get your golem to guide him?"

"I can try." In the front of the coach, the Gale figure animated and addressed the invisible creature ahead. But that meant that Bijou was no longer minding her own body; it was falling off the seat.

Havoc handed his way across and caught her with one arm. He spread his legs, wedging them against wall and seat, and clung to a ceiling handhold with his other arm. The rocking of the coach hurled her into him like a rag doll, but he was able to prevent her from flying out again. Meanwhile, his mind was working.

"Placebo, I know you can do powerful magic when you have to."

"Sometimes, Sire. But I'm out of my Chroma."

"Take back your eyes. Look around; can you see any Translucent Chroma territory nearby?"

The head turned, and the eyes gazed around. "Yes, I see one water volcano to the side."

"Bijou!" Havoc called. "Steer the steed toward that water volcano to the side."

"I'll try," the golem called back. "He's pretty spooked."

"Charm him with your girlish adoration."

"But even if we get there, you know I can't do magic," Placebo protested.

"You sure as hell can! You saved us all from the void bomb."

The coach bucked violently. There was a tearing sound. A blast of wind struck him in the face. The coach was coming apart.

There was a scream. The Gale golem had been thrown out of the coach, and was falling to the ground.

"Bijou!" Havoc cried. "Get back to your body!"

Her body came alive in his grasp. Her eyes opened. "I'll try again." Then she sagged again.

The Havoc golem animated. It pawed the seeming air, finding its way out of the torn coach. Then it leaped into space.

"Bijou!" Havoc cried.

But the Havoc golem did not fall. It landed on something and remained high. "The steed!" Placebo said. "She's on the steed."

Now the steed changed direction, heading for the water volcano. Unable to make the steed answer to the reins, she had mounted it and was guiding it directly. "You are some girl," Havoc murmured appreciatively.

"She's some girl," Placebo echoed. "I thought no one could replace Gale in my heart. No offense, Sire; I didn't know she was—"

"I know. Gale's her own woman."

"But Bijou could, I think. She's not as smart or strong, but she has determination and courage."

"That she does." They were making progress toward the volcano, though the coach was still rocking violently.

Swirling clouds were forming, boiling up and outward and fragmenting in rapid order. Dust was stirring from the ground below, shaping into an expanding funnel. This was a full fledged storm, only now becoming visible.

Then there was a much worse bump, as if the coach has smashed into a wall. It came apart, and the air rushed in around them. The invisible harness snapped, and suddenly the Havoc golem was tumbling forward and down, while the coach tumbled sideways and down. Havoc felt his hair being tugged, and his clothing. It was worse for the girl's body. He clung desperately to it. The world seemed to be spinning around them.

Bijou opened her eyes and screamed.

"We're close enough!" Havoc cried. "This is Translucent terrain. Take us, Placebo!"

"Sire, there's no—I can't—"

"Placebo!" Bijou shrieked.

That did it. A bubble of water enclosed them, stopping their fall. The storm-like winds abated. They floated toward the water volcano, which was jetting wisps of vapor and occasional gouts of hot water that puffed into roiling clouds.

"That's more like it," Havoc said.

Bijou twisted within his grip, wrapped her arms around him, and kissed him avidly on the mouth. "You saved me, Placebo," she said. "With your magic."

Havoc gave the man back his mouth. "I really didn't—"

"And you saved me, Havoc, by making him do it," she said, kissing him again.

"That about covers it," Havoc said, taking back the mouth. "Now I know you can't fly us out of this region. Land us, and we'll either walk or see if the alicorn returns."

The bubble drifted down toward the wet ground. They reorganized their clothing and combed their hair. It had been a rough passage.

"Swale's back," Bijou said. "I felt her slide into me."

"She does that," Havoc said. "I find it a bit eerie."

There was a pause. Then Swale spoke, using Bijou's mouth. "I see you aren't much of a coach driver. You lost your horse."

"What's your report?"

"Symbol says that the Invisible Chroma is completely loyal to the king, and would never countenance any such attack."

"That's what I thought," Havoc said. "But I doubt this was natural. I think my enemy struck again, and tried to make it seem the fault of the Air Chroma. This occurred beyond the Invisible Chroma territory."

"Yes. It is similar in respects to the way it was when Gale was attacked. That was within Translucent territory, but was not of Translucent making."

"So the enemy is independent of the Chroma. It can generate magic mischief anywhere it chooses."

"So it seems," Swale agreed. "But how did it know you were here, Havoc? I don't know of anything that can trace a succubus or incubus in free flight, or a soul either."

Havoc nodded. "Either the enemy has much more power than we can fathom, or there's another explanation. I think it saw this coach heading for the Air Chroma, and guessed we were after the spell of invisibility, and knew that could be mischief, so tried to take us out. It didn't know I was here."

"That makes sense," she agreed. "What now?"

"Placebo—is that air steed by any chance within the range of this water volcano?"

"I don't—"

"Don't give me that. Extend your awareness and find out."

After a pause, the man answered. "Yes, it landed at the fringe. It seems uncertain what to do, lacking human guidance."

"Enclose it in a bubble and bring it here."

"But Sire—"

"Do it," Bijou said, reading the man's mind.

"I'm doing it," Placebo said, seeming surprised.

"Now you still have the mission," Havoc said. "We've lost the golems, so you'll have to go as yourselves, acting for the king. I think they will accept you, especially since you'll be with the steed."

"But my bubble can't go beyond the boundary of this volcano," Placebo said.

"You'll ride the back of the alicorn. It seems to be competent to fly independent of Chroma, and can probably handle the two of you for the short distance remaining."

"I suppose so, Sire."

"Good enough. Swale, take me home."

"Line up," she said. She lifted Bijou's skirt.

"You know where to put it," Havoc told Placebo, and retreated to the prostate. Darkness surrounded him, but in a moment he felt a pull, and he was sucked into another place. The succubus was recovering him, having never truly let him go.

Then Swale floated into the air, leaving Placebo and Bijou seemingly on the verge of renewed sexual contact. She rose into the air, oriented, and moved rapidly across the terrain.

"How did you get a buzz from your dragon seed?" she inquired as they moved.

"I—" Then he paused. "It's with my physical body! I couldn't have heard it. Yet it gave me the warning I needed."

"Maybe you saw a warning signal, and interpreted it as a buzz."

"Maybe. But Placebo heard it too, and I doubt he has a seed." Havoc pondered. "I think the dragon seed was aware that I was entering danger, so it buzzed, because it knows danger and truth regardless of distance. There must be some tenuous connection between my body and my soul, so I was able to hear that buzz even from that far away."

"There is indeed a connection. That was why I needed my body; when my body died, I would have died, had not Gale decided to give me hers as a home. Now I am tied to her similarly, and that is the thread I am following back now. I can never get lost from my host body, if I am free to go to it."

"That must explain it," Havoc said. "So my body protected me after all."

"You seem to be very good at protecting yourself, and at making things come out right."

"It's just common sense management."

"Or a changeling talent."

He nodded, mentally. "A person can be strong and fast and smart, and still suffer because of bad breaks. My dragon seed alerts me so that I can avoid or handle some of those."

"I'm sure it's a great help. But I think also that you are the type of person who acquires special things like dragon seeds, or mind reading, or the use of a succubus, or golems or void bombs, and makes them work in ways that others might not imagine."

"It's true. Each of these things seemed like a dire threat, but became uncommonly useful. I have been fortunate."

"You make your fortune, by seeing potentials where others don't. So does Gale. It must be a changeling attribute."

"And the enemy does not want us to know about the changelings." Havoc suffered a nervous thought. "Suppose the enemy sends a changeling after me? I mean, someone who has the same strengths I do?"

"You might meet your match. So you had better complete your mission before that happens."

"I think my mission is to identify the enemy, who may also be the source of the changelings, and nullify it. But now I think this will be no easy course."

"Agreed. Yet I believe in you. I may have been your enemy, or at least an agent of your enemy, but now I love you and will do anything for you."

"You're doing it now."

"My point is that part of your talent may be to convert your enemies. So you may be a more formidable opponent than your enemy realizes."

Havoc pondered. "Or I may be typical, which is why most of the threats are inanimate. You were supposed to divert Gale by taking out

Lad Student; had you succeeded, you would not have remained long enough to become an ally."

"I underestimated Gale. Is it possible that the changeling maker does not fully appreciate the strengths of grown changelings? It seems to handle them only as incipient babies, and not touch them otherwise."

"It seems possible," he agreed. "Swale, you are not a changeling, I think, but you seem to have a rare understanding of such matters."

She laughed, unphysically. "I have recently been exposed to superior intellects. Now I draw on Gale's—and yours. I was never that insightful on my own. And that makes me think of another thing. The folk you recruit seem to be varied and ordinary, yet in your presence they become more than they were. You bring out their best, and they give you everything, as I am doing now. You have made Ennui become a formidable organizer, when she was once a creature of dullness. You have made Bijou into a princess in mind as well as emulation. Throe has become more than a bodyguard. The lady Aspect has left her grief behind and become your facilitator and defender. Even those who resist your impact, like Chief and Symbol, nevertheless perform aptly for you. Now it is happening with Placebo and Berm. You animate those around you."

"I'm just trying to do my job, so I can retire soon with honor and go back to Village Trifle with Gale."

"I don't think you'll ever do that."

"I love her!"

"And she loves you, deeply, abidingly, utterly. She trusts you as few other women ever trust a man. But it's not just that she is a changeling, so may be one you can never marry. It's that once you are out of your little village, you may be no more able to return to it than I can to my original body. You're the king."

"You mean I'm marked?"

"Yes. But also that your horizons have broadened, as mine have, and you will no longer settle for a life of farming and child raising. Neither will Gale."

Havoc wanted to argue, but there was a disturbing ring of authenticity about her conjecture. Still, he did not want to continue as king. "There must be some other way."

"If there is, you will surely find it."

"If I survive."

"Havoc, you *must* survive. Those you have touched would be desolate without you, and the kingdom would suffer grievously."

This was too much. "You talk like a love-smitten fan."

"I do. I am. And I am typical. Have a care for those you change."

Havoc had to marvel. This was a succubus, at one time merciless in her mission, now urging him to be gentle. Because he was part of her at the moment, he knew she was not pretending. She did love him, and so did the others. And he and Gale *had* wrought that change in her, and in the others. "I do care," he said. "About all of you. But I have an enemy who does not."

She made a sigh of pure emotion. "I know it."

Now they came to the coach hauled by the translucent squid. "Look at that!" Swale thought.

He looked. Inside it Havoc seemed to be having sex with Gale. How was that possible? Then he pieced it out. Gale was animating the Havoc golem, and causing it to go through the actions on her natural body, which did not have to move because it was the passive recipient. So it seemed as if two people were participating. This would have fooled any observer who did not know that one person was absent—and then it would have seemed to be the female who was gone. Gale was doing a really good job of concealing Havoc's mission.

"We will need her help to put you back," Swale reminded him.

"Contact her."

"This may not be easy. She's not moving. The golem doesn't count."

He hadn't anticipated this problem. They would have to wait until Gale finished emulating him. But that might be some time, as she was trying to mask his absence the whole time he was gone. The golem was methodically plumbing her, indefatigable because it could never climax. It was a perfect way to fool a passing observer. But it also meant it could continue indefinitely.

"Wait—we don't have to wait," he said. "The coach is moving. We're floating along with it now, but we don't have to. We can float stationary relative to the ground, and let Gale overlap you."

"So we can," she agreed, surprised. "We could have done that with the others, had we realized." She spread out ahead of Gale, then let herself drift back relative to the coach. Gale's body intersected her.

The Havoc golem abruptly withdrew and flopped on the seat, inert. Gale reached out to the Havoc body and lifted its member, which intersected Swale. She squeezed, and Havoc was flushed into his own body. In a moment he spread though it, reviving. He felt somewhat the worse for wear; his body evidently didn't like being vacated. But it remained functional.

Then he embraced Gale. "Where were we?" he asked, stroking her as if ready for sex.

"Getting sore," she said, wincing. "I couldn't feel what was happening. I discovered there was some abrasion."

"Then I won't aggravate it." He kissed her. "I'm back. I'll catch you up on what happened."

"Swale's already doing it. You animated Placebo?"

"There was a problem. We handled it."

"An air bomb!" she exclaimed. "The enemy struck again."

"Unsuccessfully, again."

"Havoc, we can't keep dodging these indefinitely."

"Soon we won't have to, I think."

The squid reached the edge of the sea. They dressed and did partial animations of their golems: just enough to reduce their weight and enable them to be guided by the hands. They got out, bid parting to the squid, and walked up the bank to the shore. As they did so, the magic of the water pills evaporated, and they returned to normal.

The land was bright yellow, with blades of flamelike grass growing. This was the fringe of the Yellow Chroma. There was a coach made of seeming fire, drawn by a fiery stallion. They approached it, and found that hot as it looked, it was comfortable for them. They led their golems in and sat down, four abreast.

The stallion moved forward, and the coach rolled across the yellow terrain. They looked out the windows, and saw that even the clouds in the sky were like rounded flames. They passed under one, and it rained: burning droplets. All the trees had golden foliage, and the trunks were burnt umber. They crossed a fiery stream, with coruscating currents around its pale yellow rocks.

"If I didn't know this is Yellow Chroma, I might guess," Gale remarked. "What are we here for?"

"A smoke bomb."

"What is that? Explosive vapor?"

"I picked up the concept from a passing mind. It forms a cloud that unmasks anything concealed by a spell of invisibility, because the smoke can't disappear."

"You suspect invisible mischief?"

"It is possible." He changed the subject. "Gale, when I retire as king, can we go back to Village Trifle?"

"Too late: Swale gave me your dialogue on that. I agree with her: we can't go back. We would no longer fit, mentally or emotionally."

"But where else can we go?"

"I'll have to see what happens to retired kings. There must be some."

"If they weren't retired by death." He changed the subject. "Swale."

"Yes, Sire," the succubus said with Gale's mouth.

"Go to Triumph and invest Spanky. Have her address Berm. Have the two of them practice with their king and queen golems. Between times, you may talk with your brother. Stay there until we return."

"But suppose you need me again, Sire?"

"You have done your part. Now you are off duty. Relax. Return to us only if you encounter something you feel we need to know immediately."

"Done, Sire!" she said gladly, and faded.

"You're giving her her reward," Gale said. "Free time with her brother."

"She did good work. I think Placebo and Bijou would not have survived had we not been there to help them navigate the air bomb."

"What was it like, riding in the womb of a succubus?" Gale asked mischievously.

"It was an interesting experience. But there was more of me in there than I normally care to put in."

"I never would have believed it. I thought there was no limit to how much of you you like to get into a woman."

He laughed. "I thought so. But henceforth I'll settle for the ordinary. Are you suggesting that I'm neglecting you?"

"No. But I wish I could throw away the wire."

"We've got to learn more about the changelings! Maybe we can marry."

"I hope so, Havoc." But they both knew this was unlikely. They did not want to risk having magically deformed babies. There were educational plays describing that problem, just as there were about the dangers of wrong sex. It was one reason for the rule of the fourth child: to ensure that there was always a fair mix of types in every village, no matter how isolated the village was.

The coach approached a Yellow Chroma village. The houses seemed to be on fire, and even the yellow children flickered brightly.

Just beyond the village was a huge golden arc stretching across to the horizon. Its near end plunged into the ground at an angle. The fiery horse galloped up to this end and onto the arc. Suddenly they were rising, balancing on the top of the arc, sliding along it with increasing velocity.

The landscape became visible below, in all its shades of yellow and orange. This was like flying, except that it was sliding. The arc was a track that guided them across the Chroma at a speed they could never otherwise achieve.

Then they saw other arcs converging on theirs. The coach descended at their common anchorage not far from the great bright volcano. There was Fireside City. It was surrounded by a palisades of leaping flames, and its buildings were in the form of towering infernos.

"It's certainly impressive," Gale murmured. "Now when we go out, do we do so as ourselves, or as animated golems?"

"Let's try the golems; that's what the others are doing, if they haven't lost their golems."

They made their bodies comfortable, and animated their golems. Then Havoc had a perverse notion. "Let's try each other's golems."

Gale, always game for his challenges, let her golem fade. Then Havoc bonded with it, and looked out through the eyes of the Gale representation. Meanwhile the Havoc golem came alive and looked back at him. "What have you been up to, woman?" it demanded gruffly.

"I'll never tell, Sire," he responded demurely.

They both laughed, but decided to see if they could carry it through. As the coach rolled to a halt, the Havoc golem climbed out, then turned back to offer a steadying hand to the Gale golem, parodying civilized mannerisms they were learning.

A small contingent of Yellow Chroma officials were on hand to greet them; three males and one lovely flaming female. "Sire," a yellow man said, bowing his head. "I am Fireman, regent of Fireside City. To what do we owe the honor of this royal visit?"

Havoc started to answer, but Gale spoke first. "I wish to obtain a smoke bomb."

Fireman was plainly taken aback. "May I inquire for what purpose?"

"No."

There was a pause. Havoc did his best to look demure; he was only supposed to be the king's lover, or perhaps more properly in this setting, the king's flame, there to look pretty. Then the female spoke. "Sire, I am Fiera. Will you allow us to entertain you while we arrange to deliver the bomb? It will take a few hours."

"By all means," Gale said.

"We have a fine relaxation resort nearby. Your coach will take you there."

They returned to the coach. "Let's switch back," Gale said. "You are beautiful, but this is wearing."

Havoc smiled with her semblance and vacated the golem.

The coach took another track—directly toward the fire volcano. It came to a stop at a high platform right next to the huge bright mountain. The coach walls faded out, so that it seemed they were sitting on nothing, and in nothing. There was the feel of intense magic in the air.

A streak of fire emerged from the great cone, flying high into the sky. It exploded into a hundred bright sparks that spread out in a star-like pattern and drifted down around the outside of the cone. Another streak sailed up, and detonated similarly. Then several more came up simultaneously, their displays overlapping.

"Oh, I like this," Gale said. "It's so pretty."

Havoc had to agree. He had never seen fire magic this close before, and it was impressive. He had not thought of non-illusion magic as a display before, as an entertainment. That was because real magic was rare in the nonChroma regions, and never wasted. Here at the fire volcano there was so much magic they could afford to waste it.

A score of streaks shot up, exploding simultaneously. The sparks formed a huge face whose sparkling eye winked at them. They laughed. "Augmented by illusion, I suspect," Havoc said.

Gale snuggled up to him. "Havoc," she breathed in his ear. "Is there a point to all this business with the couples and the golems?"

"Yes, and it's time for you to know it. Our enemy seems to know what we're doing, so we had to confuse it, not by concealment of our actions, but by concealing our purpose. I need some special tools and not others. I think our enemy can't try to stop more than one mission at a time, so now it has to guess which is the key mission. I'm gambling that it will stop the wrong ones, and that by the time it figures out the right ones, it will be too late."

"That accounts for the five missions," she agreed. "But they could have been organized without the use of all those golem copies of the two of us."

"I wanted more than one level of deception, to further confuse the enemy."

"It must have. It certainly confused your friends." She paused thoughtfully. "But if the enemy is something special, like the Glamors, that shouldn't work."

"You believe in the Glamors?"

"No. They're mythology, of course. But the way this enemy has been, it forces me to wonder."

"We can settle that in a hurry," he said. "We can ask the dragon seeds."

She smiled. "Yes. I'll make the statement: the Glamors are the enemy."

Havoc's seed buzzed. "It says no."

"Is that because they exist and aren't the enemy, or because they don't exist?"

Havoc laughed. "Because they don't exist, of course."

"I got no buzz," she said.

"That makes sense."

But she still wasn't satisfied. "If the Glamors exist, wouldn't they, by definition, have more power than the dragon seed? So couldn't they make it give a wrong answer?"

Havoc was about to demur, but paused. "The seed does have its limits. It's our most accurate guide, but I guess we can't be sure."

"And if the Glamors exist, they wouldn't be fooled by golems, either."

"That reminds me: we need more practice with the golems."

"Oh, no!"

"I want others never to be sure whether the Havoc and Gale they encounter are originals or golems. We all have to be good with them."

"All right, Havoc," she agreed wearily. "But I must say I'm tired of having sex with your golem."

"No sex," he agreed. "For now."

"For now?"

"Well who knows where my crude male passions may lead me? Maybe one day golems will develop feeling."

They animated the golems and watched the continuing fire display. It was spectacular.

Chapter 10—Glamor

"Sire."

Havoc stood to greet his visitor. "Lady Aspect."

"I am glad to see you well. Are you authentic?"

Havoc removed his crown for a moment, so that she could verify that his mind was present. He was not a golem. He was sure she could tell, but she was a careful woman. "What is your concern, Lady?" For she never bothered him without reason.

"I have completed my investigation of the lines of command. I have serious news."

Havoc braced himself for it. "I am ready, Lady."

"The majority of the officials of this kingdom are competent and loyal. Thirteen are not. Two are in doubt. And I fear there is one more who I have not been able to identify. It is that one that concerns me, Sire. He may be the one who betrayed my husband and who is betraying you."

"How can you know there is one, if you don't know his identity?"

"My husband died, and his betrayer was never known. Attempts have been made on your life."

"Perhaps they were warnings," Havoc said. "Intended to discourage me from investigating the changelings."

She paused a moment, considering. "What makes you think that?"

"The fact that I survived. The enemy has shown considerable savvy and power, and perhaps could have taken me out if it chose to. Instead it made ineffective attacks on me and Gale, and did not follow them up. It might have felt that it was better off with an ignorant barbarian as king, than with a knowledgeable civilized king. So it warned me off, hoping I would behave. But I suspect that its patience is limited."

She nodded. "This is possible. But it is also more than likely that you were simply better at avoiding mischief than the average ignorant barbarian." She smiled, for the words were no insult, and she no longer tried to conceal her fondness for him. "You were on routine business at the time of the first attempt, so should have needed no warning off. However, you were seeking a tool to investigate my husband's death at the time of the second."

"My enemy may not have realized that. But I take your point: attempts have been made, from the outset. Someone must be keeping my enemy informed of my whereabouts. And Gale's."

"There is a traitor in our midst," she agreed. "And that is the one I have not found. But this is not the limit of my news."

"There is worse?"

"Yes, Sire. I have obtained advance information on the People's Petition. It has become a Crown Assessment."

"Oh, that report on my doings as king? I thought that was routine."

"Not this time. Sire, it is negative."

Havoc was surprised. "Negative? The people don't like me?"

"The people like you, I sincerely believe. So do the Chroma Representatives. But they have no power in the face of the Crown Assessment. It claims that both the people and the Chroma voted against your continued tenure as king." She blinked, and he saw that she was crying. "I am familiar with this process because of what happened to my husband. By some devious mechanism the routine People's Petition was suborned into this deadly attack on you. It is thoroughly corrupt, but there is no effective appeal from it. Sire, you will have to resign."

Havoc felt his jaw dropping. "I thought I couldn't quit without being executed for treason. They're letting me go?"

"They will let you save face. An official will inform you privately that you have completed your mandatory term, and are now free to resign with honor. If you do, they will let you retire with honor and live as a high ranking but powerless citizen. If you do not, they will issue the report, and you will be impeached."

"Impeached! On what grounds?"

"Incompetence. They did this with my husband, and he fought it and won. Then he died. That is why I say you must resign: if you expose the speciousness of this attack, they will find another way to be rid of you."

"They are getting serious! If they can't kill me, they hope to depose me, and if they can't depose me, they'll kill me again."

"Sire, if those prior attempts were warnings, and you survive impeachment, then the next attempt will be serious."

Havoc gazed at her. "I think I need advice."

"Sire, I thought you might. I can take you to see the former kings."

"The kings?"

"The ones who resigned rather than face dishonor or death. They are not bad men; in fact I believe that they were forced out because they were trying to be good kings. They keep their opinions to themselves, but I associate with their wives, and have read their minds. They are angry, but helpless, knowing that there will be retribution if they try to make any protest. They are helpless; they have children to protect. But I think if you are circumspect, they will provide you with their thoughts."

This was her first indication that she, too, had caught the mental disease, probably by design. No, the second; he had known on some level when he removed his crown to open his mind to her. "Aspect, you are a genius! That's exactly who I need to talk to."

"No, I am merely experienced. Havoc, I don't like this business at all. I loved my husband, and I love you. I hate bringing you this news."

He stepped toward her, opening his arms. They embraced, like mother and son. "I know you do, Lady. I love you too. You have helped me greatly, and I trust you absolutely."

"I want you to continue as king. But more than that, I want you to continue to live."

"Take me to the kings."

She disengaged. "I think you should not do this openly."

"They are in the city?"

She nodded. "There are three of them. I could ask them to gather together. To join their wives for a social event to which I will also bring you. In this manner we can go to them. Sire, if you don't mind—"

"I'll be your manservant," he said.

"There are no secrets, ultimately. But for this purpose, this will do. It may mask your attendance long enough."

They were ready that afternoon. Berm activated the Havoc golem, and Gale activated the Gale golem to cover for his absence. Havoc, garbed as a husky palace servant, carried the Lady Aspect's errand box.

She took him shopping, trading a small non-magical gem stone for a nice length of cloth, and he carried it in the box. Then she decided to watch a new holograph show, and took him to her private booth at the show chamber. There were three men and three women already there. They stood when she entered, making formal bows, and she returned the gesture. "Set it down there, lad," she said to Havoc. "Then seal the door so that our entertainment is not disturbed."

"Yes, Lady." He placed the box, and closed the door, making sure it was tight. This was a soundproof chamber, for the showing of illusion holographs of the type Symbol had presented. Then he turned to face the others.

"This is King Havoc," Aspect said, without further ado. All six nodded. Then, to him: "This is King Diamond. King Enterprise. King Cheer. I leave you to your dialogue, while their wives and I enjoy the show." She took her seat and faced the holograph, which was just forming at the other side of the chamber. The three other women joined her.

Havoc realized that this was a special enactment of a regular event.

No doubt the four ex-queens formed a social group, having much in common. He couldn't read their minds, because there were too many people here, but it was clear that they were comfortable with each other. This time they had brought in the men, as requested. It would not seem remarkable to outsiders.

"I am honored to meet you," Havoc said. "Your names are in my history text."

"And we are honored to meet you, Sire," King Diamond said. He was a portly older man. He seemed to not to question Havoc's identity, though Havoc was in servant's attire and was not wearing the crown. But surely the former kings had made it their business to recognize the current king by sight, and they well understood the need for privacy.

"Please, don't call me that," Havoc said. "You are my seniors in more than one respect."

They smiled understandingly. "What can we do for you, Havoc?" King Cheer asked. He was the middle king, of pleasant mien, but his eyes were serious.

"I need advice. I am to receive a negative Crown Assessment, but am not yet ready to step down. I did not want to be king, and do not wish to remain king, but my business is not yet finished. What should I do?"

"We have heard much of you," King Enterprise said. He was the youngest king, but still substantially older than Havoc. "You are called barbarian, but you seem to be uncommonly clever."

"I am ignorant, not stupid." It was his standard response.

They nodded, understanding perfectly. "What is to be the basis for the negation?" King Diamond asked.

"Incompetence."

All three burst out laughing. "They lack imagination," King Cheer said, and indeed he did seem cheery. "You are proving to be the most competent king of this century."

"I have barely kept up with events," Havoc said.

"You should have seen *our* first months!" King Diamond said. "And we were from the cities, long conversant with the system. Our challenges were less difficult than yours, too. But we found it awkward to adapt rapidly to the sudden onset of seemingly absolute power."

"You seem to have a genius for coming up with novel but workable solutions," King Cheer said. "I suspect they expected a barbarian to be dazzled by the joys of civilization, and to indulge in much food, many women, and pointless excesses of personal power. Instead you took immediate hold, surely dismaying them."

"I had excellent advice," Havoc said, glancing toward the Lady Aspect.

"Which you sought and heeded. You won the gratitude and loyalty of almost all of the people and officials you have encountered.

Even King Deal's household staff. They had anticipated much worse from you."

"His death was no fault of theirs," Havoc said. "I felt that they could help me most, if I encouraged them."

The three kings nodded again. "So competence is not your problem," King Diamond said. "Except in this respect: you were *too* competent. You are on the way to taking back the crown."

"Taking it back?" Havoc asked. "They forced it on me."

King Enterprise gave him a straight gaze. "The king has been pretty much a figurehead in the past century. The real powers of the planet are anonymous and largely invisible. They choose the king, they run the kingdom, and they depose the king when he becomes inconvenient. It is competence, not incompetence, that makes him inconvenient. You are bidding fair to bring real power back into the hands of the king. That is why you must go."

There was substantial truth here. It answered a host of peripheral questions. "So as long as I play at being king, I'm all right, but if I try to make it count, I'm not."

"Within reason," King Diamond agreed. "You don't want to make an obvious mockery, because then it would become apparent that it wasn't real. They prefer the people to be fooled. But apart from that, you have leeway to do favors and gratify your passions."

"Which is just what you seemed to be doing," King Cheer said. "You have nice taste in women. I'm not clear why there have been attempts on your life."

"I'm investigating the murder of King Deal."

The three stared at him. "That would do it," King Enterprise said after a moment.

"And that explains how you won over his widow," King Cheer added. "Lady Aspect should have resented you, but it seems you converted her from the first."

"She's a good woman," Havoc said. "I need her."

"True. But you are the man who took her husband's place. A barbarian impostor. She was prepared to hate you, and instead she supports you. Completely. Our wives report that she has never spoken a word in your disfavor."

"In fact, you seem to have won over all of King Deal's people," King Diamond said. "And not merely because you kept them on. They really do like you."

"They are good people."

"But you asked us for advice," King Enterprise said. "We proffer it: Resign."

Havoc grimaced. "I can't do that. What other advice do you have?"

King Enterprise frowned. "King Deal was given the chance to resign. He declined. He was impeached. He fought it and won. Because his death seemed accidental, there was no disposition of his staff. It was left for the successor king to dispose of. You surprised those people, and they are now your most loyal supporters. But the point is, you can't win. If you don't resign or get deposed, you will mysteriously die. It is better to go the easy way. Then you and your woman can join us in retirement and watch holos." He glanced toward the wives with a small quirk of his mouth.

"You haven't answered my question," Havoc said evenly.

"I am arguing the case for common sense," Enterprise said. "If you are impeached and deposed, your friends and staff will suffer. If you die, they will be at the mercy of the successor king. He is unlikely to be as kind as you proved to be."

Havoc just looked at him.

All three kings nodded once more, almost imperceptibly. They were not surprised by his attitude. "We would like to have it on record that we urged you to resign," Enterprise said.

"So you did. So I will report."

"With that accomplished, we shall join our wives. We trust you will take our advice to heart, and save yourself much grief." Diamond and Enterprise walked to the chairs.

King Cheer remained. He made a small beckoning motion with four fingers and sat in a chair facing Havoc. Havoc brought up a chair and sat facing him. The two men put their heads together.

Now it was feasible to read the man's mind. *They may try to assassinate you openly*, King Cheer thought. *You have proved to be difficult to kill by covert means. You must root out all possible traitors. Your ability to read minds will help; no king we know of had that. But there's bound to be one traitor you miss; there always is. That is your worst danger. Fight the impeachment openly; make a big scene of it, so that if you die, everyone will know that it was assassination. That may discourage them; they don't like being open. Much of their power is in their anonymity. Move rapidly, to keep them guessing. And I think you must name the Glamors.*

Havoc looked at him in surprise. "They are mythical," he said only in his mind.

I am not sure they are. I suspect them of being the true powers of this planet. You cannot directly oppose them, but if you associate them with you in the popular mind, they may let you go, as they much prefer to be unknown. In effect, you will force them to prove themselves mythical by allowing you to live, at least for a while.

"What of King Deal's murder?"

Investigate it openly. Again, that may prevent the hidden powers from killing you, lest the matter be publicized too widely. I think the odds are against you, but this is our best advice, if you insist on tackling the establishment. And one more thing: check the Emergency Protocols of the Crown. They may seem dull and routine, but they have some wrinkles you may find useful. Reclaim the power of your office, if you can. Then King Cheer stood. "But come," he said aloud. "We can't sit here idly forever. We must join the women."

He had given Havoc much to think about. They joined the women. The rest of the afternoon was spent enjoying the holograph and indulging in innocuous dialogue.

Later, Havoc and the Lady Aspect returned to the palace. They did not speak of their meeting with the three former kings, and did not share it mentally. Havoc had gotten the most competent advice available, and now he had to decide how to act on it.

Chief and Symbol, the last of the five missions, returned to Triumph, bringing their prize: the timer. Havoc was ready for his next move.

"Fetch them," he told Ennui, lifting his crown to give a mental list. "We depart in an hour." She did not question him; she knew he had reason for privacy as well as speed.

They took a large coach to the site of King Deal's death: Chief, Symbol, Throe, Ennui, Placebo, Bijou, Berm, Spanky, Aspect, Gale and Havoc. All the couples who had been emulating king and consort, or who could read minds. They brought their acquisitions. None of them knew exactly how the devices were to be used. Havoc kept that secret under his crown.

But as they traveled, he spoke to them. "I am engaging in dangerous maneuvers. Your lives may be threatened. I regret this, but see no better way."

"We are all with you, Sire," Symbol said.

"I am expected to resign as king. If I do, the rest of you will be free to find other situations without prejudice, as you were before I came. If I don't, you may be under suspicion as being loyal to one who was not worthy of the office. It will be another day or two before things get difficult. I suggest that any of you who have doubts take action before then; Ennui may be able to find safe alternate positions for you."

There was a silence. Berm looked around, then spoke. "I'm really not part of this group, Sire. You rescued me from the torture cult and reunited me with my sister, and assigned a wonderful woman to be my companion. I owe you my life, and will go only if you wish me to. But I wonder why it is that you did not include the Lady Ennui among those free to depart."

"I'm free," Ennui said. "But I won't go. I'm Havoc's oath friend. If he dies, I die. He is my life."

"I thought you were with Throe."

"The king is my life too," Throe said.

"None of us are leaving," Symbol said. "We are all advocates of the barbarian."

"Then I hope barbarism prevails," Berm said. "But I must say that this is not the way I thought the king was."

"My situation is yours," Placebo said. "I'm not quite sure how I became part of this party."

"Are you sorry?" Bijou asked him.

"I am captive of his women."

"We are all his women," Symbol said.

There it lapsed. Havoc was glad for their loyalty, but felt guilty for the possible cost of it. All of them were here because they had become his closest associates. "I think you deserve to know what I'm doing here," he said. "I am investigating the death of my predecessor, King Deal. I believe he was murdered, but I don't know how or by whom. I hope to discover both on this trip. This investigation has been private; now I want the world to know it. All of you have been helping me to get the equipment and advice I need to gain the answers. Some of you have been helping by getting dummy equipment, so that my anonymous enemy could not know exactly what I was doing. You have also helped by emulating me and Gale so that the enemy could not be sure exactly where we were. I think the fact that we succeeded means that you succeeded. The enemy even struck at Placebo and Bijou. If I can now fathom the mystery of King Deal's murder, I may expose the enemy and bring it to justice."

"Why do I suspect it will not be that easy?" Symbol said. The others laughed.

In due course they arrived at the site. It was a steep mountain slope between Chroma. "Show us," Havoc said to Throe.

Throe stepped forward. "King Deal liked challenges. This is one of the rougher paths between Chroma. It mounts that slope and crosses that open chasm. There is normally a bridge, but a storm took it out. King Deal wanted to see how rapidly he could traverse it. I checked it and it seemed safe, because I knew that he was sure of foot and well able to hurdle the crevasse. I recommended against it anyway, because unnecessary risks are foolish, but he would not be stopped. This was his way of relieving the stresses of his office. He had survived a negative Crown Assessment and impeachment, and wanted to unwind."

"That's not how Havoc unwinds," Bijou said mischievously.

"On that occasion, my attentions were not sufficient," Symbol said. "If I could retrace that period, I would make sure he never got out of my bed."

"And I would have sent him back to it if he tried to leave," the Lady Aspect said. "Or taken him to mine."

Placebo looked confused. Bijou enlightened him: "The king normally has a mistress, with his wife's acquiescence. The Lady Aspect was King Deal's wife, and the Lady Symbol his mistress. Both loved him. The Lady Gale will be King Havoc's wife, if she can be, and I was his mistress for a time, and will be again if I can be. We both love him."

"Oh. Of course," the Translucent Chroma man said uncomfortably.

"You know your future lies in your own Chroma, when your business with the king is done," Symbol told him. "You would not want to be forever bandaged, as you and I are now."

"That's true." But it was evident that he would not soon be forgetting either Gale or Bijou. Havoc understood why, as well as any man could. He suspected that Placebo would not be returning to his Chroma.

"And Havoc also indulges in risky behavior," Gale said.

"The two men are similar, in such respects," Chief said. "They did not accept conventional limitations."

Throe led the way up the path. "Normally the crown would have protected King Deal, regardless. But when he fell, his flailing hand knocked it off, and so there was no barrier between him and the ground. He struck the rock below, and was dead. I failed to protect him."

Havoc stood on the brink of the chasm. The path was a ledge in the slope, and the chasm severed both slope and path. The cut was about five feet across, and widened below. There was a sheer drop of about fifty feet to jagged rocks. A fall into that could certainly be lethal.

Without warning he leaped across it. "Hey!" Throe and Ennui cried together.

"The footing is firm," Havoc said. "There should have been no trouble."

"He did not take off properly," Throe said. "He did not come close to clearing the gap. He dropped directly into it."

"He misstepped?"

"He must have."

Havoc leaped back, and inspected the path leading up to the chasm. "This is firm. There are no loose stones, no slippery sections."

"There were none then, either," Throe said.

"Could he have done it deliberately?"

"King Deal was not suicidal," Throe said stoutly. Symbol, Chief, and Aspect nodded agreement. "Neither was he incompetent. He should not have misstepped."

"That is my impression," Havoc said. "This, too, is something you all should know: he was a changeling. I am too, and so are Gale and Symbol. None of us are incompetent or suicidal. He was investigating the mystery of the changelings, and we suspect that this was the reason for his murder."

"Not his resistance to being urged to leave the office?" Symbol asked, though she knew the answer.

"His pursuit of the changelings may have been the reason for the impeachment. There's no evidence he was in trouble before he began that investigation."

"That's true," the Lady Aspect said. "My husband's tenure seemed secure. He had been seven years as king before he got curious about the changelings, and then suddenly everything soured."

"You say King Deal himself was a changeling," Chief said. "So he may have been curious about his own origin."

"He was," Symbol said. "He spoke to me about it. At that point I hadn't known he was one, and I didn't know that I am one until Havoc figured it out. Deal liked to solve mysteries, and the mystery of his origin fascinated him. The more difficult it was to learn anything, the more determined he was to fathom it. We didn't realize there was any connection to the impeachment, at the time."

"That was my conclusion," Aspect said. "After his death. It was the only thing that differed from the norm."

"And when Havoc went after the changelings, trouble came to him too," Symbol said.

"Could there be a connection between the changelings and the Glamors?" Havoc asked.

All of the others looked at him. "Sire," Chief said, "out of what planet did this notion come?"

"Call it a passing thought," Havoc said. He had no intention of getting the former kings in trouble. "We thought the changelings were mythical, and learned that they are not. We think the Glamors are mythical; could it be that they are not? Many of the qualities ascribed to the Glamors, of great personal appeal, high intelligence, physical health, and ability to handle power are also true of the changelings. If you stripped away the phenomenal reputed magic of a Glamor, which may be vastly overstated if they exist at all, don't you have something very like a changeling?"

One by one, they nodded. "Oh, Havoc," Bijou said. "If you are right, you're in double danger now. It's bad luck even to speak of a—a Glamor."

"But you know, this is an intriguing notion," Symbol said. "If there is a connection between the two, and the Glamors wish to be secret while participating in our human society, they would wish the changelings to be secret too. Maybe it is only changelings that become Glamors, so they are protecting their base from compromise or prejudice. So anyone who pursues the changelings is discouraged, and if he won't be discouraged, he is eliminated. That would account perfectly for King Deal—and now Havoc."

"It would indeed," Aspect agreed. She turned to Havoc. "Sire, maybe it's not too late. If you give up this chase right now, you may be able to live and remain king. I—I would prefer that."

"So would I," Symbol said.

"And I," Throe said. "Sire, it is my job to protect your life. This may be the single key thing to facilitate that."

Havoc looked around. "How many of you prefer that I drop this investigation?"

Slowly each nodded again. Eight of them wanted him to let it go. Only Symbol and Gale remained.

He held Gale's gaze, requiring her to answer. Her decision came suddenly. "Expletive!" she said. "That anonymous enemy went after me too."

"Amen," Symbol agreed. "If you're about to back off because it's dangerous, Sire, you're not the man I think you are."

"The vote is eight to two," Havoc said.

"Seven to three," Aspect said. "I want you to survive, but the more I consider, the more it seems to me that you have already crossed the line, and will not be spared. That being the case, I'd rather see you fight."

"Yes!" Bijou said. "You promised me my fourth. Let it be the child of a hero, and not of one who knuckled under. Six to four."

Spanky came alert. "You're giving out fourths? Five to five."

"I'm not giving out fourths," Havoc protested. "Bijou risked her life for me."

"I would too!"

Gale caught Spanky's eye. "He'll do it, when the time comes. You have my promise."

The girl was thrilled. "Thank you, Lady."

Ennui looked distressed. "I can't let all these younger women support you while I do not. I will always be in your camp, and I'm not looking for any fourth. Four to six."

"Too damn many women in the party," Throe said. "I voted with my head. Now with my heart: do it, Sire."

"Do it, Sire," Chief agreed grimly.

Placebo spread his hands. "If I have a vote, I'm changing it."

"Unanimous," Berm said. "But I hope we're not voting you into oblivion, Sire."

"You aren't," Havoc said. "I was going to do it regardless."

"As if we didn't know that," Ennui said with a weary smile.

"But I renew my suggestion that you leave my company as soon as you can. You are all being threatened."

"It's too late for us, too," Symbol said. "We are all tainted by your association, Sire."

"This very dialogue has tainted us," Throe said. "We know too much."

"I'm sorry about that," Havoc said. "I do need your support. I will do my best to survive, and to protect you." He took a breath. "Now let's be efficient about this. I suspect that events are about to accelerate. Throe, do what you have to, to ensure that we can't be taken out without making a scene that will publicize our business to the whole planet."

"Understood." Throe lifted his hand in a signal. Immediately men appeared, advancing to form a rough semicircle behind the group. Havoc was sure that others were spreading out ahead of them, beyond the curve of the mountain. Throe generally kept the protective mechanisms out of sight, but they were formidable; there was nothing casual about his mission. King Deal would have been similarly protected, but the mechanism of his murder proved to be so subtle that there was no protection from it.

"Now the enemy may be watching," Havoc said. "So I still want to mask my real effort, so that any interference has less of an obvious target. Placebo and Bijou, invoke your air spell and stand by for further action. Act as if this is a really important concern."

Placebo brought out the ball he had gotten from the Invisible Chroma. Bijou took his hand. They made a show of doing something really important, and the others duly watched. Then they disappeared. They had been rendered invisible, clothing included.

"Gale, give Berm and Spanky your smoke bomb. Make it important. Don't invoke it yet."

Gale took the yellow ball to the couple. They accepted it with great formality and paraded it around. They were being important too.

"Chief, Symbol, make your timer operative. Set it for the time of King Deal's death."

They brought out the device they had obtained from the White Chroma. It looked like a fancy clock, but was more complicated. They set it on the path and made adjustments, peering at dials and indicators as they oriented on a prior time.

"Throe, Ennui, stand ready with your mind spell."

They brought it out. This was just a translucent ball that answered to mental commands. Ennui held it, as Throe was watching the deployment of the protective force.

"And we will see what we can do with this." Havoc brought out the brown ball he had obtained from the Brown Chroma. Gale took it.

"We have the time," Chief announced.

"Orient the locator on King Deal," Havoc said.

Gale tuned the brown ball to react only to the presence of the former king. It was dull, indicating that Deal was not in the vicinity. She carried it to the timer, bringing it into the field of the past. It flickered, then glowed.

"I don't understand this," the Lady Aspect said. "We already know exactly where my husband died. What is the point of this locator?"

"This planet is in constant motion," Havoc explained. "It whirls through space, in its orbits around Vivid and Void, and orbits Planet Mystery too. The surface also changes, as Charm rotates. So this spot on the surface where the murder occurred is not close to that spot in larger space. But the locator, attuned to King Deal, is now orienting on that true spot, and will enable our other devices to orient similarly."

The Lady Aspect stared at him. "You have truly done your homework!"

"He does," Gale said.

"Now advance the timer slowly forward," Havoc said.

As they did so, the locator faded. Deal was no longer there. So she moved the locator forward on the path, and it glowed again: Deal was moving in time and space, and so the two devices had to be constantly adjusted and coordinated.

They traced him to the brink of the chasm, and to arm's reach over it.

"Move back to the spot where he jumped," Havoc said.

They did so. When the brown ball was glowing steadily, Havoc had Ennui bring the translucent ball to that spot.

"Set off the smoke bomb," Havoc said to Berm. "And drop it into the chasm."

Berm did. The smoke surged out, forming a dense ball that roiled outward and upward as the bomb fell. It bid fair to fill the chasm with its dark substance. That would surely be a distraction to whatever enemy might be watching.

"Identify any other mental presence at this site and time," Havoc said to Ennui.

She concentrated. "There's only one: Throe."

"I was jumping with him," Throe said. "I cleared the chasm; he did not. Had I realized—"

"Narrow it to Deal's head," Havoc said. "See if there is a foreign presence there."

After a moment she said "There's just a tiny trace, hardly enough to matter."

"Identify it."

She struggled. "Just one second, no more. It's not really a mind, just a—a dampening. A pushing of a switch, maybe. Then it's gone."

"What about a stun command?"

"It's not strong enough to stun a person, or even part of a person. It's just a little turnoff that at most would have made him pause. Harmless, really."

"Get the source of that push," Havoc said.

"I have copied it. But it's no one we know. It's a completely foreign trace."

"Now project that trace to my mind."

Ennui looked at him. "Havoc, if this thing somehow killed King Deal—"

"Suppose there is a switch in the mind of a changeling that can be changed for a moment by a very small push?"

"There could be. But—"

"Not lethal in itself. Just enough to make him jump not quite hard enough, and fall to his death. A seeming accident."

Both Ennui and Throe nodded, suddenly seeing it. "Yes, that could be," she said. "But to risk it on you—"

"I'm not jumping. Do it."

"Not on you, Sire," Throe protested. "Test it on me first."

Havoc shrugged. "Okay."

Ennui put the ball near Throe's head. She concentrated. Nothing happened. "No effect," Throe said.

"Now me," Havoc said.

Reluctantly, she lifted the ball, put it near his head, and gave it a silent command.

Havoc staggered, and would have fallen, but for Throe's strong hands on his shoulders. "Sire!" Throe cried.

Equilibrium returned. "I'm okay. But that was enough to set me back. So now we know: it's a switch that exists only in a changeling, not a normal person."

"That's not certain, Sire," Symbol said. "There's a normal difference between any two people."

Havoc shrugged. "Test it on others."

They did. The signal made Symbol and Gale stagger, but had no effect on Chief or Ennui or Berm or Spanky. Havoc had won his point.

"Now we know how," Havoc said. "And when that mental trace is analyzed by the Translucent Chroma professionals, we'll know who. We already know why."

"No we don't, Sire," Symbol said. "We know they don't want this matter investigated, but not *why* they don't."

Havoc nodded. "True. But maybe when we catch up to them, we'll learn that."

"I doubt we'll discover who," Chief said. "Assassins are normally apt at covering their tracks. But this does show that the originators of the changelings must be behind this, because only they would know of that special switch. They can control their own."

"So then why didn't they do it to Havoc already," Symbol asked. "Instead of going after him with crude air or fire bombs?"

"That would be suspicious," Chief said. "They can't afford to kill two kings the same way."

"Except perhaps in an emergency," Gale said.

"It wouldn't be effective anyway," Throe said. "It would have to catch him at a key moment in a key situation. It's a very specialized application."

"All the same, let's get Havoc to the Translucent Chroma and have them nullify that switch," Symbol said. "In fact, that would be a good idea for Gale and me too."

"Agreed, when I get time," Havoc said. "But first I have a date with the Crown Assessment. I don't want to be judged in absence."

They returned to their coach. "Where are Placebo and Bijou?"

Ennui asked.

"Still invisible," Placebo's voice came.

"Well, turn it off and get in here."

"How?"

Symbol smiled; this was her department. "I'm tempted to let them grow out of it. But a spell of invisibility isn't the same as natural invisibility. Just think cancellation."

Suddenly Placebo and Bijou reappeared. "That was fun," Bijou said. "We were just as solid as ever, but couldn't even see each other. So we had to keep holding hands, or whatever." She looked at Symbol. "How do you folk get along, in the Invisible Chroma?"

"We talk to each other," Symbol said. "Didn't you see how it was in my Chroma when you got the spell?"

"We got only to the fringe, so the effect wasn't complete. We could see things."

"You saw the tourist setup. The interior, including the volcano, is completely masked."

"But how do you cook or make beds, or anything, when everything is invisible?" Spanky asked. "I mean, if I were invisible, maybe I'd sit on someone's lap and he would know I was there, but at other times I should think it would be inconvenient."

"We use illusion," Symbol explained. "We outline everything we need to see with a fringe of illusion, and have no trouble." She removed one of her gloves, revealing an empty sleeve. Then a shimmering hand appeared, as she invoked illusion to outline it. "We can make ourselves appear pretty much as we wish to. But of course our reality manifests by touch when we sit in a lap."

"It certainly does," Chief agreed. The others laughed.

"So you could have shown me your body, when you first stripped," Havoc said.

"It was more fun to play Touch," Symbol said smugly.

They reached Triumph. "Relax," Havoc said. "But stay close. Things will be heating up." They were perhaps not aware just how much things would heat. He hoped his enemies were similarly ignorant.

They dispersed to their several residences. Ennui went to her office. Soon she emerged. "Havoc, it's here," she said. "The Crown Assessment."

"What does it say?"

"It's devastating. They make you look like a lascivious idiot."

"Give it here." Then he remembered something that had slipped his mind. "I need some fast and quiet research on the Emergency Protocols."

"I will see to it."

Havoc took the document and retired with Gale to review it. "Whereas: Havoc of Trifle, a barbarian rendered king, brought his ignorant ways to the crown, and has disgraced it," he read. "He spent more time away from his duties than with them, preferring to seduce the bath girl and wander alone with her." He smiled. "They certainly have my number."

"You were getting the locator so you could solve King Deal's murder," Gale said. "You had to hide so the enemy wouldn't know what you were up to."

"It seems they aren't interested in that."

Havoc read some more. "He sent his fiancée out alone on dangerous missions, without regard whether she lived or died."

"That's not true!" Gale protested. "You did your best to conceal my identity and mission, both times. It wasn't your fault the enemy was able to track me."

Havoc began skimming the list of particulars. "He pissed with women. He passed the King's Crown around to other men to wear. He left an impostor as king while he traveled irresponsibly as a minstrel, pointlessly endangering himself. He physically dueled with the Duke of Whitecrest, and with a golem warrior. Deliberately infected himself and others with a mental disease. Bungled an invasion of a torture complex. Had sex with a succubus, and let her take his soul. Paired off his male and female associates as if they were so many interchangeable bricks." He looked up again. "This is a remarkably complete detailing of my failings."

"A remarkably biased interpretation of your activities," she corrected him.

"Still, perhaps persuasive to folk who weren't there." Havoc was bemused rather than angry.

They read the rest of it together. "They don't give you any credit at all," she said. "Every misstep, every crudity is detailed. Meanwhile there's nothing about the way you handled the several early crises."

"This is a hatchet document," he agreed. "Manufactured by people who want me out. They're trying to embarrass me into resigning."

"Well, you can explain what you were doing. This stuff is garbage, and any fair minded person will see that."

"I'm not sure I want to explain. That would be fighting on their turf, and as I have been warned, even if I win, I'll get assassinated."

"Then what are you going to do, Havoc?"

Havoc smiled. "I'm going to give them a taste of combat, barbarian style. I'll need your help."

"Of course."

"Not so fast, Gale. This will be dangerous. I mean to trigger an assassination attempt, and that may be more dangerous to you than to me."

"I love you, Havoc. If I can't marry you, maybe I can give my life for you."

He shook his head. "You know I can find sex anywhere, and I

enjoy all of it. But I'll never find another love like you. I don't want to risk you."

"I know that, Havoc. I feel the same. Tell me what you need from me."

He knew she meant it. "It's like a glorified Tickle & Peek, in full public. You may not care to—"

"Tell me."

He removed his crown for just a moment and put his head near hers, focusing his thoughts. She nodded. "That will set them back," she agreed. "In more than one sense. There will be chaos."

"There will be my namesake. Havoc. That's the idea."

"Havoc," she agreed, smiling. "Yes, I will do it. For you." She was making it seem like a small favor, but it was a big favor, and a dangerous one.

He wasn't done yet. "There's something else. How did they come by the details itemized on this document? Only a close associate would know them."

"Havoc, none of our close associates would betray you. None *have*. We know each other's minds, literally. We have not contributed to this rag."

"Not consciously, perhaps."

"Do you want to take off that crown again and let me know what's on your sinister mind?"

"I think I had better keep it on. And talk with Symbol."

"Symbol," she said thoughtfully. "She's no traitor."

"That is for you to ascertain. When I first interviewed her, my dragon seed buzzed. I took it to be a warning of another nature. Now I'm not sure. I will keep my crown on; you will read her mind."

"Her mind shield is too good. She's a changeling, Havoc; she's very good at whatever she tries."

"She will let her shield down. Bring her here."

Mystified, Gale checked with Ennui, who quickly summoned the Invisible Chroma woman.

"What is it, Sire?" Symbol inquired as she joined them. As always, there was a special quality to her presence, which he now recognized as the changeling aura. Others reacted to it automatically, and it accounted for much of his own impact on people. But he was not immune to it himself; she intrigued him enormously.

"Glance at this Crown Assessment." He gave her the paper.

She skimmed though it. "This is ridiculous. 'He dallied with the Invisible Chroma Representative, who removed all her clothing and let him fondle her.' It wasn't that way. We played a game of questions and penalties as an introductory ploy. You did touch me, but only to verify my form."

She was minimizing it. Her form was seductive, and she had instilled desire in him that had never faded. But she was correct that it had not been an overtly sexual session. "Yet there are details there that only you and I could know. I did not reveal them, so you must have."

"I told no one, Sire!"

His dragon seed buzzed. "You did tell someone."

"I did not!"

"Symbol, I do not like being lied to."

Her veil looked him in the eye. "I never lied to you, Sire, and am not doing so now."

This time, surprisingly, the seed did not buzz. How could that be?

"She doesn't know she told anyone," Gale said.

"I did *not* tell anyone." But the seed buzzed.

"Symbol, there is a problem here, and we must solve it. Lower your mind shield and let Gale read your mind."

"You are suggesting that I am a traitor, Sire. I am not."

"I am suggesting that I am about to be impeached, based on information you have provided. If you did not tell anyone, and had no contact with hostile mind readers, something has betrayed *you*. I need to know what it is."

She gazed at him. "Sire, I do not want to do this. Is there no other way I can satisfy you?"

"I don't think there is."

"Havoc, that's not true," Gale said. He realized that her seed had buzzed as he spoke. His own did not buzz when he lied or was in error; he had personal immunity.

"Maybe there is a way. But why don't you want to let your mind be read? Gale is not your enemy."

"Not yet."

"What do you mean?" Gale asked, surprised.

Symbol looked pained beneath her veil. "Oh, damn it, it's going to come out anyway. Take a look."

There was a pause.

"That's enough," Gale said, evidently taken aback. "Havoc, she's no traitor to you."

"Then what's so secret in her mind?"

Gale hesitated. "Tell him," Symbol said, resigned. "I don't even want to hide it any more."

Gale nodded. "She loves you, Havoc. Really loves you, with a depth and breadth I wouldn't have believed, considering her experience with men. Mind and heart and groin. You are her Vivid and her Void. She has notions I wouldn't have thought of."

This set him back. "But she's in grief for King Deal."

"Yes, and that's real. But he is dead, and you are alive, and it really is true about changelings yearning to each other. And there's something special about you beyond that; I'm in a position to know."

"You love him the same way, Gale," Symbol said. "That's why you understand."

"I do," Gale agreed.

But Havoc didn't. "What of Chief?"

"A liaison of convenience. You're the one I want. And you have your own fiancée and your own mistress and other girls like Spanky lining up in droves. You don't need me, and I can't have you, and I wouldn't be good for you anyway, and the king's mistress does not just blithely move on to the next king, so it's impossible, so I would rather not have it known."

Havoc felt a sudden, powerful urge toward her. She had always appealed to him, and now with her declaration she appealed much more. He loved Gale and cared for Bijou, but Symbol was a *woman*. "Throe is right," he said. "This woman is dangerous."

"Havoc," Gale said, understanding too well. "You could no more marry her than you can marry me. She's a changeling."

"But I'm a changeling of a different generation," Symbol said. "A different batch, I think. You and Havoc have a family affinity, a similarity, that makes you close, but I'm probably far enough removed. I think I *could* marry him, and safely bear his children—and I wouldn't. Because my experience and notions would corrupt him in ways that your association would not. But my very presence could destabilize him, because he feels the same tidal pull. We are like Charm and Counter-Charm, squeezing each other, inciting volcanoes. You know it, Gale. That's why you'll be my enemy, and justified in it, if I don't go away in a hurry. And I can't stand the thought of leaving him." Her veil was turning wet.

Gale nodded. "You could take him from me. I always knew that. That's why I supported Bijou as his mistress."

"That's why *I* supported Bijou as his mistress," Symbol said. "I don't want to do to him what I *will* do to him if I get the chance. Because I love him, I don't want to let my love damage him."

Gale faced Havoc. "She's right. You are I are social and sexual innocents compared to her. Even Swale is impressed. Take my word."

"I resemble King Deal, in the changeling aspects," Havoc said. "You pick up on that, Symbol. But I may not live long enough for this to be a problem. So you should stay around, at least until this crisis is over, then see what remains to be sorted out. But that is not my immediate problem. Now we need to know how you gave away information. Did you mention our first dialogue to anyone?"

"No. Only—" She froze. "Oh, great planets and little gods! That must be it!"

"What must be it?"

"I keep a record, for the ages. It's done for all the kings, so that the personal aspects of their tenures will not be lost. I just write spot events in the book, and next day the page is blank. It's magic, of course. I know that the words have gone to the archives, and will never be read by any ordinary person, so privacy is maintained. I did the same for King Deal."

This was breakthrough news. "Did you record his itinerary for the day he died?"

"Yes, of course. He always told me what he had in mind. I'm a good listener, especially when I'm in love. He was taking a couple hours to relax, and he let me know the night before, after we made love. I duly recorded it—" She broke off, appalled. "I betrayed him to the enemy! I spelled out exactly where he was going, so they could set up to kill him."

"And you have recorded similar details about me," Havoc said. "So they knew where I would be, and also where Gale would be, and what her mission was."

Slowly, Symbol nodded. "I am your traitor. I have to be. I never thought—but suddenly it's obvious. I should have realized." She shook her head. "Well, at least that solves the problem of my future. You will have to find out all I know, then execute me for treason."

"I don't think so," Havoc said.

"Oh, I won't give you any further trouble. And I won't make any more entries in that record. The Invisible Chroma will replace me as their representative, and it will be done. It's the least I can do." Tears were flowing down her face; it was obvious because her veil was sodden. She removed it, leaving her face invisible, and wrung it out so that it dripped invisibly. Then she put it back on.

"No," Havoc said firmly. "You will continue as you are, and keep making your entries. But now you will be working for me instead of the enemy. We will trace the route of the pages as they travel from your book, and get a line on that aspect of the enemy. There will be no indication that you are out of favor with the king."

"I will do whatever you wish. But it won't work long." There was a catch in her voice. She had always been well controlled, but she had lost it. "The enemy will catch on quickly if the information is not accurate. And you won't want me close by anyway, considering my passion for you."

That was something Havoc wasn't yet ready to address. If he eased up at all on his own control, he would sweep her into his arms for explosive sex, with Gale watching. The worst of it was that Gale would understand. "For now there will be no change in anything." He glanced at Gale. "I think you don't want her dead."

"If you die, Havoc," Gale said grimly, "there will be no further issue between Symbol and me. If you don't—maybe you would be better off siring her children, if you can't sire mine." Her own face was wet.

Havoc did not care to address this subject either, at this time. He faced Symbol again. "Tonight write in your book that I questioned you among others, and have no idea how my enemy knows so much about me. And that I will not resign. I will fight this impeachment, and rip out the corruption we have found in the bureaucracy. I mean to name names in public, when I speak in my defense, after I tell my story."

"Sire, if you name names, they will assassinate you where you stand. These things have to be done quietly, so that the corrupt people don't realize they have been discovered. When they know they have nothing to lose, they will try to take you with them."

Exactly. "So you tried to tell me, but I wouldn't listen. I'm a wounded barbarian, and in my naïveté I think that if I only put it all out before the public, I will prevail and save my position."

Her damp veil stretched with the unseen rounding of her eyes. "I am to write all that?"

"Yes. It is true."

"Havoc, you're crazy."

"But do not write that now I know they know my plans."

"I will not," she agreed.

"Have you written of your passion?" Gale asked.

"No, and not my passion for King Deal either, though that was hardly secret. I write only about the king."

"Continue that." Havoc turned away. "I think we are done here."

"Of course, Sire." Symbol walked away, leaving him with Gale. He felt her departure much as he felt her presence; there was a place in his fancy that attuned regardless.

"Do you think this is wise?" Gale asked.

"She is no more threat to you now than she was before."

"I mean to have her write your real plans, as she knows them. I think she's right about assassination. If they are forewarned, they'll be prepared."

"Yes, I rather think they will be. But with your help, I hope to prevail. You know how."

"I know. But she's right: you're crazy."

"I'm barbarian. There's a distinction."

"I hope so." She kissed him. "Now will you spend the night with me, or would you prefer Symbol?"

"What, and spoil her notes? I had better stick with the familiar, dull as it may be."

"Dull as it may be," she agreed with a smile. But of course it was not dull at all. Possibly she had learned something from Symbol's notions as well as from the succubus.

He woke in the night and discovered a paper Ennui had left beside his bed. The report on the mental trace that had killed King Deal came back promptly: it matched no known person. So that lead too had come to little. All that work, with so many people scattered across so many Chroma, for so tiny a benefit! He had really hoped for more. His enemy was very good at covering a trail. But this contest between them was not yet over.

Next morning Havoc announced his intention to remain as king. The word was duly broadcast to all parts of the kingdom. That afternoon the impeachment court was convened. This consisted of twelve anonymous citizens whose decision would be binding. The proceedings were opened to the wider audience of the City Triumph, as had been the case when Havoc gave his first speech as king.

The Crown Assessment document was read aloud. The consternation of the masses was evident; they had believed in Havoc. Then Havoc was given his chance to speak. He was expected to resign, in which case his name would go down in the records as dishonored, but he would not be executed for treason. He had missed his chance for resignation with honor. But if he elected to fight it, as King Deal had, and lost, he would be executed. If he won, he would live for a time, but soon die mysteriously, as King Deal had. It was a fixed procedure; there was no easy way out, at this point.

But Havoc did not intend to play by their rules. He intended to impose his own rules, and thereby overthrow the existing order—or die in the attempt. He would win or lose in barbarian style. Only Gale and Ennui and Throe knew his strategy; the others were ignorant because there had to be no chance that their minds could be read and give it away.

The assemblage saw Havoc stride out onto the stage, garbed in blue traveling clothing. Only his crown showed him to be the king. Gale walked with him, also in traveling clothing; hers was silver. These were unusual costumes; normally only Chroma people wore monochrome. Ennui stood at the door to the private chamber from which they had come, garbed as the royal clerk she was. His other close associates, such as Chief, the Lady Aspect, and Bijou, were in the front row of the privileged audience, with the other notables of the realm. It was apparent that these ladies had been crying; they did not try to conceal it. Behind them the larger areas opened out below: tier upon tier of citizens of the city, gazing upward at the stage. To one side of the stage stood the ten Chroma Representatives, Symbol among them. To the other side was the Impeachment Court. Behind the stage was Throe, with a contingent of armed bodyguards: Havoc was still king, and would be protected until deposed.

"First I will tell you a story," he said boldly.

A member of the court interrupted. "King Havoc, this is not the occasion for frivolity." He was evidently the foreman.

Havoc barely glanced at him. "The content of my address is to be determined by this court?"

There were some small smirks in the audience, but none in the court. "No. But you would do best to make your case expeditiously."

"I will do best to make my case in any manner I choose, you moron." This time there were some larger smirks; the popular audience was obviously partial to the barbarian, despite the bill of particulars, and they loved seeing pompous officials set back. "I choose to begin with a story about a man, a woman, a child, and a Glamor."

There was an intake of breath throughout the huge chamber. Everyone knew that it was bad form to mention the word Glamor, if not actually dangerous. At the same time, attention focused more closely. What was this unpredictable barbarian king up to?

"The title of my tale is 'Glamor'" Havoc said, making sure that no one had mistaken the word. Gale faded back to join the company of the bodyguards.

Havoc took a moment to focus. When he spoke again, it would be as narrator and actor in a play. In his mind this was the only reality, and the stage and audience was anonymous background. It was as if one of Symbol's illusion holographs were forming the scene. He hoped the audience would picture it as he did, despite the lack of magic.

Havoc removed his crown and set it on the floor at the side of the stage, by this token indicating that during this narration he was not to be thought of as the king. In the process, he was demonstrating the very carelessness with the crown the Crown Assessment bill of particulars had claimed. But it was necessary for the tale he would tell. He was merely a man in blue, part of the story he was presenting. He walked across the stage, and back, as if hiking somewhere. Then he stopped in front of the front row audience, before Chief. He began his narration:

～∩～

A powerful, handsome young man strode rapidly toward the village. He was blue, from his skin to his hair, eyes, and clothing.

Havoc signaled Chief, who stood without otherwise moving or speaking. He was to be used as a prop, in a manner familiar to village audiences, and extremely popular, for it allowed ordinary folk to participate in the story. The narrator, Havoc, would speak all parts.

The village elder came forth to meet him. "What is your business here, Blue?"

"I am on a private mission. I wish to trade for supplies and directions, as I am unfamiliar with this region." He produced a small blue gem. "This will facilitate the taming of animals, when you invoke it in the name of the Blue Chroma. It is all I have to offer."

"The path ahead is challenging," the elder said, not taking the gem. "There are dangerous predators, not suitable for taming, and the weather is treacherous, for this is the Void season. We recommend that you wait for a better time."

"I appreciate that," Blue said. "But I must make a rendezvous at noon two days hence, and am unable to wait. Please accept my Blue Chroma stone, and provide me what I need, in your best judgment."

"Perhaps, in that case, we can arrange a service in lieu of the stone, which you will surely need on your journey. We have another traveler who is in need of support and protection."

Blue shrugged. "I am amenable, provided he does not slow me to the point of missing my rendezvous."

Gale quietly walked forward, coming to stand opposite Havoc at the front of the stage. Though her garb was for travel, it fitted very well, and she was remarkably comely.

A young woman appeared. She was silver from her skin to her hair, eyes, and clothing, and she was lovely almost beyond belief. "I am she," she said. "I have a similar appointment, and am concerned about journeying alone. If you will facilitate my progress, I will forage and clean and cook for you on the way."

Blue was taken aback. "With all due respect, Silver, I don't think you should undertake such a trip. I am not at all sure—"

"If you are concerned that I will slow you, I assure you that I will keep the pace. I walk well, and am rested; I have lost a day because these kind villagers were unwilling to let me proceed alone. I must arrive at my destination on time." She slapped her thigh, showing that she was dressed for it too, with well-fitting silver hiking trousers, and competent boots.

"This was not my objection," Blue said, though actually it had been among his concerns. "The need to sleep on the trail two nights, when it may be cold—this could be awkward."

She smiled a smile that seemed to turn the landscape silver. "I will give you my word not to seek to molest you, regardless of the necessary circumstance, if you will give me yours similarly."

"Well, of course I give it," Blue said, embarrassed, for the fact was that though she was of a different Chroma, it was impossible to look at her without fancying her embrace. "Still—"

"Then it is decided," Silver said.

"But you don't know me! I could be a brigand whose word is no good."

She lifted her hand. "Touch my stone." She held a Silver Chroma gem, much like his blue one.

Blue touched it. There was an electric tingle. He knew the stone had verified his integrity. "Then it must be all right," he said.

"Let me touch your stone."

He sifted his blue gem, and she touched it with a silver finger. It did not react, which meant that she was legitimate: it accepted her as tame.

The elder gestured to his house. "Your supplies are awaiting you."

"Thank you, Elder." Blue went to the house, and so did Silver. They packed their knapsacks, and were ready to go. Among other things, each had a shelter half, because a full shelter was cumbersome to carry.

Havoc and Gale turned their backs on the audience, and Chief, dismissed from the story, sat down.

Silver was correct: she had a good long stride, and maintained it well; she did not slow him at all. The weather was cold but good; Void was not flaring at the moment. The path was clear, and they made good progress.

The land on one side was faint red, becoming deep red in the distance. On the other side it was black. They were traveling between Chroma, as was normal. Within their own Chroma they could have used magic, but in foreign Chroma they had no such power, so it was best to stay clear of all magic. That way they would not be subject to much hostile foreign enchantment. This was also the reason that the trail wound deviously between Chroma, for all travelers preferred to avoid such mischief.

"I do not wish to pry," Silver said as they walked. "But I confess to a woman's curiosity. Do you care to tell me of your mission?"

"I have no objection," Blue said, for in truth he liked the prospect of engaging this beautiful woman in dialogue. "But I can't be very helpful, because I don't know it."

She seemed not completely surprised. "How can you be on a mission you don't know?"

"I must report to a particular place at a particular time. There and then it seems I will learn my mission."

She nodded, as if this was familiar. "But how can you be sure the mission is compatible?"

Blue shrugged. "I can't be sure. But I was made an offer I could not refuse."

"Was it by any chance the acquisition of a wonderful body?"

He turned his head to stare at her, amazed. "How did you know?"

To his surprise, she flushed; her fair silver face turned a darker shade of silver. "Because that was the offer that was made to me."

"How could you wish for anything other than what you have now? You are the most beautiful woman I have seen."

"This is the proffered body. In my natural state I am ugly, and I limp. If I achieve success in my mission, I will get to keep this lovely form. If you had seen me before, you would know why I could not refuse."

"I limp too," Blue said. "A childhood injury with a magical component, so that I never fully healed. I can walk, but only with discomfort, and I would not attempt to run fast or far."

"Yes, I am the same. I was ridiculed as a child for my infirmity, and of course no man would marry me. I am a virgin not by choice." She flushed again, less intensely.

"And no woman would marry me," he agreed. He felt his own face turning a darker blue, but he felt obliged to match her candor. "One older woman gave me one experience, because she said it would not be kind to let a succubus get me, but that was all. I did well enough in school, learning to use my mind rather than my body to solve problems. But I face bleak prospects."

"I understand perfectly." She took his hand. "It seems that someone knew how to get volunteers. How dangerous do you suppose this
mission is?"

"I have not allowed myself to think about that overmuch," Blue
said. "I will get to keep this excellent body if I succeed, so I will do my
utmost to prevail."

"Yes." She squeezed his fingers. "Let's get to know each other, as
we travel, now that we know that our only true reality is in our minds."

Blue was glad to agree. The odd thing was that he found her
more interesting, now that he knew she wasn't physically genuine,
than he had before. They talked, comparing notes about the unhappi-
ness of childhood and the delights of the intellect, and he found her
mind as ready as his own. For one of the few times in his life, he was
talking on an equal basis with a member of the opposite gender, and
enjoying it. She was neither slighting nor tolerating him; she related.
That was worth more than he had ever realized was possible.

The court foreman stood. "How long is this irrelevance to be? We
don't have all day."

Gale froze in place, putting her role on temporary hold, and Havoc
gazed out over the popular audience. He made a questioning gesture.

The audience came through. "We have as long as King Havoc
needs," one member called.

"So sit down, moron," another said.

There was general laughter as the foreman sat, disgruntled. The
court had made a mistake, allowing a sometime minstrel to play to a
large audience. Even some of the Chroma representatives were trying
to mask smiles.

Gale returned to animation, and Havoc resumed the narrative.

The path became rougher, traversing terrain that became a series
of ridges like a monstrous washboard. But Silver climbed the steep
sides as readily as he did, delighting in her strong healthy body just as
much as he did in his. "It's so much *fun* to be physically competent,"
she panted as they crested one ridge and began the descent. "I revel
in it." She ran down ahead of him, and he couldn't help noticing the
play of her fine legs and posterior. This might not be her natural body,
but it compelled attention regardless.

On the next descent, he ran ahead of her, avoiding untoward
thoughts. But then as he waited at the foot of the ridge, she came
running down, and her bosom in her silver blouse bounced just as
provocatively.

So he walked beside her, keeping his eyes forward—and a wind
came up, blowing her voluminous yet sleek silver hair across to tickle
his arm. She could intrigue his fancy from any angle.

As the day waned, they found themselves walking toward the
brother-planet of Mystery, its many colors sharply defined as it hung

low in the sky. Suddenly there was a puff of red. "Oh, look!" Silver cried. "A Red Chroma volcano is erupting."

So it was; they could see the blob of color expand. That had to be a massive effort, enlarging the territory of Red. "A lot of magic there," Blue said.

"Magic," she agreed. "Even when we're out of the Chroma, we're governed by it. Look at our colors." She took his hand again, showing her silver against his blue. "We can't escape it."

"We can't escape it," he echoed. "Even if we wanted to."

"We might want to escape it?"

"Well, you and I have not benefited much by it. Certainly I can do routine animal magic in the Blue Chroma, as I'm sure you can do electric magic in the Silver Chroma. But since everyone else is just as good at it, that's not remarkable. And when we leave our Chroma, we have very little magic."

"True." She walked in silence for a while, then spoke again. "Except the Glamors, perhaps."

"The Glamors?"

"You know. The super magicians who can do anything."

"Of course I know that. But what does a Glamor have to do with us?"

The foreman was on his feet again. "You go too far. Do not discuss that matter in public."

Havoc looked at the audience, which was plainly interested in the story.

"Tell us!" someone called. "We want to hear."

The foreman, cautioned by another member of the court, sat down again, though it was clear that none of the members were comfortable with this aspect of the tale. Havoc was addressing a forbidden subject, for all that it was mythical.

"I understand that they carry their magic beyond their Chroma. That they're like walking Chroma crystals, always magically potent. So they can go anywhere without concern."

"Oh. Yes, I suppose so. Too bad we aren't Glamors." He meant it as a joke, but it didn't work well.

"Well, they say that a Glamor can be anyone, or maybe anyone can be a Glamor. It happens entirely randomly. So it's possible that one of us–" She broke off. "But of course that's ludicrous. There's only one Glamor at a time in any one Chroma, and sometimes none."

"They erupt randomly, and glow for an uncertain time," he agreed. "Five to twenty years, I think, is the normal range. Then they fade. But in that time—"

"In that time, what a phenomenal illumination! They can do anything. They're the true rulers of their Chroma; their word is law, really by definition."

"Yet they seldom bother with politics. So they don't seem to make much difference."

"They must have something better to do," she said. "I'd give any-thing to know what they spend their time at."

"What, you'd give even that nice body?"

She was silent, and he regretted his question. "I'm sorry. I didn't mean to be unkind. I'm in the same situation myself, you know."

"It's not that. It just made me think: if you and I could not be healed by magic, how is it we could borrow these nice bodies? I mean, this *is* my body, I can feel it, but it's healed and enhanced. Could a Glamor have done it?"

That set him back. "You're right. Glamor magic might have done it, and I think not much else could have. But why would Glamor Blue bother, or Glamor Silver? We're just ordinary indifferent people, of no special account."

"I don't know. The village elder asked me if I would go on a spe-cial mission, and I demurred, being physically incompetent, and then he said the reward for success would be a perfect body. I thought he meant after I finished the mission, maybe I would have my leg healed, and I said I'd think about it, but when I woke next morning, here it was. A whole body beyond my fondest dreams. What could I do? Give it back? I found myself committed. So I set out for the address he gave me. You know the rest."

"It's pretty much my story too." He glanced across the red side of the landscape. "I hear that there's no Glamor Red now. So I suppose they couldn't get a volunteer from the Red Chroma, and had to go to others."

"But there's a Black Glamor," she said, looking across the black landscape. "Do you suppose we'll meet a black Chroma volunteer?"

"Maybe. I wish I knew what mission could be so important that it has to be done this way."

"I suspect we'll find out."

He laughed, ruefully agreeing. The prospect made him nervous.

Havoc made a signal as of time passing. The various listeners relaxed slightly, now that the discussion of Glamors had abated. Havoc had it seemed made a point: it was possible to speak openly of them without immediately summoning them. He hoped in due course to make more of a point: that they did not exist at all. They were merely folklore, dreamed up by those who longed for some chance to achieve ultimate grace and power without earning it. That would eliminate them as his enemy, and ensure that when he dealt with the political corruption, there would be nothing else to fear.

Evening came. Silver foraged for edible fruits and leaves and made a salad to go with their packed staples, and Blue gathered wood and made a fire by non-magical means. It was a good meal and and good fire, considering their handicaps of lack of Chroma magic, and they complimented each other on each.

"Do you know," Blue said, "I've never camped out with a woman before, let alone one of another Chroma."

"It is a novelty for me too," Silver said. "Now the chill of night is coming, for this is the winter season. Remember, we agreed no—"

"Of course. We'll have to share shelter, but I will lie facing away from you."

"Thank you. It's not that I find you unappealing, but there is no future in our relationship. We are of different Chroma."

"Agreed." Though he would gladly have settled for a temporary relationship, as she put it. He had never before been so fascinated by the color silver.

They unpacked their shelter halves and buttoned them together, then Blue used a rock to pound the pegs into the ground. He found repeller sticks and put a circle of them around the little tent, so that no animal would come upon them in the night. Then he crawled into the shelter, facing outward, clothed. Silver crawled in after him, also clothed, and nestled close under the blanket, her knees against the backs of his knees, her arm looping over his, so that they were as close together as was feasible. In this manner they preserved body heat. That, and the tent, and the lingering warmth of the dying fire, made sleep comfortable despite the intensifying chill. But Blue was highly conscious of her silver hair falling across his neck, and the mounds of her breasts at his back, and her firm thighs against his. He was glad that there was no mind reading, here between Chroma, for his imagination was refusing to be decently restrained.

There was a knowing murmur in the audience. The people saw Havoc lying on the floor, as he narrated the tale, with lovely Gale clasping him spoonwise, her hair disposed exactly as described. Any of the men would have traded places with him.

He woke before she did, and crawled out to rebuild the fire. Silver stretched in her sleep, taking up the extra space, unconsciously appreciating the renewed warmth of the blaze. Even disheveled, she was almost unbearably lovely.

Blue foraged for more firewood, so that the fire pushed back the cold and made the scene pleasant for the dawn. Silver woke, stretched, then climbed out and squatted before the fire, warming her hands. "That nearby stream is too cold for washing," she said. After a moment she brought out a cloth, dampened it in the stream, and removed her blouse. Blue turned politely away, not gazing at her.

Once more the court foreman protested. "This is indecent exposure. We can't tolerate such a mockery of due process."

But the larger audience was avid, for Gale's bare breasts were marvels to behold. "Shut up, moron!" an anonymous voice shouted.

"I will close these proceedings to public view," the foreman said angrily.

Chief stood. "On what authority? This is the king's public address."

The foreman stood defiantly. Then from the audience swelled a chorus: "Moron! Moron! Moron! Moron!" Women were joining in. After a moment he sat again, defeated. The tale resumed.

"You agreed not to molest me," Silver reminded Blue.

"Yes. I am trying to avoid doing so visually."

"I understand, but I think we need not be that restrictive. So you may look, if you wish. I have a good body, for now, and someone might as well see it."

"Are you teasing me?"

"I suppose I am. I never had the chance before. With anyone. So are you going to look?"

Blue didn't argue further. He turned back, and watched her wash. He tried to imagine a more enticing sight, and failed. Even when he closed his eyes, there were after images of perfect silver globes.

Once she completed her top, she donned a new silver blouse, rinsed her cloth, and bared her bottom. He had never seen a woman nude before, even in stages, and was completely fascinated by her silver perfection. If there was a heaven, it was surely populated by creatures like her.

There was a murmur of agreement from the audience. Gale's lower portion was in no way inferior to her upper portion, though neither was silver. Even the members of the court were paying close attention.

She completed her toilet, and squeezed back into her trousers. "Did you enjoy the view?"

"I could watch it forever."

She smiled. "I'm not being coy. It's hard to believe that I could ever intrigue a man, though I know this body ought to. So I need reassurance. You really do like it?"

"I really do." It was of course an understatement, but his vocabulary was not up to an overstatement.

"Good. Now it's your turn to wash."

Oops. "But it's different for a man," he protested.

There was another wave of appreciation from the audience, especially the men. The people well understood why the blue man did not want to expose his state of arousal to the silver woman. There was however a partial chant among the women: "Take it off! Take it off!"

Silver considered. "If I were in my normal body, it wouldn't bother you at all."

"Probably true," Blue agreed ruefully. "Not as much, anyway."

"Very well. I'll wash your top half." She approached him and removed his shirt and used another wet cloth to go over his face, arms, and chest. The touch of her gentle hands was its own kind of magic, especially when she reached around him to do his back. "They did give you a nice body," she said, running the cloth over a muscle in a caressing manner.

This time it was the women who reacted more, appreciating the tacit embrace. But the men were by no means lacking interest as Gale stroked Havoc suggestively.

"I hope I get to keep it."

"I do understand."

She finished, and he donned a clean blue shirt. She took the old ones and washed them in the stream. They hung them from their packs; they would dry during the day.

They hiked, again making good time, for it was a well cleared path. Then, of course, something happened. The sky brightened, and light bathed the ground. "Void is flaring," Blue said.

At first the warmth the flare brought was pleasant, but it soon got to be too much. Normally Void was a dim glow or even a darkness in the sky, sucking in the light of Vivid and leaving little for Charm. But this time Void became a full second sun, and its hot light blasted at the terrain. They had to seek cover under a widely spreading darkness tree. Normally the canopy of light-hungry leaves was so thick that almost no light reached the ground, making a patch of gloom where nothing else grew, but this time the blaze of two suns pushed a wan glow through. The tree also absorbed the heat of the rays, making it normally quite cold below, but in this case the temperature was pleasantly warm.

"How long do you think it will last?" Silver asked as they leaned against the cool trunk.

"It's a big flare. At least an hour. Then there may be weather, because of the stirring of the air."

"Then let's divert ourselves. I hate being bored."

"You know there's only one diversion a man seeks, and that's barred."

She considered briefly. "Maybe. Let's play a game of chance."

"What game to you have in mind?"

She brought out her silver gem. "Wagers. Your stone against mine."

"I don't want to lose my stone, or take yours. We might need their magic."

"Then let's give the loser a choice: the stone or the body."

Blue was suddenly interested, but cautious. "Your body? As in desire and touching?"

She nodded. "If I lose and want to save my stone."

"What if I lose?"

She laughed. "Oh, I won't really take your stone, Blue. It's just that wagers is no fun without significant forfeits."

She was right. "Very well. Wagers. Stones or bodies. How will we do it?"

"We'll each put our stone in one fist, then match fists. Even, I win. Odd, you win." This was traditional for the genders, a woman being said to have two projections, a man one. Thus she was even, he odd.

They cupped their hands together around their stones, then separated them. Blue put out his right fist, and Silver matched it with her left. They opened their hands, and each had a gem. "Even. You win," Blue said.

"But you were supposed to win."

He shook his head. "If I did, I wouldn't want to take anything you wouldn't want to give." He held out his stone for her.

"Blue, I told you I wouldn't take your stone!"

"But that's all I have."

"I'm taking your body, for this hour. Undress it."

He stared at her. "But I thought—"

"You thought you were the only one who desired intimate action. Blue, I have this body now, and after tomorrow I may not have it any more. I want to use it just once. So I changed my mind. I thought I could be demure and yield it as a forfeit, but that didn't work. So I am exposed in my unmaidenly desire for experience. I am blushing." And she was, in her monochromatic fashion. "Now come on: oblige my victory."

Still he hesitated, though torn by desire. "But you know we have no future together, regardless of the success of the mission. Different Chroma—"

"All the more reason to do it while we can. If I get to keep this body, I'll still never again get to be with a handsome blue Chroma man."

"If you're sure."

"Stop stalling!"

He was guilty of that, finding it as hard as she did to truly believe he could be desirable to the other gender. Satisfied at last that she meant it, Blue hesitated no longer. He got out of his clothes and welcomed her embrace. She was amazingly ardent, and he—he was soon in love. "Oh Silver," he said after the first round. "I wish this didn't have to end."

The foreman looked as if he wanted to put a stop to this, but the "Moron" chant began, and he refrained. The two figures on the stage clasped in obvious sexual embrace, and everyone watched. Whatever the outcome of this trial, it would never be forgotten. The barbarian was making the court pay for its procedure. If the support of the common people of Triumph had been in doubt before, it was not now; they loved this tale-telling minstrel king.

She kissed him. "I wish it too. Blue, you're a nice guy. I think that even with your natural body, you would be worthwhile. But of course I wouldn't be."

"Oh, I don't know." But there was too much truth for a strong denial. He liked her mind and spirit, but it was her body that mesmerized him. Her magical body. Surely it was his magical body that had similarly tempted her.

They lay together as the star flare ebbed. "I think we expended it," Silver said, gazing out. "Too much passion."

"That must be it. Silver, I will always remember this—this gift of yours."

"It's not a gift. I claimed you as my prize."

He was satisfied to accept that. Soon the flare had subsided to the point where they could resume travel. They dressed and left the shelter of the darkness tree, finding it still hot outside, but bearable.

"There may soon be a storm, because of the heat disturbance," Blue said. "We must keep alert for other shelter."

"The village elder did warn us about the weather."

The path came onto a swampy plain, one side of which was black, and the other side green. The fringe of the red Chroma had been left behind.

The path followed a meandering river whose banks were black and green. The water was pale red, showing its origin. There would be some magic there, but since it matched neither of their Chromas, that didn't matter for them.

"I'm not easy with this," Blue said. "There's too much cover for predators."

"I'm really not a fighter, but I can use my knife," Silver said, drawing a sleek silver blade.

"I hope you don't have to. I'll cut a staff." He found a sapling and used his own blue knife to cut it to a suitable length.

"If something threatens, and we can't avoid it, we can stand back to back and try to fend it off," Silver suggested.

"Yes. We had better have our stones ready, too."

The weather remained sultry but fair. They were nearing the far side of the plain, where a nonChroma hillside beckoned, when there was a sound. They drew together, facing opposite ways so as to watch all around, but it seemed to be a false alarm. They resumed walking—and a green tiger pounced.

Blue saw it first, as its two front legs left the ground and its two middle legs followed. The two hind legs were still springing, launching the heavy feline toward the travelers. Its great mouth was opening, showing the enormous green saber-tusk teeth.

There was no time for escape or defense. Blue invoked his gemstone. It flashed bright blue in the tiger's face, and the creature bounced to the side, somehow aborting its pounce in midair. It caught its balance, facing them, and purred.

Silver's gem was now in her hand. "I can stun it with an electric shock, but then we'll have to run, because my little stone can't handle such a big animal for long."

"No need," Blue said. "I have tamed it with my stone."

"Tamed it?"

"That is the blue Chroma specialty," he reminded her. "It is incidental magic, for us. The tiger is now our friend, while the magic of this stone lasts."

"I didn't realize that blue magic would work on a green creature."

"Oh, yes. It is the color of the magic that counts, not the color of the object of it. But the effect is temporary. We had better walk with the tiger to the far side of this swamp."

Silver nervously eyed the creature. "Walk *with* the tiger? I prefer to get well away from it. I'm glad you didn't hurt it—I do like animals—but I'm afraid it will hurt us."

"I like animals too, of course. But you are right: if the tiger goes beyond the range of my stone, it will revert, and try to attack us again. So we must keep it close until we can find defensive cover. We had better do so quickly, because I don't know how much time we have before the stone fades."

"Let's move," she agreed with alacrity.

They walked beside the docile tiger, and Silver even got up nerve to stroke its shaggy green fur. It had stripes of light green and dark green all across its powerful body and down its legs.

They had time. They reached the slope, dived behind a boulder, and faced back, guarding against pursuit. The tiger shook its head as if clearing it of an obstruction, and crouched menacingly. Blue lifted his stone, and the creature changed its mind; one encounter with that magic was sufficient. It backed away, then disappeared into the brush.

They relaxed, breathing hard. "I'm sorry you had to use your stone," Silver said. "I'm surprised there was anything left, after it tamed the tiger."

"There wasn't," Blue said. "I was bluffing." He showed her the stone, which was now almost colorless. Its blue magic had been expended. It would regain some power, in time, but not much.

"We still have my stone," she said. "And not too far to go, I think." But she didn't sound cheerful. It was hard for a Chroma person to be without everyday magic, and Blue was now bereft of his.

They moved up the slope, and in due course found a place to camp for the night: a small cave, defensible by a fire in front. They set about their evening chores, had supper, and pitched their tent in the cave.

"Tonight I'll face away," Silver said.

"As you wish," Blue agreed, gratified; it would be nice, clasping her for the night, even with clothes on. The warmth would be similar, but that was only part of it.

"It's not as cold tonight. Can we manage without clothes? I'm really not used to sleeping in them."

He looked at her. "You know I—"

"Your diffidence is so quaint. Of course I know. The rules have changed, Blue. This may be our last night together."

"In that case, I think we can manage," he agreed.

They managed more than adequately. Blue had thought there could never be another experience to match that of the day, but he was mistaken.

The audience agreed.

In the morning, as they got under way, Silver kissed him once more. "We don't know what will happen today, so I'm telling you now: I wish I didn't have to leave you. I never thought a man of a different Chroma would interest me, but this time with you has been special, and not just because of the bodies. If I get to keep this body, I could readily find a silver Chroma man, but I think I'd rather have you. You understand my inner nature."

"I agree. We have much in common, and we get along well. I think I would have loved you regardless of the bodies, but they do make it better. Do you think, if we succeed in the mission, that there is after all any way we could be together?"

She considered. "Maybe we could find a region where the Blue and Silver Chroma overlap. Our children could choose either Chroma."

"I like that notion. Silver, I love you."

She gazed at him, her lovely eyes bright. "And I love you, Blue. Then shall we agree to marry, if we can?"

"Yes, if we can."

The audience applauded.

They kissed again. Then, conditionally betrothed, they set out on the last leg of their journey.

It was not long before a storm came up. They were crossing rolling country, largely nonChroma, when a dark wall of clouds piled over the horizon. "I think the storm from the turbulence of the flare is finally arriving," Blue said nervously.

"We'd better seek cover."

They were lucky: they had passed a cave not far back. They ran for it—and were joined by several animals, including a small green bear and a black buzzard. This was a time of crisis, and there was a temporary truce between creatures. So it had always been.

They jammed into the cave, which was already well filled. The buzzard settled on Blue's knapsack, and the bear lay before the two people, at the mouth of the cave, its bulk shielding them. Smaller wild creatures filled in all around. Blue held his blue gem, ready to invoke what little remained of its taming magic if he had to, but it didn't seem necessary, fortunately.

The storm struck. Sleet and sand sluiced across the landscape, and the wind roared, but the refugees held firm. Silver reached out to grab a little bird that was in danger of being blown away, and held it carefully by her shoulder, sheltered from the savagery of the tempest.

A serpent anchored itself with a coil around Blue's foot. All of them huddled, trying to ride out the violence of the weather of the Void season.

There was nothing to do but wait. Blue slept, woke to the continuing roar and blast of debris, slept again, and then suddenly woke to something startling: silence. The storm had passed as abruptly as it came.

He opened his eyes, and found them caked with dirt and mucous. Then Silver was there with a damp pad, carefully wiping his eyes clear.

The animals stirred. The bear was half buried in wet sand, but its sacrifice had protected those behind. Blue used his hands to push much of the sand off, then took Silver's pad to wipe its eyes clear. The bear heaved itself up on six legs and launched forward, opening the cave for the exit of those behind.

Stage by stage, the cave evacuated. The serpent left Blue's foot, and the buzzard left his pack. Silver let her bird fly; one of its wings was evidently injured, but it was able to be airborne on two. A cloud of insects puffed out; they had stung no one, honoring the truce. The two people kneeled beside the cave, helping those animals that needed it, until all were gone.

"This, too, is experience," Blue said. "I would not have chosen it, but I will remember it."

"Jammed in together with a bear and a buzzard," Silver agreed. She reached across to help a spider out of his hair. "There was a time when I would not have appreciated it."

"I never had to use my stone. Even fully charged, it might not have been enough, without the truce."

"Creatures know that a blue man understands them. I think your presence protected me."

"Maybe. Or maybe they saw your stone, and decided not to antagonize you."

She laughed. "I'm not that fearsome!"

A six legged mouse was limping. Blue picked it up and examined it. "Not serious," he said, and set it by a crevice so that it could hide while it healed.

They moved on. Desolation was everywhere. Trees had been blown over and partly buried, and new ponds had formed in the hollows. The path had been almost obliterated, but they had a general idea where to go by the larger lay of the land. They had been delayed, but it was an hour shy of noon; they could still make it if they hurried.

Silver paused, listening. "A child!"

Now Blue heard it: crying.

They detoured, orienting on the sound. They found a gnarled old stonewood tree, and wedged in a hollow in its indestructible trunk was a red child.

Havoc and Gale had gone to the back of the stage, to the door where Ennui stood. From behind Ennui came a young child dressed in red. The play now had a third cast member. The child limped.

Silver lifted her out and held her. She was perhaps six years old, and her left leg was injured; it seemed to have been crushed. The girl couldn't stand on it.

"Your stone," Blue said. "Can its electricity help?"

"It can alleviate her pain, but this is beyond its power to mend. I know, for her injury is similar to mine."

"Do that, then. I'll look for her folks."

Silver nodded grimly. It was easy enough to recreate what had happened: the storm had caught them in the open, and the parents had put their child in the safest place available, and taken their chances elsewhere. They had surely sacrificed themselves for her. The chances of their survival were slim.

Indeed, Blue soon found the bodies of a red Chroma man and woman, battered almost beyond recognition and half buried in debris, still somehow holding hands. They had loved and protected each other until the end. He struggled for a moment to bring his sudden horror and sadness under control; there was no point in making things worse.

He put on a neutral face and returned to report to Silver. The red child had quieted down, her physical pain alleviated by the silver stone she held to her leg, but when she saw Blue, she knew. She screamed and buried her face in Silver's shoulder.

"I will bury them," Blue said. He returned to the bodies, checked them for any possessions that might help the girl, found nothing, and scooped more mud and debris over them. He carried stones to make a cairn to mark their place, and braced a forked stick at the top to point to the sky. One side of the fork was to signal Vivid, the other to signal Void, in the normal convention: let their souls find a home at one star or the other. The stick barely cast a shadow.

Silver and Red joined him, and they made a brief and choked ceremony of passing. "Parting, Red Man and Red Woman," Blue said. "May your spirits find solace. We will take your daughter to her kinfolk."

"Yes," Silver agreed, and the child nodded, understanding that she would not die here.

The stick's remaining shadow disappeared. The disk of Vivid was directly overhead, marking noon.

Blue's body shrank, and his left leg hurt. He knew immediately what had happened: he had reverted to normal.

He looked at Silver. She too had shrunk, her gorgeous hair turning ropy, her body becoming skinny under clothing than no longer fit. Her left leg was twisted, and she winced as she put weight on it. She was far from pretty, yet she remained recognizable.

Havoc and Gale hunched their bodies, emulating weakness and ugliness.

Red stared at them. "What happened to you?"

How could they explain? "We had something to do," Silver said. "We didn't get there in time."

"These are our real bodies," Blue said. "We are the same people as before, just not as good. We'll still help you reach your red Chroma kin."

"Oh." Red looked confused.

Blue exchanged a glance with Silver. They had used their last hour to help the child, and so had missed their rendezvous, thus forfeiting their mission. What a price they had paid! Yet what else could they have done?

Blue touched Silver's thin hand. "I love you."

She stared at him a moment, knowing that she retained no physical inducements. "You still want to—to be betrothed?"

"Yes. I know I'm no prize, but—"

She cut him off with a kiss. That was answer enough.

Blue found sticks and vines and fashioned a travois to support the child, who could not walk. Then he and Silver hauled it across the ground toward the ridge where the remnant of the path would be. It was the best they could do; with their bad legs they could not carry her. As it was, progress was slow and painful.

"We can take her back to the Red Chroma we passed," Silver said.

"No," Red said. "No one is there. We were going to another Red."

"Then we can go to the next village, and seek help," Blue said. "One way or another, we will get you there."

But Red hardly seemed comforted. She was writhing on the travois, and whimpering. Evidently the pain of her injury was returning. Yet, oddly, she did not keep the stone always at her leg; sometimes she pressed it to her head.

Silver noted his questioning look. "To abate her pain of grief," she murmured. "But the stone can't last much longer."

They tried to hurry, but it was all they could do to keep moving even slowly, and they had to stop frequently to rest. They shared their food supplies with Red, but she seemed worse, looking wildly about and shaking. "We need help," Silver murmured.

"I could go ahead and hope to bring someone back. But I don't want to leave you alone here."

She nodded, appreciating why. The truce of creatures was over; they would be highly vulnerable to predators. So they just kept hauling, not seeing any better way. At least the path was becoming clear, so they knew they would not get lost.

"Look," Silver said. "The rendezvous site."

So it was. They had been told to report at noon to a stone marker that looked like a crown. There it was. But whoever they were to meet there was gone. There was only their trail, and an intersecting one leading directly into the Black Chroma zone.

"Oh!" Red cried. She was definitely worse, and there was even a dim red glow at her skin. The silver stone was now colorless.

Silver put her arm around the girl, trying to comfort her, but it was not possible. Red gazed wildly around, breathing rapidly, and the glow intensified.

"She's not just ill," Silver said, appalled. "She's magically ill."

Something impossible had been nagging Blue. This strange ailment—could it possibly be? "Red," he said. "Maybe this isn't what we think. Stop fighting it. Let it take you."

"Take me?"

"Relax. Accept it. Flow with it. This may help."

Silver was alarmed. "Blue, are you sure?"

"I'm not at all sure. But it's obviously too strong for her anyway. If there is a chance—"

The child relaxed. Immediately her squint of pain alleviated. Her body straightened.

Then the red glow became an explosion of light that reflected off the surroundings. Rather, it imbued them, making stone, trees, and ground red. What did this mean?

Red was shining like a beacon, her hair standing out from her head. But she was no longer crying. "It doesn't hurt any more," she said, surprised.

"It is," Blue said. "It really is."

Silver's eyes went round as she caught his import, but her voice was almost controlled. "Red—can you heal your leg?"

The child looked at her crushed leg. "Of course." The red light coalesced around it, and suddenly it was whole. The girl got off the travois and stood without difficulty. "Okay?"

"Red," Silver whispered, awed. "You have erupted into Glamor."

Blue knew that she was right. The child had assumed the aspect of Glamor Red.

"Gee—what do I do now?" Red asked.

She was a Glamor—but still also a child. "We don't know," Silver said. This was beyond anything they had imagined.

"I'll go seek Glamor Black," Blue said. "I should be able to signal him not far into the Black Chroma. He'll know what to do."

"Yes," Silver said. "Hurry."

Blue ran limpingly down the path into the black Chroma. His leg hurt, but he overrode the pain. He had to get the right kind of help, for no one but a Glamor understood Glamor business.

A black woman appeared before him. "Ho, intruder," she said. "What is your business here?"

"We have," Blue gasped, then tried again. "We have a Glamor Red child. I must speak to Glamor Black."

The woman looked startled. Then she vanished.

Havoc went to stand before the Chroma Representatives, opposite the one in black. It was a minstrel's privilege to borrow freely from the audience, generating participants by his mere manner. The Representative did not move.

In a moment another black figure appeared. This one glowed, and had a phenomenal demeanor. Blue felt the aura of powerful Black magic. He knew immediately that he was in the presence of a Glamor. "Glamor, please," he said. "I beg your indulgence. We have a—"

"Yes." Then Blue floated up, supported by controlled enchantment, and moved rapidly back the way he had come, paced by the black figure.

Actually Gale and the child came to join Havoc, before the Black Chroma Representative, who was being used as an involuntary prop.

In a moment they arrived at the red-stained crown marker. Blue found himself standing beside Silver, facing the red child.

Glamour Black looked at Glamor Red. "You are in need of parents," he said. "Take this blue man and this silver woman; they are worthy."

"I know," Glamor Red agreed. "But they are ugly and lame."

"Restore them."

The child's eyes brightened. "I can do that?" Then she answered her own question. "Yes, of course I can." She looked at Blue and Silver, and suddenly they were the strong and handsome couple they had been for two days.

"But—" Blue protested, trying to grasp the significance.

"We are inadequate," Silver said. "We know nothing of—"

Glamor Black dismissed that with a glance. He knew the state of their adequacy better than they did.

"I will be your fourth," Red said gladly. Then, to Glamor Black: "Can you marry them now, and adopt me to them?"

Black faced them again. "Do the two of you, Blue man and Silver woman, agree to be married, with Glamor Red as your fourth child?"

There was no option of demurral; the overwhelming presence of the two Glamors made that clear. "Yes," they said together.

Red ran to hug them both. "Thank you," she said. "I will make you glad." That was surely a considerable understatement.

"You have already done that, dear," Silver said.

"Take them to your Chroma," Glamor Black said, and vanished with a salute.

"Yes," Glamor Red said, returning the salute to the space Glamor Black had stood. The three of them lifted into the air and moved across the landscape. It was the enormous power of her new magic, that operated not merely in the Red Chroma, but anywhere on the planet. Exactly as Glamor Black's did.

Blue realized that this suddenly and amazingly, he and Silver had found the way to be together, despite failing their mission. They would live in the Red Chroma, because Glamor Red wished it to be, and no one would question it. Whatever the child needed would be provided, because of what she was. Actually she didn't need them at all, with the incalculable power she had come into.

"Yes I do need you," Red said, reading his thought. "You loved me before I erupted. You sacrificed your welfare for me. You shared my injury. Only you can be real parents to me, now that mine are gone."

Silver seemed about to faint. "How could this happen, when we didn't even get to our mission?"

"This *is* your mission," Red said.

Blue and Silver stared at each other as the elements of it fell into place. Not the location, but the child—they had been with her as noon came and her symptoms began. They had carried her through the difficult transition so that she could emerge as a Glamor. It was indeed their mission. But by what wild coincidence had they been selected for it?

"I think it was your understanding and your good hearts," Red said. "I think not just anyone can be the parents of a young Glamor. I have power now, but you will have to guide me. I think I will need to grow up to use it wisely."

"We'll do our best," Blue said. Then he kissed Silver. It was evident that their reward was far greater than mere bodies. They had a remarkable mission ahead.

৯৯

"Now I have thoroughly invoked the Glamors," Havoc said as Gale and the girl moved back to give him the center of the stage. "I have spoken of them in full public. May they now strike me down—if they exist." He paused, raising his arms, inviting a strike from the sky.

There was a sudden hush. The tale had held the attention of the audience, especially the people of the city. But this sudden defiance of the Glamors was something else.

The Black Chroma representative spoke, plainly alarmed. "Sire, do not do this. You have no quarrel with the Glamors."

Havoc whirled to face the man. "Yes I do. Someone has been trying to kill me, and now to depose me, and I think it's the Glamors, if there are any such things. If so, I want it out in the open. I will be thrall to no anonymous power." He turned toward the larger audience again. "Witness, that I am challenging the Glamors to strike me openly, or forever let me be. For unless I am destroyed now, I mean to be king in substance as well as image."

He waited, but no strike came. "Then I declare the Glamors to be non-participatory, and will proceed to eliminate the lesser threats to my reign. By the power of the Emergency Protocols of the Crown, I

hereby dissolve the mechanism of the Crown Assessment, and dismiss this court that has presented these ludicrous charges against
me. All powers hitherto ascribed to them I hereby absorb into the
office and person of the king. Henceforth the king shall answer to no
anonymous entity, but only to the will of the people and the Chroma."

"That will has already been expressed," the foreman of the court
said. "Both have decided against you."

Havoc's dragon seed buzzed, as it had the first time this announce-
ment was made. "So you claim," he said. "But I say this is false. They
voted *for* me, and you faked the tally."

The foreman's mouth opened, but for a moment he could not
speak. He was plainly outraged by the accusation.

"I will prove it." Havoc spread his arms toward the huge audience. "What say the people?"

There was a massive roar of applause and support. There was
no question: the barbarian had won the loyalty of the ordinary citizens.

He faced the Chroma Representatives. "What say the Chroma?"

There was consternation among the Representatives. Then Symbol spoke. "Sire, we cannot answer without consulting our home
Chroma."

"Yes you can. Take an individual tally now: how did each Chroma
vote? We will compare that to the tally the court claims."

The foreman of the court jumped to his feet. "You can't do this!
You're a mere figurehead. *We* hold the power."

Beautiful: he had succeeded in rattling the man, who was now
speaking from anger. "Not any more, moron," Havoc said. "I have
taken it back."

"You can't do that. There is no basis."

"Study your Protocols," Havoc said. He glanced at Ennui, who
walked across the stage and presented the man with a scroll. "Your
faked tallies will be exposed. The people support me, and so do a
majority of the Chroma. I am assuming emergency crisis power, in
accordance with the Protocols; even if you manage to depose me later,
you can't stop me right now."

The foreman opened his mouth to protest further, but another
member of the court cautioned him again. Havoc was indeed within
his rights. He had outmaneuvered them on their own turf, thanks to
the hint given by King Cheer.

"Now to the next item of business," Havoc continued, giving them
no chance to recover. "The rooting out of corruption. There are many
good officers in the king's service, but some bad ones. I shall now call
out the names of the bad ones, who shall be immediately arrested and
held in detention pending confirmation of their crimes, and execution
for treason." He paused, but this time there was no protest; the members of the court and the Chroma Representatives were staring at him,

stunned by his audacity and the headlong rush of surprising events. They weren't accustomed to barbarian warfare. This also spoke well for the Lady Aspect, who had managed to get the data without alerting anyone.

"Purser Downbeat," Havoc announced. "Embezzlement of royal gems."

Throe signaled, and two men detached from his formation and went rapidly to take hold of one of the prominent members of the front audience. The man's mouth was hanging open; this had caught him by complete surprise.

"Officer Cornrow. Rape of civilian women under false arrest." Two more guards went after another man in the front audience.

Havoc continued calling out names, and the arrests were publicly made. The larger audience, at first amazed, began to greet the names with applause; they knew of much of the corruption, having suffered by it, and were gratified to see it so suddenly ending. Even a few of the Chroma Representatives were nodding appreciatively; they too had known of the bad men. Symbol was openly smirking under her veil; she was holding it tight against her face so that it outlined her mouth.

Suddenly an arrow flew from above the audience. It struck the figure of Havoc in the face, and exploded. Gale and the child in red screamed and clutched each other. The king's head became a fireball. Then the body fell, headless.

The crown that should have protected the king was still sitting at the side of the stage, supposedly forgotten.

The audience stared for a moment, aghast. Then it erupted into chaos. "Murder! Murder!"

"Trace that shot!" Throe cried, righteously furious. "Bring me that king killer!" His men, well trained, leaped to obey. The assassin would very soon be in custody, or dead, if the audience got to him first.

Havoc smiled. The dragon seed had not buzzed again, knowing that he was in no immediate danger. He was standing behind a screen, in the room behind Ennui, able to see without being seen. They didn't know that it was his golem that had been destroyed. Havoc had been operating it from the chamber Ennui guarded. Gale was real, but the king wasn't. She had treated the golem throughout exactly as she would have treated Havoc, even to the extent of enduring sex with it. No one had suspected. Only Gale, Ennui, and Throe had known. Havoc had done his best to trigger an assassination attempt, and had succeeded. The one person the Lady Aspect had not been able to identify had not realized that he remained anonymous, and had acted before his name was called out. He had given himself away, and would soon be caught unless his hired assassin managed to die before being questioned. Even then, there were ways to trace the connection; he would not escape. The worst danger had been handled. Once that threat had been eliminated, Havoc would reveal his ruse, and be king.

The court foreman was on his feet. "The king has been assassinated! Power devolves on us, in this emergency!"

Havoc smiled. The man had a disappointment coming.

But before anyone else could move, a black male figure materialized in the center of the stage. It glowed with a phenomenal presence. "This annoys us," he said.

For a moment, the anarchy abated. Court members, Chroma Representatives, and audience froze in place. All heads turned to stare at the surreal figure. So did Havoc. How could this be? *The Glamors didn't exist.*

Then the Black Chroma representative cried out desperately: "Glamor! Spare them! They know not what they—"

The Glamor merely gestured. All the men who had been arrested imploded, leaving only drifting flakes of black ashes. Several more in the audience, not yet identified but on the list, disintegrated similarly. Two members of the court also collapsed. Those surprised Havoc; their corruption must have been beyond Aspect's power to penetrate. The foreman, however, remained; he might be misguided, but not corrupt.

Glamor Black stood for a moment more. The Black Chroma Representative spoke again. "Glamor, how many Chroma support the king?" It was a curious question, in the circumstance, since the king was supposed to be dead. Unless the Black Chroma Representative somehow knew the truth.

The Glamor made a dismissive gesture. "All of them."

"But King Havoc is dead!" another Representative cried.

Chroma Black frowned. "Red will come." Then he faded out.

But in his place another figure appeared. This one was red, and female. She too glowed with the aura of her power. "Thank you, Black," she said, her voice dulcet yet possessed of vital authority. Then she looked at the chamber Ennui guarded. There was a flash of red, for a moment blinding Havoc. He felt dizzy.

Suddenly Havoc was no longer in the chamber or behind the screen. He was lying on the floor at Chroma Red's feet, where the dead golem had been. She had seen through the ruse, and brought him to her. The crown was back on his head.

"Rise, King Havoc," she said. "Rule, with our blessing."

Havoc got to his feet. People all around him stared; to them it seemed that the Glamor had just brought him back to life. That would have been an impossible feat, even for a Glamor, had it been his real head lost. She evidently knew how to use what was available.

She looked up at him. She was red throughout, and stunningly beautiful. "You intrigue us." Her personal magnetism enfolded him. It was not possible to resist. The crown provided no protection against her evocative power. She was not only real, but overwhelming. In a moment he would be her complete love slave.

"Glamor!" he cried. "Don't take me! I have business to accomplish. Don't take me!"

She nodded. "Not yet," she said, with mixed humor and regret. "And we must not help you find your enemy." She faded away.

Havoc stood unsteadily, staring at the place she had been. His doubt about the existence and power of the Glamors had been banished. Yet he was amazed. They had ignored his arrogant summons, then appeared in their own time and manner—and publicly supported him. This was not only dramatic, but generous. What kind of entities *were* they?

Then others were around him, his women, escorting him away from the chaos of the stage and audience, while his men set about reestablishing order. They took him unresisting back to the king's apartment.

The Lady Aspect carefully wiped his face with a silken handkerchief. "You are fortunate," she murmured. "Glamor Red was about to take you."

"I know. I would have gone gladly."

"You did it, Havoc," Gale said. "You took power and destroyed the enemies."

"The enemy," he said thoughtfully. "I thought the Glamors were the enemy, if they existed."

"Now we know," Symbol said. "They do exist—and they are not your enemy. They proved that."

"Yet Glamor Red told me that they must not help me find my enemy," he said. "Which means that this day's cleanup has not yet done the job."

"*Must* not help you?" Ennui asked.

"They must know something we don't," he said. "This must be more complicated than we know."

"Your story must have summoned them," Bijou said. "You spoke of the Black Glamor, and the Red Glamor, so they came."

"I thought it was random," he said. "I didn't know their ages or genders, or if they ever participated in mere human events. I thought I was making them up."

"Maybe they put themselves into your mind," Ennui said. "It looked as though you liked Glamor Red, who might be the age of the child you described, if your story happened a few years ago."

"She—you know the personal attraction the changelings have?" He shook his head. "She has so much more of it that I love her already. But I have to finish the job I started."

"I think you did intrigue them," Symbol said. "So they played your game, to a degree. And they were annoyed that others were trying to interfere with you, so they interceded."

"Of course your story was nonsense," Ennui said. "It presumes precognition, which is a form of magic that surely doesn't exist. But if they had it, why would they have let the Red Chroma parents die, orphaning the child? They would have saved the parents, instead of going to all that trouble to put together a new family."

"Nonsense," Havoc agreed. "But it served its purpose: to evoke the Glamors, or prove that they didn't exist. I thought it would be the latter, but I wasn't sure."

"And now we are back to square one," Symbol said. "We still don't know who killed King Deal and tried to kill you, and we have no suspects. We have to start all over."

"And I still don't know whether I can marry Gale," Havoc agreed ruefully. "And I can't resign as king until we solve these mysteries."

"You should have asked the Glamors," Gale said.

"I should have," he agreed. "I didn't think of it."

"Poor thing," Bijou said. "Let me comfort you." She embraced his head, drawing it into her soft bosom.

"Hey, don't leave us out," Symbol said. In a moment Havoc was buried in bosoms. It was fun—but he knew that the challenges remaining were unlikely to be any fun at all. He had hardly gotten into this business of being king, but he had already discovered how hard it was to get out of it intact.

What did his future, and that of the kingdom, hold? He anticipated it with mixed fascination and dread. The havoc he had generated at the court hearing was but a reflection of what was in his mind and heart at the moment.

Author's Note

In 1997 I had been seeing Xanth novels published for twenty years. I like Xanth; it put me on the map as a bestselling writer. But I never wanted to be limited to it. Xanth was humorous because at first I just couldn't take fantasy seriously, but with more experience that changed. It was time to move on.

So I conceived the ChroMagic series. That's Chroma as in color: magic color. At first I thought there would be a number of different moons casting their colored light and bringing their flavors of magic, but my researcher of the time informed me that that had already been done in a game related series. Oh. So I pondered a while, and thought of volcanoes: had that been done before? No. Okay, so volcanoes it was. And the fact is, that worked out so well that I'm glad of it; I love the colored world. I was an aspiring artist before I was an aspiring writer; that's long behind me, but I retain a visual mode when writing. I actually see the scenes I am creating; I am in them. I love it when readers tell me they see them and are in them too; we have truly connected. So in this series I painted my words in magic colors.

I have a number of analogies for writing. It is like building a highway: first you have to survey the terrain to see not only where you want it to go, but what the lay of the land is, so you can guide around a mountain, avoid a lake, and keep it fairly level. Then you have to obtain the rights to the land you need, which may mean buying and destroying some houses or cutting through someone's ranch. It gets complicated before you ever bring in your construction equipment. Then you have to bulldoze, fill, level, pound, and get it in shape on a deadline despite the inclement weather, a threatened strike by workers, and a lawsuit by someone who claims mineral rights to your key section. Only then can you start work on the surfacing. It's a big job. When you do build it, critics who never made a highway will carp endlessly about the details of it. Thus a regular novel.

But a major series is worse. For that I think of a pyramid. An enormous area has to be cleared and leveled. Then huge stones must be hauled in and laid in regular courses. The foundation has to be right. Spectators will remark on how they could build a higher structure faster by laying blocks on top of each other, rather than beside each other. But the entire base must be worked out before the second course is started. It's a slow business, but necessary to make sure everything is consistent. Years may pass before the grandeur of the whole slowly becomes apparent. This is true regardless of the genre or type. Big projects require big vision and a lot of patient work.

Here, in capsule, is the genesis of this big novel and series, subject to whatever analogy seems comfortable. On March 1, 1997, while wrapping up the Xanth novel *Zombie Lover*, I started a new file titled "Colors." "Realizing that GEODYSSEY [my historical series] may be finished after this year, to my deep regret," I wrote, "and that Xanth is being run into oblivion by [the publisher], [my wife] suggested that I try a different fantasy series, quarter million word novels of the scope of those by Goodkind, Brooks, and Drake. Heroic fantasy is the one type I haven't done. Such a series would not require heavy research, so I could complete a novel within six months, and I could do as good a job at it as anyone. This might enable me to rebuild my career, if I had the right publisher." I continued surveying and laying blocks, and by the end of the month had 12,500 words of notes, and no text. I had the series title, ChroMagic, but not the novel title. I considered *Crown of Thorns*, because Havoc did not want to be king, but when I checked BOOKS IN PRINT I discovered there was already a book by that title. I wrestled with it, and decided on April 16 to try *King Havoc*, as relevant and suggestive.

With that, the last preliminary detail was in place, after a month and a half and 21,000 words notes. That day I started with my first 1,000 words of text. "One thousand years ago a ship of space orbited a luxurious world girt by many colors, and landed a colony of its own kind. One thousand individuals, male and female, together with initial supplies, tools, and cells of many supplementary species. The ship departed, and the colony fended for itself." Well, as you may have noticed, that didactic prologue did not survive; reconsideration and editing returned me to my normal mode, which is to get the hell on with the action. "The boy made his way swiftly but carefully through the forest, stepping in patterns reminiscent of a game." That opening sentence survived unchanged. The second was "It was as though there was a path that only he could see..." That survived too, but a description of his staff was added before it. This is the way revision and editing work. After another month, and further discussion with my wife and my researcher Alan Riggs, I concluded that the existing title would not do; there were other titles galore that were similar, like *King Conan*, making this unoriginal. Damn it, I prefer to be original; it's one of my failings as a prospective best-selling novelist. How about *The Charm of Havoc*? Or maybe *Key to Havoc*, as that started with a K so I wouldn't have to change the location of my King Havoc directory. It was the last one that stuck, after a while.

I completed the first chapter in April, and wrote a summary of the remainder in May. I revised and edited it, and sent it to my literary agent as a sample for marketing. Meanwhile I got to work on my GEODYSSEY novel *Climate of Change*, hoping that series was not yet dead. Unfortunately it was, and in mid April 1998 I resumed work on *Key to Havoc*, though it had not found a publisher. I'm a writer; I write, and this was a project I really liked, market or no. It moved well, and I completed it in August, a thousand manuscript page, 250,000 word novel, and sent it to my agent. Two years later, in 2000, I wrote the sequel, *Key to Chroma*, of similar length, that picks up where the first leaves off, and after another two years, in 2002, I wrote the third, *Key to Destiny*. Two more are projected, if the success of the first three make them viable: *Key to Liberty* and *Key to Survival*.

Not only did none of them sell, most publishers declined even to look at them. All they wanted from me was Xanth, and if they couldn't have that, too bad, and I was on my own. I think three publishers did look, and bounced: this wasn't Xanth. It's no secret that I consider publishers as a class to be idiots, stupider than any person within them, like a mob. They chase baying after last year's bestsellers and are blind to what may be next year's successes. Editors seem not to trust their own judgment—which may mean they aren't entirely ob-tuse—so don't like to take chances on anything that isn't a clone of last year. They follow rules that look crazy to ordinary folk, such as that no real sex is allowed in fantasy, or big novels cost too much to print. There's only so much of this nonsense I care to put up with. After five years of unsuccessful marketing of the big sexy ChroMagic series, I'm doing an end run around this witless blockade and putting it into print via a small press publisher, so that readers can decide for themselves whether it is worthwhile. We'll see, in due course.

Meanwhile, some stray notes. I want it known that I wrote Chap-ter 2, with the survival motif, in 1998, before the TV *Survivor* series started; I didn't copy it from anyone. The idea of telepathy as a dis-ease was suggested to me by a reader. To my tooth-gnashing frustra-tion I can't find the letter after 5 years so can't give proper credit for a great idea. I used the name Shrapnel in my earlier Space Tyrant se-ries and forgot, but I suppose I can get away with it here also.

Some themes of the series are not given the play in this first novel that they are in later ones: the linguistic convention of making a one word initial statement is indicated here mainly by "Greeting" and "Part-ing," but that's just the beginning. Folk say "Expletive!" instead of cussing, as Gale does once, and "Excitement," "Disbelief," "Wonder," "Outrage!" and many other terms, followed by more detailed discus-sions. When a man says "Curiosity" or "Question" he is asking for information or clarification. When a woman says "Love" to a man, she's not fooling. When a child says "Obscenity" he gets punished. It is my secret hope (don't tell!) that readers will like this descriptive shorthand as I do and start using it in role playing games and maybe even reality, much as they did with Robert Heinlein's grokking and sharing water. There's more than one way to change the world.

Then there is no fault. When Chroma folk need to travel beyond their Chroma, they don't want to be helpless targets for brigands, so they generally arrange to travel in company, in guarded caravans or at least with other people. Men tend to be better at hauling loads and defending themselves with weapons; women know the domestic arts like cooking and sewing. So a man may travel with a woman he has never met before, and for the duration of the hike he protects her as if she is his wife, even risking his life on her behalf, and she cooks for him and gives him sex as if he is her husband. When they arrive where they are going they separate and say no more about it, having no further obligation to each other. It is no fault. No one else questions this; it is understood. It's not limited; there can be no fault friendship between two men, as no fault brothers, or no fault parent and child association. Whatever works. But there are those who seem to love to travel, for some reason.

I also use inset stories in this series, as seen by several examples in this novel. The stories use similar conventions to those of the general culture, sometimes with special twists, such as man-woman no fault travel that turns into real love though both are married elsewhere. That's forbidden love that can keep the audiences of minstrels rapt. I came to know and like the art of the inset story in the Arabian Nights tales, and have used it on occasion in Xanth and notably in *Firefly*. I have more ideas than I can use, being a natural story writer who writes novels instead; I have a huge Idea file listing hundreds of notions, and when I need a story, I go there. That's where the story of the paralyzed teacher and his ardent student came from, and the illusion video Symbol shows of the handsome young man and the disfigured older woman. Some are substantial; one in the second novel, "Dancer," about the journey of an old man and girl child, no fault grandfather-granddaughter, runs 14,000 words and I think could be the basis for a great motion picture, had movie moguls the wit to see it.

Thus this series, which I regard as my best serious fantasy. The sequel goes into the Glamors in much more detail, and the third one explores the sister world Mystery or Counter-Charm, each novel wilder than the preceding one. The driving force is Havoc's determination to solve the riddle of his origin, and to complete his necessary service as king so he can settle down with Gale, if their status as changelings does not prevent it. Yet some mysterious and powerful force opposes him. There are spectacular revelations coming. But at heart it's the realm of ChroMagic with its adventure and its culture—a realm I love to immerse myself in, regardless what's happening there. I hope you do too.

About the Author

Piers Anthony is one of the world's most prolific and popular authors. His fantasy Xanth novels have been read and loved by millions of readers around the world, and have been on the *New York Times* Best Seller list many times. Although Piers is mostly known for fantasy and science fiction, he has written several novels in other genres as well, including historical fiction, martial arts, and horror. Piers lives with his wife in Central Florida.

Want to learn more about Piers Anthony?

Piers Anthony's official website is HI PIERS at **www.hipiers.com**, where he publishes his bi-monthly online newsletter. HI PIERS also has a section reviewing many of the online publishers and self-publishing companies for your reference if you are looking for a non-traditional solution to publish your book.

Piers Anthony's largest fan-based website is The Compleat Piers Anthony at **www.piers-anthony.com**. The Compleat Piers Anthony contains extensive information about all the books and stories that Piers has written, as well as up-to-date information about forthcoming books.

Printed in the United Kingdom
by Lightning Source UK Ltd.
120741UK00001B/350

9 780972 367066